D1596082

[УПЫРЬСКИЙ ЗАГОВОР]
THE NOSFERATU
CONSPIRACY

BOOK TWO: THE SOMMELIER

KDK 12 Press • Miami, FL

[УПЫРЬСКИЙ ЗАГОВОР]

THE NOSFERATU CONSPIRACY

BOOK TWO: THE SOMMELIER

BRIAN JAMES GAGE

2022

First Printing: 2022
978-0-578-98963-1

Also available in electronic format
and hardcover:
979-8-482-75944-8

KDK 12 Press
Miami, FL

brianjamesgage.com
nosferatuconspiracy.com
instagram.com/brianjamesgage
instagram.com/nosferatuconspiracy

For Kimberly Roth.

ACKNOWLEDGEMENTS

Special thanks to the following people who either inspired or
supported my journey in writing this novel:

Anne Horowitz, Niels Feder-Sværdpiil,
Andrew R. Deutsch, Lukas-Lowery Ross, Kane Oueis,
Skander Ladjimi, Alevtyna Kugushyna, Anne-Lise Langmeuer,
Svenja Keller, John Jihanyan, Jennifer Surprenant, Amey Rene,
Stanley Kubrick, Bram Stoker, Holly Randall, Humphry Knipe,
Suze Randall, Kevin Kocur, John Beauregard, Jowell Doughly,
Shannon Maher, Angie Del Rosario, Troy C. Ford, Jo Roderick,
Jordan Freid, my parents, my sister, and the venerable
Ryan J. Hyde.

Summary of the Nosferatu Conspiracy, Book One

The Sleepwalker told of the censored, true story behind the fall of the Romanov dynasty at the hands of the vampiric witch Grigori Rasputin and a shadowy cabal of occultists called the Black Hundred, along with several Rasputin loyalists. Most importantly: the dark warlock Olaf, Grand Duke Dmitri Pavlovich, and an erratic and eccentric sycophant named Charles Vondling.

But Rasputin had other plans as well.

Prince Felix Yusupov was pulled into these events after he was framed and jailed for the brutal murder of his fiancée Irina—an act actually committed by a notorious killer named the Sleepwalker, who we learned was the vampire Rasputin. It seems that Irina's murder was a means for Rasputin to isolate Felix and alienate him from the royal family for reasons known only by Rasputin and Olaf.

Wanting answers, Felix escaped jail and sought out Rurik Kozlov, the district coroner and amateur vampire hunter. To keep Felix safe from Rasputin, it was decided he would travel to Bucharest by train and convince Rurik's twin brother, a reclusive and genius vampire hunter named Denis, to return to Saint Petersburg where the real fight was brewing.

During his harrowing journey, Felix was rescued from a train full of vampires by a young innkeeper named Mary and her gargantuan sidekick Sebastian, who bore terrible stitching scars across his body. They then led Felix to Denis, who was badly mauled by Rasputin in a previous altercation.

After an ill-fated quest to Loch Dracul deep within the Carpathians with the help of Denis's friend Florin, Felix and Denis realized Rasputin's plans were on the precipice of unfolding. They quickly returned to Saint Petersburg by biplane and reunited with Rurik to stop the pending Nosferatu attacks. But Rasputin proved too clever and on the evening of December 16, 1916 (OS), the vampiric tsarevich Alexei attacked and murdered his father, Nicholas. With Alexei's human bloodlink destroyed, the Nosferatu were unleashed across the city.

Rasputin killed Denis after the group made their last stand within the Winter Palace. Felix managed to deliver mortal blow to Rasputin, but it was finally empress Alexandra who vanquished the Nosferatu by sacrificing herself and tsarevich Alexei through self-immolation, destroying the blood thirsty creatures' vampiric ballast in this realm.

Upon reaching his palace, where he gathered supplies, Felix declared his intention to find and kill Dmitri Pavlovich, who had been converted to a vampire by Rasputin and was on a train to Bucharest to assert control over Charles Vondling's handling of the cabal's mysterious operation there.

Act 1 ended with Felix and Rurik setting out on foot from Saint Petersburg bound for Bucharest.

And now—act two, *The Sommelier*.

PART I:
DIE TODESHEXE

Chapter 1

1

STAATSGEHEIMNIS [STATE SECRET]
OPERATION ZITADELLE [OPERATION CITADEL]
IM DIENST VON KAISER WILHELM II
[IN SERVICE OF KAISER WILHELM II]
27, MÄRZ 1917 [MARCH 27, 1917]

At approximately 5:20 a.m., Berlin operatives of the Prussian Secret Police entered the Altes Museum undetected. All archived documents relating to eyewitness accounts of the disappearance of REDIGIERT [REDACTED] in 1614 have been located and destroyed. Documents burned as directed. Further actions included ████ ████ naming ████████ and ████ of Austria as belligerents **RESTLICHER BERICHT ZENSIERT [REMAINING REPORT REDACTED]**.

*

The Nosferatu attacks that ravaged Saint Petersburg, Russia, in December 1916 were merely a dress rehearsal—a failed supernatural incursion eventually covered up and historically cited as the Bolshevik Revolution. The clandestine cabal behind the conspiracy viewed it as nothing more than an ancillary loss to the master clockwork still ticking in the shadows. A veritable powder keg of darkness still awaited ignition.

Their true ambitions were far more sinister and protracted, and their operatives were actively working far beyond Russia's borders to bring the next phase of the operation to fruition. The epicenter of this activity was rooted deep inside the Prussian Empire's headquarters in Berlin, and their alignment with a secretive coven of witches hidden within the Baden-Württemberg region of Germany near the base of Mount Hohenzollern.

The top of Mount Hohenzollern had remained undisturbed for over three hundred years. Derelict foundational ruins were the only indication that upon the mesa there once sat a castle stronghold for the Counts of Zollern during the Middle Ages. Coveted for its strategic position—perched nearly nine hundred meters above sea level and surrounded by a dense deciduous forest that grew from Mount Hohenzollern's base all the way to the peak of its steep incline—the castle once served as an imposing admonition to anyone who questioned the strength and majesty of House Hohenzollern.

The acropolis on the pike was constructed in several phases.

The first inception was utterly destroyed in 1423 after a year-long siege by the Swabian League of Cities. New construction began in 1454, but once completed, the castle fell into a deep state of disrepair due to the depletion of upkeep funds and was essentially abandoned by 1505. The inhabitants of the surrounding countryside grew to think of the decaying structure as nothing more than a monument to what was, and what would never be again.

That was until the morning of September 4, 1614, when several hundred residents of the Baden-Württemberg region awoke to find the castle had disappeared entirely from the top of Mount Hohenzollern, and a large garrison of Holy Roman Emperor Matthias's personal soldiers had surrounded the area, forbidding anyone to pass upon the bluff.

Traditional historians acknowledge the stories surrounding the castle's decay; however, owing to the unexplained nature of the complex's disappearance from its foundation in 1614 and subsequent reappearance in 1917 shortly before German surrender in World War I, the vanishing of Hohenzollern Castle is now considered fringe conspiracy right in line with Sasquatch and the Loch Ness Monster.

Dozens of eyewitness accounts of the mysterious event did, in fact, exist in the archives of Berlin's Altes Museum until the early morning of March 27, 1917, when the Prussian Secret Police quietly entered the institution and seized the documents at the behest of Kaiser Wilhelm II. The operation included scrubbing from the records any mention of the involvement of Emperor Matthias and one Radu cel Frumos.

Radu was an ancient warlock with ties to the bloodiest portion of the Crusades—the holy war waged by the Vatican, not to claim the holy lands as history speculates but rather a genocide co-ordinated in tandem with powerful imams and rabbis to eradicate witchcraft and anyone who practiced or supported the art. This epoch was branded 'The Inferno of the Witch' by those who survived the purge.

During the Inferno, Radu was one of the few magick wielders authorized by the pope to lead the Vatican's secret service of anti-witchcraft inquisitors known as Opus Spiritus Sancti. His modus operandi: to discover, destroy, and subsequently cover up all para-normal activities from the public purview.

But Radu had his own agenda, driven by a dark secret.

Unbeknownst to most, Radu was the younger brother of Vlad the Impaler—a powerful warlock of light who, in the 1400s, led the charge of hunting down and containing the demons of Solomon at the pope's command. But the mortal religious leaders of the time had no intention of stopping at demons, and once Vlad and his order of archangel warlocks vanquished the seventy-two demons, im-prisoning them forever, phase two of the Vatican's plan was set in motion to eliminate any and all supernatural entities. In response to this betrayal, Vlad fell to darkness and unleashed the first wave of Nosferatu attacks in the mid-1400s as revenge against the leaders of the Abrahamic religions.

Forced to kill his brother to end his dark reign, Radu purportedly collected Vlad's remaining blood in a bottle, hoping to one day res-urrect and redeem him. But he knew the dangers that threatened humanity should the bottle fall into evil hands and Vlad be resur-rected by factions of darkness.

Still suffering from grief and guilt over the loss of his brother, Radu vowed to protect the bottle and to bring back Vlad only if King Solomon's demons ever escaped their prisons. Until then, Radu quietly slipped into hiding and spent his time in the shadows, creating a string of false identities over the centuries while continuing to secretly serve the Vatican as an inquisitor—but always to his own advantage. For he knew, what started during the Inferno was far from over.

In the early 1600s, Radu was quietly tracking an evil entity known as the Death Witch—an elusive remnant of the Inferno who single-handedly slaughtered Vlad Drăculea's collective of seventy-one warlocks as revenge for imprisoning her demon father, Bael. But the Death Witch was hunting Radu as well, taunting him and luring him from hiding with a string of heinous murders designed to attract his attention. For in Radu's possession were two items she coveted: blood of the only archangel who'd escaped her wrath, and a mystical sword that confined Bael's soul within its hilt—the latter being the sine qua non of her father's resurrection; the former being the gravest of threats to her malevolent agenda.

A series of gruesome and unsolved child murders that plagued Romania, Hungary, and Slovakia for the better part of the fifteenth and sixteenth centuries were rumored to be perpetuated by the Death Witch, and Radu emerged to investigate—an investigation that would lead him to the castle doorstep of land baroness Elizabeth Báthory of Hungary and forever change the course of history.

On August 26, 1614, Radu requested ownership of Hohenzollern Castle from Holy Roman Emperor Matthias of Austria, five days after unmasking Elizabeth as the Death Witch and beheading her for her crimes. Being a demi-demon, Elizabeth wielded powers that far exceeded Radu's, and he knew what remained of her needed to be contained until he could discover such magick to vanquish her forever.

Matthias seized the mount at Radu's request, and the warlock placed a concealment spell upon the castle. As legend would have it, he also secured Elizabeth's remains inside with a banishment hex—blood magick so dark and binding that only upon Radu's death could it ever be broken.

Whatever was left of Elizabeth had no hope of escape, and for now, Radu retained the advantage.

In addition to casting the spells, Radu demanded that the Holy Roman Empire quarantine the entire mount, and that no person, nobility or otherwise, be permitted to pass. After a secret meeting between Matthias, Radu, and Pope Paul V, the Vatican chancery issued a papal bull decreeing that trespassing on the mount was considered a sin—punishable by death. Afterwards, Radu seemingly vanished, but as his spells remained intact upon the mount, he was assumed to be alive.

The decree was handed down and enforced over the centuries by German rulers, but it wasn't the death sentence that kept the curious away. Rather, it was the lore that spread throughout the Kingdom of Württemberg that something far worse than capital punishment was lurking atop Mount Hohenzollern—and indeed, from 1615 to 1917, Württemberg, Germany, carried the dubious distinction of more missing persons per capita than London, Paris, and Berlin combined.

For something wicked now resided at the top of Mount Hohenzollern—a revenant of evil that whispered its name into the wind to lull passersby into the forest, unfortunate souls who were never seen again. In time, the trees upon the mount and the thorny shrubbery at its base answered to the whisper. They answered in appearance, growing gnarled and ebon and devoid of any leaves, as if the voice were some unholy rot emanating from within the invisible castle's walls. They answered in service, becoming carnivorous and athirst for any animal or human flesh that happened upon their path.

And the foliage surrounding the mount did feast, but only in service of *her*.

After the branches and brambles drank their fill, the animal or person was hoisted to the top of the mount by the trees as an offering to the devil sequestered at its peak. The venison and vermin captured by the black briars were always delivered to her partially gored, for it was blood the herbage craved, but for her—the ravenous one—blood was mere sustenance.

It was their souls for which she hungered.

The vile forest that became her guardian would merely batter and sip from the people, often feasting on their tongues and other soft tissue about the face to disorient and weaken them before passing their bodies from tree limb to tree limb to the top of the mount. And then the vines would shove and most times drag them into the castle, where they would wander only to soon find themselves once again ensnared and forever helpless. The people were always left mostly unscathed, for she desired to savor them whole. And savor them she did—savored their harrowing screams at the sight of her, savored the fear in their bloodstream, and savored their souls as she swallowed them day by day and night by night into her black abyss of infinite torture.

And once the dread had finally proliferated to all living things throughout the terrain, and the brush's quarry had run dry, that is when a single solemn man astride a single solemn horse appeared at the base of Mount Hohenzollern—but this was not just any man, and his steed was not just any horse.

A fiendish warlock by the name of Vago Vakól and his undead mare known as the Hellhorse arrived one misty morning in 1693 to the mount's briar patch after decades of searching for her—the black witch sequestered at the peak.

Vago held out his open palm and sensed that the powerful hex upon the plants bore the psychic imprint of Elizabeth's magick.

"She's cursed the forest," he said to himself, patting the Hellhorse on its bony, exposed rib cage. "They bring her prey to feed."

The Hellhorse reared and let out a ghoulish whinny as a thorny vine shot from the briar patch and sunk its wooden teeth into Vago's leg, pulling him off balance toward the brush. He reached for a knife on his belt and slashed the plant until it recoiled and slithered away. Crawling backward on all fours, Vago watched as the voracious vines rose into the air, blocking his view of the summit.

Ensuring he was far enough from the briar patch, Vago stood and calmed his steed. He now understood the hex upon the forest: Radu cel Frumos, by choice or necessity, had exiled what remained of Elizabeth instead of destroying her and—whatever his reasons—might very well still have plans for her. The accursed forest would prevent Radu and any of the enemies she had made over the centuries from reaching her in a vulnerable state; conversely, the banishment field prevented any of her allies from communicating with her telepathically or teleporting onto the castle grounds—a trek through the bloodthirsty plants was the only feasible means of reaching her.

Vago grew frustrated as he glanced upward to the peak.

Breaking Elizabeth's magick was far beyond his skill, and he too would be prevented from ever contacting her. He closed his eyes and clenched his fists, cursing his predicament. And as the rage welled within him, causing white and red dots to flash on the insides of his eyelids—that was when a vision emerged. A witch born of the purest magick. One raised to serve father Bael and trained as a warrior in the dark arts—why, yes! Such a witch could potentially overpower the spell and breach the mount.

Vago opened his eyes and sucked down the country air with vigor. He glanced behind to a dense forest not too far in the distance, tugged on his horse's reins, and sauntered toward the darkened woods.

There, he walked to a blackened tree.

In its shade was a horse-drawn cart containing an ornately carved vanity. As he knelt before the mirror, a burly man wearing an executioner's hood with no eyeholes appeared within the glass.

"I have found her, Master," said Vago. "She is alive. Our work can now begin."

"Not until I am free from this prison," said the hooded man.

"I have located a likely replacement, Master—a greedy and wrathful young witch who lives deep within the Black Forest."

The dark wraith nodded in agreement then dissipated, leaving Vago to gaze into a mirror that did not cast his reflection.

His eyes moved to the tree canopy and he was satisfied with its density. Considering their proximity to the mount, he decided these woods would suffice. Vago would start his coven here. He would breed a witch of the purest stock who could break the spell. Radu cel Frumos would be captured and killed. Elizabeth would be reclaimed.

Vago stood and raised his arms high.

"The demon king, Bael, shall be resurrected," he shouted, his booming voice echoing through the woods. "The Black Sun will rise once more!"

And from this quiet forest in the middle of the German wilderness, Vago would serve his dark masters to set in motion a dire and cataclysmic series of events that would lead to the most pervasive supernatural deception in human history. A deliberate, coordinated censorship campaign perpetuated by covert factions within leading world governments to cover up what started during the Crusades, crescendoed during the Nosferatu attacks on Saint Petersburg, and rose to a harrowing and violent apex at the Battle of Arras in World War I.

2

March 22, 1917

Peace can be found even in times of war, thought Hershel Güterbach.

Hunched before his rustic kitchen's sole window, he placed his liver-spotted hands on the rim of a deep basin sink as his pupils reflected the picture-perfect spring day. A cloudless sky of radiant blue crowned a hardy forest in the short distance, which shifted ever so slightly with the stirs and lulls of a gentle breeze.

On days like this, Hershel could see all the way to Mount Hohenzollern far off in the distance. He was not a superstitious man, but ever since childhood, a local nursery rhyme rang through his mind whenever his eye caught the mount's distant silhouette:

> *Lock your doors and try to hide.*
> *She always finds a way inside.*
> *When blue skies fall to ashen swirls—*
> *The Death Witch comes for boys and girls.*

After eighty-two years of living in Zimmern, Hershel wanted to believe he was immune to the legends ingrained within his community, but a small shiver always pricked him center spine when he recited the rhyme.

He knew missing persons had been reported over the years, but nearly all of them were outsiders, vagabonds, or drunkards. Hershel had never heard of any kidnappings in his town. It was merely folklore. Silly superstition. He recalled the numerous times he and his childhood friends ran for their bedroom closets and slammed the doors tight when rain clouds appeared in the sky. So far as Hershel remembered, all of his friends had grown into happy and healthy adults—most staying right here in Zimmern. He came to believe the nursery rhyme was told to children to keep them from getting caught in the rain and catching a cold.

And as for rumors of the Thule Society? Hershel had never seen any evidence of the fabled apocalyptic cult that supposedly lived near the base of Mount Hohenzollern and offered human sacrifices to its haunted forest. Indeed, no. A stand-up leader such as Kaiser Wilhelm—a brash, fearless emperor who declared war on Serbia after they assassinated his dear friend Archduke Franz Ferdinand of Austria-Hungary—would never allow such criminality to fester within Germany.

Kaiser Wilhelm was a man of God.

Hershel continued to stare out the window, transferring his gaze from the mount to his backyard and the tree branches shifting leisurely against the azure sky.

A sense of optimism welled within him.

Today was Hershel's big day.

His wife and daughter had left for Berlin to visit relatives, and he was acting as guardian to his grandson, Oskar. He'd planned a busy schedule of activities for the boy—everything from cooking hearty meals together, to playing *Schafkopf* by candlelight while drinking hot cocoa, to teaching him how to bait a hook before their Saturday visit to the local fishing hole, and especially teaching Oskar the infamous family secret of using bologna to catch fish.

Knowing his health was in steady decline and treating each day as if it could be his last, Hershel had every intention of making the weekend memorable for Oskar. When his wife and daughter returned, they would marvel at what a wonderful guardian he was. The house would be tidy, and Oskar would gush over the endless fun he'd had with Grandpa. No more talk of Hershel losing his faculties, no more quiet whisperings about his incontinence, and no more speaking down to him and coddling him as if he were Oskar's age. Hershel would put an end to the heated debate as to whether it was safe to leave Oskar alone under his care.

He wondered for a moment where Oskar had run off to and decided to finish his chores before checking up on the boy. The cold water pouring over his hands triggered his arthritis as he washed his morning teacup, and he scornfully wished his wife had cleaned before leaving for Berlin. While watching the water pour from the faucet and swirl down the drain, Hershel was reminded of a new invention he'd heard of from America that heated water before it came from the faucet. He envisioned what the device might look like and how the warm water would soothe his arthritic hands. He then questioned whether he could afford such a device, and where it might fit in his modest kitchen.

"Grandfather, look!"

Hershel peered down to see his grandson standing outside, just below the windowsill. The golden-haired child held his hand high— a black butterfly perched on his finger. The insect flapped its wings as the boy extended his reach, and Hershel noticed an unusual marking on its pinions. He placed his teacup on the counter, released the window latch, and opened the pane. Hershel then pulled up the spectacles hanging around his neck and placed them on the bridge of his nose.

"Very good, Oskar. Gently, bring it closer."

Oskar crept toward his grandfather and stood on his tiptoes, holding the butterfly as high as he could.

Hershel inspected the bug. He believed it to be a swallowtail, but had never seen one with such a marking on its wings. The white oval spanned both wings with a small black circle on each half, giving it the appearance of black eyes on a white face. Toward the insect's posterior, the oval grew narrow and jagged like sharp teeth. Hershel was convinced the shape looked like a human skull. Marveling at the strange marking, he grinned and glanced back to his grandson's face.

"Look at that," he said. "I believe you found yourself a swallowtail. Very beautiful and unique, this one. Swallowtails are good luck— today must be your day."

Oskar smiled, revealing his missing two front teeth. "I want to name her Klara."

Hershel reached for a dish towel next to him and dried his hands. "A lovely name for a lovely—oh!" His blue eyes shot upward as he watched the swallowtail fly from his grandson's hand. "There she goes."

"I'll catch her," said Oskar. He turned and ran after the tiny black body.

"Careful, Oskar. Be delicate with our new friend."

Hershel leaned into the basin and felt at ease as he watched his grandson give chase to the butterfly. He was pleased his daughter had come back to live with him while his son-in-law was away on the front lines. The country air would be good for Oskar, he thought, watching the child race after his catch. This weekend would indeed be perfect.

Hershel's gaze moved to the trees and a sensation of worry came over him.

The forest looked suddenly ill.

The verdant greenery and healthy wood appeared morose, as if the leaves had fallen limp and the bark had grown to black scabs.

Something's not right.

Hershel pushed his glasses higher on his nose and studied the woods. The idyllic weather from moments earlier darkened, and a fog began emanating from the trees like some toxic, sullied exhale. The mist swirled into his backyard as clouds formed above the tree line, churning ashen and tin.

When blue skies fall to ashen swirls . . .

"Oskar!"

Oskar, still intent on the butterfly, ran into the fog.

A violent gust of wind blew the window shut.

Hershel was startled yet relieved to see the panes remained unbroken. He hobbled away from the sink to the back door and snatched his cane. The moment he opened the door, growing winds tore the knob from his hand. He planted his cane on the ground and shuffled after his grandson.

"Oskar! Away from the fog!"

The whipping wind felt almost rabid upon Hershel's arms as he aimlessly wandered into the thickening fog. He felt disoriented and nauseous while breathing in the misty air.

Tastes like decay.

Hershel gagged as the stench became more pervasive, and he wondered if the vapors were some chemical attack. After stumbling around for another moment, he noticed a gray lump on the ground just ahead. Hershel walked closer and positioned his glasses to see Oskar huddled on the earth, his hands domed above the grass.

"Oskar, obey me, boy! Come back inside."

"I caught her, Grandfather," said Oskar, peeking into his hands. "Come see!"

Hershel had nearly reached his grandson when a strange sensation came over him. The more he struggled toward the boy, the farther away Oskar seemed, as if some invisible force were stretching the earth between them.

"Oskar, quickly now. Come with me," he said, extending his hand.

Oskar released the butterfly and it sailed into the air against the turbulent winds before disappearing into the fog. The boy stood, but appeared rigid. He ran his hands over his forearms.

"I feel cold, Grandfather."

Hershel again tried walking closer to Oskar, only to see the ground between them push the child farther away.

Hershel stood still.

Am I having a stroke?

The thought vanished when he saw the hooded figure emerge from the fog. It was tall. Lean. Black. Its angular skulled face was crowned with the horns of a twelve-point buck that rose into the murk like bony lightning rods.

Hershel shivered at the sight.

"Oskar, *now* . . . come now."

He motioned Oskar toward him, hoping the child would not look back.

The boy tried to take a step forward but froze, seemingly gripped by some ghostly force. Panic filled his eyes as he once again tried to move forward. He raised his fists and slammed them against the air, banging his hands onto an invisible barrier.

Hershel dropped his cane and stood shaking as he watched the figure fully materialize behind Oskar. Its black cloak flowed outward from its body and slithered over the ground toward the child, who looked down and whimpered as its slender tendrils enveloped him.

"Grandfather, help—"

The boy was silenced as the cloak swallowed him, his entire body disappearing into the black mass. Hershel attempted to yell, but let out only a frightened grunt as saliva dripped from his dentured mouth.

The slim iota turned to him and raised its long white index finger to its skeletal mask, revealing a decayed fingernail.

"Give me back my grandson."

Quiet, it seemed to say as it placed its finger to its bony mouth.

"Please," whispered Hershel, his voice quivering. "I can't lose him."

The figure lurched over Hershel and seemed to grow taller against the drab fog. He fell to his knees and cowered as its horns extended toward the heavens, conveying the sense that he was a captive—the gnarled spikes now his prison bars. It then reached upward, pulled back its hood, and removed the mask.

Hershel shook violently at the sight of her pale, gaunt face and spindly hair sucked of its color. Arthritic pain ripped through his knee and finger joints as the convulsions ground his feeble bones together. What sounded like a murder of crows shrieking in unison rang out all around him and he covered his ears. A wet sensation warmed his thigh as he stared at her. Nausea chewed into his stomach when he noticed she had no eyes—only sockets scarred dark blue with blackened varicose veins that spread onto her cheeks and forehead, shifting like earthworms just beneath her skin.

She did not speak, but her intentions were clear. She had no eyes, yet her gaze pierced the deepest part of his being. In that moment he knew—he knew exactly what she was.

The Death Witch comes for boys and girls.

As she moved closer to Hershel, he felt no cold, no warmth—only an unfathomable void. Hershel saw inside her mind, a sadistic psyche born of a million tiny, razor-sharp mouths with silvery fangs grinding onward to infinity. She feasted upon all mirth and devoured all joy that encircled her rapacious heart, only to regurgitate some fragment of light before swallowing it back whole until only vacuity remained.

Hershel grew transfixed upon her. He felt the urge to worship her—to offer something unto her.

"Why yes," he wheezed. "For you . . . yes!"

Hershel smiled and calmly raised his hands to his face before forcefully ramming his index fingers into his eyes. Hooking his fingers around the back of his eyeballs, he could feel his fingernails scratching the insides of his sockets. He then shoved his middle fingers into each eye and found the leverage.

Then he pulled.

White and blue flashes filled his vision the harder he tugged, reveling in a pain that he knew pleased and fed her. Squeezing both optic nerves between his fingers, Hershel let out a great wail and tore his eyeballs clean from his head. Blood ran down his cheeks as his eyeless face peered up to her. He took in large, lingering breaths and extended his hands, holding his eyeballs before her like some grand offering.

Her black cloak snaked over the grass onto his skin and embraced him up to his shoulders with a sensation of damp, vile hopelessness.

"Yes," said Hershel, his neck falling limp. "Take everything."

The Death Witch glared at Hershel for only another moment with no expression on her face before placing her deer skull helmet back upon her head. Her cloak released him, and her cruel shadow melded into the mist.

The winds calmed, the fog dissipated, and the sky turned blue once more.

The sedate spring day returned, shining its hopeful rays upon Hershel's withered, pallid corpse still kneeling on the grass. Black and broken capillaries blossomed across his body, and in his out-stretched hand sat only a black butterfly, gently flapping its wings.

The swallowtail took flight, and Hershel's body crumbled to ash.

His dentures fell to the ground as gray, dusty whispers of a man who once was floated across the perfectly manicured grass. Catching the breeze, the winged silhouette fluttered upward against the calm sky and sailed on toward the distant shadow of Mount Hohenzollern.

Chapter 3

3

STAATSGEHEIMNIS [STATE SECRET]

The eagle with two heads shall perish below two hills,
Near the valley where the bridged river flows.
The Prussian's ruse will spark revenge for blood that spills.
A peasant and the White Demon shall breed her storm of crows.
—Michel de Nostredame, *Les Prophéties*, 1555

**ZENSIERT—ALLE KOPIEN IM DIENST VON KAISER
WILHELM II AUFGEFUNDEN UND ZERSTÖRT
[CENSORED—ALL COPIES LOCATED AND
DESTROYED IN SERVICE OF KAISER WILHELM II]**

*

March 20, 1917, night

Two evenings prior to Oskar Güterbach's disappearance, Vago Vakól's hooded figure marched along the narrow center line of his congregation. He held a golden scepter in both hands across his body as he strode forward under the starry night, crushing the dew-kissed grass beneath his yellowed toenails.

It smells sweet, he thought as he inhaled the nighttime spring air, focusing his gaze on the darkness before him. Even under the fragment of light cast down from the waning crescent moon, Vago could discern the blanched shadows of the accursed forest shifting unnaturally in the near distance. He looked to the thorny bushes that surrounded the mount and took notice of their overgrowth, pouring much farther outward into the fields even within the last few weeks.

She's ravenous.

Vago grinned, revealing his large square teeth, and looked upward into the night where the castle once reigned.

Sporadic torch lamps on the grounds illuminated his kneeling followers in bubbles of flickering orange light. To his left were fifty of his coven's elders, all wearing blood-red cloaks that masked their faces; to his right knelt nearly one hundred novices, all in white hooded cloaks. The timpani pulsed a slow, deep resonance from behind him, matching every step of his rhythmic gait.

Tonight was the night—the vernal equinox.

Vago concentrated on his heartbeat, slowing his pulse to the beat of the drums and allowing the Void to enter his consciousness. His eyes widened when he felt it—nothing more than a mere splinter shift in the Void's equilibrium. The tiny vibration pulsed through his very marrow, and he knew: after more than three hundred years of waiting and fourteen failed attempts, this eve would swing the Ether's balance back to the Void.

Elizabeth would be reclaimed.

As he reached the front of his congregation, Vago paused and looked to the long row of perfectly aligned posts that poked from the ground, each hung with a sterling white banner adorned with a black circle containing a rounded swastika—the symbol of the Thule Society, known as the Black Sun. The banners rippled in the breeze as Vago's eyes moved once more to the top of the mount, and that's when he saw it—the shimmer. In three hundred years, it had never been seen, yet there it was: Hohenzollern Castle revealed as a slight ghostly phosphorescence in the night sky. As quickly as it came, the image was gone.

Vago knew it was the sign.

He turned to his congregation, removed his hood, and raised his scepter into the air. The drumbeats stopped and a quiet settled over the field. The torchlight illuminated Vago's dark green cloak with white ornamental stitching around the sleeves and cast a flicker upon the golden lamen hanging from his neck with the engraved letters *B-A-E-L* encircling the ornate symbol at its center. Vago rubbed the medallion between his thumb and forefinger, then planted his scepter in the ground before him. The torches carved striking shadows into his unusually elongated facial structure—an unsettling amalgam of masculine and feminine features accentuated by a stark white, wispy mustache and beard that grew patchy and coarse about his jawline, which was cracked, dry, and riddled with eczema.

"Come forward!" commanded Vago.

The timpani resonated once more as two red-cloaked elders rose from the ground and proceeded into the aisle that separated the congregation. They advanced to Vago and knelt before him.

"Remove your hoods," said Vago.

The figures pulled back their garments, revealing themselves as a blond man and woman in their midthirties, both with an air of eagerness radiating from their bright blue eyes. The woman smiled as Vago looked down to her.

"Yes," he said, reaching to caress her face. "Yes, my child. Tonight shall be a joyous affair."

The woman looked to her husband, and the two exchanged a loving glance.

Vago held out his scepter's orb to the woman. Upon it was a golden idol split into three parts: the face of a crowned man with pointy ears, a frog's head, and the face of a cat. The base of the sculpture was adorned with eight spider legs.

"Worship your master," said Vago.

The woman planted her lips upon the frog.

Vago moved the scepter's orb to the man. "Worship your master."

The man closed his eyes and kissed the face of the crowned man.

"Now join hands," Vago said, pulling the scepter away. "Do you obey Father Bael?"

"We obey," they said in unison.

"And is your blood of Prussia? Swear by it."

"Our bloodline is pure. By this, we swear."

"And was your daughter conceived to be pure in service of him? To serve at the altar of his will and might? To obey him, his son and minions, and his daughter confined at the top of this mountain?"

"She was."

"Loudly, into the night," commanded Vago, "exactly as we prepared."

The couple raised their heads high and in unison professed, "Our daughter was conceived of pure Prussian blood to serve unto thee— the Bornless One! We give her soul to thee! Our union brought forth to right the wrong delivered unto thy daughter, thy blood. Our seed thy servant, our blood thy well. Drink from us. Drink for glory! We are bound to thee as it is now and ever shall be."

Vago shoved his scepter into the soft earth and placed his hands upon their heads. The couple's eyes rolled back into their heads, and their eyelids twitched as their bodies shivered with frenzy.

"For it is blood that binds us!" Vago's voice grew in volume as he lifted his face toward the sky, exposing his unusually large Adam's apple. His eyes shot to the crescent moon and his bony fingers gripped the elders' heads more firmly. They continued to convulse in his grasp as the drums grew to a near-frenetic tempo.

"*Blut und Boden!* Grant purity unto our bloodline. Fertility unto our soil. We—the chosen order of the Second Reich!"

The congregation erupted in a chant.

Blut und Boden. We are the order. We are the chosen.

"Thee, I invoke! The Bornless One. Thee that did create the earth and the heavens! For tonight we cast unto you our very own blood—a daughter of purity. So that she of holy Prussian blood may pass. To break the hex. To climb the mount. To commune with your daughter. O mighty Bael! Thee, I invoke! Thee who are imprisoned and shall be free once more by our toil's blood!"

The congregation followed: *With our blood covenant, thee, we invoke! The Bornless One. We offer our blood, our souls unto thee and thine.*

"Bring forth the witch!" yelled Vago.

He thrust his palms into the elders kneeling before him, and they fainted to the ground. Vago raised his hands as two white-hooded novices rose from the front of the congregation and pulled their limp bodies away. Looking to the back of the line, Vago saw her seated upon a pale, emaciated horse that ambled toward the front of the congregation. Her white gown flowed freely over the animal's body, and her long blonde hair was visible even under the antlered deer helmet she wore.

"Behold, an ashen horse!" shouted Vago. "And the name of her who sits upon it is Death!"

Part I: Die Todeshexe

The congregation chanted, *And Hell shall follow close behind with authority to rule the earth. To kill with sword, with famine, with death, and by beasts of the land.*

*

Ten minutes prior, Hanne Nauhaus stepped from her low-lying hut into the warm spring night. In the short distance she could see Master Vakól walking toward the front of her coven's congregation. Tonight was Hanne's seventeenth birthday, but that was not the cause for this celebration.

Her white ceremonial gown flowed about her as she walked barefoot across the grass. She plucked one of the wildflowers from her braids and held it tightly for luck as she continued toward the line of coven elders awaiting her.

The last purity test was attempted three years ago with a young and talented witch named Gunter Hess, who was Hanne's third cousin. He was supposedly pure—he and Hanne shared almost identical bloodlines—but when he stepped into Mount Hohenzollern's bramble patch, the thorns must have tasted some impurity. In front of the entire coven, Gunter was immediately mauled by the brambles and then tossed to the mesa's top by the tree branches, where he met his grim and final fate. Days later, the only remnants of Gunter recovered from the perimeter briar patch were a ceremonial deer skull helmet and two swords sheathed in a black metallic material that he'd worn as he entered the brush.

Tonight would be different.

Hanne's blue eyes appeared hopeful as she sauntered to the emaciated, ashen horse before her. Upon arriving at the line of elders, she stopped and waited for instruction.

"Proceed, my child," came a voice from the red-hooded figure nearest to her.

Hanne walked down the pathway that split the congregation in two, with seven elders on each side.

"Your covenant is of blood," said the first two elders as she passed. The invocation was repeated by each pair she passed.

When Hanne reached the Hellhorse, two elders hoisted her by her shoulders and placed her bareback upon the bony animal. Hanne could feel the horse's exposed ribs and torn flesh as she gripped its body with her calves.

"My child," came a voice from below.

Hanne looked down to see two elders bowing before her, both holding offerings in their hands.

The first elder looked up and handed Hanne two scimitars sheathed in a unique material that resembled a blend of black leather and a metallic onyx. The pommel of each sword was fashioned into a broad, circular loop where a gray bulbous gem glowed ever so slightly, appearing as a dull opal that had nearly lost its shimmer. Hanne took the blades one by one and wrapped their harnesses around her waist so that the scabbards fell to either side of her hips.

"Your crown," said the other elder as he held a deer skull to her, each of its antlers with four sharp points.

Hanne accepted the skull and saw that its interior had been fitted with a leather-padded helmet with blackened metal meshing that covered the eyes from within. With the tip of her finger, she poked the top of one of the antlers, and it was apparent that each spike had been sharpened by hand. The skull's face had several flat metal fastenings affixing the various cracks and broken portions that riddled the object.

This was a battle helmet.

Hanne closed her eyes and placed her hand on the skull's forehead. She whispered a spell and called upon her psychometric abilities. A vision of an ancient warrior wearing the helmet in a forest engulfed in flames seared into her mind. The helmet was cracked across the lower portion of the skull, and Hanne could see that the warrior was female as she raised two scimitars into the air—the black blades had a dull electricity about them and pulsed a low, deep hum into the air. The woman let out a battle cry as she stood over multiple slain adversaries at her feet, all missing large portions of their torsos and limbs, but there was no blood—the wounds were entirely cauterized.

"This belonged to the Death Witch," Hanne said quietly, stroking the skull.

Hanne placed the helmet upon her head and fastened the leather straps around her chin. She shook her head vigorously, trying to displace the skull, and was surprised at how snugly it fit. A nervousness grew in her stomach as she looked ahead to see her parents passed out on the grass before Master Vakól. Their part in the ritual was complete. Now it was her turn.

"Bring forth the witch!" she heard from the distance.

Hanne drove her heels into the zombie horse, and it crept toward Vago Vakól.

*

The drums beat steady and low as the Hellhorse trotted slowly toward Vago with Hanne upon its back. As Hanne reached the front of the congregation, Vago patted the horse's snout. The animal huffed in protest, then gave a short whinny. The old warlock offered his hand to Hanne, who took it and dismounted.

Vago led her a short distance from the congregation—her menacing figure standing nearly eleven inches taller than Vago's six-foot stature.

"You're doing masterfully," he said, placing his hand on the small of her back and rubbing her softly. "The ritual is proceeding exactly as we rehearsed."

"Thank you, Master Vakól. I can't wait to meet her." Hanne grew disgusted at the sensation of his hand moving to her buttocks.

Vago smiled. "And meet her you shall."

"Is she as beautiful as you say?"

"Even more so, my child. You will see."

The two stood together, staring at the bramble patch. Even in the dark, Hanne could see the thorny vines shifting slightly as if they were agitated and anticipating a meal.

"Don't let it frighten you. You are prepared for this. Remember, you are not to unsheathe the swords. They are offerings to her."

Hanne nodded and Vago removed his hand.

"Your time is now. Proceed forward."

Hanne took in a few deep breaths, and slowly extended her right foot forward. She swore a millennium passed before the soft pad of her foot greeted the damp grass. Her hands fell to her waist and she gripped the sword hilts—the feel of the leather material comforted her as she proceeded toward the briar patch.

The drumbeats were low and deep behind Hanne as the congregation chanted a prayer in her name. As she reached the perimeter of the thorny bush, she stopped once more and watched as the sharp tendrils snaked toward her, extending as far as they could into the air, trying to reach her. Knowing what awaited her if the thorns tasted but a sliver of impurity in her bloodline, Hanne tried to calm her nerves.

The drumbeats stopped.

The chanting ceased.

It was time.

Hanne took one last breath and placed her bare foot into a bushel of low-lying brambles. Instantly, the vines wrapped around her feet and calves, sinking their thorns into her flesh and tasting her blood. She relished the pain, knowing it would be only another moment before her fate was sealed. Her soul was prepared for any outcome, but it was not death she wanted—it was not death for which she had prepared. Hanne winced once more as the thorns slithered upward to her thighs and tore more deeply into her legs. A warm, wet sensation coated her legs as the foliage fed upon her blood with abandon.

The thorns crept higher across her body and fear swept Hanne as they pulled her down into the bush. An audible gasp erupted behind her as the congregation stared on in shock. Hanne was on the ground, smothered by the harsh wooden spikes sinking into her flesh. She tried to struggle, but their voracity was too intense. Tears filled her eyes as she realized she had failed, and that a more painful death awaited her at the top of the mount. The sharp brambles reached her face and slid under the deer skull helmet, feverishly swarming about her chin and trying to shove themselves into her mouth. Hanne forced her lips closed as the barbs cut into her face, and in that moment of panic, she felt a release.

The vines retreated from her body, leaving her in an empty patch on the ground.

Hanne stood.

Her gown was shredded, barely clinging to her punctured flesh. She reached up and positioned the deer helmet. Before her, the bushes had created a clear path to the tree line. Her insides tumbled as she took in the implication. She was pure. She was chosen. A hopeful shiver crept across her body as she looked once more to the peak, and there she saw it—the ghostly shimmer of Hohenzollern Castle.

Hanne glanced downward to see deep lacerations across her skin and streams of blood dripping down her body, staining what was left of her gown a deep crimson. She lifted her head high and smiled as her antlered shadow walked confidently toward the trees, knowing that at the top, *she* was waiting.

*

"Praise unto Bael!" shouted Vago as he watched the trees surrounding the mount lift Hanne into their grasp.

The elders and the novices broke the lines, and Vago watched them embrace and congratulate one another. A knot hardened in the pit of his stomach as Vago looked to the top of the mount.

Now the real test begins.

He thought for another moment about the implications of the evening's events. Revisiting a memory of Hanne levitating a stone table at age three, a feat even his older students were barely capable of after years of study, reassured him that his plan would succeed.

Hanne would return in morrow's eve. But Vago knew that *what* returned would not be Hanne Nauhaus.

*

The tree limbs cradled Hanne as they pushed her toward the peak, keeping her in an upright, seated position. She thought back to a memory of her childhood when she first learned to ride a galloping horse, and believed this sensation to be far more thrilling. Hanne tried to crane her neck to look back toward her coven's encampment, but the helmet blocked her peripheral vision.

As she reached the peak, the trees placed her upon the earth with an ease that felt almost nurturing. She stood looking at the barren mountaintop, where some crumbled stones were the only indicator that a castle still occupied the grounds. Moving her head slightly from side to side, she noticed a strange phenomenon. The castle's behemoth structure was there—directly in front of her. Hanne's eyes could sense the illusion as if the night sky and surrounding forest were projected through the castle's structure, which stood like some giant stone chameleon.

A series of vines began moving around her and crawled up her back, pushing her toward the phantasm. Hanne could now make out the outline of an arched wall. The vines had grown up along the stone, so that they seemed to hover in midair. The opening of the arch was devoid of any plant life, and Hanne assumed it was her way through. She turned, pushed the aggressive plants back with her hands, and sent a signal with her mind for them to allow her to pass unfettered.

"I don't need any help," she said with an air of frustration.

The vines obeyed and fell to the wayside.

Hanne walked to the opening, which was framed by what she recognized as decayed red valerian. From there, she could see to the other side of the mesa's clearing. A strange shimmer before her gave the notion that something was there, but in the darkness it was difficult to see. She reached her hand outward to the threshold and pushed her arm through, watching her limb disappear into the field up to her elbow. A giddy excitement came over her. Hanne closed her eyes, inhaled deeply through her nostrils, and stepped forward beyond the entrance.

Most witches began to know their talents in their late teens or even twenties, but Hanne was a rare witch who showed such capabilities as a very young child. She had been practicing spells and enchantments for nearly fourteen years, but none of that work had prepared her for the thrill of watching the night sky blend seamlessly into the massive Gothic grounds of Hohenzollern Castle.

She stood for a moment, short of breath, feeling as if the wind had been sucked from her lungs—gooseflesh rose up across her arms as she stared at a square bastion directly in her path. The structure, which sat just across a drawbridge, had an arched passageway with five parapets at its peak. The center parapet had a dilapidated stone carving of the House of Hohenzollern's seal, and above the archway was a relatively well-preserved carving of a warrior with his sword drawn, riding a horse in full battledress.

Hanne proceeded forward across the drawbridge and through the east gate's peaked arch. Upon exiting, she was prevented from continuing by the plant growth covering a winding path that ran along a stone wall leading to the main courtyard of the castle's grounds. She closed her eyes, spoke softly to the plants, and they created a walkway for her to advance.

As Hanne reached the top of the winding path, she noticed that her feet were becoming badly cut from the sharp stones embedded in the mud, but she was too delighted by the sweeping courtyard to pay the pain much mind. The darkened castle now sat before her like some befouled leviathan waiting to be awakened.

She stood dead center upon the pathway that halved Hohenzollern Castle, taking in the architectural authority of the U-shaped, spired structures, and wondered what the panorama must look like during the day. To her right was a striking Gothic cathedral with a golden cross hanging upside down upon its frontage. Hanne quietly laughed at the symbolism. To her left was another structure that rose from a squat base to a peaked pinnacle and extended into the distance, where the entire castle was conjoined by a soaring, singular bastion topped by a thin, towering spire. As her eyes took in the drab beauty of the fortress, even in the night, Hanne could see it was in a terrible state of disrepair with large portions of the roof caved in.

She felt overwhelmed by the expanse. "Where do I go?"

The vines before her slithered away, creating a path that led up the slight incline to the larger cathedral structure to her right. Hanne placed her hands upon her swords and walked toward the spiked and decayed structure, marveling at the massive arched stained-glass windows that remained mostly intact.

As she walked along the pathway, Hanne noticed that the vines began to intermingle with dense spiderwebs, and multiple carcasses of deer or horses—she could not discern which—were entwined in the webs.

She remembered Master Vakól's words: *Once you enter the grounds, the vines will show you the way. Present yourself with humility and hope she communes with you. Only then will you know her power.*

In her coven, the history surrounding the banishment spell was forbidden speak. From the quiet whisperings of the elders, Hanne had learned that a very important noblewoman, rumored to be an extremely powerful witch, a demi-demon, and the only daughter of

Bael himself, had been banished inside Hohenzollern Castle toward the end of the Renaissance—and she must be freed to initiate the next phase of Master Vakól's secret plan.

Hanne had heard a name once—Elizabeth Báthory.

After all her years studying witchcraft, Hanne was still largely ignorant of the happenings surrounding the Death Witch's banishment. Other than the general story, all she knew was that contacting the Death Witch was somehow integral to resurrecting Father Bael and his legion of demons. The specifics of these events were reserved for Master Vakól, for it was he—and only he—who was powerful and brave enough to carry the burden of such esotericism.

Hanne thought back to his descriptions of the Death Witch and envisioned kneeling before her in a display of submission and gazing upon her beautiful face. The ancient enchantress would smile down upon Hanne, recognizing her humility and also her potential for breaching the spell mostly unscathed. The Death Witch would order her to rise, and the two would embrace. Hanne's talents would be acknowledged, and they would commune together. Having every intention of being an apt student, Hanne fantasized that a mutual respect would kindle between them, and in time she might finally have someone to call a friend.

Hanne was determined to learn the Death Witch's secrets and return as the envy of her coven. She saw herself standing over all as they bowed before her—trembling at her might, quivering in fear of her wrath. At last, she would be strong and empowered enough to lash out at those who abused her. She would then walk away, create her own destiny, and never return. There would be no more manic scoldings from her unhinged mother, no more ruthless beatings from her narcissistic father, and no more ostracization from her so-called peers for her unusual height. But most importantly, Hanne envisioned a future where she never again endured the repulsive hands of Master Vakól and the other coven elders on her body.

As the unpleasant memories from her youth invaded her thoughts, Hanne grew anxious. She had to succeed. There was no other way. Finally, after all these years, she would be the one with power, and she had every intention of wielding it against all who caused her harm—then, now, and forevermore.

Part I: Die Todeshexe

Following the path laid before her, Hanne passed the dilapidated cathedral on her right. The plants appeared to lead her toward the larger central structure. She looked up to the sky and found her favorite constellation, Ursa Major, hovering just above the bastion's pinnacle. The closer she moved to the castle, the more the plant life became entwined with dense spiderwebs, which reflected the crescent moon's light and shimmered ever so slightly.

Hanne now found herself standing before the darkened stone archway that led into a grand hall. A rancid breath blew from the entrance's peaked arch, overwhelming her with the centuries of death and decay that had crept into the castle's mortar like rotting plaque. Hanne's mind was racing. There was no turning back. Even if she wanted to, Hanne knew the vines would revolt and drag her into the castle.

Searching for some source of bravery that would enable her to cross the threshold, Hanne thought back to an estival solstice celebration four years ago, when an athletic older boy named Karl tried to force himself upon her behind one of the mud huts in her village. Instead of screaming or crying as the boy muscled her to the ground, Hanne simply allowed him to pull down his trousers, then grabbed his testicles and squeezed them with such might that he passed out cold on the grass. After the encounter, the boys in the village kept a good distance from her. Hanne was raised to fight, and believed herself to be fearless. Whatever was waiting for her inside those walls, Hanne convinced herself that she was ready. She stepped forward and entered Hohenzollern Castle—the shadows appearing to swallow her lonely figure whole.

*

The change in temperature upon entering the castle was immediate. The mild spring air shifted to a dull freeze on Hanne's skin, and she noticed slight condensation from her breath rising from her mask. She stood very still for a moment and took in the bleak majesty of the decrepit expanse.

The vaulted ceiling of the once-stunning hall was partially destroyed—the moonlight flooded the darkened interior in a somber blue glow. Every portion of the hall was covered in spiderwebs.

Even the marble flooring was barely visible under its blanket of cobwebs. Hanne's bare feet were soon sticky with webbing as she walked into the main hall, which opened up into a bone graveyard with piles of animal and human bones stacked and strewn haphazardly about the floor.

The webs reflected a bluish-gray sheen as Hanne's eyes found Ursa Major through one of the larger holes in the ceiling. Some of the thin, beamed arches remained intact, and from them hung wrought-iron chandeliers that appeared decayed, as if the rust itself had oxidized to black from being encased in the dense webbing. Hanne looked to her left and counted five such chandeliers dangling from the ceiling, each slightly off its gravity's center. She envisioned one fierce gust of wind easily crashing the hanging lamps to the cracked marble floor.

Hanne's eyes followed the slight glimmer from the ceiling's faded gold-flecked inlays to the end of the hall. Despite the webs and decay, the structural integrity of the hall's perfect geometric lines remained intact, framing the scopic, arched windows aligned with gilded Corinthian columns that ran symmetrically along both sides of the gallery.

"Hello?" Hanne's voice echoed through the chamber.

Silence.

She turned to her left, where the webs grew more dense. At the very end of the hall, she could make out a short and wide staircase consisting of five stairs with an opening at its top. She closed her eyes and concentrated, but the room did not speak to her.

Hanne crossed the expanse to one of the broken arched windows and placed her hand upon the Corinthian column next to it. She peered down to the floor to see portions of skeletons strewn about, all tangled in webbing. Physiology was not a subject taught in her coven, but Hanne was certain the bones were human rib cages, pelvises, and either leg or arm bones. She remembered some of the outsiders her coven had kidnapped over the years to feed to the briar patch, and she wondered whether these bones belonged to anyone she'd witnessed in the past.

Hanne pulled some of the web apart and inspected it. The dense, sticky substance had the appearance of a very thin blanket, and it reminded her of the funnel spiderwebs she had grown accustomed to near her home. As she applied pressure to the webbing, it glowed faintly, and Hanne swore she could hear singing, as if some tiny ghoulish choir were crying out between her fingers. She rolled the web into a tiny ball and flicked it on the floor after several attempts to shake it free from her hand. She then pushed her hand more firmly upon the column and closed her eyes.

"What happened here? Where is this Death Witch?"

Hanne stood leaning into the column as a faint ringing resonated from somewhere above her. She opened her eyes to see the chandelier farthest from her swaying back and forth.

"Is it you?"

Hanne's only answer was her own echo.

She closed her eyes once more and concentrated on the column. The stone gave her no information, and Hanne almost ripped her helmet from her head in frustration. The only vision that flashed in her mind was of shadows of men and women entering the hall— limping and frightened, then becoming confused and entangled in the spiderwebs. Their harrowing screams resonated in her mind as she pulled her hand from the column.

"I'm over here," came a soft, feminine voice. Hanne thought it sounded almost musical.

She stepped away from the column and stared down the expanse toward the darkened staircase.

"Who enters my domain on her own volition?" came the voice once more.

This time, Hanne was certain the voice was resonating directly into her mind—it sounded angelic and hypnotic with the transient weightlessness of a mezzo-soprano.

Hanne walked to the center of the hall, trying to avoid the mounds of animal bones, debris, and random decay that riddled her path, her eyes still intent on the shadows at the hall's dead end.

"I've come to meet the Death Witch," called Hanne, her voice quivering slightly.

She continued toward the staircase, trying to perceive what lay in the shadows. Someone was there. Hanne was sure of it. A figure of a woman, she thought, stood in the darkened doorway.

"Reveal yourself!"

Hanne's impatience surged.

She tore the deer skull helmet from her head and tossed it to her feet.

"*Luciedeus!*" she yelled. A small ball of yellow light flew from her fingers and lit the darkness. The magick flare arced upward to the ceiling and fell slowly toward the floor. Nothing—no woman, no witch, only an empty, web-drenched doorway before her. Hanne watched with disappointment as the ball of light drifted to the floor. Just as the light extinguished itself, the hair on Hanne's neck grew rigid and a forceful shiver clamped her vertebrae—*it* was to her left.

She saw the shape in her periphery for certain: a white body the size of a mare with numerous black circles for eyes. Hanne's entire being seemed to calcify, as if her muscles had morphed to heavy, immovable granite. She craned her neck to the left as her eyes became accustomed to the dark once more.

It was there, lurking in the dark.

Nothing—nothing she had studied or learned—had prepared her for the grim vision before her. It skulked in the shadows, staring back at her with eight black eyes just above its sharp, ebon fangs. All eight of its legs tucked perfectly together as it concealed itself between two columns, camouflaging seamlessly with the webbing around it.

The creature moved its palps and stroked its face.

Hanne took in short, fierce breaths, trying not to hyperventilate as the massive white widow spider displaced its front two appendages into the moonlight and crept gracefully toward her. She tried to turn and run, but in her haste fell backward into a pile of bones, becoming quickly entangled in the spider's web. Hanne struggled, and in her panic, lost any semblance of a spell she might cast to free herself. But it was too late. The spider now hulked directly over her as she squirmed and whimpered, becoming helplessly entwined in the sticky mass.

"Now, now. Struggle, and I will only love you more."

With a slow, fluid motion, the spider extended its front appendage and plucked open the webbing covering Hanne's face with its claw. Hanne could feel her intestines cramping as she lay still and stared at the monstrosity before her.

Part I: Die Todeshexe

The pure white spider gazed back with black, emotionless eyes. It then reached its palp outward and caressed Hanne's face—the soft spindly hairs felt almost soothing upon her supple skin.

"My name's Elizabeth," said the spider. "What's yours?"

Chapter 4

4

March 21, 1917, 12:47 a.m.

Kaiser Wilhelm snapped awake from a deep sleep.

His head lay flat against the mattress, and he turned on his side to find his pillow on the floor next to his plush bed. He grabbed the plump cushion and placed it back underneath his head, then shifted to conform the down feathers to his head's shape. He ran his right hand through his thick, curled mustache and let out an extended exhale as his gaze moved to the darkened chandelier hanging from the domed ceiling of his living quarters.

The pins and needles in his left arm were causing him great discomfort. With his right arm, Wilhelm pulled the lame limb from underneath the duvet. Running his hand across the silken fabric, he grabbed the covers and pulled them upward, covering himself to his chest. The bubble of warmth under the blankets comforted him, but his feet were freezing. He positioned his left foot closer to his wife's body in hopes of warming his cold digits without disturbing her sleep.

"What's the matter, my darling?" asked Empress Augusta.

"Did I wake you?"

"You did."

"I'm sorry. I'm feeling troubled. I—"

"There's nothing to be done now," she said, rolling on her side to face him. Augusta reached out and caressed his face. "Such worry, such worry."

Wilhelm held her wrist and brought her hand to his mouth, placing a gentle kiss upon her knuckles.

Still a beauty, he thought, noticing how smooth her skin appeared in the moonlight shining through the west windows.

"The moonlight suits you, my beloved," he said. "I don't believe you've aged a day since we married."

Augusta smiled and grabbed his hand more firmly. "And once your goals are achieved, neither of us will ever age again."

Wilhelm let go her hand and sat at the edge of the bed.

Augusta shifted to him and wrapped her arms around his waist.

"What is it, Friedrich?"

Wilhelm knew well enough that when she used his first name, she was on to him.

"It's nothing. I felt something. A disturbance."

"For a mortal man, your intuition has never failed you. Are you certain you do not know?"

Wilhelm shook his head. "It's just a feeling I have. There's been a shift. I . . . I can't describe it."

What he couldn't tell her was that she would play no part in his quest for immortality because of her age. His seers had confirmed: at fifty-nine years old, one year his senior, she was too old to bear children. Her womb was barren. Not even a sip from the bottle would invigorate her so. He thought to his younger mistress, Nette, who would serve as his surrogate for the child once the bottle of Drăculea's blood was obtained, and a rare moment of guilt pricked his heart when he thought of the implications for Augusta.

Deep down, he knew she hid her suspicions about her part in his plans, but the two never spoke of it. Sensing that she might broach the subject, Wilhelm stood and moved to the Italian Renaissance mahogany chair that sat next to their bed. He grabbed his robe and slid his feet into his slippers.

"Where are you going, darling?"

"I need some air."

Wilhelm leaned over and planted a kiss on her forehead. "I'll be back soon. Rest for now."

*

Kaiser Wilhelm felt rattled as he leaned out the third-story window and flicked ash from his cigarette into the pleasure garden below. He scanned the lush garden for his personal security detail, knowing they had advised him time and again about smoking before an open window—especially since the beginning of the war. Deciding the heavy cloud cover provided enough darkness, he pulled the cigarette to his mouth and inhaled deeply. He watched the smoke rise and focused on the Berliner Dom in the short distance.

Gorgeous building. Simply magnificent, he thought.

Wilhelm looked to the dome's pinnacle and scowled, silently cursing the golden cross at its top.

"How hard is it to find a goddamn bottle of blood?" he lamented aloud. "Millions of marks wasted. And this conventional war will certainly deplete the treasury in less than three years . . . Nothing that won't be solved with more taxation, Wilhelm. Calm down . . . once France and England fall, their hoards are yours. You'll be the wealthiest man in the world in a year or less."

Wilhelm took a long drag from his cigarette, decided he was finished, and flicked the butt into the garden below. He pulled the window closed and flipped the latch, then jumped at a ghostly reflection appearing in the glass.

"Hello, Wilhelm," said Archduke Franz Ferdinand.

His ghastly specter stood behind Wilhelm, still wearing the white formal attire he was buried in after his assassination three years ago. The rotten flesh from a bullet exit wound on his neck hung over his collar, exposing his decayed thyroid cartilage and windpipe. His eyes appeared covered by thick cataracts and his face was gaunt—even skeletal—save his broad mustache, which remained as bushy and vibrant as it was on the day he was laid to rest. "Trouble sleeping?"

"Not you again," said Wilhelm, shaking his head while keeping his eyes on Franz Ferdinand's reflection. "Aren't you the one who should be sleeping? Goddamn permanently? Christ! How many more times must I suffer these intrusions?"

"Until you tell the truth."

Wilhelm placed his hand against the cool glass and leaned forward, grinding his teeth. "I don't think so, Ferdy. It's you who owes the confession. You attempted to betray me. It was you."

"I was always your most steadfast ally."

"Lies! Always with the lies. You just happened to be in Sarajevo for your health? Sure, Ferdy, sure. Nothing says 'summer holiday' like a very public and reckless visit into unfriendly territory. Some good it did you. Have you seen yourself lately?"

"Confess," said Franz Ferdinand, wheezing through his decomposing lips.

Wilhelm placed his right hand in his pocket and stood with a casual air, rocking on his heels as he glared at Franz Ferdinand.

"Fine, then. If you will leave me alone. Yes. I did it . . . I set you up. Happy?"

Franz Ferdinand moved his jaw, exposing lower teeth that were stained to black.

"And you know what?" continued Wilhelm. "I'd do it again and again, as it will never be traced to me. The public outcry surrounding your assassination has immeasurably strengthened my position. When my spies alerted me that you were seeking to steal Drăculea's blood behind my back, can you imagine my fury? So, yes—my secret police made you believe that Radu cel Frumos would meet with you and sell you the bottle for a small fortune. A ruse, Ferdy— one you eagerly fell for in a craven attempt to usurp me. Don't go blaming me that the Black Hand was wise to that! You moron."

"You alerted them to my arrival."

"And you stupidly remained after they bombed your car procession upon your arrival. Can you imagine?" Wilhelm laughed. "Just envision my chagrin when I heard the operation was botched. You fall for the setup, arrive to meet Radu, the Black Hand attempts to blow up your car . . . and you survive! The rage! I was planning to kill everyone involved for that failure. And then I get word that you decided to stay. How greedy were you? You and Sophie just had to have that bottle, life and limb be damned. Don't blame me the Serbs came back and put a bullet in your neck."

"And my leg."

"I wish it were your stupid face! I'm sick of staring at your rotten skull every time I cross a reflective surface. It's very annoying, Ferdy. You must stop."

"They shot my innocent wife."

"Ha! Innocent?" barked Wilhelm. "A ruthless hypergymist if there ever was one. She brought this on herself. A fate truly deserved—the both of you. And now, after all the mourning and anger? I declared war on Serbia. And the French? No. No. The French didn't like that one bit. So I said to them, 'We'll gladly pull our forces back if you hand over Radu cel Frumos.' They hemmed and they hawed and swore that no such person exists. So, hell! I went ahead and invaded Belgium and declared war on them too. I'll take that bottle by goddamn force if I must."

Wilhelm stared at the carpeting and a pursed grin appeared on his face. He glanced up at Franz Ferdinand's reflection.

"And the best news? I almost have it. My seers have predicted that we will locate the bottle any day now. And then I will drink half and Nette will drink half, and we will be granted immortality. Our child will be the most powerful entity on this earth, groomed to serve darkness, and my empire shall eclipse any rule that has ever been. You will rue the day you ever went behind my back. In fact—no. Don't go away. Bring the whole undead House of Habsburg-Lorraine with you, for all I care. I want you all to witness me march into Vienna with a legion of darkness in tow, then watch as your feckless nephew Charles is forced to bend the knee and hand over the Austria-Hungary Empire to me. The one true emperor of the world. You hear me?" Wilhelm was shouting. "Emperor of the goddamn world!"

He spun around to confront Franz Ferdinand, only to find his finger pointing into the air.

Wilhelm exhaled and ran his hand over his nightclothes. As he calmed himself, he looked to his desk, sitting toward the back of his neobaroque study.

What woke me? I wonder.

He decided the disturbance was related to a name he recalled from a summary document he'd read the day before. He walked to the desk and switched on a small desk lamp, then pulled a document from a folder that bore the title "FINAL REPORT OF

THE SECRET COMMITTEE TO STUDY INTELLIGENCE FAILURES OF OPERATION NOSFERATU WITH RESPECT TO KAISER WILHELM II." Wilhelm selected a black marker from the shot glass to his right that also contained several pencils and pens.

"They'll trace this back to you as well," came Franz Ferdinand's voice.

Wilhelm groaned and threw his head onto his arm on the desk. After resting for a moment and mumbling into his sleeve, he shot up and stared at Franz Ferdinand, whose reflection was cast in the desk's polished oak surface.

"Who? Who will, Ferdy? The French? The English? Nobody but me has the foresight to use supernatural technologies for hegemonic purposes! My spies tell me the Allies view paranormal activity as no more than quiet curiosity. So, tell me, who's going to believe that a bunch of vampires overran Saint Petersburg, after it's all covered up? Not even the Bolsheviks have figured it out. By the time this war is over, it won't matter. Darkness will rule the earth."

"What you did to that poor little boy and Empress Alexandra . . . she was practically your sister."

"My sister? Hmpf! Blame Ernest Louis for that. She was his actual sister."

Wilhelm and Franz Ferdinand continued to stare at one another.

"What?" screamed Wilhelm. "I gave you your confession. Can't you finally rest now? Filter on to the great beyond or whatever it is you ghouls do?"

"You'll pay for this, Wilhelm. You will see. A Romanov will be your demise."

Wilhelm slammed his fist into the table. "The Romanovs are dead! All of them. The whole wretched and expensive Nosferatu operation saw to that. Your part too has been played. Be gone!"

Franz Ferdinand's apparition slowly dissipated with a ghoulish, disembodied wail, and Wilhelm caught himself staring into his own face. He quickly slid the document before him to block his reflection.

"Finally," he said, letting out a breath and perusing the summary report on the failed Nosferatu operation.

Wilhelm gripped his marker, using it to redact all mentions of his name. After reaching the end of the document, he went back and paid particular attention to the summary of key assets and belligerents to ensure his name was blacked out. Satisfied that the document was scrubbed, Wilhelm returned the marker to the shot glass and grabbed a pencil. He then circled the name Felix Felixovich Yusupov several times before snapping the lead.

"What's his place in this? He wasn't Black Hundred. Nor was his family to my knowledge."

Wilhelm leaned back in his chair.

He pulled his limp left arm onto his lap, then placed his right hand behind his head while tapping his foot on the plush carpet. He watched the shadows from the lamp's flickering filament shift slightly on the ornate ceiling.

"How does a Russian aristocrat with no ties to this operation become a bona fide belligerent? Something's amiss."

Deciding his subconscious had pushed this bit of information to the forefront of his mind while he slept, Wilhelm pulled a piece of paper from his drawer. He plucked a pen from the glass holder.

I order immediate attention to this matter. I want a full dossier on the background of Prince Felix Yusupov of Russia, his family, and his conspirators delivered to me personally in twenty-four hours. Consult the seers.

He scribbled his signature upon the memo, returned the pen, then positioned the paper exactly center desk. Wilhelm switched off the light and walked back to his bedroom where Augusta was fast asleep, snoring face-first into her plush silk pillow.

*

TOP SECRET—CIPHER BUREAU EYES ONLY
Summary report recovered post-WWI from
Kaiser Wilhelm II archives
STAATSGEHEIMNIS [STATE SECRET]
ZUSAMMENFASSENDER BERICHT DER
PREUSSISCHEN GEHEIMPOLIZEI
[PRUSSIAN SECRET POLICE
SUMMARY REPORT]
MÄRZ 1917 [MARCH 1917]
ABSCHLUSSBERICHT DES GEHEIMEN
AUSSCHUSSES ZUR UNTERSUCHUNG VON
BETRIEBSFEHLERN DER OPERATION
NOSFERATU IN BEZUG AUF ▮▮▮▮▮▮▮
▮▮▮▮▮▮▮
[FINAL REPORT OF THE SECRET
COMMITTEE TO STUDY INTELLIGENCE
FAILURES OF OPERATION NOSFERATU WITH
RESPECT TO ▮▮▮▮▮▮▮▮▮

EINFÜHRUNG [INTRODUCTION]

Operation Nosferatu commenced on October 4, 1893. ▮▮▮▮▮▮▮▮ (now ▮▮▮▮▮▮▮▮) and Ernest Louis Charles Albert William, Grand Duke of Hesse and by Rhine entered into a pact with Russian operatives of the Black Hundred to overthrow the Russian aristocracy and decimate the Russian Empire through use of supernatural technology discovered through writings of Vlad Tepes (Vlad Drăculea, Vlad the Impaler).

ABSICHT [INTENT]

Operation Nosferatu is a dual-objective operation conceived to deliver supernatural technologies into the purview of the Prussian elite with certain vetted Russian aristocratic factions brought into the fold.

Objective one: To summon ancient vampires (Nosferatu) to the mortal plane for use as supernatural weapons in service of the Prussian Empire. Through the intended union of Princess Alix of Hesse and by Rhine (Alexandra Fyodorovna, empress of Russia) and Grand Duke George Alexandrovich of Russia, the operation's goal was to convert the aforementioned assets into prime vampires by infecting them with the bites of giant vampire bats that spawn in the blackwood forest of Loch Dracul deep within the Carpathian Mountains. Once converted, Alexandra and George would then procreate a vampiric child, who would be the human bloodlink for the bats to transform into Nosferatu. The intended purpose of this objective was to suppress the global populace by controlling and wielding Nosferatu and, in turn, render Russian leadership as a proxy government beholden to the Prussian Empire.

Objective two: To procure the last remnants of Vlad Drăculea's blood contained in a bottle harbored by his brother Radu cel Frumos, a.k.a. the Sommelier. The bottle was to be delivered to ███████████ to initiate a blood magick ritual outlined in Drăculea's writings, which would grant immortality to anyone who drinks from the bottle and reincarnate Drăculea as their child. For this objective, the intended vessels of the blood magick ritual were ███████████ and ███████████████. Seers of the highest order confirmed that the reincarnated Drăculea, upon reaching maturity, would wield the ultimate power over all supernatural entities, including the Nosferatu, giving those who controlled him total authority over all operations. With Drăculea and all subsequently acquired supernatural technologies at their command, the Prussian Empire would thus achieve global hegemony.

STATUS DER OPERATION [OPERATION STATUS]

Objective one: Defunct.
Results: Failed operation.

Objective two: Ongoing.

Results: Pending further ground invasion into Paris, where the Sommelier is rumored to be in hiding.

ZUSAMMENFASSUNG DER OPERATION [OPERATION SUMMARY]

Through multiple intelligence and infiltration misalignments, Operation Nosferatu, phase one, extended well beyond its initial intended timeline of two years into a twenty-three-year undertaking due to operation infiltration by Grigori Yefimovich Rasputin and Khlysts loyal to his agenda. Phase one concluded in failure on December 17, 1916 (OS), with confirmed deaths of Grigori Rasputin, Alexandra Fyodorovna, Alexei Nikolaevich, and Nicholas Aleksandrovich Romanov II. No further actions to resurrect the operation have been attempted or discussed.

Based on both intensive intelligence gatherings of the Prussian Secret Police and assistance from supernatural seers loyal to the German Empire, advisors cite no existing possibility or necessity to restart the operation. Bolshevik seizure of the Russian government removes the nation as an existential threat to German wartime operations.

Phase two is still underway and salvageable. Although it was agreed that the bottle would be delivered to ▮▮▮ ▮▮▮▮▮▮, Archduke Franz Ferdinand of Austria made a preemptive attempt to obtain it in secret and usurp ▮▮▮▮▮▮▮▮. After receiving intelligence of Franz Ferdinand's intention to interfere, ▮▮▮▮▮▮▮ created a plan to acquire the bottle by force from Radu cel Frumos and any persons harboring him in France.

In accordance with this plan, the Prussian Secret Police created a ruse, leading Franz Ferdinand to an undisclosed location in Sarajevo, Bosnia and Herzegovina, where he believed he would meet Radu cel Frumos. After the Prussian Secret Police alerted the Serbian organization the Black Hand of Franz Ferdinand's presence in the area, he was assassinated in Sarajevo. As restitution, ▮▮▮▮▮▮ demanded that the French government hand over Radu.

French authorities refused, claiming no such person existed, and one month later, the German and Austria-Hungarian Empires declared war on France and Serbia, citing Franz Ferdinand's assassination as the inciting event.

Owing to the inability of the Prussian Secret Police to acquire the needed supernatural technologies, the war has carried on for nearly three years and is currently at a stalemate. Royal seers have projected there is no foreseeable end to the war besides a truce, unless Drăculea's blood or some other dominant supernatural technology can be identified and procured.

SAMMLUNGEN VON INFORMATIONEN ÜBER SCHLÜSSELVERMÖGENSWERTE UND BELLIGERANTEN [INTELLIGENCE GATHERINGS OF KEY ASSETS AND BELLIGERENTS]

SCHLÜSSELVERMÖGENSWERTE [ASSETS]:

Alexandra Fyodorovna Romanov [TSARITSA OF RUSSIA, DECEASED]

Alexei Nikolaevich Romanov [TSAREVICH OF RUSSIA, DECEASED]

Nicholas Aleksandrovich Romanov II [TSAR OF RUSSIA, DECEASED]

Ernest Louis Charles Albert William [CABINET MEMBER OF ███████████████, ALIVE, BERLIN]

███████████████ [███████████████████, ALIVE, BERLIN]

Kir Oltan [BLACK HUNDRED OPERATIVE, STATUS UNKNOWN]

Dmitri Pavlovich [RUSSIAN GRAND DUKE, STATUS UNKNOWN]

Olaf Volkov (a.k.a. Olaf the Kind) [SUPERNATURAL, ALIVE, LOCATION UNKNOWN]

Charles Christopher Vondling [SUPERNATURAL, ALIVE, BUCHAREST]

BELLIGERANTEN [BELLIGERENTS]:

Grigori Yefimovich Rasputin [SUPERNATURAL, DECEASED]

Radu cel Frumos (a.k.a. the Sommelier) [SUPERNATURAL, ALIVE, ASSUMED TO BE IN PARIS]

Franz Ferdinand Carl Ludwig Joseph Maria [ARCHDUKE OF AUSTRIA-HUNGARY, DECEASED]

Rurik Borovitch Kozlov [RUSSIAN CORONER, VAMPIRE HUNTER, STATUS UNKNOWN]

Denis Borovitch Kozlov [EX OKHRANA AGENT, PROFESSOR OF CHEMISTRY, VAMPIRE HUNTER, CRYPTOZOOLOGIST, REANIMATOR, DECEASED]

Felix Felixovich Yusupov [RUSSIAN PRINCE, STATUS UNKNOWN]

ENDBERICHT [END REPORT]

*

"Hanne, my name is Hanne! I was sent by Vago Vakól."

Elizabeth withdrew her palp from Hanne's face and scurried backward.

"Vago Vakól is dead." Elizabeth sounded agitated.

"No!" protested Hanne with a quivering voice. "He's alive. He worships you. We all do."

Hanne could feel her heart thumping against her rib cage, her muscles growing tingly and numb. She now had a clear view of Elizabeth—eight gangling legs spread wide from her giant white body, ready to pounce.

"We?" she questioned.

Hanne's mouth was parched. She closed her lips and forced her tongue into her front teeth in an attempt to generate saliva.

"Yes, our coven," she said, gagging a bit. "We worship Bael and the Death Witch. But—"

"But what?" Elizabeth raised her legs slowly, vibrating the webs around them as her clawed appendages moved toward Hanne.

"He never told me . . . any of us . . . he never said—"

"That I, the Death Witch, was a spider?"

Elizabeth was close.

Hanne made out what appeared to be a clear liquid dripping from her black fangs. She closed her eyes, trying to think of any words that might convince Elizabeth to free her.

"No," was all she could muster. "He never mentioned . . . he never said what you had become."

"Become?" Elizabeth's voice was calm and soothing.

She crawled near Hanne and her eight eyes seemed to scan the young witch up and down, as if she were deciding what to do with her.

"I was sent here to commune with you. To let you know you still have allies!"

Elizabeth was silent.

"I am pure. I passed the test!"

"So you know I was once a woman?"

"Yes! Your name was Elizabeth Báthory. You—"

Elizabeth charged at Hanne, gripping her with her two front appendages.

"I am still Elizabeth Báthory, child!" she said angrily.

Hanne sobbed into hysterics.

Elizabeth released her grip on Hanne, crawled backward, and positioned herself to Hanne's left.

"Although you might be pure, fearless you are not."

Hanne took in a few deep breaths and calmed herself. "I *am* fearless," she said, sniffling. "I want to learn your powers. It's my destiny."

Elizabeth's head tipped to the side as she studied Hanne.

"I see you have brought my old battle helmet and scimitars. Do you take me for a fool?"

"No, of course—"

"Radu cel Frumos sent you here, did he not?"

"No, it was Vago . . . I swear!"

"The coward Radu. Not powerful enough himself to break my spell . . . Instead he sends a child to finish his—"

"Please!" begged Hanne, twisting to look at the scimitars. "Let me wield them in your name!"

"In my name? You? A mere blubbering girl? Hanne the assassin? Hanne the sneak? The moment I free you, you will plunge those blades into my heart and vanquish me forever!"

Elizabeth crept across Hanne's field of view until her white body sat directly before her. She lifted one leg at a time, placing each one closer to Hanne as she clambered near.

"My fangs are razors, my legs a vise, my heart black as a raven's talon! And you—you dare to slay me?"

"Please. I swear! What do you want?" shouted Hanne with tears rolling down her face.

"Oh, my poor, poor child. I want only one simple thing from you."

Elizabeth loomed over Hanne.

The liquid dripping from her fangs was now fully apparent as she rubbed her palps over her eight eyes, preparing to feed. Silence pervaded the room until Elizabeth shifted slightly, agitating the surrounding webbing and causing the chandeliers to sway—a chime rang out as their dangling crystals settled.

Elizabeth's black eyes were now intent on Hanne's webbed figure.

"Name your price. I'll do anything. What do you want?"

"Everything!" growled Elizabeth as she seized upon Hanne, wrapping the girl in her slim legs and sinking her fangs deep into Hanne's eye sockets. Hanne screamed and writhed from the pain, but the webbing had grown so tight around her that she was rendered immobile. Elizabeth placed her mouth over Hanne's face, silencing her screams, and began to suck the essence from her young body. A dull bluish-white light shone from Elizabeth's jaws and suffused her translucent body as Hanne's soul slid down her esophagus and into her blackened stomach.

After another moment, it was done.

Elizabeth backed away from Hanne's corpse, rubbing her palps across her face. A sullen quiet settled on the great hall as she crept to her hiding spot and tucked herself away.

Of all the souls Elizabeth had swallowed, Hanne's felt the most satisfying—the most powerful, nearly exceeding those of the arch-angels she had consumed when she was still in human form. Elizabeth repositioned herself, finding a more comfortable pocket in her webbed lair to support her abdomen, and continued to stare at Hanne's lifeless, entangled body.

Three hundred and three years this August.

She thought of Vago and her heart welled with an emotion she hadn't felt since becoming trapped in the spider's body. What if it was true? What if Vago was alive? What if this young witch had been sent to commune with her? Elizabeth recalled a previous visitor—a young boy who arrived before her, gravely mauled and delirious with gaping flesh wounds across his body. As with most who arrived at the castle, his jaw was partially torn off, hanging by a single condylar process, and his tongue had been shredded by the thorns. The boy was muttering unintelligibly before she attacked and consumed him, but there was powerful magick within his blood. There had been several such victims over the centuries. Perhaps those too were sent by Vago?

And then she remembered the day she first awoke in Hohenzollern Castle, realizing she was no longer human; realizing that a mere war-lock with powers nowhere near her own had bested her.

Radu cel Frumos!

A rage kindled inside Elizabeth and her mind flashed back to their duel. Radu was beaten. She merely needed to finish him off. And in that moment of calm confidence, Radu released the wretched spider from his ethereal cloak. Shock and dismay crippled Elizabeth as the white arachnid attacked her face and wrapped its powerful legs around her head, sinking its fangs deep into her eye-balls. The spider sucked down her soul and forever entwined her consciousness within its body. Vertigo, blackness, then finally—fear. For the first time in her life, Elizabeth knew terror upon waking in a burlap sack on the castle's cold marble floor, her spider legs still wrapped around what was once her own head, now decay-ing and rancid. But there would be no furs, no hearth to warm her.

Instead, Elizabeth found what would become her only source of comfort in her new prison: hatred. An ever-present animus that festered beyond mania as she came to understand exactly what she had become.

Elizabeth cleared the thought and focused her energies on the Void. Although the static surrounding the banishment hex had been growing weaker, her ability to commune with the Void was still greatly hindered. Elizabeth hadn't felt its true power for centuries—tonight was no different.

Realizing that Hanne had not been aggressive, Elizabeth began thinking of her arrival as a sign.

Certainly Radu would have prepared the girl better for confrontation.

Vago. Oh, my Vago. Could it be true?

Sensing that she could very well have allies beyond the castle's walls and that she had not been forgotten over the centuries, Elizabeth fused together a vision—a plan to escape these walls once and for all.

Her black eyes settled on the purebred witch, one—if she was to be believed—conceived and raised to serve her. One who proved her merit by breaching the darkest of spells Elizabeth had cast upon the forest. She now understood Vago's intention, as before her lay a vessel strong enough to withstand and carry her power.

And with one forceful breath through her thorax, the white widow spider who was once the Hungarian noblewoman named Elizabeth Báthory decided it was time.

"Rise!" she commanded. Her disembodied voice rang through the expanse. "Rise now, my harbinger of death!"

Hanne sat up at once, easily freeing herself from the webbing.

She glared at Elizabeth.

Her skin had grown pasty, her hair the texture of dry, crazed silage. The deep, cratered scars carved below her brow shimmered, coagulating to black as melanoid varicose veins spread from her eye sockets to her cheeks and forehead.

"What now, Mother?" asked Hanne, her voice low and hoarse.

"Now . . . ? Why, now we have my revenge."

5

March 21, 1917, midday

"Withdrawal to the Hindenburg Line is complete as of five o'clock this morning, Kaiser," said Minister of War Hermann von Stein. "As you so brilliantly strategized, the shorter line will strengthen the front with fewer units necessary for defense. I envision this will free as many as thirteen or fourteen divisions."

"Which?" asked Wilhelm, seated at the head of the monolithic polished black table. His mustache pointed sharply downward and his blue eyes seared into Stein.

Stein swallowed, aware that the eleven other cabinet members were equally focused on him, as all knew—the more sharply downward Wilhelm's mustache pointed, the more furious his mood.

"Which what, my Kaiser?"

Wilhelm's jaw pulsed and his pupils contracted to tiny specks.

"Yes . . . yes, of course," stuttered Stein. "Fourteen, Kaiser. Fourteen."

Wilhelm continued to glare at him in silence.

"Hermann, do you dye your mustache?" asked Wilhelm, cocking his head.

Stein appeared surprised.

"Kaiser, I—"

"Stop doing it. Appears as if shoe polish is slathered upon your lip. It's an embarrassment."

Stein hung his head as quiet chuckles ran round the table.

"Then, you're certain," continued Wilhelm. "Fourteen divisions?"

"I feel moderately certain."

Wilhelm stood, knocking over his high-backed chair and planting his right fist onto the table's black surface.

"Kaiser is standing!" yelled General Hindenburg.

The twelve seated men grabbed their pickelhaubes, placed them upon their heads, and stood at attention.

"You feel, or you know?" asked Wilhelm curtly.

Stein produced a short, quick nod. "I know. I—"

"Fifteen thousand men per division. That is why this matters," said Wilhelm in a quiet, calm voice. "There is quite a large difference in actual manpower between thirteen and fourteen divisions. Another perfect example of the sloppy estimations that have kept this war raging for three years."

"Yes, Kaiser. But that was my predecessor."

"Cowards blame others. Cowards do not sit at my table. Understood?"

Stein hung his head once more. "Yes, Kaiser."

"'Yes, Kaiser.' It's always 'Yes, Kaiser.' Then you all simply slink away to your respective purviews and continue to drag out this war. Always telling me what you think I want to hear and nothing else. Now, Minister, with your firm estimation that we have freed fourteen divisions instead of thirteen, that gives us fifteen thousand more infantry to place at Arras. Now tell me why that is important."

"It's important because of the bombardment of Vimy Ridge—"

"Enough!" yelled Wilhelm. "This is for all of you. Except General Hindenburg and Prince Henry." He shot out his finger and pointed in turn to each and every one of his council, standing with their broad mustaches and piked helmets upon their heads. "You are to be the ones telling me answers. Not estimations. Not 'hopefully.' Not 'probably.' 'Hopefully' does not win battles! I am starting to find very little value in advisors when it is always me doing the advising. I command you all, shore up your respective authorities, and no more sloppy estimations. Numbers matter!"

Wilhelm punctuated the statement with a short, frustrated breath from his nostrils. Scowling, he leaned over the map on the table, paying specific attention to the line defining the western front, which ran a jagged red just east of Dunkirk at its north all the way south to the Swiss border just east of Belfort, France.

His index finger moved to Arras.

"This!" he said, while tapping on Arras. "This is why numbers are important. One hundred seventy-eight kilometers. Three years. In three years, the closest we have broken the line to Paris. One hundred seventy-eight kilometers from that stinkhole filled with filthy, weak Parisians mocking us at every advance. Arras is their last line of defense, and it's finally in our sights. If we take Arras, Paris will fall. When Paris falls, so does London—easily. And then New York. The favor will be ours. Tell me you understand."

"I understand, Kaiser," said Minister Stein.

"And?" Wilhelm questioned the remaining cabinet.

"We understand," they said, nearly in unison.

"Excellent. I take it you will pass along this attitude to your field marshals. You may be seated." Wilhelm turned around and repositioned his chair. The sounds of wooden chairs sliding upon the marble and the shuffling of polished patent leather boots filled the gilded expanse of Knights' Hall as the cabinet members settled.

Wilhelm rested his left arm on his lap and placed his right hand on a folder marked "Staatsgeheimnis."

"Prince Henry," he said, looking to his younger brother. "I believe you have something to show us."

All interest moved to Henry as he walked to a large box draped with a purple velveteen curtain just to Wilhelm's right. He was dressed in a perfectly crisp military ensemble, and his gray beard shone to near silver in the light pouring in from the hall's windows. Henry gripped the fabric over the top corner of the box, then looked to Wilhelm.

"May I, Brother?"

"Proceed," said Wilhelm, exuding an air of pride.

Henry pulled the curtain from an open wire-rimmed cube to reveal a long torpedo propped a meter from the floor, upon metal posts.

A hushed chatter filled the room.

Wilhelm stood at his brother's side, placing his hand atop Henry's golden epaulet.

"Come," said Wilhelm, moving toward the smooth cylinder. "Join us. I want all to see the next phase of our naval operations—designed and engineered by my brother himself."

Wilhelm's council members moved to the display, their pickel-haubes giving them the appearance of a crash of formally dressed rhinoceroses as they flocked around the torpedo. A few of the men ran their hands over the smooth metal surface, while others squatted to inspect the propeller system.

"This!" said Wilhelm, tapping the nose of the torpedo, "is what will finally deliver us high-seas superiority."

"Tell us," said Stein, hoping his interest would find some favor with Wilhelm.

"Our torpedo arsenal fails far too often," began Wilhelm. "Better than the Allies, but not good enough. Currently, once a torpedo is fired and reaches its target, three in ten will merely leave a nasty dent in the side of their mark. No longer."

"Pure potassium," interjected Henry. "Guaranteed to explode upon every impact."

"How can you guarantee this?" asked General Ludendorff.

"Elementary chemistry," said Wilhelm. "Pure potassium in contact with water creates a fierce chemical reaction. No need for wires or switches. The moment the hull is breached, the potassium explodes, causing the rest of the payload to ignite and obliterate any target. It's light, compact, and three times faster than our previous arsenal. None have failed thus far." Wilhelm placed his hand on the torpedo's shaft. "Interestingly enough, the reaction will cause a massive purple explosion. Hence the code name: Purple Demon."

"Can we use it on land?" asked Ludendorff, sounding excited.

Wilhelm shot him a curious glance. "Did you not hear the part about reacting with water, General?"

Ludendorff slouched and shuffled off behind General Hindenburg.

Wilhelm grimaced. "Since annexing Romania, we are now in possession of their vast natural resources. With the assistance of our operative in command of the Bucharest operation, we have managed to seize and upgrade a small and remote mining operation in Zănoaga, eighty kilometers north of Bucharest, where we discovered likely one of the largest potash deposits in the Eastern Hemisphere."

"And through that," continued Prince Henry, "we can refine not only an endless supply of potassium nitrate for our explosive needs, but a voluminous load of pure potassium for our Purple Demon arsenal. No more blockades. The seas are ours, gentlemen."

"Hear, hear!" shouted Stein as a less-than-enthusiastic round of applause rose from the group.

Ludendorff poked his head from behind Hindenburg. "Might I ask, Kaiser, where have we come about the labor resources for a sustained mining operation capable of meeting such demands? It is my understanding there is only one division stationed outside of Bucharest—and that is mostly specialized tank operators."

"Labor has been accounted for," said Wilhelm. "Our operative in Bucharest has devised a method to man the mines. We are now producing . . . let's just say, the clock's hands will spin and there will never be a lag in output."

"Excellent news," said Ludendorff. "And might I ask when we will be privy to the information surrounding this Bucharest operative? He's not military, to my understanding."

Wilhelm stared at him with a cool, commanding gaze. "No. He is not." His right arm swung wide. "Meeting adjourned. You are all dismissed."

The advisors saluted Wilhelm and shuffled from Knights' Hall through the massive brocade-coffered entrance. Wilhelm watched as the last of his men exited the hall, then he returned to his chair. He looked down to the folder before him, opening it to a document titled "Staatsgeheimnis: Dossier über Prinz Felix Felixovich Yusupov."

*

Empress Augusta glided down the Schlüter staircase in her white silken gown. Holding her suede pouch close to her abdomen, she reached the bottom of the sweeping Italian baroque stairs and took a lingering glance down the passage that led to Knights' Hall. Even in the distance, she could hear the booming echo of her husband's voice as he chided his cabinet. Two armed soldiers stood at attention just before the sealed doors leading to the hall, and Augusta made a mental note to remind Wilhelm that others could eavesdrop on his meetings unless he kept his voice at a more respectable volume.

She turned right and entered her favorite parade room, the Chamber of the Black Eagle—one of the few remaining designed by Andreas Schlüter himself. Wilhelm had expressed interest in renovating the room several times, citing his annoyance at its pro-Catholic themes, but Augusta refused, saying the chamber was her favorite space within the palace. She briefly looked to the rich ceiling fresco. Framed by ornate golden baroque crown moldings, it depicted the Siege of Aachen in 1614, featuring Count Wolfgang Wilhelm as a fierce hooded rider, sitting high on his black steed as he smashed a morning star down on a mob of his Protestant enemies.

Her eyes fell upon the grandfather clock in the room's corner.

Watching the golden pendulum sway back and forth, Augusta swore it seemed to quicken in step with her own rising pulse. She reminded herself there was still time to turn back, but she also knew time was her enemy. Augusta overheard the seers herself: the Kaiser would locate the bottle of Drăculea's blood in less than one week. She knew acting with expediency was the only means to keep these unfolding events tipped in her favor—immortality was still within her grasp. Her red blood cells chilled as she imagined the catty whispers behind her back if Wilhelm were to conceive a child with his younger mistress. Augusta had no intention of becoming a laughingstock within the royal court. She and Wilhelm had been kinder and more patient with one another lately, but paranoia claimed her—for all she knew, his kindness was a façade and his secret cabal was drafting up divorce papers this very instant.

Augusta peered back into the hall to ensure none of her staff had followed her, then moved to the gold-flecked grandfather clock. She opened its glass face and proceeded to set the clock hands to midnight. The clock chimed and Augusta pushed her weight onto it, sliding it slightly to her left until she heard a click. The tips of her fingers ran along the red and golden velveteen damask wallpaper behind the clock and found a circular iron handle. She pulled on it, revealing a slim corridor that led to a descending stone stairwell.

She stared into the darkened passage—her heart now a fist, mercilessly boxing her rib cage. Knowing there was no turning back once she engaged, Augusta took one final inventory of her decision. She had to secure her place as Wilhelm's sole consort. A kidnapping or a contract killing would certainly be traced back to her. Especially once General Hindenburg became involved. This was the answer. Nobody, not even her personal seer, seemed to have any notion of her past summonings. Augusta believed someone or something was concealing them, and she was convinced that today would be no different.

As her slight figure stood before the secret door, Augusta thought to the nightmare that woke her earlier that morning—the hooded man had appeared to her once again. The dream had grown fuzzy as the day wore on, but she remembered a portion of the vision where the hooded man moved in behind her and placed his hands upon her belly, whispering to her as her abdomen grew plump with child. *Summon and sacrifice unto her and ye shall conquer, else . . .* came the hooded man's words as the pressure of her ballooning stomach became too much to bear. Her flesh burst open and a quiver of asps slithered from her pelvis, violently waking Augusta as she sat up in bed, gasping for breath. Despite the dream's horrific ending, and her alarm at the reappearance of the hooded man, she felt a strange tinge of satisfaction at the fading reality of feeling pregnant. The sensation dissipated when she looked to her nightstand to see a pair of pliers sitting upon the polished wood.

With lead in her heart, she picked up the pliers. The mirror beneath the palace was calling her.

Augusta swirled her tongue along her teeth, trying to remind herself that she was brave enough to continue. Opening her pouch, she pulled out a small whiskey flask and downed its entire contents, shaking her head at the alcohol's sharp bite. She returned the flask and as the booze coated her esophagus, sending warm shivers over her shoulders, Augusta found her resolve. A few brief moments of agony were nothing compared to a life of shame, pity, and ridicule—and in her mind, momentary physical pain was far preferable to the lifelong malady of losing out to a younger woman of lesser noble status. But most importantly, Augusta would not lose her chance at immortality. She gripped her pouch and crept down the darkened stairs. Upon reaching the bottom, she pushed a rusty iron lever, and the door above slid quietly shut.

A snap echoed through the cramped stone corridor, and light emanated from Augusta's hand. She lit four candles on a bronzed candelabra that stood in the hallway, which she carried to her secret room at the end of the corridor. Augusta pulled open the rusty barred entrance to the tiny room. Only about five square meters, its sole decoration was an ornately carved alderwood vanity holding a foxed mirror adorned with a silver frame carved with trumpeted cherubs and wide oak leaves.

Augusta placed her pouch upon the vanity alongside her candelabra. She inhaled through her nose and tried to ignore the room's overwhelming musty smell. Reaching into her pouch, Augusta produced a small vial filled with lavender essential oil and dabbed it on her wrist. She rubbed her wrists together as the smell eased her senses. She corked the vial and stared into the mirror that did not cast her reflection.

At fifty-nine years of age, she was still a striking beauty. Her hair of pure silver was pinned into a neat bun, and her aura was that of a younger, confidant woman. She ran her fingers along her crow's feet, silently cursing the wrinkles as anger welled within.

"I will not be shut out," she said, looking into the mirror with defiance in her tear-filled eyes.

Augusta took a few calming breaths, then reached into her pouch. She removed the pliers, a lock of brown hair, an athame with a carved ebony handle, a picture frame, a small silver ashtray, and a beige bandage. She arranged the items on the vanity, then closed her eyes and clenched her fists.

It had to work this time. The hooded man in her dreams had confirmed it: there was a powerful and greedy witch named Gunda trapped in the mirror, who could make Augusta's wishes come true if only she paid a price. Yet, time and time again, the small cuts she riddled her body with yielded no magical spirit within the glass. Augusta had been studying the grimoire that had mysteriously appeared on her nightstand just before her discovery of the clock's secret passage. She now knew the invocations by heart, but more importantly, she was prepared to follow the hooded man's instructions and sacrifice whatever was necessary to Gunda's greedy desires. Augusta took a deep breath, opened her eyes, and stared into the infinite black of the mirror's surface.

"I do invoke and conjure thee, O spirit." Her voice was low and rhythmic, echoing in the tiny stone enclave. "And being with power armed from the Supreme Majesty, I do strongly command thee by him who spake and it was done, and unto whom all creatures be obedient. Unto thee imprisoned and banished from this realm,

I say reveal thyself upon this enchanted glass. Grant me your power, your wisdom. The great one, mighty and strong—thrice I invoke thee! Greedy Gunda, Greedy Gunda, Greedy Gunda. My offering is of blood to thee whom I invoke."

Augusta opened her eyes, disappointed to see nothing but reflectionless glass. She held her athame in her right hand and ran the blade along the meaty portion of her left hand's thenar eminence, careful to avoid the thin white scars from her previous cuttings, believing the mirror preferred a fresh rupture of the flesh. Gripping her hand tightly, Augusta held her bleeding palm over the silver ashtray as the red liquid dripped into the vessel.

A frost began crystallizing upon the rim of the mirror, exciting Augusta.

"Thee I invoke," she said, quietly.

Augusta closed her eyes and squeezed her fist as the blood dripped into the tray. "Greedy Gunda, Greedy Gunda, Greedy Gunda."

With her eyes still closed, Augusta found the bandage and wrapped it around her hand, satisfied her blood offering was sufficient. The room grew cold, and the sensation of rime ice pelting the back of her neck sent a quivering chill over her skin. Augusta opened her eyes and nearly yelped to see a version of herself reflected in the mirror—one with pale, rotting flesh and exposed teeth through her torn cheek. Augusta noticed the image was missing several molars on both the top and bottom of its mouth as well as its left eye.

"Who summons me?" said the reflection, barely moving its mouth.

Augusta placed her hands on the rim of the ashtray and bowed her head.

"I am humbled before you, O Gunda, spirit of greed. I beg thee— accept my offering of blood."

The rotting reflection peered down to the offering with its horrifically bloodshot eye.

Augusta held the picture frame with a photo of a young dark-haired woman before the spirit in the mirror, who flashed its smile filled with blackened and missing teeth.

"Her name is Nette. She is my rival," said Augusta. "Young and very beautiful. She has usurped me in the affections of my husband. And for that, I command thee to curse her womb and drown her in sorrow and agony. I don't care what you do to her, but it can never be traced back to me."

Augusta grabbed the lock of hair and held it to the candle, igniting the strands.

"A lock of her hair, inflamed and drowned in blood," she said, before dropping the flaming hair into the ashtray.

The horrific reflection watched with a mocking smile.

"For such dealings, I require more," it said, staring down to the pliers. "You know exactly what I desire." Gunda ran her rotten fingers over the gap in her cheek as she clicked her teeth together.

Augusta stared at the ghostly reflection for a long moment. Although frightened and reluctant, she was committed to her decision. Her hands felt for the pliers on the vanity. She took a breath, then inserted them into her mouth as their metallic essence spread across her taste buds. The tool found its way to her upper first molar, and Augusta squeezed the tooth, twisting and pulling with dire force. Pain seared through her skull and quickly consumed her with white-hot pangs nipping at her toes, shocking her system so greatly that she felt the sudden urge to urinate. Augusta accepted the pain as best she could, continuing to yank and pull as tears filled her eyes before she finally plucked out her molar with a great wail.

She dropped the tooth into the pool of gore.

The spirit stared on with an unsatisfied gaze.

"You require more of me?" asked Augusta, wiping the tears and snot from her face before placing her hand upon her jaw and massaging the soreness.

"I always require more."

Augusta's mouth thumped with incredible misery. Certainly, she could take no more.

She thought to run away—to close the passage and never return. Instead, she stared at the ghastly apparition as it faded to a wispy vision within the mirror, transforming itself into Nette. Her young rival looked radiant, standing next to Wilhelm, who raised their newborn child into the air as cheers and applause erupted from a small circle of royal admirers. Augusta saw herself standing behind them, appearing much older—even gaunt—as she slunk toward the tapestries and hung her head. All the while, her petty noblewoman peers and servants seated at the gathering pointed at her and covered their mouths, quietly snickering at the washed-up, barren empress.

"Throw the relic in the attic where she belongs!" came a voice, causing all in attendance to burst out in mockery toward Augusta.

The vision dissipated and Gunda reappeared.

"Fine," said Augusta, sniffling a bit. "Have it your way."

Augusta thought over the vision while swallowing the salty blood slowly filling her mouth. Deciding she would not be reduced to some pitiful, royal joke and slowly succumb to old age as Wilhelm lived forever, she raised the pliers once more—this time finding her bottom second molar on the opposite side. She gagged and choked as blood streaked down her chin, staining her porcelain skin a ruby red. A terrible cracking filled the room and with one more forceful grunt, Augusta plunked another molar into the offering tray. She moaned and breathed heavily, again moving her hand to her jaw to apply pressure to her wounded gums.

Never taking its gaze from Augusta, the spirit reached from the mirror and plucked a bloody tooth from the tray with a pale, rotting hand missing its ring finger. Augusta watched as it shoved the molar into the side of its cheek, filling an empty space. The specter jerked its neck and the sounds of bones cracking bounced from the chamber walls. It then reached for the remaining tooth, again inserting it into a space among its bottom molars. Through its torn flesh, Augusta watched as the spirit ground its jaws together while adjusting its new teeth into place.

"Bring this rival before me," said Gunda, before vanishing to blackness.

Augusta was alone, staring into the reflectionless mirror.

She stood, woozy from the throbbing pain stabbing her gums. Lifting the candelabra, she proceeded back down the darkened corridor.

Chapter 6

6

March 21, 1917, evening

Night settled over the Berlin Palace.

"Emperor, I advise you once more to stay away from the window when smoking," said General Hindenburg. "I sense there are bad intentions nearby."

Wilhelm rolled his eyes and looked at the shadows cast by the waning crescent moon upon the pleasure garden below.

"I've been sensing bad intentions ever since my coronation, General."

Realizing the moonlight was brighter than he'd expected, Wilhelm decided Hindenburg was correct. He flicked the cigarette out the window and returned to his council.

Wilhelm stared across his desk to his four closest advisors: General Hindenburg, his younger brother Henry, Grand Duke Ernest Louis, and Minister of Arts and Sciences Friedrich Schmidt—the Council of the Black Eagle, as they had named themselves. Thumbing through several folders, Wilhelm removed the dossier regarding Felix Yusupov and placed it in the center of his desk.

"Now," said Wilhelm, "before we begin, update me on Bucharest."

Hindenburg shifted slightly in the small chair barely able to contain his bulk. He folded his blocky hands on his lap, and Wilhelm thought momentarily as to what power the burly man must generate with a punch.

Missed his calling as a pugilist.

"Vondling has Bucharest overrun," began Hindenburg.

Wilhelm listened intently for a moment, then lost interest as Hindenburg went on one of his usual long-winded and overly specific tactical analyses about the division surrounding the city and which exact inlets and outlets they guarded—and why. Wilhelm was pleased to hear an entire tank garrison now guarded Bucharest's perimeter, making it essentially impregnable. Hindenburg assured him they could hold the territory indefinitely. Especially since the allies and surrounding areas were under the impression that, in addition to being fiercely guarded by German forces, Bucharest was also suffering from a horrid plague.

Hindenburg continued on and Wilhelm rolled his eyes at his brother Henry.

Taking the cue, Prince Henry interjected, "And you truly believe this new operative, Charles Vondling, can be trusted?"

"Under no circumstances can Vondling be trusted," said Hindenburg. "He is what we call a belligerent asset. He will turn on us the moment a higher bidder comes along."

"Then we kill him," said Wilhelm. "Seize the operation."

Hindenburg raised his wide palm. "Not so fast. Richthofen and members of Jagdstaffel Eleven arrived only this morning. Their conversion is taking place as we speak."

Wilhelm nodded in approval, knowing his air command would soon dominate the skies.

"With our loss of the Nosferatu in Saint Petersburg," continued Hindenburg, "vámpir are currently the next-best weapon in our arsenal until we complete our trial runs with the Romanian ustrel. And as we have experienced in the past . . . well, vámpir are a wayward technology. Self-serving, even potentially timid in lesser numbers. Terrible soldiers, but excellent for overwhelming a city.

"Perhaps a vampiric witch could oversee the operation, but until one is located, Vondling is enthralling the Romanian vámpir to his will through the blood magick defined in the Impaler's grimoire. For now—he stays. He loves gold as much as he does power. We have provided him with both."

"And if he goes wayward?" asked Wilhelm.

"Then we fumigate the entire city," said Hindenburg. "In our inquiry into the failed Saint Petersburg operation, my seers and I put together an image of one of the belligerents, a vampire hunter named Denis Kozlov. Obviously, we became curious as to how three vampire hunters broke the defenses of the Nosferatu within the Winter Palace. Turns out this Kozlov fellow had invented a new weapon to be used against vampires—a novel and noxious gas."

Wilhelm cocked his head. "A gas?"

"Yes. A phototoxin created from a plant called giant hogweed—one that behaves as a light accelerant. Essentially vaporizes vámpir, Nosferatu, or ustrel upon contact."

"A gas we can easily deploy from biplanes if and when necessary," said Ernest Louis.

Wilhelm smiled. "Clever. And you can procure this gas?"

All eyes shifted to Schmidt, whose unruly mustache covered his upper lip and bobbed outward as he spoke. "Why, yes," he said. "General Hindenburg and I have already begun the necessary steps to procure the hogweed and produce the gas. We will have a batch ready for deployment in two days or less."

"Minister," said Wilhelm, "I am going to command you one more time. Trim your goddamn mustache! I can't take anything you say seriously with that unsightly hair curtain blowing with every syllable. It's very distracting."

Schmidt nodded.

Wilhelm leaned back into his chair, feeling satisfied. "Ustrel," he said.

"Kaiser?" questioned Hindenburg. "What of them?"

"How are they different from vampires?"

Hindenburg patted Schmidt on the forearm. "That would be Minister Schmidt's area of expertise."

Schmidt sat forward.

"I would very much appreciate the chance to do my presentation for you, Kaiser. I feel it's important we are all clear on the variety of these technologies so that there are never any muddled commands or operations. I have created a very enriching slide show on my magic lantern, and—"

"A quick summary will do," said Wilhelm, sounding bored.

Wilhelm noticed Schmidt slump his shoulders and place his hand on a leather-bound carrier box at the side of his chair as the rest of the group cocked their heads, seemingly curious about the contents of the box. Realizing that Schmidt's presentation might provide some much-needed amusement and camaraderie, Wilhelm relented.

"On second thought, Minister, please proceed. I have become suddenly curious about this magic lantern."

Schmidt lifted his head and his eyes brightened. "Why, of course, my Kaiser."

The men all shifted in their chairs, trying to find a comfortable position as Minister Schmidt opened his box and pulled out a blocky device that had a small silver cannon with a glass lens sticking from its front. He then removed a cylindrical metal object that he unfolded and set up a projection screen.

"May I use your desk, Kaiser?" questioned Schmidt.

Wilhelm slid his chair back, making room, and Schmidt set down the device, pointing the metal cannon toward the screen. He reached down to unplug Wilhelm's lamp from an electrical outlet under the desk, and the room fell dark for a moment until he connected his device and flipped a switch on its top.

A burning smell filled the air, followed by a hum as a blurry image projected onto the screen.

"Very interesting," said Ernest Louis. "But it's mechanical, is it not? I thought you said it was magick."

"Oh," said Minister Schmidt. "No. Not magick. But new technology that might seem magical to mortals, so I assume that's how it was named. Emerging technologies of mortals are but a small hobby of mine, and I am quite enamored with this device. See for yourselves." Schmidt wrapped his fingers around the metal cannon and fumbled with a dial until the image came into focus.

Prince Henry looked to Wilhelm and both men nodded in wonder to see a clear illustration of a giant white bat hanging upside down from a dark tree.

"And here it is!" said Schmidt, smiling. "The Holy Upir—the giant vampire bats that spawn in the blackwood forest of Loch Dracul. And now—" Schmidt pressed on the slide sticking from the lantern's side and a new illustration appeared on the screen, this one of a man and woman with bite marks on their necks, kneeling before a giant bat hovering above them.

"Amazing!" said Ernest Louis.

"The bats bite a man and woman, who then become the prime vampires in the ritual to spawn Nosferatu." Schmidt moved the slide to an illustration of the man and woman holding up a child.

Behind them stood an army of fanged Nosferatu. "Once they mate and give birth to a human-formed child, then the Holy Upir can transform to Nosferatu—"

Wilhelm slammed his fist on the desk. "This I know! You're reminding me of Saint Petersburg . . . Ustrel!"

Schmidt nodded. "Of course." He flipped quickly through a few slides before settling on an illustration of a fanged man in a high-collared black cloak. "But, firstly—vámpir. Vampires created by other vampires via a venomous injection in the nape of the neck, deep into the spine. Vámpir are never created by accident. Culturally, it seems vámpir regard this transfer as a great gift—"

"Did you just say 'culturally'?" interjected Wilhelm.

"Well, yes, Kaiser. I believe that's the best way to understand how these creatures behave, so that we may control them."

"They're savages," said Wilhelm. "Don't speak in such a manner again. Sounds like something a Communist would say."

"Yes, Kaiser. But vámpir are a wide class, you see," said Schmidt, pressing the slide so that a bulleted list of text appeared on screen. "There are human vampires—they have magical abilities, can transform between their human and hunting forms, perform some environment manipulation—but it is the vampiric witch who wields the power over other vámpir due to their extraordinary abilities. Very powerful entities."

"Rasputin?" asked Wilhelm.

"Vampiric witch," affirmed Schmidt.

"Vondling?"

"Human vampire or simply vámpir," said Hindenburg. "That is not to say he could not acquire further skills, but for now, he is not as great a threat as he may seem."

"Not entirely reassuring," said Wilhelm. "But proceed, Minister."

"I must warn you, gentlemen," said Schmidt. "What you are about to see next is not only historic but terribly horrific." He pushed the slide fully into the lantern and a new image came into view. "Behold—the first and only photograph of a living ustrel."

Gasps.

"My God!" exclaimed Wilhelm.

"This is an ustrel our forces captured in Romania," said Schmidt, his finger casting a shadow across the projection screen as he pointed to the creature's jagged teeth.

Wilhelm stood and walked to the screen.

"That is the most harrowing image I have ever seen," he said, stooping slightly and looking over the photograph of a gaunt-faced, fully nude ustrel. It was collared by the neck with a chain being held by an unknown person standing out of frame.

Wilhelm was disturbed by the lean, muscular body, short pointy ears, and protruding jawline with barbed teeth haphazardly spread nearly ear to ear. "And those beady, soulless eyes." He shivered a bit. "I've never seen such a wretch."

"Look at those teeth," said Prince Henry. "Horrid creature. Utter depravity."

"Depraved is exactly what they are," said Schmidt, standing next to the screen. "This is a more mature ustrel. A newborn ustrel often shares a closer resemblance to the person it was in human form. But as they feed, their teeth grow and their jaws protrude."

Wilhelm returned to his chair as Schmidt explained the differences between vámpir and ustrel. Vámpir, he said, could largely choose their hunting form, but ustrel were forever stuck in their gruesome appearance. Schmidt rattled off more specific and precise physiology surrounding the differences, which caused Wilhelm to lose focus, but he came to understand that ustrel were essentially infected survivors of vámpir attacks, and their increased prevalence in Romania was a direct result of the onslaught of vámpir in Bucharest and the surrounding region.

The only other tidbit from Schmidt's presentation that piqued Wilhelm's interest was that, true to their reputation in folklore, ustrel were naturally timid, preferring to attack weak prey from the shadows—unless engaged in a larger hive.

A hive, explained Schmidt, was extraordinarily savage once provoked, comparing them to a swarm of killer bees.

"How then do we contain them?" asked Wilhelm.

"It's simple, really," said Schmidt. "The same method a ringmaster uses to tame a tiger. We subdue them, starve them, then reward subservient behavior with fresh blood."

Ustrel retained their human psyche, Schmidt explained, and could be moderately reasoned with thanks to their voracious cravings. Schmidt and his team had been experimenting since discovering the Romanian ustrel and found the creatures were obedient and relatively tame toward whoever supplied them with blood. Else, the wretches would revert to their solitary ways and forage for food in graveyards, digging up the freshly dead to feed or occasionally attacking the sick or elderly if desperate or feeling bold.

Wilhelm blew out heavily from his lips.

"Some existence," he said. "But clearly there is a danger that a larger hive might easily overwhelm our operatives."

Minister Schmidt calmed the concern, stating he was actively researching all practical means to control the hive mind and assuring Wilhelm that ustrel were a far better technology to employ in close quarters with human handlers. Vámpir were willful and clever and often quite difficult to destroy—prolonged exposure to direct sunlight, beheadings, hogweed gas, and blackwood through the heart or brain being the only definitive means. But, ustrel? Any piercing of the heart would do. Along with blackwood stabbings, fire, beheadings, direct sunlight, and of course—hogweed gas.

Wilhelm grew impatient as Schmidt continued on.

"Nosferatu the king, vámpir the rook, and ustrel the pawn. Understood," he said, before ripping the cord from the electrical outlet.

The lantern fell to black as Wilhelm fumbled beneath his desk and plugged in his lamp.

"Apologies, gentlemen," he said. "I couldn't bear to stare at that thing for another moment. It was sickening."

"Agreed," said Ernest Louis.

"I hope that was the end of your presentation, Minister," said Wilhelm.

"It was, Kaiser." Schmidt pulled the magic lantern from Wilhelm's desk and placed it on the floor.

Wilhelm glanced to Hindenburg. "And how are the ustrel performing thus far?"

"Flawlessly. Their output is outstanding."

"Finally, some good news," said Wilhelm, leaning forward. "And, speaking of news . . . " He opened the folder and pulled out the Yusupov document. "This is what is troubling me. I take it you've all had time to review this?"

"We have," said Hindenburg. "I am curious as to why this subject has captured your attention. I have taken the time to scan the Ether on Felix Yusupov and have found nothing other than Rasputin and the Black Hundred's interest in him. Well, that and he was a socialite and a lush. No threat to anyone. It seems to me he was accidentally swept up—"

"You and I both know there are no such things as accidents in matters of conspiracy."

Hindenburg sat back in his chair and motioned for Wilhelm to continue.

"Firstly, his parents," said Wilhelm, as he thumbed to the second page of the dossier. "Murdered when he was twenty, leaving him alone with the second-largest personal fortune in Russia. But! What I find particularly curious is their corpses were discovered beheaded and burned to a crisp."

"Sounds like typical Russian operations to me. They likely owed the wrong people," said Prince Henry.

"If only it were so simple," said Wilhelm. "Normally, I would concur with such an analysis if it weren't for Rasputin and the Black Hundred's eventual interest in him. Beheadings and burnings—those are methods reserved for killing immortals, are they not?"

"My Kaiser," began Ernest Louis, "my sister, Tsaritsa Alexandra, and Felix were very close. I actually met him and his family one time when he was a teenager. In no way were his parents immortals."

"Not in the classical sense," said Wilhelm. "But I believe they became immortals. And then I believe that someone or someones wanted them out of the way to—"

"Forgive me for interrupting, dear Kaiser," said Hindenburg. "But I feel this is a fruitless exercise."

"Do you?" Wilhelm was agitated.

"As your key advisor on the supernatural, may I suggest that our inability to locate the bottle of Drăculea's blood has frustrated you so greatly that you are looking under the wrong stones?"

"The wrong stones, you say?" Wilhelm's mustache was pointing downward. "Tell me, then, General. How is it a drunken aristocrat gets swept up into the most secretive supernatural coup d'état ever attempted? How is it he survived for one moment? How is it he then somehow bested Rasputin—a powerful vampiric witch—and an army of vicious Nosferatu with a crew of two lowlife vampire hunters? There's more to this man than any of you see. This is not by happenstance or luck. I don't have anything solid to present to you. But my intuition is suffocating me on this matter."

The room fell to silence.

Wilhelm stood and leaned over his desk, making firm eye contact with his advisors.

"I have a gut suspicion that the Sommelier has tricked us once again," he said.

"Brother, just say what's on your mind," said Henry.

Wilhelm thought to spill his suspicions about Yusupov right then and there, but held back. He believed his inklings were correct, and he was not going to be talked out of this conviction.

Still, he needed more time and information if he was to convince his supernatural advisors.

"What's on my mind is that both of the wizards on this council will now focus any and all resources in locating this Felix Yusupov, who is believed to still be alive. I want him captured and brought before me. Is that understood?"

General Hindenburg and Minister Schmidt stared at the carpet, appearing forlorn.

"What?" asked Wilhelm, pausing briefly. "Fine! The two *witches* on my council. Is it truly that big an issue for you two?"

Schmidt continued staring at his boots. Hindenburg lifted his gaze to Wilhelm.

"You see, Kaiser . . . It's demeaning, the term 'wizard.' Implies a warlock who has lost his senses—a bumbling, uneducated conjurer."

"Yes, yes," said Wilhelm. "Pejorative term. You've reminded me in the past." He considered the two men, and a fleeting sensation of camaraderie took him by surprise.

"My apologies, gentlemen. I greatly admire and respect what you both offer to this council."

General Hindenburg and Minister Schmidt nodded. "Thank you, Kaiser," they said in unison.

Wilhelm sat down and exhaled before vigorously running his hand over his face in frustration. He looked to his advisors, who were still seated.

"Dismissed!" he yelled as a vein in the middle of his forehead throbbed.

*

"He's losing his mind," said Schmidt, leaning over a small wrought-iron balcony that extended from Hindenburg's personal study within the Berlin Palace. "I worry this may muddy our objectives."

"Relax, Friedrich," said Hindenburg.

Hindenburg thought about confessing his desire to slit Wilhelm's throat, dump his body somewhere along the Spree, and launch their coup early. But such action was far too precarious, and commenting on it would only alarm Minister Schmidt due to Hindenburg's reputation as a ruthless, calculating operative who always followed through on his objectives.

Eliminating Wilhelm now? The impulse of a younger, impatient man.

Hindenburg had long suffered for the rashness of his youth.

He would not make those mistakes again.

Besides—the mechanisms to dispose of Wilhelm were well underway and would play to their advantage far better than a very public and mysterious assassination. The sheer panic and disarray of such an event would batter, if not entirely terminate, his covert efforts.

Hindenburg still needed the lumbering Kaiser exactly where he was.

He cleared his mind and continued, "Wilhelm's clearly still in shock over his losses in Saint Petersburg. Lots of time and money wasted for an operation to just go poof. My assumption is this Yusupov fellow being alive—he feels that will give him answers. In two days, he'll be wildly speculating about some other matter."

Minister Schmidt still appeared worried. "Oh, Paul. I told you we should have looked into the Black Hundred more closely before they were exterminated. They were on to something with Felix Yusupov. Wilhelm's correct—Rasputin's interest in him. Certainly Olaf knew something and was hiding it."

"Darling, calm your mind," interrupted Hindenburg. "Wild speculation of a desperate Kaiser and that's all. I will inquire with Olaf. I'm certain it's nothing." Hindenburg placed his hand over Schmidt's and squeezed it gently. "Just take in the view." His free hand motioned to the Berliner Dom sparkling in the night. "It's a beautiful night."

Schmidt smiled, relaxed his shoulders, and leaned into Hindenburg. "Careful . . ."

"No one is about," said Schmidt. "As the more talented seer, I figured you'd know."

Schmidt leaned his head onto his lover's shoulder.

"You're right about Wilhelm," said Schmidt. "But his new obsession with Yusupov could cause problems if it takes us too far off course."

Hindenburg gripped the railing. "It won't. As usual, we placate Wilhelm's inclination until it subsides—if he thinks Yusupov is a problem, then Yusupov is a problem. He is alive, but I cannot locate him for some reason."

"Concealment spell?"

"Possibly. But until I can acquire either a physical sample or a personal item, tracking him alone is challenging." Hindenburg smiled. "But now that Wilhelm is eager to capture the man, I can use the royal seers. As a group, we should be able to generate the psychic energy needed to untangle such magick. You see—this is how we should always frame our agendas. Place it in Wilhelm's head and let him think it's his idea. Sneaking around in the shadows so that we may be together is enough to keep track of. I prefer our political operations to be a tad more . . . straightforward, I suppose."

"I agree," said Schmidt, turning to Hindenburg. "But I know you didn't shuffle me out here for just a peek at the dome."

"Indeed, I did not," said Hindenburg, pulling a split bottle of champagne from his jacket pocket.

Schmidt appeared amused as Hindenburg twisted the wire from the cork and popped it off into the night.

"Vago has broken through."

Schmidt's eyes widened. "What?" he shouted, embracing Hindenburg.

89

"Keep your voice down." Hindenburg eased him away and handed him the bottle.

Schmidt took a large swig and peered out over Berlin. "I—I . . . I'm speechless," he said, handing the champagne back to Hindenburg. "He did it! That crazy old wizard actually did it."

Hindenburg laughed. "Now, that assessment I can agree with. That old kook is the epitome of a wizard. But, don't get too excited. We don't know if the witch he sent survived her encounter with Elizabeth." Hindenburg took a long, lingering gulp of the bubbly liquid and wiped the remnants from his thick white mustache.

"Has Vago spoken to her?" asked Schmidt.

"I haven't sensed so. But the girl breached the trees. Once Elizabeth realizes she has allies, she should relax the spell on the forest and allow others to pass upon the mount . . . If not, then I may have to finally step in. I'm waiting to hear on any further developments."

"I feel you should go. You need to see her. Elizabeth will eventually discover you are still alive, and will be furious that you didn't attempt to free her."

"I love you. But do not question my actions on this matter. I could not have her interfering until everything was to our advantage."

"Of course. My apologies." Schmidt held on to the railing and bounced a bit. "A purebred witch! I never believed . . . Do you have any idea the implications of this? And she is Aryan, correct?"

"She is," said Hindenburg, handing the remaining alcohol to Schmidt.

"Praise Bael," he said, finishing it off and placing the bottle on the balcony.

"Praise Bael."

Hindenburg stood behind Schmidt and held him close. Being nearly a foot taller, Hindenburg placed his chin upon his lover's head as they stared out into the Berlin skyline.

"So you see, my Omega," began Hindenburg, "we learned a very valuable lesson tonight. If this young witch happens to be fortunate enough to commune with Elizabeth, then the next phase of the operation will begin tomorrow."

"Splendid," said Schmidt, leaning back into Hindenburg's arms.

Everything was falling into perfect alignment.

The timing, thought Hindenburg, felt nearly serendipitous. Wilhelm would certainly be informed of the kidnappings within a day. Then, all he had to do was convince the Kaiser to cover it all up and bring Elizabeth into the fold.

Hindenburg felt a rush of excitement as he reflected on the budding outcomes.

Soon, Radu would be killed and Bael would be reborn. Wilhelm and the monarchy would be destroyed and Hindenburg would seize the German war machine. Channeling Bael's power and Elizabeth's magick, he would bolster the German forces and unleash the most indomitable fighting force the world had ever seen.

By the time anyone figured out who he truly was, Hindenburg would rule over all.

The living. The dead.

The Veil and the Void.

Gaze upon me and tremble, oh ye abject, oh ye stalwart—for I am the Alpha and the Omega.

Hindenburg pulled Schmidt close. "Soon, you and I will never have to be apart. For now, we let the Kaiser bustle on with his little quest to obtain Drăculea's blood while we acquire the one true path to global domination right out from underneath him. I feel this Felix Yusupov is the perfect distraction."

Schmidt reached down and squeezed Hindenburg's hands. "Wherever he may roam."

Chapter 7

7

March 21, 1917, near dusk

Felix gasped as the air was punched from his lungs.

He quickly composed himself and wrapped his legs around the ustrel's waist before it could straddle him. Reaching to his belt, Felix grabbed a blackwood stake and held it horizontally across his neck while the creature chomped its fangs toward his jugular vein.

The ustrel shrieked as its jaws crushed the stake, shattering the blackwood to a mouthful of caustic splinters. A glowing, greenish-gray smoke swelled from its fanged mouth. It broke Felix's guard, then fled, gagging and hissing while rushing up the short staircase, across the rickety porch, and back into the squat house riddled with broken windows and a dilapidated door hanging from its hinges.

Rurik yanked Felix from the ground.

"You hurt?" asked Rurik.

"I'm fine." Felix brushed himself off. "Hurry, back to the horses."

The two men dashed about fifty meters to their steeds.

"Sorry to be right on this one," said Felix. "But there's definitely someone in the house."

"Some*thing*, my friend. Some*thing*. I pray that wasn't Florin," said Rurik, looking over the docks in the distance that sat destroyed and partially aflame.

After three solid months of traveling mainly on foot from Saint Petersburg to Romania, both men were gaunt, bearded, and haggard, with random garments strewn over their bodies in an attempt to fend off the early spring cold. Various camping supplies and pelts hung from their horses' saddles. They had crossed the Romanian border over two weeks prior in hopes of reaching Denis's compound in the Bucharest outskirts, but due to the German annexation, their situation had grown far more precarious. They were exhausted and badly in need of supplies. As they hugged the foothills of the Carpathians on their journey south, their nerves became frayed and their stomachs grew empty.

Other than the occasional German garrison they had to avoid near more populated areas, Romania was quiet—eerily quiet—as if vast swaths of the population had packed up or simply disappeared the farther south they traveled. Small towns sat boarded up and abandoned, and they found no opportunities to trade. After an unexpected encounter with an ustrel hive near Focşani, they decided to check in on their old friend Florin in the outskirts of Verneşti for some much-needed shelter and hopefully a hot meal before embarking on the final leg toward Denis's farmhouse.

Things were now worse.

"They'll come for the horses first," said Felix, scanning the sky and dreading the oncoming night. "We need to move them. I'm certain there are more in the house."

"There's not enough time. If it's a hive, they're now agitated. They'll swarm us."

Felix looked back to the house and swore he could see multiple shadows moving about just past the windows. Even in the waning light, he could make out the faint yellow specks of their glowing eyes. "It's a hive, all right. They're watching us—at least five of them."

"It's dusk in less than ten," said Rurik as the last beacon of sunlight began to slip behind the Carpathian summits.

"As I've just proven—I don't think they really care if it's night or not."

"Then what the hell are they waiting for?" asked Rurik. He reached behind his neck and tightened the knot on the leather strap that kept his glasses from falling off. "Let's not find out, good?"

"Great."

Rurik and Felix pulled their hogweed canisters from their horses' rumps and slung the contraptions over their backs.

"These things spit?" asked Felix, gripping a gas mask hanging from his horse.

"The last ones didn't, but I'd prefer not to chance it."

Felix tossed Rurik the gas mask, then grabbed his own and pulled it over his head.

Both men fumbled through the various supplies on their horses, pulling two blackwood stakes each and slinging them into their belts before slipping on leather gloves and pulling canvas hoods over their heads.

"You ready?" asked Felix.

"Huh?"

Felix pulled up his gas mask. "I said, 'Are you ready?'"

Rurik held out his hands wide. "Don't I look ready?" he mumbled.

"Wise guy," said Felix, brushing past him and pulling down his mask.

"Hold up!"

Rurik walked behind Felix and ensured the nozzles on his canister were fully open. He spun around. "Check mine."

Felix reached to the nozzles and dialed them to their fully open positions.

They walked toward the house as night settled upon the remote area, stopping about twenty meters from the darkened structure.

"You rushing? Or me?" asked Felix.

"I've been in that house. Let me handle the ones inside. The second I pop this off"—Rurik shook his hogweed nozzle—"any I miss will burst outside, so be ready. We have no idea how many there are and we can't risk the horses. I'll rejoin you the moment I can."

"Do it," said Felix, pulling his nozzle gun into position.

"And away we go!" yelled Rurik, sprinting toward the house.

Felix stood defensively and watched Rurik near the house.

As Rurik reached the stairs and sprung up onto the porch, his weight proved too much for the rotting wood and his right leg broke clean through the planks, causing him to fall forward and lose his grip on his hogweed nozzle. He shot upright and struggled to pull his limb free.

"Not good," said Felix.

He immediately tore toward the house, screaming at the sight of three ustrel bursting from the front door and seizing upon Rurik, who pulled a blackwood stake from his belt and shoved it clean through an ustrel's mouth. The creature fell forward off the porch, wailing as its body burst into flame. The remaining two lunged toward Rurik.

Felix was close.

He pulled the trigger and doused the two ustrel in a thick cloud of hogweed gas that shone with a green light as it vaporized them and their screeches dissipated. Upon reaching the porch, Felix pulled Rurik out of the hole. The two men backed away from the house, aiming their nozzles forward in case more ustrel attacked.

"So much for surprise," said Rurik, laughing a bit.

"Nothing fazes you, does it?"

Rurik shrugged. "Ustrel, vámpir, Nosferatu . . . all in a day's work, my friend. OK—here goes for real."

He ascended the stairs once more, avoiding the hole he'd made on his previous advance, and disappeared into the house.

Felix backed away and listened as sounds of breaking glass were followed by the hiss of Rurik's canister being deployed. Ghoulish wails erupted from the house, and Felix watched as its interior glowed green for a moment before falling to black. He gripped his nozzle, breathing heavily and waiting for Rurik to reemerge.

Silence.

"Rurik?"

A crow cackling in the distance rattled Felix's nerves as he walked a few paces forward.

"Rurik?"

No response.

"Run!" screamed Rurik as he suddenly burst from the front door, leaping over the porch entirely. He rolled onto the dirt and, as he landed, turned the motion into a sprint by using the momentum to stand and dash past Felix, who took one last look at the house, then ran after Rurik.

Felix looked behind them in horror as at least thirty ustrel rushed from the house, breaking through what remained of the windows and door.

"Go! Go! Go!" yelled Felix, firing off hogweed gas haphazardly over his shoulder as he ran.

They mounted their steeds and tore off down a narrow path that led away from Florin's house.

The horses galloped at full speed as Felix pulled up his gas mask and looked right to see Rurik doing the same while twisting at the waist and peering behind them. Felix craned his neck to see the shadows of the pursuing ustrel. The hive was gaining on them with every stride.

"Not tonight!" yelled Rurik, who gripped his saddle's horn with his right hand and cantle with his left. He fed his right leg over the seat and rode sidesaddle for a moment before swinging his left leg over the cantle. Rurik was now riding backward. He leaned forward, gripping the cantle while trying to feed his feet back into the stirrups.

"What the hell are you doing?" yelled Felix.

"Watch!"

Rurik steadied himself firmly in the stirrups. He then pulled down his gas mask and readied his hogweed nozzle, pulling the trigger and dousing the trailing ustrel in a thick cloud of gas, vaporizing them on contact.

"Nice thinking!" yelled Felix.

Rurik's gas offensive eliminated over a dozen ustrel, but the remaining hive was undeterred. They continued on, sprinting toward Rurik and Felix at a shocking pace, howling and hissing all the while.

Rurik sent off another blast of hogweed gas, vaporizing more ustrel.

"It takes two to tango," shouted Rurik.

Felix nodded. He twisted around and gripped the cantle with both hands while feeding his right foot over the seat. Just as his foot cleared the pommel, his bootlace looped itself over the horn, causing Felix to lose his balance and nearly fall from the horse. He struggled, pushing and pulling his foot, to no avail. He tried to sit upright and free his boot, but his horse became spooked from the shift in weight and bucked her hind legs outward to rid herself of the burden.

Felix was thrown from the saddle and landed hard on the dirt with his left foot still stuck in the stirrup. The landing crushed his hogweed nozzle and knocked him unconscious as the steed continued to barrel forward with Felix's limp body in tow.

"Oh, no!" screamed Rurik as he watched Felix fall from his horse and slam into the dirt.

Felix's horse slowed and veered off to the path, the trailing ustrel nearly upon him.

Rurik's steed continued on at a brisk gallop. He pulled his feet from the stirrups and leaned into the cantle, then swung his legs over the seat and flipped himself forward in one fluid motion.

"You're getting good at this," he said to himself.

Rurik yanked the reins, stopping his horse. He turned the beast around and pulled up his gas mask, squinting at the shadows of the charging ustrel, who were less than ten meters away from Felix. Rurik looked down to his hogweed nozzle and fancied it as a medieval lance. He drove his heels into his horse and snapped the reins.

"Go, girl!"

Rurik tore toward Felix.

Just as the first wave of ustrel attempted to seize Felix's unconscious body, his steed whinnied and bucked, jolting her hind legs into two ustrel and sending them flying backward.

Rurik was gaining on them, but he knew the wind would blow the gas back into his face if he pulled the trigger. Instead, he positioned his trajectory just left of Felix's horse as the remaining ustrel reached Felix. With mere seconds remaining, Rurik's horse barreled through the hive, knocking them in all directions like screeching, fanged bowling pins as their bodies slammed into the mud before they scurried off into the thicket.

Rurik pulled the reins and slowed his steed, yanking left as he turned around then trotted toward Felix. He dismounted, knelt next to Felix, and aimed his hogweed nozzle outward into the darkened forest. Both horses let out disgruntled neighs and snorts, alarming Rurik, as he envisioned they'd panic and tear off into the darkness. He stood and reached to his animal, patting her nose and tugging on her reins to keep her in place.

"Stay still, girl. Stay still," he whispered as both horses settled.

Rurik pulled down his gas mask and stood over Felix. The quiet forest path mocked his senses as he feverishly looked back and forth to gather a sense of his attackers' position, the mask narrowing his peripheral vision and making it almost impossible to see.

All was still.

Rurik had very little experience with ustrel, other than a small hive he and Felix had uncovered upon crossing the Romanian border. He understood they were rumored to be timid hunters when solitary, but quite fearsome when gathered in larger numbers.

All Rurik really knew for certain was that he was definitely being watched.

"You know what?" asked Rurik aloud. "To hell with it!"

He pulled the trigger and sent a cloud of hogweed gas into the trees, illuminating three ustrel crouched behind a fallen log a mere five meters before him. Felix's horse whinnied and galloped off a short distance, pulling Felix with her as Rurik's horse trotted away, huffing and snorting, before settling center path. Once the horses were clear, Rurik spun around and sent more hogweed gas flying into the air just as two more ustrel seized upon him from the darkness. Their bodies melted into pools of glowing green ooze, casting a light just bright enough to illuminate the wooded path.

Rurik was breathing heavily, spinning in all directions as he scanned for the slightest movement in the shadows. Sensing motion to his left, he turned and pulled his trigger.

Click.

"Of course," lamented Rurik.

He pulled up his gas mask, then tore the hogweed canister from his back before retreating toward Felix's horse. Trying his best not to telegraph his movements, Rurik knelt and began to remove Felix's hogweed canister, cursing when he noticed the nozzle was bent beyond repair. He removed the remaining blackwood stake from Felix's belt, then quickly gripped the last stake from his own waist holster. Turning away from Felix with a stake in each hand, Rurik's eyes moved to his horse's shadow.

"Two or three left . . . I bet they go for my horse," he said, believing ustrel preferred an easy kill.

Rurik crept forward, putting equal distance between him, his own horse, and Felix. Standing center path, he waited for the remaining ustrel to make a move.

"Come on, you stinky rats!"

Three shadows burst from the woods toward Rurik's horse.

The steed whinnied and galloped toward Rurik with the creatures in fast pursuit. Rurik roared and ran toward them, focusing his gaze on the leading ustrel. Just as he reached the fanged creature, Rurik sidestepped and swung his arm wide, striking the ustrel in the heart with his blackwood stake. The creature howled as it disintegrated to dust.

The remaining two continued after his horse.

Rurik sprinted toward them.

The two ustrel jumped on Rurik's mare and muscled her to the ground, gnashing their teeth toward her neck. Rurik leapt into the air and sailed down on an ustrel, sending his last stake clean through its neck. The creature choked and gagged as its body ignited into flames and fell into the muck, quashing the fire.

The last ustrel abandoned the horse and tackled Rurik, knocking him over and straddling him. Rurik reached up and wrapped his hands around the creature's neck, using all his might to keep its jowls away as the monster lashed its claws toward his face. At that moment, a clang rang out.

The ustrel slumped to the mud, then scampered away.

Felix stood over Rurik with a cast-iron frying pan in his hand.

Rurik looked up at him. "We have to cook with that, you know?"

"If it works—it works," said Felix, spitting dirt from his mouth. He extended his hand to Rurik and pulled him from the ground.

Rurik's horse writhed on the path for a moment before standing upright. She then trotted toward Felix's steed.

The two men stood close, never taking their eyes from the remaining ustrel that sat crouched on the path, slightly illuminated by what remained of the glowing green pools—even in the shadows its fearsome jowls reflected the light and shone green.

"I hate these things," said Felix. "They're all teeth."

Rurik reached down and grabbed his blackwood stake, noticing Felix wrap his fingers more firmly around the cast-iron pan. They looked to each other, nodded, then crept toward the ustrel.

"Really not happy about this weapon," said Felix.

"I'll take this one. Just give it a good whack in the mouth if it happens to overpower me."

Felix and Rurik slinked toward the ustrel as it hissed at them and backed away on all fours. Realizing it was now alone and outnumbered by its intended prey, the ustrel let out a rage-filled howl that echoed for miles before it slithered off into the forest.

"Distress call?" asked Felix, listening to the branches snapping farther in the distance as the creature scurried away.

"Could be, but we just took out its entire hive. Let's just get out of here and assume it won't come back for more." Rurik turned to him. "You OK?"

"Possible broken rib," said Felix, holding his hand at his side. "From now on, I'm leaving the trick riding to you."

"Wise choice," said Rurik. "Let's get the hell out of here. I know a place near town that should provide us with enough privacy and shelter."

"Suits me," said Felix, spitting more dirt from his mouth.

*

Felix leaned against moss-covered bricks and held a telescope to his eye. With his body partially hanging from the crumbling stone window, he scanned Verneşti's darkened town not too far down the hill.

"Pronounced 'Verneshti', right?"

"Close enough," said Rurik, casually gazing at the plant overgrowth and charred interior of the Annunciation Church.

He stood in a broken portion of the wooden floor and set up a hanging boiling pot over a kindling fire before wrestling some of the overgrowth away from the flame.

"What's it translate to?" asked Felix.

"No idea."

"I bet it means 'creepy, abandoned town with no one in sight,'" said Felix, sliding the telescope into his pocket. "Or at least, it should."

"Told you."

"So this is it, huh?" asked Felix, walking past Rurik and fumbling through a satchel on his horse's rump.

"This is it," said Rurik. "The infamous church where Denis and Rasputin had their fateful duel."

"How are you OK with being here?"

"No idea," said Rurik, shaking his head. "I mean, at least it's as deserted as I expected. Sorry about the roof—guess my promise of shelter didn't pan out."

"What's shelter?" Felix laughed. "Never heard of it."

Rurik smiled and scanned the destroyed roof. "I just had to see it again, I suppose. Twenty-some years ago, and I'm still riddled with guilt. I was supposed to be with Denis, you know. But my nerves were too much, so I had to have a drink first. That led to another, then another. I basically left my own brother alone to be maimed by that monster. What troubles me the most is had Orna not been there to heal him, Denis would have ended up as an ustrel. Can you imagine?"

Felix was silent for a long moment. "You have to forgive yourself. Maybe laying off the booze would help—even as a symbolic gesture?"

"Ha! If you hadn't noticed, I ran out of vodka over three weeks ago. So, now I'm fortunate enough to sit here sober—inside the literal embodiment of the shame and regret I've carried with me for decades. I don't know. I figured maybe I could finally let it go. Confront your fears kinda thing."

Felix closed the satchel and returned to the fire. "Five potatoes and a day-old dead rabbit," he said, tossing the items next to the fire.

"Just be thankful we still have salt. The meat should be fine—weather's cold enough."

Felix sat next to Rurik, who threw the potatoes in the water.

"Shouldn't we wait till it boils?"

"Suddenly you're a chef?" asked Rurik, looking to Felix with humor in his eyes. "Haute cuisine this is not, garçon." He watched their horses begin to nibble on a small tree that sprouted from the charred and rotting wooden floor. "At least they're seemingly well fed."

"Another week of this and I'll be joining them. We're out of bullets. Anything we eat from now on, we have to trap. That's the last of the potatoes."

"We need supplies badly," said Rurik. "Since Florin's was a bust, we have to make it to Denis's. It's remote enough from Bucharest, and we can't keep scrounging through one abandoned town after another—too risky. Out of hogweed gas and down to one blackwood stake. The next chance encounter with urstrel could be our last."

Felix lay on the floor and placed his hand under his head, massaging the tender and pronounced lump on the back of his skull. He moved his other hand to his ribs and pushed on the bones. "I think I'm just bruised, but I'll tell you—that was a hard hit."

"Indeed it was," said Rurik. "Thought you were done for, to be honest."

Felix tried to ignore his pounding headache and stared past the caved-in ceiling into the open night. Dilapidated stone spires rose up on all four sides of the church, giving the appearance that he and Rurik were contained within a decaying stone claw that glowed orange from within.

"Not a good idea—Denis's. Could be another ustrel hive. Besides, did you notice Florin's docks? Still embers. They were set ablaze in the past twenty-four hours, I'd estimate."

"Agreed. But the question being—by whom?" Rurik shrugged. "One thing's for sure. If it was the Germans, then we should be traveling in the trees from here on out. Maybe they're just burning down everything in sight. We get caught on an open road, there's no telling what they'll do to us."

"That reminds me," said Felix, reaching into his pocket and producing a tattered piece of paper. "What's this say? Found it in the graveyard on our way in—a cluster of them."

Felix handed Rurik the flyer, which had several lines written in Romanian.

Rurik positioned his glasses and inspected the paper.

"What it says is—we're about to get a decent meal."

Felix's eyes widened. "Do tell."

Rurik cleared his throat and postured as if he were reading an official decree.

"All men of working age. Come to Zănoaga—twenty five kilometers south west of Ploieşti. Serve the Kaiser. Work, fair wage, food, and shelter for all who come." He folded the paper and looked to Felix. "What do you say? Ready to serve the Kaiser?"

103

Felix bobbed his head, thinking over the proposition. "Well, I suppose a few days of labor never hurt a man, so long as food is part of the equation."

"Don't forget the shelter," said Rurik. "How far is Zănoaga?"

Felix walked to his horse, unfastened a saddlebag, and returned with a map. He spread it out near the fire and traced his finger from their position to Zănoaga.

"Day and a half maximum. Should be easy to find—right off the Teleajen River."

"Since Denis's is a bit of a gamble currently," said Rurik, "we head there. How far is it from Bucharest?"

"No more than a day."

"That's the move."

"At least it will be populated. Maybe even have a trading post. Very frustrating to have a saddle stitched full of gold and nowhere to spend it. Ever since we crossed into Romania, seems the whole world has gone into hiding."

Felix folded the map, then lay back on the floor and looked to his horse, who seemed content munching on the leaves.

"I've decided to name her Nima," he said.

"Who?" asked Rurik.

"My horse. She seems like a Nima to—"

"I wouldn't get too attached if I were you," said Rurik, handing Felix a knife and motioning toward the rabbit carcass. "How about it?"

Felix took the knife and began to skin the small animal. After a short minute, he plopped the fur onto the floor and placed the carcass on top of it. "How's that for speed?"

"You certainly can skin a rabbit . . . oh, I nearly forgot," said Rurik, pulling a small patch of canvas from his back pocket and handing it to Felix, who noticed it was tied with a piece of red yarn. "Happy birthday."

Felix looked surprised. "How did you know?"

"You've been talking in your sleep."

"It's actually in two days, but thank you." Felix smiled, then suddenly winced. He reached to the back of his neck and massaged the area where he had been bitten by Rasputin.

"Still troubling you?" asked Rurik.

"It is. Bad nightmares too. But this"—he pushed his fingers into his neck—"still flares up. Any idea what that means? You're the expert on all things vampire."

"I don't. Probably just like any other wound. Bound to flare up." Rurik pointed to the gift. "I hope that will brighten your spirits."

Felix placed the small parcel in his lap and stared at it. "It's great. I really appreciate it."

"Well—open it!"

"Of course," said Felix, shaking his head. "I swear I'm losing my wits."

"We both are."

Felix pulled the red string and opened the canvas patch to find a needle and thread inside.

"I noticed your knee could use a patch. Sorry. It's the best I could come up with."

Felix sat for a moment, looking at Rurik's gift. He grimaced and his upper body shook slightly as he exhaled through his nose. "It's very thoughtful. Thank you." Felix pulled his legs to his chest and buried his face in his knees.

"What's the matter?"

Felix looked up at him with tears in his eyes. "I—I want to go home, Rurik. I don't know how much more of this I can take. I feel we're at the earth's end. I mean, the first two months were mostly fine . . . extreme camping. I actually was starting to enjoy it. But ever since Romania, this new sense of dread has taken me. And if that ustrel hive was any indicator—we have no idea what we're walking into. Throw a German war campaign into the mix, and this is about to get far more dangerous."

"Calm your mind. We'll figure a way out of this."

"I think we should just gather what we can at Zănoaga, then head to Zurich. I can access my accounts. Then we can reassess on exacting revenge on Dmitri Pavlovich with actual funding. This feels fruitless, and we have no idea how or where this ends. I've lost my home. With Irina, Alexandra, and Alexei gone—any semblance of a family I had. We're going to starve or end up refugees, or . . . worse."

Felix lay on the floor.

Rurik walked to his horse and returned with a blanket and a canteen.

"Here, try to relax," he said, handing the items to Felix. "I've lost everything too. We're in this together."

"I'm sorry," said Felix. "I didn't mean to minimize your—"

"I understand. Just let it out. We'll be fed and well supplied in less than two days. Then we can decide if we want to try for Denis's or head to Zurich. I'm leaning towards Zurich too. What we really need to do is contact Zazlov—that'll be easier once we're away from the Germans and back to civilization."

"Who's Zazlov?"

"Funny enough, an old student of Orna's. Or, at least he was for a short amount of time. She always seemed a bit suspicious about him for some reason. But he's the warlock who assisted me in sending you and Denis the messages once Orna was . . . well."

The two were silent for a moment as they remembered Orna's harrowing murder at the hands of Rasputin.

"Is Zazlov in Saint Petersburg?" asked Felix.

"No idea. He seems rather peripatetic. I think of him as the Cheshire Cat."

"How's that?"

"It's . . . something about his way. Popping in and out of the Ether when it serves him. Always cheerful and charming—extremely put together and articulate, but secretive. Helpful, but a definite sinister undertone about him. Who knows? He's an ancient warlock, so my guess is he's simply haunted by something in his past."

"Aren't we all?"

Rurik nodded.

"Think we can trust him?" asked Felix.

"Seems. He's always behaved as an ally. No love for creatures of darkness, that's for sure. I just can't shake the sense that he's engaged in a chess game nobody else knows they're playing. Hard to describe."

"Can't hurt to have a wizard on our side once we're out of this mess, I suppose," Felix said.

He took a swig from the canteen.

"Ugh," he said, wincing. "Tastes like a barnyard. We're going to end up with dysentery if we keep this up."

"I boiled it yesterday. You're fine."

Felix capped the canteen and threw the blanket over his shoulders. He held out his hands and tried to warm them against the fire. A hole in his sleeve caught his eye.

"Have you ever seen a vagabond and wondered how he became that way?" asked Felix.

"Come to think of it, I've actually never pondered it too deeply."

Felix pulled the blanket more snugly over his shoulders. "Before all of this started, Dmitri and I were traveling back to my palace in my limousine. It was one of those frigid days. Simply freezing. We were at an intersection waiting to cross the Moika, and outside the window is this old man—and I mean old, just engrimed with the dirt of ages. Scraggly gray beard, not too different from ours, currently." Felix ran his fingers through his beard.

"And he's staring at me, smiling through the glass with huge gaps in his rotten teeth . . . and the weirdest part is, there's this fat one-eyed pigeon sitting on his head, as if his hair had become its nest. So we make eye contact and he starts screaming, 'I was the king of Belarus!' over and over. The driver then pulled away, but it stuck with me."

Felix took another sip from the canteen, then shook his head and stuck out his tongue in protest of the taste. "Anyway, I've been thinking lately. What if that's me now? What if, say, a year from now, I'm merely some scraggly vagabond wandering the streets of Bucharest or wherever, mumbling on about how I used to be a Russian prince? People will stare at me, thinking I'm crazy. And I wonder—when does one lose the ability to tell between reality and fantasy? What if I'm simply slipping past the point where I—"

"You're tired and hungry," said Rurik, patting him on the boot. "Lie back and rest. I'll handle dinner tonight. Consider it your birthday party."

Felix forced a smile. He rolled on his side and faced the fire while running his thumb over the canvas patch Rurik had gifted him. "It's a really great present, Rurik. Thank you. I'll sew it in tomorrow morning."

"It's your patch and thread. Do with it what you wish."

Felix settled and tried to relax, noticing his feet were much less sore at the day's end since they'd acquired the horses.

"One thing's for certain," he said. "We should have stolen horses three months ago."

"Borrowed, my friend. We're simply borrowing them without permission."

Rurik tossed the rabbit carcass into the boiling water and began to stir their vagabond stew as somewhere far in the distance a harrowing ustrel howl echoed through the country quiet.

8

March 21, 1917, night

Vago Vakól stood outside in the crisp evening air, his gaze set upon the peak of Mount Hohenzollern.

Tonight. She returns tonight. I can feel it.

His thoughts turned to the last time he saw Elizabeth and a despondent pressure squeezed his heart, constricting the blood flow entering and exiting his ventricle chambers. He placed his fingers firmly against his rib cage, attempting to calm his pulsations. Vago hadn't been himself ever since the day Elizabeth was beheaded by Radu cel Frumos. He missed her. He missed her cunning, her beauty. He missed her dark intentions.

His life had felt dreary and grueling ever since she'd been gone, and even the coven he'd groomed and bred over the centuries barely gave him a sense of purpose any longer. Every day his true love stayed sequestered in that castle, a tiny piece of him drifted into the Void. Vago wondered how many more days would pass before he'd simply be a mindless dolt with the body and psyche of a man, but the soul of a corpse. The guilt he harbored about his actions on that fateful day pulsed through him, and he realized the sensation had become his default emotion. Vago ground his teeth and reminded himself that he had done everything within his power to free Elizabeth from her prison, over the centuries. Alas, he knew much more work lay ahead—that was, if Elizabeth hadn't slaughtered Hanne on sight. Elizabeth seemed to let out a slight laugh *Hanne will return tonight.*

With one more gaze into the evening's shadows upon the mount, Vago turned to the candlelight dancing in the circular windows of the clay huts that encircled his small encampment.

All was quiet.

"If this fails," he told himself, "I'll simply walk away. I'll rise early in the morning and go—walk the earth until I find the edge."

Despite the doubt and anxiety pervading his mind, Vago knew nothing more could be done. It was time to retire and wait.

Vago entered his circular, domed hut and sat at a desk opposite his hay mattress. He kindled a flame between his fingers, which he used to light four candles before him. His ears perked up and he listened to the rising wind howl as it sailed through the nearby trees. His quarters fell to silence once more and he sat staring at the wall, tapping his fingers upon his desk's wooden surface.

Only a few moments passed before Vago stood and began pacing, his mind awash with the events from last evening. Certainly, she passed the test. Praise to Bael, she passed the test.

Vago muttered to himself and clenched his fists while fluttering his fingers and grinding them into his palms—his impatience had grown unbearable. He sat upon his hay mattress and stared at the circular opening in the center of his ceiling.

"*Flamuetur*," he said, motioning his hand toward the clay fire pit below the aperture, and a fire ignited within the pit. He watched the smoke rise from his dwelling.

Vago sat upright with a rigid spine at the sound of approaching horse hooves.

He shot to his wooden door and listened as the galloping grew louder. A hellish whinny resounded through the air and his door burst open with a shower of splinters, knocking him backward, almost into his fire pit. He gathered his senses and looked to the door. Hanne's horned, ghastly figure now stood before him. Her deer skull helmet glowed orange as it reflected the light from the fire pit, and Vago noticed her tattered gown was stained brown from her dried blood. She tore the skull from her head, unsheathed the swords harnessed to her back, and charged at Vago.

Knowing the blades' power, Vago closed his eyes and cowered, raising his arm before him in self-defense.

"You lied to me, old man!" she wheezed. "Look what I've become!"

The twin blades were mere inches from Vago's hand, and he could feel their inherent gravity pulling upon him. A thundering bass resonated through the room. Realizing she had not struck him down, Vago opened his eyes and positioned his back against the wall of the fire pit. He knew no spell in this realm could defend against such weapons, so he slowly lowered his arm and gazed up to Hanne. Her black, scarred eye sockets seemed to stare right at him.

"Hanne, my child. Please," said Vago. "Lower the blades. You'll accidentally—"

"There are no accidents here," said Hanne calmly, crossing the blades before Vago's neck as if she intended to behead him.

Vago slowly raised his hands in surrender, all the while staring at the blades in horror. He could feel the weapons pulling upon his flesh as his blood was forced to his skin—any closer and the swords would begin to absorb him.

The pure black scimitars hummed and flickered, and churning within them was a distant white light with spindles reminiscent of a galaxy whirring around a bright center. Shallow bolts of silver electricity shimmered across the blades in random patterns. The static resonance emitted from their tips seemed to bend light and space around the razor-sharp, black-mirrored blades.

"You're endangering yourself as well. Please, lower the blades. I— I have something very important for you."

Hanne remained unmoved as Vago assessed his situation and studied her strikingly gaunt and pallid appearance. Knowing that Elizabeth now ultimately controlled Hanne, but the banishment field made their connection sporadic, Vago gambled that Elizabeth would not send her minion to kill him. Hanne's actions were bluster based on fear and frustration. He relaxed slightly and began to stand.

Hanne backed away, keeping the blades upon him.

"Sheathe your swords, Hanne! I command thee!" Vago's voice was low and booming.

Hanne's posture conveyed that she was shaken by Vago's command.

"I understand you are confused and angry, child. But I have made you more than any witch could ever be. May I show you?"

Hanne stood silently, then sheathed the blades behind her back.

The room fell quiet.

"Tellius!" said Vago, and the splintered door re-formed itself and sealed them both inside.

"Now," he said. "Let us complete your transformation so that you may effectively wield such weapons."

Hanne was silent.

Vago moved to a large metallic chest next to his desk and opened it.

Hanne turned toward the chest as a black, wispy specter rose from its interior.

"Remove your gown," said Vago. "It is time for you to adorn yourself in your new mother's garments."

Hanne hesitated, but was mesmerized by the black cloud floating toward her. She removed her gown and the black ether swarmed over her, encircling her pale body. The cloudy essence materialized over Hanne, covering her body in what appeared to be leather and metal, before finally settling itself in the shape of a hooded cloak upon her head.

"Now you are what all men will come to fear," said Vago. "From this point forward, you are oblivion incarnate—the Death Witch."

Vago watched her new coverings conform to her body and sensed a notion of strength and resilience rise within Hanne. Her legs and torso were covered in a firm patent leather that shone against the various black metal fastenings over her forearms and chest. The cloak flowed around her, completing the dark vision standing before Vago.

"This garment is your symbiote—your ally and protector. Forever bound to your command. Wield it powerfully against those who oppose you."

Hanne looked over her ethereal garments and began to speak.

Vago raised his hand to her. "Silence!" he bellowed. "For now it is time for you to obey."

Hanne scowled at the command.

Vago placed his hand on her cold, clammy forehead.

"Ride now, my child. Bring her children of the purest Prussian blood so that our destiny may unfold."

Hanne backed away and turned to the door.

She forcefully pulled it open and stood outside Vago's hut. Reaching to the ground, she picked up her helmet and placed it on her head before pulling up her hood. She unsheathed one of her swords and pointed it toward Vago.

"She commands your presence."

Hanne's horned figure turned to the Hellhorse, and she mounted the steed. The horse reared its front legs and screeched into the night. Upon landing, it tore from the encampment into the forest with hooves echoing a clamorous thunder throughout the village.

Vago watched from his door frame as the Death Witch's shadow fused into the dark. Several of his coven had exited their abodes and stood staring at him.

"Return to your homes, my children," he shouted. "Father Bael will be reborn once more!"

*

Vago arrived at the top of the mount as nighttime had taken its hold. The vines in the vicinity immediately swarmed upon him as an intruder. He allowed them to wrap around his green robe before gripping some of the plants in his hands.

"Release me," he said softly. "She is expecting me. You will show me the way."

The creeping plants continued to swarm him as if they were sensing his intentions. Then they fell to the ground and opened up a path before him. Vago proceeded beyond the concealment field. He continued up the winding path until he came upon Hohenzollern Castle's sweeping courtyard. Closing his eyes and raising his hand, he sensed Elizabeth's presence and walked toward the bastion at the castle's center.

Vago entered the darkened castle, his flat-soled boots collecting spiderwebs as he moved into the main hall. It was quiet save a faint ringing from the chandeliers being disturbed.

"My beloved," he called.

"Go away," came Elizabeth's disembodied voice.

Vago crept toward the end of the hall as giddiness filled his stomach. "You sent for me, my love."

Chapter 8

"I've changed my mind. I refuse to let you see me like this."

Vago stood at the short staircase at the end of the hall. He could sense Elizabeth to his left. He turned slowly to see her body hidden in the shadows and walked closer.

"Come," he said, holding out his hand. "Fear not. I will never turn away from you."

Elizabeth raised her appendages and crept into the moonlight. Vago fell to his knees at the sight of her and began to cry. "I'm so sorry, my beloved," he bellowed.

Elizabeth now loomed over him. Vago raised his hands to reach out to her, and she scuttled backward.

"Please," he said. "Let me touch you once more. It's been an eon. I care not of your appearance."

Elizabeth seemed to glide toward him, and Vago reached out to touch her front leg.

"I did everything I could, Elizabeth. Please forgive me. I should have been there that day."

She extended her palp and ran it down his elongated face.

"There, there," she said. "Dry your tears."

Vago stayed on his knees, staring up at her with soft blue eyes.

"I bred them. The witches—I believed only a purebred witch could pass your enchantment. And now—"

"And now we let bygones be."

Elizabeth crawled away from him, and Vago slumped on the ground, taking in her horrific appearance as she moved back to her hiding spot.

"It was you all this time, wasn't it? Sending people up the mount for me to feed."

"Yes. I even attached letters to some. I knew you likely would not find them, but I—I just didn't know how to reach you. Your spell upon the mount was far beyond my powers. I tried everything, even using carrier pigeons for a short while."

"I'm certain the vines appreciated those." Elizabeth seemed to let out a slight laugh. "Oh, my Vago. If it were not for you, I might have starved to death long ago, or been trapped here until Radu's natural death. Eventually this castle will be rediscovered and demolished—

me along with it. You have given me a second chance. And for that, you will be rewarded. Come to me."

Vago stood and walked to her. He stared into her black eyes.

"May I?" he said, reaching out his hands.

Elizabeth seemed to nod her body downward and Vago wrapped his arms around her head, embracing her.

"We can do this. Together. We will bring back your father and his allies. We will find and kill Radu. You will be freed."

"There is much to be done. But I confess, I do not know the state of the world now. I can tell by the manner of dress of my new victims that much has changed."

Vago let go his embrace and stood before her.

"It has, my sweet. But there is a great war now ravaging the world. With fantastic war machines like you have never seen—even ones that can fly. I believe we can acquire new allies if you will allow me to lobby on your behalf."

"How can this be?"

"Kaiser Wilhelm—the German emperor. He's an occultist. He too seeks the bottle, as you once did. But his intentions are not to destroy it. He intends to make himself immortal, and to resurrect Vlad Drăculea and raise him to serve the darkness."

"Never! Far too risky. Should Vlad grow back to the light, he will crush us all."

Vago extended his hands. "I beg you. Hear my plea. Kaiser Wilhelm has shown himself to be a resourceful and wise tactician. I believe once he is informed of your power and what your agenda can bring to his empire, he will ally with our cause. Vlad Drăculea be damned—the Demons of Solomon combined are far more powerful. And we share a common enemy in Radu. Once we obtain his patronage and acquire the blood and the sword, my allies within his camp intend to remove him from these dealings, and you may assert your dominance over these affairs."

"The banishment spell contains most of my power within these walls. I can't perform so much as a conjuring in this wretched body. Had the plants not grown inside the compound, even that spell would not have taken hold. I am essentially powerless here."

"But now we have spawned your proxy—a new Death Witch."

115

"My communication with her is quite sporadic. Although the banishment field is weakened at times, it still interferes with my ability to maintain sustained communication with her . . . For now, we must rely upon her remaining loyal."

"She will. She has nowhere else to turn. And once she delivers the vessels to you, we can hunt and kill—"

"Radu!"

"Yes. Radu. He has been in hiding for centuries. He is now known as the Sommelier to all who seek him."

Elizabeth shifted. "Then bring this Kaiser before me. We will use his empire's might to reclaim the blade imprisoning my father and resurrect him. And once Radu is killed, we will smash that bottle to ensure Vlad Drăculea never returns to threaten our endeavors again."

"Yes, my darling," said Vago, stroking her front leg.

"For now, my Death Witch is on the hunt . . . and once my father is resurrected, we shall reign. You actions were wise, Vago. You've given me hope."

"I would do it all over again for you, my Queen." Vago crouched. "May I?" he asked.

"But of course, my darling."

Vago knelt upon the floor and slid into position underneath Elizabeth's abdomen. He curled up below her, and she embraced him in her legs as he ran his hands gently across her smooth underside.

"That feels nice," said Elizabeth. "It's been so long since I've been caressed."

Vago smiled and continued to run his fingers lightly across her body.

"Vago?"

"Yes, darling?"

"In your travels, over the centuries, have you encountered a shape-shifter?"

"I don't believe I have. They are extremely rare. Born maybe once a millennium. Why?"

"I've been thinking. Once we succeed and the banishment spell is released, I would like to have my body back. That is currently an impossibility. I am forever trapped inside the body of this spider. But that impossibility could be broken if I consume the soul of a shape-shifter and absorb its magick. Then I can transform into any-thing I choose."

Vago patted her on the abdomen. "Consider it done. I will rest at nothing to see we find such a witch. With my eugenics studies, I may even be able to breed one."

"I promise that one day you will hold me in human form again."

"It matters not. You are my queen in any shape."

Elizabeth rested her body upon the floor, and Vago curled up to her. She placed her legs more snugly over him and pulled him close.

Vago was soon asleep, breathing peacefully in the arms of his one true love.

Chapter 9

9

March 23, 1917, 10:47 a.m.

"It looks unusually put together," said Felix, holding the telescope to his eye.

"How so?"

"A perfectly manicured mining town, like one of those Hollywood motion pictures. Everything looks new. Structures have new timber. Even the mine carts seem better for wear." Felix scanned the foreground to their right. "That's a huge reservoir. They've dammed the river—all new construction, but looks shoddy. If that thing breaks . . ." Felix panned his scope up and down, inspecting the dam, and could see the top part of a large mill wheel spinning before it. He took a moment to inspect the two-story brick building next to the wheel. "Look at that. They're generating their own electricity."

"Let me see!" Rurik said, pawing at the tarnished telescope.

"Hold on." Felix swatted away his hand. "Six oil derricks scattered through the grounds. They're definitely pumping out some volume on raw materials. Wonder what they're mining in the caves?"

"Any sign of Florin? German soldiers?"

"No Florin. Hard to say on the soldiers. Doesn't seem to be any military vehicles." Felix quickly counted the bodies in the scope's circular field of view. "Twentyish people. Mostly workers. Two seem to be barking orders. Then some mules."

"My turn," said Rurik, pulling the scope away.

Felix slid down the bank and made sure his head was below the sight line.

"This looks too good to be true . . . well, look at that."

"What?" asked Felix.

"There's an entire stream of oil just flowing down the side of the main street right through the quarry. They must be swimming in it."

"You sure it's not runoff from the dam?"

"Not sure. But it's running downward to town, so it's not coming from the derricks. Besides, too black and shiny to be water—it has to be seep. They're swimming in it."

Rurik continued to scan the terrain. It appeared the main road opened right into the quarry, which split the mining operation in two halves. Six mines on the left were dug right into the rock and six more on the right rose from the ground. The path then led to a small town center with a series of ramshackle buildings. The entire operation appeared to have been artificially plopped into the mud in the middle of a dense deciduous forest. Beyond the town, Rurik made out a moderate-sized tent encampment. He decided it must be for the workers, then refocused his gaze upon a horse tied in front of a small storefront at the town center. He watched as a man exited the store, holding a sack of grain and loaves of bread.

"Trading post," said Rurik, slapping Felix's shoulder with his free hand.

"What?" Felix sounded excited.

"My friend! We have a trading post . . . which I hope means alcohol!"

Felix reached over and snatched the telescope. "Lush," he said, raising the glass to his eye. "Well, look at that . . . trading post, indeed. OK—what's the plan?"

The two men sat at the bottom of the mound and looked to their horses hidden in the trees.

"They stay here," said Felix.

"Are you crazy? The moment we leave, that's the last we'll see of them. How much gold do you have hidden in that saddle?"

"Enough to last us until we can get to Switzerland and access my funds." Felix looked down to his tattered and dirty clothing. "Going to be a real fun time convincing anyone I'm me, though."

"We'll worry about that later. Here's what," said Rurik. "We take the horses and ride them into town. Right to the trading post. Trade gold for supplies and we're gone. Sound good?"

Felix laughed. "No. We're not riding into town on horseback like the goddamn Kaiser. We need to be more inconspicuous. They're expecting migrants and refugees—showing up on horses and bartering with gold? We'll be robbed and likely murdered. The gold is a problem. The horses are a bigger problem."

"So we walk into town *next* to our horses. We're not leaving them here."

Felix pondered the plan and pulled his foot to his knee, revealing a sizable hole in the middle of his sole.

"As long as I get new boots out of this, I'm ready."

*

Felix and Rurik walked down the embankment and onto the narrow muddy road that led into Zănoaga, holding their horses' reins. They proceeded along the slope as a stone wall rose from the earth to contain the artificial reservoir above, and then through a large stone archway that fed into the quarry.

As they emerged from the arch, they passed by the wooden dam on their right and were surprised to see it was much taller than it appeared from the distance. Felix guessed it was forty meters high. The clinking and clanking of the mill wheel was almost deafening as they came into the main throughway.

They walked past a series of mine shafts on both sides of the road. Felix noticed the mines carved into the quarry wall on the left all had barred gates, then looked to the mines popping from the ground on the right to see the same cage-style openings on their entrances. He wondered if the mines were for precious metals. The workmen were busy unloading reddish-brown rocks from the mining carts onto open-air mule-drawn carriages and seemed to pay them no mind.

"What did I tell you? Crude oil running right down the road," said Rurik, pointing to the stream of black viscous liquid to their right. "There must be an ocean of it below our feet."

Felix looked to the line of wooden oil derricks to their right in the short distance and didn't notice any runoff coming from that direction. "That's a lot of seep. No wonder the Kaiser seized Romania."

They continued through the quarry until they reached a row of wide and long tin troughs in the middle of the road opposite two mine shafts. Felix noticed their interiors were stained a deep brown and riddled with scratch marks. Even more curious were the U-shaped clamps that lined the troughs' brims, with rusty padlocks hanging from them.

"You men! You men, there! Away from the troughs!" came a voice in Romanian.

Felix and Rurik turned to see a heavyset man with a turban and dirty overalls racing toward them.

"What's he saying?" asked Felix.

"He wants us away from the troughs."

The man arrived before them, catching his breath.

"Are you here for work?"

"Supplies, actually," said Rurik. "We were hoping to barter at your trading post."

The man took them in, paying particular attention to their horses.

"We're not currently keen on trading. We need manpower. What are your names?"

"I'm Nicholas. This is my traveling companion, Eli," said Rurik.

"Very fine to meet you gentlemen. I'm Alexandru," he said, extending his hand.

All three men exchanged greetings.

"He doesn't speak Romanian?" asked Alexandru, motioning to Felix.

"No. But we are both fluent in Russian and English. He also speaks German."

"Half the men here speak German." Alexandru shook his head. "We need more Romanian foremen, not Germans. But we can always use more horses—perhaps for those we can barter," he said, eyeing their steeds once more.

"The horses aren't for trade," replied Rurik.

"That's too bad. Where are you men headed with such fine animals?"

"What's he saying?" questioned Felix.

"He wants to know where we're heading."

"Real bad idea to tell him. Just pretend we're here for temporary work."

Rurik nodded and turned to Alexandru. "We found one of your flyers offering food and shelter, but we also need some basic supplies. If we can't trade . . . well, we're good workers."

Alexandru clapped his hands together. "Wonderful. Wonderful. Follow me."

Rurik followed Alexandru as Felix turned and took a lingering glance at the operation behind them. The place felt too well run for something in the hinterlands, and suspicion swept over him as he eyed the poorly constructed dam once more.

"Come on, girl," he said, tugging on Nima's reins.

"What is it you're mining?" asked Rurik.

"Drilling for oil, obviously," said Alexandru, pointing to the petroleum seep. "Romania is now under German control, and our new emperor Vondling has seized control of this operation in service of—"

"I'm sorry. What?" interrupted Rurik.

"I was saying . . . in service of the Kaiser. And in addition to oil, we are mining potash for conversion to both pure potassium and eventually potassium nitrate for gunpowder. Really makes you proud if you—"

"Did he just say Vondling?" interjected Felix.

"You don't want to know," said Rurik.

Alexandru appeared annoyed at the interruption.

"As I was saying. Really makes you proud to think that our efforts are going to serve the Kaiser and win the war. They say we supply over forty-five percent of the potassium nitrate that goes into German explosives and gunpowder."

"Excellent," said Rurik. "Long live the Kaiser."

Alexandru smiled and squeezed Rurik's forearm. "So wonderful to hear you say that. I have my suspicions about some of these men's loyalties. Too bad. We're given a great deal of freedom here, so long as our quotas are met. The only time we see soldiers is when their trucks come to pick up materials."

The three men continued on toward the town center and passed what appeared to be a large refinery on their right.

"What's that?" asked Rurik.

"Ah! That is where we refine the potassium. Are either of you men familiar with the electrolysis process?"

"Actually, I am," said Rurik. "I minored in chemistry at university."

"Splendid!" said Alexandru. "Then you are of great use to us. And I suppose we can find some janitorial duties for your friend at the camp, since we're overstaffed on miners. Come, hurry. It will be evening soon, and I want to finish our business so that you men can be fed and prepped to begin work tomorrow at sunrise."

"Say," said Rurik as the men resumed walking. "You don't happen to have a bar in town?"

Alexandru swung his arm around Rurik. "Let me guess— vodka?"

"Yes, of course! But my friend and I also enjoy the company of women," said Rurik.

"There are no prostitutes here."

"Dear heavens!" said Rurik. "I think you have us all wrong. Believe it or not, I happen to be a bit of a ladies' man—"

"For that, you will have to go elsewhere." Alexandru removed his arm. "Women and alcohol are forbidden in Zănoaga." He sounded stern.

He turned his back on them and continued toward town.

*

Rurik and Felix sat at a well-fashioned table next to a wide bay window inside the trading post, trying their best to ignore the lean dirk of a man standing beside the door to the back room. He stood with his gaze transfixed upon the pair and never budged, except to occasionally run his thumb and index finger over his broad black mustache.

"Excellent craftsmanship," said Rurik, inspecting the table.

Felix was too intent on the shelves filled with breads and tins and various other supplies. "I'll eat that whole can of beans with my bare hands right now," he said, staring at the dry goods section.

"We'll be eating in no time. Calm down."

"I am calm. For once," said Felix, still looking at the beans. His gaze shifted to Rurik. "So?"

"So?"

"Vondling?"

Rurik shook his head and looked to the man standing beside the door. "Alexandru said that Romania is now ruled by an Emperor Vondling," he whispered.

Felix turned white. "You're joking."

"I am not."

"Well, those bodies in the loch now make sense. Vondling's building an army."

"Like you said—we have no idea what we're walking into. And that ustrel hive we encountered . . ."

Felix stared at him blankly as Rurik gathered his thoughts.

"Here's the thing," continued Rurik, lowering his voice further. "Ustrel are extremely rare or, in theory, they should be. According to the vampire bible, they are only created by vámpir who do not finish their prey, or somehow the prey escaped after being bitten. So they become infected by the bites, but don't fully become vámpir, as the conversion process is different. They're not quite a vampire and not quite human. They're something—"

"Worse. Those things disgust me. The one that attacked me when we approached Florin's had teeth growing on the roof of its mouth. Horrific. Like someone took a mangy, rabid rat and fused it with a human."

"That's about right," said Rurik. "How many did we kill? It was close to thirty."

"Well, seeing as how I was unconscious for half the encounter, I lost count, but yes—close to that."

"Then it seems fair to assume, based on the voracity with which vampires feed and the low likelihood of a person surviving such an attack, that they're being created on purpose."

Felix nodded. "Can ustrel create other ustrel?"

"Of course."

"So it's possible that hive spawned from one who escaped an attack?"

"Reasonable," said Rurik, scratching his beard. "But I still find it troubling due to the fact that ustrel by themselves are mostly timid if confronted. They generally feed on freshly dead bodies and will only attack the living in large groups as we experienced. If they're being created on purpose, the question is—to what end?"

"Well, throw an Emperor Vondling into this mix and there could be a variety of depraved reasons—especially if the Kaiser is behind this."

"Switzerland is sounding better by the minute."

The door to the back room swung open.

Felix and Rurik ceased their conversation and pretended to be focused on their horses tied up just outside the window.

Alexandru appeared with two plates teeming with mashed potatoes and ham.

"Will you?" he said to the mystery man, handing him the plates. Alexandru disappeared momentarily to return with a glass pitcher filled with crystal-clear water.

"Here we are—for our new friends," said Alexandru.

The two men placed the food and pitcher on the table, then stood back, crossed their arms, and stared at Felix and Rurik with wide, forced smiles.

"Thank you," said Rurik.

"Tell them I said thanks," followed Felix.

"My friend says—"

"You're quite welcome," said the taller gentleman in Russian.

Rurik cast a surprised glance to Felix.

Felix inspected the man and felt a sense of intimidation about him. He was lean but muscular with several blotchy trinket tattoos inked across his forearms. His black mustache contrasted against his tanned, sun-creased face and added an air of martial intent to his domineering posture.

"You speak Russian," said Felix.

"I do," he said. "I am from Chernivtsi."

"I see . . . Ukrainian. Do you speak Romanian as well?"

"Fluently. German too. Just a friendly warning—you should keep your misgivings about Emperor Vondling to yourselves. In Russian or otherwise. Enjoy your meal."

The man turned and walked to the back storeroom. Alexandru remained with his arms crossed. Felix noticed he now had a revolver holstered to his belt.

"Well?" asked Alexandru. "Aren't you going to eat?"

"Yes, yes, of course," said Rurik, looking to Felix while grabbing a fork. "Dig in."

The two men fell upon their meal, barely chewing the food before swallowing.

"Oh," said Felix with a mouth full of potatoes. "This is incredible."

"My compliments to the chef," said Rurik to Alexandru as he continued to devour his meal.

Felix lifted his head, still chewing. He swallowed his food, then grabbed the pitcher and poured himself a glass before downing it in one large gulp. Extending his arm across the table, he poured a glass for Rurik.

Alexandru remained uncomfortably close to them, inspecting their every movement and continually checking his watch. Rurik and Felix did their best to ignore the awkwardness of Alexandru's watchful stare.

Two minutes passed. Then three.

At seven minutes, Alexandru turned and called, "Yegor, they're out!" The lean Ukrainian man exited the storeroom and moved to Rurik first, who was facedown in his mashed potatoes.

"That one to the refinery," said Alexandru. "Says he's a chemist. If he lied, chuck him in the mines."

"What about the other one?" Yegor said, looking to Felix, who was passed out on the floor.

"Keep him locked up until the drugs are out of his system. Skander can assist you."

*

Felix opened his eyes as a great sense of confusion overtook him. Everything was spinning.

He looked around the small cavern with no understanding of where he was or why, only that the shadows of dusk were upon him. Cool stone pressed against his back and soft mud sat beneath him.

Felix tried to focus his gaze forward on the bars imprisoning him, and through them, could see early evening's cobalt sky blending to twilight with a small yellow star poking its light through the hazy blanket of navy and purple.

Felix discerned that his neck was constrained to a wall and he was naked, seated with his legs outstretched before him. He tried to move, but his appendages were numb. A pungent mixture of feces, urine, and decayed flesh overwhelmed him, and he tried breathing through his mouth to avoid the stench.

Where am I? What the hell is happening?

Felix tried to shake off the tingling in his arms and lifted his hand to feel the fetter clamped around his neck. His eyelids became heavy. Somewhere between consciousness and the oblivion of whatever drug cycled through his system, Felix registered that he was trapped in a mine foyer—most likely one of the shafts he and Rurik had passed on their way into Zănoaga. There were, in fact, bars on the entrance, two strange men also constrained and sitting on each side of him, and someone else seated on the far wall past the shaft's opening. He tried to lift his head, only to relax his jaw and drool all over his bare chest.

Come on, Felix . . . snap out of it, old boy.

Felix fell to darkness once more.

*

Rurik woke upon a cool dirt floor with his back against a metal barrel.

His hands fumbled across his chest until he found his glasses hanging from the strap around his neck. He pulled them to his face and as his surroundings came into focus, he noticed he was sitting in a small enclave encircled by other such barrels and a workbench to his left. Through his grogginess, Rurik's senses were immediately overcome with the chemical bite of kerosene, and his eyes watered a bit. He reached up and pulled on the rusty metal collar fastened tightly around his neck as his eyes traced the metal chain that ran from the collar to a position behind the barrel. He pulled on the chain until it became taut.

"Definitely fastened to something," he said, realizing there was no give.

He dropped the chain, then stood and scanned the vast expanse beyond his small enclosure.

Its ceiling was supported by heavy metal beams reminiscent of a rib cage, which caused Rurik to reflect on the story of Jonah and the whale. A series of domed lights hung from the rafters and cast cones of flickering orange light over sporadic pockets within the dispiriting interior. The space was mostly open air: the front and back entrances ran the entire width of the structure, which was supported by its east and west walls, constructed of sturdy brick. Just below the ceiling's arch, a series of opaque glass windows ran along both sides.

Noticing the crude electrolysis station on the workbench before him, Rurik pieced together that he was imprisoned within the refinery. He then noticed five other such stations, each with its own circle of barrels. He inspected the electrolysis tools before him.

"Back away!" came a voice from behind him.

Rurik turned around to see a laborer—a filthy man with filthier coveralls, who clearly had been taking the lion's share of any meals being rationed to the camp workers.

"Alexandru says you understand the electro-sis?"

"Yes," said Rurik. "I do, but—"

"Then show me."

Rurik thought to knock him out cold. He scanned the man's belt for keys that might unlock his neck's padlock, but didn't notice any. With escape currently not an option, Rurik decided it best to earn his captor's trust.

"This is for potassium, correct?" asked Rurik.

"Does it matter?" The heavyset man removed a baton from his belt and leaned in toward Rurik.

"I—I haven't done it in many years. Allow me to inspect the tools."

"Well, you better remember real quick. Name's Pavel, by the way, and let me just say you'll do yourself right to get on my good side. I'm a pretty big deal around here."

Rurik nodded and turned to the workstation.

"Let's see. Metal bin with anode and diode sides. OK. Where's the power source?"

"Under the bench," said Pavel, pointing underneath Rurik's workstation.

Rurik bent over and almost fell forward as the lingering drugs in his system rushed to his head. He steadied himself, focusing on a fat black battery with two cables running to alligator clamps clipped to a rubberized pole. He pulled the clamps from underneath, inspected the metal jaws, then returned them to their insulated resting place.

"It's a bit archaic, but I can do it. Where's the potash?"

"In that bin there. Bucket holds five kilos."

Rurik poked his head over the brim to see reddish pulverized potash. "I think that about does it then. What am I supposed to do with the pure potassium once complete?"

Pavel opened a barrel next to Rurik's workstation that was filled with black petroleum.

"Drop them in here. Each barrel will hold about twenty bricks. And do it fast—the potassium will react with moisture in the air if you leave them sitting out. Last guy who manned this station blew his damn arm off waiting too long. Seal the barrel, ring the bell, and we'll push it to the side and bring you a new one."

Rurik scanned the floor of the refinery and noticed at least two hundred sealed barrels. "That's a lot of pure," said Rurik.

"Not really your business," said Pavel.

Two men walked past the front entrance with German shepherds on leashes and rifles in their hands. Besides Pavel, Rurik was the only person inside the refinery.

"Am I the only one?"

"For now. You're night shift. Alexandru wants me to inspect your work. If you're good, maybe you can train some of the others in camp."

"And if I'm bad?"

Pavel smiled, his plump cheeks widening his already ample facial features.

"Trust me, friend. You don't want to be bad." Pavel tapped his baton in his palm a few times. "Five barrels minimum tonight, or we'll throw you in the mines. I'll be back in an hour to inspect your work." His portly frame began walking away.

"Excuse me, sir?" beckoned Rurik.

Pavel stopped but did not turn. "Yes?"

"My traveling companion. Can you tell me if he's all right?"

Pavel stood silently for a moment with his back to Rurik. He then forcefully shoved his baton into his belt holster and sauntered off into the shadowy refinery.

*

Felix was wandering through a dense, dark forest. He knew this place—the black woods of Loch Dracul.

Having no certain idea as to the way out, he spun around, searching for some source of light. He saw a sliver in the distance and proceeded in that direction. The forest became more sparse, and he could see the clearing that led to the cliffs in the distance. As Felix emerged from the darkness, he saw her—standing in the same red dress she wore the last time they were together.

"Irina?" called Felix.

Her head jerked slightly backward, signaling she'd heard him.

Felix dashed into the clearing as the sweeping expanse of Loch Dracul opened before him. The drab, silvery cloud cover painted everything beneath it a solemn, cinereous color, save Irina's red dress at the cliff line. Felix continued toward her as a strong breeze flattened the low-lying smug-grass before him.

"Irina!"

She turned to him as he approached.

Felix stopped a few paces in front of her and noticed her face was wet with tears.

"You lost me, Felix. How could you let them take me?"

She leaned backward with her arms outstretched and cast herself over the cliff.

Felix sprinted to the edge, expecting to watch her body fall into the murky waters below, but there was nothing. His eyes scanned the surface, searching for bubbles from her entry point.

The loch was black and calm.

A flicker of red caught his eye, and Felix looked down to his left to see Irina walking toward the end of the nearly submerged dock where he and Denis had landed when they arrived at the island. Her pace was slow and resolute as she neared the dropoff to the bottomless waters.

Felix stood and ran to the camouflaged stairwell—the missing portion of the top stairs that had crumbled upon his and Denis's previous ascent lay before him. He stepped back about three meters and dashed forward, jumping over the pit and landing on the hard stone stairs, tumbling down a few before regaining his balance. Felix continued down the stairwell as quickly as he could before emerging on the long stone dock.

Irina was now standing at the very end.

"Irina! Stop!" he yelled, outstretching his right hand.

He raced toward her, the water sloshing about his feet as the loch's depths ebbed and flowed over the stone surface. Felix was nearly to Irina when he noticed a froth begin to gather upon the loch's surface a short distance from her, quickly approaching the dock.

"Irina, come back," he called.

It appeared as a small black lump at first—barely breaking the surface. Felix stopped and fell backward when the tentacled leviathan burst from the black waters. The beast seized upon Irina, wrapping its massive tentacles around her slim body and pulling her into its circular mouth lined with barbed teeth.

With another foamy splash, the briny beast was gone.

Felix screamed.

He ran to the edge of the dock, searching for some speck of red in the darkness below, only to be faced with his panicked reflection wriggling before him.

"And that is where she is to remain," came a calm, cool voice at his back.

Felix stood to confront the voice, and his arms went numb at once. Before him stood none other than Grigori Rasputin.

"You!" growled Felix.

Rasputin placed his arms behind his back and cocked his head. "Still have that temper, I see."

"Why am I here?" asked Felix. "Is this hell? Is this my mind?"

Rasputin let out an enthusiastic laugh. He looked around with wide, amused eyes. "Why, yes! I would say both are a very accurate description of what this place is."

The thought of his hands around Rasputin's neck, drowning him in the onyx waters, flashed into Felix's mind, but the mystic stood too far away—Felix knew he would never take him by surprise.

"Felix. Really? Drowning me? Do you still not know what this is all about? Why do you think this, of all places"—Rasputin spread his arms wide—"is indicative of your mind?"

Felix glared at Rasputin.

"Allow me to show you," said Rasputin, as giant tentacles rose from the waters on both sides of the dock. He charged at Felix with great speed and pushed him into the loch.

Felix floated downward, finding himself unable to swim. The water around him felt viscous, almost syrupy. His lungs screamed for air as he sank lower into the murk, the black suctioned tentacles of the behemoth loch monster swarming all around him.

The slithering appendages faded away as unfamiliar ghostly images floated past him: his parents' headless and charred bodies, Alexandra's lacerated nude flesh, and an old tarnished shield covered in brown algae bearing a red dragon emblem with golden flames rising from behind the beast.

Felix tried once more to swim to the surface, but some unnatural force kept dragging him farther down. His vision began to fade as he looked upward to see a male figure standing at the edge of the dock—the stranger's image rippling and contorting on the surface. Felix was certain the man was not Rasputin—he was bald, with a shorter, striped beard.

He knelt on the dock and extended his hand below the surface toward Felix.

"You are more powerful than you know," came the stranger's voice. "Take my hand and you will see."

Felix extended his hand but was too far under to reach the stranger—the black, bottomless waters slowly enveloping him.

"Just breathe, Felix," came the stranger's voice. "The Veil will show you the way."

Felix closed his eyes, opened his mouth, and inhaled the loch's murk into his lungs.

Chapter 9

He snapped awake.

Still confined by the neck to the mine's stone wall but with a new sense of clarity about him. Felix sucked in great pockets of air as the effects of the drug seemed to dissipate from his mind.

It was nighttime.

Felix looked to the cage that confined him and three other men inside the mine as a shadow appeared on the other side of the bars.

A jingling rang out as the shadow unlocked the gate and opened it.

"Wake up, gentlemen," said the shadow in German. "It's feeding time!"

The shadow was joined by another portly man, and they moved to the person confined on the opposite side of the mine foyer just past the shaft entrance. They unlocked his collar, and the man began kicking and struggling.

"*Nu, vă rog nu!*" yelled the man.

Felix watched as the shadowy man pulled a baton from his belt and thumped it down several times on the prisoner's rib cage, beating him into submission until he lay whimpering in the mud.

"*Ia-l cu ceilalți,*" said the shadow, and his counterpart dragged the man by his ankles as he desperately dug his fingernails into the muddy road while begging to be freed.

By the light of a string of incandescent bulbs that hung from makeshift posts along the road, Felix watched as the portly man, who he could now clearly see was Alexandru, forced the nude man's face into a trough, then locked a curved clamp over his neck. Felix noticed eight such clamps on each side of the trough.

Felix's eyes settled on the shadowed man inside the foyer—it was Yegor.

He hulked over the naked prisoner to Felix's left and began to unlock his neck harness.

"No!" screamed the man in German. "I'll go back. I'll fight. Long live the Kaiser!"

"Silence!" yelled Yegor, whacking him with the baton.

The prisoner, seemingly resigned to his fate, stood, and Yegor yanked him by the nape of his neck, leading him to the trough.

Alexandru opened the bars wider, taking a moment to ensure they stayed in place before flashing a mocking smile at Felix.

I'll get you, you son of a bitch, thought Felix.

Felix was hyperventilating as he watched two other men lead a row of fourteen nude prisoners and corral them around the trough. Craning his neck, Felix could make out a portion of another trough with more men being locked into that one as well. They all looked filthy, and Felix couldn't discern if their appearance was due to dirt or bruises or both. He tried to calm himself and looked to the remaining man chained next to him.

"Do you speak German?" asked Felix.

The man turned his dirty, beaten face to Felix.

"I do. Infantry. Deserter," he said.

"What's happening here?"

The man was silent with a heaviness about him that resonated as shame. He hung his head.

"Them . . ." began the man, motioning his head toward the mine opening. "They're using these monsters to mine potash. The savages don't need any rest or light to see in the dark. All day, all night, those devils mine down there in the pitch black." The man's blue eyes focused on the trough. "Their only payment is blood."

Felix immediately thought back to his conversation with Rurik.

"Ustrel," he said.

"What?"

"Like vampires, but more . . . depraved. No semblance of humanity."

As Felix tried to position himself for a better view of the outside, he became aware of stones underneath his hands. He looked down to see he was seated upon a decaying body embedded in the mud, and what he first took for stones was in fact a pelvis bone.

"Ah!" he yelled, trying to move his naked flesh from the corpse beneath him.

He then noticed the entire floor of the foyer was littered with human bones.

"Sometimes they don't wait," said the soldier. "They come from the mines and feed."

"What's your name, friend?" asked Felix.

"I am Jonathan."

"Jonathan. I'm Felix. I'd say nice to meet you, but—"

"Ha!" yelled Jonathan, smiling unexpectedly.

Felix seemed taken aback by his sudden exuberance.

"Nice to meet me? You're a madman."

"Listen, Jonathan. What do you know about this place? The timing of their activities—anything."

"Devising escape?"

"Aren't you?" Felix sounded agitated.

Jonathan shuddered a bit as snot began to drip from his nose. He reached up and wiped his lip. "There is no escape," he whispered. "Anyone who's tried always returns to the trough. They have those monsters, men with guns, and dogs . . . German shepherds. They'll hunt you. You either work or you die."

Felix took in his own predicament. "Apparently, sometimes you're just given a death sentence."

"They're running out of men to use for feed. Most new arrivals are drugged and locked up unless they're extremely useful. They have taken to kidnapping people from their homes all over the countryside."

Felix reached up to his collar and yanked on it as hard as he could.

"It's no use," said Jonathan. "We all try, but they're well fastened into the stone."

Felix took a few deep breaths and shifted his gaze back to the trough. Each of the nude men was forced to his knees and locked into the metal trench. Felix looked to Jonathan to see he was purposely looking away from the happenings.

Felix saw one remaining naked man standing on the opposite side of the trough, and his heart sank.

"Florin!" he yelled.

Florin looked up in surprise. He squinted and stared into the mine holding Felix.

"Who's there?" called Florin.

The words were no sooner from his mouth than Yegor's baton found Florin's knee. He shrieked in pain, fell to the dirt, and was fettered by the neck into the trough.

"Your friend?" asked Jonathan.

"Yes."

"Best look away then."

Outside the mine, Yegor walked around the trough, inspecting the neck fetters. He reached to a holster on his thigh and produced a silver taiga machete. As if murder were his first nature, Yegor then proceeded to circle the trough and whack each of the prisoners in the back of the neck with his blade, severing their cervical columns as their heads still hung from their bodies by the flesh at the front of their necks. One by one, the men slumped to lifelessness as their blood flooded the trough.

At first, Felix averted his gaze, but something inside him welled and he turned to watch the slaughter. An intense anger brewed in his gut. Yegor finally made his way to Florin. He raised his taiga high into the air and turned to Felix.

"Tomorrow this will be you, Russian!" he said, never breaking eye contact. He swung the blade down on Florin's neck, severing his head completely from his body.

Felix grunted and looked away.

Yegor took another lap around the trough as it filled with blood. Deciding he was satisfied with his endeavor, he looked to Alexandru.

"*Suna-i,*" he said in Romanian.

Yegor sheathed his taiga and walked off into the night.

Alexandru stood next to a post on the opposite side of the road and pressed a large button on a metal box.

A screeching siren rang out.

Alexandru looked at his watch for several seconds, then silenced the alarm.

Silence pervaded the country air as the blackest of nights settled upon the mining town with a sense of cruelty and woe. Felix could feel his heart thumping with such fury, he believed his blood vessels might burst.

"What happens next?" he asked, kicking Jonathan's leg. "What now?"

Jonathan had turned his face to the wall as far as he could and whimpered softly.

"What happens—"

It started as a rumble, bouncing and ricocheting off the shaft's walls from deep within the mine—the sound of a thousand starving rodents scurrying and shrieking out for blood swelled from the darkened stone pharynx. The harrowing call grew to a near-deafening volume, sending a freeze across Felix's skin as his hair stood up to sharp pointy bristles.

The shadows of the ustrel seemed to explode from the shaft's entrance as they shot past Felix and swarmed upon the troughs. Felix squeezed his eyes closed, then slightly opened his left to witness the bloodbath. Some of the damned were clothed in the very manner of dress as the miners Felix had seen earlier in the day, some wore mere tatters, while others stood completely nude.

All were fanged, horrifying creatures.

Felix watched as their lean, muscular bodies crowded the pool of blood while others took to feeding on the kneeling carcasses. Gurgles, crunches, and ghoulish shrieks filled the air as at least fifty of the depraved feasted upon the offering.

"You've worked in these mines?" asked Felix, short on breath, kicking Jonathan's leg.

Jonathan nodded.

"OK. I need you to think. Hard. Tell me anything you know."

Jonathan was sucking erratic breaths into his mouth, unable to speak.

"You're a goddamn soldier! Think. Anything. Tell me!"

"They're all connected," said Jonathan. "This shaft leads to the main cavern where they mine. They all do. And then each shaft is connected to the others about forty meters in."

"Anything else? Anything?"

Jonathan paused for a moment as the feeding frenzy outside calmed.

"Um . . . inside each there's a stockroom toward the front of the shaft."

"Which side of the shaft?" questioned Felix.

"Uh, left, I think."

"You think?"

"Yes. Left side," said Jonathan.

"And?"

"And what?"

"And what's in them?"

"I don't know! Just . . . just a workbench. Small tools. I don't know what you want from me!"

The words were no sooner from Jonathan's mouth than the siren reared up again. After a moment, it ceased.

"*Suficient!*" yelled Alexandru from a distance, cracking a bull-whip on the backs of several ustrel.

The monsters hissed at him and backed away.

"*Revino la îndatoririle tale!*" he screamed, cracking the whip into the air.

The body of ustrel began to disperse, scurrying back into their respective mine shafts. Two others ignored the command and continued to lick the bloodstained trough clean. Alexandru flipped open his trench coat and pulled a long wooden stake from his belt. He charged upon the disobedient ustrel, continuing to scream at them in Romanian while shoving his stake into their faces.

The ustrel licked the blood from their hands and backed away toward the mine where Felix and Jonathan sat. Alexandru brandished the stake like a ringmaster confronting unruly tigers, forcing the ustrel inside before slamming the bars shut and locking them in.

The two ustrel gripped the bars and shoved their faces between them, holding their clawed hands out as if they were begging for more blood.

Alexandru whacked his stake across the bars. He spit at them, then muttered something in Romanian before sauntering off to lock the remaining mines.

The ustrel stood at the bars for a moment before turning their attention to Felix and Jonathan. Even in the shadows, Felix could see their yellow eyes and rows of jagged teeth nearly bursting from their mouths.

"Any other exits?" asked Felix, speaking rapidly.

Jonathan was shaking.

"Quickly! Any other—"

"I don't know! I think."

The ustrel fell upon Felix and Jonathan, extending their clawed hands and gnashing their sharp teeth.

Jonathan let out a quick gurgled whimper as the ustrel ripped open his throat and began to feed.

Felix, acting on instinct, raised his foot into the air, blocking the other ustrel's initial attack. The rodent-like creature recovered, wrestling with Felix's legs and digging its claws into his torso as it lusted for his neck. He slammed his fists repeatedly into its face as the creature chomped its teeth, trying to bite Felix's hands.

The ustrel wrapped its arms around Felix and subdued his strikes. Realizing he was done for, Felix turned his head away from the pending attack.

Suddenly, the ustrel's weight was gone.

Felix looked to the gruesome face mere inches from him as sucking and biting sounds continued from his right—Jonathan was no longer struggling. The ustrel before Felix simply stared at him, curling its peaked nose and sniffing. It moved toward his jugular vein. Sensing the sodium diethylbarbiturate still in Felix's bloodstream, the creature hissed at him and dove toward Jonathan's legs, sinking its fangs into his thigh and chewing on his muscle before finding his femoral artery and guzzling from the blood-engorged pipe.

Felix tried to remain perfectly still as the two ustrel fed upon Jonathan. Only another moment passed before a high-pitched screech echoed from deep within the shaft. The ustrel ceased their feast, looked at one another for a brief second, then fled down the darkened corridor.

Felix clenched his fists and thumped them into the mud, struggling to not go entirely mad from fear. As his flesh hit the ground, he remembered the corpse bones beneath him. He placed his hands on his thighs and in his periphery could see what was left of Jonathan. Not daring to look, he could nevertheless see pockets of white from exposed bones and deep reds from mangled muscle contrasted against Jonathan's flesh. A wet sensation coated the back of Felix's thighs as what was left of the man's blood seeped onto the ground.

OK, Felix. Figure this out . . . figure this out.

He once again gripped his collar and tried to pull it from the wall. Convinced it would budge with more pressure, Felix pressed his neck into the device as hard as he could, hoping to find some leverage. His vision began to fill with sparkles of blue and red as he constricted the blood flow to his head.

Felix would find no quarter.

He relaxed his neck and took a moment to catch his breath.

Knowing that removal of the neck collar was his only means of escape, Felix ran his fingers across the curved metal to find that, in addition to the padlock, a bolt was secured on each side. He tried to loosen the bolts, but his flesh was too soft to counter the torque by which they were fastened. Felix then rammed his open palms upward into the collar, hoping to force it loose. He gripped the device once more, pulling up and down on it, noticing a very slight wobble, but nothing indicative of structural weakness. Feeling defeated, Felix dropped his arms and let his hands fall into the blood-soaked dirt.

Felix was alone now, his breath and rampant heartbeat his only semblance of companions save Jonathan's corpse and the carcass beneath him—and that was when an idea formed in his mind.

Lifting his legs from the muck, Felix found the pelvis bone beneath him. He ran his fingers along its bulbous shape until he found what he believed to be the thighbone. Inch by inch, Felix forced his fingers into the soft mud until he was able to wrap his hand around the cylindrical bone. He pulled, unearthing the entirety of a leg with decaying flesh and a nearly intact foot clinging to the marrow. Gagging from the excavated stench, Felix wrapped his feet around the knee joint still held together by decaying cartilage. He gripped the circular notch of the hip joint and pulled forcefully until the leg snapped at the knee.

Felix then grabbed the thighbone by both ends and placed his foot at the center of the femoral shaft. Yanking with all his might while forcing his foot into the weakest center portion of the bone, Felix snapped it in two.

His fingers found the stone wall behind him and he pulled half the leg bone upward, trying to grind it to a fine point upon the stone. He stopped for a moment, realizing he was exhausted. After composing himself, Felix looked at the bone and was heartened to see that the tip was beginning to come to a fine, sharp point. He then returned to filing it against the stone wall.

"OK, OK," he said aloud, inspecting the bone once more. "This could work."

Deciding it was sharp enough, he used his right palm to force upward pressure onto his clamp. He then slid the sharp portion of the bone into a small gap between the wall and the collar.

It fits. Thank you. Thank you!

Felix twisted and shoved the bone farther into the gap, trying to dislodge the collar as bits of stone residue cracked and fell from the wall. The metal continually dug its way into the marrow, and Felix was forced to reshape it several times. Each return loosened his fetter as the collar began to bend the bolt and the stone gave way to dull force.

He continued this action for some time before deciding he could do no more.

Felix placed the bone on the ground and rested.

Now. Just be still for a second, and then give it every ounce of strength you have.

Felix lifted his hands to the collar and gripped it. He then raised his body slightly and hung himself on the collar, using his fingers to protect his windpipe. The collar gave, but he was still stuck. Felix then pulled his heels beneath his buttocks and forced as much up-ward pressure on the collar as he could before dropping his legs and all his weight with them. He feverishly continued this action until he felt a snap and, from the corner of his eye, watched a bolt head fly from the screw and tumble into the mud.

Felix pushed the collar from his neck and stood.

Taking in the carnage of Jonathan's mangled remains, he tried to steady his breath and remain calm. Felix moved to the bars, then pushed and pulled on them with all the strength he had left. Realizing they had no give whatsoever, he relented and looked to the headless gored bodies and severed limbs strewn about the road.

A sense of resolve kindled inside him as his eyes settled on the mostly skeletal remains of Florin's corpse.

Tomorrow this will be you, Russian! came Yegor's earlier threat.

"We'll see about that," said Felix.

He reached to the ground, picked up his makeshift bone stake, then proceeded into the darkened abyss of the damned.

10

March 23, 1917, evening

The carved ivory hearth appeared as a glossy white beacon in the candlelit dining salon of the Berlin Palace. The roaring fire within cast a cozy radiance over the formally dressed company, who mingled as champagne flutes occasionally clinked above the soft chamber music arising from an orchestra quartet situated in a corner just right of the grand Neo-baroque entrance.

A repeated ringing pierced the calm as General Hindenburg stood at a circular table in his formal military uniform, tapping a spoon upon his glass. The chamber music ceased and the fifty-odd guests hushed as the giant man raised his flute into the air.

"A toast!" he called. "Our siege of Arras is nearly complete. Paris is within our grasp."

"Hear, hear!" chimed the crowd.

"My special congratulations to our minister of war, general of the artillery, Hermann von Stein and his excellent field marshals who have held the advance. Take a bow, Minister."

Stein walked around the various circular tables adorned with white tablecloths and stood center room, just beneath the ornate crystal chandelier that crowned the dining salon. He looked upward and moved slightly to his left to ensure no candle wax would drip on his immaculate uniform as he gave his speech. Stein took an exaggerated bow, hoping Wilhelm was watching, then stood with a proud smile as the guests offered a polite round of applause.

"Hail to the Second Reich," he said, holding his glass above his head and purposely in the direction of Wilhelm. "None of our ingenious victories would have been possible without the deep wisdom, perseverance, and extreme intelligence of our supreme commander, Kaiser Friedrich Wilhelm II. France will be ours. Long live the Kaiser!"

"Long live the Kaiser!" repeated the guests.

"Please, Your Eminence, grace us with a few words," finished Stein.

Kaiser Wilhelm leaned into Augusta and planted a firm kiss upon her cheek. He reached to his left hand, hooked a loop on his glove around the hilt of his saber so that his lame limb would stay in place, then proceeded to the center of the room.

An obedient hush quieted the hall.

"Not too very long ago," began Wilhelm, his uniform hanging heavy with medals, "our great ally and my dear friend Archduke Franz Ferdinand was brutally murdered by Serbian swine. And that left our people, our friends, and our monarchy with a choice: Do we continue to allow our divine monarchy to suffer the slings and arrows of outrageous fortune, as a great man once wrote?"

A hushed, pleasant laughter filled the room.

"Very nice," said Wilhelm. "As some of you know, Shakespeare is nearly sacred text to me. Sadly, he was not Prussian . . ."

More laughter followed.

"But I often turn to Shakespeare for inspiration. Do I treat my power as King Lear did? Squandering it, spreading it among our ungrateful or weak allies to the point that it is watered down to nothing? Only to be paid back with such flagrant disrespect that filthy rebels in Sarajevo can assassinate a great man? A great friend to Germany? Or am I to be Henry V and assert supreme power over not only our holy monarchy, but France and England and any nation that dares defy me?"

Wilhelm was silent for a moment as a quiet fell upon the gathering.

He smiled and held his glass outward. "'Once more unto the breach, dear friends, once more; or close the wall up with our—*Prussian*—dead!'" He raised his glass. "To Germany, to victory . . . to the breach, dear friends!"

The audience erupted in cheers.

Stein moved in close and placed his hand upon the Wilhelm's shoulder. The Kaiser shot him a glare and distanced himself. Stein, feeling embarrassed, looked back to his wife at their table, only to see her standing far too close to his rival, Heinrich Adolf Wild von Hohenborn, in all his handsome exuberance.

"General Hindenburg, please," said Wilhelm, beckoning Hindenburg to join them.

Wilhelm stood so that Hindenburg was between him and Stein, whose shoulders slumped in defeat. He tried holding his head high, but his repeated blinking belied his shaken confidence.

"To the greatest general our nation has ever known!" said Wilhelm.

Hindenburg took a short bow and turned to embrace Wilhelm as Stein stood back and applauded softly.

"Now," said Wilhelm in a voice low and calm, "let us celebrate. Enjoy the wine and food. Paris will be ours by summer!"

Chamber music and applause rose into the air, and the guests returned to mingling.

*

"And you all know my lovely Nette," said Hindenburg, throwing his arm over the shoulder of his comely young daughter.

"Of course," said Wilhelm, kissing Nette upon the hand.

Augusta reached out and yanked on Wilhelm's arm, pulling him back to her side. The small circle of advisors and cabinet members fell momentarily quiet, trying their best to ignore the tussle.

"Pleasure to see you all again," said Nette, bowing her head slightly.

Augusta took in Nette's slinky white silken gown, then rolled her eyes.

"Nette," began Wilhelm, "how are your university studies?"

"Wonderful, Kaiser. As you know, I—"

"How could I know? That is why I asked."

Hindenburg shot a curious glance at his daughter as Augusta seemed to stiffen.

Sweat beads gathered on Wilhelm's brow. With his mind racing for something to say, he spotted Friedrich von Berg, his head of secret police, standing in the parlor entrance, appearing studious in his round-rimmed glasses as he checked his watch.

"What's he doing here?" asked Hindenburg, leaning into Wilhelm and whispering.

"Pardon us for one moment," said Wilhelm to the group. He leaned his head sideways, motioning Hindenburg to follow him.

"You stay hidden, remember?" said Wilhelm, approaching Berg. "I want no one to know who you are or what you do. As far as anyone's concerned, you're a low-level treasury associate. Seeing you here—"

"Understood, Kaiser. But it's urgent. My men have made a horrid discovery." Berg took a deep breath. "Kidnappings. Many of them. Started yesterday morning in and around Zimmern."

"That entire area is known for missing persons," said Hindenburg.

"Not like this," said Berg. "All children. Rich, poor. Twenty-five have gone missing in the past thirty-six hours."

Wilhelm's eyes grew wide. "Twenty-five? You're certain?"

"Yes."

"It's the French," said Wilhelm. "An intimidation tactic!"

"I don't think so. We have two eye-witness accounts of *something* materializing and stealing the children."

"Something?" Wilhelm looked to Hindenburg. "Are you aware of this?"

"I am not."

The men stood silently.

"I feel there is something you're not telling me, Paul," said Wilhelm. "I can see it on your face."

Hindenburg closed his eyes and bowed his head, his short white hair appearing to glow in the candlelight. "I have a very strong suspicion . . . We should discuss this matter in private."

Wilhelm looked back at the small gathering and decided the patrons were likely drunk enough not to notice his departure.

"To my study," said Wilhelm.

The three men marched quickly through the main hall, up the Schlüter staircase, and across the palace to Wilhelm's private study.

Augusta watched as Wilhelm left the parlor with Hindenburg and Berg in tow, then turned her attention to two rambunctious little girls who dashed into the parlor, engaging each other in a game of tag.

"I think we'll have to remind our patrons that, although lovely, little children should be left at home next time," said Augusta to polite smiles from her circle of admirers. "Don't you think so, Nette?"

Nette seemed taken off guard by Augusta's sudden warmth. "Why—why yes, Empress. Of course."

"You're close enough to their age," said Augusta. "Perhaps you can watch them for a bit, before your father returns?"

Nette turned to see the small girls now crawling under the chafing table, disturbing the serving platters.

"I'm not certain my father would approve," said Nette. "He said I was to stay engaged with the party."

"And why would that be?" Augusta sounded stern once again.

Nette appeared uncomfortable. She swallowed and ran her hands across the front of her gown as she averted her gaze to the entrance.

The children suddenly crashed into Nette and hugged her around the waist.

"You're it!" they cried. "You're it!"

Nette bent over and playfully tried to grab them as they howled with laughter and scurried off to the dining hall's entrance. One little girl poked her blonde head around the threshold's molding and pointed at Nette. "You're it," she called. "Come and catch us!"

Nette looked to Augusta.

"Well? " said Augusta. "It appears as if you're it. Do us all a favor, would you? Go gather the children and find out who their parents are. We can't have them running amok through the gathering."

Nette bowed her head and curtsied. "As you wish, my Empress."

She then followed the two small girls as they dashed into the grand halls of the Berlin Palace.

Augusta watched with a vengeful glare as Nette's slim frame approached the door and disappeared after the children.

"That's strange," said Stein, sliding in next to Augusta to join the group. "I don't recall any guests arriving with children."

Augusta ignored him and stared toward the entrance in a near trance.

"Is everything fair, my Empress?" asked Stein.

"It will be soon enough," she replied flatly.

*

"Come out, come out—wherever you are!" Nette crouched over and crept toward the back of a teal rococo sofa with gold trim.

"Gotcha!" she exclaimed as she reached over the sofa, only to find it empty.

Quiet laughter echoed from the parade room behind her, followed by the chime of a grandfather clock.

Nette hunched to the marble floor and peered under the sofa— nothing but bare floor. She stood and turned back around to see the silhouette of a little girl dash past the doorframe.

Nette gave chase.

That's curious, she thought as she entered the Chamber of the Black Eagle. The grandfather clock in the corner had been moved to the side, revealing a dark passage cut into the wall. *It wasn't that way when I entered before.*

Feminine, infantile laughter rose from the passage. "Down here! Come and get us."

Nette's heart thumped as she neared the grandfather clock—its ticking rattled her nerves even further. She leaned into the passage to see a stone stair leading downward and flickering candlelight below.

"Girls!" she called into the dark. "Come up at once! I am not amused."

"Come find us," echoed a small voice.

Nette bit her lower lip, growing frustrated. She thought to turn back and alert the palace guard, then considered that this impromptu game of hide-and-seek was still preferable to shivering in the chill of Augusta's gaze and her continual passive aggression.

"I am to be a mother soon," she said, projecting confidence— certainly, she was brave enough to walk down a dark stairwell to check on the well-being of some misbehaved kids.

"You can't leave them down there," she said to herself.

Laughter echoed from below, raising the hair on Nette's arms. She took one last look around the chamber and stepped into the stairwell, crouching a bit to see into the passage.

"Girls, please—"

The door behind her slammed shut.

Nette shot up the stairs and banged on the wall. "Let me out of here. Hey!"

"We have a surprise for you, Nette. Come find us!"

Nette turned around and ran her hands along the front of her rumpled dress. She took a long look at the passage below, where the flickering candlelight casting shadows upon the stone walls. Her immediate thought was to bang on the door until the palace guard found her, but first she needed to collect the children before they ran any farther. Nette winced, thinking of the chiding she would receive once her father found out she had left the party and trapped herself in a strange passage. And what if the Kaiser found out? Perhaps he'd think this blunder showed she was too irresponsible to bear his child.

"I'll never hear the end of this," she said, descending into the dark. "Little girls! You'd better come up here right now."

The corridor blew cool, humid air over her flesh. Nette swallowed and rubbed her hands over her forearms, attempting to quash her oncoming chill. Her frustration turned into anger as she reached the bottom of the stairs. "You two are in big trouble!"

She lingered in the passageway for a moment, looking toward its end.

"Who's there?" she questioned.

Nette angled her head and realized it was her own reflection in the distance.

Is that a mirror?

Step by step, Nette crept toward the small chamber at the end of the passage. She entered to see an ornate vanity with a distressed mirror at its top. The candelabra on its surface cast enough light for her to see a picture frame sitting just before the mirror. She reached for the frame, and dread constricted her windpipe as she stared at her own photograph.

The bars to the room slammed shut behind her with a horrid clang.

Nette dropped the frame and shot toward the rusty iron. She gripped the bars, pulling and pushing upon them to no avail.

"Hey!" she yelled. "Let me out!"

"Nette . . ."

The voice was feminine and calm.

Nette froze.

She slowly turned around while keeping her back firmly pressed against the bars. Nette covered her mouth at the sight of her own bloodied reflection in the mirror. She looked down to see there was no blood on her own gown. Her eyes darted back to the looking glass, and she shuddered as the reflection moved on its own.

The bloodied specter reached from the mirror and slid the candelabra to the far side of the vanity. It then pulled itself through the glass in an unnatural motion as its joints appeared to move in the opposite direction, cracking and distorting to fit itself through.

The ghoul stood motionless before her as its brown hair waved about its shoulders.

"What are you?" breathed Nette, looking to the gaunt, pale version of her own face.

The grisly doppelgänger remained rigid.

Nette focused on its abdomen as blood gushed onto the floor, staining the lower portion of its silken gown. It then reached to its stomach and tore open the gown to reveal a gaping flesh wound across its abdomen.

"Help me! Please, someone help!" yelled Nette, never taking her eyes from the intruder.

The apparition simply stared at her with black, soulless eyes, plunging its fingers into its open abdominal wound—a rotten smile conveying a sense of pleasure as it wrapped its hands around its womb and squeezed tightly, further bloodying its bony hands.

Nette slid to the floor in hysterics.

"Please don't hurt me! Please don't—"

The doppelgänger grinned at her once more.

It then turned, grabbed the ebony-handled blade upon the vanity, and blew out the candles.

*

"You mean to tell me that Elizabeth Báthory is alive?"

"She is, Kaiser, yes," said Hindenburg with a solemn air about him.

"And the legend is true? She's the only daughter of the demon king Bael?"

"Yes, Kaiser."

"What exactly is she capable of?"

Hindenburg placed his elbows on his knees and leaned forward. "Currently, due to the banishment spell, very little. But were she to roam free, immeasurable destruction. She's a demi-demon. Her mother was mortal. Elizabeth was a terribly powerful entity before she was banished. Human witches and warlocks draw their power from the world around them, and grow tired after casting too many spells or holding a powerful spell for too long. Demons or even demi-demons have no such limitations. Their power is fueled continually from the Void. They are unstoppable forces of pure menace. Never tiring, never daunted."

Wilhelm leaned back in his chair and stared blankly off to his bookshelf as he pondered the news.

"Kaiser," said Berg. "What are your orders?"

Wilhelm continued to sit in silence. He glanced to Hindenburg and his mouth fell agape.

"I—I honestly have no idea how we respond to this," he said.

Hindenburg and Berg both bowed their heads. They folded their hands and placed them in their laps.

Wilhelm stood and leaned onto his desk with his right fist. "A demi-demon alive in Germany. I . . ." He blew out a big breath and sat. "Paul?"

"Yes, Kaiser?"

"How long have you known?"

Hindenburg shuffled in his chair, trying to find a more comfortable position.

"I've known for a very long time, but—"

"How long?" questioned Wilhelm, raising his voice.

"I've known since the late 1600s. But—"

"Treachery!" Wilhelm slammed his fist upon the desk.

"Kaiser, please," said Hindenburg. "You know my loyalties are with you. And I simply can't go bothering you with every ghost story in Germany. Some legends are simply that. But it has been rumored since the mid-1600s that an extremely powerful witch—

namely Elizabeth Báthory—was sequestered at the peak of Mount Hohenzollern. It wasn't a matter to concern you with until . . . well, it became one."

Wilhelm nodded. "My family owned a castle atop the mount before it decayed to nothingness in the 1600s."

"That's just it, Kaiser. It didn't decay. The castle still stands, hidden by a concealment spell that Radu cel—"

"Don't even speak his name!" yelled Wilhelm. "That bastard has wormed his way into my affairs far too often. Is he alive? Does he even exist? I've been chasing after this ghost for the better part of thirty years."

"Kaiser—"

"My grandfather spoke to me of this legend. That a castle belonging to our family disappeared into the ether upon the mount. As I grew older, I came to believe the castle crumbled away and he was merely telling me a scary story before bed—family folklore. You're telling me it's real? Hohenzollern Castle still stands?"

"It does, Kaiser," said Hindenburg.

"And Elizabeth Báthory has been living there in seclusion for nearly three hundred years?"

"That is a fact."

Wilhelm stood and walked behind his chair. He pushed and pulled upon it before standing upright and shooting his fist to the ceiling. "Now what in hell's name am I supposed to do with this information?" he screamed, his face flushing. He glared at Hindenburg. "Well, Paul? What? Tell me what!"

Hindenburg held up his palms. "Kaiser, please. We must address this with caution. You see, there's more. You should sit."

Wilhelm slumped into his chair.

"During the Inferno of the Witch—"

"The what?"

"What you would know as the Crusades," clarified Hindenburg. "But as those of us who deal in witchcraft know, it had nothing to do with reclaiming the holy lands—rather, it was a Vatican-sponsored genocide of supernatural entities."

Berg shifted and opened his notebook.

"Commander, this is fully off the record," said Hindenburg, glancing at the pen in his hand.

Berg capped the pen and placed it in his breast pocket. "Understood."

Hindenburg continued, "Magick was prevalent back then—often encouraged. And a variety of what you would call supernatural technologies existed that are now long defunct. Some forgotten, others banned or annihilated."

"I'm uncertain what I need right now is a history lesson," said Wilhelm, having regained his composure.

"I'm afraid you do. The story of Elizabeth Báthory is a tale far more gruesome than simply being confined at the top of Mount Hohenzollern. You see, in that time—the Inferno—a society of warlocks known as the Order of the Dragon initially allied with the Vatican to eliminate the seventy-two demons of Solomon—the most powerful and vile of all demonic entities. At that time, the demons roamed free, inflicting untold death, suffering, and destruction upon mankind. And there was only one method to kill, or should I say immobilize, such power."

Wilhelm leaned into his desk.

"*Latrodectus anima,*" said Hindenburg. "Or, more colloquially, soul spiders—a genus of arachnid that fed not on the bodies but the souls of its prey."

Berg suddenly crossed his arms and gripped his biceps as he shivered and let out a quick high-pitched wail.

Wilhelm and Hindenburg gazed at him in silence.

"Sorry," said Berg, dropping his arms. "I hate spiders."

Hindenburg grimaced. "Well, you'd have loathed these devils. They have since been eradicated, but back then they spawned from an inter-dimensional plane located in the Russian necropolis of Dargavs." He spread his hands wide in front of his body. "Leg span the size of a large dinner plate. Fangs that could tear right to the bone through the tip of a reinforced leather boot . . . and extremely aggressive. They fed not only by immobilizing prey in their webs, but also by hunting them in the wild, sinking their fangs into their victims' eye sockets and drinking their souls—man, beast, no matter."

Wilhelm appeared enthralled by the tale. "Go on."

"The Order of the Dragon used these spiders to capture the demons' souls, and through this action made a discovery. Normally, the spiders would feed upon mortals and simply continue on. There are legends saying they then spun the souls into their webbing, and plucking one, you could hear the cries of their victims resonating from the silk."

Wilhelm chuckled. "Delightfully grim!"

"But the Order discovered that upon consuming the soul of a more powerful entity—a demon, for example—the spiders would petrify, become hard as stone, then crumble to dust, leaving behind only their oblong abdomens as a gray jewel of sorts with the demon's soul trapped within. Something that might look like a porous stone at first glance . . . You've seen an opal?"

"My favorite stone, in fact," said Wilhelm.

"Now imagine an opal but with a dull gray shield around it. Only when holding and turning it in the light would you notice the sparkle."

"What do these spiders have to do with Elizabeth Báthory?" asked Wilhelm.

"I'm getting to that. My, my . . . how do I put this?" Hindenburg reached up and patted the perspiration upon his brow. "Elizabeth Báthory *is* one of these spiders. The last remaining one."

Wilhelm and Berg stared at him with open mouths.

"We don't have the specifics," continued Hindenburg. "But what has been handed down from elder seers is that she entered a duel with Radu cel Frumos, who somehow unleashed a soul spider on her. And since she is the daughter of Bael but only half demon, instead of her soul being consumed outright as it would have been if she were mortal; or petrifying the spider as it would have had she been a demon, her consciousness became entwined with the spider's body. In time, she's grown quite large."

"How large?" questioned Wilhelm.

"From our scans, we have gathered that her body is about the size of an adult stallion with the leg span to match."

Berg coughed. "I'm speechless. Kaiser, I . . . I know myself and our higher operatives are privy to your dealings in the paranormal, but this . . . this is unprecedented. I'm uncertain our men—"

Wilhelm held up his palm, silencing Berg. He grabbed a pencil with his right hand and scribbled a star doodle upon a piece of paper before him, tapping the pencil several times before the lead snapped.

"Let me see if I have this correct," said Wilhelm, looking to Hindenburg. "Elizabeth Báthory is currently alive and living in Germany atop Mount Hohenzollern which is now invisible. Her consciousness is trapped inside a . . . soul spider, you say?" Hindenburg confirmed with a nod. "And now she has sent forth some kind of entity to kidnap children to bring back to her lair for her to feed upon?"

Hindenburg shook his head. "Partially correct. She's not feeding on the children. She's . . . collecting them."

Wilhelm leaned his head to the side. "Collecting them? To what end?"

"Mind you, I have some very knowledgeable witches I must consult, but it seems she is preparing to resurrect her father and the remaining demons of Solomon." Hindenburg paused, scanning the ceiling as if he were carefully choosing his next words before settling his gaze on Wilhelm. "A mystical Japanese swordsmith named Masamune gifted every member of the Order a blade forged from a very peculiar material—one that exerted a magnetic force on the petrified spider abdomens, attracting the jewels to a circular fastening on its hilt. Once the sword and jewel were connected, the blades became immensely powerful weapons. The Order now carried their mortal enemies upon their belts, wielding them as weapons and ensuring the demons would never escape. That is—unless the blades were cast into a soulless void.

"It is my belief that Elizabeth plans to drink down the souls of these kidnapped children so that their vacuous bodies may serve as vessels for the demons' resurrection once the blades are plunged into their hearts."

"Elizabeth possesses the blades?"

"She did, Kaiser, but no longer. Most have been missing for centuries. The blade containing Bael is not. You see, when he was still a warlock of light, Vlad Drăculea imprisoned Bael and wielded the blade until he was killed by his brother. So, both the bottle of Drăculea's blood and the blade containing Bael are in Radu's possession."

Wilhelm leaned forward and banged his head on the desk with a loud whack.

"My Kaiser!" said Berg, rising to check on Wilhelm.

Wilhelm sat up, blinking and appearing dizzy. "Apologies, gentlemen. My frustration is peaking. Next thing you'll tell me is that Radu is also leading the French and British armies. I'm tired of this trickster." Wilhelm massaged his temples with his right thumb and middle finger, groaning a bit. "Demons! Ustrel! Spiders. What next, werewolves?"

"Yes, werewolves too," said Hindenburg. "But they are hardly a problem. Reclusive lot."

"So, Elizabeth is also hunting Radu?" asked Wilhelm.

"She is, Kaiser. And it could affect our plans greatly," said Hindenburg. "Especially considering these kidnappings—she's making a move. Which leads me to believe she intends to capture and kill Radu, then escape her prison. When Elizabeth was in human form, she hunted under the moniker of the Death Witch, a soul stealer herself. She cleverly ambushed or oftentimes seduced each member of the Order of the Dragon, devouring their souls and forever imprisoning them in her blackened stomach—revenge for vanquishing her father.

"She managed to kill and consume all but one: Vlad the Impaler. By then, Vlad had been betrayed by the Vatican. He had converted himself to a vampiric witch and unleashed the Nosferatu. He was essentially untouchable. That is, until Radu confronted and be-headed him. Mind you, these are just visions from elder seers; the specifics may differ."

"I'm not interested in the specifics. Elizabeth."

"Well, if she succeeds in her plans, there will be no forces of light powerful enough to counter her—unless Vlad Drăculea, after all his final evil deeds, is resurrected and brought back to serve the Veil. After capturing and killing Radu to obtain the blade containing her father, Elizabeth will absolutely destroy the bottle to ensure Vlad never returns."

Hindenburg paused as Wilhelm closed his eyes and pieced together the information.

"Well," said Wilhelm, opening his eyes, "if she thinks she's getting to that bottle first, then let's just squash this bug right now."

"There may be a better solution," said Hindenburg. "I believe you and I and Minister Schmidt can devise a strategy to turn this situation to our advantage. This never-ending search for Drăculea's blood is taking far too long. A conventional war will only end in more death for our people and likely a stalemate. Yet, within our grasp we now have a demi-demon—the daughter of Bael himself. Imagine, just for a moment, what a power like that would bring to the crown if wielded properly. You read it yourself in Berg's summary on the Nosferatu operation: this war moves no inch in either direction unless some other supernatural technology is located and procured. What if the German Empire could resurrect and harness King Solomon's demons?"

"How, then?" asked Wilhelm. "How do we harness such power? Certainly, demons could overpower you and even Minister Schmidt."

"Not exactly," said Hindenburg, leaning back in his chair. He placed his hands together and brought his fingertips to his mouth.

"Don't be coy with me, Paul."

"It's quite simple, actually," said Hindenburg. "We will convene a council of powerful witches under my command who understand the spells and methods of governing such entities— mainly through sacrifices made to their carnal demands. As King Solomon himself once proved, we can contain and wield them. You see, sophisticated demons do not behave like more visceral entities— vampires, for example, or lesser demons, which can be quite savage and base in their actions. Their evil is subtle, yet far more dangerous.

"Although they thirst for human flesh, they are shadow creatures and parasitic in nature, preferring to allow surrogates to carry out their agenda while they remain hidden, secretly feasting upon the misery they unleash. A true monster is one that devours and cannot be seen. There is no defense against the invisible." He looked up. "You've heard of a virus?"

"Yellow fever is a virus, correct?"

"Exactly. Now, imagine a virus that does not infect the body, but rather the soul. This is how a high-level demon behaves: seducing and possessing its prey. They are masters at turning brother against brother, enslaving all who encounter them into unknowing, lustful thrall as evil metastasizes within their hearts and minds.

Envision ruling over a supremely ignorant and fearful populace—one easily controlled and manipulated, obsessed with the material, the sexual, and the mundane . . . A black sun will rise, and its woeful rays will scorch the psyches of all men. There will be no more illumination; no more joy. Those delicacies will be reserved for those of us in control, while the rest of humanity bends to our will, turns on their neighbors, and eagerly feasts on its own squalor as if it were a savory, substantive bread. This is what harnessing demons will bring to you."

Hindenburg gazed solemnly at Wilhelm, who appeared enraptured by his words.

"If you could only see what I see, Kaiser, then the choice would be clear. May I show you?"

"Not another slide show," said Wilhelm.

"No, my Kaiser. Allow me to enter your mind, where I can show you a possible future."

Wilhelm glanced at Berg, who raised his eyebrows and stuck out his lower lip, appearing curious. Not one to back away from a mystery, Wilhelm nodded. "Please, Paul—show me."

Hindenburg stood and leaned over the desk. He wrapped his large fingers around Wilhelm's head.

Wilhelm's eyes widened and he froze, entranced, as the room around him faded and he found himself floating through large, puffy clouds illuminated by the full moon. The landscape below was lit up with specks of orange light, spreading outward in haphazard grids against the darkened earth. His heartbeat resounded through his mind as it thumped slowly in his chest. Floating closer to the ground, Wilhelm recognized the Berlin Sportpalast. He neared the building, picking up speed. As he shot quickly toward its roof, Wilhelm threw his hands over his face and yelled, expecting an impact.

He pulled his hands away to find himself standing on a red carpet, center aisle, inside the Sportpalast. Squinting against the bright spotlights that encircled its expansive ceiling, Wilhelm saw that the arena was bursting with people from the floor to the upper bleachers. His heartbeat faded and his eardrums filled with chanting as the audience shot their right hands into the air, saluting a man standing at a podium at the front of the rally.

The chants calmed as the man screamed a manic and impassioned plea into a microphone. Wilhelm proceeded down the aisle to see a golden Prussian eagle hanging behind the man with its talons wrapped around a swastika. Below him hung a red banner with the symbol dead center. Wilhelm now stood before the man, noticing his very peculiar mustache—it was black and trimmed perfectly so that it did not extend beyond the sides of his nostrils.

"The greatest means to enslave is to convince the indentured they are free!" shouted the man as he slammed his fist into the podium. Great cheers erupted from the arena. "This is what our enemies have done to our sovereign people! The Jew, the Gypsy, and the dissident—all destined to serve and tremble before our rising fist!"

Wilhelm grew excited as he spun around, the cheers and chants now becoming rhythmic thunder. He noticed a long line of young men in the aisle wearing brown uniforms that stood out against the body of attendees, who were dressed in crisp, dark gray attire—all with red armbands displaying the black swastika on a white circle. They were enamored with this man, seemingly entranced and more frenzied with his every word.

"They will bend to our will. Our God-given might!" shouted the man. "It is intolerable for us to be the puppets of other nations and to have them prescribe for us how to govern. No more! For, we are the masters. We are the chosen Reich! A power that will march and conquer! A power that will ascend to rule over all! And once our might is unleashed, this dissonance will cause our enemies to self-immolate, broiling their own minds with our creed of dominance over the weaker races. We will incinerate any opposition and crush their free will with idolatry like some jagged, rusty bit in their mouths as they plow our fields, toil in our factories, and build our Kaiser's empire!"

The crowd stomped their boots repeatedly, and the arena seemed to shudder and quake.

The man continued, "But they will never look up, never understand who truly controls them. The dissidents who do will be ostracized as liars, traitors, and unpatriotic cowards! The lesser races will turn upon each other and cower as they come to worship and obey the exact mechanisms of their oppression. Always riddled with fear and misery! Poverty. Famine. Slavery. That is the fate bestowed on any and all non-Aryan people. We will shove our boot into their necks, and they will praise us as they beg for our scraps. Hail to Germany! Hail to Kaiser Wilhelm! Hail to the Eternal Reich!"

The man banged on his podium several times before making the flat-handed salute. The rally followed the gesture. They shouted in unison, "Sieg Heil! Sieg Heil! Sieg Heil!"

The cheers and revelry grew to an unbearable volume.

Wilhelm covered his ears and fell to his knees.

The vision around him faded and he found himself standing on a cobblestone street as tanks rolled past him, followed by more soldiers bearing swastika armbands. A series of armored trucks followed the procession with wheeled cages in tow, all holding haggard prisoners with the Star of David stitched on their armbands. Beautiful blonde women and strikingly handsome blue-eyed men lined the street in perfectly tailored dresses and suits, smiling as they cast slurs and rotten vegetables at the cages rolling past.

Wilhelm ascended into the air as a flurry of visions filled his mind: threadbare citizens with brown skin fighting in a town center over a loaf of bread while swastika-adorned Aryan soldiers stood laughing, smoking cigarettes and taking bets on who would prevail; a long line of emaciated prisoners standing behind barbed-wire fencing before a squat, square building with smoke rising from its chimney and harrowing screams echoing from within; then gold-drenched palaces that rose into the sky with Prussian eagles at their peaks. There was order in the streets, oppression in the fields, and death to anyone who opposed the might of the Eternal Reich.

Hindenburg pulled his hands away, and Wilhelm's consciousness was back in his study.

"Are you all right, Kaiser?" asked Berg.

Wilhelm sat silently, and a thick tear fell from his eye. "It's beautiful," he said, wiping his face and glancing to Hindenburg. "But I don't understand. Who was that man? What did it all mean?"

"That man is currently an unknown soldier in your army. One whom the Void thrust into your consciousness. Possessed with demonic power, he shall infect all those around him with our ideology, destroy any who oppose, and command the empire for your glory."

Wilhelm took a few moments to consider the implications. "We would become the Eternal Reich."

"Yes," said Hindenburg. "The Eternal Reich."

"Well, then," said Wilhelm with wide, eager eyes, "I would like to meet with Elizabeth personally. How exactly does this banishment spell work? Can I enter the castle to see her?"

"You can," said Hindenburg. "A banishment spell is powerful blood magick. Extremely draining on the witch who maintains it. But it is only Elizabeth who is confined by the hex—and now that she has relaxed her own magick over the surrounding forest, we can enter her domain."

"Can you or Minister Schmidt guarantee my safety in her presence?"

"Most definitely," said Hindenburg. "We will send a heavily armed garrison, along with tanks and Minister Schmidt. We already have an envoy in the region who can arrange a meeting and inform Elizabeth that any attempt to harm you will result in her outright obliteration."

Wilhelm nodded. "Then do it. Immediately. But! The bottle is mine. As soon as Radu is captured or killed, it is to be delivered to me. I will become immortal, and my child will be the most powerful of all—ruling over demons and men. Elizabeth is not to come in contact with it under any circumstances. If she agrees, then I will allow her to live and offer her all the resources in my empire to resurrect her father and Solomon's demons under our command. Can it be done?"

Hindenburg crossed his arms against his powerful chest.

"That, my dear Kaiser . . . is where I come in."

*

The harmonic warmth of Beethoven's String Quartet in A moll, op. 132, filled the dining hall as the guests carried on with pleasant chatter from table to table. Stein closed his eyes for a moment and allowed the deep tone rising from the cello to wash over him.

I love this movement, he thought.

He opened his eyes, looked to his wife, Maria, across the small circular table, and delighted in the pearls hanging around her neck as she sipped from her champagne flute. The pearls were a gift for her twenty-eighth birthday, and Stein was certain to remind her periodically as to their expense.

Heinrich Adolf Wild von Hohenborn's broad, tall frame appeared behind her, and Stein watched him place his hands upon her shoulders, massaging them slightly. Maria closed her eyes and leaned back into his grasp.

A sharp rage welled within Stein.

"Unhand my wife!" he said, glaring at Hohenborn.

Hohenborn raised his hands in the air and backed away a few steps. "My apologies," he said, swaying a bit from drunkenness. "I simply don't know what came over me."

Maria looked up to him with a wide, lingering grin. She then turned to her husband. "Darling, stop being silly. Heinrich was merely—"

"Merely being handsy with my wife!" Stein was agitated and jittery. "Let me remind you, Heinrich. It is I who am now minister of war, not you," said Stein, puffing out his chest in a display of dominance. "I succeeded you in a position you failed in."

"And I am merely succeeding you in a position *you* have failed in." Hohenborn held up his index finger and thumb, several inches apart.

"How dare you!" Stein stood back and placed his hand upon his saber, his action causing Hohenborn to move backward several paces and do the same. The two men squared off against one another, slightly unsheathing their sabers.

"Hermann, please!" said Maria.

"Gentlemen, gentlemen!" came Grand Duke Ernest Louis's voice. "What is the cause of this disturbance on such an evening of revelry?"

He stood between the two and folded his arms.

"He insulted me!" shouted Stein.

"What's happening here?" asked Augusta, joining the small circle.

Stein looked back and forth between Hohenborn and Ernest Louis as the music continued in the background. The vast majority of the guests paid the confrontation no mind.

Ernest Louis turned to Hohenborn. "Heinrich, please," he said. "I see there is currently no line at the bar. How about we all just drop this and you go and fetch yourself another?"

"Heinrich, this way," said Augusta, gripping him by the wrist and leading him away.

Hohenborn sheathed his saber and turned toward the bar, keeping his gaze on Stein until it was no longer physically possible to do so.

"Hermann, please. Let us enjoy the evening," said Ernest Louis. He threw his arm around Stein and walked him back to his wife's table.

"I'll get that son of a bitch."

"You already have. You're the minister of war now. You embarrassed him. You're the better man. The Kaiser loves what you have done."

"It doesn't seem like the Kaiser appreciates me," said Stein.

"He does. It's Wilhelm. What can you expect? He's never happy with anyone—you know that."

Stein was still shaking a bit as he grabbed his champagne and downed the glass, still glaring across the room at Hohenborn, who was being chided by Augusta.

"He's lucky you showed when you did. I'd have stuck him right in his fat—"

Stein became aware of his wife tugging on his sleeve.

"Darling, isn't that General Hindenburg's daughter?" she asked, pointing toward a figure who had entered the dining salon, walking with a slow, stiff gait.

Nette von Hindenburg appeared disheveled with her dark hair mussed down over her face and deep purple bruises around her neck and biceps as if she'd been in a struggle. Her silken gown was torn and tattered.

"She's even lost her shoes," said Maria, laughing nervously. "Poor child can't handle her liquor!"

Stein and Ernest Louis turned to watch Nette cross the floor and approach the chafing table.

Nette stood before a portion of the table where a plump prime rib roasted under a heating lamp. She reached for the lean carving blade, then turned and faced the party. Standing perfectly erect with wide eyes and an open, exaggerated grin upon her face, Nette plunged the blade into her lower abdomen and slowly pulled it up toward her belly button.

"Oh my God!" screamed Maria, watching as blood stained the lower portion of Nette's gown.

Nette raised the blood-soaked blade once more—the wretched grin still frozen on her face.

Several other screams filled the hall, followed by the clanging of serving trays. The chamber music stopped and the entire room fell to a sudden horrified hush.

"I've been very bad!" shouted Nette, appearing entranced. "Shame on me!"

She plunged the blade into her stomach, stabbing herself over and over in a slow, mechanized motion like some demonically possessed doll. "Curse this wretched womb!"

Stein and Ernest Louis dashed toward Nette as she buckled to the floor and moved her hand to her open wound. Several servants in their white livery joined to assist in restraining her as she shoved her hand into the slice in her abdomen.

"Someone call an ambulance!" shouted Ernest Louis, grabbing Nette's wrist and wrestling the knife from her hand.

Nette continued to kick and growl as the men forced her bloodied hands to the floor, her abdominal wound spurting blood upon Stein. Several onlookers choked and gagged at the gruesome spectacle and ran from the room.

Augusta watched from the distance. She quickly ducked her head and made her exit.

A voice resonated behind Stein. "I'm sorry, I'm so sorry! She just grabbed the knife from my table."

Nette began kicking.

"Grab her legs!" shouted Stein.

It took five full-grown men to restrain Nette upon the marble floor, where she continued to struggle and gnash her teeth toward the men pinning her wrists.

"Let me go! I must obey!"

Her high-pitched growl sent shivers across Stein's neck.

"Grab a tablecloth!" shouted Stein, ripping open the slash in Nette's gown.

Stein had seen plenty of broken limbs and bullet wounds in his past as a field medic, but he winced and averted his eyes from the sight of Nette's stomach sliced open with her womb partially sticking from her gut.

"What's happening here?" came a male voice.

"She's cut herself open. Quickly, I need to apply pressure!"

Stein was handed a tablecloth. He bunched it up and placed it firmly upon Nette's stomach, the fabric rapidly soaking with blood.

"Keep her steady! Has someone called for a doctor?" yelled Stein.

Nette continued to suck in full and frenetic breaths as her strength waned.

"Just be calm, Nette," said Stein, keeping pressure on her wound. "We'll get you to the hospital."

"You," growled Nette in a low and grumbling voice. "How dare you interfere. A weak man with a whore wife who will never love him—"

"Hold her steady!" said Stein, his hands wet with blood. "My child, what has come over you?"

"You will see," snarled Nette. "You will all see!"

The bystanders continued to hold her down as the royal palace police entered the hall and Nette passed out on the marble.

*

Augusta sat in her bedroom before her brushed vanity, wearing a silk nightgown. She stared into her own eyes, taking in short calming breaths as she tried to slow her pulse. A mixture of worry and excitement flushed her cheeks.

"Just be calm," she said. "Be calm—you'll get away with this."

She removed the hairpins from her bun and shook her head as her silver locks flowed down to her shoulders. Her fingers ran through her hair to untangle any knots and grabbed a brush to smooth out the right side, which was frazzled. After placing the brush on the vanity, Augusta leaned forward and plucked her false eyelashes from her eyelids, marveling at how realistic they appeared.

Looks like the Americans are good for something after all.

Augusta's mind flashed with grisly images of Nette cutting herself open, and she raced to piece together an alibi. Her ear curled as boots approached, and she looked in the mirror to see Wilhelm's shadow emerging from the hall. She quickly gathered a small glob of night cream on her fingertips and began rubbing the moisturizer into the wrinkles on her forehead.

Wilhelm's hand suddenly gripped her wrist.

"Have you lost every ounce of sense in your body?"

Augusta turned on her small swivel stool and stared up at him. "Unhand me."

Wilhelm flipped her wrist over and glared at the bandage on her palm. "Back at it again, I see."

Augusta shook free her hand.

Wilhelm reached to her vanity and opened its top drawer, removing a thin hardbound book—*The Grand Grimoire* stamped onto the cover's tattered gray fabric.

He held it to Augusta's face.

"You think I don't know?" he said, tossing the book haphazardly upon the vanity, knocking over her makeup brushes and jars of facial creams.

A hot rage snapped across Augusta's nervous system as she watched her cherished beauty products splatter over the vanity and onto the floor. At that moment, the offense became a clear metaphor for her marriage. Augusta decided her needs would no longer be dashed aside by this boor she shared a bed with, nor would her deeds remain hidden from him. It was time Wilhelm knew exactly who he was dealing with. Augusta felt certain the best way to keep her actions secret was to make Wilhelm her knowing accomplice.

She placed the grimoire back into the drawer and slammed it closed, then forced a pursed smile and stared willfully at Wilhelm, blinking repeatedly.

Wilhelm thrust his finger in her face. "That text is extremely dangerous in the wrong hands."

"Is it now?" she said coldly, grabbing his finger and lowering it to his waist. "So I hurt your plaything. Find another."

"How dare you!"

Augusta stood and pushed past Wilhelm, knocking him a step backward. She walked to her cherry wood wardrobe and feigned sorting through her evening gowns. Listening as Wilhelm walked toward her, she turned and pointed at him.

"No! How dare you, Friedrich!"

Wilhelm was taken aback by her forcefulness. He raised his hand and opened his palm in a display of submission. Feeling empowered, Augusta pressed on.

"I will not be shut out!" she yelled. "You can go stick yourself inside your little whores, but I will not . . . I will not be cast away like some used-up dishrag. You promised me immortality when we wed, and it's immortality I will have."

Wilhelm relaxed his hand. "Do you have any idea what you have done? Any at all?"

There was silence between them.

Augusta scanned Wilhelm's eyes and sensed his genuine and grave concern. She believed she even saw a hint of fear reflected from his pupils. To her surprise, this further invigorated her. She took a quick inventory of her surging emotions and felt only anger waiting to be released—a powerful mental climax she'd been holding within her for the better part of two decades. Her lack of guilt felt freeing, as if she'd removed an age-old python constricted around her neck and her true self was breathing for the first time in a long, long while. The only regret she felt—a heavy and solemn regret—was that she had not acted sooner and unleashed the mirror's powers on more of her enemies.

"So now that I have asserted just a smidgen of say in these affairs—suddenly you're concerned? Suddenly, I matter?"

"A smidgen?" said Wilhelm, swirling his tongue across his inner cheek. "Goddamn you, Augusta!" he shouted. "You stubborn . . . Clearly you do not understand what you have done. Firstly, her father is the most powerful seer—"

"Oh, spare me!" she said, throwing her hands in the air. "Hindenburg is a joke! Where's this bottle of Drăculea's blood then, Friedrich? Isn't that his big task? He's taking you for a fool.

We'll be dead in the grave before he figures it out. He'll never know what I've done." She walked to the other side of their bed and sat with her back to Wilhelm, who ground his teeth at the sight of her relaxed shoulder blades.

"I noticed your jaw was swollen at the reception. What exactly is it that you have done? What did you summon, and where?"

"That's none of your business. You and your secret council play with ghosts. Why can't I?"

Wilhelm stormed to her side of the bed and stood over her.

"Augusta! You are engaged in a very dangerous game. I have consultants—seers and even goddamn wizards!" He looked to the vaulted ceiling and composed his thoughts. "Have you ever, in your existence, heard of a story where a mortal summons a spirit and that story ends well? You must cease whatever it is you're doing."

Augusta looked up at him with closed, quivering lips.

"No."

"No?"

"You heard me. No. Not until I'm fertile again. You keep promising the bottle is just within our grasp. I'll be immortal soon, will I not? What, then, does it matter?"

Wilhelm clenched his fist. "It matters because at some point in this investigation, a seer will trace this back to you."

"How? Seers are forbidden from reading your mind, are they not?"

"Augusta—"

"And if I'm not mistaken, that applies to any ruling monarch. So they are forbidden from my thoughts as well."

"Hindenburg will know!" shouted Wilhelm. "A perfectly healthy young woman suddenly ups and gives herself a hysterectomy in the middle of a—"

"They'll say she was drunk."

"Oh, Augusta. What has happened to your mind? You have no idea what you are summoning."

"I know exactly what I am summoning—a means to reclaim my rightful place at your side. Now that you've witnessed how far I'm willing to go, maybe it's time you reconsider your doting wife's role in these affairs? I demand a seat at your council."

Wilhelm slumped next to her on the bed. "My dear Augusta, you have damned us. This ... everything ... our entire plan will be cursed by inviting this entity into our affairs."

"It's trapped in a mirror," she said. "It can project itself from the mirror but cannot escape."

Wilhelm looked to her with a sober, listless expression that smoothed the wrinkles across his forehead.

"I don't know exactly what you are doing or how you came across such magick. Since you won't tell me, and especially since I can't consult Hindenburg or Minister Schmidt on the matter, all I will say is this—stop. Immediately. Before it's too late. You will unleash a curse upon this family that may never end. If you're using an enchanted mirror to commune with this spirit, smash it. Then bury the glass."

"Not until I'm fertile. The mirror has that power."

Wilhelm let out an exaggerated groan. He took a few steps away from her and stood, facing down the hall.

"I command that you do this. It's for your safety. Nette may recover, and when that child wakes—"

"Oh, so you agree that she's a child?"

Wilhelm kept his back to her, and she noticed his hand become a fist.

"What is it you want, Augusta?"

"It's very simple, my darling. I want what you want. To rule—forever."

The words were barely from her mouth when Wilhelm marched from their bedroom and slammed the door behind him.

*

It was not quite dawn when General Hindenburg arrived back at the Berlin Palace from his daughter's hospital bedside. The entrance guards were surprised to see him at such an early hour.

"The morning bird feasts the best," he said while passing them.

He walked to the dining hall to find the room had been largely cleaned and evacuated. The tables were free of cloth and set along the wall next to a series of stacked chairs. Hindenburg stood over

169

the marble where Nette had cut herself open and could still sense traces of her blood upon the floor.

Reflecting on Nette's frailness at the hospital rattled him as he tried to quash the memory of gripping her frigid hand—the poor girl barely clinging to life, begging him to make the pain stop. Her sedative-addled words came to him: *The last I remember, I peeked under a sofa looking for the children, and when I stood, I must have knocked my head into a table or something. Then I woke up here.*

Hindenburg knew full well there were never any children inside the palace, and he cursed himself for not sensing the ghoulish astral projections in time to save his daughter. Nette's words echoed through his mind as he exited the hall and walked toward the parade rooms. He thought to the gruesome black stitches across Nette's belly and further cursed himself for behaving like a typical dark warlock and never seriously studying the healing arts—for not heeding Minister Schmidt's advice to employ at least one witch within their council who specialized in advanced healing spells. Hindenburg had always looked down upon healers, considering them overrated—nothing more than do-gooders too unskilled for more powerful magick. The faint rumblings of Schmidt's advice reminded him that hubris had often prevented him from reaching his full potential by making him mistake-prone. He quietly swore to be more careful and open-minded from this point forward as his goals came closer to alignment.

Hindenburg entered the Chamber of the Black Eagle and peered up to the fresco upon the ceiling. Standing before the grandfather clock, he opened the glass and set the hands to midnight. When the chime rang out, he pushed the clock to the left and pulled on the lever that opened the passage. He stepped in and shut the door behind him. His footsteps echoed in the stone passage, and he blinked repeatedly until his night vision made the darkness clear as daylight. He then walked to the small room at the end of the hall.

Hindenburg picked up the silver offering tray on the vanity and inspected it, noticing the dried blood. He placed his hand over the flaky, brownish remnants and sensed it was Augusta's. Looking to the stone floor, Hindenburg grew angry to see Nette's photograph marred behind the broken glass of its frame. He sat upon the small stool and stared into the reflectionless mirror's infinite black.

A dark figure materialized in the looking glass, eventually taking the shape of a young woman with tattered flesh, missing an eye and a finger on her right hand.

Hindenburg looked to her torn cheek and noticed she now had two new molars.

"I suppose you think that was clever," he said.

Chapter 11

11

March 23, 1917, night

A hot, foul breath blew upon Felix's naked flesh from deep within the mine shaft. Sweat poured so heavily down his face that he closed his eyes to avoid the sting of salt. He leaned into the left wall to find his bearings in the pitch-black and used the mine cart tracks at his feet to ensure he wasn't accidentally wandering off the path. His hope was to find the storeroom Jonathan had mentioned. With any luck it would be filled with tools—a claw hammer or shovel to dig under the entrance bars and, with some real fortune, a flashlight.

Every meter or so, his hands would locate a vertical wooden beam, and he hoped to find an entrance to the storeroom on the other side. The sounds of machinery and human voices yelling echoed from the dark, but Felix could not see any source of light.

He moved past three more beams, and upon reaching to the other side of the fourth beam, Felix's hand fell into an open space. He gripped his bone stake and ran his free hand along the wood, confirming it was a doorframe. Kneeling to the ground, he found a stair and traced it to the entrance of the storeroom's ligneous floor. Felix crawled inside and kerosene filled his nose.

On his hands and knees, he traced the perimeter of the room until he found the workbench Jonathan had mentioned, knocking over its stool as he moved along the length of the bench. Felix fumbled his hand across the desk's surface and then the wall.

Small hammer? Screwdriver? Cloth!

Felix gripped the cloth, then released it and continued to feel around the workbench.

"Please let this be what I think it is," he said when his hand came across a metal cylinder. He traced the object to its top to find a flint wheel and wick. "Goddamn miracle. Please work. Please work."

With one flick of his thumb, a small flame erupted from the lighter. Felix could now see around the tiny space. He searched for something that might be useful for his predicament. Realizing the screwdriver and small ball-peen hammer were essentially useless, he let the objects be. He shook the kerosene lighter. It was nearly full.

Felix blew out the flame and unscrewed the lighter. He then dipped the cloth he'd discovered into the cylinder and wrapped the kerosene-soaked fabric around the tip of the leg bone. Placing the bone torch on the workbench, he found the top of the lighter and began flicking the flint wheel toward the cloth.

"Come on, come on . . ."

The cloth ignited at once, followed by Felix's kerosene-dampened hands.

"Ah!" he yelled, shaking his hands vigorously and rubbing them on his stomach until the flames extinguished.

The flame on the workbench burned bright and filled Felix with more hope than the rays of a bright sunny morning. He grabbed the bone and held the flame before him. Looking down to the tipped stool, Felix lifted his foot and smashed it into the flimsy wood, cracking a leg from its body. He reached down for his new wooden stake and slipped back into the mine, ready for battle.

Back in the shaft, his torch proved only bright enough for Felix to see several meters in front of him. He continued down the corridor, placing his bare feet on the rail ties to save them from the sharp gravel between the wooden planks. The walls and ceiling seemed to constrict the farther Felix traveled into the shaft, and as best he tried to ignore it, his claustrophobia welled.

He reached a cross in the path and hoped it was the interconnecting tunnels Jonathan spoke of.

Felix shined his torch to the right and noticed the path banked slightly upward. He turned to the left to see a corridor that sloped sharply down. The sounds of grunting and machinery grew louder by the minute. Deciding up was better if he hoped to discover a way out, Felix turned right.

There were no rail tracks on this path, and the hardened mud and occasional sharp piece of gravel tore into Felix's feet.

"Who's there?" crackled a voice before him in German.

Felix froze. He knew the torch was his only salvation—extinguishing it was certain death.

"Stop!" hissed the voice.

Felix heard a scurry of footsteps from the darkness in front of him, followed by a choking gurgle that grew in volume and number as it neared him.

Ustrel.

He turned and dashed in the other direction as the wretched sounds echoed behind him. They began screeching as they pursued him, alerting all others below that an intruder was among them.

Felix ran past the rail tracks and into the portion of the connecting tunnel that sloped downward. The drop was steeper than Felix had realized, and he tumbled to the rock, dropping his stake and bone torch. He quickly gathered the objects and ran once more down the path, listening behind him but never turning back.

As he continued down the path, Felix noticed that the tunnel became more cavernous with small holes in the walls and stalactites forming from the ceiling. Ahead of him in the darkness, he made out a flickering light. He turned with his torch, unable to see his pursuers but able to hear them approaching fast.

"Stop! Stop!" hissed a voice among the oncoming ustrel.

Felix turned to the path's bottom to see several shadows emerging from the distant light. They sprinted toward him, howling and wailing as they approached. Felix twisted and turned both ways, extending his torch into the darkness.

He looked to a hole in the cave's wall and decided it was just big enough.

This is your last goddamn chance.

With no idea whether the small cavern led anywhere but no other viable options, Felix shoved his stake and torch into the hole and crawled inside.

He felt his larynx constrict almost immediately upon entering the small circular cavern—a combination of his claustrophobia and the acerbic smoke he was inhaling from the torch. The flame was growing dim and he wondered if he should just extinguish it, but decided against it. Felix lurched forward, holding the torch in one hand and the wooden stake in the other, using his elbows and the sides of his ankles to shimmy through the narrow tunnel. Every inch deeper into the blackness gave him the feeling he was climbing down a python's constringing esophagus.

The sounds of choking and hissing resonated from behind him and filled Felix with a deep sense of dread that at any moment he would feel an ustrel's claw grab on to his ankle and drag him backward. At times, the tunnel narrowed so tightly around his body that Felix believed he was stuck—panic and exhaustion taunted him as he squirmed and struggled to push his mass through the ever-astringing rock.

Felix coughed and gagged. Tears filled his eyes. He tried to lean a bit to the left, away from the torch's smoke, but found little relief. Finally, he lowered his face to the bottom of the tunnel and was able to find some fresh air as he slinked along, the smoke enveloping the top portion of the tunnel before him.

He crawled ten meters, then twenty, with no end in sight as the hissing and gurgling crept closer. As Felix pushed his way through the shrinking space, the flame suddenly brightened. He looked up to see the bone sticking into a cavern and quickly pulled himself through.

His predicament was no better.

Felix stood on a narrow ledge with nothing but a steep drop below. There was no path to his left, and across the pit was a sheer wall of jagged rock. Felix turned to his right and extended his torch as the light began to flicker. It was too dark to be certain, but he swore that a short climb in the distance there was a bridge connecting two tunnels.

Knowing he'd have to abandon both his tools to attempt the climb, Felix turned back to the tunnel from which he escaped. He placed the torch on the cave floor and stood just before the opening. The sounds of the slithering ustrel approached. Felix grew focused, tightening his grip on the wooden stake.

You have one shot at this.

The moment the first ustrel popped its head from the opening, Felix drove his stake deep into the creature's temple with great force. Careful to not fall into the crevasse, Felix placed his back against the cave wall and pushed on the stake, dragging the ustrel from the hole by the pike impaled in its head. The monster screamed as it fell on the ledge where it writhed and kicked against the stone— its last moments of life were struggle and pain. Felix then grabbed the dying torch and ignited the ustrel's tattered clothing, causing the rest of its body to burst into flames.

A second ustrel crawled from the tunnel, managing to avoid its burning counterpart, and rose up to confront Felix, who shoved the flame-tipped bone stake into its chest. Felix kicked the ustrel square in the gut, causing it to fall backward into the flames. Its final howls bounced from the stone as the fire grew.

Felix stood back and took a moment to admire his impromptu bonfire, which extended up toward the crawlway's opening. He could see the face of another ustrel trying to poke through the flames. It hissed at him before retreating back into the tunnel. Felix turned around and looked up. The fire cast enough light for him to clearly see a wooden bridge connecting two shafts. He shuffled along the narrow path, which ended in a series of jagged stalagmites. He shimmied through and mapped out a ridged pattern on the wall that he thought he could climb. Then he began his ascent, slipping occasionally on some slimy moss. The incline was fortunately not too steep, and he managed to reach the bridge.

With all his might, Felix pulled himself up and rolled onto the bridge's railed surface. He looked to the tunnel that he believed led back to the mine's opening and then down to the smoldering ustrel to see two more force themselves from the hole as the fire abated. They howled while scurrying to Felix's position. Knowing he'd be trapped if he ran back to the entrance, Felix turned and dashed through the opposite shaft, which led deeper into the mines.

The tunnel was pitch-black and the heat felt oppressive. After a few moments, he made out a flickering light in the distance and heard the sounds of machinery, drilling, and yelling. As he approached the source of light, the shaft opened to another bridge. Felix crept out along it and stared down in horror at the massive gulch laid out below him with ustrel miners laboring away. He positioned himself against the cave's wall to conceal himself in the shadows.

The cavern was mostly dark, save for the beacons cast from lamps on the human foremen's helmets. Countless ustrel were hunched over with pickaxes and shovels as they pulled the potash from the earth and dumped it into bins fastened upon the backs of other ustrel laborers. Occasionally, a human foreman would snap his signal whip onto the backs of the undead. Felix stood only for a moment, taking in the mining operation until the sound of his ustrel pursuers echoed from the tunnel behind him. Deciding he'd seen enough, Felix dashed across the bridge into the opposite shaft.

Felix once again resorted to using the rail ties to keep his naked feet from grinding on the gravel. He kept his hands extended to prevent himself from running into any mining carts or other objects on the track, his main fear being running right off an unforeseen cliff.

Lights flickered in the distance.

Felix kept his pace until he finally came upon a cart that was banked at the end of the tunnel. He swung around its opening to see more mining caves below. Before him was a pulley system used to raise the potash bins from below to where they could be loaded into the mine carts, and directly across the well was another caged opening with its bars halfway open. Felix devised a plan to jump on the pulley system, then swing to the open gate—the bars of which appeared just in reach.

At that moment, a horrid high-pitched screech rang out through the caverns, and Felix looked behind him. Through the darkened tunnel, he listened as the two ustrel chasing him howled to the laborers below. The sounds of pickaxes and shoveling stopped, and a heavy silence settled inside the cavern. Then, all at once, as if the creatures were some hive mind, they screeched back in unison.

Knowing the cries spelled certain doom, Felix leapt onto the pulley system, his feet landing almost perfectly inside one of its bins. His weight immediately sent the device downward, and he reached out to the opposite chain to stop his descent.

"You, stop there!" came a voice from below in German.

Felix looked down to see several human foremen pointing at him, their headlamps shining directly on his bruised and dirty body.

"Grab that man!" echoed another voice.

The next thing Felix saw was what appeared to be a sea of ustrel rushing from the cavern below. They began scurrying up the walls toward him as the sounds of cracking whips and ustrel gurgles bounced off the stone walls.

Felix tugged on the chain, elevating his position slightly. He did this several times until he was directly across from the barred cage to the next tunnel. He extended his hand to find it was just out of reach. Leaning into the chain, he sent his legs backward, then forward, trying to generate some swing momentum. After he repeated this action a few times, his hands gripped the gate. Felix swung his body onto the rickety door and it opened outward, slamming his back into the hard cave wall.

"Figures," he said.

He pushed himself away with his foot, and the bars swung around to the opening. Felix placed his foot upon the cave wall, opened the gate, and slipped inside. He latched the bars closed.

The tunnel before him was nothing but pure darkness.

I'm dead. There's no way out.

He leaned against the rocky wall and slid to the ground, peering through the gate as the heinous sounds of ustrel neared from below and flashlights flickered from the tunnel across the gap.

A sense of defeat swept over him and he half-heartedly congratulated himself for making it this far, but he knew his time had come. His mind flashed back to the morning he and Rurik broke into his palace after defeating the Nosferatu in Saint Petersburg and how invigorated and optimistic they had felt despite the losses suffered by both men. Together that morning, they decided to embark on this ill-fated journey to settle the score with Dmitri Pavlovich and Charles Vondling, and in the short months that followed before they'd reached the Romanian border, every bit of that quest felt righteous and just—even wise.

But now, as he sat with his back to the cave wall, naked and sweating, seemingly bruised and scraped over his entire body with impending doom upon him—that version of himself felt distant, strange, and terribly naive. Felix thought to one of his favorite books by H. G. Wells and envisioned all the things he might be able to change if only he had a time machine. His mind raced with all the moments in his life when he could have prevented this ending. Where exactly did he go wrong? Was it his drinking? His devil-may-care attitude? Was he so spoiled and blinded by his wealth that he had overestimated his ability to survive such a dangerous expedition?

After thinking it over, Felix wished he could travel back to the evening he and Irina went to Dmitri's party. He closed his eyes tightly and imagined warning his past self of the dangers that lay ahead: of Dmitri's imminent betrayal; of Rasputin's plans for the royal family. He would warn himself to hold Irina tight and never let her go—to gather what things he could and flee Russia forever. As he sat in the darkness, that was the version of himself Felix longed to be: alone with Irina on some gorgeous tropical island— far away from this horror, this carnage, this death.

Alas, there was no time machine.

The darkness found him as it always did, and he would never hold Irina again.

The sharp claws of ustrel soon pawed at him through the gate as flashlights flickered across their bodies, casting shadows. Felix decided he didn't care if they figured out how to unlatch the gate. He slumped against the wall and watched their bloodlust unfold just out of reach.

"What?" he yelled in protest and spit at the ustrel. Then he placed his head in his hands and waited.

This entire venture was bound to end this way. I'm sorry, Irina. I failed you.

A gunshot rang out and Felix snapped from his dire thoughts.

"Off the gate, you savages!"

Two ustrel fell from the bars as three more gunshots echoed, causing the rest to scurry away along the cave walls. There was another bang, and Felix felt the dirt next to his leg kick up. As the beacons across the drop shined through the gate, casting vertical shadows upon his naked, filthy flesh, he forced himself as far into the wall as he could. Two more shots came—one ricocheting from the gate while the other whizzed past. He turned into the tunnel and took a deep, healing breath at the sight illuminated by the flickering lights: a rickety wooden ladder leading to a shaft in the ceiling.

Felix dashed for the ladder and scaled it while several more bullets buzzed by him.

The wobbly ladder seemed ready to snap under Felix's weight as he moved up the shaft, finally reaching the top, which dead-ended into a metal ceiling. He banged on the metal to feel it pop agape. He then pushed upward, and the hatch swung open to the great starry sky above. The rush of cool spring air filled his lungs and cradled his flesh. He pulled his body through the opening, slammed the hatch closed, and collapsed on the ground. Steam from his sweaty body rose into the air while he looked up to the stars.

"Holy hell!" yelled Felix while running his hands across his body to ensure there were no serious cuts or bullet wounds.

Realizing he was still in danger, he looked around the encampment for a better place to hide. He could see the lampposts on the main road and two more lights from the refinery in the short distance. He was now over three hundred meters from the mines' openings, and the shadows of two oil derricks peaked up before him. The slow metallic rhythm of the drills filled his ears, and a panic brewed in his mind. Felix opened the hatch, grabbed the ladder, and pulled it out. He let it fall to the ground, then lay back in the dirt.

I have to find Rurik.

*

The rusty metal collar around Rurik's neck dug into his flesh. He reached up and tried to loosen it a bit, but the padlock on the back of the clamp gave no leeway. The heavy iron chain connected to the collar was agitating him as well—every time he settled, the chain would sway slightly and tap his spine. After hours of such minute abuse, Rurik's nerves were rattled, and a migraine seared into his head.

He walked to a bin containing pulverized potash and scooped up five kilograms into a tin bucket, then returned to his extremely crude electrolysis station. He dumped the mineral into a metal heating receptacle and lit the large Bunsen burner under the hopper.

Several minutes passed before Rurik pushed his glasses up the bridge of his nose to inspect the chemical reaction, noticing the potash had become molten. He reached below his workstation and pulled out the lead clamps attached to a battery, holding one in each hand. With his eye on the color of the potash, he gripped the leads, opening and closing them like tiny alligator mouths in an attempt to amuse himself. Once satisfied the potash was hot enough, he attached the leads to metal lips on opposite sides of the receptacle.

He quickly extinguished the burner and watched as the molten potash became metallic, collecting mostly on the side of the anode. Rurik pulled the lead clamps and returned them to their insulated resting position beneath his workbench.

As he cleaned and organized his area, Rurik tried to envision a variety of solutions for escape, but with each option, his mind filled with images of armed men and guard dogs chasing him down as he searched for Felix and they ran from Zănoaga.

He wiped the sweat pouring down his face and grabbed the glass water jug on his workbench. While taking a big gulp, he regarded the cooling potassium. Rurik knew full well the explosive power of pure potassium when combined with water. His mind raced with ways he could use this reaction to his advantage. His jug was a quarter full, so at best he could only devise a diversion.

A rustling sound came from the barrels just in front of him, and between a slim crack separating them, he spied a sliver of Felix's dirty face.

"You're alive!" whispered Rurik.

He spun around to see a few guards standing at the entrance and Pavel walking toward his area. Another guard patrolled the perimeter of the refinery with a rifle slung over his shoulder.

He quickly turned to Felix. "Stay low, the foreman is coming," he whispered, feigning organizing his tools. "Another guard that way."

Felix crouched low and slipped into the shadows.

Knowing it was best to appear focused on his labor, Rurik stayed close to his workstation as he took another swig from the jug.

"Don't spill it!" came Pavel's voice as he poked Rurik in the back.

A small amount of water splashed down Rurik's chin. He placed the jug on his desk and turned to Pavel.

"Very clever, boss," said Rurik, pretending to be entertained.

"Know what it's for?" asked Pavel, pointing to the cooling potassium.

Rurik couldn't decide which was filthier, Pavel's face or his tattered overalls. "Well, I can assume it's more stable in pure form than as a hydroxide or nitrate, so . . ."

Pavel jabbed him in the gut with his baton.

Rurik bent over, absorbing the blow.

"I didn't say 'speak'."

Rurik nodded, then shrugged.

"Torpedoes!" Pavel was smiling. "Kaiser has developed a new torpedo that explodes every time underwater."

Rurik remained silent.

"Well?" questioned Pavel.

"Well, what?"

"Don't you think that's genius?"

"I do!" said Rurik. "Long live the Kaiser."

Pavel's brown eyes scanned Rurik up and down. "I know some pretty important things around here. It's top secret, so keep your mouth shut."

"I certainly will, boss," said Rurik, saluting him.

Pavel appeared surprised by Rurik's salute. "I like that. Do that from now on. If you stay on my good side, I have enough power to make things much easier for you."

"I will, boss. Thank you."

Pavel turned away and Rurik relaxed. "Boss?"

"Yes?" he replied, turning to Rurik.

"I am hoping, if you find it apropos—"

"Apro what?"

"Um, agreeable. If you find it agreeable. After this batch cools, I very much need a break to—"

"Gotta piss? Do it in the bucket." Pavel pointed to a bucket on the floor.

"Actually, I—"

Pavel raised his hand. "Understood. Just ring the bell when you're ready."

"Will do, boss."

He placed his fists upon his hips and stared at Rurik. "Well?" His eyes dropped to Rurik's hand.

"Yes, of course," said Rurik, saluting him.

"Much better."

Pavel shimmied around the petroleum barrels surrounding Rurik's station and walked toward the refinery's front opening.

Rurik returned to his workbench as a siren rang out across the camp. He perked up his head and turned to see several guards enter the refinery, grab their rifles, and dash into the night. Pavel tried to join the group but was admonished to stay behind.

"I assume that's for you?" asked Rurik.

"Definitely," came Felix's voice from behind the petroleum barrels. "Is he gone?"

"Yes," said Rurik. "But he's still at the entrance. Stay where you are."

"Now what?" whispered Felix, poking his head from behind the barrel.

Rurik noticed the bare flesh of his shoulders.

"Felix! Are you naked?"

"I can't get into it right now."

As best he tried to avoid it, Rurik began laughing. He quickly cupped his hand over his mouth and calmed himself, casting a glance over his shoulder to see if his outburst had been noticed by Pavel.

"Not funny at all if you knew what I've just been through," said Felix.

"Sorry. It surprised me is all."

"Can you get that chain unlocked?" asked Felix. "We can make a dash out the back—it's wide open."

Rurik shook his head and stroked his bearded chin. "They'll chase us down. But something just occurred to me moments ago. Can you make it to the dam undetected?"

"They're swarming the place, but I'll try. What's on your mind?"

"What's on my mind is—if we make a run for it, the entire mining town will pursue us. Unless, of course, there is no mining town."

"How's that?" asked Felix.

"Simple, really. You're going to take several bricks of this pure potassium and blow the dam. Flood the entire operation. The chaos should give us enough cover to slip away."

"You honestly think that can work?"

"As decent a chance as anything else," said Rurik. "In fact, better. They'll never expect this." He pointed to the open barrel.

"Now, here's what I need you to do. Reach into that barrel and remove a brick of potassium. Each is about five kilos."

Felix, who was well concealed between rows of sealed barrels, stood slowly as he scanned the perimeter for any guards. Pavel was at the front entrance, staring out into town with a rifle in his hand.

"In here?" asked Felix, looking to the petroleum-filled barrel before him.

"Yes," said Rurik. "It's stored in oil as it's reactive to moisture."

"Whatever you say," replied Felix, who reached into the barrel and produced a misshapen block of metallic potassium. It slipped from his hands immediately and sank back into the barrel.

"No way I'm carrying those. Too slippery."

Rurik looked around his workstation for some fabric. Not finding any, he removed his yellowed lab coat. "Here, use this. Now, carefully . . . remove the potassium, then place it on the coat. It will work well as a satchel if you bundle it then tie the sleeves as handles."

Felix grabbed the lab coat and spread it on the floor. He then reached into the petroleum barrel and produced a metallic gob, carefully lowering it to the lab coat.

"How many can you carry?" asked Rurik.

"They all the same size?"

"Roughly."

"It'll be tough, but I think I can do four. Maybe five."

"Five!" said Rurik. "Oh, boy. Some fireworks tonight!"

"You sure that's enough?"

"My friend, twenty-five kilograms of pure potassium reacting in water will create an explosion like you've never seen. That rickety dam has no chance. Just scale it any which way you can, drop the potassium, and flee. With the oil coating, you have at best ten seconds before these things go boom. Fifteen if you're lucky."

Felix seemed satisfied with the answer and retrieved four more slabs of potassium. He placed them onto the coat and bent over the barrel once more. "Are they safe to carry?"

"Not particularly, but you should be fine. There's enough oil coating them. Just do it as quickly as you can. Speaking of which, how long do you think it will take? There's no way I'm getting this collar off without the key, so I need to time my break."

Felix thought for a moment.

"It's roughly two hundred meters to the dam. With the load and a few rests, say ten minutes? Anything longer, assume I'm captured."

"Then ten minutes it shall be," replied Rurik. "Best get to it."

Felix stood once more and looked to Rurik. "You have no idea what we've stumbled onto."

Rurik reached up and grabbed his collar. "I can imagine. You can tell me all about it once you blow the dam. I'll meet you behind the trading post."

"Just be careful—they're using ustrel as miners."

Rurik slapped his own forehead with a loud whack. "Of course the Kaiser is using ustrel."

"So, watch out."

Felix sat on the floor and tied the lab coat into a satchel, taking care to double-knot the arms as a makeshift handle. He stood and picked up the oil-drenched coat. After shaking it a few times to make sure it could carry the weight, he slung the satchel over his back.

"See you at the post," said Felix.

Then he scampered through the long row of barrels that led to the back entrance of the refinery.

Rurik leaned over a barrel and watched Felix's nude frame scurry through the darkness.

Interesting fellow, that Felix.

*

Felix dashed into the night.

He hid behind a small storage silo and poked his head around it to survey his predicament. The grounds were crawling with armed men with flashlights, and the sound of barking dogs rose up over the alarm siren. Felix covered his eyes as several giant spotlights near the main road lit up and started flashing across the quarry. He squatted back behind the silo.

Knowing his time was short, he decided it was best to sprint for the dam. He surmised the guards must have released ustrel to join the hunt, and his hunch was soon confirmed by the gurgling and shrieking that accompanied the barking of dogs. He peered around the silo once more and noticed a gathering of guards at the main road, where Yegor was issuing orders to about a dozen men before they scattered in different directions.

Now!

Felix made a straight line for the dam. He crouched and modified his gait so that, in the darkness, he might appear as an ustrel to a guard. The twenty-five kilos of potassium were much heavier than he had expected, and upon reaching the escape hatch from the mine, Felix dropped the satchel and shook out his legs to ease the fatigue. He ducked low as a group of shadows with flashlights centered on his position.

Felix was now a little over fifty meters from the dam, and even from a distance, the sheer wall seemed impossible to scale—especially with a heavy sack in his grip.

"Footprints. I think he's this way!" came a voice.

Felix picked up the potassium bundle and ran for the dam.

"I see him! He's there!"

A gunshot reverberated through the night and a bullet buzzed past Felix.

"This way! Bring the ustrel."

Felix was now sprinting as fast as he could—the dam just before him. He stood beneath the giant spinning mill wheel and scanned the towering barrier, trying to devise a means to scale it. Bullets hit the wooden wall before him, and Felix crouched to the dirt.

"Halt! Stop right there!"

The lights from the brick building next to the mill wheel and the searchlights now locked onto him. He turned to see at least twenty shadows bolting toward him. They released their German shepherds and the dogs tore after Felix, followed by the gruesome faces of ustrel emerging from the shadows at full sprint.

Now or never, Felix.

He slung the satchel over his shoulder and climbed up on a short brick wall that led to the mill wheel. Above him, water gushed from a pipe over the wheel's planks. Felix scurried to the ascending side of the wheel as another bullet struck the wood in front of him. He hung the lab coat around his neck and grabbed the wheel's sides, placing his feet on the planks that connected its front and back discs.

The wheel shot him upward. Due to the planks' downward angle, it was incredibly difficult to hold on, but Felix managed to find enough leverage by grabbing a plank directly in front of him as his fingers screamed for rest.

Two more bullets struck the wheel, sending splinters into his face.

The howling ustrel and barking dogs were now just below. The ustrel began scaling the dam wall just as Felix reached the wheel's pinnacle. He could now see over the dam and into the massive reservoir that fed from the Teleajen River.

"Bring him down!" called a voice in German.

Felix looked down to see Alexandru standing next to Yegor, who had two muzzled ustrel on leashes at his side.

"Get the Russian," he said, removing their muzzles and letting go their tethers.

They scurried along the ground to join a pack of thirty other ustrel trying to climb up the wheel. Their weight was so great that the water pouring from the opposite side was not enough to keep the wheel spinning clockwise. The gyre moved in the opposite direction, Felix descending with it.

Without another moment's thought, Felix sprung from the top of the wheel and landed on the dam's slim wall as a bullet tore through his right thigh. He yelled and fell forward, holding his leg as the weight of the potassium on his back dropped him into the reservoir full force. The cold water shocked his system, and his lungs howled for air. But Felix had bigger problems—namely, the twenty-five kilograms of highly explosive potassium bricks strapped to his back, sinking him to the bottom. It would be only another moment or two before the oil coating them was breached. He tore the satchel from his neck and let it sink. He then quickly surfaced and swam toward the dam's wall.

"Of course," griped Felix as he watched what seemed to be countless ustrel breach the dam and jump into the reservoir.

Felix swam away, then treaded water roughly fifteen meters from the dam's brim. He took a big breath and dove underwater, still able to hear the howling and hissing from the ustrel above as he swam just under their kicking legs.

Felix cupped his hands and pulled as hard as he could, swimming nearly to the dam's wall when a forceful purple flash erupted from the depths. An enormous, violent explosion knocked the air from his lungs and sent him flying from the water, pinning him against the dam's inner wall—what was left of it.

Grabbing on to a post in an attempt to fight the powerful draining current, Felix watched as the dam caved in and toppled the mill wheel, pouring a veritable tidal wave onto the quarry and surrounding grounds. His pursuers, including Yegor and Alexandru, drowned instantly. Felix pulled himself along the brim of the dam as the structure caved in further. The wood planks nearest him popped from their fastenings and disappeared into the newly formed rapids.

Felix was no match for the ruthless current. He knew he'd be swept away if he didn't exit the water quickly. With every bit of strength left in him, he pulled himself onto the wall and attempted to run along the top of the dam, though he was limping from his bullet wound. Another burst of purple light filled the dark as more potassium reacted, causing a second massive wave that obliterated another large portion of the wall tailing Felix. He crouched over and grabbed on to a plank of wood to steady himself as the dam behind him exploded with a third and fourth purple flash gurgling from the water.

Felix managed to steady himself and shimmy along the top of the dam as the remaining structure bowed and flexed from the aftershock and flowing water. Finding a portion that seemed moderately sturdy, he paused and surveyed the destruction below.

The gush had now mixed with the petroleum seep throughout the grounds, and the water's surface burst into flame as the potassium reaction continued to bubble with shocks of purple light from below. The flaming waters filled the quarry and poured into the mine openings as the force of the caustic liquid obliterated everything in its path. Next, it would sweep the oil derricks and on to the refinery. He covered his eyes as an explosion detonated from the first oil derrick and caused a chain reaction, igniting and toppling the two other derricks nearby.

The reservoir was relentless, thrusting a seemingly never-ending tsunami of chaos and destruction onto the encampment. Felix watched as the spill moved toward the perimeter of the refinery. He guessed it would still flood the facility with a foot or so, even though the majority of water was now being absorbed by the openings of the mine shafts on both sides of the quarry, drowning their entrances and submerging them entirely.

Felix inspected his bullet wound. Although he had initially believed it to be moderately superficial, he was dismayed to see an alarming amount of blood running down his right leg. He applied pressure to the wound and limped along what remained of the dam as the sounds of screaming and struggle rang out from below. Felix reached the perimeter and crossed along the top of the stone archway that extended over the quarry's entrance. He entered the trees on the opposite side of the arch and keeled over, trying to catch his breath. His eyes traced the flood, which seemed to dissipate just toward the town's center, and he noticed several dozen men running from the tent encampment in the distance toward the commotion.

At that moment, the refinery exploded in a gargantuan purple shock wave, sending Felix hard to the ground. The bursts continued for nearly a minute while he lay low, covering his ears.

"I hope you made it out in time," he said, thinking of Rurik as he rolled over to see that the refinery had been vaporized in the blast.

The sounds of rushing water still engulfed everything around him and Felix stood, silently purveying the destruction—his blackened, nude silhouette stark against the lake of fire that now consumed nearly every portion of the mining operation. The oil derricks were aflame with giant fire columns shooting from below. Even the force of the water pouring in around them could not stop the igniting crude oil from gushing through the surface. The shadows of men and ustrel swimming and becoming engulfed in flames filled his vision, and a queer silence settled into the air. Felix looked down to see several German shepherds paddling along the quarry's wall to avoid the flames, which were mostly spread across the flood's center. He traced their figures as they swam toward the safety of town, and was glad to see they would survive.

A giant creaking noise filled the air as the electricity mill suddenly caved in and its roof sank below the water's surface. The town was now dark, save for the lake of fire that flooded everything in sight, sending black caustic smoke into the night sky.

Felix bent over with his hands on his knees, still breathing heavily. He felt invigorated—mostly from the water cleanse, which had washed all the grime from his body. His bullet wound was still bleeding profusely—cuts and scrapes covered his body. The crisp air nipped at the wounds on his elbows and ankles, and Felix covered his elbows with his hands. The motion brought no comfort.

He placed his arms at his sides and stood upright.

Felix stood strong as the firelight washed him in an orange glow. He looked to the ridge just above the flooded mines on the left side of the quarry and decided it was his best path to the trading post. He stepped farther into the tree line and slinked along the shadows toward town.

*

"I hear you. I hear you!" came Pavel's voice.

Rurik ceased ringing the bell next to his workstation and turned to see Pavel approach with a rifle in hand.

"You must do this now?" asked Pavel.

"Please," said Rurik.

Pavel gave him a curious look. "Say, where's your lab coat?"

"My what?"

Pavel leaned into him. "Your lab coat. The one I gave you."

"Um, boss . . . I was never given a lab coat," he said, saluting Pavel, who looked him up and down with great suspicion.

"Someone's escaped," began Pavel. "I assume that I will be needed shortly to assist. I'm probably the only one here who can catch him."

"Most certainly, you are," replied Rurik, lowering his salute. "I promise to make it quick so you can get out there."

Pavel nodded and proceeded to unlock the neck collar. Rurik leaned away, trying to avoid the permeating stench of Pavel's overwhelming body odor.

Has this man ever bathed?

The chain clanked to the ground and Pavel poked Rurik's back. "Let's go," he said.

Rurik walked to the left of his workstation and slid between two barrels as Pavel followed, barely able to fit his gut through the space.

They moved to the far wall of the refinery where a quarter-cut barrel sat—the smell hit them before they could actually see the squat bin.

"Thank you," said Rurik, turning his posterior to the barrel and undoing his belt.

Pavel rolled his eyes and turned his back to Rurik, standing just a short distance away.

Rurik squatted over the bin and grunted a bit.

"Keep it quiet," complained Pavel, whose gaze was focused on the shadows of men running past the refinery's opening. He placed the butt of his rifle on the floor and held on to the barrel.

Pavel slouched. "It's just not fair," he said, letting out a distressed breath. "Carry this, Pavel, shovel that. Pavel, Pavel, Pavel." His voice rose in volume. "Oh, don't worry, Pavel, you can do it next time!" He reached up and pulled on the brim of his cap. "There's never a next time."

He turned around. "I can be smart sometimes too, you know!" he yelled, looking directly at Rurik. "Why am I always the one left behind?"

Rurik opened his mouth, but no words came out.

Pavel frowned and turned back around.

"Picks on me . . . tells me I'm . . . and I'm the one who . . ." Pavel's words fell to muttering and Rurik could no longer make out his grievances.

As Pavel continued to drivel on about his mistreatment among his peers, Rurik thought back to his dealings with the hapless Constable Petrov in Saint Petersburg.

Long-lost twins?

As he plotted his next move, Rurik envisioned Pavel as a small child—one likely ignored or abused by his parents . . . kicked around by older kids . . . poorly educated, and definitely rejected by every woman he ever encountered. Rurik frowned a bit and his heart filled with guilt as he stood and quietly pulled up his pants, knowing full well Pavel's evening was about to get much worse.

Rurik held his breath as he grabbed the rim of the barrel and tipped it slightly. He then gripped the bottom of the metal bin, picked it up, and ran forward before dumping the befouled barrel over Pavel's head.

Pavel shrieked and dropped his rifle.

Rurik kicked the back of his knees, sending him falling to the ground with a resounding thud.

"Why? Why?" screamed Pavel.

Rurik snatched the rifle and drove its butt forcefully into Pavel's kneecap as the chubby man screamed and pulled the barrel from his head.

"I thought we were friends," cried Pavel. His corneas seemed to shine in contrast to his filth-covered face.

"Best friends," said Rurik, ramming the butt into Pavel's forehead and knocking him unconscious.

Rurik turned around and scanned the interior of the refinery. Sirens still blared from outside.

The windows on the east side of the building suddenly imploded with the sound of a mammoth explosion.

"Felix!" yelled Rurik, covering himself from the flying glass. He proceeded to jump up and down in a brief moment of celebration.

Rurik slung the rifle over his shoulder, ran back to his workstation, and used all his might to tip three unsealed petroleum-filled barrels. The oil-covered potassium bricks spilled out all around him. He quickly surveyed the number of potassium nuggets lying on the ground.

"Each barrel holds roughly one hundred kilos. That's three hundred. Should be spectacular."

Rurik turned to run out the back entrance, but paused as he became entranced by the dozens of sealed barrels before him.

"Let's give them a real show!"

Knowing he was extremely short on time, Rurik unsealed as many barrels as he could on his way out and tipped them over.

More explosions rattled from the distance, rocking the refinery's walls.

By the time Rurik was on his way out the back entrance, another seventeen barrels lay on their sides with unrefined petroleum covering the floors and 1,700 kilograms of pure potassium awaiting Felix's flood.

Just as he exited the back, Rurik stopped in his tracks. He looked to his right to see the fiery flood rushing toward the refinery.

"Holy smokes!" he yelled.

The oil derricks exploded, and against the light of the lake fire rising in the distance, Rurik saw what he assumed to be Felix's shadow running across the top of the dam as the structure caved in behind him. Rurik gasped, panicked by the flaming waters rolling toward the refinery—much faster than he'd envisioned. He turned to dash away, then froze as a tinge of guilt poked at him.

"I'll never forgive myself," he said.

Rurik looked to the onrushing waters and estimated he had roughly two minutes before they breached the refinery and reacted with the potassium. He turned back and ran toward Pavel, who still lay unconscious upon the floor. Grabbing Pavel by his overalls, Rurik dragged him out the back as quickly as he could, pulling the slovenly oaf another sixty meters from the refinery until exhaustion caused his knees to buckle. Rurik crawled up a short embankment and took a moment to catch his breath. He then pulled Pavel toward him, believing they were far enough away to keep safe.

A purple flash ripped through the night as the refinery seemingly evaporated, sending Rurik flying to the ground from a forceful concussion.

Standing slowly, Rurik tried to balance himself as a terrible ringing in his ears caused him to wobble a bit. He pulled his glasses to his face and shook his head while trying to focus on the spot where the refinery once stood—the flaming waters still rushing toward him. Rurik placed his hands on his knees to balance himself and determined he was on high enough ground to avoid the flood. He swung around to see Pavel had been blown another five meters from their position and lay facedown, unconscious in the dirt. Rurik looked him over one more time, decided his due diligence was done, and hurried off into the darkness.

*

Rurik made his way to the town center, surprised to see the flood had covered the road in an ankle-deep river that ran almost to the encampment, which appeared deserted. He heard yelling in the distance from the perimeter of the flood, but it was far enough away not to cause concern. He crouched at the side of a building and peered into the road—it was desolate. The fiery lake still burned in the distance, and several underwater explosions sent deep-bass reverberations into the air. Rurik dashed across the street to the trading post to see that all of the windows on the small squat buildings were blown out, most of them leaning to one side or the other from the structural damage sustained in the refinery blast. He slid to the side of a building and found dry ground once more.

Upon reaching the back of the trading post, he saw Felix lying in the dirt, resting and holding his thigh with one hand while covering his genitals with the other.

"Felix!"

Felix looked up at him.

"How hurt are you?" asked Rurik.

"Shot in the leg," he said, removing his hand from the wound.

"Oh, dear. Is it—"

"Mostly superficial, but they took a chunk of me. Hurts like high heaven."

"Anything else?"

"Just banged up in general."

Rurik looked around to ensure they were alone. "Stay here. I'll grab some supplies."

"We need to find our horses," said Felix, pointing to the corral nearby.

Rurik positioned his glasses and looked to the corral to see a few mules and about six horses. "We'll grab some horses. Maybe not *our* horses. Be right back."

"Hey!" called Felix, causing Rurik to pause. "'Flood the operation'? Seems we—"

"Blew it to smithereens." Rurik shrugged, then scratched the back of his head. "Seems in my haste, I forgot to factor in the petroleum seep. Unintended consequences, I suppose."

"That was absolute genius. You amaze me."

Rurik smiled. "Ha! Me? You're the maniac who just blew up an entire mining town. I merely planted the seed." Rurik knelt to him and they gripped hands. "Glad to see you alive, my friend."

He released Felix's hand, walked to the back of the trading post, and kicked in the back door.

Felix lay on the earth, staring into the night sky. He wondered when he should tell Rurik about Florin's fate. Knowing Rurik was unaware of Florin's imprisonment within the mines, he decided it best to wait until they were away and had set up camp. He placed firm pressure on his leg and counted his breaths until Rurik returned.

"Jackpot," said Rurik, throwing Felix's saddle on the ground next to him. "Mine's in there, too. Everything else is gone."

Felix sat up and ran his hands under the saddle. A moment later, he produced a small gold bar.

"They didn't even check the saddle," said Felix.

"Tonight's our lucky night."

Rurik walked to the store, emerged with his own saddle, and dropped it next to Felix.

"One more trip," he said.

Felix waited for about ten minutes before Rurik returned with a duffel bag filled with various supplies.

"Pirates' booty, my friend."

"What did you get?"

"Anything I could. Those beans you wanted, for one. And even some spoons!"

Felix laughed. "I'm still open to bare hands."

"Here, let me help you." Rurik knelt to him and wrapped a bandage around Felix's thigh. Felix winced as he tightened it. "Too tight?"

"No," said Felix, running his hand along the cloth. "It's perfect. I'm mostly worried about infection."

Rurik reached back in the duffel bag. "And now, ladies and gentlemen—the pièce de résistance!" He stood and unrolled canvas overalls. "Your brand-new suit!"

Felix lay back on the ground and relaxed. "Amazing. Hand it over."

Rurik threw him the garment and Felix quickly suited up, buttoning it all the way up his chest.

"Oops," said Rurik. "I forgot the best part." He dashed back into the trading post and returned with a new pair of boots. "Try these."

"You know—that patch you gave me was real thoughtful, but these are officially the best birthday presents I've ever received."

Felix slipped on the boots and laced them. "A bit tight, but they'll do. Let's get the hell out of here."

*

An hour later, Felix and Rurik were on a small path about ten kilometers south of Zănoaga, having been reunited with their horses. There was no moon, but the starlight provided them just enough illumination to carry on. Both sat upon their steeds with expressionless faces and an open can of beans between their legs, spoon in hand, quietly shoving legumes into their mouths.

Felix couldn't tell if he was in shock, malnourished, or both, as he swore the beans were the most delicious thing he'd ever tasted.

"Drina," said Rurik with his mouth full.

"Huh?"

"I've decided to name her Drina." Rurik patted his horse on her mane.

Felix pondered the name. "Drina and Nima? Don't you think that's—wait . . . after your deceased barmaid girlfriend, Hedrina?"

"Just go with it."

Felix laughed. "You're certainly a glutton for punishment, Mr. Kozlov."

Rurik clicked his tongue and trotted slowly past him. "You just worry about those birthday beans. You've earned them . . . Another few kilos, and we'll set up camp."

Felix watched Rurik's shadow move into the path before him.

"That I will," he said, digging his spoon into the can. "Happy birthday to me."

Chapter 12

12

March 24, 1917, 11:28 a.m.

"Engage the flamethrowers! This is madness!"

Panicked yells filled the country air as First Lieutenant Erwin Jünger marched along the semicircular formation of armored trucks arrayed before Mount Hohenzollern's briar patch. He thrust his hands onto his hips and surveyed the destruction before him, silently cursing his superiors for commanding him to clear a path to the top for the Kaiser without any debriefing as to what he truly faced.

The plants may be unruly was the only warning he and his troop received.

"Some intelligence briefing that was," said Jünger, before spitting on the mud.

"Sir, what's happening?" came a voice from behind him. "Is the forest alive?"

Jünger turned to the soldier's boyish face and watched as the young man slipped a bit in a muddy patch beneath his boots.

"Seems that way, Private. We need to engage the flamethrowers."

"We only have two, sir!"

"Then engage them . . . now!" screamed Jünger.

The soldier saluted him.

"Put your stupid hand down and do as you're goddamn commanded!"

The young man turned on his heel and gathered two other soldiers before sprinting to the supply tent stationed just behind the row of armored trucks.

Jünger squinted into the light drizzle past the trucks to the dozen or so of his men who were entangled and struggling against the vines. Four other men lay bloodied and beaten along a small footpath leading up the mount to their overturned truck. The plants swarmed upon the men, sinking their thorns into their soft flesh as the truck rolled farther down the hill—its gas line ruptured and gushed over the voracious plants.

"Go! Go!" yelled Jünger as he watched two soldiers emerge from the supply tent with flamethrowers in hand and canisters strapped to their backs.

"What about us, sir?" questioned a soldier leaning against the back of a truck with four of his men crouched beside him, their rifles aimed at the forest.

"Hold fire. Hold position." Jünger marched past them and stood in front of a truck, watching as the two soldiers with flamethrowers ran to the briar patch's perimeter. They knelt and unleashed their flames upon the angry branches, which ignited and thrashed about like a pool of flaming asps. His eyes widened when one of the men began spraying too close to the overturned vehicle.

"Watch the truck!" yelled Jünger.

He turned and jogged to the supply tent.

"Sir!" A soldier saluted as he entered the tent.

"Where are the blades?" asked Jünger, moving toward the back of the tent.

"In that trunk there, sir."

Jünger opened the trunk. "Trench knives. I need something I can swing."

The soldier opened another locker.

"Here, sir," he said, pulling a long blade from the box. "From the captured French soldiers."

The soldier handed him a French coup-coup machete.

Jünger looked it over and decided it would suffice.

"How many more in there?"

"Only four, sir."

An explosion rattled through the air, followed by a spattering of gunfire.

"Hand me another and grab the remaining two. Follow me."

"Sir, I'm to stay on my post."

"Damn your post, son! Follow me."

The two exited the tent and took in the sheer mayhem before them. The truck was completely engulfed in flames as the vines burrowed beneath it and lifted it into the air. What appeared to be a small tidal wave of thorny branches thrust toward the vehicle, and it was thrown from the briar patch toward the soldiers with flame-throwers. The men dove out of the way, barely escaping the path of the flaming truck as it rolled and bounced past. Another two dozen men crouched behind the line of armored trucks and fired their service revolvers and rifles into the plants as the brush continued to feast upon and dismember the remaining soldiers trapped in the patch—their screams ripped across the field. Jünger approached a soldier firing a Mauser C96 and tore the weapon from his hand.

"That serves nothing! Here," he said, handing him the coup-coup machete. He turned to the rest of his men. "Cease fire!" he yelled. "I said, 'CEASE FIRE!'"

The call resonated down the line of trucks and the gunfire stopped. The two soldiers carrying the flamethrowers returned to Jünger.

"What are our orders, sir?"

Jünger glared at them. "Your orders were to hold the line and engage the flamethrowers. Get back out there!"

He looked to the briar patch to see the brambles shaking and moving on top of the burning plants, smothering the fire.

"Hold! Hold!" he yelled to the flamethrower operators.

Gray smoke slithered through the line of vehicles as a calm settled upon the field, the overturned truck still smoldering in the short distance.

"Sir?" Three of Jünger's men knelt before him, awaiting orders, each gripping a machete. Jünger looked to the briar patch to see it rising into the air like some foul thousand-tentacled monster.

"We have orders to clear a path to the top for the Kaiser's arrival. That is what we will do. Where's this goddamn liaison Commander Louis spoke of?" Jünger gritted his teeth in frustration. "You men, there. Where's your driver?"

A soldier with muddied knees dashed toward him.

"Corporal Uttz reporting for orders, sir!"

"I need you to drive, Corporal. That truck, there. You two!" he said, pointing to the flame-wielding soldiers. "In the back. Aiming forward—clear the brush around the truck."

"Sir!" The three men moved into position.

"Now, you men! Follow the truck and hack any vines that try to get into the wheels to overturn it." Jünger noticed their eyes widen and their expressions turn to confusion.

"Well? What are you waiting for?"

They continued to stare, and Jünger realized they were focused on something behind him. He turned to see an elderly man with striking long white hair and a spotless green robe standing before him with a pursed grin on his face.

"Who are you?" questioned Jünger, lifting his machete.

The man bowed slightly. "My name is Vago, young master. Perhaps I can help."

*

Wilhelm paced around the large oblong table in Knights' Hall, his left sleeve looped upon his saber.

"Arras is ours, gentlemen. We have pushed our naval fleet to the second meridian east, which you should know is .23522 degrees west of Paris. We will now begin staging operations from Arras to push toward the second meridian upon land. With our fleet position, nothing can flank us. We are primed to begin striking the English coast via sea, and we may now move forward into a full land offensive operation to annex Paris." Wilhelm stopped and turned to his advisors seated around the table. "Congratulations. Final victory is within our grasp."

Applause erupted from the council with several men standing to salute Wilhelm.

"Please be seated."

The hall's massive door creaked open, and a soldier approached the table. He clicked his heels and bowed at the waist, extending an envelope to Wilhelm.

"What's this?"

"Urgent news from Bucharest. It commands your immediate attention, Kaiser."

Wilhelm accepted the envelope.

"Dismissed," he said, and the messenger scurried from the room.

Wilhelm walked back to his chair at the head of the table. He fidgeted with the envelope slightly while trying to open it with his right hand, occasionally looking to his council to ensure none of them were staring as he struggled.

"What does it say, Kaiser?" asked Stein.

Wilhelm pulled his reading glasses to his face and held the telegram close to his blue eyes before peering up at his advisors.

"It says, dismissed."

"Dismissed?" questioned Stein.

Wilhelm shot a cold glance to Stein. "It says dismissed. Everyone. Out. Now. Save my inner council."

A murmur arose in the hall as the advisors stood from their chairs and shuffled away. The giant door closed as the last man exited and a chilly silence fell upon Knights' Hall.

"And who are you, exactly?" asked Wilhelm, glaring at the uniformed young man seated next to Hindenburg.

The man bowed his head. "Forgive me, Emperor. I was told you were briefed about my attendance."

"I was not."

The man stood. "Allow me, then, to formally introduce myself. I am Ludwig Otto. I am Charles I's liaison from Vienna. I am here to—"

"Did you not hear me say 'dismissed'?" Wilhelm sounded stern.

Ludwig swallowed and shifted, clearly aware of the unfriendly gazes around the table.

"I—I did, Kaiser. But I assumed that was for the lesser staff. Emperor Charles has been feeling our contributions have been . . . how should I say? Sidelined? And I was sent in his place—"

"Sidelined?" asked Wilhelm calmly.

"Yes, Kaiser. And I was sent in place of Charles to be a contributing—"

"Get out," said Wilhelm. "Now."

"But, Kaiser, I—"

"Herr Otto, since you're new here, I will make things clear for you. First: if the youngster Charles wants to contribute to our war efforts on the western front, he can come to Berlin and sit in that chair himself. Two: I told you to leave . . . I do not repeat myself."

Ludwig appeared pale. He grabbed the folders before him on the table. "As you command, Kaiser," he said, nodding, then hurried from the hall.

"Lock it," said Wilhelm, motioning to the door.

Prince Henry walked to the hall's entrance with expediency, locked the door, and returned.

Wilhelm was reading over the document he'd received.

"Kaiser?" questioned Hindenburg.

"What does it say, Kaiser?" followed Minister Schmidt.

Wilhelm cleared his throat. "It says, well, it says a lot, actually. Apparently, Charles Vondling has taken it upon himself to execute King Ferdinand and Princess Marie of Romania, and has declared himself emperor. That's what it says, firstly."

He continued to peruse the document. His hand let go the parchment as he reached the end, and the paper floated softly to the floor. Wilhelm stared blankly at the table's ebony surface for several moments.

"It also says," he began, "that the entire mining operation in Zănoaga has been obliterated."

"Impossible!" shouted Prince Henry, rising from his chair to retrieve the fallen paper. "Let me see."

Wilhelm closed his eyes and swallowed. "Where's Ernest Louis?"

"Sire, he's overseeing the Hohenzollern operation to prepare for your arrival."

Wilhelm nodded and leaned back in his chair.

"So," he said, looking to Hindenburg. "What now?"

"I will need to meet with the royal seers."

"No!" shouted Wilhelm. "No more information gathered in secret without my presence. I'm no longer certain I am being told the truth. I was informed that anything south of Buzău was under our control. I was told that the Allied forces were under the impression that Bucharest was suffering from a horrid plague and would not dare operate in the area. I was told that Zănoaga was remote enough that we would continue to operate in secret. I was also told that Vondling would not become a problem. So, how did the Allies destroy an entire mining operation with no forces in the area? And to what extent have Vondling's actions been made known to anyone outside our circle?"

"Sire, without the assistance of multiple—"

"You're a seer, are you not? In fact, aren't you both gifted with second sight?" Wilhelm pointed to Minister Schmidt.

Hindenburg sat in silence.

"Paul. Friedrich. It's time. No more secret warlock meetings. No more secondhand information. Tell me. Right here. Right now. What is going on with this operation?"

Schmidt sat quietly staring at Hindenburg. He nodded and Hindenburg returned the gesture.

"Very well, Kaiser," said Hindenburg. "For clarity's sake and for the betterment of our long-term mutual trust, we will do it now."

"Excellent," said Wilhelm. "Proceed."

"Prince Henry," said Schmidt. "Would you mind drawing the curtains?"

Henry nodded and walked to the wall of large windows that ran nearly from floor to ceiling. Window by window, he pulled the drapes closed and darkness fell upon Knights' Hall save small slivers of light framing the windows. Prince Henry sat next to his brother, and the two men focused on Hindenburg and Schmidt.

The two warlocks bowed their heads and began breathing deeply. Hindenburg was humming softly. Schmidt lifted his head and opened his eyes to reveal pure white corneas that glowed ever so slightly. Hindenburg followed.

Schmidt and Hindenburg mind scanned the Void, following its dark reverberations, which led their vision to an unsteady static surrounding the events near Zănoaga. Schmidt sucked in a quick and audible breath as Hindenburg began to quietly growl, gnashing his teeth.

"Do you sense it?" asked Hindenburg.

"I do," said Schmidt.

"Follow me," directed Hindenburg.

The two men snapped their necks backward and opened their mouths wide—their white eyes focused on the ceiling. Their minds melded upon a vision of Felix Yusupov struggling through the mines of Zănoaga. Images of fanged mouths, purple explosions rising from churning, black waters, and a lake of fire flooded their thoughts. Next came the image of Charles Vondling biting deeply into the Red Baron's cervical spine as four other men dressed in pilots' uniforms knelt around them. A goat skull. A bottle of blood. The seal of the Order of the Dragon burning to ash. A final vision of Felix Yusupov kneeling as a cloaked figure slowly approached, holding a black scimitar radiating in the darkness. *It's you*, came a voice.

Hindenburg tensed and closed his eyes, lowering his head. Schmidt followed.

They appeared unconscious.

Wilhelm studied both men, wondering if he should intervene. He looked to Prince Henry, who shook his head in silence. A full two minutes passed before Hindenburg and Schmidt opened their eyes.

"You may open the curtains," said Schmidt.

As Prince Henry complied, Wilhelm became impatient. "Well?" he asked.

"Well, indeed," said Hindenburg. "I'm uncertain how to begin. None of what I will tell you is pleasing."

"Tell me now," said Wilhelm.

"Zănoaga was destroyed by two men and only two men. The specifics are murky, but it appears they used the pure potassium deposits as an explosive agent that blew up the dam and flooded the operation."

"Clever men," said Wilhelm.

"A Rurik Kozlov, who was mentioned in the Nosferatu dossier, and—"

"Prince Felix Yusupov," interjected Wilhelm.

"Yes, Kaiser."

Wilhelm bit his lower lip and bounced his right leg beneath the table.

"My Kaiser," began Schmidt. "I can sense your displeasure—"

"Can you, Minister? Can you also sense that my displeasure is focused upon you? And you?" He pointed to Hindenburg.

"There's more, Kaiser," said Hindenburg.

"Proceed."

Hindenburg let out a short, erratic breath. "Our last trace on Radu cel Frumos was December 26 of last year."

"I recall. You sensed he had broken his silence and tried to send a psychic message from Saint Petersburg to Bucharest."

"Yes, Kaiser. But his message was cloaked. Five of us could not break the psychic encryption. And afterward, he went dark once more. We then found some static pointing to him being back in Paris shortly thereafter, so we believed it all to be a misnomer."

"We believe now," said Schmidt, "that it was no false alarm. We just picked up his mental fingerprint again. Radu is in Romania. We have a solid understanding of his location."

Wilhelm stared in silence.

"He is tracking Felix Yusupov," continued Schmidt. "Who, from our understanding, is gravely wounded. He was shot in the leg. Difficult to predict entirely, but it seems he will die in a matter of days from septic shock. But . . . most importantly . . . Radu has the bottle of Drăculea's blood with him."

"Or at least near him," finished Hindenburg. "The bottle is in Romania."

Wilhelm raised his fist to his mouth and bit down on his index knuckle. He stood slowly as his chair skidded away from him. Raising his head in a proud and dramatic fashion, Wilhelm swallowed as his blue eyes widened and he looked to Hindenburg.

"If Radu gives Yusupov the bottle, can it save him if he drinks it?"

Hindenburg considered the question. "Well, I suppose—yes. But I find it hard to believe Radu would harbor this bottle for centuries only to waste it so."

"No matter," interrupted Wilhelm. "I will say this once and only once. I want Charles Vondling terminated. Immediately. Let the remaining vampires overrun Bucharest for all I care. We can fumigate it later."

"My Kaiser," said Hindenburg, "I will handle this objective personally."

"Very well," said Wilhelm. "As for the rest, Yusupov and Radu being in the same vicinity is no accident. I don't know why Radu is tracking him, but I will not allow this opportunity slip through my grasp. From this point forward, we will use every available resource of my empire's might. Every ounce of cunning in my very marrow.

"Let it be known!" he yelled, slamming his fist into the table. "The German Empire and its allies—supernatural or otherwise—have officially declared war on one Prince Felix Yusupov. Bring him before me, dead or alive. I want that bottle and the head of Radu cel Frumos. Deploy Jasta Eleven."

"Understood, Kaiser," said Hindenburg. "But you should also know that earlier, Minister Schmidt and I scanned and analyzed Elizabeth's movements—and her intentions are exactly as I surmised. The entity she is using in the child abductions is essentially a proxy of her own consciousness—one that can operate at her behest outside the banishment spell. As Elizabeth was known during the Inferno, so now is this entity known as—"

"The Death Witch," finished Wilhelm.

"Yes. The Death Witch," continued Hindenburg. "Once Ernest Louis makes contact with Elizabeth's liaison, Vago, our first order of negotiation will center around hunting and killing Radu. Her Death Witch would essentially be at your disposal. It's an entity of immeasurable power—and wrath."

Wilhelm turned and stared out the windows as a sense of optimism welled inside him.

"My Kaiser, what would you have us do?" questioned Schmidt.

Wilhelm spun around with a broad smile on his face. "Well, it's obvious isn't it? We send in the Death Witch."

*

It was 4:21 a.m. when Jünger and eleven of his best soldiers reached the peak of Mount Hohenzollern. The previous seventeen hours ascending the mount had been sheer hell, and the troop was badly beaten, bruised, and exhausted. The light drizzle from earlier had turned to a heavy downpour about midday, causing multiple delays as their two armored trucks repeatedly became stuck in the mud while they tried to clear the age-old path that led to the castle. Vago was able to keep the carnivorous plants mostly at bay, but even with his presence, three additional men were lost to the bloodthirsty foliage.

It was pitch black when they reached a clearing at the top of the mount.

"Fire up the generators!" shouted Jünger.

Several of his men switched on their flashlights as others pulled the heavy, gas-powered generators from the rear of their trucks. Another group of six soldiers set up telescoping towers with flood-lights wobbling at the top.

A thunderous rumble filled the mountain darkness as the genera-tors rattled to life. A moment later, the floodlights came on to reveal nothing but scattered castle ruins and a clear view to the other side of the mountain.

"Is this a joke?" asked Jünger, turning to Vago.

"Why no, Commander. I see no humor in this whatsoever."

"It's First Lieutenant," said Jünger. "You said Commander Louis sent you to assist us. For what? What are we doing up here?"

Jünger felt disgusted as he looked to the truck where Ernest Louis sat ghost-faced from the harrowing ascent.

Typical royal coward, he thought.

Vago bowed. "I am under the impression that your Kaiser is coming to visit, and that a path up the mount was to be cleared. The spell upon the plants has been relaxed, but they are still aggressive."

"*Schwachsinn!*" shouted a soldier near Jünger.

Jünger turned to him. "Hey! You want to hike back down alone?" Jünger noticed a cigarette between the soldier's fingers. "Finish your goddamn cigarette and keep your mouth shut."

"Sir!" bellowed the soldier.

"So, what?" asked Jünger, looking to Vago. "We just stand here until the Kaiser arrives?"

"I am not privy to your operations. I was only enlisted by your commander to keep you safe from the vines."

"Some good that did. He won't even leave the truck," said Jünger. "We lost three men on this climb."

Vago flashed his blocky teeth. "Apologies for your losses," he said, bowing his head slightly. "Although there is something that might make this worth your while."

"Yeah? What's that?"

"Take a better look at the vines before you," said Vago, extending his hands toward the invisible field.

Jünger studied the foliage. The vines running along a foundational stone seemed to rise up into the night air with no support to form an arched opening.

"Walk through that arch," said Vago.

Jünger squinted and shot Vago a distrustful glance.

"Please, see for yourself."

Jünger kept his eye on Vago as he hesitantly walked toward the soldier he had chided. The two men exchanged quiet words, and the soldier handed Jünger a cigarette. He placed it in his mouth without lighting it and looked back to Vago, then swaggered insouciantly toward the arched opening.

Jünger sauntered toward the invisible field, his gray and muddied uniform a perfect match against the muck before him. He stood for a moment at the threshold, looking up to the vines in midair. He then took one step forward and disappeared from sight.

"Lieutenant!" shouted several soldiers, pulling their rifles from their sides.

A group of six soldiers immediately turned their rifles on Vago, who threw his hands in the air.

"What did you do to him?" screamed one of the men.

"Now, now, gentlemen," said Vago calmly. "Your lieutenant is fine."

"I'm fine, men. I'm OK!" came Jünger's voice from beyond the field.

The soldiers turned slowly with a palpable sense of disbelief and caution as they positioned their rifles outward and crept toward the invisible field.

"Get in here! Now!" came Jünger's voice.

The soldiers continued to slink toward the field as Vago watched, slowly lowering his hands.

One by one, they disappeared into the enchanted grounds.

"Is it safe?" came Ernest Louis's voice from the truck.

Vago turned to him. "Very much so, Commander. Please . . . join me."

*

"What in holy hell is that?"

"It's a giant castle," said Jünger, his cigarette hanging from his lip.

The dozen soldiers stood at the east gate, which led up to the main grounds of Hohenzollern Castle. The floodlights were just bright enough to illuminate the red brick façade—the entrance beyond the drawbridge remained in shadows.

"Sorry about my outburst earlier, Lieutenant," said the soldier who had given him the cigarette. "But I didn't sign on for this—"

"Quiet," commanded Jünger, raising his hand. "What's that?"

"Where, sir?"

"There—just past the drawbridge. I saw something in the archway. Hand me your flashlight."

The soldier reached inside a pouch on his belt and handed a flashlight to Jünger.

Jünger flicked on the light and shined it into the archway.

"There! You see it? Someone's in there. Follow me. Rifles up." Jünger lurched forward and his men followed—all ready to fire.

"I see it, Lieutenant."

"Shhhh," whispered Jünger, shining his light into the darkness. "Is that a kid?"

They crept onto the drawbridge, and the flashlight revealed a small child sitting alone inside the arched pathway, halfway toward its exit.

"Lower your weapons," said Jünger, rushing toward the child.

Even in the darkness, Jünger could see something was wrong with the child's skin—the small boy appeared almost pure white with a chalky texture to his pale hair. The child sat against the wall, holding his knees to his chest with his head buried in his lap.

Jünger believed he was whimpering.

211

"Little boy," said Jünger, extending his hand to the child. "Little boy, what are you doing here?"

The child reared up his head to reveal deep black scars where his eyeballs once were. He grabbed Jünger's hand and pulled the man downward, sinking his sharp teeth into Jünger's palm. Jünger shrieked and fell backward, hitting his head on the brick wall and dropping his flashlight. The archway fell to shadows as the filament split in two.

The remaining soldiers raised their rifles. Even in the dark, they could see the exit from the archway was now blocked by the shadows of seven other children—their pale, eyeless faces appeared to glimmer in the dark. The soldiers huddled together as the child who bit Jünger scurried away through the exit.

The floodlights cast a splinter of light into the first quarter of the pathway, and it was soon overtaken by multiple silhouettes approaching the entrance. The soldiers turned to see another group of ghostly children now standing behind them.

Blocked on both sides, the men fired their guns.

*

Vago stood smiling and cackling on the other side of the banishment field, listening to the gunshots and screaming.

Ernest Louis exited the truck and stood next to him.

"Will the gunfire harm the children?" he asked.

"Not one bit," said Vago.

Ernest Louis grinned.

They waited until the commotion ceased, then entered the field.

Vago and Ernest Louis proceeded to the drawbridge and peered into the passageway to see all twelve soldiers lying on the ground—each of them shivering, alive, and riddled with gaping bite wounds upon their hands, necks, and faces.

The children had vanished.

"What—what's happening here?" asked a soldier, barely able to muster the words.

Vago stood over him and several pale children scurried in behind him and Ernest Louis, wrapping their hands around the warlocks' legs and peeking at the soldiers.

"You will see, my son," said Vago. "You will see."

Chapter 13

13

STAATSGEHEIMNIS [STATE SECRET] ZENSIERT—ZENSIERT—ALLE KOPIEN IM DIENST VON KAISER WILHELM II AUFGEFUNDEN UND ZERSTÖRT [CENSORED—ALL COPIES LOCATED AND DESTROYED IN SERVICE OF KAISER WILHELM II]

Clipping from *Vossische Zeitung*
Child Kidnappings Ravage Württemberg Region

Bisingen, Mar. 25, 1917—A state of emergency was declared in the Kingdom of Württemberg and its surrounding areas this morning in response to a rash of sudden and unexplained child abductions. The kidnappings began on Thursday afternoon in Zimmern with the abduction of six-year-old Oskar Güterbach, followed by the abductions of another 11 children in the surrounding area the same day. Several guardians of the children are also missing.

A total of 72 children have disappeared since then. Whoever is committing the bold kidnappings seems unconcerned with discretion or time of day, and most of the abductions are reported to have occurred in the morning or mid to late afternoon.

The Kingdom of Württemberg finally declared a statewide emergency Saturday morning after three more children of noble families disappeared just east of the Black Forest.

Compounding the mystery is the decision to call off the search for the missing children. The XIII Royal Württemberg Corps were enlisted to carry out the search, but the operation was unceremoniously terminated within 24 hours by a direct order from Kaiser Wilhelm II. The order cited a drain on the army's resources. War, it seems, is taking precedence.

Worrisome stories have emerged from the now-disbanded search and rescue committees. Although children were reported missing in all areas of the 17,000 square miles of Württemberg, the accounts were the same: the children were taken by someone in black.

Niels Hermann of Zimmern reported witnessing the abduction of his granddaughter from his family's front yard early Saturday morning. According to Hermann, the morning became suddenly foggy, and a tall, lean figure appeared out of the mist. The figure, dressed in a black cloak and white mask, quickly approached the child, who fell unconscious upon its touch. The masked abductor then wrapped the cloak around the child and disappeared with her into the Zollerhalde nature reserve, which borders the family's property, in the direction of Mount Hohenzollern. According to the heavily redacted report, when asked why he didn't follow the child or shout for help, Hermann simply stated, "Because of what lurks upon the mount."

The abductions have led to a swirl of rumors, including unconfirmed reports of tanks, armed transports, and several dozen elite soldiers arriving at the base of Mount Hohenzollern on Saturday morning under no publicly disclosed orders from Berlin. There was no official announcement in the press for such a measure, and any military activity connected with the abductions has been ordered a state secret by Kaiser Wilhelm.

(CONT. A-14)

*

March 25, 1917, 4:23 p.m.

Kaiser Wilhelm stepped from his personal armored vehicle and walked briskly past the small encampment of soldiers and vehicles for a clear view of Mount Hohenzollern. The journey from Berlin had been nearly eleven hours, and he was eager to stretch his legs.

"Kaiser on the grounds!" a commanding officer announced.

The twenty or so troops seated in the area sprung to attention while trying to get a good view of their Kaiser.

Wilhelm looked down to his muddy boots and realized his white garments were a poor choice for such a rain-drenched environment. Taking in the foggy majesty of the mount, Wilhelm adjusted his black and gold pickelhaube before turning to his armored vehicle. He waved to the driver as two men exited the back of the vehicle and rapidly approached him with a black canvas tarp in tow.

The two soldiers unfolded the canvas and raised it behind Wilhelm, blocking him from the onlooking soldiers. He then proceeded to unzip his fly and urinate on the fresh mud as he took in the destruction surrounding the briar patch, specifically focusing on the burned-out metal skeleton of the armored truck strewn across the field.

"Gentlemen," said Wilhelm with a sense of duty in his voice, as he zipped himself up and turned to the encampment.

The soldiers folded the canvas tarp and followed Wilhelm toward the gaggle of troops waiting to meet him. There were eager faces all around.

Minister Schmidt and Ernest Louis stood next to Wilhelm as he took a moment to look over the ragged soldiers.

"Brave men one and all!" he bellowed. "At ease."

The soldiers relaxed and politely applauded him.

"Very well. Thank you," began Wilhelm, then spoke directly to a field lieutenant. "It is my understanding that you lost nearly twenty of your own on this operation?"

"Yes, my Kaiser," said the soldier. "Our first lieutenant Jünger and all the men who ascended the mount last evening. None returned."

"They were heroic men," interjected Ernest Louis. "I, too, bravely faced the dangers of that climb. They saved both me and Masker Vakól several times in clearing a safe path to the top for our Kaiser."

Wilhelm nodded and stepped closer to the line of soldiers.

"I grieve with you, gentlemen, for these losses. I want you all to know that no matter how strange this operation may seem and how this unexpected turn of events must shock you, your brothers did not die in vain. You will all be debriefed by your senior officers before you depart, but I want you to hear it from my mouth first. None of you are to discuss what you have witnessed here over the past twenty-four hours. This operation is of the highest importance to our success in this war and is now officially a state secret. I thank you from the bottom of my heart for your service to our fine empire. Minister Schmidt thanks you. My advisor and your command of this operation"—he placed his right hand on Ernest Louis's shoulder—"thanks you. And Empress Augusta sends her love and admiration to you all. Hail the Second Reich!"

"Do not salute your Kaiser on a field of battle!" shouted a commanding officer.

The soldiers stood more rigidly at attention.

"At ease, my sons," said Wilhelm.

He and his brass walked toward the soldiers, then shook hands with the service members eager to touch the hand of their Kaiser.

*

"Kaiser Wilhelm II, I give you Vago Vakól of Bad Boll," said Ernest Louis, bowing at the waist.

Vago remained kneeling upon the muddy grass. His lips quivered as he looked up to Wilhelm.

"Praise unto you, Kaiser. I give you the highest praise! Praise unto Prussia! Praise unto the House of Hohenzollern. Praise—"

"You may rise," said Wilhelm.

Vago's eyes lit up as if he'd been spoken to by Bael himself. He stood to face Wilhelm and was noticeably taller than the Kaiser. An awkward silence ensued as Vago simply stood, smiling at Wilhelm, who broke eye contact and looked to the low-lying circular domed huts of Vago's wooded encampment.

"Bad Boll?" inquired Wilhelm.

"Sire?"

"The name . . . it's unique. Ernest Louis tells me you founded this small village here in the forest."

"Yes, Kaiser. We are far enough away from civilization that we are left to ourselves. My coven generates enough dark psychic energy that we remain essentially cloaked from prying eyes, and I suppose the superstition surrounding the mount also helps."

"Not really a superstition, though. Is it?"

Vago laughed. "No, Kaiser, it's all very real. But as for the name— I founded this community, and I simply liked the sound of it. So, yes! Welcome to Bad Boll, home of my Thule Society." Vago bowed slightly.

"Very well," said Wilhelm, noticing a line of young coven members forming near their gathering. His eyes moved over their eager faces and lingered on several of the young women dressed in white ceremonial gowns.

"They are all pure Prussian, my Kaiser," said Vago.

Wilhelm turned his attention back to Vago. "Pure Prussian?"

"Why, yes. I've bred them all. Only from the heartiest Prussian lineage. We are the chosen order of your Second Reich."

Wilhelm furled his brow. "Are you? I wasn't made aware." He felt vaguely disgusted by Vago's groveling demeanor.

"No?" asked Vago. "I am very sorry to hear that. All that I have done here in secret has been for the betterment of the empire."

Vago's inflated perception of his coven's importance made Wilhelm uneasy, and he became suspicious about his inner circle's quiet dealings with this unusual man. Certainly, they had been in contact for some time. Wilhelm thought back to Hindenburg's seemingly offhand assertion that he knew of a liaison to establish contact with Elizabeth, and took a mental note to confront him on the matter. As far as Wilhelm was concerned, Vago and his clan were nothing more than useful idiots in his master plan, and he found himself at a loss as to how to respond to Vago's claims. He slid past the strange warlock in silence and inspected the rest of the small encampment.

Ernest Louis, Schmidt, and the soldiers in Wilhelm's entourage followed as several young children approached and offered the Kaiser a bouquet of dried flowers. A blonde woman then came before Wilhelm, bowed, and placed a dried daisy in the leather strap of his pickelhaube. She kissed him on the cheek and scurried off to her friends, who embraced her and smiled with the hushed giggles of nervous schoolgirls.

"Apologies, Kaiser," said Vago. "They are very excited about your visit."

"It's quite all right," said Wilhelm, handing off the bouquet to Ernest Louis.

"Anything you desire is available to you here, my Kaiser," said Vago. "The women, the children—the men, if you so desire. You as well, Grand Duke. I personally train them all from youth to submissively serve their betters. Any demand you have they will gladly oblige."

Vago flashed his obsequious grin.

"I am loyal to the empress, Master Vakól," was the only response he could muster before he shot a surprised glance to Ernest Louis.

"Very well, Kaiser," said Vago. "And please do not take offense at my comments about our society being your chosen order. I have tried to contact you for years to tell you of my work. I am breeding pure witches of Prussian descent. Imagine the power they will bring to your—"

"What about the spider, Elizabeth?" asked Wilhelm, turning to him.

"What of her, my Kaiser?"

"When can I meet her? We have much to discuss."

"I am certain. She is eagerly awaiting your meeting, as well. But it is late. Tomorrow morning is better. Especially considering the plants—they grow unruly at night."

"Ah, yes," said Wilhelm. "The vegetation is quite a surprise. I was briefed, but seeing it in person is another story. You can guarantee my safety as we ascend?" He scowled. "There will be grave repercussions for you and your entire coven if I am harmed in any way."

"I guarantee your safety with the utmost assurance," said Vago. "It is how she survived, you know. When she awoke in the castle, she had no allies, and no other choice. Elizabeth cursed the mount so that no one—friend or foe—could pass. The plants protected her. Fed her for centuries. She has since relaxed the spell so that I and other loyalists may pass, but the plants still must feed."

The group stopped near a larger hut with ceremonial carvings atop its threshold, and Vago bowed.

"This is my home. I would be honored if you came inside so we may discuss these matters in greater detail. I promise you that my hut is quite comfortable."

Wilhelm looked the structure up and down, and was impressed by its quaint sturdiness for something essentially built from the nearby woods. He took in the encampment once more, his eyes finally settling on the mount in the distance.

"She cursed the mount so that none could pass," said Wilhelm. "And you, as her loyal follower, set up camp here to attempt to free her."

"Yes, Kaiser. I was intent on breaking the spell. Eugenics are a complicated and time-consuming endeavor, but I knew only a witch of the purest stock could pass and break the spell. There can be pure witches of many ethnicities, of course, but I chose witches of Prussian descent, as, well, myself being Prussian . . . and I believe we are the master race."

"Master race?" said Wilhelm. "I like that phrase—there is truth in those words." He looked Vago over once more, still unsure if he despised him outright or was merely put off by his eagerness. "You spent centuries breeding witches to break this spell?"

"Why, yes. My loyalty knows no bounds, and Elizabeth, in resurrecting her father, holds the power to rule over all mankind. A power that you may now harness for your Prussian Empire. Tomorrow, when we ascend the mount, you will see."

Wilhelm brightened, invigorated at the thought of harnessing such power. He reached out and opened the door to Vago's meager hut.

"Come," he said, laying his right hand firmly upon Vago's shoulder. "Tell me everything."

Minister Schmidt raised his eyebrows and exchanged a glance with Ernest Louis as the four men entered Vago's hut.

Chapter 13

*

It was mid-morning when Kaiser Wilhelm stood at the opening that led into Elizabeth's lair. He craned his neck and stretched his arms, marveling at how rested he felt after sleeping the night on a hay mattress in Vago's guest hut. He wondered whether the hay had some magical properties, as even his lumbar region, which generally troubled him, was feeling loose and relaxed.

The morning air was crisp, and Wilhelm enjoyed a few deep breaths as he watched dismal rain clouds roll in, crowning their gathering. He looked down to the sweeping panorama below and counted fifteen tanks on the grounds—all with their guns pointing upward.

Vago and Ernest Louis stood next to him.

"My Kaiser," began Ernest Louis, "may I advise that artillery fire may crumble the structure."

"Simply warning shots near the foundation, and only if necessary." He glared at Ernest Louis. "Your men are well trained, are they not?"

"Yes, Kaiser."

"Then shooting the side of a mountain should be no problem at all."

"Kaiser," said Vago, "do you truly feel that having the tanks here is necessary? I briefed her earlier about their presence and what they are capable of. Elizabeth found their placement here to be adversarial, even offensive."

"Good," said Wilhelm. "She is to be considered an adversary until proven otherwise."

"My Kaiser," said Vago, bowing his head.

"They are merely a reminder that I am to return safely down the mount." Wilhelm looked up to the sky. "Minister Schmidt. Can you hear me? I am authorizing you to scan my mind for the duration of the mission."

A short moment passed, and Wilhelm nodded his head after connecting telepathically with Schmidt.

"If you sense any pain or panic on my part, fire with fury."

Wilhelm nodded once more and proceeded to the entrance.

"Kaiser!" protested Ernest Louis. "Certainly you aren't going in alone?"

Wilhelm stood with his back to them and stared into the web-festooned entrance. After a moment, he turned around. "She's expecting me, is she not?"

"Yes, Kaiser," said Vago. "But—"

"And she knows I have the means to blow the castle to smithereens if she even attempts to harm me?"

"Kaiser, please," said Ernest Louis, moving toward him.

"This creature needs to know who she's dealing with. Stand ready at the entrance to intervene if I call for you. I'm going in alone."

"Kaiser—" interjected Vago.

"I'm negotiating with her. Not you," said Wilhelm.

He then turned and strode fearlessly through the web curtains.

*

Wilhelm was immediately disgusted by the stench of death and decay as he entered the hallway that led into the main chamber. He unsheathed his thin saber and held it before him as he crept along the webbing on the floor, taking in the stacks of bones and other debris strewn about his feet.

As he entered the main hall, Wilhelm froze in his tracks at the sight of the sweeping expanse—all the while thinking back to the stories his grandfather told him about this supposed castle that had disappeared into the night. He was delighted to see that some of the arched stained-glass windows on the far wall remained mostly intact. His eyes followed the damaged ceiling to the webbing along the chandeliers. At the very end, he noticed a series of webbed pods that hung from the vaulted arches.

He quickly counted in fives—thirty in all.

Wilhelm headed toward the end of the hall, continually scanning all sides and occasionally turning back to make sure nothing was creeping up on him from behind. There was no giant spider to be seen. As he reached the end of Elizabeth's lair, he wrinkled his nose upon closer inspection of the pods, noticing the faces of small children just behind the webbing. Wilhelm had been dabbling in the occult since before his coronation. He'd witnessed many hair-raising events over the years in his dealings with warlocks and seers, but he was simply unprepared for the horror before him. Nausea poked at his stomach as he stared up at the ghoulish young faces behind the webbing.

He looked to the floor and took in a breath, trying to quell his disgust.

Where is this creature?

Elizabeth was hiding in a web pocket in the vaulted ceiling, watching Wilhelm as he passed beneath her and stood looking up at the entombed children. Leg by leg, she emerged from her hiding spot, then lowered herself from the perch by a sturdy strand of web.

As she landed on the floor, her weight disturbed the webbing and the chandeliers rattled a bit, causing Wilhelm to cock his head.

Elizabeth crept more closely to him.

Wilhelm sensed the disturbance and steadied himself. Before he turned to confront her, he reminded himself that Vago and Ernest Louis were a short sprint away, that Schmidt was scanning his mind, and that over a dozen tanks sat ready to blast the castle. He was emperor of these lands, and she was an unwelcome houseguest—a mere insect, drained of her powers and trapped in this castle. Wilhelm was the dominant one, and it was time Elizabeth knew.

He puffed out his chest and swung around to see Elizabeth slinking toward him. A shock rolled over him as he stared at her giant white body and eight soulless black eyes. He thrust his saber toward her.

"Ah! Ah!" he said. "Unless you want seven eyes, I suggest you stand back, creature."

"Creature?" said Elizabeth in a calm, soothing voice. "Is that any way to greet—"

"I said, 'Stand back.'"

Wilhelm stepped forward and held his saber mere inches from Elizabeth's face. He looked her over, realizing her voice had projected directly into his mind, and a strange sense of calm enveloped him as he thought back to his teens when he'd confronted a large brown bear on a hunt in the Bulgarian Rhodope Mountains.

Despite her gruesome appearance, Wilhelm realized he had been far more frightened of the charging bear he'd easily gunned down.

He now felt back in control.

Elizabeth took a few soft steps backward, and Wilhelm lowered his saber slightly.

"So, it's true," he said, his eyes wide as if he were witnessing some mythical beast. "The Blood Countess herself. Quite a predicament you've found yourself in. You've seen better days, Elizabeth."

Elizabeth seemed to chuckle quietly. "You're shorter than I expected."

"And you are far uglier."

Elizabeth crawled to Wilhelm's right. He tracked her every move with his saber extended.

"Here I thought you'd come for pleasantries."

"I certainly don't see any tea and crumpets in this hellhole," said Wilhelm. "I came here only to tell you that I will not have your agenda interfering with my plans." He raised his sword and pointed to the web tombs hanging from the ceiling. "Unless you submit and begin operating in the service of my empire, this stops now."

"This will not be stopped. Certainly not by some mortal in a strange pointy cap."

Wilhelm was amused by her bravado. He lowered his saber. "You've been away a long time, Elizabeth. Much has changed. Allow me to show you a preview of what's to come if you do not bend to my will."

"Your will? How dare you!"

Elizabeth seized upon Wilhelm, who thrust his saber at her, causing her to rear her front legs and recoil.

"Do it now!" said Wilhelm, looking to the ceiling.

What sounded like a thunderclap resounded through the hall from the fields below, followed by an ever-growing whistle that culminated in a jolt to the castle walls. The chandeliers bounced as bricks from the decayed ceiling fell in around them—a large brick striking Elizabeth on the top of her abdomen. She scurried off between the columns and tucked herself away.

Wilhelm turned to her.

"Now then," he said. "It is my understanding that although you are a witch and essentially immortal, your powers are gravely weakened and you may be killed by conventional means. Do you know what I do with bugs?"

Elizabeth backed farther into the wall without responding.

"I squash them. If I do not leave here safely, that was just a warning of the destruction I will rain down upon this structure. I will obliterate this castle and you along with it. Do we understand one another?"

Elizabeth was quiet.

Wilhelm crept toward her, careful not to become entangled in any of her webbing or trip over the mounds of bones. He stood just in front of Elizabeth and held his saber to her eyeballs.

"Well, creature? Will you submit to the Crown?"

At that moment, Wilhelm heard fast-approaching footsteps from his right. He turned, only to have the wind knocked out of him as he flew to the floor from some unseen blow. He quickly composed himself and turned on his back as the sound of a low bass filled the expanse. He peered up to see a black-clad figure in a horned skull mask standing over him, pointing two black scimitars at his throat. Elizabeth was now crouched directly behind the figure.

Wilhelm sat up and tried to shake the webbing from his clothing and hands while staring up at the radiant blades and the skulled face.

"Send another," he said.

A boom resonated from below and the castle walls shook once more, raining bricks upon all of them.

The figure sheathed its blades and removed its helmet. It glared at Wilhelm, who stared back dazed and horrified at its gaunt, pale face with blackened scars where its eyes once were. A strange sensation came over him as a horrid, high-pitched wail seared through his mind, filling his vision with gruesome images of infinite razor-sharp teeth tearing through everything in their path. He gripped his head and wanted to scream—to cast these visions from his psyche.

Wilhelm had the notion that he was shrinking in the presence of this looming figure. He became overwhelmed with the desire to worship it—to offer something unto its dark presence. The figure then spoke to him telepathically in a voice low and hoarse. Wilhelm now knew the only way to cease the calamity overtaking him was to obey its command.

"Why, yes," he said. "Yes!"

Wilhelm reached up and began to stick his index fingers into his eye sockets as Vago and Ernest Louis ran into the hall. They tackled him, holding his arms at his sides as he thrashed about and tried to claw at his face.

"Stop this!" yelled Vago. "Hanne! Put your mask back on at once!"

Hanne placed her deer skull helmet back on her head, and Wilhelm calmed as he came back from his trance. After Ernest Louis helped him from the floor, Wilhelm continued to shake his head, trying to expunge from his mind the memory of melding with Hanne. He blinked in an exaggerated fashion several times before looking back to her.

"The Death Witch, I presume," he said, trying to convey he was unrattled by the exchange.

Hanne's horns dipped slightly in acknowledgment.

"Your reputation precedes you," said Wilhelm, eyeing the hilts poking from her shoulders.

Hanne stood back and postured as if she were protecting Elizabeth.

"Well, creature," said Wilhelm, looking to Elizabeth. "It seems we are at an impasse."

"Please, please!" said Vago, moving in between them. "This is supposed to be a union. Not a confrontation."

"I will decide that," said Wilhelm, taking another moment to admire Hanne's intimidating appearance. "I say," he continued, looking to Ernest Louis, "that would make a fine new uniform for our front-line soldiers, don't you think? The French would lose their minds."

The group was quiet with all eyes on Wilhelm.

Wilhelm let out a booming laugh and patted Ernest Louis on the back.

Vago smiled at the unexpected moment of levity, and Hanne appeared to relax, casually placing her hands on her hips.

Wilhelm ran his hand across his uniform, trying to free it from any web remnants as he approached Hanne.

"Step away," he commanded.

Hanne stood firm for a moment, then relented.

Wilhelm placed himself before Elizabeth and stared into her black eyes.

"Well then, creature," he said. "It seems you and I have a common enemy and similar goals." He looked to the vaulted ceiling. "And since you've been living rent-free in my family castle, how then do you propose we work this out? Certainly, we can strike a bargain."

Elizabeth's head dipped in agreement. "Most certainly," she said.

14

March 26, 1917, 3:12 p.m.

It was late afternoon. Felix lay in his makeshift tent, finding a moment of calm as he listened to the repetitive thumps of fat raindrops pelting the canvas. He grabbed the lid from his canteen and moved it into the open in hopes of gathering some rainwater to boil.

Rurik had fortunately acquired two canvas field ponchos in his trading post run that could be used as small field tents or as rainwear, and Felix was feeling glad to have some shelter as he watched the rain begin to fill the lid. A stone underneath his back was troubling him and he dislodged it, wincing as he moved his right leg. He thought to look under his bandage but didn't feel like removing his coveralls and knew from the pain pounding his leg that it wouldn't be a pleasant sight.

It had been nearly thirty-six hours since they fled Zănoaga, and neither man felt comfortable moving from their concealed position in the forest until they were certain they had waited out any search parties.

Rurik flipped open Felix's tent.

"We have big problems," he said.

Felix sat up, pulled the tent over his head, and wrapped it around his shoulders.

"At least an entire division and two tanks rolled by. I have to assume they're headed to Zănoaga. I'm certain they'll be tracking us soon, if they aren't already."

"Did they see you?"

Rurik gave him a curious glance. "Of course they didn't see me. How's your leg?"

"Not good," said Felix, holding his knee up as he extended his leg and placed it gingerly on the ground. "I can walk. Running is out of the question. Very sore."

"We're going to have to move deeper into the forest. Only a matter of time before they send back scouts, once they see the damage—" Rurik perked up his head. "You hear that?"

Felix looked to the gray skies and became aware of a distant buzzing. "Get the horses," he said, hobbling to his feet.

Felix limped and scurried around, trying to displace last night's fire pit as Rurik led the horses to tree cover. The leaves were only just beginning to bud, and Felix worried the cover wasn't thick enough. He grabbed his duffel bag and slid it on the mud to Rurik's location.

"You have the spyglass?" asked Felix as the buzzing grew louder.

"They took it at the camp. But I did manage to snag us some very nice and very new binoculars."

Rurik stood next to Drina and pulled the binoculars from her saddle pouch. He handed them to Felix, who scanned the sky.

"Terrible flying weather," said Rurik. "It's my understanding that pilots stay grounded during storms. Denis wouldn't dare fly with a cloud in the sky."

"Seems that would be the protocol," said Felix, scanning the murk. "Especially with this visibility . . . oh! There they are."

Felix focused the binoculars in line with the shadows of five planes that poked through an opening in the clouds. "See for yourself," he said, handing the binoculars to Rurik.

Rurik watched the sky as the plane engines grew louder. After a moment, he stiffened and cried out, "Oh no. Oh . . . no!"

"What?"

"It's the Red Baron."

"No chance," exclaimed Felix. "Let me see."

Felix took back the binoculars and focused on the five shadows buzzing through the rolling, wispy clouds. When they emerged, his jaw dropped at the sight of a bright red Fokker Dr.I triple-winged plane with a bold black balkenkreuz painted on each wing. The Red Baron was flanked by four unmarked matte black Fokker E.I Eindecker monoplanes, flying in a perfect V-formation.

"You think that's for us?" asked Felix.

"Absolutely. No way he'd be out here in the sticks otherwise. The fact they even pulled him off the western front is—"

"Stay low, then. Throw the ponchos over the horses. Anything shiny that needs hidden? Here," said Felix, handing Rurik his rain poncho.

Rurik threw both ponchos over the horses, who huffed in protest.

"Well, I suppose congratulations are in order," said Rurik, kneeling next to Felix.

"Congratulations for what?"

"We're now being hunted by the world's most famous pilot."

"A dubious distinction indeed," said Felix with the binoculars pointed to the sky. "Get down!" he said, suddenly yanking Rurik to the mud.

The planes hummed low over their position as the two men huddled against a large oak tree. Felix swore the planes were mere meters above the tree line as they shot past. Rurik and Felix waited until the engine sound was in the distance before moving a toe.

"That was close," said Felix.

"How they're even navigating in this visibility is beyond me."

"They're circling back," said Felix, listening as the engine growls neared.

Felix and Rurik lay close to the ground, covering themselves in muddied leaves as the Red Baron and Jasta Eleven circled for nearly twenty minutes.

"Do you think they saw us?" asked Felix as the planes shot off into the distance.

"I don't know," said Rurik, sitting up. "It's clear now we're being hunted from the land and the sky. Good thing for the rain, as it should wash away our hoofprints. One thing's for certain—we're traveling by night from now on. We have to make it to Denis's. It's our last hope for sanctuary."

Felix winced as he moved his leg.

"Think you can make it?"

Felix nodded.

"We need to clean that leg soon, or I fear the worst," said Rurik. "May I see it?"

"Later. We need to get the hell out of here. How far are we from Denis's?"

"No idea." Rurik walked to Felix's horse and returned with the map. "You tell me, Mr. Military Academy."

"Hold the poncho, will you?"

Rurik removed the poncho from Drina and held it over Felix as he opened the map. Felix ran his fingers across the latitude and longitude lines several times while counting aloud.

"From what I can tell? Twenty kilometers out. But here's the problem. Thanks to our new friends in the sky, we can't go this way and come in from the north. That's all open fields. We'll have to skim the Bucharest outskirts and come up from the south. It appears a bit rocky in elevation with lots of trees. But as long as my leg doesn't give out, we should be good."

Felix tucked the map away, and Rurik draped the rain poncho over Felix, who pulled it close as he shivered a bit.

"And what if we get there and it's razed or . . . occupied?" asked Rurik. "We don't have anywhere else to go."

"Honestly," said Felix with a note of exhaustion and dismay in his voice, "I have no earthly idea."

15

March 27, 1917, 2:02 a.m.

Augusta gasped and shot up in bed.

She threw her hand to her chest and felt her heart's rapid pulsations. The royal doctors had diagnosed her with sleep apnea just shy of her fifty-sixth birthday, and Augusta couldn't remember the last time she'd had a decent night's sleep. Tonight's awakening felt particularly abrupt, and she wondered if there would come a time when she would simply stop breathing entirely and never wake.

Her jaw was still sore from her molar extractions, and she massaged her cheek as she reached to her nightstand for her glass of water.

That's strange, she thought, noticing a rather large white feather lying on the floor just before her nightstand.

At first, Augusta believed it to be a rogue feather from her down comforter, but upon second glance, the feather was too large, appearing as if it had fallen from a full-grown swan.

She plucked the feather from the floor.

The plume was quite thick with a quill nearly the texture and sturdiness of bone. She ran her finger along the quill, then shrieked and dropped the feather upon her duvet when she realized the tip was soaked in blood.

Augusta dropped the feather to the floor and leaned back in bed, pulling the covers all the way to her chin. She lay breathing deeply, trying to calm herself. Ever since the incident involving Nette, she'd been on edge. The image of the young woman slicing herself open in front of the palace guests had begun to fill her with guilt day by day, more than the satisfaction she'd hoped for.

Revenge is only pleasant in thought, she reminded herself.

Her mind raced back to her argument with Wilhelm and she looked to his empty side of the bed, wishing to see him rather than the perfectly fluffed pillows—a glaring reminder that she was alone.

"He'll be back from Mount Hohenzollern tomorrow, relax," she said quietly aloud.

Her thoughts turned once more to Wilhelm's warning about engaging with the spirit in the mirror, and she momentarily fancied herself rising from bed, finding a meat tenderizer in the chef's kitchen, and smashing the mirror to pieces for good, casting out any darkness along with it. Wilhelm was correct: she was not a witch, and stories of mortals dabbling in witchcraft *never* had happy endings.

Since the hooded man had first appeared in her dreams and guided her to the mirror, Augusta had spoken to the enchanted looking glass and made offerings many times. For small things: good weather for a garden party, Wilhelm's safe return from afar, even snow on Christmas morning—but especially for fertility.

Time and time again, she made small cuts across her body and begged for fertility, but the mirror never answered, and after her last encounter, she understood why: the spirit in the mirror wanted more. Augusta's mind filled with dread as she recalled the morning she awoke to find the pliers on her nightstand.

It's been calling you, Augusta. You should be careful.

Augusta closed her eyes and quietly promised never to visit the mirror again. She thought briefly to pray for forgiveness and protection, but the idea was wiped from her mind when her eyes fell upon the ceiling's fresco.

"Where are the cherubs?" asked Augusta, sitting up in bed.

The fresco was now barren—only a painting of dark foreboding clouds, drab and dreadful.

Augusta wondered if she was dreaming.

She looked to the floor, searching for the white feather—nothing but bare marble.

Augusta became aware of movement beneath the comforter on Wilhelm's side of the bed. She moved herself to the edge of the bed as small lumps formed under the blankets, slowly moving toward her.

Just as the lumps reached Augusta, she screamed and threw herself over the bed, landing hard upon the marble. Her ankles were suddenly constricted as if gripped by the jaws of a powerful animal, and her lower torso was pulled underneath the bed frame.

We want more! came tiny, disembodied voices.

Augusta shrieked as she gripped the bedframe, fighting and kicking to keep herself from being dragged under the bed. From underneath the comforter, six chubby, stumpy arms reached out to her hands and tried to break her grasp. Augusta could see their glowing red eyes and fat cherub faces peeking from under the blankets as they plucked at her fingers, releasing them one by one. Realizing she had no grip left, Augusta panicked as the devils under the bed pulled on her legs to the sound of mighty trumpets blasting her eardrums from every direction.

Burn the witch, burn her! they screeched. *We want you!*

The cherubs underneath the comforter emerged and pinned Augusta's hands to the floor as their surprisingly powerful wings struck her face and blue flashes filled her vision. Augusta watched as one of the cherubs handed a harp string to another and they placed it across her throat, then slowly began sawing the wire back and forth, cackling all the while.

Augusta wailed once more as the metal wire cut into her hyoid bone and sliced into her jugular veins. As she watched in horror, the hooded man appeared over her and folded his arms.

"Majesty! Majesty!" came a voice from her bedchamber's entrance, and the lights turned on.

Her night servant Harold dashed into the room, still in his nightgown. He found Augusta on the floor—her head poking from underneath the bed and both her hands wrapped around her own neck.

She was sobbing uncontrollably, but otherwise unharmed.

"Majesty, what's happening?"

"Help me. Help me!" she screamed, reaching out to him.

Harold reached down and grabbed Augusta's wrist and pulled her from underneath the bed.

"What on earth, Majesty?"

Augusta stood and pointed to the ceiling, only to find the cherub fresco as it always had been—comely, plump cherubs playing their horns and strumming a harp upon perfectly white, fluffy clouds.

"I—I! I don't know what's come over me," she said, lowering her hand. "Maybe they're still under the bed?"

"Who, Majesty?"

"The cherubs! Please. Will you check?"

Augusta watched as Harold dipped slowly to his stomach and peered under the bed.

"Nothing but some cobwebs and lint . . . oh. Wait a moment."

Harold reached under the bed and pulled out a sterling silver cigar cutter. He held it up and inspected it. "Curious. Has the Kaiser been smoking cigars in bed?"

"I don't believe so. No. I'm . . ." Augusta was shivering.

"Majesty, please. You're hysterical. Let's get you back to bed."

Augusta leaned into him with all her weight and he walked her to bed and tucked her in. Harold placed the cigar cutter on her nightstand and handed her the water glass, ensuring she drank every last drop.

"There, there, Majesty. Perhaps you were having a nightmare?"

Augusta nodded. "Yes. I think so. I'm still very upset over that poor girl at the reception."

"I understand, Majesty. Quite a tragedy. A horrific end to a wonderful engagement."

Augusta placed the glass back upon the nightstand.

"Shall I fill you another?"

"No, thank you. I'm just overextended these days and never like it when Wilhelm is gone."

Harold patted down her comforter. "Please try to get some sleep, Majesty. Remember—just breathe and count the cherubs," he said, pointing to the ceiling.

He exited the room and turned out the light.

Augusta lay in bed for several more hours, waiting for daybreak and never taking her eyes from the cherubs painted on the ceiling. After noticing the harp in the painting now had four instead of five strings, she knew what she'd just experienced was no nightmare.

Augusta picked up the cigar cutter from the nightstand and held it, wondering where it must have come from. She opened and closed it a few times, then slid the opening over her ring finger. She gently depressed the blade to her flesh. And in that motion—the tiny cellular sliver between flesh and blood—Augusta realized that although she was done with the mirror, the mirror still wanted more from her.

Burn the witch. We want you.

PART II:
DER DOPPELGÄNGER

Chapter 16

16

STAATSGEHEIMNIS [STATE SECRET]
ZENSIERT - ALLE KOPIEN IM DIENST VON GENERAL
PAUL LUDWIG HANS ANTON VON HINDENBURG
AUFGEFUNDEN UND ZERSTÖRT
[CENSORED—ALL COPIES LOCATED AND
DESTROYED IN SERVICE OF GENERAL PAUL
LUDWIG HANS ANTON VON HINDENBURG]

"Der Doppelgänger" von den Brüder Grimm 1812
["The Doppelgänger" by the Brothers Grimm 1812]

Once upon a time there lived a greedy little witch named Gunda. Her clothing was stitched of the finest threads, her hair was braided with the most expensive silk ribbons, her shoes were fashioned by the finest cobblers, and yet—Gunda wanted more.

"I want them all!" she screamed at the baker, then kicked him in the shin when he offered her only one cake.

"Yours is better than mine!" she yelled at the magistrate, then scratched his face after he gifted her a fine steed to ride on.

"My room is too small!" she barked at her parents and yanked out their hair before taking their room as her own.

Her parents and siblings and all the townsfolk were terrified of Gunda's raging fits. She incessantly pleaded, and nagged, and begged—then scratched, and kicked, and took. Throughout the town and throughout the day,

Gunda wandered, always wanting and howling for "More! More! More!"

One summer day, a single solemn man astride a single solemn horse appeared from the forest and trotted into town. Behind his withered steed was a simple wooden cart that held a beautiful vanity. The man's wispy white hair flowed over a green robe so splendid that not one stitch hung fray upon him. But 'twas his vanity and his boots of the shiniest shimmer that caught the eye of young Gunda as she skipped through town on that bright sunny morning.

The townsfolk were wary of this odd man in green as he tied his ghoulish steed to a post at the town center, but not greedy Gunda, who approached him with aplomb.

She stood before the vanity and admired its beauty. It was carved from the finest wood, adorned with the richest of inlays, and the mirror atop it shone with the purest of silver—it was far superior in every way to her own vanity.

"Who are you? And what are you doing in my village with your sickly horse?" asked Gunda.

The old man stared down at her with wide blue eyes. "Hello. My name is Vago, and I am only a humble traveler in these lands. What is your name?"

Vago extended his hand to little Gunda.

"My name is Gunda," she said, shaking his hand, "and I want your mirror!"

"Fair child, that is a request I cannot honor. I am bound to protect this mirror, for it is enchanted."

Gunda frowned. "Enchanted how?"

"Why, it is a wishing mirror, you see. A magic mirror that imprisons a very powerful warlock who will grant any wish, so long as the wisher trades in kind. But one must be careful and choose one's words wisely—for the warlock in this mirror craves escape, and the malevolent spirit guarding the glass demands a prisoner. If that spirit is ever angered, its wrath knows no bounds."

Gunda looked over the vanity.

"I'm not afraid of a silly mirror," she said. "And I wish for everything!"

242

"I'm sorry, my child. It simply doesn't work that way. If you wish for everything, then to the mirror everything you must give."

"That's not fair!" yelled Gunda. "If you and your ugly horse can't give me my wish, then I will see you cast from my town or I will turn you into a toad."

"Very well," said Vago. "I see that I am not welcome here."

Vago untied and mounted his steed. "*Der Doppelgänger,*" he whispered to Gunda, then trotted back into the forest with his illustrious vanity in tow.

Greedy little Gunda stared at him as he rode away, her eyes never leaving the wishing glass.

"I wished for everything, and it's everything I shall have!" she screamed, running into the forest.

And through the gnarled branches Gunda ran, intent on finding this old man and his enchanted mirror. But very soon, she became lost and frightened, unable to find her way home.

Just as she was ready to give up hope, the smallest of glimmers caught her eye.

Gunda peered around a trunk to see the magic mirror resting beside a black and gnarled tree. She marched toward the mirror and stared at her reflection.

"I wish for everything!"

While Gunda stood still and scowled, her reflection moved independently and smiled at her. "Then it is everything I require in return," it said.

Gunda pouted as she pondered this answer.

"You can't be me. I see that your dress and the ring on your finger are prettier than mine!" she yelled. "Your hair more golden. Your eyes more blue. Your skin more fair and your teeth more white! Give them to me!"

The Doppelgänger spoke softly. "But it cannot be true, for we are the same."

"Liar! If you will not give them to me, then I will smash you to bits!"

Gunda reached to the ground and grabbed a round rock. She thrust it at the mirror, and to her surprise, her arm extended through the glass and she struck the Doppelgänger's mouth, shattering its teeth. The specter simply smiled a bloody grin and conveyed no sense of pain. The mockery sent Gunda further into a rage. She snapped a sharp branch from a tree and poked out the Doppelgänger's eye.

"Your skin is still fairer than mine!" cried Gunda as she gouged the flesh from the Doppelgänger's cheek. "And I'll have that pretty ring."

Gunda grabbed the Doppelgänger's hand from the mirror and pulled it to her mouth, biting and chewing its ringed finger until the digit snapped from its hand. As she pulled the ring from her mouth, Gunda noticed there was blood dripping all over her own white dress. Her mouth was sore, her eye was missing, and her hand had one finger less.

Gunda looked to the Doppelgänger, only to see it morph into a giant man in black with an eyeless hood over his face.

"Please," begged Gunda, looking over her bloodied body. "What have I done? Give me back my teeth, my eye, my skin, and my finger!"

"But I cannot," said the hooded man, "for they are mine now."

"Liar! I wished for everything. And now you owe me."

"But you have not given me everything. Only then will your wish come true."

"Then, I beg you! I'll do anything. Name your price."

"My price?" asked the hooded man. "Very well. I will give you the opportunity to earn back what you have lost. But first, you must swap places with me so that I may roam free once more."

Gunda panicked as she looked at her hand that was missing a finger.

"I agree," she said. "Please! What must I do?"

"It is simple, my child. You must simply wish it."

"Then I wish to swap places with you so that you may roam free!"

In a flash, the Doppelgänger stood free upon the forest floor, and greedy Gunda was trapped behind the glass.

"What about my wounds?" she asked. "My teeth, my eye, my skin, and my finger! You promised I could have them back."

The giant warlock turned to her.

"I promised you might *earn* them back. In time, little one . . . in time."

The Doppelgänger snapped his fingers and the sound of horse hooves upon the earth came from the distance. Vago soon appeared, riding his steed with his cart in tow.

The Doppelgänger placed the looking glass on the cart and sat beside it as Vago rode off into the darkened forest. All the while, the Doppelgänger smiled under his black hood as he watched greedy Gunda paw against the mirror's surface where she would remain evermore, consumed by vanity and greed—and always wanting more, more, more.

THE END

*

March 27, 1917, 6:48 p.m.

Hindenburg sat at Nette's bedside in a private hospital room reserved for the aristocracy. It had been four days since her breakdown at the reception, and three hours since she had been declared dead from septic shock. All his attempts to heal her had failed, and he knew the black magick within the mirror had taken its final hold upon Nette. He held her hand tightly, closed his eyes, and began chanting quietly to himself. After a few moments, he released her and ground his teeth as he watched her arm fall limply to her side.

"This is what comes of dabbling in mortal blood," he said to himself, quietly questioning his wisdom in conceiving a child with Nette's mother.

Hindenburg had never truly loved Gertrud. He merely married her for status and to keep up appearances with the ruling elite. On making his pact with Wilhelm that his daughter would be the vessel for Drăculea's return, Hindenburg had hoped his offspring would be born a magick wielder.

Alas, her mother's genes took dominance despite his multiple attempts at seances and invocations to achieve otherwise. For years, he looked upon Nette with disdain for her mortality, and saw her as valuable only as a means to align himself more closely with the anticipated reincarnation. But as he stood over his dead daughter, Hindenburg thought to the times that Nette, as a small child, had warmed his icy heart with her curious nature and wide-eyed wonder. His chest grew heavy and he realized he had come to love his mortal child. He believed he had taken every action available to ensure she would lead a happy and healthy life, eventually becoming Wilhelm's wife and the immortal empress of Germany.

Hindenburg knew Gertrud would be arriving at the hospital soon, and he had every intention of avoiding her. Their union now felt entirely hollow with the death of Nette, and his mind fell to thoughts of eliminating his spouse. Hindenburg thought to the enchanted mirror, for it had been he who placed it in the palace, he who quietly led Augusta to it, and he who ultimately endangered the life of his only daughter by failing to foresee a long-overdue coup from the witch he'd trapped inside it long ago.

He reflected on his reasoning for placing the mirror in the palace and decided his intentions were well-conceived. Royal seers were forbidden from reading the minds of the mortal ruling class, and, at the time, he'd believed the glass would provide insight into the private thinking of Augusta and Wilhelm. Over the years, Augusta's requests remained mostly innocuous—she'd once even asked for Wilhelm to have more vigor in the bedroom, as she put it.

Bastard has two lame limbs.

As Hindenburg continued to assess his intentions, he realized his decision to escalate Augusta's summonings was a grave miscalculation. He had believed that by invading her dreams—filling her with panic and fear—he could influence her to beg for fertility, each time harming herself as she extracted, cut, and chopped off pieces of herself as offerings to the mirror. Eventually, her wounds would be impossible to conceal. Augusta would be hospitalized, diagnosed as insane, and locked away. Hindenburg would seal off the passage so the mirror would never be discovered. Nette would marry Wilhelm and be officially installed in Augusta's place.

After Nette conceived, Hindenburg believed he could convince the Kaiser to take residence in Doorn Manor—the monarchy's private getaway in the Netherlands—where Wilhelm's influence over the unfolding events would be eliminated. It was to be a slow and protracted maneuver, one he and Minister Schmidt were convinced would play to their advantage as they called upon the Void to affirm their actions time and again.

Alas, none of it mattered. Fate, it seemed, bucked even the plans of the mighty.

As he stood looking over Nette's corpse, a rage kindled inside him and he plotted his next actions. Gunda would be destroyed. But due to his history with the mirror, Hindenburg knew he would not be the one to take this action. Instead, Augusta would suffer.

There was a knock at the door.

"Come in."

A fresh-faced soldier opened the door and poked his head in.

"Your car is ready for you, sir."

"Very well. I will be down shortly."

Hindenburg watched as the door closed. He then pulled his deceased daughter's hand to his chest.

"I will see you avenged, my child. Of this, I assure you."

He then pulled her sheet over her face and tearfully exited the room.

*

Hindenburg arrived at Berlin's airfield forty minutes later, just as dusk had settled upon the grounds. He exited his limousine and looked to the four soldiers standing before a massive bomber transport, holding their rifles across their chests. They placed their guns at their sides and saluted him as he approached.

"At ease, gentlemen," he said, approaching a soldier with lieutenant markings on his shoulder. "I sense she's aboard?"

"She is, sir. Her horse too. It's a tight fit, but we can fly. The pilots can depart whenever you say."

"Very well. I remind you all of the utmost secrecy of these affairs. Any mention of this aircraft leaving or landing is to be scrubbed from the records. I trust you can carry out that order?"

"Absolutely, sir."

"Excellent. You will all be handsomely rewarded once these operations are complete."

"Sir!"

Hindenburg slid through the line of soldiers and walked along the runway to the waiting transport. The grumble of a fast-approaching automobile caught his ear. He turned around and raised his hand to shield his eyes from the glaring headlights. A shadow emerged from the back door of a limousine.

"Leaving without saying goodbye?" asked Minister Schmidt, holding an envelope in the air.

Hindenburg's broad shoulders relaxed, and he waited as Schmidt pressed his way through the soldiers and jogged toward him.

"Hitching a ride, I see," said Schmidt, looking toward the airplane.

Hindenburg nodded. "Teleporting such a great distance will alert anyone scanning to my actions. I must take Radu by surprise."

Schmidt held out the envelope. "Understood. But, really? A letter?"

Hindenburg pursed his lips and looked into Schmidt's blue eyes.

"I'm sorry. I—I simply wanted to be on my way . . . Did you read it?"

"I did."

"Augusta surprised me with her actions, and I did not foresee that Gunda would take it so far," continued Hindenburg. "The outcome is not exactly what we planned, but these events still provide an opportunity to pull Wilhelm away."

Hindenburg's mind flashed with the image of Nette lying dead upon her hospital bed. "This is all my fault," he said, forlorn. "And it will escalate to madness once Gunda is destroyed. I cannot be near, or I fear the mirror will come for me instead. Augusta will satisfy its desire for a prisoner. I'm certain you can handle the rest."

"From what you described in the letter, yes. Finishing this is perfectly within my skill set. But I'm concerned . . . we can't simply murder—"

"Who said anything about murder?" said Hindenburg. "Berg will reassign the palace guard that evening and have her personal staff away from the palace. Then we simply allow the mirror to do what the mirror does. It will all be Augusta's own undoing. I say let her suffer." He crossed his arms. "We now have the narrative in place. Wilhelm will suspect nothing and will soon be out of our way."

"Then, so be it."Schmidt stood closer to him and attempted to hold his hand.

Hindenburg pulled his arm away and his eyes darted to the pilots inside the cockpit. "Have you lost your wits?"

Schmidt stepped back a few paces. "It seems I have. I can't help it when you're so serious and brooding."

"How can I not be? You saw what I saw."

"Most clearly."

"I need to see Yusupov in person for myself. I still question the vision. It's simply stunning that Radu managed to conceal it. And it seems Rasputin still haunts us from the grave."

Schmidt bit his lower lip and shook his head slightly. "I'm sorry, my love. I don't like any of this. We promised . . . swore . . . that after escaping the mirror, all our actions were to remain in the shadows. You said yourself that we would use our powers to manipulate others into doing our will. Putting yourself in danger to see this through . . . I—I'm concerned. You're certain you must do this alone?"

Hindenburg nodded. "I must. This is a culmination of events that started a long time ago, and it's my duty to see them finished. After centuries, I finally have a lock on Radu's exact location. Although what he did to Elizabeth has served me in many ways, it's time for me to seize the advantage—for both our sakes."

"Will you kill him?"

"No—unless he presents a grave threat to me. Currently, he's too valuable to be killed. I have no intention of freeing Elizabeth until the time is right, and I will not allow her new proxy to change that.

Using her as a shield as I carry out my agenda will keep me safe enough."

Schmidt looked to the plane. "I can sense her on board. She's full of anger."

"That she is. Despises both Vago and Elizabeth. With nowhere to turn, I believe I can gain her loyalties. The first leg of the flight is short, but long enough to earn her trust. By the time I disembark in Slovakia, I will have made her promises I have no intention of keeping."

"Elizabeth will scan her mind. She'll discover you."

Hindenburg knew there was a chance, but he believed he could cloak his communication with Hanne. Even though the banishment spell had weakened as Radu aged, Elizabeth's telepathic connection to her proxy would still be tenuous. He intended to take every precaution to ensure his dealings and identity remained undiscovered.

"Never," he said. "The only information I will share will be the bare minimum required to make her believe her mission is legitimate. Unfortunately, I will have to inform her of Yusupov's importance to ensure she doesn't harm him in any fashion. Radu and Yusupov will soon be trapped near Bucharest on all sides. If they happen to escape Romania, the Death Witch will drive them toward Čachtice. The moment I trap them, I will dispose of her too."

Schmidt raised his eyebrows. "Sounds precarious."

"We deal in the precarious. It's no matter."

"Please tell me you will be careful. I couldn't bear to lose my darker half."

"Elizabeth's proxy is a mere child, and Radu is more clever than powerful. From what I gathered during our scan, holding the banishment spell for so long has exhausted him beyond measure—he's practically become a bumbling conqueror. And I'm . . . well, I'm me. In no uncertain terms are the advantages mine."

The two stood staring into each other's eyes for a long moment.

"Then I'll leave you for now, General. But I expect you back the moment you're finished."

Hindenburg dropped his gaze to the runway and frowned.

"I've been aligning this for centuries. Now, when all the pieces are finally in place, I take no pleasure in any of it."

"Stop. You lost your child. Turn your grief into revenge upon those who have stood against you. Remind yourself that you're about to usurp this entire chain of events and seize control. Centuries of careful planning, finally come to fruition."

"Thank you," said Hindenburg, looking up at Schmidt. "No matter how heavy my burdens feel, it is always you, my lighter half, who brings me perspective."

"Your burden is the world, it seems. And my burden is you—an onus I gladly carry. For, if not for your wisdom, I would have never existed."

Hindenburg relaxed.

"Off with you then," he said. "I sense the prison warden you call a wife is wondering where you've gone off to."

*

Wilhelm lay awake staring at the cherub fresco on the ceiling. Even in the darkness, a curiosity caught his eye.

I never noticed that, he thought. The cherubs' harp was missing a string.

Augusta was snoring.

Wilhelm rolled over and placed a pillow over his head to block the noise. His meeting with Elizabeth was still at the forefront of his mind. Not only was it agreed that he would retain the bottle once Radu and Yusupov were captured, but experiments were already underway to enhance German soldiers with Elizabeth's venom, a prospect that filled him with excitement.

France had no idea what was coming, and it would only be a matter of hours before the test subjects were unleashed on Arras. Between his natural excitement over the possibilities of their pact and Augusta's snores, sleep was a far way off. Wilhelm sat up and walked to the chair where he had hung his robe.

"Off to make more plans?" came Augusta's voice.

Wilhelm looked to her. "Did I wake you?"

"You did. But my sleep has been troubled of late. I'm seeing the hooded man again when I dream."

Wilhelm nodded. "I'm sorry, my darling. Those recurring nightmares sound frightening."

Augusta sat up. "Please forgive me," she said. "I've taken this too far."

Wilhelm raised his eyebrows and sat back upon the bed. He grabbed her hand.

"I do," he said. "I should have been more forthright with you in my dealings."

Wilhelm noticed her eyes unexpectedly filling with tears.

"But what you did to that poor—"

"Oh, here we go," she said, tensing a bit before wiping her eyes and rolling over.

"My darling. I'm not certain you understand the gravity of your actions. She was the daughter of a powerful warlock. This will not go unanswered if Hindenburg discovers the truth."

She turned to him, glaring. "What then? He will simply assassinate me?"

Wilhelm sighed. "Of course not. He'd be a fool to take any action our royal seers could detect. It's what they can't detect that worries me."

Augusta rolled on her back and stared at the ceiling.

After a moment, she said, "Something horrible happened when you were away." She gestured toward the ceiling. "The cherubs came alive. They attacked me in my sleep."

Wilhelm became direly worried. She'd been overwrought lately. He felt mostly to blame—he had driven her to the edge with his secrets and leaving her too much on her own. "I'm certain it was simply a nightmare."

"How do you explain this, then?" she questioned, reaching to her nightstand and handing him a small silver object. "The cherubs left it for me. Harold found it under the bed when he came to save me. Don't you see the position you've put me in? They want me to hurt myself, Friedrich—it's the only way I can become fertile."

Wilhelm grew alarmed at her ramblings. He took the object from her and turned it over in his hand, recognizing it as the cigar cutter Hindenburg had gifted him on his birthday. He was now gravely concerned that Augusta was losing her grasp on reality.

"Harold saved you?" he said. "From what?"

"You're not listening!" she said, pointing to the ceiling. "The cherubs." Her eyes filled with tears once more. "They tried to cut off my head, for Christ's sake!"

Wilhelm stared at her. She looked pale, worn out. Her eyes, which once reflected a certain sense of command, now appeared dull. Wilhelm felt as if he were witnessing her mind shatter into jagged shards that left delicate scars of paranoia and frailty across her psyche. He pulled himself farther into bed and held her hand as a nursery rhyme rang through his head.

All the king's horses, and all the king's men . . .

Wilhelm swallowed. "My beloved. Please. You're worrying me. Firstly, I warned you about summoning this entity. I will delicately broach the subject with Minister Schmidt to see if he can vanquish it from the palace. But Hindenburg must not know. Until then, burn your grimoire and stop what you're doing. The rest is all very explainable. You had a bad dream. I perhaps misplaced the cutter and it was knocked under the bed when—"

"Fine. Don't believe me," she said, pulling her hand away and rolling over. "Go make your plans. It's clear I do not have any part in them."

"Augusta. Augusta, please. Of course you do."

Augusta turned back around and stared him in the eyes. "Oh, then when you acquire the bottle of Drăculea's blood, I will still be the vessel for the child? I too will be granted immortality?"

Wilhelm sat with an open mouth, but said nothing.

"Exactly . . . exactly, Friedrich." She turned away from him once more. "I wish you'd quit taking me for a fool."

Augusta held the cigar cutter to her chest as she felt Wilhelm's weight rise from bed. She listened to him shuffle from the room in silence as a veritable avalanche of dread smothered her heart.

I've lost him, she thought. *I've lost everything.*

Feeling alone and abandoned, she racked her mind for a way to escape her predicament. She'd taken it too far. Her husband was now a stranger—her vengefulness and vanity had boxed her in with no means to pivot. Augusta's fury turned to fear, and she knew at that moment her only means of salvation was to vanquish Gunda's spirit, no matter the cost.

Augusta turned on her back and looked to the ceiling.

The cherubs had changed their positions in the fresco and were now staring directly at her with mocking, evil grins upon their faces as childish giggles and discordant trumpet blasts filled the room.

"Leave me be!" she yelled, gripping the cigar cutter and throwing her hands over her ears. "I'll give you whatever you want!"

Burn the witch. We want you.

17

March 27, 1917, 11:43 p.m.

Mud. Everything smelled of fresh, wet mud. It was the only scent he'd known for the past ninety days. His uniform, his haversack, and the equipment he hauled day in and day out reeked of fresh earth—even his rations had begun to taste like dirt. Corporal Raphael Brodeur of the French Fourth Army stood in his small enclave, taking one last look at the map sprawled out before him upon a flimsy wooden table. At forty-two, he had been having trouble with his eyes of late, and he moved his table lantern directly over his command's position in hopes of easing his eye strain. He then lifted a tin mug to his mouth and inhaled—mud. *How is it the coffee smells of mud?*

Brodeur tipped the cup, swallowed the last of his cold coffee, and winced at the bitter taste and the grinds that coated his mouth.

"Trench coffee is the devil's coffee," he griped to himself, thinking fondly to the last time he'd been to a quiet and clean Parisian café. *What I wouldn't do for a croissant and a nice creamy noisette.*

A dull movement along the wall caught his attention and he looked to see a large rat attempting to climb up the muddy surface, rocking its head back and forth as if a scent other than fresh earth had caught its senses. Brodeur waited until he felt the rat's eyes were away from him and then chucked his tin mug at the animal, nearly striking it. The rodent shrieked, scurried along the wall, and fled through the open door that led into Brodeur's quarters.

"Where's the goddamn dog?" he yelled.

A young soldier slid into the room.

"Sir?" he said, saluting Brodeur.

"At ease. Where's Poppy?"

"I believe they pulled her back a few trenches. She's a barker."

"Yes, yes. I know. Make sure she's back at daybreak. Best rat catcher in the trenches."

"Yes, sir."

Brodeur flipped his wrist and checked his trench watch—23:47. Thirteen minutes till strike. He snatched his Adrian helmet from the table and fastened it under his chin. After buttoning his trench coat, he grabbed his rifle and exited with the soldier following him.

"Corporal in the trench!" yelled a soldier, his breath rising into the cool, crisp night.

Even in the dimly lit trench, Brodeur could see the fear and worry in his troops' eyes as they rose to attention, all holding their rifles vertically at their sides. They looked weary and filthy, yet alert.

Brodeur marched past the long line of young faces, keeping his eyes dead ahead. He knew they needed to see him marching forward proudly and firmly. Any eye contact, any semblance of human connection, was a disaster at this point. They needed to see a leader who knew exactly what he was doing and exactly how he was going to achieve it, despite what misgivings were telling him.

The time for comfort and camaraderie was over.

For now, it was time for war.

Brodeur looked to the waxing quarter moon and silently cursed his commanding officers for planning this assault around a forecast of cloud cover. Tonight brought nothing but a few wispy clouds that shone against the pitch-black sky. Frustration welled as he remembered his pleas to launch the attack four days ago and to put the British on point since this was technically their offensive.

No matter—orders were orders.

Brodeur marched another twenty meters along the narrow walls, barely skimming past the uniformed soldiers who lined the trench before him. A small bubble of light glowed in the distance. He halted upon reaching the lookout station where two soldiers seemingly caked in dried mud crouched into the sandbags that walled them off from no-man's-land.

A spotter hugged a periscope to his face as he scanned the darkness for any movement while another huddled, ready to poke his rifle through the small opening in the sandbags.

Brodeur reached down and switched off the lantern's kerosene latch.

"You trying to get your head blown off, soldier?"

The young man with the periscope turned and immediately stood at attention while the rifleman continued to stare through the small opening.

"Moonlight's enough," said Brodeur, realizing he didn't recognize the soldier.

"Yes, sir. Apologies, sir!"

"Apologies won't cut it, Private. A light like that is a beacon in the darkness. Next thing you know, they'll be lobbing mortars at it. Every time you light that thing, you're endangering yourself and all your fellow soldiers."

"Yes, sir!"

"Now, who are you, and where's Private Laurent?" Brodeur was annoyed.

"Private Moreau, sir! Sixth Army!"

"Sixth? Very well. I hope you brought some of their guts along with you, as you clearly didn't bring any wits."

"Sir!"

"At ease, Private. Back to your post."

Private Moreau relaxed and returned to his periscope.

"Trench foot," said the soldier with the rifle, never taking his eyes off the opposing trenches. "They had to amputate Laurent's foot earlier today."

Brodeur swirled his tongue in his cheek and frowned.

Damn good soldier, that kid.

"Wow, sir. Much better without the lantern light," said Moreau, scanning the darkness.

Brodeur thought to reprimand him once more for lighting the lantern, but instead leaned into him. "What can you see?"

"There's no one there, sir. Haven't seen so much as the tip of a pickelhaube. I believe they've retreated a few lines. Not even a glimmer of a spyglass in the past ten hours."

Brodeur checked his watch—23:54. Six minutes remained.

"Listen up, men!" he shouted into the night. "Your actions over the next twenty minutes will define who you are for the rest of your lives.

The Fritzies have overwhelmed Arras. This is our last stand. If we do not succeed and overtake their position, then onward to Paris they will roll. We are the last line of defense."

Raphael's eye fell on a soldier in his proximity who had a dirty white fabric band around his helmet.

"Trying to make yourself a target, Private?"

"No, sir!"

"What's your name?"

"Private First Class Frank Longuemare, sir!"

"The white band is nonissue."

"Sir, I placed it on my helmet in tribute to—"

"It's your ass, Private. Wear it if you want."

Brodeur turned and looked to Private Ladjimi, who stood pale-faced with a whistle in his mouth.

"This is it, men! There will be no mortar cover tonight. This is a surprise attack. Two waves. The first wave over the top, to overwhelm. When you reach their trenches, I want grenades lobbed in before you enter. It's dark. Be mindful of your brothers. Nobody dies by accident tonight. Once you've taken your position in their trenches, I want flares up. The second wave will then be sent—only then are you to enter the tunnels. Everyone carrying your flashlights?"

"Sir!" "Yes, sir!" "Ready, sir," came a barrage of replies from a gaggle of soldiers with flashlights strapped to the bottoms of their rifle barrels just beneath their bayonets.

Brodeur looked to his watch—23:59 and counting.

"On my command! Careful of snipers. Do not step in any puddles —could be a bomb crater deeper than your head. Any wounded between the lines, you pull back upon your return. No man left behind!"

The soldiers along the back wall of the trench leaned across the sandbags, ready to charge over the top. Brodeur raised his hand in the air and kept his eye on his watch's second hand. When the slim lever ticked to twelve, he dropped his hand, and Private Ladjimi blew his whistle.

Grunts and the shuffling of boots filled the nighttime air as the first wave shot over the trench and into the muddy void. Brodeur stood next to Moreau and the rifleman, who had now positioned his rifle through the peephole.

"You see so much as a hint of a pale face or a pointy helmet over their wall and you fire," said Brodeur.

"Sir!"

Brodeur nudged Private Moreau away and grabbed his periscope, squinting through it as he watched the first wave of soldiers navigate the moonlit hellscape before them. A heavy rain two days prior had left the field slippery with mud, and he could see several soldiers struggling to keep their footing as they avoided large puddles and the random charred posts jutting from the earth that were once vibrant trees.

The lead soldiers were roughly one hundred meters into their two-hundred-meter journey. Brodeur's pulse was pounding. He reached up, swatted the sweat from his brow, and continued to scan the advance. Something wasn't right. No shots fired. He'd never seen a surprise attack go this smoothly.

"How's your scope, Private?" asked Brodeur of the rifleman.

"Bit foggy, but I can see. Nothing yet, sir. Looks deserted on the other side."

The front-line soldiers in Brodeur's field of view had nearly reached the opposing trench and began to find position behind various debris that riddled no-man's-land. Most crouched or ducked to the ground as they reached to their belts and removed their grenades.

"Grenades up," said Brodeur. "Come on, come on."

He could barely make out their movements in the distance but noticed several soldiers swinging their arms upward. A moment later, blast concussions lit up the German trenches.

"They're going over!" yelled Brodeur, watching a wave of his comrades leap over the barbed wire and sandbags that lay in their path.

Brodeur reached to Moreau's shoulder and gripped his uniform, shaking him a bit.

"Sir?" questioned Moreau, turning to him.

"Oh, nothing. Just releasing some tension . . . Where's the goddamn gunfire?"

"I don't know, sir," replied Moreau.

The words were no sooner from his mouth than the night sky lit up with a pink haze as nearly a dozen flares shot into the air.

"They did it, sir!" said Moreau.

"Hold. Something's—"

Private Ladjimi's whistle rang through the air, followed by the cheering of the second wave as they rallied over the top.

"No! No!" yelled Brodeur, pulling the periscope from his face. "Hold position. Hold position!" He thrust his fist into a sandbag as the last of the second wave disappeared into the muck. "Goddamn it, soldier!" he screamed, looking to Ladjimi. "I said, 'Hold'!"

"Sir! I was obeying orders. The flares are up," said Ladjimi, pointing to the falling pink lights trailed by smoky arcs in the sky.

Moreau moved in and pulled the periscope to his face. "They're fine, sir. Advancing quickly," he said.

Brodeur removed his helmet and sat next to the rifleman.

"Looks good to me too, sir. They're going to make it."

"Let me ask you something, Private," said Brodeur to the rifleman. "How many assaults have you seen?"

"This is my eighteenth, sir."

"And in how many of them have you witnessed two entire divisions making it past the German line without a single casualty? Not even a bullet fired?"

"Second wave is over the wall, sir," said the rifleman. "But none, sir. Never."

"Exactly . . . wait. Do you hear that?"

All three men perked their heads up as a curious sound rose from the German trenches.

"Growling dogs?" said Moreau. "Hand-to-hand fighting?"

"Out of the way, soldier," said Brodeur, grabbing the periscope. He scanned the bleak shadows of no-man's-land, which glowed with pink light from several dying flares that lay upon drier portions of the earth. The smoke from the flares slithered through the burned-out trees and various mechanical debris, making it difficult for Brodeur to see a straight line to the German trench. "Wait a minute," he said. "Wait a minute."

"What is it, sir?" asked Moreau.

"They're coming back," said Brodeur.

"You're certain it's our men?"

"Confirmed," said the rifleman with his eye seemingly glued to his scope.

"I see Longuemare," said Brodeur. "Damn white band turns out to have some use. What the hell are they doing? . . . Take the tunnels, you morons!"

Brodeur continued to scan the field as more and more shadows of his men crawled back over the German trench and came sprinting back to their position.

"They're getting a court martial over this, so help me God."

The rifleman started firing at once, taking out Longuemare and two other soldiers before Brodeur dropped the periscope and pulled him away from the sniper perch.

"You lost your mind?" screamed Brodeur.

"Sir! We need to retreat. Now."

"What? Why?" demanded Brodeur.

"It's not them. It's—"

"What do you mean, it's not them? I saw Longuemare with my own eyes."

"I could see through my scope. It is them, but they're—they're changed."

Brodeur meant to reprimand the rifleman once more, but something in the man's tone with the word *changed* gave him pause.

"Shhh! You hear that?" questioned Moreau.

They froze in position and listened as the soldiers ran back toward their trench. The silence soon filled with the sounds of gurgling and grunting coming from no-man's-land.

"What the hell?" Brodeur reached down to his flare gun and slowly crawled up the sandbags. He popped his head over the line and fired the flare into the night, illuminating his oncoming men, who had hollow, gaunt faces and torn flesh hanging from their ripped uniforms.

"Run. Run now!" yelled Brodeur, grabbing his rifle. "Follow me."

They dashed along the narrow trench to the next sniper position, where three other soldiers crouched along the sandbags.

"Sir! What are we—"

Growls and grunts crashed on them from above, and Brodeur hit the ground hard as someone pinned him to the earth. Screams of terror filled the trench as Brodeur tried rolling onto his back. A searing pain tore through his wrist as an undead soldier chomped down upon his hand, then continued to chew the flesh from his ulna bone.

Brodeur cried out as he felt the blunt pierce of human bites rip into his hamstrings and calves—the monsters chewing his muscle clean from the bone with their dull, rotten jaws.

"Help, Mother!" were Brodeur's last words as his face was pushed into the muck and he began drowning in a puddle of mud. Another bite tore into the back of his neck and his vision fell to black.

Brodeur would reawaken moments later—starving, rabid, and thirsty for human flesh.

*

Vago sat with his legs crossed and his hands placed neatly in his lap, hovering several meters above the courtyard of Hohenzollern Castle. As his mind scanned the Ether, the surrounding vines swarmed about his body and face in a curious and playful manner, as if they were inspecting their new ally. His eyes of the purest white glowed softly as he stared upward into the starry sky and the visions filled his mind.

He watched as Wilhelm and his cabal arrived back in Berlin and eavesdropped on their positive and encouraging comments about their meeting with Elizabeth, then shifted his mind to the Void to channel the happenings in Arras. A wretched grin emerged while he watched the French soldiers run directly into the trap he had devised.

They were completely overrun. He derived particular pleasure watching the French corporal, one Raphael Brodeur, torn nearly limb from limb as he was converted by the erstwhile Lieutenant Jünger. The plan was a flawless success, and the French were now among their undead army. Soon, more would follow, and they would control every soldier on the western front as Elizabeth's plague spread. The Kaiser would be pleased, but more importantly— Elizabeth would welcome the news.

Vago's glowing eyes faded to blue, and he lowered his legs to the ground, gently brushing the vines away from his body.

"No time for play, my children," he said.

He entered the castle and found Elizabeth, who was tucked away in her usual hiding spot.

"I just received word from Arras. Your thrall have completely overwhelmed the French offensive. They stood no chance."

Elizabeth rubbed her palps across her face and remained quiet.

"What is it, my Queen?"

"That boor of a man is the matter."

Vago sat on the marble floor before her and looked up to her fearsome fangs.

"Kaiser Wilhelm is only a temporary problem. Once Hanne captures Radu and Vlad Drăculea's blood, they will be brought before you first, despite what we promised. You can have your vengeance upon Radu and finally free yourself."

Elizabeth crawled past Vago toward one of the castle's broken windows. She extended her front leg to where the glass once was and a small ripple of blue light emanated from the invisible field that had contained her for centuries.

"I long for escape, my Vago. I want to see the stars again. Even the sight of a mere cloud against the blue sky would lift my heart. These recent events, initially reviving my long faded hope, have turned to agonizing frustration and impatience."

Elizabeth crawled up the wall a bit and peered out the window, as if she could take in the night sky—though Vago knew she could see nothing but a hazy gray field.

"My children succeeded? Infected the soldiers so that my influence shall grow?"

Vago stood and walked to her, placing his hand upon the back of her abdomen.

"Yes, my Queen. Soon you will have an unstoppable army that obeys only your command."

"This cursed banishment hex is interfering. I can sense my thrall but can barely communicate with them. Hanne too. Her mind feels distant and far away. I can only sense great anger in her."

"Yes," Vago said, remembering Hanne's rage when she broke down his door. "Indeed, she is angry . . . with me, mostly. But it will pass. We've made her more than any witch could ever be."

Vago felt a true sense of optimism about the future. His plan with the thrall was a success. Soon, he and his true love would walk through the grassy fields of Bad Boll, holding hands and staring up at the stars together as they discussed their plans for global domination.

Elizabeth tapped upon the field once more and a fleeting blue light reflected from her pale body.

"The Kaiser will be pleased, no?"

"Most certainly," said Vago. "He's been attempting to use the supernatural to his own ends for over two decades. When he hears of the success at Arras, I am certain he will expand the program. In any case, actions are being taken to remove him from these affairs."

He stood next to Elizabeth and gazed out the window.

"This reminds me of the last time I held you in your human form. Do you remember?"

"I do."

"Several nights before—"

"Enough!" protested Elizabeth, who crawled back to her hiding cove. "I don't like to be reminded of it. How that hapless wizard breached my castle walls will confound me until the day I pass."

"I understand, my Queen," said Vago. As he walked toward her, a sense of calm came over him, and he thought of ways to ease Elizabeth's angst. "I'm so sorry," he said. "It was shocking to me, as well, when I heard the castle alarm sound."

Elizabeth froze. "What did you say?"

Vago became tense. "I—I was saying, when I heard from the castle guard days later that the alarm had been sounded. It must have been quite—"

"You were there that night."

"My Queen. I merely misspoke."

Vago had spent the better part of the last three centuries fretting over his alibi concerning these events, knowing the wrath he would face if the truth were ever known. But whether it was his overwhelming optimism, the ease he felt at being near Elizabeth again, or a surrender to the pressure of centuries of bottling up a lie, his subconscious had revolted against him.

Elizabeth emerged and crept toward Vago, and he began to sweat.

"You're lying, Vago. I sense it."

Vago knew her intuition was as keen as it ever was.

His mind raced for answers, a way out of the conversation. Although her telekinetic powers were weakened by entrapment in the spider's body, and her ability to unleash a spell upon him was hindered—her rage knew no such bounds.

"You didn't leave that morning, as you said. You were there when Radu entered the castle, weren't you? You heard the alarm yourself."

Vago raised his hands as Elizabeth crept toward him. "My love, please. I—"

Elizabeth seized upon him and knocked him to the floor, pinning him with her front appendages.

"What did you know?" she growled.

Vago remembered it all—remembered sneaking to the castle depths and showing Radu the secret way in. He tried to block the memory of standing in the forest and listening as the castle alarm sounded, knowing he'd betrayed his lover. Vago brought himself back to the here and now—he'd corrected his actions, atoned for them. Surely Elizabeth would forgive him.

"I searched for you for years! I waited for centuries. I broke the spell!"

Elizabeth leaned into him as her fangs dripped clear sticky fluid—all eight of her black eyeballs were now staring at Vago's face.

"You lying little traitor! I see it. I see it in your mind. You let Radu in!"

"Please, my love! Please! Allow me to explain. I merely let him in to trap him. I swear!"

"Then why was I not told of your little ruse? Why pretend you were away?"

Vago curled his chin and began crying as Elizabeth tightened four of her legs around his body—the motion squeezing his suppressed memories to the forefront of his mind. Driven mad with jealousy upon discovering she had taken a new lover, Vago was indeed the one who betrayed her. And now, bereft of all other options, he would finally tell the truth.

"Because I was jealous!" wailed Vago. "Because I love you and didn't want you in anyone's arms but mine!"

Elizabeth lashed her front claw at Vago's face, cutting a wide gash across his nose.

"You deceived me."

As he continued to cry, Elizabeth let out a great scream and thrust the silver stinger on the back of her abdomen into his stomach.

"Liar! Traitor!" she howled, while stabbing him repeatedly.

Vago began foaming at the mouth as Elizabeth expelled webbing from her abdomen, turning Vago over and over and wrapping him in the stringy fluid up to his neck.

"I'll show you what I do to traitors!"

Elizabeth dragged Vago's paralyzed body to a corner of the hall and climbed partway up the wall before turning and hoisting him upside down and hanging him facing outward into the expanse. She crawled down and stared into Vago's wide-open blue eyes as foamy saliva dripped from his mouth.

"And here you shall remain, Vago the faithless. Vago the false. Forever a fixture in this tomb, as I am. You will starve, but never eat. Your eyes will grow dry and painful, but you will never blink. You will yearn for sleep, yet never rest. And once I am freed, I will keep you with me as a reminder never to trust again. You were once my lover and confidant. You betrayed me, Vago, and this is how I deal with snakes. Now, imagine what I will do to all others who slither behind my back. Suffer now, mighty warlock. Suffer eternally."

Vago watched as Elizabeth crawled away and spoke to several of her thrall children who had entered the hall. The ghoulish thrall took her commands and crawled away into the night. Elizabeth then hoisted herself up to her web pocket in the vaulted ceiling and disappeared from Vago's sight.

Vago could feel the blood rushing to his scalp as intense pressure built up in his eyeballs. He tried to move, but his body would not respond. He wanted desperately to scream—to beg for forgiveness.

His eyes remained open, his mouth was sealed shut, and although he could feel his entire body, his limbs remained paralyzed. Dread swept over him as he realized that never again would his feet touch dew-kissed grass; never again would he taste a strawberry or enjoy the sensation of a fresh spring breeze; and never again would he hold Elizabeth in his arms.

For the rest of his existence, Vago would remain a living, web-encrusted statue, hanging upside down—alone, immobile, and in a perpetual state of torture.

*

Luna Nauhaus lay upon the hay mattress inside her round, modest hut. She felt her husband, Walter, place his hand on her back and rub her shoulder softly, trying to quell her sobs.

"Luna . . . Luna, I beg you. Come back. You've been a wreck for nearly a week."

"Can you blame me?" she cried, turning to face him. "Our daughter . . . our . . . poor child!"

Luna buried her face in her pillow. Her sobs devolved to near blubbering as she thought about Master Vakól's lies and how he had torn her family apart.

"My sweet," said Walter.

"No!" shouted Luna, pushing the hair from her eyes. "They made Hanne a monster! They took her soul . . . her innocence."

"Luna, please. It was our duty to—"

"Duty to whom? To Father Bael? Where is he now? Where, Walter? She was our child, and we betrayed her. Don't you see that? And why do you think a garrison showed up? And the Kaiser himself? This is beyond why we came to Bad Boll."

"What, then? We are to abandon our community, our home?"

Luna grew incensed at *our*—the word her husband always used to manipulate her into thinking she had any say in their marriage. This was not *our* community; it was his. Walter wanted to be a part of the Thule Society. She had grown sick of his endless spouting of praise at Master Vakól's power and wisdom; his turning into a limp sycophant anytime the old warlock came near and inserted himself into their family matters as if he owned both her and Hanne.

Luna thought to the countless times Walter had dismissed her concerns about Master Vakól's constant lingering gaze, about how she had caught him groping young Hanne during her lessons. This had to end. These events were no longer about practicing witchcraft safely away from prying eyes. This was now about treachery. A panic grew inside Luna as she realized these events were far more sinister than she could begin to fathom, and she wondered why she had ever agreed to be a part of it.

"We should have stayed in Berlin," she said. "I'll never forgive you for this. I'll never forgive myself."

"We signed a pact. We pledged our souls, our powers."

"You think I don't remember?"

Luna did remember. She remembered the surprise and dismay she felt returning that day to their small home outside Berlin to find that Walter had packed all their belongings onto a horse-drawn cart without ever discussing the matter with her. She remembered his promises that he'd found a haven for magick wielders to live in quiet harmony—a refuge for Aryan witches, as he put it. She felt the urge to vomit as she recalled the moment she and Walter signed their names in blood to Master Vakól's pact, swearing their souls and attesting their veins flowed with pure Prussian blood.

"We produced an Aryan child of the purest witch lineage, Walter! For what? He used us, then butchered our angelic baby into a horrifying ghoul for his own benefit!"

A scream and the sound of breaking glass came from outside their hut, followed by a growling dog. The barking continued for a moment until the dog squealed and fell silent.

"Did you hear that?" asked Walter, standing from the mattress.

Luna shot up in bed, wiping the tears from her eyes as a rough, fevered scratching came from the door.

"Someone's outside," she said.

Walter crept to the central clay fire pit and took up an iron poker, then made his way to the door. The scratching turned to banging, then ceased. Walter turned his blue eyes to Luna, who pulled a blanket to her chest and watched as her husband placed his hand upon the wooden plank that locked the door.

"Don't, Walter. I sense—"

Walter whipped the door open, only to be faced with a clear, calm evening.

"You see," he said. "It was nothing."

Luna watched Walter step outside and look around the village—all seemed quiet. She closed her eyes and sensed no danger. Walter turned to enter the hut and suddenly yelped. Luna shrieked and backed against the wall at the sight of the rabid, white-skinned boy biting into her husband's Achilles tendon. Walter fell to the ground and the eyeless child climbed on top of him, chewing on his cheek and ripping the flesh clean from his face.

"Alpartio-duté!" yelled Luna, sending a ball of yellow light toward the child.

The enchanted bubble struck the child and absorbed into his body with no effect.

The boy turned his attention to Luna as another thrall child dropped from their chimney opening. Elizabeth's thrall children crouched on the ground, raising their faces in the air as if they were sniffing for Luna's whereabouts. They crawled on the ground toward her as her mind raced for another spell to cast. Luna gasped at the sound of more screams rising from outside as the quiet village became engulfed in chaos.

Walter stood fiercely and suddenly from the floor. Gaping flesh wounds hung from his face and neck, and his skin had turned near white. The children scurried to Walter, placing their bony hands upon his legs, their rabid faces peeking out at Luna.

Walter clenched his fist and the door slammed shut.

The rush of air extinguished the candles, and the interior fell to darkness.

Pain and panic coursed through Luna as the rabid children seized upon her and tore into her flesh. She lay screaming, her last waking memory was the sensation of her own husband clamping firmly upon her wrist as he growled and chewed her dainty fingers clean off her hand.

Chapter 18

18

March 28, 1917, early afternoon

Felix bobbed back and forth on a makeshift stretcher fashioned from a rain poncho and a series of thick tree branches. He was harnessed to Nima's rump and fastened to the stretcher by two leather straps around his shoulders and a rope tied over his midsection. Unable to ride for the past day, he shivered and his pallid, chalky face dripped with sweat as Rurik pulled Nima by the reins up a steep wooded embankment.

Upon reaching more level ground, Rurik patted Nima on the bridge of her nose and released the reins. He turned to Drina, who kept struggling forward while her hooves slipped on the rocks.

"Drina, stop!"

Drina continued on to the flat ground that opened up to a clearing at their right.

"Damn horse. Wait here," he said to Nima.

Rurik dashed after Drina, who had stopped next to some low-lying rocks at the top of the hill.

"Come on, girl. We can't be out in the open," he said, pulling on her reins.

He quickly ducked to the earth when he took a look to his right. The clearing at the top of the embankment opened up to a wide plane with Bucharest's cityscape in the background.

"That's not good," he said aloud.

Rurik crept up on the rocks and peered over them to see a line of German tanks roughly three hundred meters below stretching along the field, all their guns faced outward from the city. Various tents and military vehicles dotted the field behind the tanks, and German soldiers walked about the grounds. Rurik crawled to Drina and reached up to her reins. Just as he gripped them, he looked to see Nima exiting the forest with Felix in tow.

"No, no, no!" he hissed at Nima as Felix's stretcher became destabilized on the uneven ground and started to tip.

Rurik crouched and shot toward Felix, catching him just before the stretcher turned over.

"You still with me?" he asked, steadying Felix.

Felix half-opened his eyes and nodded. "I need water."

"One moment."

Rurik sorted through a few bags hanging from Nima's saddle and found Felix's canteen. He returned and tipped it into Felix's mouth.

"Where are we?" said Felix after he swallowed. His voice was timid and hoarse.

"Just outside of Bucharest. Ten kilos from Denis's."

"I think I can make it if—"

"We have big problems. Massive German encampment just below this ridge. And Drina's currently standing right out in the open. We'll have to wait for nightfall, as the only way out is up that ridge." Rurik pointed to a ridge beyond the clearing. "They'll see us for certain if we try now."

Nima became unsettled and started marching toward Drina.

"Damn it!" yelled Rurik, pulling on the stretcher as Nima lurched forward. The stretcher came unfastened from her rear and Felix crashed to the ground.

"Are you hurt?" asked Rurik, crouching over him.

"All over, actually. But not from that."

Rurik looked to see the two horses casually standing next to one another in full view of the encampment below.

"We're screwed," said Rurik, pulling Felix to the line of rocks.

"Just unstrap me. Unless you intend on pulling me yourself."

"Let's not worry about that until we know if we've been spotted."

Rurik undid his binds, and Felix sat up, swaying a bit from dizziness. "Help me, I want to see."

Rurik assisted him as he slid along the mud and rolled over on his stomach to survey the fields below.

"Binoculars?" asked Felix.

"They're on Drina's saddle."

"Can you get them without being seen?"

"Let's hope," said Rurik, shaking his head. He crawled to the side of Drina facing away from the soldiers and stood slowly, then fumbled inside his pouch and returned with their binoculars. He held them to Felix.

"Actually, you do it. Best I can do is lie here," said Felix, turning upon his back and groaning at the pain in his leg.

Rurik put the binoculars to his face and scanned the encampment.

"Looks like they've set up a perimeter of tanks around Bucharest. Far as I can see in the distance . . . I count at least twenty tanks. Tents seem to be barracks. Then, just some trucks and armored vehicles."

"Any idea what they're doing?"

"None. But the guns are facing in our direction, so they're definitely poised to defend the city. We're in bad shape. It won't be long until those scouts catch up with us. We can't turn back."

Felix took a few big breaths and rested his head on the ground, just as Rurik noticed a black butterfly land on Felix's chest.

"Looks like you have a visitor," said Rurik, inspecting the strange white markings upon the butterfly's pinons. Another black butterfly landed just atop the rocks. Felix seemed uninterested, barely able to retain consciousness.

"Oh, no. Not now!" said Rurik as the sound of biplanes echoed from the distance. "We need to hide under the trees."

He visually traced the path before them that led to a rocky forested ledge that jutted from the ridge, and he evaluated it as a means of escape. Fog emanated from the forest, and Rurik grew uneasy at the sight of the wispy vapors slithering through the trees. A figure emerged from the gloom, and at first glimpse of its antlered head, Rurik believed it to be a deer. His eyes opened wide when he realized the figure was human.

"Uh, Felix," he said, nudging him and finding to his dismay that Felix lay unconscious. "Felix, wake up!"

Rurik looked back to the ridge as the horned figure emerged fully from the fog and stood at the rocks' edge.

"What is that thing?" he asked aloud, looking up to the shadow.

273

At that moment, the figure unleashed two black scimitars from its back and leapt into the air with the blades hoisted overhead, then sailed down to Rurik's position and landed with a dull thud just before him.

Rurik raised his hand in the air as the female figure lifted her blades and swung them down upon him. He twisted out of the way and slid down the slope as the sound of deep bass and crackling followed him. He rolled over to see a crater in the earth where her blades had made contact. Nima and Drina whinnied at the intrusion and galloped away toward the ridge as the shadows of five airplanes roared overhead, shooting past them by several hundred meters.

The horned warrior turned to Rurik with her blades extended as he scurried backward over the mud and pressed his spine against a tree. Her attention turned back to Felix, and Rurik watched as her cloak spread outward from her body and enveloped Felix up to his torso. Quickly scanning the ground, Rurik found a fat, round rock and chucked it at the attacker, striking her in the helmet.

She released Felix from her cloak and marched toward Rurik with her blades at her side. The sound resonating from her scimitars grew lower and louder, and Rurik swore he could feel it vibrating the fillings in his teeth. He found another rock and threw it full force at the fearsome figure. She raised one of her blades to deflect the projectile—the sword absorbed the rock entirely.

Rurik cowered at the base of the tree as she reached him and raised her blades into the air. He closed his eyes and awaited his fate, but just then, a sudden white flash and crashing rang out.

"Not today, devil," came a low male voice.

Rurik opened his eyes to see another black-clad figure standing between him and the attacker. He crawled away and turned to see that the man wore a metallic goat skull mask with metal mesh bolted across the eye openings. The stranger stood deflecting both of her blades with his own black scimitar. The weapons shot white sparks into the air as the mystery figure leaned into the attacker and blocked her advance before kicking her in the gut and sending her backward. After a few clumsy steps, she composed herself and steadied her blades.

Rurik felt confused and panicked. He'd seen plenty of ghosts and ghouls in his day, but this confrontation was decidedly unexpected, and he had no means of defense against either of these dark warriors. He thought to grab Felix and drag him back into the forest, but it was useless—there was no means of escape from the ridge.

"And now I send you back to hell," shouted the goat skull as he charged toward the antlered attacker.

She raised her blades to a defensive position and blocked the strike as he thrust his blade down toward her head.

"You're not Elizabeth," said the goat skull. "Who are you?"

"All that matters is I know who you are," she said as her cloak wrapped itself around his feet and sent him tumbling to the ground.

She leapt into the air and descended upon her enemy as he positioned his scimitar across her blades' strike path. More sparks shot from the weapons as she thrust all her weight onto her opponent.

Hoping the man was his ally, Rurik stood and sprinted to the rock he'd previously thrown at her. He gripped the stone, dashed back to the female warrior, and struck her clean in the back of the neck, causing her to fall forward. The man on the ground raised his foot into her stomach, then extended his leg and sent her flying into the trees. He sat up and shot out his hands, releasing a white shockwave that caused her to tumble farther down the wooded embankment.

The man extended his hand and Rurik pulled him up.

"Thank you," he said, sheathing his blade. "Hurry. We have to move Felix."

Rurik watched the tall, broad stranger run to Felix. "Wait. How do you know his name?"

"No time. Hurry."

Rurik stood cold in his position, then looked to the encampment below to see three tanks rolling forward and pointing their guns upward. Atop the tanks sat spotters with binoculars in their hands, tracking the commotion upon the ridge.

"Now! Help me!" said the masked figure.

Rurik snapped from his daze and ran to Felix just as the Red Baron and Jasta Eleven circled back, seemingly diving straight for the ridge.

"Excuse me . . . sir," said Rurik, tapping the man on his back. "We need to hide."

The Red Baron pulled into point and the formation shot toward them. The thunderous sound of gunfire erupted from the sky.

"Stand behind me!" shouted the man in the goat skull. He pushed Rurik back and stood over Felix.

He unsheathed his black blade and stood in a defensive position as the bullets tore into the turf before them, sending mud and grass into the air. The goat skull crouched low and tracked the path of the projectiles. He thrust out his scimitar and absorbed three bullets that would have struck Felix.

The Red Baron and Jasta Eleven shot past them once more over the tree line.

"Grab him!" yelled the goat skull.

Rurik refastened the rope around Felix's midsection. Both men took a side of the stretcher and ran as quickly as they could, making it nearly to the other side of the path before Rurik had to rest. He placed his hands on his knees, winded, and looked to his new ally.

"What's your name, friend?" asked Rurik.

The man removed his mask.

"Zazlov!" yelled Rurik, overjoyed to see his old friend. "What the hell are you doing here?"

"Later! We have to get to the horses," said Zazlov, hooking the helmet upon his belt. "I like your beard, by the way."

Zazlov turned back toward the field below as the horned figure reemerged from the woods with her scimitars unsheathed. She set her sights upon Zazlov and sprinted toward them as a rumble erupted from the field below. Rurik looked down to see a circular plume of smoke explode from the barrel of a tank, followed by another as Jasta Eleven once again zipped overhead.

"Get down," said Zazlov, pulling Rurik to the ground and shielding both him and Felix with his black cloak.

The earth around them rumbled and massive chunks of rock and dirt rained down on them as the tank projectiles found their mark. Zazlov moved off them and Rurik saw that the entirety of the ledge had been blown off the ridge. The mystery assailant was nowhere to be seen.

"Did it cave in on that thing?" asked Rurik.

"No time," said Zazlov, bending over Felix. "Into the trees— now!"

Rurik lifted the other side of Felix's stretcher and they sprinted into the woods at the top of the ridge as two more bursts of tank fire resonated from below. Deep into the forest they ran as the shells found their mark upon the ridge, followed by the sounds of the Red Baron circling overhead.

They placed Felix on the ground.

Zazlov closed his eyes and held out his hand.

"What are you doing?" asked Rurik.

"Calling your steeds."

After another moment, both Nima and Drina appeared in the distance. The horses galloped toward them, and Rurik jumped up on Drina's saddle. Zazlov pulled the rope away from Felix, picked him up, and slung him over his shoulder in one powerful motion. He mounted Nima while still carrying Felix's unconscious body and drove his heels into her ribs.

"Kya!" he yelled, and the horses were off.

*

"Well, that's it. We have nowhere to turn," said Rurik, spying Denis's farm compound in the field below. To his dismay, the grounds were overrun with German soldiers.

"You can put those down. I can sense what's happening."

Rurik lowered his binoculars and looked back to Zazlov, who hunched over Felix.

"Can you save him?"

"I can," said Zazlov, tearing open Felix's pant leg.

Felix lay unconscious as Zazlov undid the bandage around his leg wound. Every portion of his right leg below the wound had turned black and purple save a green-and-yellow ooze around the point of the bullet wound.

"Oh, my," said Zazlov, taking in the pronounced red streaks running up Felix's leg toward his inguinal lymph node.

Rurik took a few steps backward as Zazlov rubbed his hands together, then applied them to Felix's wound with great pressure. He began whispering in tongues as a green light emanated from underneath his palms, causing Felix to take in a deep breath.

Zazlov continued to lean into Felix for another moment, then released his hands. He sat back on the ground and Rurik planted himself next to Zazlov, watching as Felix's wound began to close and his leg blossomed back to flesh color.

Felix remained unconscious.

"You're lucky I found you when I did," said Zazlov. "Two more hours and he'd be dead."

"Thank you," said Rurik, placing his hand upon Zazlov's broad shoulder. "But how do you know Felix? And why were you tracking us . . . and what on earth was that thing you were fighting? And where'd you get that sword?"

Zazlov held his hand up to Rurik, silencing his rambling questions. He looked up to the gray sky and blew out, puffing out his cheeks. "There's a lot converging right now—and none of it is good. The mayhem you faced in Saint Petersburg is nothing compared to what is transpiring. We'd better find a safe place and I'll inform you of our predicament."

Rurik looked back to Denis's. "We're not finding any shelter here. They've commandeered the entire grounds."

"I hate to inform you, but we'll be finding no shelter anywhere in Romania, after your little Zănoaga excursion. Excellent work on that, by the way—we're surrounded on all sides. There's another large encampment of Germans to the north, and the garrison we just encountered in Bucharest is deploying scouts as we speak . . . they're closing in quickly. But since they won't expect us to hide among German soldiers, I sense they won't look here. Your brother's home is our only means of staying hidden in the short term."

"What about that thing that attacked us?"

"That thing is an entirely different problem. I've cloaked us for now. But she will find us."

Planes buzzing overhead rattled the quiet of the dense forest, and Rurik ducked low to the ground. "They've followed us!"

"Hold on," said Zazlov, perking his head up. "No. They're stationed here."

Rurik and Zazlov watched as the Red Baron and Jasta Eleven circled over Denis's farm grounds, then landed one by one upon the small landing strip that Denis had installed for his planes. They taxied along the strip and parked next to three other biplanes and one massive aluminum-plated bomber with black balken-kreuzes painted on the tail and wings.

"Take a look at that," said Rurik.

Zazlov held out his hand and closed his eyes. "*That* is an experimental bomber transport ... a modified Siemens-Schuckert Forssman, if I'm scanning correctly. Can hold a crew of seven or more. It's what transported our horned friend from the ridge here from Germany. Her nasty horse, too."

"How'd they fit a horse in that thing?"

Zazlov continued to move his hands in circles. "Compression spell, I assume." Zazlov opened his eyes. "That bomber is our only ticket out."

"Can't you just teleport us?"

"If only it were so easy. I would need rest for a spell of such magnitude. In any case, teleporting any distance is too simple to track for anyone scanning. Traveling by mechanical means will give us a better chance of concealing our path and confusing our enemies. At least in the short term."

"You can fly?"

"I cannot. We'll have to kidnap a pilot."

Rurik lay upon the mud and peered through his binoculars. He scanned the grounds and watched as the Red Baron and his troop hopped from their airplanes and headed to a series of tents next to Denis's barn.

"That's weird," said Rurik, noticing all five pilots were suited in head-to-toe black canvas coveralls with no goggles or eye openings on their suits.

"Not for vampires."

Rurik looked to him. "You're joking."

"I wish I were. Converted by your friend Charles Vondling not too long ago."

"No wonder they can fly with such precision in horrid conditions."

"Their echo-calling is a real problem. They'll follow us day or night. And it's my guess their marksmanship in the air is terribly accurate. We'll have to disable their planes before we escape. That gun on the top of the bomber will help, but not against five of them operating with such deadly precision."

"Can't you do some magick to put them off?"

Zazlov smiled. "I believe I can muster something. But I will need some rest after today's exertions. A few hours will do."

"I don't think that's happening," said Rurik, scanning Denis's residence. "Looks like four officers out front of Denis's house. Who knows how many are inside."

"Three more."

"Three more," continued Rurik. "Just great."

"Not a problem. I can handle them. There are another dozen soldiers in the tents and fifteen human pilots on reserve. So far as I can sense, they are not to enter the main house. Restricted to officers."

Getting any closer to the compound seemed like madness to Rurik, but he decided to trust Zazlov's instinct. "Now what?" he asked.

"Now we wake Felix and head to your brother's."

Zazlov clapped his hands together and Felix shot awake. He looked to Rurik with a great sense of confusion about him. "Where am I?" He then took in Zazlov's hulking frame. "Who are you?"

Rurik crouched to Felix and helped him up. "This is Zazlov, Felix. Remember, I spoke of him at the church? He used to work with Orna."

Felix nodded and massaged his leg. He looked to Zazlov. "It doesn't hurt. Did you . . . ?"

"I did, Mr. Yusupov, and you're welcome. Now, gather your things. We need refuge."

*

"I would be remiss if I didn't express my grave misgivings about this plan," said Rurik, pulling Drina by her reins.

Felix followed with Nima in tow as Zazlov walked before them both.

"Keep quiet and follow my lead," said Zazlov.

They approached Denis's home and passed by three armored vehicles before catching the attention of the four German officers casually leaning against the hood of a truck, smoking cigarettes and drinking coffee from tin cups.

"Halt!" shouted one of them, dropping his cigarette and coffee on the ground and removing his service revolver. The remaining three officers followed suit—all pointing their guns at Zazlov.

"I said, 'Halt!'"

Zazlov stopped and held up his hands, signaling to Rurik and Felix to stop.

The officers approached and encircled them with their pistols cocked.

"Who are you? State your purpose."

"I am here," said Zazlov, lowering his hands, "because I was concerned as to where my chickens had gone."

The officer in the front suddenly jerked his head. "Ba-gawk!"

"Now that I've found them," said Zazlov, waving his right hand in a circle, "I want all my good little chickens to run up that ridge over there—deep into the forest. And once they reach the deepest part, I want them to go deeper still, where a nice mound of feed awaits such hungry little chickens."

All of the officers were now bobbing their heads while clucking and cooing.

"Go now, my little chicks. Find your dinner. And do not return until you are well fed."

The officers dropped their guns and hobbled past while tucking their hands under their armpits and flapping their elbows.

"Good little chickens," said Felix, barely able to contain his laughter. He stood next to Zazlov and watched the officers shuffle off toward the ridge that led to the forest. "I would give anything to watch them eat feed off the ground."

"Just wait, Master Felix. I'm merely finding my pitch," said Zazlov, winking at him. "Come, we must hurry. Grab the guns."

Zazlov led the way to the front of Denis's home as Rurik scanned the perimeter to ensure no one else had seen them.

"I have some bad news, gentlemen," said Zazlov. "It's time you said goodbye to your loyal steeds."

Felix stood close to Nima. "But—"

Zazlov raised his hand to Felix. "I'm sorry. Their journey ends here. If you need peace of mind, I can sense they will be safe and well attended to. Best to tie them there." Zazlov pointed to a piece of piping that ran along the façade of Denis's house.

Felix pulled Nima to the pipe. He tied her reins and ran his hand across her forehead as she flicked her ears. "You're a great partner, girl. I promise to come back and find you when this is all over." He placed his forehead firmly to her neck and embraced her before turning away, trying to hide the tears in his eyes.

After collecting himself, Felix unfastened Nima's saddle and placed it upside down on the ground. He traced the stitching with his fingers and tore it open, revealing a cache of gold bars and coins. He picked them up and held them toward Rurik.

"You mind putting these in your bag?"

"Free gold? I thought you'd never ask."

Rurik placed the gold in a small satchel hanging from Drina's saddle, then swung it over his shoulder. He secured the mare and gave her a warm scratch along her mane. "Take care of yourself, Drina. Sorry I had to steal you . . . uhh, Zazlov?"

"Yes, Master Rurik?"

"Seems that leaving the horses out in the open is a bad idea."

"Indeed it is," said Zazlov. He snapped his fingers and the horses disappeared. "How's that?"

"Whoa," said Felix. "Where'd they go?"

"Still here," said Zazlov. "The spell will last nearly a day. They'll be fine."

Felix walked closer to Drina and could see her hoofprints shifting in the mud as she settled. He thought to reach out and touch her but, not understanding the sorcery behind the spell, decided to keep his distance. He followed Zazlov and Rurik to Denis's front door, where he caught sight of himself in the mirror embedded in the wood. Having not seen his own reflection in well over three months, he was a bit dismayed at his scraggly beard and gaunt cheeks.

You've seen better days, old boy.

"Is it safe to enter?" asked Rurik.

"Hold," said Zazlov, making a fist. "I need you both to listen to me carefully. I'm going to cast a cloaking spell. It will create roughly a five-meter bubble around us where we cannot be seen or heard.

I've grown a bit exhausted after all of today's events, so I must stress in no uncertain terms the field limitations. Stick close."

"How long will it last?" asked Felix.

"As long as I have the energy to maintain it. It's not binding magick, so if I should become unconscious or injured in any way, well . . . run."

Zazlov closed his eyes. "There are three men in Denis's kitchen. One of whom is about to drop a cooking pan in . . . three . . . two . . . open the door!"

Felix opened the door to the sound of a pan being dropped from below. He stood to the side of the stairwell that led down to Denis's comfortable sitting room. Zazlov and Rurik pushed past him and Felix closed the door.

"Lock it?" he asked, looking to Zazlov.

"Please."

The three men crept down the long staircase lined with various-sized mirrors before coming to the main floor. They came to the lower level, which opened into Denis's sitting room, and took in the black-wood furniture that adorned the small space, and the spiral stair that led to the upper floor.

"Stay by me," said Zazlov, moving to the back wall toward their right. He removed the goat helmet and sheathed scimitar from his belt and placed them on a table next to the sofa before plopping himself upon the cushions.

"Gentlemen, just a word of caution. Do not handle this blade under any circumstances. It will kill mortals upon touch."

"Fine by me," said Rurik. "But care to explain that thing?"

"In time," said Zazlov, resting his head.

"So what? We just wait here?" asked Felix, kneeling next to Zazlov as Rurik sat in a sturdy chair fashioned from blackwood.

Zazlov pinched the bridge of his nose with his thumb and index finger while opening and closing his eyes. "Sorry. All these spells are causing me quite the migraine. I don't know how much longer I can hold this field. I need to devise a soft technique to deal with our friends in the kitchen."

"Maybe we can convince them they're pigs?" joked Felix.

Zazlov smiled. "If only I weren't so exhausted. At best, I could enthrall one of them."

Felix looked back to the bookcase they had passed upon entry and noticed a very strange and blocky lamp placed next to it that was not constructed of blackwood. It had been months since he'd visited Denis's, but the peculiar lamp still stood out to him—he didn't recall seeing it before. He then focused his gaze on the opening cutaway between the sitting room and the recessed kitchen, which was viewable through open accordion-style wood paneling.

"You sure they're in there? I don't hear anyone."

"Stand up," said Zazlov.

Felix stood and peered into the recessed kitchen from this better vantage point. He could see two German officers seated at the long blackwood table, talking quietly with another who was out of view. Scanning the tall glass planes that led to Denis's greenhouse on the opposite side of the kitchen, Felix noticed a mammoth man with gray, ashen skin wearing a white shirt that was riddled with stains and torn to fit around his hulking biceps. The man stood very still, doing his best to camouflage himself behind a row of giant hogweed plants—but he was too tall, and his head poked over the stalks.

"Uh, Rurik? You better see this."

Rurik stood next to him and gazed into the kitchen. "What?"

"Remember when I told you about Mary and Sebastian, who saved me from Vondling on the train?"

"Yes."

"In the greenhouse. You see him?" said Felix, pointing to the perimeter of hogweed plants.

"Oh, dear. Zazlov. We have a big problem," said Rurik. "Very big."

Zazlov joined them and looked to the plants.

"Interesting," said Zazlov. "I couldn't sense him. You know this man? . . . Is he a man?"

"So far as I know," said Felix. "I met him last time I was in Bucharest. Rurik?"

"His name is Sebastian," said Rurik. "Denis, uh . . . how do I put this? Denis reanimated him almost a decade ago."

Zazlov appeared surprised. "I warned him about such endeavors," he said. "Explains why I couldn't sense his life force. I feel he's a friend?"

"He is," said Rurik. "And a good one at that. I once witnessed him hoist a horse over his head using one arm—didn't even seem to grunt. So now we just have to guess where Mary is hiding."

Felix noticed Rurik cock his head and take a sudden interest in the blocky lamp next to the bookcase.

"Anyone else notice that lamp has no electric cord?" said Rurik. "Zazlov, would you mind standing a bit more toward the center of the room? We need to envelop the lamp in the cloaking field."

"Oh," said Zazlov. "Indeed we do. I am truly slipping. I didn't sense her either."

Zazlov took a few steps forward. "You're hidden now," he said to the lamp.

Felix leapt backward as the lamp shimmered with a white translucence, then transformed into a lean, athletic woman with dark hair and big blue eyes, wearing plain farmers' clothing. She stepped forward and dashed toward Rurik.

"Uncle Rurik!" she said, hugging him deeply.

"What the hell?" said Felix.

"Felix, you remember Mary, from the inn?"

Felix remembered her well, becoming a bit dazed as he realized she was even more comely than he recalled. "I do."

"Incredible!" exclaimed Zazlov. "It's been eons since I've seen a shape-shifter in action. Pleasure to meet you, young Mary. I am Zazlov."

Mary nodded. "The pleasure is mine. Your beard's reputation precedes you."

"Very kind of you," said Zazlov, stroking his sharp black beard with white-stripes along the sides.

"Why are you away from the inn?" asked Rurik.

"It seems our German friends are annexing everything in sight. We fled three days ago, when they arrived. Then they just showed up here unexpectedly."

Rurik moved close to Mary and put his hand on her shoulder. "I'm sorry about your father," he said. "I've been meaning to reach out to you, but have been in the middle of nowhere for months."

"It's fine, Uncle. He led a brave, dangerous life. It was only a matter of time."

Mary stood away and lowered her gaze.

"Are you aware that Sebastian is in the greenhouse?" asked Rurik.

"I am. They arrived so suddenly this morning. We barely had time to scatter."

Zazlov, Mary, and Rurik stood at the cutaway and inspected Sebastian.

"I mean," said Rurik, "he is pretty well camouflaged."

"Other than we can completely see him from here," said Zazlov.

"Excuse me!" said Felix, and all three turned to him. "Can we take a moment here? I just witnessed Mary transform from a lamp, and did she say 'Uncle Rurik'?"

"I thought I told you Mary was a shape-shifter when you told me the train story," said Rurik. "And yes—she's my niece. Denis's daughter."

Felix took a few steps backward and sat in a blackwood chair. "No. You failed to inform me of either of those details."

"Oh," said Rurik, casually. "Well, Mary is my niece and a very rare witch." He wrapped his arm around her and squeezed. "And a brilliant one at that!"

"From my mother, Elda's side," said Mary. "My father was as mortal as they come."

"Denis was your biological father?" questioned Felix. "*Denis* Denis? The cranky old vampire hunter Denis?"

"Yes," said Mary, scrunching her face. "Why are you acting so strangely?"

"It's—it's just a lot to process."

Mary shrugged and joined Rurik and Zazlov at the cutaway.

"So, what's the plan?" she asked.

"I cannot hold this field for much longer," said Zazlov. "Do you mind?"

"Please," said Mary.

Zazlov extended his hand to her and placed it upon her neck. Felix noticed a warm glow illuminate Zazlov's hand.

"Thank you. But I should still sit. I'm feeling spent." He sat upon the sofa, joined by Rurik and Mary. "Give me a few moments," he said. "I'm sure something will occur to me, but I need to meditate on the future outcomes."

"We can just rush them," said Rurik.

"Terrible idea," said Felix. "We can't risk any gunfire. And what if we're shot?"

"The prince is right," said Mary, smiling playfully at Felix. "We have to be subtle."

"Zazlov?" said Rurik, turning to the warlock, who was now passed out, snoring quietly.

"Oh, no," said Mary.

"Um, earlier Zazlov mentioned something about being unconscious," said Felix. "Does this mean the cloaking spell is broken?"

"That's exactly what it means," said Mary.

"Can you make one?" asked Felix.

"I'm a shape-shifter, not a conjurer."

"That's not true," said Rurik. "I saw my little niece do several spells when she was a teenager. Felix, you should have seen this one as a child. You were saying how beautiful she is, but you should have seen how adorable she was back then."

"Not now, Uncle!"

"I never said that," interjected Felix.

"Yes, you did! When you told me about the train encounter. You said Mary was stunningly beautiful, I think you said, and that you felt something toward her you hadn't felt since—"

"Can we reminisce about that some other time?" snapped Felix, keeping his voice hushed. "We're in serious danger."

Despite their predicament, Mary gave a coy glance to Felix, who diverted his eyes to the hallway.

"We've been in serious danger for months," said Rurik. "What's the difference?"

A motion caught Felix's attention, and he looked to see a German officer enter the room from the kitchen hallway. The man held a plate of eggs before him and a fork in his right hand. He appeared stunned to see the four of them in the room.

Everyone became stiff.

"*Guten Tag*," said Felix, smiling.

"*Ja! Guten Tag*," said Mary.

"*Tag*," followed Rurik.

"Intruders!" yelled the officer, spitting out a mouthful of scrambled eggs.

He dropped the plate and pulled his revolver from his hip. Felix dove for the floor and covered his head. The sound of animal hooves and snorting filled the room, followed by a loud bang. Felix looked up and was astonished to see the officer being gored against the wall by a large boar with sharp tusks. The man looked panicked and surprised as he slid down the wall, finally falling unconscious.

From the kitchen came the clattering of silverware on plates and the shuffling of wooden chairs against the floor. The sound of boots scurrying up the recessed kitchen's stairs resonated from the long hallway as the other two officers rushed toward the sitting room.

The boar transformed back into Mary. "Hide!" she hissed before turning herself back into a lamp against the bookcase.

Felix dashed toward Rurik, who was grunting as he struggled to pull the sofa from the wall. After clearing enough space, they stood over Zazlov. Felix grabbed him by his ankles, and Rurik took him by the wrists. They heaved, but the mighty warlock proved too heavy for their grasp, and they dropped him to the hardwood floor, disturbing his rest.

"Uhh," said Felix, looking to Rurik.

"Halt!" came a voice from the hall as the two German officers entered the room and drew their revolvers.

Felix and Rurik dove to the ground, pulling their guns from their jacket pockets.

Zazlov sat up and cast his hand toward the officers as they fired a barrage of bullets.

A white burst flashed from Zazlov's hands and everything fell into slow motion.

Felix's eyes traced the decelerating bullets headed directly for him and Rurik. Both men rolled out of the way as Zazlov stood and reached outward, calling his blade to his hand. He unsheathed the sword and swung it toward the projectiles, absorbing the incoming bullets before slashing the black scimitar vertically downward. The blade sliced the lead German officer in two perfect halves and swallowed what remained of him into its dimensional field. Zazlov then thrust the sword into the remaining officer and held the weapon in long point, twisting it slowly. The horror on the man's face chilled Felix as he watched the officer's body slowly contort and compress while being sucked into the flickering blade.

Zazlov stood back, sheathed his weapon, and all motion resumed a normal speed.

"Where'd they go?" asked Felix, standing next to Rurik.

Zazlov tapped the oblong jewel set into his blade's hilt. "They're demon food now," he said, turning to Mary, who was back to her regular form.

She stood with arms akimbo, glaring at him.

"Young Mary?" questioned Zazlov.

"I thought you were to be meditating, not sleeping."

Zazlov hung his head. "My apologies to you all. My life force is growing weaker, overburdened by a variety of dark spells that I must maintain. I fear that from this point forward, I must ask you all to keep a watchful eye on me to ensure this doesn't happen again."

"It's fine," said Mary. "I'm sorry I snapped at you."

Felix pocketed his revolver and gave Rurik a curious glance. "How are we constantly in over our heads?"

Rurik twirled his gun around his index finger, shoved it in his pocket, and shrugged. "This is normal for me."

Zazlov walked to the unconscious soldier upon the floor. "Best to be rid of him as well," he said. He unsheathed his sword and brought it down upon the German officer.

Felix's mouth fell open as he witnessed the blade absorbing the man, whose bones bent and cracked as if his full body were being crammed into a breadbox.

After another moment of humming and snapping, the officer's body was gone.

Zazlov sheathed his blade and turned to Felix. "I suppose I owe you an explanation, Felix."

289

Rurik raised his hand. "Uh, me too, please."

Heavy footsteps came from the hallway and Sebastian emerged, shooting past Zazlov and embracing Mary.

"We're all right, Sebastian," she said.

Spotting Felix and Rurik, Sebastian flashed a wide grin, lumbered across the room, and lifted the two men in a bear hug.

"*Unk Rur. Fele!*" Sebastian's voice was deep but quiet.

"Nice to see you, Sebastian," said Rurik, grunting from the hug.

"Sebastian!" called Mary. "Put them down before you suffocate them."

Sebastian placed Felix and Rurik on the floor, then turned to Zazlov.

"My, my! You are an impressive specimen," said Zazlov, inspecting Sebastian's bulky frame and the brown stitch scars that riddled his body and bald head.

Sebastian stooped slightly to avoid scraping his head on the ceiling and glanced shyly at Mary.

"He's a friend, Sebastian," she said.

Sebastian looked Zazlov up and down, unsure of the warlock's dark appearance. He reached down to a leather pouch upon his belt and removed his sawdust rabbit doll.

"Dollie," he said, extending the floppy doll to Zazlov. "Dol-dol, fren."

"Very nice," said Zazlov, staring at the one-eyed rabbit. "It's nice to meet you, Dollie."

Sebastian smiled, pulled the doll close to his chest, and gave it a squeeze.

Zazlov looked around the room and exhaled.

"Well then," he said. "It looks like you're my cohorts from here on out: a shape-shifter, an angry prince, a—what exactly are you, Rurik? Not a coroner any longer."

"Vampire hunter will do."

"A vampire hunter, and"—Zazlov looked to Sebastian—"a giant, jovial dead man."

There was a long pause among them as they looked back and forth to one another.

"Well, let's go save the world, shall we?" said Zazlov, placing his hands upon his hips. "We have much to do and very little time to do it." He moved into the hallway toward the kitchen. "There's much to explain if we are to be prepared. My chickens will return tomorrow after daybreak."

"Chickens?" questioned Mary.

"Just go with it," said Rurik, following Zazlov down the hall.

Mary looked to Felix, who shrugged. "Definitely just go with it."

Chapter 19

19

March 28, 1917, night

"Presume not I am the . . . presume . . . the thing I . . . presume not I the thing . . ."

"Hold! Actors hold," screamed Charles Vondling, glaring at the eleven nude actors onstage as he stood from his plush velveteen seat. "You're chewing the scenery and you can't say your lines correctly? I've dealt with some divas in my day, but you, Carol, you!"

Vondling wagged his finger at Carol II, heir to the Romanian throne now that his mother and father had been deposed days prior in this very same theater by way of Vondling's unique interpretation of *Macbeth*. For tonight, Vondling had chosen *Henry IV, Part 2*, and the audience full of vámpir eagerly awaited their master's follow-up production.

The gold-flecked finishings of the grand hall shone against Vondling's silhouette as he approached the stage.

"Now then," said Vondling, his fangs fully apparent. "Your mother was a native English speaker, so I—for the life of me—do not understand how you can butcher Shakespeare so badly. I will remind you once more, it's: 'Presume not that I am the thing I was; / For God doth know, so shall the world perceive, / That I have turned away my former—'" Another actor's movement caught Vondling's attention. "Nicholas, step forward. I need you to cheat out a bit more. Zizi, you as well. The audience cannot see you." Vondling turned to the packed theater. "And you do want to see them, do you not?"

The vámpir howled and hissed, gnashing their sharp teeth in agreement.

"You see! I'll make stars of you yet."

Vondling pulled himself onstage and walked toward Carol. He extended his riding crop toward the nude royal and slapped his cupped hands away from his genitals.

"Not the actor's way! You must give your all to the audience—your everything. Only then will you truly touch their hearts. Of course, with *that* display. . ." said Vondling, pointing his riding crop to Carol's crotch. "Well, as we say in the theater, 'There are no small parts—only small . . .' Well." Vondling shrugged and moved past Carol.

Carol's chin quivered and a tear ran down his face. He stood shivering, embarrassed and ashamed, as he squinted against the bright floor lights and tried to ignore the rabid faces staring back at him from the gallery's shadows.

"Same with you both. No more covering up. Zizi! Come, come now. Let them see the goods, young lady."

Carol's wife, Zizi, and his younger brother, Nicholas, dropped their hands to their sides and stood completely nude before the lights illuminating their pale, bruised bodies against the black backdrop.

"Now," continued Vondling, "where's my script?" He looked to the edge of the stage, where his fang-faced assistant stood holding out a thick manuscript. He grabbed the playbook and thumbed through it. "I'm going to give you all one more chance. If you're to be my rivals and challenge my rule, then it's only fair to see how you perform under pressure. Don't we agree, audience?"

The vámpir became raucous with saliva visibly dripping from their mouths.

"Let's just make sure everyone knows their blocking," said Vondling as he moved among the actors and positioned them. "Pistol looks good. Falstaff, excellent. King, let's have you a bit more forward. Chief Justice, Prince Henry, and her attendants, offstage." Vondling pushed Zizi and Carol's younger sister Elisabeth off stage right as the remaining six nude actors followed and stood behind the curtain.

"For taking on male roles, you both are simply delightful. I truly mean it. And to the attendants—more crying, more tears. The audience will eat that up . . . literally. I think this will be a command performance. Don't miss your cues, and no fluffing!"

Vondling returned to the stage and took a deep bow to wild applause from the vámpir. He tucked his riding crop under his elbow before jumping back into the auditorium and taking his seat. After positioning his round-rimmed glasses upon the bridge of his nose, he opened his script.

"And . . . action! Enter Prince Henry and his train, the Lord Chief Justice among them."

Vondling watched as Zizi, Elisabeth, and the others shuffled onstage.

"Falstaff says!" shouted Vondling.

Carol's other sister Maria stood shivering as she called, "God save thy Grace, King Hal. My royal Hal."

"Excellent. Now, Pistol."

"The heavens thee guard and keep, most royal imp of fame," said Prince Nicholas.

"Very convincing, Pistol. Very nice. Falstaff says—"

"God save thee, my sweet boy!"

Vondling pursed his lips. "You trailed off there on 'boy,' but we can keep it. And now the king! Let us have it!"

Carol shuffled a bit and looked into the shadowed audience. "My Lord Chief Justice, speak to that vain man."

"Wonderful! Wonderful!" cheered Vondling. "Chief Justice—to Falstaff. Let's not miss the beats."

"Have you your wits? Know you what 'tis to speak?" Zizi took in quick and erratic breaths as she tried to steady herself.

"A bit flat. More inflection next time—more inflection . . . Falstaff says—"

"My King, my Jove. I speak to thee, my heart!"

"And now King Henry!" said Vondling, crossing his legs. "Let us have it! Mind your blocking."

Carol took a small step forward and lifted his head, appearing proud.

"I know thee not, old man. Fall to thy prayers. / How ill white hairs become a fool and jester. / I have long dreamt of such a kind of man, / So surfeit-swelled, so old and so profane: / But being awaked, I do despise my dream. / Make less thy body hence and more thy grace: / Leave gormandizing. Know the grave doth gape / For thee thrice wider than for other men."

"Here it comes," Vondling whispered to his assistant, tapping his sharp fingernails together.

"Reply not to me with a fool-born jest. / Presume not I am the th–thing I was, / For G–God doth know and *show* shall . . . and *so* shall the world perc . . . so shall the . . ."

"No!" screamed Vondling. "No! No! No!" He threw his script on the floor, then strode toward the stage. "As your mother and father proved several days ago—it seems that special flair for theater simply does not run in the family."

"Please, no, please spare us," begged Carol, dropping to his knees.

His brother, sisters, and the remaining actors crowded in around him, shivering and whimpering. The mass of nude, quivering bodies huddled more closely together center stage as groups of hungry vámpir appeared on both side exits.

The actors' sobbing and begging grew louder.

"Finally! Finally some raw emotion," said Vondling, mocking them. "Where was this earlier?" He flashed his fangs. "To paraphrase the immortal bard himself, 'Exit, pursued by vámpir!'"

Vondling turned and walked up the red-carpeted aisle.

"Devour them," he commanded, clapping his hands together several times. "Now!"

Screaming, gurgling, and a grinding echo of bone crunching filled the ornate theater as the audience of vámpir charged the stage. Vondling continued up the aisle, never looking back. He opened the double doors with an exaggerated push from both hands, then descended the wide stair that led to the grand lobby.

He exited Teatrul Naţional Bucureşti and stood on the plaza outside the behemoth structure. Four vámpir dressed in dark gray military uniforms rushed to his side as he scanned the surrounding streets and listened to the disquieting sounds of human screams that beckoned to him from every darkened cranny of the city.

"Your Highness," one said as all four knelt before him.

"How was the performance, Majesty?" asked another, looking up to Vondling.

Vondling flashed his fanged grin. "Simply delicious. Another fine evening of *Death by Shakespeare*. And now . . . is *our* time to feed."

A black, wispy cloud formed around Vondling as he transformed into mist and shot into the starry night.

His security detail quickly followed.

*

Vondling materialized behind a tree a short distance from the stairs leading toward the Royal Palace of Bucharest. His four security officers popped from a charcoal-colored ether just behind him. He poked his head around the thick tree trunk and inspected the main entrance.

"I sense foul intentions afoot," he said.

"I feel it too, Sire," said an officer as his pointy ears twitched.

Vondling looked to his first officer. "Remove your uniform."

"Sire?"

"Swap with me. Do it now."

Without further hesitation, the vampire took off his uniform and boots while Vondling took his time removing his flamboyant velour suit and black leather pants. The two exchanged outfits, and Vondling placed his top hat upon the officer's head, adjusting it slightly so that it was perfectly vertical.

"Now. Approach the stair," said Vondling.

"Yes, Emperor."

The Vondling decoy started across the cobblestone lot toward the front of the palace.

"I meant all of you!" Vondling cast a disdainful glance to the remaining three officers.

"Sire!" they said almost in unison.

Vondling stayed hidden behind the tree and watched as his security detail sauntered toward the palace's entrance. Just as they arrived at the foot of the stairs, four German soldiers appeared at the top with gas masks and cylindrical tanks strapped to their backs. They pulled what appeared to be cattle prods from their hips and sprayed a thick white fog over the four shadows, enveloping them entirely.

Howls erupted from the fog, which shone with a haunting green glow as the vampires melted inside the cloud of hogweed gas. The gas dissipated and the soldiers walked down the stairs to inspect the pool of bone soup that glowed with a sickening verdancy upon the cobblestone path as the remnants of the vámpir melted into the brick.

One of the soldiers removed his mask and spit into the illuminated pool.

"Kaiser Wilhelm sends his regards. Traitor."

The soldiers sprinted away along Calea Victoriei, sticking close to the palace walls along the sidewalk.

Vondling scurried up the tree and watched their shadows blend with the dark. He folded his hands around a branch and ground his teeth together before snapping the thick sprig.

"I've been betrayed!" hissed Vondling, releasing the heavy branch and sending it crashing to the ground. He let out a frustrated growl as he watched the embers of the green slime die out.

"Kaiser Wilhelm sends his regards, does he? Does he now?"

His psychotic mind flooded with rageful thoughts as he tried to piece together any viable reason why Wilhelm would dare betray him. Vondling was a leader now—a great man of vision and initiative, who had done Wilhelm a favor by eliminating King Ferdinand and his entire family. There was now a power vacuum within Romania, one that ensured the Allies would never regain its strategic position. Certainly it was Vondling's right to seize the throne—it was simply how monarchies worked: whoever kills the king becomes the king. Clearly, Wilhelm was jealous of such bold action—perhaps even intimidated and fearful of what Vondling could achieve as emperor.

He could still sense the German mercenaries not too far in the distance. They would pay, he thought to himself. Images of tanks, biplanes, and explosions filled his imagination, capped by a grand vision of his vampiric army marching upon Berlin. "It's war the Kaiser wants," he said aloud. "Well, then. Our fragile truce ends here."

Vondling let out a howl so great that its echo resonated for several miles throughout the city. He waited as a quiet breeze brushed through the newly budding tree leaves. A moment later, a chorus of unsettling screeches arose as his minions ravaging every portion of the city replied to their master.

His shadowy figure leaped into the sky to pursue the fleeing Germans.

More vámpir joined his flight as hundreds more scurried below him in the city streets, crawling on the sides and tops of buildings when the roads became overrun with vámpir.

Moments later, they would tear into the mercenaries sent to assassinate their emperor. Hours later, every tank, every plane, every soldier, and every weapon of war surrounding Bucharest would be under the command of Emperor Charles Christopher Vondling and his rabid, fanged army of the undead.

*

A round bead of sweat gathered upon Augusta's philtrum, and she wiped it away. She then touched her finger to the grandfather clock's minute hand and rotated it to twelve, silently dreading every single minute marker as the hand crept closer to the witching hour.

A chime rang through the Chamber of the Black Eagle.

Augusta clicked the secret door's mechanism, pushed the clock from her path, and opened the passage. Candlelight emanated from the stairwell, and she knew—the mirror was waiting. Gripping her suede pouch, Augusta descended into the darkened passage.

The candelabra had been lit and sat on the enchanted vanity. Augusta sat before it, and Gunda appeared as her ghoulish doppel-gänger with a wretched grin upon her face. Reaching into her pouch, Augusta produced the silver offering tray, her ebony-handled athame, and the cigar cutter. As she began to remove the bandage from her palm, the witch wiggled the four remaining fingers on its hand.

"A finger for fertility, perhaps?" questioned Gunda.

Tears streamed down Augusta's face.

"Do I have a choice?"

"Not any longer."

"Very well, then," said Augusta. "I wish for fertility so that I may bear my husband's child."

Gunda waved her hand with the missing finger, taunting Augusta once more.

Augusta removed her wedding ring and slid open the cigar cutter. She placed her left ring finger inside the hole and positioned her right hand to squeeze the device. After closing her eyes and taking a few deep breaths, Augusta suddenly glared at her rotten reflection.

"I think not. I choose, instead, to vanquish you."

Augusta pulled away the cigar cutter, then reached into her pouch and grabbed a half geode she used as a paperweight. She thrust the stone into the mirror, attempting to smash it—not single solitary crack. Gunda reached from the mirror and grabbed her wrist.

A scream echoed through the small chamber as the apparition forcefully twisted her arm until Augusta dropped the geode. With her free hand, Augusta reached to the candelabra and lifted the flames to the Gunda's lace sleeve, igniting the spirit at once.

She let go Augusta's wrist and howled as flames engulfed her body.

Augusta ran from the chamber, scampering up the stairs and slamming the passage door closed. As she leaned against the wall trying to catch her breath, a faint rumbling came from her back. Augusta listened as the sound grew louder. The wall behind her erupted with fierce banging, causing her to stumble forward and lose her balance. She sat up and looked to the grandfather clock as its chimes swayed from the commotion. In another moment, the clock broke from its wall bracket and crashed to the hard marble floor.

Placing her hand to her chest as she tried to slow her sporadic breaths, Augusta watched as the wall to the secret passage buckled from the fierce blows within.

Suddenly—all was silent.

Augusta crawled backward on the cool marble, eventually pressing her spine against a plush sofa. She wiped the sweat from her forehead and peered around the darkened room. It appeared calm.

Glancing to the room's entrance to see if any of the commotion had alerted her staff, she was relieved to hear no one approaching. Augusta stood, patted down her gown, and began to walk from the room, her eyes scanning the fresco above her. The ceiling once adorned with a battle scene was now painted with a skeleton inside a silver pool, pulling a likeness of Augusta into its reflective waters.

Augusta gasped.

Her eyes darted to the paintings hanging on the walls to find that the once supple subjects now appeared gaunt and hollow—the victims of some horrid skin disease as they came alive and turned their attention toward her. Augusta dashed for the entrance and steadied herself at the threshold of the next parade room, checking that nothing was waiting to pounce. A shiver ripped upward along her neck and she felt a presence behind her. She heard the sound as she slowly turned, searching for its source in the shadows of the Chamber of the Black Eagle.

Clip-clop. Clip-clop.

Horse hooves echoed through the chamber.

Augusta watched its intimidating shadow creep toward her before it was finally illuminated by the moonlight entering the chamber. A hooded Count Wolfgang Wilhelm, who once adorned the ceiling fresco, now stood before her mounted on a large black stallion, whirring a morning star at his side.

"Oh, God. No. Please. No!"

The black steed let out a piercing whinny, reared its legs, then galloped toward Augusta, barreling through the furniture in its path.

"Help me! Help me!" she screamed as she ran from the parade rooms as quickly as her feet would carry her.

As she ran through the next parade room, the paintings began to move and the ghoulish subjects crawled from their ornate frames and chased after her.

Augusta reached the main hall as hooves clacked upon the marble, coming nearer and nearer. Sprinting along the hallway that led to the Schlüter Stair, she stopped dead in her tracks as another horse burst from the grand painting hanging just before the ascent. It turned to her, huffing and snorting, staring at her with glaring red eyes. She looked to its skull-faced rider, who unsheathed his saber and pointed it at her, just as the black steed entered the hall from behind, skidding on the smooth marble surface.

Augusta was cornered.

Before her stood the hulking white steed with the armed ghoul in its saddle, and behind her crept Count Wolfgang on his horse, whirling his morning star round and round. With nowhere else to go, she backed up to the wall adorned with a painting of her mother-in-law, Princess Victoria.

Augusta yelped as Victoria's hands reached from the painting and wrapped around her neck. She spun around, knocking away Victoria's hands, to see her skeletal face and bony hands furiously reaching for her. Augusta sprinted toward the white horse as Victoria emerged from the painting and joined the pursuit.

The black steed whinnied and gave chase, and the specter on the white horse swung his blade downward upon Augusta as she shot past, missing her neck by mere inches.

Augusta made her way to the grand stair and gripped the banister as she ascended to the second floor, all the while looking back to watch the ghouls from the palace's paintings following her. Upon reaching the top of the stair, Augusta shrieked at the sight of the vanity sitting before her. More paintings lining the walls became undead caricatures and emerged from the frames as their ghoulish groans echoed through the hall.

Augusta scampered toward her bedroom, screaming for help.

Upon entering her private quarters, she slammed the door to find that the entire space was empty save the vanity sitting dead center. She quickly scanned the ceiling to see the cherubs were missing and the clouds had turned to charcoal as they churned above her, occasionally flashing brightly with lightning flickers.

She ran past the mirror and exited into the darkened passage reserved for her staff.

As she reached the passage's end, Augusta opened the door and poked her head into a barren, expansive hallway. In the distance to her right was a doorway that led to another hall that exited to the palace roof. To her left was the Schlüter Stair and a shadowy hall that led to the front of the palace.

She closed the door and remained in the passage, breathing heavily and taking a moment to consider her predicament.

I have to make it to the roof.

Her eyes became accustomed to the dark, and she spotted a swarm of small glowing red eyes staring at her from the other end of the passage. A trumpet blast rang out in the corridor, followed by infantile laughter as the incandescent bulbs flicked on, revealing the cherubs crawling toward her over the floor, walls, and ceiling. Augusta opened the door and entered the grand hall. She slammed the door behind her and turned right, only to see the vanity blocking her path to the next hallway.

She spun around and hurried toward the Schlüter Stair as the cherubs broke down the door behind her. Two of the devils held a long harp wire between them.

"Give us your head!" they taunted. "We want your head!"

Augusta stopped cold in her tracks as the sounds of horse hooves clambered up the marble stair, and she stood facing the shadows of hundreds of zombified ghouls marching toward her from the hall that led to the front of the palace. Trapped on both sides, she backed into the wall and looked to the long line of windows across from her, wondering if a jump through the glass was her only means of escape. Water began pouring about her feet and Augusta turned to see a floor-to-ceiling painting of a seafaring vessel being attacked by a gargantuan tentacled monster—the high seas splashed over the ship's hull, and dark storm clouds whirled above it.

The seawater gushed from the painting, flooding the hall and sending Augusta sliding toward the row of windows on the opposite side. She managed to find her footing and squirmed past the cherubs toward the vanity at the hall's end—the rushing waters coming closer and closer as the tempestuous seas expelled the leviathan and the ship from the painting. The boat crashed into the windows, tearing a wide gash in its hull and snapping its mast as the beast gripped the walls with its giant tentacles and pulled itself closer to Augusta, its jaws opening and closing like a rabid lamprey. Just above its briny head hovered the cherubs, and around it, a throng of zombified ghouls flailed in the oncoming tsunami.

Augusta dashed past the vanity and made it to the next hall. She slammed the door behind her and thrust her weight into the wood as the force from the crashing waters on the other side nearly sent her flying forward. The door rattled and shook—cascading waters poured in over its threshold, further soaking her slippers. She threw her hands into the door and forced every ounce of strength backward as the sea monster's growls taunted her from the other side.

The banging stopped.

Augusta lifted her eyes down the empty hall to once again see the vanity sitting before the exit door that led to the palace roof. She then turned to face the door and backed away slowly.

The rushing waters ran dry from the other side.

She stood soaking wet, whimpering and casting her gaze between the mirror at her back and the door, trying desperately to think of an escape.

Where are the bloody palace police?

A rapping came at the door, followed by a single, solitary bang. Augusta yelped, then calmed herself and focused her eyes on the wood. She swallowed, taking a moment to pat down her drenched gown.

The door swung open.

Augusta shrieked at the sight of Nette's pale-faced corpse standing in the doorway, her torn white gown stained brown at the abdomen. In her hand, she held Augusta's ebon handled blade.

Augusta backed away slowly, staring at Nette, whose hair hung disheveled about her face.

"I made a mistake," said Augusta, crying. "Please. Please don't . . ."

Nette rushed Augusta in a motion so quick and unexpected that Augusta had no time to react as Nette thrust the blade deep into her stomach.

Augusta buckled over and Nette pushed her to the floor, straddling her. Nette raised the blade high above her head, and as Augusta lifted her hand to block the blow, the blade pierced clean through her palm.

The cherubs entered from behind Nette and seized upon Augusta, pinning her arms to the floor and feeding the harp wire across her mouth. They began pushing and pulling the steel, severing her cheeks as they sawed to the back of her throat. Nette raised the blade into the air and brought it down into Augusta's alabaster flesh time and again with a repetitive splashing thud. Augusta tried to scream, but was choking on her own blood as the cherubs continued to saw her jaw from her face—their infantile laughter growing louder and more fevered with each and every slice.

A trumpet blast punctuated the mayhem as the pain and panic inundating Augusta's body became too great. She fell to blackness just as a remaining body of ghouls entered the hall, swarmed upon her, and began feasting on her flesh.

"Empress! Empress!" came a male voice.

Augusta opened her eyes and stared at Minister Schmidt.

"Minister! Help me! Help!"

"Majesty, what is the matter? Why are you writhing upon the floor?" Schmidt knelt to her and assisted her from the marble.

Augusta stood and looked down the perfectly well-lit passage. There was no mirror, no ghouls, and thankfully—no Nette.

"I—I!"

She turned her tear-filled eyes to him in a panic.

"I did something I shouldn't have," she said, sobbing. "Wilhelm said I can trust you. That you wouldn't tell Hindenburg. Can you keep a secret? Please. I beg you!"

Schmidt looked to her with concern.

"My Empress, but of course. What is it? How can I help?"

"There were ghosts, and the paintings—they came alive . . . the sea monster, the cherubs, they—"

"There, there. Please, be calm. Everything is fine."

Augusta scanned the empty hall once more.

"But . . . I saw them."

"I think you were merely having—"

"No! This is real. I can prove it."

*

"An odd place to hide a vanity," said Schmidt. "How did you find such a thing?"

"It—it's just been calling to me in my dreams. But look, don't you see? There's no reflection. I have to summon the—the—"

"Ah, yes," said Schmidt, looking over the mirror. "I will agree that it is enchanted. But it seems perfectly harmless now."

"Then, you believe me? Please. You must help me. You must vanquish the spirit from these halls."

"Let me see what I can discover." Schmidt closed his eyes and held out his hand to the mirror, waving his palm in circles before the reflectionless glass.

He opened his eyes and looked at Augusta.

"You were right, Empress. There was a witch trapped in the mirror. But it seems you vanquished her by fire. She's gone now and will trouble you no more."

Augusta stood before the mirror and peered into it.

"You're certain? Then why did the paintings come alive? What did I just witness?"

"You see, the mirror is an entity of its own, and after you vanquished the spirit within, it was merely lashing out—as it craves a prisoner." Schmidt moved behind her.

"What do we do?" asked Augusta. "What does it want?"

"Interestingly enough, it told me exactly what it wants."

"Yes?"

"It wants you."

Fear pricked Augusta's senses, and she turned to confront him.

"Back away," she said, trying her best to sound forceful.

"Or what, Empress?" said Schmidt calmly and quietly, stepping in close. "Back away or you'll do what, exactly?"

Augusta became off balance.

She placed her backside against the vanity, looked behind her, and grabbed the ebon handled blade that was still on its surface.

"Stay away from me!" hissed Augusta as she held the blade to him.

Schmidt had no discernible reaction. He moved in close and placed his hand before the blade's tip.

"Allow me to help," he said, slowly forcing his hand onto the knife so that it stabbed through his flesh.

Never wincing, Schmidt forced the blade clean through his hand until his fingers gripped the handle. He then tore the blade from Augusta, pulled it from his flesh, and casually dropped it to the brick floor. Schmidt grinned and grabbed Augusta's wrists—she noticed he had no knife wound.

"Unhand me!"

"Oh, my poor, poor empress. Have you ever heard of a tale where a mortal summons a spirit and that tale ends well?"

A shiver seized Augusta over her shoulders as she realized that her conversations with Wilhelm had not been private—that her endeavors had been doomed from the start, and that she had unknowingly played her part in a scheme far more sinister than she had envisioned.

Schmidt let go her wrists and thrust her backward, her body appearing to blur as she fell into the mirror and disappeared. Standing back and folding his arms, Schmidt watched with a pursed smile as Augusta materialized behind the glass. She banged and pawed at the mirror's surface, screaming for release. Schmidt turned and walked down the darkened pathway, eventually sealing the passageway shut from above.

Augusta fell into madness, screaming as she banged against the glass. But there would be no escape. She would remain in the mirror evermore, consumed with pride and envy—always waiting for the next hapless soul who happened upon the looking glass, begging for more, more, more.

*

Minister Schmidt entered the top-secret hangar at Berlin's airfield and walked briskly toward Wilhelm and his men.

"My sincerest apologies, Kaiser. I was attending to another matter and time slipped away from me."

Kaiser Wilhelm scanned Schmidt from head to toe, then turned his back on him.

"Don't be late again," said Wilhelm, walking with Prince Henry and Ernest Louis to a nondescript metal door toward the end of the hangar.

Schmidt shuffled past the three men and removed a key from his pocket. He stood before the door as his blue eyes passed over the series of biplanes and three large bombers lining the hangar. Satisfied they were the only people present, Schmidt inserted the key into the door handle and pressed a large round button. A loud buzzer rang out through the arched expanse.

"After you," said Schmidt, holding his arm outward to the steel stairwell before them.

Wilhelm and his cabal descended the stairs—ten flights in all—before reaching the bottom.

"Isn't there an elevator to this thing?" complained Wilhelm.

"There is, Kaiser, but it's quite slow."

Wilhelm huffed.

Schmidt stood before a heavily armored door and looked to Ernest Louis, who stood next to him. Each man took his key and inserted it into a separate keyhole.

"On three," said Schmidt. "One, two, three."

The two men turned their keys and another buzzer sounded, followed by a latch release. Schmidt pushed on the door and entered a narrow hallway, the rest following him. Behind them came the sounds of the entry door closing and latching as they reached another reinforced metal door.

"Now, I warn you all," began Schmidt, "what you are about to see may shock you to your very core, but your understanding of my findings is essential to our future operations. Please do not touch anything, and I request you leave any sympathies you may have in this hallway. My discoveries are grim, but they will change the tide of this war."

"On with it," said Wilhelm.

Schmidt yanked on a large lever at the center of the door and pushed it open to reveal a brightly lit room that was a cross between a madman's laboratory and a sterile mortuary. Various beakers containing multicolored liquids sat on the shelves encircling the room and in its center sat four metal slabs—two of which were encircled by white curtains.

A soldier wearing a gas mask and canisters on his back stood next to the door and saluted them as they entered.

"At ease," said Schmidt. "Any escape attempts?"

"No, sir. The blood infusions seem to be working. They're completely docile."

"Very well."

Wilhelm watched as Schmidt walked to the rightmost slab and stood before the curtains.

"I warn you again. This is not for the squeamish. There will be no shame in turning back now."

"Proceed," said Wilhelm, stepping forward.

Schmidt pulled back the curtain to reveal a dissected human figure bound to the metal slab by its wrists and legs with a steel cage covering its face. He pulled a small metal pointer from his pocket and extended it.

"Now then," he said. "I give you a fully dissected vámpir. Careful—it's still alive."

The men circled the slab, each trying their best to maintain composure at the sight of the specimen. Wilhelm showed particular interest in the sawed-off ribs sticking from the creature's chest, which seemed to have the texture of brown, hardened jelly— appearing more like cartilage than bone.

Prince Henry backed away. "You're telling me that thing is alive? Can't it transform or something?"

"No, no. We are safe. The clamps over its wrists and legs are entirely of blackwood, which burns them and can be potentially lethal. Hence the stake." Schmidt motioned to the blackwood stake hanging from the ceiling, positioned directly over the vámpir's heart. He reached down and produced a wire from the table attached to a red button. "One small move and I press this. The hydraulic clamps the fetters further into the skin, and this button will thrust the stake into its heart. The bottle is filled with blood, which feeds intravenously into the creature's stomach, keeping it satiated and docile." Schmidt looked to them. "Please. Join me. It's important you understand."

Wilhelm and the rest surrounded the table as Schmidt stood near the vámpir's shoulders. The creature lifted its head slightly. Its black eyes seared through the metal cage enveloping its head, and it hissed at them.

"Oh! Excellent. Excellent," said Schmidt. "Look here." He pointed his metal rod to two green glands sitting in front of the esophagus in the vampire's neck that expanded like balloons.

"These are their venom sacs. It was preparing to spit, you see—the glands are filling." Schmidt swatted the cage with his pointer. "*Destul!*" he ordered in Romanian.

The vámpir relaxed and the glands receded.

"*Elibereaza-ma,*" it gasped.

"They can speak?" asked Prince Henry.

"Indeed they can. This one is relatively newborn. Arrived three days ago from Bucharest—it only speaks Romanian, so you may speak freely. I'm certain it has no understanding of its powers, or I fear we would not be able to contain it . . . Now, before we move on to the next, please take note here." Schmidt pointed to the vámpir's abdomen. "The entire intestinal tract is in the process of atrophy. Soon it will waste away and completely detach from the stomach, which by my estimation has grown over two and a half times the size of a normal human stomach—all for the sole purpose of digesting blood. See here, notice the tendrils." Schmidt hovered his pointer over the blackened veins extending in all directions from the vampire's stomach to various parts of its body. "But notice here," he said, pointing to two larger veins that ran to the creature's appendix and gray beating heart. "Bigger pipes to the heart and, interestingly enough—the appendix."

"Why the appendix?" asked Ernest Louis, regarding the engorged organ at the base of the large intestine.

"Vestigial organs in all creatures of the supernatural are quite active. The appendix, for example, essentially behaves as a secondary brain in most witches and supernatural creatures. The saying, 'I had a feeling in my gut'—well, that is your appendix speaking. But without any further experimentation, I can only assume this is what gives vámpir their power to change between hunting forms, and vampiric witches obviously the ability to do much, much more." Schmidt placed his hand to his gut. "My appendix, for example, is quite pronounced. I can feel it generate a great deal of heat, specifically when I am engaged in clairvoyant or telekinetic activities."

"That's quite interesting," said Wilhelm. "Does that mean we are all capable of witchcraft?"

Schmidt shook his head. "I believe at one point in time, historically—yes. Even mortals had the ability to perform magick. There are some residual talents most mortals retain due to their appendixes—

intuition and even prophetic dreaming is believed to generate from the appendix. But after the Inferno and the vanquishing of witchcraft, I fear the dormancy . . . Well, let's just say your appendix is about as good to you as whatever is left of this creature's intestines. Now!" Schmidt pulled the curtain closed and moved to the next slab. He pulled back its curtain and Prince Henry gagged at once.

"The stench!" he said.

Ernest Louis and Wilhelm raised their elbows to their faces, hoping to inhale the smell of their own garments.

"Gentlemen—I give you an ustrel. The most wretched of all creatures."

The ustrel was fettered to the metal slab in a similar fashion to the vámpir.

Wilhelm and the rest backed away as Schmidt stood next to the dissected creature.

"Nothing to see here, really, other than . . . well, as you might expect, there appear to be no physiological changes to the internal organs from when it was human. The only difference being the coloration change to black among the organs—they appear in every way to be rotten from the inside out."

The ustrel began thrashing about, and Schmidt pressed a button on the slab that caused its blackwood fetters to sink further into its legs and wrists. An acerbic yellowish-gray smoke rose from the points of contact, and the creature howled in pain. Schmidt rapped his rod upon the cage around its face.

"Are you ready to behave?"

The fanged face behind the metal wiring appeared to nod, and Schmidt pressed the button once more, releasing the pressure of the blackwood fetters.

"This one is from Zănoaga. A deserter from our own ranks."

"Fitting end," said Wilhelm.

"Agreed," said Prince Henry.

"Now," said Schmidt, walking to a reinforced metal door along the sidewall with a porthole at its center. "This is where things get interesting." He stood next to the widow. "Please gather round and see for yourselves. This is one of the soldiers converted from Elizabeth's thrall children—I had it flown back before the remainder were deployed to Arras. See for yourself."

Wilhelm peered through the porthole to see a zombified soldier standing alone in a room. It appeared as any other German front-line soldier save its rotting gray flesh and blackened teeth, which stood out as most of the flesh had been torn from its face.

"Ghastly," said Wilhelm, who suddenly stood back from the window.

"What's the matter?" questioned Ernest Louis.

"The damn thing saluted me," said Wilhelm.

"Indeed it did," said Schmidt. "I wanted you to see for yourself that the plan to convert our soldiers worked better than we pre-dicted. The thrall retain their wits for the most part. They can be reasoned with, take orders—even fire a rifle."

"You're kidding me," said Wilhelm with wide eyes. "I thought they would only be used as cannon fodder."

"As they will," said Schmidt. "But now that I have had time to inspect this specimen, I believe the thrall will be the perfect soldier in every practical sense of the word. They never sleep, never tire, and are incredibly vicious. They can move about during the day but are naturally nocturnal . . . and so long as they have fresh meat to feed on so they do not fall into rigor mortis, they seem relatively immortal. Fire, brain injuries, outright obliteration are all that seem to kill them, but it takes quite a bit. Allow me to demonstrate." Schmidt looked to the rest. "You might want to stand back for this." He stood at the door and opened a small blast window. "Private Gantz!"

The zombified soldier looked to him slowly and saluted. "Sir!" it wheezed through its shattered teeth.

"I want you to take that grenade on your belt and pull the pin."

"Yes, sir," it seemed to gurgle.

Schmidt closed the latch and all four men stood away from the door.

"Is this safe?" asked Prince Henry.

"The glass is blast proof," said Schmidt, appearing confident.

The men positioned themselves to see into the porthole and watched as the soldier removed the grenade on its belt and pulled the pin. It held the bomb at its side as it exploded, splattering the window with a thick green ooze.

Wilhelm and the rest crouched and covered their ears as the blast resonated through the room, shaking the lamps hanging from the ceiling.

Wilhelm looked to Schmidt. "He did it with no concern for his personal safety."

"That's not all," said Schmidt. "See for yourself." His eyes motioned toward the window.

Wilhelm crept toward the blast window as the green ooze slowly dripped down the glass. He peered in to see the soldier in bits, with chunks of its body strewn across the room. All that remained intact was its head and the upper right portion of its torso as it clawed itself along the floor and growled.

"It's still alive! Incredible!" Wilhelm turned. "We'll have battlefield superiority in weeks!"

"Not so fast," said Schmidt. "The issue is this: thrall create more thrall. Once bitten—if not devoured alive—the human attacked by a zombie will in turn become one. But they are hive-minded to a degree, and ultimately they answer to one master."

"Elizabeth," said Wilhelm, slumping his shoulders.

"Exactly. It seems she will have ultimate control over any and all generational converts, once the banishment hex is removed. But!" Schmidt thrust his finger into the air and walked to another blast door. "I have taken the liberty to do some grand experimentation, and believe I have solved this problem. Join me."

They hovered around the porthole to see a young man sitting on a chair. He looked to the widow and stood up at once, yelling at them in French.

"Who is this?" asked Wilhelm.

"This is a French prisoner, and what I believe will be our very first successful attempt at creating an unstoppable soldier directly in service of the German Empire."

"How so?" asked Wilhelm.

"Watch and see," said Schmidt, reaching to a button at the top of the door seal. "Just be reminded that this subject is fully human and entirely loyal to his nation."

Schmidt pressed the button and the chamber filled with a bright yellow cloud, enveloping the French soldier.

"You see. Telepathy is a simple yet fragile form of communication. It's relatively easy to put someone under a trance, but difficult to prevent interference from another psychic signal and maintain dominance. And though Elizabeth can communicate with these soldiers, command them to some degree, and see through their eyes if she so chooses, the banishment shield does hinder her ability to have full control—especially if a new form of psychic static is introduced into the connection."

Wilhelm kept his eyes on the porthole as the yellow gas began to dissipate.

"So, what I have done is taken the blood of the thrall and mixed a portion of it with the blood from our ustrel subject. I then gasified it—one whiff of this incredibly noxious gas, and a human subject will be immediately converted to our command."

"Why is it yellow?" asked Prince Henry.

"Oh," said Schmidt. "I assume it is merely the natural chemical reaction. Which is why I have named it 'mustard gas'."

"I can control this thing once it's transformed?" questioned Wilhelm.

"Not exactly," said Schmidt. "As I mentioned, the gas is composed mostly of ustrel blood. Ninety-four point eight three nine percent, to be exact, which does unfortunately leave us limited to mostly nocturnal operations. They can survive during a cloudy day better than ustrel, but direct sunlight will destroy them in a matter of hours. The benefit being that the dominant telepathic connection now spawns from our subject here."

"Behold," Schmidt said, walking toward the fettered ustrel. "Are you hungry?" he asked.

The creature hissed and gnashed its fangs. Schmidt reached to the dial above its IV bottle filled with blood.

"I will release all of this blood if you command the man in that chamber to bash his head against the glass until he bludgeons himself," said Schmidt.

The ustrel nodded.

"Very well," said Schmidt, turning the dial so that the red liquid filled the tube and gushed toward the ustrel's gut.

At that moment, Prince Henry jumped at the sound of the French soldier banging his face into the glass.

Wilhelm turned to see the hollow-faced soldier, now visible through the yellow cloud, repeatedly bang his face into the glass, splattering the window with dark green blood until its skull caved in and it could no longer continue.

A palpable sense of shock and surprise filled the room as Schmidt stood before the blast door, appearing proud.

"You see, it works! I have broken the psychic channel. We gain the ferocity of thrall through Elizabeth's venom and retain control of the soldiers through our ustrel. I have essentially engineered our very own Nosferatu."

Wilhelm stroked his mustache and considered the implications. "Do you mean to tell me that you intend to put an ustrel in command of our armies?"

Schmidt extended his hands palm outward, intending to brunt Wilhelm's qualm. "Let's not forget," he said, "these super soldiers, if I may coin the term, will remain mostly independent and obedient to their field commanders so long as they have enemy soldiers to feed on. Every enemy soldier who is bitten by our hybrid Nosferatu will, in turn, awaken under our command. I still need to do more experimentation on the generational psychic downflow of the hive mind, but it does seem that unless a, shall I say, master ustrel is killed, all converts under its dominion will ultimately answer to its call.

"Once we deploy the gas to the western front, we will convert any French or British to our armies of the undead, and it will be our master ustrel who controls them. In time, we will destroy any of Elizabeth's converts and maintain ultimate control of an unstoppable army."

"And if the Americans finally join? It's heading that way," said Wilhelm.

"They, too, will become ours. I cannot stress enough how quickly the gas works—the slightest inhalation. Our enemies will become our thrall, and our forces will grow exponentially. Nothing will stand against your might, Kaiser. We simply need the hive mind to be centered in an entity that we ultimately control."

For a moment, Wilhelm seemed entranced—but then shook his head. "No," he said. "I'm afraid it's impossible. I cannot allow our forces to be controlled by some random undead deserter, and no loyalist in his right mind would volunteer for such a thing. I am not risking any backlash from forcing a trusted advisor against his will to become a savage monster."

"Nor shall you have to," answered Schmidt. "There has been a development, my Kaiser. One that I needed to hold secret until the time was right and my experimentation proved fruitful. As it turns out, we have managed to locate and procure such an ustrel. One who, with some coaxing, should be relatively sympathetic to your cause. And who, with a steady supply of fresh blood, should be relatively easy to control."

All eyes were on Schmidt.

"Well?" asked Wilhelm, just short of shouting.

Schmidt pulled out his pocket watch and checked the time.

"Perfect timing," he said. "Please . . . follow me."

*

Minister Schmidt led Wilhelm and the rest from the secret room at the back of the hangar as an immense triple-winged transport plane taxied into the hangar and parked.

Wilhelm covered his ears as the quadruple engines stuttered and eventually came to a stop with the sound of a loud backfire.

"What's all this?" asked Wilhelm, looking to Schmidt.

"It's wonderful news, Emperor. I promise."

The side door of the plane popped open, and four soldiers dressed in black, non-patched uniforms ran down the plank to the giant hangar doors. With two men on each side, they pushed the doors closed, then positioned themselves in front of the transport plane and saluted Wilhelm as he approached.

Wilhelm and his gaggle lazily saluted the soldiers as they passed, and Schmidt led them to the ramp extending from the plane.

A man emerged at the side door of the plane.

"I don't believe it," said Wilhelm, as Dmitri Pavlovich strode down the ramp and knelt before him.

"My Emperor," he said, reaching out to plant a kiss on Wilhelm's gloved hand.

Wilhelm retracted and stood back a few paces.

"You have some gall showing up here, young man."

"Emperor, allow me to explain," said Dmitri, staring up at Wilhelm with his boyish blue eyes.

"Explain what? How you and your ilk took my funds, then botched the entire Nosferatu operation?"

Schmidt moved between them. "Emperor, I believe you should listen to what he has to say."

Wilhelm glared at Schmidt. "And I believe you have forgotten your place, Minister. Henry, Louis? Am I not correct here?"

"We should hear him out," said Ernest Louis.

Dmitri stood. "Please, Emperor," he said, extending his hands forward. He turned and walked up the ramp to the plane.

A moment later, Dmitri's back appeared in the plane's entrance as he tried to steady a giant crate shrouded in a black curtain that was about a foot taller than he. Dmitri guided it down the ramp with the assistance of another burly, bearded man Wilhelm did not recognize. They navigated the wheeled crate before Wilhelm as another older gentleman appeared at the top of the ramp.

"Oh, no," said Wilhelm, recognizing him. "No. No. All of you. I want you to board that plane and head back to where you came from. Do you have any idea the trouble you have caused me? The misery?"

"Pleasure to see you too, Emperor," said Olaf, bowing deeply. He proceeded down the ramp, joining Dmitri and the burly man.

"Who is this?" asked Wilhelm, looking over the muscular man in black.

"Kaiser," said Dmitri. "This is Kir Oltan. He was head of security for the Black Hundred."

Wilhelm raised his hand. "Enough. I recognize the name from a report I read on your botched operation."

Kir bowed. "It's an honor to meet you, Kaiser."

"I'm serious!" yelled Wilhelm. "Back on the plane immediately. If you're not clear of German airspace in two hours, I'll send a squadron to shoot you down. Back to the Bolsheviks with you!"

"Kaiser," said Schmidt. "Please. You must hear them out."

Wilhelm's face grew red and his mustache pointed directly to the floor. He turned around for a moment, composed himself, then faced Dmitri once more. "Fine. You have two minutes."

"Thank you, Kaiser," said Dmitri, bowing. "I want you to know that during the Saint Petersburg operation, both Kir and myself were merely following orders. I was, in fact, turned to vámpir in the early morning of the day of the Nosferatu spawning and sent on a train to Bucharest. I was on orders to rein in our operative, Charles—"

"Vondling. Yes. Wretched fellow. He has been neutralized."

"Very well, Kaiser," said Dmitri. "Much to my sorrow, when I awoke from the transformation process aboard the train, I knew something was wrong. I was still human—I had no special powers. And then I learned of the failed operation. It turned out my master, Rasputin, was destroyed before I was able to take my first human life. Thus, my transformation did not stay."

"If this is some attempt at garnering my pity, you've come before the wrong person."

"No, Kaiser. You see, I made my way back to Saint Petersburg as quickly as I could—about a day or so. I avoided the rioting and looting, and eventually sneaked my way back into the Winter Palace in hopes of finding any survivors. And find them I did." He placed his hand upon Kir. "Kir and I were searching the palace room by room when we came upon *this*, feeding on the corpse of a palace guard." Dmitri rested his hand upon the curtained crate. "At first, I couldn't believe it, and certainly had no means to contain it, so we summoned Olaf, who assisted us in trapping it."

"Enough of the goddamn mystery," barked Wilhelm. "Trapped what?"

Wilhelm pulled down the curtain to reveal a bearded ustrel in a bloodstained white uniform, trapped inside a cage constructed of blackwood. Wilhelm looked to its fanged face as it hissed and slashed its clawed hands outward, trying to grab Wilhelm.

Wilhelm placed his hand over his heart the moment he recognized the ustrel.

"Why—why, no. It . . . cannot be," gasped Wilhelm. "How is this even possible?"

"This is a curse," said Prince Henry, backing away.

"It's true, Kaiser," said Olaf. "His blood was consumed. Technically, he was murdered and the human bloodlink to Alexei was destroyed. But due to the foul biology of a vámpir bite—it seems that this was not the end of his tale." Olaf bowed, twirled his hand, and announced in a mocking voice, "I give you the venerable Nicholas Aleksandrovich Romanov II, Emperor and Autocrat of All the Russians."

As he backed away, all eyes turned to Nicholas.

Wilhelm looked over Nicholas's face, encrusted with dried blood. He placed his hand on his knee and bent over slightly as he inspected him. Finally, a smile appeared upon Wilhelm's face. He stared at the sickly, desperate-looking tsar, who cowered at the cage's far side as the seven men surrounded him.

"Hello, cousin," said Wilhelm.

Chapter 20

20

March 28, 1917, 11:41 p.m.

Felix sat in a hot bath, taking solace in the warmth surrounding his body as he finished shaving his beard. Gripping the straight razor in his hand, he fantasized about slicing it across Dmitri Pavlovich's neck and watching him bleed out. Of course, now that Dmitri had been converted to vámpir, Felix knew the final confrontation would require much more than a razor blade to the throat.

No matter the method, Felix believed he was prepared.

He sat with his knees to his chest and inspected his jawline in a hand mirror. Despite a few nicks that mixed his blood with the remnants of white foamy lather dripping from his face, he felt relieved to be looking at his reflection again—even if he appeared a bit more hollow and even slightly emaciated than he remembered.

"I'm going to look fifty in a week if I don't watch it."

He placed the straight razor on the tub's rim and splashed some hot water upon his face, rinsing the remaining lather before reaching over and setting the hand mirror on the tiled floor. Felix then lay back and submerged himself under the water, blowing bubbles from his nose as he swayed his head slightly to feel the water flow through his waving hair.

He emerged from the suds, and the cool air of the tiny washroom felt refreshing on his skin. He cupped his hands and threw water over his shoulders, attempting to prolong the sensation.

A knock came from the door.

"Yes?"

"Clean clothes outside the door," came Rurik's voice. "You're bigger than Denis and me, so I hope you can squeeze into them. Sorry, no underwear. You'll—uh—have to free-wrangle."

"I'm sure it's fine. Thanks."

"Don't mean to rush you, but dinner is almost prepared, and Zazlov says we only have about six hours before more Germans come looking for our feathered friends. We want to move before dawn."

"I'll be out shortly."

"Don't take too long. I miss you, buddy!"

Felix smiled and listened as Rurik's footsteps moved down the hall.

He relaxed, draping his left leg over the rim. Felix couldn't remember the last time he had felt so overjoyed just to have a roof over his head. Knowing a bona fide home-cooked meal was coming his way shortly, he reveled in the fleeting hopefulness that swept over him.

"A bottle of Drăculea's blood," he said, waving his arms under the warm water. "All this chaos and war over a damn bottle. That Kaiser is a real bastard."

He thought back to the conversation with Zazlov in the kitchen, and how nonchalant and accepting both Mary and Rurik had been of the news. Just when Felix thought his predicament couldn't possibly become more peculiar—well, it had certainly become far more peculiar. Zazlov had informed the group about the urgent hunt for the bottle of Drăculea's blood and the Kaiser's reason for seeking it, but he was oddly evasive when pressed on why the Death Witch had attacked Felix and why Zazlov had been tracking both him and Rurik, arriving just as the encounter occurred.

I sensed my friends were in danger, so I sought you both out, was all Zazlov would say.

Zazlov explained that the Death Witch had been enlisted as a mercenary in service of the Kaiser to bring them to justice for their actions in Zănoaga and Saint Petersburg.

You're wanted men now, said Zazlov.

Felix hadn't seen the Death Witch, but Rurik's description of her sounded terrifying. He was rather glad he'd been unconscious for that part. The Red Baron and his Jasta Eleven pilots were now vampires who could hunt them day or night from the sky. The Kaiser was trying to reincarnate Drăculea. And to top it all off, Elizabeth Báthory was alive and attempting to conjure demons.

Hold up, he told himself. *Say that aloud, and try not to sound like a crazy person.*

Felix sat up with a slosh of the water.

He retrieved the mirror from the floor and stared into it. "Elizabeth Báthory, as in the Blood Countess from the 1600s, is alive and she's trying to summon her demon father to enslave humanity. Oh! Felix, just wait! That's not all. She's also a giant white widow spider sequestered inside an invisible castle. And she too is seeking the Sommelier to free herself from a containment hex."

Hex? What the hell was a hex, anyway? Some type of spell?

Felix stared into his own eyes, then dropped the mirror into the water.

"This is utter insanity."

He lay back, took a few deep breaths, and massaged his scalp with his nails, trying to relax.

After the group discussed their options, Zazlov said he believed escaping to Paris was in everyone's best interest. Drăculea's blood was in Paris with the Sommelier, who Zazlov revealed was also Vlad Drăculea's estranged brother, Radu cel Frumos. It was urgent that they locate both the man and the bottle. Felix wondered why Zazlov hadn't attempted to obtain the bottle sooner.

When pressed on this point, Zazlov became curt: *The bottle is no longer safe with the Sommelier. I was in Paris seeking him out and sensed my friends were in danger, so I came to seek you out as quickly as I could. Now we must return so I may finish what I started.*

Felix didn't care.

His only thoughts were of making it to safety. With the supernatural entities now hunting them and the Germans quickly closing in on all sides, Romania had become a pressure cooker—Felix felt as if he were the meat.

It would be good to get to Paris. They'd be safe—finally. No spiders. No Drăculea. No demons. Felix could secure transport to Zurich, access his funds, and then he was out of this mess. South America. He envisioned making it to South America.

Somewhere tropical, far away from this disaster, where he could use his funds and resources to finally hunt down Dmitri and devise the best means to capture and kill him. Felix wondered briefly if Rurik would come along. Maybe they could bring Mary with them.

"What did she say again?" he said aloud, thinking of Mary's contribution to their escape plan. "Psycom-something? Psychometry?" She could simply touch a pilot, ingest his memories, and fly a plane. "No way. No way . . . I don't care."

Whatever her talents, it beat walking across Europe again. She'd morphed into a goddamn lamp for Christ's sake! And a boar? God, this was crazy.

Felix sat up and thought over Zazlov's words. *The Kaiser now knows where the bottle is. We must find our way to Paris and destroy it before his mercenaries obtain it.*

Something felt amiss.

Felix reflected on Zazlov's continued deflections of their pressing questions and wondered if the warlock was telling the truth. Rurik was right about Zazlov—he was hiding something.

"Why the hell doesn't this Sommelier character just smash this bottle himself? I didn't sign on for any of this."

The Inferno of the Witch, came Zazlov's words once more.

Felix ran through Zazlov's harrowing tale of the Crusades—the death, destruction . . . the terror. As he pieced it all together, he began to believe that the devils of the past were about to explode into the present in a very real and destructive way. What if the Kaiser succeeded? What if Elizabeth Báthory escaped? What if this Bael demon was reborn?

He envisioned the world overrun by ghouls and demons, and the hair on his neck spiked.

A panic swelled within him.

This will never end. South America may not be far enough.

He thought to what he had been through over the last four months, and became worried his predicament would worsen. He pulled his legs to his chest and wrapped his arms around them.

"I can't do this anymore. I think I'm done."

His mind fell to his slain parents. The grief that had haunted him most of his life stalked him once more, seeming to bubble up from the soapy water itself and crush his spirit in a hopeless vice.

Irina. Alexandra. Alexei. Even Denis. Florin? The kid? Hedrina?

Considering their current predicament, the list of the dead would soon include Rurik, Mary, Sebastian, and Zazlov—hell, likely himself.

His frustration over his inability to exact revenge upon Dmitri Pavlovich was almost unbearable.

"I'm such a failure," he said aloud.

Felix pictured himself standing upon the cliff at Loch Dracul, placing as many heavy stones in his pockets as he could cram in, then walking to the ledge and dropping into the murky depths—one painful breath in and it would all be over . . . sinking endlessly in peace forever and ever.

He'd lost everything he had because of these events.

He thought to lower himself into the tub once more and breathe out until no air was left.

His eyes fell on the straight razor resting on the bath's rim.

He reached for it and opened the blade, placing it gently against the supple flesh of his forearm. Closing his eyes, Felix imagined a short, quick pain, then the peace of lying back in the hot water—a final respite, a permanent escape.

He thought to Irina and how very badly he wanted to hold her again, to join her forever. Felix pressed the razor into his wrist with just shy of enough pressure to break the skin.

One quick slash. Do it. Just one quick slash.

The thumping of his heart seemed to grow in volume and silence all ambient sounds as Felix's gaze became transfixed on the razor's edge against his flesh. He took in a calming pocket of air and held it before letting out a despondent groan.

"In three . . . two . . . one . . ."

Cool air swept the room as the door swung open. Felix dropped the razor and stood to confront the intruder—the suds dripped down his soapy body.

Mary stood in the doorway, looking abashed.

"Do you mind!" yelled Felix, cupping himself with both hands.

"I'm so sorry," said Mary, averting her eyes. "I knocked three times."

"It was locked for a reason, you know!"

Felix noticed Mary's finger was in the shape of a skeleton key as she quickly hid her hand behind her back.

"I was worried when you didn't respond. So I—"

"Can you at least close the door?"

Mary reached for a towel hanging on the wall and threw it to Felix. "Dinner's almost ready. Again, I'm really sorry." She exited and slammed the door.

Felix stood for another moment before tossing the towel on the floor and sitting back in the tub.

He shook his head and smiled. "That was something," he said.

His hand found the razor's handle and he pulled it from the water.

"Stupid idea," he said, casting it on the towel.

He lay in the warm water, and his mind fell to Mary. It was true, what Rurik revealed. Felix definitely felt something toward her. She had a certain charm that invigorated him whenever she was near— an undeniable chemical reaction that radiated from his very bones. He'd felt it immediately when meeting her at the inn and again earlier in the day despite the shock of watching her transform from a lamp. No matter how beaten or bruised he was, Mary's presence made him feel alive in a way he hadn't experienced since Irina.

Mary, he thought. Mary was worth fighting for. And so was Rurik. No way. No way was this over. And in no universe was he going to sit back and allow these dark forces to harm or murder any of his friends.

"I'll smash that goddamn bottle against the Kaiser's face if it's the last thing I do."

He grew angry as he cupped his hands and splashed warm water on his face—the baptism of warmth further cleansing his despair.

Felix felt alive.

Felix was ready to fight.

*

Tsar Nicholas II winced as Minister Schmidt inserted the twenty-two-gauge straight needle into his median cubital vein.

"Does this hurt you?" questioned Schmidt.

Nicholas shook his head, his eyes fixed upon Schmidt's jugular vein through the cage bars.

"I assure you, Nicholas," said Schmidt casually, never taking his eyes from the cc tick marks along the metal needle's small glass window, "attacking me in any fashion would be the worst mistake you've ever made"—he studied Nicholas's sharp teeth and filthy face, briefly inspecting the crusty dirt lining Nicholas's wrinkles, before looking him dead in the eye—"in a life obviously full of wretched mistakes."

Schmidt pulled the syringe from Nicholas's arm and capped it, then held it aloft and inspected the volume markers. "Just enough blood that I can replicate its chemical makeup," he said, pocketing the syringe and turning to Wilhelm, who stood next to Ernest Louis and Prince Henry.

The three men held their noses and leaned into an empty metal table just past the curtained slabs containing the vámpir and ustrel specimens.

"Is there anything you can do about his smell?" asked Wilhelm.

"I suppose we can bathe him," said Schmidt.

"It's just piss and shit and decay, all at once. My God," said Ernest Louis.

Nicholas reached beyond the bars, careful not to touch the blackwood, and tugged at Schmidt's blazer.

"Can I have it now? You promised." said Nicholas in a thick Russian accent.

"Very well," said Schmidt as he walked to a noisy refrigerator and pulled out a glass jar containing seven hundred milliliters of blood. He returned to Nicholas, who became agitated as the bottle neared, thrashing his arms out of the cage and trying to grab it.

"Stop!" yelled Schmidt, pointing at Nicholas. "If you break this or drop it, I will give you no more. Do you understand?"

Nicholas cowered away from the bars. "Yes. I'm sorry. I'm simply starving."

Schmidt handed him the bottle. Nicholas turned his back to the room and began guzzling the cruor.

Wilhelm stepped forward and leaned into Schmidt. "You're certain this will work?"

"I am, Kaiser," he said, lowering his voice. "We should discuss our approach to this in private. It will be complicated to—" Schmidt turned to Nicholas to see him still feasting on the blood and licking it from his fingers.

"It's fine," said Wilhelm. "His German is terrible."

"Even still," said Schmidt. "We will have to create a new reality for him to believe in. I'm not certain we have honed the proper narrative yet."

"We will. He is my cousin after all. Despite our falling out, I believe I wield all the influence to keep him ignorant and behaving as we need."

Nicholas lowered the bottle and opened his mouth, letting out a long and extended belch that sounded more like a growl.

Wilhelm covered his nose once more. "Disgusting creature."

Nicholas looked to him. "Please, cousin. I'm sorry. I should have sided with you instead of Serbia. Is that what this is about? I don't understand. Please help me."

Wilhelm stared down at Nicholas with revulsion reflecting in his pupils. "I *am* helping you."

A telephone rang.

Nicholas appeared startled and stood, searching for the source of the intrusion as if he'd never heard such a sound. Schmidt walked to the phone as Wilhelm stood closer to the cage.

"It's a telephone, Nicholas. Certainly you remember what a telephone is?"

Nicholas nodded, wrapped his clawed hands around his bottle, and clutched it to his chest.

Schmidt pulled the phone receiver to his ear. "It's Schmidt," he said. "I see . . . yes . . . He's standing right in front of me . . . He's safe."

Wilhelm turned around to face Schmidt.

"What is it, Minister?"

Schmidt continued speaking into the phone in hushed tones. He turned and his eyes grew wide as Nicholas reached out to Wilhelm and pulled him in toward the cage, his fangs intent on Wilhelm's trapezius muscle. Wilhelm hit his head upon the bars and lost his footing, sliding to the ground as Nicholas followed and pulled his arm into the cage, attempting to bite his forearm.

"*Inpedious-balactum!*" shouted Schmidt, holding his arm out as if he were lifting something from the ground.

Nicholas choked and gagged, grabbing his throat as an invisible force lifted him and slammed his head into the top of the cage, burning his cheek. Wilhelm slid away as Ernest Louis and Prince Henry ran to his assistance and pulled him from the floor. Schmidt continued toward the cage, never lowering his arm.

"Foul creature," he said, clenching his fist. "I warned you."

Nicholas continued thrashing about. Schmidt relaxed his hand, causing Nicholas to crash to the floor and cower upon his knees, placing his face in his hands and weeping as a yellowish smoke rose from between his fingers. Schmidt stood before the cage as the rest backed away to the empty metal slab.

"Do that again, and I'll tear your head clean from your body. Do you understand me?"

Nicholas looked to him with tears running down his face. "Please help me. I don't understand what's happening." His desperate eyes shot to Wilhelm. "Pray for me, cousin. I feel so sick."

Schmidt kicked the bars with his polished black boot.

"Enough, savage."

Nicholas looked up to him with a quivering chin. He closed his eyes, then buried his face in his hands, continuing to weep.

"What was the message?" asked Wilhelm. "It sounded urgent."

Schmidt turned to him.

"My Kaiser," he said. "I regret to inform you there has been an assassination attempt at the palace."

"Augusta?"

"She's gone missing. The palace guard killed some of the French mercenaries responsible, but so far they have not located her. She's definitely been taken from the palace."

"Damn these French!" shouted Wilhelm. "I should have been there. She doesn't deserve to be caught up in this."

His anger appeared to give way to panic as he placed his hand to his stomach and leaned back against the slab.

Ernest Louis and Prince Henry moved next to Wilhelm and rested their hands upon his shoulders.

"Come," said Schmidt. "Your security detail is awaiting upstairs. We have to move you to a secure location."

Wilhelm shook off his daze and stared at Nicholas.

"What about him?"

"He'll be safe here until we find something permanent," said Schmidt. "Oh, and Nicholas," he said, opening the curtains to reveal the vámpir and ustrel specimens.

Nicholas's yellowing eyes followed him.

"Next time you lose your senses, this will be your fate."Schmidt reached down and pressed the button on each slab, activating the blackwood hydraulic devices, which descended with the sound of an air piston and fired into the hearts of the undead.

A searing wail came from both monsters as their bodies disintegrated to dust.

*

Felix entered the kitchen wearing Denis's nondescript clothing. The only remarkable element of the garments was their sheer starchiness, which caused him to shift them constantly, trying to keep them from chafing his still open scrapes.

"They fit!" said Rurik, who was busy stirring a large pan full of food. "Baby face," he said upon noticing Felix's beard was gone. "I've decided to keep mine."

"It's a good look for you," said Felix, adjusting his garments once more.

Felix walked to the table and sat next to Mary, and the two exchanged a pleasant but uncomfortable glance. He looked across the table to Zazlov and once again found himself questioning the warlock's intentions. He shook off the thought when Rurik moved from the stove with a pan full of chopped sausages and vegetables.

"This was the best I could muster," said Rurik, circling the table and dumping a ladleful of his concoction onto each person's plate. He returned the pan to the stove, then sat at the table, plopping a large bread basket down in the middle.

"Smells pretty tasty," said Felix. "I've become used to your stew, so this is fine dining as far as I see it."

"Hey!" said Rurik, pointing at him. "That stew kept us fed for nearly three months. Pretty sure there's still a can of beans in my sack if you'd prefer."

Felix raised his hands. "No, no. This is great."

"Marvelous meal," said Zazlov, reaching for some bread.

Felix looked around the kitchen. "Where's Sebastian?"

Zazlov motioned toward the greenhouse.

Felix turned to see Sebastian sitting upon the greenhouse floor with his legs crossed. His head hung low and he appeared to be breathing deeply.

"He feels safe among his own kind," said Mary.

"How's that?" asked Felix.

"Plant life. When my father reanimated him, he infused Sebastian's cellular makeup with embryophyta and hogweed. Apparently aids in circulation of any necrotic tissue and also healing wounds. Sebastian is actually quite a talented healer. And with the hogweed infusion . . . well, just watch him touch a vampire and see what happens."

"That's incredible," said Felix. "Isn't he going to join us?"

"Doesn't need to," said Mary. "He essentially runs on sunlight."

"Photosynthesis," said Rurik. "Quite genius, if you think about it. Denis was trying to devise a way to integrate it into human cells, but obviously . . . well."

Mary interjected, "Sebastian is an amalgam of plant, human, and . . . wait for it . . . yeti."

"Yeti? Like a menk?"

"Menk, Bigfoot—whatever you want to call it," said Mary.

"Why's he hairless, then?" asked Felix.

"I'd venture the three hundred million volts of electricity my father shot through him had something to do with it."

Felix stared at Sebastian for another moment, then picked up his silverware. As everyone around the table dug in, Felix watched Mary fumble with a blunt wooden fork.

"Here, use mine," he said, playfully tapping his fork on Mary's wrist.

"Na!" screamed Mary, freezing in position at once with her eyes wide open.

"Felix!" yelled Rurik, reaching across the table and slapping the fork from his hand.

Mary immediately shot up from the table and backed away from Felix with fear on her face.

"You clumsy oaf!" she yelled.

Felix raised his hands. "What did I do?"

"Calm down, Mary. He didn't know," said Rurik, sitting back down.

Mary walked back to the table and sat next to Felix. She angrily grabbed her wooden fork. "The reason I use wooden utensils is because I'm direly allergic to silver. It immobilizes me."

Felix was pale. "I—I'm so sorry. I had no idea. Can it kill you?"

"No. A silver stake to the heart—yes. But I can't even touch it or my system simply freezes. I can't move at all."

"I'm so sorry, Mary. I had no—"

"Let's move past it," said Mary.

"It is known that silver can disable shape-shifters," said Zazlov, chewing on a mouthful of carrots and sausages. "All witches have a weakness unique to their own persona. I once knew a witch who was so allergic to water that she lived alone in the middle of the desert. Too much moisture in the air would melt her skin."

"What about you?" asked Felix. "What's your weakness?"

"A genuine smile and a fat cut of steak." Zazlov grinned. "A true warlock never tells."

Felix seemed deflated as he turned his attention back to his plate.

"Well," continued Zazlov, "silver is problematic for us all to some degree. Silver fetters are a very common means of containing a rogue witch. Bare minimum, it will turn one's skin a wretched green and deaden one's powers. Molten silver—oh, boy. Now, that will destroy most any supernatural."

"Not me," said Mary. "But it would certainly turn me into a nice wall decoration."

"You'd make a pleasant addition to any sculpture garden, young Mary."

Mary laughed.

"Don't laugh," said Zazlov. "I haven't told you the story of Baphomet."

"The goat demon?" asked Mary. "I know of this one. He disappeared around the time Drăculea unleashed the Nosferatu."

"That's correct," said Zazlov. "But he was far more dangerous than suggested by the Sabbatic Goat symbol by which he is now depicted. Master of the bloodthirsty Knights Templar during the Inferno. And lucky for you that he did disappear, young Mary, as he kept a pool of molten silver in his dungeon. Baphomet would make his enemies walk the plank, then save whatever remained of them for his grotesque collection of silver statues. He preferred to keep his true identity a secret and was known primarily as the Doppelgänger, as he swapped in and out of many identities to confuse and manipulate his enemies. The Black Butcher was probably his most famous. Baphomet is an anomaly in demonology as he spawns not from the Void but was the rare offspring of two demons—Queen Kimaris and King Bael."

"King Bael, as in Elizabeth Báthory's father?" asked Felix.

Zazlov remained silent as the implication spread around the table.

"Baphomet is Elizabeth's brother," said Mary, appearing pale.

"Half siblings," said Zazlov. "Elizabeth's mother was mortal."

"Did he have a peg leg and parrot to go along with the plank?" asked Rurik, clearly trying to lighten the mood.

"No, no," said Zazlov. "Poor parrot wouldn't last ten minutes. When Baphomet embodied his Black Butcher persona, he was terribly cruel. Although he did shepherd and protect a pack of werewolves during the Inferno. They in turn acted as his guardians, but I question the alliance. Werewolf blood holds many magical properties. It is my assumption he was keeping them close to feed on them and grow his power. The tales surrounding him are quite heinous."

Felix listened intently as Zazlov explained that Baphomet's core power was similar to Mary's shape-shifting. The difference being that the demon was a mimic—a heinously destructive shadow entity that absorbed cloned copies of people by touching them, then impersonated those individuals down to the smallest inflection in their voice. But being a demon, Baphomet could maintain that identity indefinitely. Felix's mind raced with suspicious thoughts of people from his past as Zazlov told them that mimics thrived on misery—destroying families, communities, and as witnessed in the Greek and Roman Empires, world governments.

Baphomet had earned the Black Butcher moniker during the Inferno from being a merciless eugenicist. The demon grew obsessed with creating a master Aryan race of humans who would rule over the rest of humanity as proxies for Solomon's demons. Baphomet was apparently so driven to create this master race that he was known to behead people if he didn't like the shape of their nose. The descriptions of this entity chilled Felix, especially the detail of his executioner's hood with no eyeholes in the fabric. The Black Butcher slaughtered for sport and, like all demons, was a voracious cannibal.

"That's quite a rap sheet," said Felix, looking over his sausages and wondering if he'd lost his appetite. "What happened to him?"

"Our invisible friend, the Sommelier, trapped him in an enchanted mirror."

The sounds of silverware hitting the plates rang through the kitchen.

"Trapped in a mirror?" asked Rurik.

"Indeed," said Zazlov smiling broadly. "Radu is a clever man. Not particularly the most powerful warlock, but the mind of a fox—according to the historical records, anyway."

"Where's the mirror?" asked Mary.

"No one can say. It was rumored Radu buried it somewhere deep in the Black Forest. Baphomet has never been seen since, but if he ever arises—the world is in grave danger. Until then, it's just one of those wonderful ghost stories I tell to frighten mortals."

"Gives me the shivers too," said Mary.

"I'm beginning to wonder if Radu even exists," said Felix. "All these stories. Nobody has ever seen him. Sounds like a bit of a jerk. Selfishly holding on to this bottle when he could just smash it. Would have saved a lot of lives."

Zazlov became suddenly stern. "That bottle contains the blood of his only brother. What would you have done if you had the chance to resurrect your brother—redeem him? Just smash it to oblivion? Certainly, Radu had his reasoning. He's a cunning warlock, and through the centuries has proven himself to always do the right thing at great cost to himself—even ostracism by his brethren."

"I didn't mean to offend," said Felix, looking sincerely to Zazlov. "I simply don't understand why he hasn't smashed the bottle, considering all the carnage around it."

"Because it has as much power to do good as it could evil," said Zazlov, raising his voice. "Do not mistake his patience for selfishness."

Felix raised his hands. "I won't."

"You speak as if you know the man," said Rurik with a curious gleam in his eye.

Zazlov hung his head and relented. "Forgive me. My frustration is getting the better of me. But have faith. I sense we will meet him soon enough."

"I'll take your word for it," said Felix. "I was actually more interested in the warlock weaknesses."

"Oh. Well, there's silver. Moving water will also gravely wound most witches. Rivers, waterfalls. It's very rare to find a witch living near a moving body of water. Some are immune. Myself, for example. Nothing I love better than a refreshing swim in a pristine river. Then there are immolations, beheadings, mortal wounds, dark witchcraft—all wonderful things to be discussed over dinner."

"Hey," said Felix, "you're the one bringing up butchers and cannibalism—"

"Felix!" said Mary, slapping him on the arm.

"What? Zazlov started it."

Felix picked up his fork and dug into his sausages. "Rurik," he said with a full mouth, "you've done it again."

"I'm starting to realize my culinary skills are best suited for the starving."

The company returned to silence and finished their meal.

Afterward, Rurik removed everyone's settings and piled the dirty dishes high in the sink.

"No sense in washing. I don't believe we'll be returning."

"No. We will not," said Zazlov, closing his eyes. "We have five hours before anyone comes looking for our chickens. I suggest we all try to get as much sleep as we can, as we will need it. We move just before dawn. Is everyone clear on their respective duties?"

Rurik and Mary nodded.

Felix raised his hand. "I do have a question. If I'm to man this gun on the bomber . . . how am I supposed to do that? I've never handled anything other than rifles and revolvers."

"You can fire it once briefed?" asked Zazlov.

"Most likely."

"No issue, then. I can merely touch the weapon and acquaint myself with its mechanical workings."

"I sure would love to acquire that skill myself."

"Careful what you ask for," said Zazlov. "Psychometry is not a skill to be taken lightly. Absorb the wrong info from the wrong person or object and . . . well, I've seen witches and warlocks of the highest caliber driven insane."

"Very true. I hold several memories that I wish I didn't have," said Mary.

"Best to stick to your marksmanship," said Zazlov.

Felix nodded, his eyes moving to Zazlov's sword, which was sheathed and leaning against the cabinetry. "Speaking of weapons . . ."

"I know where you're going. And the answer is no. Some things are better left unknown to mortals."

"Come on, Zazlov!" said Rurik. "Give us something. We promise not to touch it."

Zazlov looked to both men, and a faint smile appeared at the corners of his mouth. He swayed his head back and forth, considering their request. "Fine. But then no more of it!"

Felix, Rurik, and Mary leaned forward with great curiosity as Zazlov casually sauntered to his blade. He looked to the table with wide eyes and unsheathed the weapon. A low humming and crackling filled the room.

"Wow," said Felix. "It looks like stars."

"It *is* stars," said Zazlov, holding the blade outward. "Technically this blade is its own entire universe. Powered by this nasty fellow." He pointed to the glowing gray jewel at its hilt. "Each of these blades is named after the demon imprisoned within its jewel."

"There's more than one?" asked Felix.

"Seventy-two of them, to be exact," said Zazlov as he gripped the gem and struggled for a minute, finally popping it from the pommel. The sword fell to dark gray at once and ceased humming.

"Now you may touch it," said Zazlov, handing the blade to Felix. "Be extremely careful though. A mere cut from a Masamune blade will sever your soul right from your body."

Felix stood and held it before him, practicing a few parry positions he'd learned from fencing in military academy.

"Very good, Felix. I see you can handle a blade."

"Eighth place in my class fencing tournament."

"That's not really something I'd brag about," said Mary.

Felix relaxed his arm and handed the blade back to Zazlov.

"Better than ninth place," said Felix.

"But not quite as good as the seven other people who'd flay you in battle," said Mary.

"Now," said Zazlov, moving the jewel to the hilt. "Watch."

As the jewel came closer to the hilt, it began to shift and vibrate in Zazlov's palm, finally thrusting itself onto the pommel and igniting the blade.

"Now, that's impressive," said Rurik.

"Incredibly dangerous weapon," continued Zazlov. "You see, it doesn't cut—it absorbs. If I were to place it near your skin, you would feel the blade's gravity pulling you toward it. And once that happens, you're sucked into its dimensional field, and essentially food for the foul creature imprisoned in the hilt. Hence, the name: demon blades."

"It's quite mesmerizing," said Mary, watching as Zazlov waved it with a few slashing movements.

"I don't get it, though," said Rurik. "When the Death Witch came at me and hit the ground with her blades, I looked back to see a huge crater in the earth. What happens if you drop it? Just falls to the center of the earth? Absorbs the core?"

"Ha!" said Zazlov. "A very astute observation. Behold!" He cast the blade into the air, and the rest watched as it sailed to the floor and hovered just above the tile.

"Whoa," said Felix. "How the—"

"It's repelled by the earth's magnetic field. Mind you, the un-sheathed blade can breach the field with great force as Rurik witnessed, but not for long. It will always return to its natural magnetic resonance point outside the earth's magnetism. And say you happen to be in a two-story building and drop the blade. Naturally, you'd think it would sink to the basement. Alas—it seems the blades are somewhat bound to their masters. It would stay in a position near the witch who wields it."

"That's one of the most amazing things I've ever witnessed," said Felix. "How did you acquire it?"

"Op!" said Zazlov, raising a finger. "I've said too much. No more questions." He extended his hand and the blade shot into his fist. Zazlov sheathed it and placed it back against the counter. "Another reminder—do not touch it under any circumstances, or you too will meet the demon."

Felix and Rurik nodded.

Zazlov sat at the table. "Now that our little demonstration is finished, I will remind you again that our main concern when we approach the airfield is the vampires. I foresee they will be resting as it will be near dawn, but just be prepared." He looked to Rurik. "Ensure that your new canister devices are full."

"Aye-aye, Captain. But what about this Death Witch? If she arrives and interferes—"

"I can see she put quite a scare into you," said Zazlov.

"Well," said Rurik, "she is terrifying."

"Agreed," said Zazlov. "A proxy spawned and controlled by Elizabeth Báthory is a grave threat to us all. Very foul intentions are afoot. I cannot currently sense her, but if she does happen to re-emerge, leave her to me. Under no circumstances are you to engage. In short—run."

"Understood," said Rurik.

"Excellent," said Zazlov, squeezing Rurik's forearm with his powerful hand. "And to the rest of you, good luck. I foresee gray around this operation, but there is light . . . I sense we will be successful. Once airborne, we will head for Paris. It's imperative we make it there—for our safety and for any hope of finding this bottle before the Germans do. For now, I'm exhausted. Let's rest as best we can, and I'll waken us before dawn."

21

March 29, 1917, 6:32 a.m.

Felix scrunched his face and inhaled sharply through his nose as a falling sensation woke him. His eyes roamed Denis's kitchen for a moment until the happenings of the past several days came back to him and reminded him where he was. Felix sat up from the kitchen floor, pulled away his blanket, and tried to click his spine into place as he caught sight of Sebastian, who was standing in the greenhouse, basking in a direct beam of light from the early morning sunrise.

A loud bang came from Denis's front door, startling Felix.

I'll wake us before dawn, came Zazlov's words.

Felix's exhausted mind quickly threw the events together: *Sunbeam, loud bang, Zazlov not waking us at dawn.*

Two more bangs erupted from above and Felix began to panic. He looked at Mary and Rurik, who were still asleep next to the large iron door that led to Denis's basement.

"Guys," whispered Felix. "Guys, wake up."

Rurik stirred as another bang rang out, causing him to sit upright.

"Mary," said Rurik, shaking her shoulder.

Mary turned over and watched as Sebastian entered the kitchen from the sunlit greenhouse. Then she sat up quickly. "Where's Zazlov?"

Everyone stood and ran into the sitting room to find Zazlov snoring on the sofa.

"Zazlov!" yelled Mary. "Wake up! It's past dawn."

Another intense bang came from above, followed by the wooden door tumbling down the stairs, shattering the mirror embedded in its façade.

"Oh, dear," said Zazlov, widening and blinking his eyes. "It appears I've overslept."

Bootsteps thundered down the stairs as three German soldiers entered the premises.

"*Tilmarius!*" said Zazlov, freezing the soldiers in place upon the stairs. "Hurry," he said, turning back to the group. "That spell won't last."

Zazlov strapped his demon blade around his waist as the rest filed into the kitchen.

Felix and Rurik slung their new hogweed canisters appropriated from Denis's greenhouse over their backs, then hoisted smaller supply pouches around their shoulders as Mary and Sebastian slipped on larger duffel bags.

"Hurry! In here," said Mary, opening the large iron door to the basement.

Felix and Rurik entered first, followed by Mary, and they made their way into the musty, cavernous basement filled with Denis's reanimation equipment.

Zazlov turned to see Sebastian standing by the kitchen table, seemingly frozen in his stance.

"Well?" said Zazlov. "Come on!"

Sebastian shook his head and backed away. The sound of the soldiers shuffling down the stairs could be heard from the kitchen.

"Sebastian. Now!"

"He's afraid of the basement," came Mary's voice from below. "It's where he was—"

"Sebastian!" shouted Zazlov as the rushing soldiers sprinted down the hall toward the kitchen.

Zazlov looked to the pouch on Sebastian's belt and extended his hand—Dollie sailed across the room and flew into Zazlov's fist. He dangled it in the air as Sebastian tore after the doll. Zazlov tossed it down the stairs and Sebastian followed.

Three German soldiers entered the kitchen—the lead soldier firing at Zazlov, who pulled out his blade in a flash and absorbed the bullets. He then threw the weapon end over end into the line of soldiers, piercing the lead through the gut and impaling the soldier behind him. The third man backed away in horror at the sight of his comrades being absorbed by the blade, screaming and choking as their bones cracked and snapped into the black sliver. He turned quickly on his heel as Zazlov pushed the blade through the other two soldiers and stabbed him in the spine.

Zazlov lifted his arm and the blade shot back to him. He sheathed the sword and watched as the perfectly cauterized heads and shoulders of the three men fell on top of what remained of their calves and boots—their torsos and thighs had completely disappeared. Zazlov pulled on the heavy iron door, sealed and locked it, then descended into the basement.

"What the hell is the matter with you?" yelled Mary, charging toward Zazlov. "This big plan of yours is ruined!"

Zazlov leaned against the wall and looked to Sebastian, who held Dollie close to his chest.

"I'm sorry. I let you all down. I'm terribly exhausted."

"Unbelievable!" Mary clenched her fists and let out a near growl as she turned and made her way to a ladder on the opposite side of the basement.

"It's all right, Zazlov," said Rurik. "We'll figure a way out."

"Sebastian. You OK, buddy?" asked Felix.

Sebastian shook his head and backed farther into the moss-covered bricks near the stair.

"Oh, Sebastian," said Mary, coming back to the group. She approached Sebastian as his scared eyes scanned the darkened laboratory. The moment he was able to make out a rickety iron slab with a strange-looking arrow device hanging over it, he turned and pressed his face into the wall.

Mary placed her hand upon Sebastian's protruding triceps. "Hey. It's me. Sebastian, come on. We have to go. You know I would never hurt you. I've always looked out for you, and I need you to climb that ladder over there with me. Your friends need you. Can you do it for us?"

Sebastian shook his head and turned to face the corner.

"Those men up there," continued Mary. "They're very bad men. And they intend to hurt me and all your new friends. But especially Dollie. If they catch us, nobody will be left to protect her."

Sebastian turned at once, knocking Mary back a few steps. Felix looked to Sebastian's face and became a bit unnerved at the sense of resolve shining from his eyes. The giant man placed Dollie in his leather pouch and buckled it closed. He then marched past the group, right to the ladder.

"Careful, Sebastian," said Mary, as he turned the wheel to an escape hatch at the top of the iron ladder.

After a few small rotations, a latch swung downward and doused Sebastian in water pouring in from a well above. The water continued flowing with great force until the portion of the basement they were standing in was flooded nearly ankle-deep.

Mary leaned into the ladder and looked upward. "It looks clear . . . Zazlov?"

"Reveille is in five minutes. We have time. Go. Everyone to your posts once we surface."

Mary led the charge up the ladder. Sebastian followed, barely able to squeeze himself through the tight space.

"Mortals first," said Zazlov, with a chivalrous bow.

Rurik and Felix scurried upward.

Zazlov took one last look around the basement and ascended the slippery ladder.

*

Felix slumped over the well's brick wall and lay low against the ground next to the others as Zazlov's bald head rose from below. The burly warlock pulled himself over the well and lay on the ground next to Sebastian.

"I just realized I left my helmet behind," he said.

"You mean that goat skull?" said Mary. "Leave it. What's the point of it, even?"

"Long story. Mostly for intimidation."

"Well, color me unimpressed," she replied.

"I thought it was pretty scary," said Felix.

"Gave me the creeps," said Rurik.

"You see!" said Zazlov. "It works."

Mary shook her head. "You are the strangest lot I've ever met—for the record." She looked to Zazlov. "Am I clear?"

"You are clear," said Zazlov. "Remember—the tent on the right. Left tent is the vampire roost."

"Well, here goes," she said, pulling off her duffel bag and handing it to Sebastian. Mary then ran toward the tent barracks, intent on completing her mission to pull memories from a pilot.

Felix watched her form shimmer and break into pieces as she transformed into a dozen large rats. He lost sight of her in the tall grass, but could see the tips of the stalks swaying as the rodents scurried through.

"Amazing," he said.

"How long?" asked Rurik, turning to Zazlov.

"Reveille in two. Mary arriving at the barracks in one. We go on three . . . two . . . now. Go now."

All four men ran for the airfield.

"The red plane first, Sebastian! That's the important one," Zazlov shouted after Sebastian's hulking frame.

Rurik, Felix, and Zazlov dashed toward the bomber at the end of the runway as Sebastian headed toward the line of airplanes along the track. He made it to the Red Baron's triplane, reached up, and pulled down on the right wing, collapsing all three wings to the ground. He then turned and tore the wings from a matte black monoplane.

A siren rang through the grounds.

"That's enough, Sebastian," yelled Zazlov from across the field as the rest reached the bomber.

Sebastian nodded and ran to one more monoplane. He wrapped his powerful hands around the propeller and tore the entire engine clean from its bracket before rejoining his friends.

"How do we get in?" asked Felix, looking up to the door on the side of the plane.

"Here. On my shoulders," said Rurik.

343

Rurik crouched and Felix climbed on his shoulders, careful not to disturb the hogweed canisters on his back. Rurik's knees buckled a bit as he lifted Felix.

"It's locked!" said Felix, looking to Zazlov.

Zazlov raised his palm, and Felix heard a click. He opened the door and crawled inside the plane. After ripping his canister and satchel from his back, he lowered a metal staircase that extended to the ground.

Rurik and Zazlov ascended the stair to join him.

The inside of the bomber was much more spacious than Felix had expected, yet somehow still felt cramped. There was enough room for two people to stand side by side in the hollow corridor that stretched nearly from tail to cockpit, and just about four meters of space from the floor to the roof. A platform hung from the ceiling, and slim metal pegs jutted from the corridor wall. Felix hoisted himself up on the platform, using the pegs to support his feet. After flipping open the semicircular roof hatch, he tried to acquaint himself with the Maschinengewehr 08 machine gun before him. He practiced swinging it around its lever device, which sat in the center of a U-shaped cutaway, providing him with a nearly three-hundred-degree firing swoop from tail to nose.

"Uh, Zazlov?" he called below.

Felix looked into the distance and watched Sebastian rounding the plane as Zazlov squeezed into the gunner perch and placed his hand on the machine gun.

"Here," he said, flipping open a latch on the gun. "Feed for bullets is here. Unlatch this. Place them in so." Zazlov reached to a box at his feet and opened it to reveal an ammunition belt. He pulled the string of bullets into the feed and slammed the latch.

"Now what?" asked Felix, grabbing a pair of goggles hanging next to the ammunition box and strapping them over his face.

"Now you pull the trigger and cover us," said Zazlov, pointing to a group of soldiers emerging from the tents in various states of undress.

Gunshots rang out, and several bullets whizzed by Felix and Zazlov.

"No time like the present," said Zazlov, disappearing below.

Felix swung the gun to his right and pulled the trigger, unleashing a salvo of bullets at the soldiers exiting the tents. He looked to the grass below to see a mischief of rats jumping along the airfield as their bodies morphed back together one by one, eventually reforming into Mary dashing toward the plane.

"I did it! I did it!" she shouted.

"Hurry, then!" screamed Felix, firing relentlessly into the tents.

Mary entered the plane and moved toward the double-seated cockpit. She slid into the left seat and smiled as Sebastian wedged himself into the seat next to her. He smiled and bobbed with excitement.

"Copilot. I like it!" she said, flipping a few levers on the console before stopping suddenly. "Uh, Zazlov?" said Mary.

"Yes?"

"We have a slight problem. Huge, actually."

"What is it?" he asked as he shuffled toward the cockpit.

Mary continued running her fingers along the console as if she were looking for a certain button or lever.

"So, the pilots I touched"—Mary turned to him—"well, as it turns out, they were backup pilots here on reserve . . . and have never flown a plane like this." She banged her fists into her lap. "I knew I should have taken my father up on flying lessons!"

"You psyched trainees?"

"It was dark in there! I didn't know. I can't even figure out how to fire the engines."

Zazlov shook his head as Sebastian planted his palm to his forehead.

"Watch it, you!" said Mary, pointing at him.

"Sorry," said Sebastian raising his hands.

Zazlov closed his fist, touched the pilot's console, and the engines spun to life.

"OK, OK . . . we can do this," said Mary, rubbing her hands together. "Plane's a plane, right?"

"Just get us off the ground," said Zazlov.

"Guys—we need to get airborne now!" came Felix's voice from above, followed by more gunfire.

Rurik joined Zazlov at the front and they both peered out the cockpit's left window to see the Germans setting up two Maschinengewehr machine guns toward the side of the runway.

"Would be a great time to display those marksmanship skills of yours," Zazlov called up to Felix.

"This thing has zero precision!" shouted Felix as he spattered more bullets into the distance. "Can't you zap them or something?"

"So you're the warlock now?" yelled Zazlov. "How about you point and shoot and I'll worry about the witchcraft?"

"Temper, temper," replied Felix.

The plane lurched forward as Felix noticed sudden cloud cover darkening the otherwise sunny morning. He set his sights on the two unscathed monoplanes and opened fire on them, completely destroying the craft with explosive fury as the bullets tore through their engines and ruptured the fuel lines.

"Nice thinking!" shouted Rurik from below.

Felix angled his gun toward the remaining three biplanes as the bomber gained speed. He managed to obliterate the first in line before losing his balance as his plane bounced along the grassy field. Two biplanes still sat completely intact and ready to launch. He steadied himself and positioned to fire as he saw a horseback rider emerge from the woods in the distance.

"The Death Witch," cursed Felix, swinging the gun toward the back of the plane. He watched with dread as she advanced toward them on her ashen Hellhorse.

"Hit the throttle!" yelled Felix. "We have some very bad company!"

He tried to target the Death Witch, but she was tracking them directly behind the tail. Fearing he would blow the tail to bits, Felix turned the gun once more to the barracks as a barrage of bullets whizzed by him, tearing through the plane's roof just near his chest. He dropped from the perch and ducked on the corridor's floor, watching as the end of the runway approached quickly through the cockpit glass.

"Get back up there!" yelled Zazlov.

"That witch! She's charging us," said Felix.

"Oh, no," said Zazlov, moving to the gunner perch.

Zazlov emerged at the plane's roof and thrust his hand at the Death Witch, who was nearly upon them. She unsheathed one of her demon blades and pointed it at Zazlov, who shot a purple bolt of lightning at her as three bullets buzzed by his head—one of which nipped his cloak. The enchantress raised her blade and absorbed the electrical beam, pressing even faster toward the plane.

"Get us off the ground!" shouted Zazlov as the plane skipped and bobbed just above the grass.

He dropped from the perch and moved to the cockpit, pulling Rurik and Felix behind him.

"Here!" he yelled, thrusting downward on the throttle lever. "Now, pull up!"

"I'm trying," grunted Mary as she leaned back and pulled on the control yoke.

The plane lurched upward, barely clearing the tree line as a metallic bang came from the plane's starboard.

"What was that?" shouted Rurik.

Zazlov looked starboard and peeked down to see that the landing wheel was entirely missing.

"There goes any semblance of a safe landing," he said.

"We hit a tree?" asked Felix.

"No. We were struck by her blade."

"I have this. I have this," said Mary. "It's not so bad once in the air."

"Get us as high as you can," said Zazlov. "We need cloud cov—"

Everyone suddenly slid toward the cockpit with Rurik and Felix piling onto Zazlov, who was pinned to the back of Mary's chair. The plane seemed to collide into an invisible wall. Its engines screeched as the craft tried to lurch forward—a shower of electric white lightning enveloped the windows.

Zazlov heaved himself from the floor and leaned into the cockpit, gripping the throttle. "Keep pulling up."

"Doing all I can!" yelled Mary.

"What's happening?" asked Rurik.

Zazlov grunted. "Traction spell. She's pulling us back."

"Can't you—"

"Leave the witchcraft to the witches!" scolded Zazlov, who struggled against the throttle lever as it appeared to push back against him. "Keep aiming up. We're heavy and the engines are powerful enough, so just a little more oomph."

The sky before them became more visible as the white static started to dissipate. The interior continued to rattle and shake.

"Just a bit more," groaned Zazlov. "Strap yourselves in, gentlemen! We're about to go boom."

Felix and Rurik scattered to the plane's tail and braced their backs against the corridor's end.

The static was nearly gone from the windows. "And now!" shouted Zazlov, clenching his fist and breaking the remainder of the spell. He gripped Mary's seatback as the plane shot forward with incredible speed.

A few moments passed and the aircraft settled to a normal cruising speed.

"Hoo! That was close," said Zazlov, relaxing as the plane settled. "Clever one, this new Death Witch—goading me into combating her, knowing full well the Pyrrhic nature of traction spells."

Mary gave him a curious glance. "What the hell does that mean?"

"Had I countered her to break free, we'd have been stuck in battle until one of us ran out of energy. Psychic tug-of-war, essentially. She's a chess player, this one."

"Everyone OK?" shouted Felix from the back.

"We're fine, Master Felix. Back to the perch."

Felix climbed back to his gunner position and peered down at Denis's farm. He could see twenty or so soldiers moving onto the field and aiming their rifles at the Death Witch, who sat on her Hellhorse at the end of the runway, looking upward to the bomber as it escaped. Felix then noticed a series of shadows emerge from the vampires' tent and run toward the Red Baron's squadron planes. A few of them banged their fists into the planes' metal sides. Felix focused on the pilot he believed to be the Red Baron, but it was difficult to discern because of their canvas-covered bodies. His eyes widened as two human pilots dashed along the line of destroyed aircraft and hopped into the last two working biplanes, firing up their engines.

Felix swung down into the corridor.

"We're about to have a serious problem!" he shouted.

Mary leaned from the cockpit and made eye contact with Felix. "In case you haven't noticed, Your Eminence, we've been having nothing *but* serious problems!"

"Two biplanes, incoming," said Felix. "So . . . do pilot stuff! I'll man the gun." He popped back to his weapon.

Mary gripped the controls and tried to steady the plane as they ascended.

"Do pilot stuff," she grumbled, looking to Sebastian.

Sebastian shrugged and forced an awkward smile. He then placed his hand in his leather pouch and pulled out Dollie, gazing into its one-eyed rabbit face.

"Don wor, Dol-dol. I keep safe," he said, patting her head.

*

Roughly ten minutes had passed.

Zazlov and Rurik stood behind Mary and Sebastian as they all nervously scanned the horizon.

Zazlov walked to the gunner perch.

Any sign of them?" asked Zazlov.

"Not yet," shouted Felix.

"You feel that shaking?" yelled Rurik over the sound of the sputtering plane engines.

"I think that's just how flying feels," said Mary. "Hold on."

She ran her fingers across the console, then settled on pulling back upon the throttle as they continued to ascend into thicker cloud cover.

"There. I think that will do it," she said. "Too much stress on the—"

The engines sputtered and choked.

Rurik looked out the window to see them both spit black smoke from their exhaust.

"That can't be good."

"You think so, Uncle?" said Mary, agitated.

She looked on in horror as the propellers jerked to a sudden stop. The plane sailed downward.

"Hold on. I have this. I have this." Mary flipped a few switches on her console.

Zazlov stood next to Rurik and looked out to the dead engines.

"One moment," he said, closing his eyes and holding out his hands. The engines sputtered to life and then stopped again. Zazlov shrugged and tried once more, to the same effect.

"Must be the fuel line," said Mary, scanning her instrument consoles. "Says we're half-full. This teleportation plan of yours better work! No way we're making it to Paris on half a tank."

Mary reached over to Sebastian and placed both her hands upon his forearm. She closed her eyes for a moment and squeezed his arms as she transferred the piloting instructions into his mind.

"Do you have it?" she asked.

Sebastian nodded.

"Just hold it steady."

Sebastian grabbed the yoke, and Mary hopped up from her seat.

"You mind?" she said, sliding past Rurik and Zazlov to a console near Felix's gunner perch. "Any sign of them?" she asked, looking up to Felix.

Felix poked his head down. "Why are the engines stopped?"

"You worry about the planes. I'll worry about the engines."

Felix shook his head and returned to his machine gun.

"What seems to be the problem?" asked Zazlov, squeezing in next to Mary.

"Luckily, one of the pilots I touched had some mechanical experience," said Mary, pulling a metal plate from the wall. "My only guess—well, his guess, technically—is the fuel pump might be plugged. Can you scan it to confirm?"

"I cannot sense it," said Zazlov.

"Well, here goes." Mary peered into the fuse box opening and sorted through some wires. "No . . . no . . . no . . . damn it!"

"What are you searching for?"

"There's a manual pump. When I scan the memories, I can see a fuse box and then a lever for the fuel pump. Maybe there's another?"

"No. You have it," said Zazlov. "Here." He reached into the fuse box and forced his hand upward into the console. "Yes. It's there . . . up here. Try it."

Zazlov backed away and Mary pushed her hand into the console. "Found it," she said, and began jerking the lever back and forth. "You OK up there, big guy?" she said, looking to Sebastian.

Sebastian turned to her, stuck his thumb in the air, then returned to steadying the craft.

"Can you do your thing again?" Mary said to Zazlov as she pumped the lever as fast as she could.

Zazlov held out his hands and squeezed his fists. The engines sputtered, backfired, then fell silent again.

"This thing is killing me!" yelled Mary as she stood and shuffled back to the cockpit. She came to a halt and glared at Rurik, who was blocking her path.

"Sorry, kiddo," said Rurik as he let her go past. He slinked down the corridor past Zazlov and took a seat on a raised portion of the corridor underneath Felix's gunner perch.

Mary sat back in her seat. She pressed a raised fuel pump button a few times, then wrapped her fingers around the choke. "I need you to do it again on three," she said to Zazlov. "Ready? One . . . two . . . three!"

Mary pulled the choke lever as Zazlov clenched his fists.

The engines whirred to life once more as Mary released the choke.

Zazlov and Mary kept a tentative watch on the propellers' blur, which seemed to steady after a few false starts.

"Excellent work," said Zazlov, squeezing her shoulders. "Now for my part."

He lowered his head and began breathing deeply through his nose.

"What are you doing now?" called Rurik.

"I was trying to teleport us as far away as I could. But it's a complicated spell that requires deep concentration," said Zazlov, looking back to Rurik with a scornful glint in his eyes.

"Why couldn't you have just teleported us from the farm again?" asked Rurik.

"For all the non–magick wielders aboard," commanded Zazlov, sounding stern, "as much as I value your concern, I would appreciate from this point forward if you would keep the witchcraft advice to yourselves. Can we work on that?"

Rurik nodded.

"I needed rest to prepare for such a feat," continued Zazlov. "The farthest I've teleported myself was a record 450 kilometers . . . I was much younger and sending only myself. So if you do not mind, I am trying to save our lives."

Rurik hunched back against the corridor and folded his arms.

Zazlov closed his eyes once more and began humming slightly.

Mary peered into the distance as the clouds began to swirl and connect themselves in a bluish-purple haze that formed a circle and streaked past the plane.

"It's working!" she said.

The clouds returned to puffy white and Zazlov opened his eyes.

Mary looked at him sheepishly. "Sorry, Zazlov."

"Any more magick tips?" asked Zazlov, looking back to Rurik and then to Mary and Sebastian. "Any more affirmations you'd like to expel before I try again?"

They all quietly shook their heads.

"Now then—"

The plane shook and rattled as bullets tore through the fuselage.

"Christ!" yelled Mary, seizing upon the control yoke and veering left.

Zazlov turned and strode to Felix's position.

"Can you see them?"

"Indeed I can!"

Felix scanned the clouds behind the bomber—two gray specks broke through the silvery-white plumes in the distance. He noticed small white flashes bursting from their silhouettes before more bullets whizzed by. He returned fire at once, unable to tell if he was remotely on target.

"I can't hit them! They're too far!" he yelled downward.

"They seem to be having no issue hitting us, so try harder," said Zazlov.

"Easy for you to say," grunted Felix, squeezing the trigger and swinging the gun wide in hopes of hitting either plane. He noticed one of the planes jerk to the left and dip before it steadied and rejoined its formation next to the other biplane.

"I think I hit one!"

"You think, or you know?" shouted Zazlov.

"Can you give me a break?"

Zazlov ascended and squeezed in next to Felix, pressing him against the rim of his gunner perch.

"What are you doing?" asked Felix.

"Saving our lives, as usual."

Zazlov scanned the sky as the fast-approaching biplanes popped in and out of the tailing clouds. He waited until he saw the white flashes from their guns and raised his hand. Felix noticed a soft yellow glow envelop the back of the bomber, as if it had deployed a drag parachute. A moment later, the glow lit up with white specks as the bullets struck the near-invisible field.

"Now. Return your fire," said Zazlov, dropping below as the field vanished.

Felix grew intent and focused on the biplane to his right. He aimed just above its wings, thinking he could lead the gunfire enough to strike the plane, and at that moment, black smoke erupted from the aircraft and it shot downward in a nosedive.

"I hit him! I hit him!"

"Good! Now the other," said Zazlov, returning to the cockpit. "I can't do this by myself. I'm going to need your energies."

"Whatever you need," said Mary.

Zazlov placed his hands upon Mary's and Sebastian's shoulders. Sebastian reached up and patted Zazlov's hand.

"When I say so, I need you to conjure as much emotion in your gut as you can," Zazlov said, leaning forward. "Now, hold on to me."

Mary steadied the control yoke with her knees and turned to Zazlov, embracing him, as Sebastian did the same.

Up in his perch, Felix tried to steady himself against Mary's erratic flight pattern. He found it difficult to target the biplane for fear of striking the bomber's tail. He occasionally shot a spattering of fire in hopes of intimidating or distracting the trailing pilot.

The lone pilot seemed to steady his flight pattern and throttle forward—Felix could see the plane clearly gaining on them. He continued to fire random bursts but knew his marks were nowhere close. His senses became overwhelmed with white and purple flashing, and he looked to the front of the bomber to see a bluish-purple light glowing dead ahead. Felix turned to see white flashes from the biplane followed by the sound of gunfire as a wave of purple-white light enveloped him entirely.

And then . . .

The sky was clear.

Felix looked over the edge of his perch to see an entirely different landscape below. It was hilly and smattered with farmland. "What the hell?" he said aloud.

He scanned the perfectly clear skies—no enemy plane in sight. He dropped from the perch and moved to the cockpit to find Zazlov seated on the corridor floor just behind Mary's seat. The warlock was pallid and sweaty.

"Are you shot?" asked Felix, hovering over him.

"No," said Zazlov. "Just the aftereffect of the spell."

Rurik stood behind him. "Best give him some air. Here, help me." Rurik reached down and assisted Zazlov from the floor. He and Felix shepherded him to the tail portion of the corridor, where Zazlov lay back and placed his head on Felix's discarded supply satchel.

Rurik returned to the cockpit. "Any idea where we are?" he asked.

"No clue," said Mary. "Zazlov?"

"We should be over Switzerland. Give me a few more moments, and I can perform a scan."

Mary looked to the landscape. "I don't know, Zazlov. Sure doesn't look like the Alps. Compass says we're headed northwest." She looked to the fuel gauge. "We have just under half a tank, so as long as the engines don't cut, I think we can stay airborne for a few hours."

Rurik knelt to a duffel bag that had been dislodged during their skirmish, and reached in to produce a canteen. As Mary turned and watched him carry it to Zazlov, she made eye contact with Felix, who was helping the warlock find a more comfortable position.

"You all right?" asked Felix.

"Oh, you know me," said Mary, winking and saluting him with her index finger. "Just up here doing pilot stuff."

*

Hanne scowled underneath her mask as she sensed the biplanes ascend after her targets. The warlock aboard the bomber had proved to be more cunning than she expected. Even so, it was she who had won the battle of wits, thanks to the centuries of skill and knowledge she had absorbed from Elizabeth. Her anger gave way to calm as she reflected on her actions. Her traction spell was merely a misdirection—a tactic of chaos magick discharged to confuse and ultimately conceal a parasite hex now embedded in the bomber's metallic body. Hanne would be able to track the plane anywhere, but more importantly: if they teleported, their craft would materialize over Slovakia, exactly where the hooded man had commanded she deliver them.

As best she tried, Hanne had not been able to uncover the true identity of the mysterious hooded warlock who had accompanied her on the first leg of her travels, but she felt his power and believed it was even greater than Elizabeth's. Although she intended to keep her meeting with this warlock a secret from her master, Hanne decided to relay her potential discovery around Felix Yusupov to the spider in hopes of finding favor. She could only hope this dark witch would keep his promise to break her psychic bond to Elizabeth if she delivered Felix and his companions to him—a task she still had every intention of completing.

Her directive was to capture them in Romania and bring them to Čachtice Castle, so now she had to improvise. Teleporting to Slovakia would be too draining with the parasite spell in place, and would run the risk of alerting Elizabeth of her movements.

Scanning the sky once more, Hanne sensed the biplanes trailing the bomber. She decided the damaged planes along the runway were her only means of following her bounties—her new powers would see to the rest.

A sensation of being watched pricked the back of her ear, and she turned the Hellhorse toward a line of German soldiers and several pilots draped in canvas coveralls who were staring at her. The human soldiers began arguing with the canvas-covered pilots. A moment later, the mortals walked away from the heated exchange and positioned themselves behind their machine guns set up at the edge of the makeshift runway.

Hanne dismounted her steed and walked a few paces in front of the animal. Sensing the foul intent of the gunners, she unsheathed her blades and crossed them defensively before her.

Gunfire erupted through the country air as smoke rose from the machine guns, sending gray streaks raining upon Hanne. She knelt to the ground on one knee and placed the crossed blades directly in front of her, absorbing the barrage of bullets. The gunfire continued for another twenty seconds before their ammunition belts ran out and the gunners scrambled to reload.

Hanne marched toward the line of gunners as other soldiers knelt to the ground and fired their rifles at her. She tossed one of her blades at a rifleman, striking him center chest. It absorbed his shoulder and head upon contact, sending the remainder of his body limply to the grass.

The blade returned to her in a flash.

She then raised both blades over her head and hurled them at the machine guns, absorbing the blunt weaponry in a shower of sparks and molten metal. Raising her hands into the air, Hanne caught the swords as they shot back to her end over end. She marched toward the line of soldiers, alternately blocking a rifleman's bullet and choking others by clenching her fists in their direction.

As she reached the troop line, many of them abandoned their rifles and ran off into the distance. The canvas-covered pilots huddled behind a taller man draped in black.

Sensing they were undead, Hanne stood before him and sheathed her blades.

"Whose man are you?" she questioned.

The leader confidently crossed his arms.

"I am Captain Manfred von Richthofen. Commander of the Jasta Eleven Squadron. I am in service of Kaiser Wilhelm and the German Empire. Whose man are you?"

"I serve no man," replied Hanne.

"Then who are you?"

Hanne folded her arms across her chest. "I am Death."

"Clearly," said Manfred, stepping back a few paces. "What was your business with the fugitives on that bomber?" Having been sworn to the utmost secrecy, Hanne thought to ignore the inquiry and cut them all down. But realizing she needed a means to follow the bomber, she relented. "I am on command to capture two of them."

"We are on the same orders. Kill or capture. They are enemies of the German State."

Hanne walked past Manfred, and his squadron backed out of her way.

In the distance, some of the soldiers were returning. She could sense that they were frightened and curious, no longer a threat. She stood at the long line of destroyed airplanes.

"It seems to me," said Hanne, "that your mission has stalled."

Manfred stood by her side and surveyed the damage.

"Yes," he said. "We have three mechanics on site. But not enough replacement parts to repair the craft."

Hanne noticed an engine buzzing in the distance and turned to sense a speck of a biplane returning from above. She, Manfred, and his squadron stood at the edge of the runway as the human pilot landed the craft and taxied to their position. He turned off the engines and hopped from the plane, running to Manfred.

"Lieutenant Freiherr. He was shot down, sir," said the pilot, kneeling before him.

"And you abandoned the kill?"

"No, sir! They vanished. I—I had them. In my sights. And then there was this . . . this purple flash. It was so bright, I had to close my eyes. When I gathered my senses, the bomber was nowhere in sight. It was simply gone."

Manfred turned to Hanne.

"What sorcery is this?" he asked.

"Teleportation," said Hanne. "Get me in your flying machine and I can track them."

"You're not going anywhere with our last working aircraft," said Manfred, stepping between her and the kneeling pilot.

"Is that so?" said Hanne, turning to the destroyed airplanes. She walked a few steps forward and scanned the damaged craft. "Best stay back now."

Hanne raised her hands into the air and called out to the sky—her chant echoing through the country quiet. A dull white glow emanated from her hands, and she thrust the light at the planes. The energy beam spread apart, crackling and flashing as it struck the damaged fuselages. Hanne cried out once more, sending another shock wave from her body that floored everyone standing around her and caused the planes to nearly topple over backward.

The planes thumped down to the mud—two of them losing what remained of their intact wings.

Manfred pulled himself from the ground and stood next to Hanne.

"Well done," he said. "Now they're worse."

Hanne held up a hand to silence him. She then leaned forward and hovered over the grass at an angle well past forty-five degrees, while extending her hands like gnarled claws. The planes began banging and shaking as if some sudden earthquake had erupted beneath them. The wings popped back into their sockets, splintered wood repaired itself, and various bolts and metal screws shot from the ground and refastened themselves into their sockets. An engine torn from one of the planes rose into the air and popped itself back into position, and the bullet holes riddling each craft seemed to cure themselves and spit the projectiles back onto the earth.

Hanne floated back to vertical and lowered her hands. Realizing the monoplanes and Manfred's triplane were single-seat aircraft, she turned to the biplane and sensed it had seats for the pilot and rear gunner.

The human pilot backed up a bit as Hanne approached him.

"You! Back to the barracks," she ordered.

The pilot wasted no time in obeying and jogged off into the distance.

"You!" Hanne pointed to one of the Jasta Eleven pilots, then motioned to the biplane. "You're flying this one."

She stood before Manfred. "Get the rest of your squadron airborne now."

Manfred folded his arms, the rest of his team standing firmly behind him.

"We don't take orders from you," he said.

Hanne unsheathed her blades and held them wide at her sides.

"Captain, do I truly need to explain myself?"

*

The bomber rattled once more.

Mary looked out to the engines and watched the propellers as they sputtered briefly before once again purring with their normal rotations. She relaxed a bit and looked back to Felix and Zazlov.

For a spoiled prince, he's actually quite sweet, she thought, watching him help Zazlov tip the canteen to his mouth.

Sebastian leaned into her. "I like Fele. He good for Mare-mare."

"Knock it off!" said Mary, slapping his arm and returning her attention to steadying the plane. She looked out over the deciduous landscape below and began to worry, not knowing if they were flying over enemy lines—or where they were flying at all. She kept their bearing northwest and looked back to see Zazlov stirring. Relief washed over her, and she returned to steadying the craft.

Zazlov walked to the cockpit, followed by Rurik and Felix.

"Thank you both for assisting," said Zazlov to Mary and Sebastian. "There was no way I could have completed that spell on my own. I'm, well, getting older I suppose."

"Happy to be of service, Captain," said Mary, saluting him. "So . . . where are we?"

Zazlov squinted as he took in the green, hilly panorama. "Certainly not over Switzerland."

He closed his eyes for a moment and scanned the Ether to track their position.

"No," he said, opening his eyes as his complexion grew ghostly. "I'm an old fool."

"This we know," said Mary, keeping her eyes forward as she smiled tensely and anxiously tapped her fingers on the console..

359

"No time for joking. We've been deceived," said Zazlov. "This is northern Slovakia. Directly over the lair of an old adversary." Zazlov ran his hand over his beard. "Veer west. We need to get out of here. Now." He leaned in and pushed the throttle forward.

Mary pressed on the yoke and the plane banked left.

"What's happening?" asked Rurik.

"The Death Witch cast a parasite spell on us—usurped my teleportation and put us here on purpose. We have to clear the area immediately. Hurry, Mary!"

"Hurry? This is as fast as she goes."

Zazlov appeared gravely worried.

"We don't have enough fuel to make it to Paris," said Mary. "Not even close."

Zazlov exhaled deeply. "Paris is due west. Another thirteen hundred kilometers. Even at top speed and a full reservoir of gas, we'd need to refuel."

"How are we going to refuel?" asked Rurik. "Can you scan for an airfield or something?"

Zazlov hung his head. "I cannot. We are close enough to Vienna, but I fear they must have telegrammed ahead to warn of a stolen bomber."

"No way," said Felix. "They still use carrier pigeons to send messages from their tank squadrons."

"I do not envision a clear chance of us landing and refueling without very serious repercussions," said Zazlov, turning to him. "I see only death or capture."

"So, what? We just fly until we can't? We're missing a landing wheel," said Rurik.

"Our best chance at survival is to find a lake or river and get as close and slow as we can," said Zazlov. "With some rest, and by combining our group energy fields, I may be able to teleport us out into the water."

"Don't we have any parachutes?" asked Felix.

"Have you ever used one?" replied Zazlov.

"No. But how hard can it be?"

Zazlov rolled his eyes. Just as he opened his mouth to respond, the left engine erupted in fire.

"Something hit us!" yelled Mary, trying to steady the craft.

"Kill the engine!" said Zazlov.

Felix dashed to his gunner post as Mary frantically flipped levers. The propeller came to a stop with thick black smoke pouring from the back of the engine.

"It's the Red Baron!" screamed Felix from above. "They followed us."

"Damn that foul witch," shouted Zazlov as he moved toward the perch. He pulled himself up and watched five planes approaching fast from behind.

"Listen, son," he said, turning to Felix. "I need you to think like a warlock."

"How's that?"

"With their echo-calling, they'll be impossible to hit by conventional methods. They'll sense your gun movements almost before you make them. You need to think in random abstract terms. If you intend to fire right, move left, then turn quickly right and fire. Might just be enough to confuse them."

"I don't—"

"Think and do in opposites! You'll be more . . . more . . . Just shoot!"

White flashes from the noses of the trailing planes lit up Felix's vision as he pulled the trigger and returned fire. The bullets whizzed past them, two striking the top of the fuselage.

Zazlov dropped below. "Anybody hit?"

"We're good!" yelled Rurik.

"Mary!" called Zazlov. "Do the opposite of what your brain is telling you."

"What?" she said, turning to him.

"If you think to veer right—go left instead. Up is now down!"

"Why?"

"Just do it!" he said, as three more bullets ripped through the cabin—one nearly striking his boot.

"This is no good," said Zazlov, returning to the gunner perch.

"Can you do that shield thing?" questioned Felix.

Zazlov was already extending his hand, generating a yellowish field that appeared behind the plane. He placed his hand on Felix's shoulder. "I'm going to need to draw some of your life force for this. Do you consent?"

"I encourage," said Felix, as a series of glowing white circles reverberated across the yellow field.

"Now," said Zazlov. "I'm going to pull the field for your return fire. Follow my commands."

Felix steadied the gun.

"Swing left. Now swing right. Up, down. Fire!" Zazlov lowered the field. "Diagonally right, then low left . . . fire!"

Felix followed the instructions and Zazlov regenerated the field behind their tail—it was shrinking as Zazlov tried to hold it in position. They watched as Jasta Eleven scattered and a puff of smoke erupted from a monoplane on the far right. It quickly broke formation and began a nosedive as its engine flew into overdrive and screamed with a harrowing low growl.

"I nailed him!" yelled Felix.

"Good. Now, we do it again."

The Red Baron and his remaining pilots re-formed to a tighter position and pulled slightly below Felix's gun trajectory.

"I can't target them," he said as more white whirlpools pocked across Zazlov's shield. "Mary! I need you to dive!" he yelled.

"What?"

"I need you to dive!"

Felix gripped the rim of his gunner post as the bomber shot downward, and Zazlov's field shrunk to a small point. He looked to the warlock, who appeared pale and exhausted, barely able to hold on to the railing as the turbulence kicked up. Felix tried to hold him, but Zazlov's weight proved too much.

"Get below! I have this," said Felix.

Zazlov nodded and slipped down into the corridor.

Felix turned his guns on Jasta Eleven, firing in sporadic and random patterns. The trailing planes looked like a horde of agitated gnats as they dodged Felix's gunfire.

The shield was now gone.

Bullets shot from the Jasta squadron, causing Felix to duck below. He saw Zazlov resting toward the plane's tail and Rurik kneeling behind Mary, holding on tightly to her chair.

"You hanging in there, Zazlov? We need another shield," said Felix.

"Just another moment," said Zazlov, panting heavily.

Felix poked his head above once more to see that the top of their tail was blown to bits. He glanced to the front of the plane, where sections of the top wings were also riddled with bullet holes.

More bullets shot into the fuselage.

"Enough of this!" shouted Mary as a bullet shot past her shoulder and tore into the center control panel. "Take over," she said to Sebastian, jumping from her seat and reaching toward Rurik.

"Do you mind, Uncle?" she asked, placing her hands on his temples and transferring a pilot's memory into his mind. "Just in case."

Rurik appeared dazed for a moment.

"Do you have it?" she asked.

"I—I do, actually."

"Good. Now, hop in."

Rurik shimmied around her and hopped into her seat. He looked to Sebastian, who seemed to have a solid grasp on keeping the plane flying in a sporadic pattern.

"Out of the way, hotshot," Mary said to Felix as she emerged next to him on the gunner perch.

"What the hell are you doing? You're supposed to be flying the plane."

"Remember when you asked how I saved you from that train?" she said. "Well, here's the big secret. Mind if I use you as a ladder?"

She placed her foot on Felix's knee and jumped up on his shoulders before leaping from the aircraft.

"Mary!" screamed Felix as she transformed into a large black bird of prey, diving downward. Mary's ethereal garments wrapped around her winged body and formed a leather harness across her back and breast.

The Red Baron and Jasta Eleven took immediate notice of the new bogey and hovered into position, firing again upon the bomber. Mary assumed the planes' fixed guns could only shoot dead ahead, and she dove sharp and low to avoid their range.

Her real concern was the Death Witch.

Mary had abandoned her witchcraft studies in her early teens to focus on her psychometry, but she still carried some basic knowledge. She cursed herself for not keeping up with her conjuring skills as she tried to summon the spell. Mary locked in on the Death Witch's psychic energy and cloaked herself. Knowing the spell would only affect the dark enchantress, she hoped the invisibility would hold long enough for her to bring down the Red Baron.

She turned her head left and spread her wings wide as she glided with great speed toward their formation—all the while calculating the angles where their guns could potentially target her.

The Red Baron and his squadron kept their formation tight, still intent on the bomber as they continued to fire upon the damaged craft.

As Mary reached the outer left periphery of their formation, she craned her neck to the right and forcefully flapped her wings, climbing above Jasta Eleven. She then extended her neck, tucked her wings into her body, and descended upon them, aiming for the Red Baron.

Because of his triple wings, a frontal assault would prove troublesome, and Mary occasionally pulled her wings from her body to correct her path, in hopes of plotting an exact path to his cockpit.

She positioned herself once more as her trajectory became clear. Just as she cleared the top wings of the triplane, she spread her wings wide and extended her claws, striking the Red Baron directly in the head. She ripped the canvas covering clean from his head and left several claw marks across his face.

Hope you're well fed, you bastard, she thought as she shot left and dove beneath the squadron.

The Red Baron growled as the bird's talons tore into his face and ripped off his canvas covering. It had been two days since he and his squadron had a proper feeding, and the sparse cloud cover was not enough to protect him from the sunlight. His flesh burned, and acerbic smoke rose from his skin. Manfred raised his gloved hands to his face as he tried to protect himself, and his plane started to descend.

Following his sudden movements, his squadron descended with him.

Manfred tried to pull the rest of his coveralls over his head, but only managed to protect half his face as his exposed head boiled and oozed in the sunlight. He called out to the landscape below, hoping to locate some tree cover, but more importantly, a place to land. Sensing a small stretch of land that was sufficient, he hammered on his throttle and targeted the area.

"Stay on that bomber!" screamed Hanne, as the canvas-suited airman piloting her biplane veered after the descending Red Baron.

"I am bound to protect my commander," yelled the pilot, turning back to her.

Hanne thrust a demon blade forward and held it near the pilot's neck. "I said, 'Stay on that bomber.'"

The pilot nodded and turned back around. "As you command."

"They're badly damaged. Get over top of them."

Hanne sheathed her blade and held on to the rim of the gunner pocket as the pilot increased the throttle. From the corner of her mind, she sensed a large black streak and deciphered the shape of a giant bird, flickering as it attempted to hold a cloaking spell.

"Clever girl," said Hanne, annoyed she didn't sense this amateur conjurer earlier.

The winged creature dove for the bomber's gunner perch, transformed into a woman, and disappeared back into the plane.

I'll capture her too, thought Hanne, believing that bringing the shape-shifter before Elizabeth would find her favor.

Below them, Felix poked his head through the opening and aimed the machine gun upward, firing immediately. The pilot took evasive maneuvers, and Hanne extended her hand, casting a glowing red shield before the biplane.

"Steady yourself," said Hanne. "Do not fire upon them."

A series of pink circles reverberated across the field as Felix's bullet barrage found its target. The biplane sailed toward the bomber, which rattled and shook, expelling thick black smoke from its bullet-riddled engine—its wings losing more and more of their structure as the damaged engine wobbled in its setting.

Hanne thought to teleport directly into the bomber's fuselage, but due to the multiple moving bodies inside the craft and its erratic flight, she deemed the attack too precarious. She could very well end up fusing herself within the body of the plane—or worse, melding with one of her bounties.

"Get to their right and just in front of them!" ordered Hanne as she peered below to see that they were directly over the bomber.

The pilot increased his speed until they were flying just in advance of the wounded craft. Hanne stood from her seat and looked backward, gauging the distance to the gunner perch still occupied by Felix. She leapt into the air and unsheathed her demon blades as her body sailed toward the gunner opening, causing Felix to duck back into the fuselage.

"She's coming!" yelled Felix as he crashed onto the corridor's walkway. He dashed toward Zazlov, who was still resting.

"Who?" asked Rurik, scrambling after him.

"Stand back, Rurik!"

The Death Witch crashed in from above, cracking two of her antler spikes off her helmet and tearing the gunner perch from its rivets. Her extended blades ripped two gaping holes in the side of the bomber as the perch came down hard upon Rurik, knocking him toward the cockpit and pinning his leg beneath the metal grating. He screamed as his ankle cracked, then passed out when his head struck the metal walkway.

The Death Witch stood in the fuselage as wind and chaos surged through the corridor.

The bomber shook—the tail portion now holding on only by the floor of the craft. She sensed Zazlov attempting to stand. Extending her hand, she cast a containment spell that shrouded him and Felix in a glowing red webbing, then threw them onto the corridor floor. Satisfied they were neutralized as Zazlov struggled to free them from the spell, the Death Witch turned to the cockpit.

"No you don't!" said Mary as she hopped from her seat and transformed into a panther.

The Death Witch looked down to Rurik and thrust her hand at him, causing his body to fly toward Mary. They both crashed back into the cockpit, disturbing Sebastian, who steadied the plane as it continued to crack apart. Mary composed herself as Rurik's body fell limply over her seat.

She growled at the Death Witch and gnashed her teeth.

The horned specter raised her blades, extending them past the cutaway in the ceiling. She then turned and sliced the floor clean from the fuselage, sending Felix and Zazlov, trapped in the tail portion, sailing to the earth below. The plane jerked forward, arcing into a nosedive as the remaining engine roared from the descent.

Mary slipped and tried to use her claws to steady herself as the Death Witch quickly sheathed her blades. She extended her arms as her cloak slid protectively over her hands. The Death Witch then conjured a web of pure silver and cast it over Mary, freezing her upon contact.

Pulling Mary's frozen figure toward her, the Death Witch leaned backward and sailed into the blue skies with Mary in her grasp.

What remained of the plane now screamed downward in a vertical descent with Sebastian and Rurik pinned in the cockpit.

Chapter 22

22

March 29, 1917, 10:32 a.m.

Two matte black Fokker monoplanes circled the small landing area where the Red Baron's empty Dr. I triple-winged craft had come to a stop. They made two passes, searching for Captain Richthofen, but because of the heavy tree cover in the surrounding area were unable to locate him. They descended upon the short landing strip, clipping their engines as they approached.

After a series of bumps on the uneven field, each aircraft came to a slow stop. Lieutenant Hilder jumped from his cockpit and ran to greet Lieutenant Guntz. Both men sprinted to the Red Baron's plane.

They inspected it, clicking and squealing from their mouths as they searched for footprints leading from the red craft.

"Here," said Hilder. "He went that way."

Following audio disturbances created by the muddy footprints, the pilots jogged into the forest and came upon an uprooted oak tree. The sounds of Manfred grunting in pain came from an area behind a massive hunk of mud clinging to the tree roots. They circled around to find him cowering at the bottom of a muddy pit left by the toppled tree.

"Commander!" yelled Hilder as he jumped into the gulch.

Manfred moved his head in the direction of Hilder's voice, and Hilder could sense that one of Manfred's eyes had melted away and the other was victim to the black bird's claws.

"Hurry. Help me," mumbled Manfred, extending his arm. "I need blood. I can sense a deer or something nearby. Bring it to me . . . quickly!"

The two pilots shot into the forest in search of sustenance for their commander.

Manfred sat in the shadows, trying to bear the pain of his facial wounds. Most of the flesh on his face had melted away, and he could feel that portions of his jawbone had also succumbed to the direct sunlight, leaving his tongue to hang from the side of his mouth. Having had a very short period of time to understand his new vampiric powers, his mind raced with terrible thoughts about these being his final moments.

I'm going to die out here.

He remembered the day he had agreed to a direct order from Kaiser Wilhelm and General Hindenburg to travel to Bucharest and be converted, and he cursed himself for his ambition. He was already the world's greatest pilot, and the opportunity to become *more*—to become immortal—was simply too appealing.

Manfred sensed his lieutenants emerging from the wood with a large body in tow. They arrived at the top of the gulch and dropped a gored wild boar before him—the animal was still breathing. Without another thought, Manfred gnashed his fangs and tore into the animal's sternum as the beast let out one final gasp.

He drank eagerly from the boar's heart and could feel his body surging with pleasure as the warm, almost sugary liquid poured down his esophagus. An itching sensation began on his scalp and jawline, and Manfred sat back into the shadows with fresh blood dripping from his chin. He tore off his glove and felt his scalp—the flesh and hair was beginning to re-form. His head jerked up to his lieutenants.

"Where's Lieutenant Haas?"

"We don't know, sir," said Guntz. "When you started to descend, all of us followed. Haas broke formation at the last moment and kept on the bomber."

"That damn witch," said Hilder.

"If that's what she was," said Manfred as his wounds continued to heal. "I need cover. Do either of you have anything in your storage?"

"I do," said Guntz. He ran in the direction of his monoplane and returned after a moment with a wide sheet of green canvas, which he handed to Manfred.

Manfred draped it over his head as his skin continued to materialize upon his face. He then reached to his waist, removed his leather belt, and slung it around his neck, tightening it just enough to ensure the canvas would stay on his body and protect him from any sunlight.

A plane engine growled in the distance.

Manfred crawled from the pit and all three of them waited near the edge of the forest as Lieutenant Haas landed his biplane. After a short taxi to the other parked aircraft, Haas dropped to the ground and ran toward them.

"Commander! You're alive," said Haas, approaching them.

"What happened?"

"That *thing* is crazy! It had me fly over the bomber. It then jumped into the sky and crashed into the bomber through the gunner perch. Tore the entire plane apart with those swords."

Manfred sat upon the forest floor and leaned his back against a tree.

"Such power," he said. "I've never witnessed such hateful abandon."

"Do you think she was on Wilhelm's orders?" asked Guntz.

"I cannot say. My suspicion would be Hindenburg. Both he and Schmidt are masters of the dark arts. Wilhelm has no clue that he is merely their puppet." Manfred paused for a long moment. "Do any of you have a track on Lieutenant Schintz? I cannot sense him."

"No, sir. None of us can," said Guntz. "His craft was hit pretty hard. I believe he perished."

Manfred clenched his fist. "Good pilot, that kid. With our new powers, he could have rivaled anyone."

"Should we search for him?" asked Hilder.

"We will, yes. We'll take another pass once airborne, but in the short term—we need to figure out where the witch teleported us." He took stock of their surroundings. "We'll have to wait until nightfall. The stars can help give us a sense of our position."

"Then what, sir? Our mission failed," said Hilder.

Manfred grew angry at the suggestion of failure and thought to reprimand Hilder, but deep down he knew the man was right.

"I don't think we should return to Berlin," said Manfred. "Our bounties are clearly dead, if what you say is true. And our core mission remains intact—an objective we will complete by transforming an entire legion of airmen into the most deadly pilots the world has ever known. For now . . . we rest. I sensed a village not too far away when I landed. We feed at nightfall. Then we head to Arras."

*

Felix watched in amazement as the protective bubble shielded he and Zazlov from the shower of wood and metal as the detached tail broke to bits while they sailed through the trees and crashed toward the forest floor.

They hovered above the ground, suspended safely within the bubble before Zazlov opened his eyes. The shield dissipated and their feet gently touched the forest floor.

"Holy shit!" said Felix, looking over the wreckage strewn about their crash site.

"Indeed," said Zazlov, scanning the heavily forested ridge.

"What happened to the others?" asked Felix.

Zazlov closed his eyes. "I cannot sense them," he said with a despondent exhale. "As much as I hate to say this—I fear we must prepare ourselves for the possibility that they did not survive."

"I'll kill that witch," said Felix.

"You may just have your chance," said Zazlov. "She's not done with us yet. For now, we have far graver concerns." He walked to a toppled log and slumped upon it. "The Black Butcher I spoke of?"

Felix sat next to him.

"These are his lands," finished Zazlov.

"I thought he was trapped in a mirror."

"As did I." Zazlov peered into the darkened forest. "But it seems he has escaped and brought me here for a confrontation."

"Then we have to flee—find the others."

Zazlov stood and walked a short distance into the forest.

"Zazlov?" called Felix. "We have to find the others."

Zazlov stood at the cliff's edge, watching the rapids rage in the rocky gorge below.

"Easily two hundred meters down," he said, walking back to Felix.

"What are you doing? We have to get out of here."

Zazlov stood before him.

"There will be no escape this time, Felix. At least not for me. I must confront this evil once and for all, or neither of us will leave these lands alive."

"Can I help?"

"No. I must ensure you remain safe," said Zazlov with a caring look in his eye. "I wanted to wait until you were safely in Paris to divulge this, but it seems I have no choice."

"You can tell me whatever secret you're holding. We're in this together now. I can handle it."

"That's just it, Felix—I'm not certain you can."

Felix stared up at Zazlov. "I can. Tell me."

A black butterfly landed on Felix's knee, and a motion caught his eye at the forest perimeter. He turned to inspect, noticing the horns before anything else. Then, inch by inch, the Death Witch emerged from the hill.

Felix stood and backed away. "Zazlov!" he shouted.

The butterfly scout fluttered back to the Death Witch and absorbed into her cloak as Zazlov unsheathed his demon blade and held it defensively.

She marched up the slope with both scimitars extended at her sides.

"Stay back, young man," said Zazlov, pulling Felix behind him.

Felix stood frozen in place as he watched the Death Witch sail into the air with her blades raised above her head.

"Radu!" she screamed. "I have you now." Then she flew down to Zazlov, striking his blade defense with both her scimitars. A bright shockwave burst from the swords as they clashed, followed by a deep bass resonance that caused Felix to duck and cover his ears. He searched the forest floor for a weapon and noticed a thick, blackened branch poking from some leaves. He grabbed the branch and ran at the Death Witch as she and Zazlov continued to trade blows.

Felix raised the blunt branch and yelled as he charged her.

The Death Witch thrust a blade into Zazlov's strike, blocking it, and with her other hand sent Felix flying backward with an invisible blast. He landed hard on the forest floor, getting the wind knocked out of him and dropping his branch. While attempting to catch his breath, Felix rolled over and watched as the Death Witch swung her free blade back toward Zazlov, who crouched to the ground, spun around, and swept her legs out from underneath her with a wide swoosh of his leg.

Zazlov stood quickly and swung his scimitar downward onto the Death Witch, who blocked the blow with both her blades. The giant warlock forced his weight onto her and began to overpower the Death Witch, sending her blades closer and closer to her torso as white sparks showered her deer skull helmet. A portion of her cloak extended out from her body and struck Zazlov, pushing him back a few paces.

Felix rose to his feet and gripped his branch once more. He watched as the Death Witch dove toward Zazlov, spinning horizontally over the ground with her blades extended before her like two spears. Zazlov appeared surprised by her unique attack and parried left, deflecting it. The Death Witch landed gracefully on the earth and darted toward Zazlov, extending her scimitars and spinning like a fevered dust devil.

Zazlov jumped backward and blocked the initial strike, but the Death Witch's rotation was much too fast and too fierce for him to counter.

A harrowing howl rang through the forest.

"No!" yelled Felix, dropping his branch as the Death Witch struck Zazlov on her final rotation, her blade absorbing his forearm clean from his body.

The mighty warlock fell to his knees and his demon blade hovered over the grassy knoll—the hand of his severed arm still gripping the hilt.

Zazlov's hand slipped from the blade and fell to the ground.

"I'll have that bottle and I'll have that blade," said the Death Witch, standing over him.

"Never," said Zazlov, falling back upon the ground.

"Radu cel Frumos! Then I give you oblivion!" screamed the Death Witch as she raised her blades over her head.

Felix zeroed in on Zazlov's blade hovering just above the ground. He wanted that weapon—to snatch it and drive it deep into the heart of this creature who had maimed his friend.

He extended his hand toward the blade, craving the feeling of its hilt in his hand.

The blade rattled for a moment, then shot to Felix, who clenched it in his fist. He looked to the powerful weapon in his grasp—stunned it had flown to him, stunned it did not kill him upon contact as Zazlov had warned. Felix looked to Zazlov, still kneeling before the Death Witch. As she slowly turned to face Felix, the back of her cloak slid around Zazlov's neck and tightened.

After a moment, Zazlov's limp body slumped to the earth.

The Death Witch locked in on Felix.

"So it's true," she said.

Felix swallowed and quickly looked back to make sure there were no branches or rocks that might trip him. Realizing he was standing too close to the cliff's edge, he scurried a few paces forward, turning his attention to the Death Witch and gripping the demon blade tightly while wiping the sweat from his dirty face.

Her horned figure rose into the air and landed several meters before Felix, who backed away with his blade extended. The Death Witch charged him, striking his blade with several jabs as he blocked her advance. His mind raced to his fencing lessons, but not single technique presented itself—Felix was simply outmatched. A forceful blow came from one of her blades, causing Felix to lose his grip. The black weapon was cast from his hand and struck a tree, absorbing a portion of the wood before falling toward the earth. The large oak toppled, separating Felix and the Death Witch.

Felix lost his balance and fell to the ground.

The dark witch alighted on the fallen oak, extending her blades in Felix's direction. He lay on the ground and raised his hands in surrender.

"Vehuiah," said the Death Witch. "It seems you have forgotten yourself."

A strange pulsing sensation warmed Felix's temples as he stared at the Death Witch—his mind seemed to scan her psyche. He saw her as a young blonde girl shrieking in pain, tears streaming down her face as a male hand repeatedly beat her backside; her small frame running through a grassy field, looking back in terror as a group of white-cloaked figures tackled her and pinned her to the ground, punishing her for attempting to flee; images of nude people dancing around a fire while she sat in the shadows with bruises encircling her neck and arms; a horse with torn flesh, then spider fangs piercing her vision.

"Hanne! Your name is Hanne!" yelled Felix, looking up at her. "They tortured you!"

The Death Witch recoiled, seemingly surprised by Felix's discovery. She then sheathed her blades and lept high in the air, aiming toward Felix.

A thunder clap pierced the air, followed by a series of flashes as the Death Witch became suspended in a field of white lightning. Zazlov marched toward her, shooting silvery beams from his hand and shouting in a strange tongue. Felix slid away from the Death Witch's attack trajectory as Zazlov clenched his fist and cast a massive white blast that sent her flying over the cliff into the rocky gorge below.

Felix turned and crawled on his hands and knees. He peered over the crags and watched as her body flailed limply into the river below. A white splash rose from the brown waters, and then her figure was gone. Felix turned over and looked at Zazlov, whose eyes were glowing a striking white. The warlock stood at the cliff and watched the rapids, unable to find any indication that the Death Witch had survived.

"The raging waters should do her in," said Zazlov, sounding stern. "Good riddance."

"Your arm!" yelled Felix, looking up to Zazlov's missing hand.

Zazlov's irises returned to brown. He held out his cauterized arm and inspected it.

"Long time coming, I suppose."

"Long time coming? Zazlov! You need a doctor."

"This wound is far beyond a mortal doctor. I'll be fine."

"Does it hurt?"

"Quite so," said Zazlov, wincing a bit as his ethereal garment moved along his arm and covered the wound. "But events like these are to be expected in matters of the sword. No sense in fretting about it."

Felix was stunned by Zazlov's blasé reaction to the maiming.

The warlock extended his left hand and the demon blade returned to him. He sheathed it and held his hand out to Felix.

"Are you hurt?"

"No," said Felix, gripping Zazlov's hand. "I touched the blade. It didn't kill me."

"Come. Sit with me."

Zazlov pulled him up and walked back to the log, pinching his sinuses between his thumb and index finger. The hulking warlock sat upon the bole with a thud. He looked up to Felix with tired eyes.

Felix followed Zazlov and sat before him, his mind piecing together the unfolding events.

"You're Radu cel Frumos."

Zazlov smiled. "Radu Drăculea, actually. *Cel frumos* means 'the beautiful.' I was . . . well, much more handsome in my youth. And who am I to argue if the nickname sticks?"

Felix's molars were on full display as he sat slack-jawed.

"I don't understand. Why the big charade?"

"Secrecy was and is paramount. I have lied, slaughtered, betrayed, and . . . probably every other terrible verb you can think of, to countless people over the years—mortals, immortals—all in the name of protecting humanity from the reincarnation of my brother. I've had many names over the years. Zazlov to some. Lord Rufe Camus to others. The Sommelier to most."

"Camus?"

Radu flashed his perfect teeth. "Lord Rufe Camus IX by now, actually. That's the one that actually surprises me the most. Nobody ever figured it out. It's merely an anagram for Radu cel Frumos. In addition to my Parisian haberdashery, I also own the largest winery in France—Camus Estates. Children become parents, then grandparents . . . and over the years, I just became Camus the first, second, and onward. As the generations passed, I was told, 'You look so much like your father or grandfather.' No one ever suspected. I was staying very well hidden right in front of the world."

"But, why?"

"There's far more at play here than you realize, and it's time you knew the truth." A strong sense of concern shone in Radu's eyes, and he blew out a heavy breath. He reached inside his thick animal-pelted cloak and pulled out a sturdy and aged wooden box, which appeared to materialize from deep within the garment. "I carry this with me everywhere I go."

He handed the box to Felix. "Open it."

Felix unlatched the box to find a green corked bottle with a red wax symbol of a dragon pressed into its hull.

"This is it. This is the bottle."

Radu took the vessel from Felix. He studied a rock jutting from the mud. With one forceful swoop of his arm, Radu raised the bottle into the air and smashed it upon the rock, sending glass shards and red liquid splattering about his feet.

Felix was stunned.

"You smashed it. We . . . we won!"

"It would be a truly wonderful world if only that were so."

Felix grew confused.

"It's a decoy—fermented pig's blood. And it has been a decoy ever since a young apprentice of mine stole the real bottle from underneath me several decades ago."

"Then we still have to get to Paris. We have to find it before the Kaiser—"

"We will find no bottle there. I merely needed you all to understand what we were up against, and I intended to disclose this all once we were safely in Paris."

"Where is it, then?"

"Felix. I don't believe I've told you yet, but one of my favorite qualities about you is your steadfast passion to do the right thing. You seem to throw yourself with abandon in the direction of righteousness and loyalty to your friends. Your bond with Rurik is truly wonderful for me to witness—your natural inclination to be a friend to those around you, to bravely help others. I find it endearing. It's a trait you carried when I knew you in the past. One I was sad to see go once you were betrayed by the Vatican."

"What are you saying?"

Radu became stern as his dark eyes bored into Felix.

"The real bottle was stolen from me thirty-one years ago by a very crafty young warlock named Grigori Rasputin—you remember him. He then gave it to your parents, who consumed it nine months before you were born."

Felix grew pasty.

"You're the bottle, Felix," said Radu. "The reincarnation of my brother, Vlad Drăculea."

Felix slumped upon the dirt and raised his fist to his mouth. A dark emotion welled inside him, as if some massive black tidal wave born of tar crashed into his heart, drowning him in fear and betrayal.

"And this, as it was in the past, I suppose is yours now," said Radu, extending the demon blade to him.

"I don't want it," said Felix, standing and walking a few paces away.

He kept his back to Radu for a long moment, then turned to him with tears in his eyes.

"How is this true? How?"

Radu slouched. "They hid you from me, you know—Rasputin and Olaf. I only began to sense you right around the time of the Nosferatu attacks. I traveled to Saint Petersburg to find you, but you were already in Bucharest. That's why I was tracking you and Rurik. Do you know when I knew it was you?"

Felix shrugged.

"It was your preauricular pits," said Radu. "When I found you lying unconscious yesterday. I still couldn't sense my brother in you, but the moment I saw them, I knew—you were the one."

"I don't know what that is."

"Those dimples on your upper ears. Only witches have them. They are what give us our extrasensory perception . . . well, among other things."

"You're telling me that I'm Vlad the Impaler? Impossible. Then why am I not a vampire?"

"My brother became a vampiric witch—he was not born one."

"So is that why Rasputin converted me to vámpir? To control me?"

"Yes. That was his precise intention. It's why they took your parents away from you, and why you were thrust into these events. After inserting himself into the Nosferatu operation, Rasputin was always at grave risk of being eliminated by the Black Hundred. With Alexei having ultimate control over the Nosferatu, it seems

Rasputin worked to reincarnate you for his advantage, knowing that Vlad would rule over all." Radu looked to the sheathed blade. "And it's why you were able not only to handle this weapon but to call it telekinetically. You're a warlock, Felix . . . and the most powerful one in the world at that."

Felix sat upon the ground once more. "I . . . I can't accept this. I can't do any magick."

"You will have much to remember if we are to survive."

"I don't believe you," said Felix. "I simply can't. This is insanity."

"I understand," said Radu, rising and walking toward him.

Felix stood and they both stared into the darkened forest as faint howls echoed from the distance.

"I look forward to a time when I may explain this all for you, to help you accept it and understand."

More howls ricocheted through the woods.

"The Butcher must know by now that I have bested his mercenary," said Radu. "He's sending his werewolves to capture us. Baphomet has been scheming in the shadows—this is checkmate."

"So what, we run?"

"No. If we flee, the Butcher will never relent. I sense he too has become wise to who and what you are. His intention now will be to capture and torture you until you become twisted and evil. More death and destruction will follow, more innocents slaughtered."

"How do we fight this Butcher?" asked Felix.

"*We* don't. I do."

Radu stood quietly for a long moment.

"I'm sorry, young man, I can't risk you."

Felix suddenly froze in place, unable to move as his body slowly dematerialized.

"What's happening?"

Radu held his hand outward and lifted Felix from the ground, pushing him toward a fat oak tree that grew at the crest of the ridge. He lowered Felix into a seated position beneath the tree, watching as Felix finally disappeared.

"Radu!" grunted Felix.

"Listen to me. I'm placing you under an immobilization and protection spell. It will keep you invisible and resting comfortably here until I return. If you find yourself free, then you will know I perished. At that time, you are to climb down this ridge to the river. There is an old ally of mine who lives downstream not too far from here. Her name is Boryana. Once you reach the river, call out to her. She can assist you in finding my confidant Albert in Berlin, who will know what to do from there."

Radu sensed Felix struggling.

"Please. Be calm. This is the only way." Radu faced the darkened woods. "I must face this devil alone."

Radu walked into the forest with werewolf howls stalking his every step. He summoned what remained of his energy and cast a cloaking spell over himself, knowing he couldn't hold it long or he would tire before his confrontation with the Butcher.

Radu reflected on the calamities of the past and couldn't decide if it was irony or destiny that his path had come full circle— thrusting him back toward Čachtice Castle where the fate of humanity teetered on his actions once again. But he was old now. Tired and missing a limb. Holding the banishment hex for so long had finally worn his fabric thin. He felt frayed, near his end. It stalked him every day, creeping closer and closer. For the first time in his life, Radu understood frailty.

Not far through this werewolf-infested forest, high upon a crest, sat Čachtice. Once the stronghold of Elizabeth Báthory, it was the place where Radu had trapped her in the body of a soul spider so very long ago. It now lay in ruin, its abandoned appearance enough to keep outsiders away through the sheer force of dread it instilled into anyone who happened to gaze upon it.

Dismay overtook Radu as he scanned the Veil for any pending outcomes. Everything resonated in bursts of gray and onyx with no discernable answers. What Radu did know was that he had sworn an oath to protect the reincarnation of his brother from the clutches of darkness. All that mattered now was Felix. And in that moment, Radu swallowed what remained of his doubt and pressed on toward the castle.

For now was not the time for worry—now it was time for battle.

*

Mary's entire muscular system relaxed and she sat upright, transforming back to her normal shape. She looked her body over to see that the silver webbing had disappeared.

The Death Witch must have been wounded . . . or killed. After the horror aboard the bomber, a lucky break.

Mary stood and brushed herself off.

She took a careful look at her surroundings, and wondered if any of her friends were still alive. Closing her eyes, she reached out to the Veil and concentrated on a cluster of bright pink illumination still lingering about their recent calamity. Nothing. Damn it. She really should have studied remote viewing more seriously.

Mary looked into the valley and saw a large lake in the distance, then turned and sensed the Death Witch's trail which led to a dense forest.

Mary arrived at the woodland's edge soon thereafter and immediately felt drawn to a toppled oak tree. From the color of the split wood, she guessed it had crashed over recently. She walked to the tree and placed her hand upon the bark.

Her mind flashed to Felix, holding his ground as the Death Witch attacked him, sending his blade into the tree. Felix on the ground. Zazlov striking the specter with white lightning. The witch sailing over the ridge. Felix and Zazlov conversing.

Mary opened her eyes and traced a visual path to the log Zazlov had sat on. She looked to the ground where a green bottle lay shattered, with remnants of red liquid still splattered across some of the shards.

Mary reached down and held a shard of the bottle in her hand— her mind immediately filling with a series of confusing images.

Zazlov entering a hulking castle riddled with decay.

Werewolves bowing before a man wearing an eyeless executioner's hood.

Dungeon walls coated in silver.

Then Felix kneeling before Zazlov, followed by the words *You're Radu cel Frumos.*

"No," said Mary. "How can this be?"

Zazlov's face flashed before her. *You're the bottle, Felix. You're the reincarnation of my brother.* The glass shard landed on the rock with a clink as Mary stood speechless.

"Holy smokes!" said Mary. "Tricky fellow, that Radu."

As the implications rang through Mary's mind, then faded like the decaying echo of a church bell, a wave of terror swept over her.

"Felix is in grave danger," she said, looking deeper into the dense woods.

Anger welled inside her as she scanned the forest floor for footprints, and that was when she heard quiet grunting.

Mary, a voice seemed to say.

Mary spun around, trying to locate its source.

She followed a single set of footprints to a wide oak tree.

"Help me," came Felix's muffled voice.

Mary knelt to the tree. "Felix! Where are you?" She scanned the bark, wondering if Felix was somehow trapped inside the tree.

As she reached outward, she felt his boot.

"Felix!" Mary stood and leapt back.

"I'm stuck," came Felix's voice.

Mary knelt to him once more and ran her hands over his legs, finally making out the shape of his body as her hands ran along his arms, which were pinned to his sides.

"This is a new one," she said.

"Help me up."

Mary blew out a big breath.

"Today has been one hell of a day for not keeping up with my witchcraft studies. That much I can tell you."

She sensed Felix continuing to struggle.

"Just sit tight. Let me think this over."

Mary closed her eyes and placed her palms against Felix's chest, concentrating while absorbing Felix's memories.

"OK, I have it. Protection and immobilization spell. Hmm."

She gritted her teeth and tried to recall her lessons.

"Til'ranius!" she said, watching a shimmer of light run from her hands and take the shape around Felix's body.

Mary waited for a moment as the light bounced over Felix's invisible shape, believing she had cast the right spell, only to see an orchestra of crickets materialize on his body. They swarmed over him as they chirped and leapt away.

"Uh . . . sorry, Felix."

Mary tried to piece the spell together—*til* was the word for manifestation. It was *tol* she wanted. *Tol* meant to scatter or break apart. *Ranius*? Didn't mean crickets. It meant to invoke fear. Mary's eyes widened.

"Let me guess—you hate crickets."

More grunting.

"Sorry. I'm trying," she said as several of the bugs hopped along Felix's imprint.

She reached in and brushed the rest away.

It wasn't *ranius*. It was . . . something close. *Ra'lium*? No. Come on. What was the word for 'bonds'?

"I have it!" she said. "OK, just a word of warning. This is either going to work or put you to sleep for a good decade, so . . . buckle in."

Mary stood back and clenched her fists. "*Tol'ra'minum!*"

A sliver of yellow light ran from her hands and absorbed into Felix's body. After a few seconds, Felix appeared and slumped to the mud.

He shook his head and finally looked up at Mary, appearing a bit dazed.

"Well, hello there, handsome. Busy day?"

Felix stood and embraced her at once.

"Thank goodness you're alive," he said.

"Close one, for sure."

They let go the embrace.

"Any hope on Sebastian and my uncle?"

"Nothing. I'm sorry. Radu said they likely . . . oh," said Felix, pausing. "I suppose you don't know yet."

"I do. I pieced it together from holding the broken bottle. Are you OK?"

"I am, but . . . I can't believe it."

Mary looked into the woods, and noticed the day begin to darken.

"Seems it gets dark early in these parts. I think Radu went that way," she said. "We can't let him fight this thing alone."

"Agreed. But the forest is teeming with werewolves. They protect the Butcher."

"Just as Radu mentioned."

"Can you transform into a horse or something?"

Mary blinked up at Felix in surprise. "Why, Prince Felix! I hope you weren't thinking of mounting me."

Felix blushed. "Uh, no . . . I . . . well, yeah. I suppose—just to travel more quickly."

Mary laughed.

"Shape-shifting doesn't work that way. It's mass for mass. I mean—I could transform into a horse, just not one big enough to ride. I can't transform into anything bigger or smaller than myself."

"We need to be swift," said Felix.

"Here's what. Ravens. I can transform into multiple birds, fly above the forest—locate the castle and track the wolves as I go. You keep to the crest, and I'll alert you if you need to climb down. Pretty sure this stone tomb is that way."

Felix rubbed his hands together. "Sounds as good as any."

"See you at the castle."

Mary leapt into the air and shimmered as her body broke apart into a dozen small ravens and flapped above the canopy, cawing all the while.

Felix looked into the darkened woods, dreading the prospect of huffing it.

"I sure miss Drina," he said, then jogged off along the ridge.

*

Sebastian tugged on Rurik's unconscious body, pulling him from the brown waters. The giant man dragged Rurik to dry grass and sat beside him, taking a moment to enjoy the radiant sunlight and rolling up his tattered sleeves past his shoulders. Sebastian reached down to his leather pouch and removed Dollie's waterlogged body.

"All fine, Dol-dol. You dry now," he said, closing his eyes and tilting his face to the sky.

385

Sebastian's chin curled as he thought to the crash.

He was ashamed he had not acted in time to save Mary—aside from Dollie, his only true friend.

He still remembered awakening in Denis's basement on the evening of his resurrection. Disoriented and in great pain, he had nearly killed the strange man before him in a fit of rage, tearing the lab apart and cornering Denis. Then suddenly, feet rumbled down the stairs and there she stood. His savior. The moment he took her in, sensing her kind energy, everything felt better. He remembered Mary standing at the foot of the basement stairs, screaming at her father for his madness.

How could you! You're torturing this poor thing!

She then reached out to Sebastian and his fear and confusion gave way to a sense of calm—a sense of belonging. He gripped her hand, and she led him away from Denis's farm. Sebastian had gone to live with her at the inn, where they shared their days together in peace and occasionally answered the call to fight dark entities. Mary had taught him to read and helped him learn to speak again.

It was she who named him Sebastian, as the memories of his previous life had become fuzzy and washed away, causing him to forget his own name. *We'll call you something regal*, she said. *A name fit for a king!*

When Sebastian's psyche grew too oppressive and cast him into pits of self-loathing, loneliness, and disgust, quashing his attempts at a full night's sleep, it was Mary who showed up with a big box wrapped in red paper. Sebastian remembered opening the box to find a fluffy rabbit doll with two of the shiniest black buttons for eyes. Dollie—his forever companion, who turned all his nightmares to restful slumber. As the rest of the world cowered at his appearance or pointed in mockery, Mary had always stood up for him and looked upon him with loving care.

And now . . . she was gone.

Sebastian thought over his actions and realized it had all happened too fast for him to do anything. He decided he was lucky enough to have grabbed Rurik, scaled the inside of the bomber, and leapt into the lake before the fuselage impact. He meditated for a few more minutes, swearing to himself that he would find Mary and see her to safety no matter the cost.

"Wha—what happened?" came Rurik's voice, soft and timid.

Sebastian looked down at him and shrugged. "Everyone lost."

"If we survived, I'm sure they did too. We'll find them."

Rurik winced as he tried to reach down to his leg. "Wow, that smarts," he said, looking down to his right foot, which was twisted unnaturally to the right.

Rurik tried to sit up, but the pain was too great. He lay back on the grass and threw his arm over his face. "It's broken! That's it . . . I'm dead."

Sebastian reached over and patted him on the chest.

"It get better, Unk Rur. I help."

Rurik squinted up at Sebastian through one eye.

"I appreciate your optimism, but unless we find a doctor real fast, I'm in serious trouble. The wounded don't last long in circumstances like ours."

Sebastian placed Dollie on the grass and knelt to Rurik's broken ankle. His brown eyes looked to Rurik. "I sorry, Rur. This hurt now. I make heal."

"No! No!" shouted Rurik, then gave a terrible screech as Sebastian yanked on the ankle and gripped it to set the bones.

Rurik lay back on the grass. He let out a loud grunt and kicked Sebastian with his other leg. The blow barely disturbed the giant man, who continued to grip Rurik's ankle with great force as a soft green glow emanated from his hands. Rurik twisted and shook, trying to pull his leg from Sebastian's fists, finally scurrying away on his back when Sebastian let go.

"You're magick?" asked Rurik.

Sebastian shrugged. "No maj. Sebastian heal good."

Rurik calmed himself and rotated his foot in a circle. It was still painful, but felt more like a bad sprain.

"Help me up," said Rurik, extending his hand to Sebastian.

Sebastian pulled him to his feet, and Rurik winced as he tried to put weight on his foot.

"I think it's still broken."

"No more break. But still need heal."

Rurik leaned into Sebastian and gingerly applied more weight to his foot. A moment later, he was limping freely over the grass.

"OK, OK," said Rurik. "Not great, but we can work with this. Thank you."

Rurik hobbled next to Sebastian and surveyed the lake—its surface scattered with debris from the crash.

"You see that?" asked Rurik, pointing to a section of debris that appeared like a big green glob floating in the water.

Sebastian looked to the lake. He curled his nose, then ran into the water and swam toward the floating object. He returned a moment later, emerging from the lake with a hogweed canister entwined in a canvas duffel bag.

"No way," said Rurik, sitting once more to rest his ankle. "Quick, let me see!"

Sebastian dropped the hogweed canister and duffel bag before him. Rurik inspected the device, checking to see if all the hosing was still secured properly.

"Better stand back," said Rurik, twisting one of the canister's nozzles and holding the trigger.

Sensing a light breeze at his back, Rurik pulled the trigger. A white fog shot from the nozzle's tip.

"We're in business, baby!"

He set the hogweed canister on the grass and pulled the mostly empty duffel bag to him. He opened it to find two blackwood stakes and a can of beans. A rattling at the bottom of the bag caught his attention, and he shoved his hand in the bag and dug out a handful of Felix's gold coins.

"Jackpot," said Rurik, looking up at Sebastian. "Great news. We have money and can at least defend ourselves should any vámpir be on the loose."

Sebastian shrugged. "Vamp easy," he said, reaching down and picking up Dollie from the grass. He squeezed the doll in his hands, wrung more water from her body, then placed her back in his pouch.

A bell rang out in the distance, and both men gazed across the lake as the chimes continued for a short minute.

"There's a town nearby," said Rurik. "We might be in luck."

Sebastian walked to the water's edge. He placed his hand to his brow and squinted from the sun reflecting from the lake's surface.

"Small tower," said Sebastian.

"I think we should head that way."

Sebastian turned and shook his head. "No good. People scare of Sebastian."

Rurik relaxed on his elbows and took in Sebastian's mighty frame.

"Of course. Well . . . hmmm. I assume we're still in Slovakia, but we need to make sure. And we'll eventually need shelter. There has to be a barn or something abandoned in that town. Let's just get some rest here, and we'll head that way after dark, to see."

Rurik perked up his head as something yelped from the forest behind them.

"Do you hear that?" he asked.

Sebastian looked to the trees.

"Rur stay. I check."

"Be careful. If something happens to you, I'll rot out here."

Sebastian walked past Rurik and into the forest.

As he entered the wood, he heard something whimpering to his right. He navigated around a series of trees to see a headless boar hanging from a rope and a wolflike creature clamped in a trap below it, struggling to free its leg from the shiny silver device.

Sebastian carefully approached the trapped animal.

It watched as Sebastian neared, gnashing its fangs and emitting a low growl. Sebastian extended his arms outward and spread his hands as a means to convey he intended no harm. As he neared the animal, it tried to drag itself away from him with its front append-ages, only to be fettered by the thick chain attached to the device. Sebastian noticed that its paws appeared like clawed human hands and its coat suffered from a horrid mange—its hairy body was more human than beast.

Sebastian knelt to the animal.

It positioned its body toward him, growling as he crouched just out of reach. Sebastian studied the animal with a great sense of curiosity. It had a lean, muscular body and the head of a wolf, but its face resembled that of a human female with wide blue eyes.

A foreboding growl resonated from the creature as Sebastian ex-tended his hand slowly toward the trap. He took two more crouching steps toward the wolf and gripped the mouth of the circular contrap-tion, pulling it open. The beast lashed its claws across his forearm, growling as it tore open his flesh. Sebastian conveyed no sense of pain as he ripped the trap open, snapping its springs.

The she-wolf scurried away.

It stood upright and dashed on two legs into the wood, turning to look at Sebastian before it became one with the dense woods.

Sebastian looked into the forest for another moment, convinced there were others like the animal he'd just freed, staring at him. Deciding it was merely shadows from the thick canopy, Sebastian walked back to Rurik.

"You're a madman!" called Rurik, when he caught sight of Sebastian. "Are you wounded?"

Sebastian held his forearm, dripping with dark green blood.

"I told you," said Rurik. "Best to leave things alone. What was it?"

"Hurt dog," said Sebastian. "I help." He looked to his forearm, which was badly gored, and gripped his hand tightly around his shredded flesh and muscle.

Sebastian closed his eyes as a light green glow shone from his arm. When he pulled his hand away, the limb was mostly healed, save visible indentations from the wolf's claws. The marks slowly returned to his normal ashen skin tone.

"That's really something," said Rurik.

"What now?"

"Well," said Rurik, "I think it's best we take cover near the tree line until dusk. A giant plane crashing into a nearby lake is certain to pique the interest of the locals."

Rurik peered back toward the forest and swore he saw the shadow of a wolf standing on two legs, watching them. He squinted, then blinked a few times before the image dissipated.

"Then again, maybe staying out in the open is our best option after all," he said.

"Don care. Sebastian never scare. Only basement." Sebastian reached into his leather pouch and pulled out Dollie. He extended it to Rurik. "Hold Dol-dol. She make brave."

Rurik begrudgingly accepted the rabbit doll, still damp with lake water, and held it to his chest.

"Much better. Thanks, big guy."

23

March 29, 1917, dusk

The first-quarter moon had just breached the horizon when Radu arrived at the outer perimeter of Čachtice Castle. He crouched in a sparsely wooded area at the foot of the castle and stared at the darkened shadow cast against the cobalt sky.

Looking up at the imposing relic, Radu was reminded of the story of David and Goliath.

Howls echoed through the dark woods.

Radu took a few steps forward before dashing toward the castle's foundation.

More howls rang through the darkness, seemingly closer than before.

Radu walked around the rocky embankment until he came to a small stream that led into the rock. He bent down and inspected the half-circle opening. Pulling himself through a series of broken and rusty iron bars that once protected the sewage outlet, he was able to rise to a stooped position once in the corridor. The small amount of water trickling past him smelled fresh. Radu shimmied along, careful not to twist his ankle on the various round rocks strewn along his path, which grew darker the farther he trod.

He continued for another two hundred meters before coming to a rusty and corroded ladder that led to a round doorway. Radu looked upward to the opening and placed his remaining hand on the ladder, the motion reminding him just how ill prepared he was for this encounter.

Radu felt his throat constrict—there was nowhere left to run. He knew it was his duty to confront this evil, but he began to question himself.

"This is the way of the warlock," he said aloud. "There is no turning back."

He reached down and gripped his demon blade. The last time he squared off against the Butcher, he had only his wits and an iron sword. He'd bested this demon once before. Baphomet was a shadow creature; although proficient in hand-to-hand combat, it was not his forte. He preferred to allow others to do the fighting and weaken his prey. Radu knew the Butcher was expecting him, but by cloaking his actions, he believed he held an element of surprise that might tip this confrontation to his advantage once more.

Radu concentrated on his amputated limb, and his ethereal garment formed itself into a metal hook. He secured the grapnel on a rusty bar, then ascended the ladder, taking care not to lose his grip on the slippery metal.

He emerged into a dilapidated brick corridor lit by sporadic torches. It was nearly as he remembered it, except there was something new. As he peered down the long hallway, Radu noticed a row of animal skulls that lined the wall about twenty meters away.

He walked to the long line of craniums that hung along the bricks. As he neared the first skull, he spotted a sheathed demon blade hanging below it. He began to count the skulls, each with a sheathed blade just underneath. He stopped at twelve, knowing the fabled scimitars were missing no longer.

"Excellent discovery," he said.

Radu looked back and forth down the darkened corridor. He knew these walls. It had been nearly three hundred years since his last incursion into Čachtice Castle, but its diabolism still resonated from the very rock—even the musty air hung heavy with an age-old malevolence that smelled of death and decay.

To his right, the hall extended to a darkened entrance. Radu was well aware of where it led—to the Butcher's dreaded dungeon, where a pool of molten silver waited to claim the demon's enemies. Sensing the Butcher was lurking above and knowing a duel near the molten pool was far too precarious, he proceeded left toward a circular room that glowed with an orange light shining from above.

Radu pushed ahead, crouching as he walked. He reached the circular dead end and peered up a shaft that led to the castle's main floor. He gripped the hilt of his blade and realized his palms were sweating as the stone floor beneath him rumbled before slowly ascending.

Time turned to sludge as the stone elevator moved up the shaft.

Radu kept his eyes on the orange glow above.

In a matter of moments, he would arrive in the castle's grand hall. What awaited him there, even his clairvoyance could not determine. As the vaulted ceiling of the grand hall came into view, Radu fixed his eyes dead ahead and watched the bricks slide downward. The torchlight from above died out and everything fell to black, save a sliver of moonlight cast through the hall's arched windows.

Radu's head breached the threshold to the main floor as the stone platform beneath him came level with the grand hall. Sculpted bronze sconces shaped like dragon heads popped from the walls encircling the shaft as the elevator mechanism clicked into place. Radu peered into the darkened hall through an opening hung with stone dragon's teeth.

He focused on slowing his breathing as he took a step forward. A few paces more and he stood in the grand hall of Čachtice Castle, just underneath an ornate sculpture of a dragon's head—its mouth the entrance to the elevator shaft.

To his left was a massive fireplace carved of stone and a series of peaked windows, which were cracked and broken. Above the mantel was a tattered white tapestry stitched with the emblem of House Báthory—a serpentine dragon curled around a red circle containing a portion of a wolf jawbone with three sharp fangs. The rest of the walls hung heavy with the pelts of flayed werewolves.

To Radu's right, a flight of six wide stairs ran the entire length of the hall, leading up to another hall with a smattering of columns. Before him was a long, wide table carved of heavy slate.

Radu wrapped his hand around his blade, trying to sense the Butcher. His eyes ran along the darkened stone table, which was partially illuminated by the moonlight shining in from the opposite end of the shadowy hall. He stood in the gloom until his night vision acclimated him to the darkness.

And across the expanse, at the top of the stairs, there he stood—his age-old enemy, Baphomet as the Black Butcher. Draped in black leather with his arms folded across his chest, he appeared like a burly statue carved of matte obsidian, an eyeless executioner's hood covering his head and shoulders. Bass pulsations and crackling filled the hall as the Butcher unsheathed a demon blade from his waist and held it at his side.

"The years have been unkind, Radu. I can sense your quiver."

The Butcher's voice was low and commanding.

"You mistake my tremble, for it is rage. Soon you will join your father, imprisoned in my grasp." Radu unsheathed his scimitar and stood before the stone table. "I bested your Death Witch," he said, pointing the weapon toward the Butcher. "And now I've come to finish this."

The Butcher grunted. "Ah, yes! I watched the encounter remotely. A rather Pyrrhic victory, wouldn't you agree? Let us not forget Felix's little distraction, which took her attention from you. You were lucky, Radu. No more. I fear your luck has run dry."

"Then try me."

The Butcher stood silently as the sounds of their black scimitars seemed to vibrate the castle's walls. He extended a gloved hand across his hooded figure and telekinetically pushed the massive stone table from between them—rock grinding on rock screeched through the hall. The Butcher flipped his hand and sent the slate mass flying into the hearth, cracking it into large sections.

"You were saying . . ." said the Butcher, walking down the short flight of stairs until he was level with Radu.

The two warlocks stood in the darkness, silently facing one another as the white sparks encircling their blades flashed against their silhouettes.

Radu felt the Butcher scanning his mind. This was positive, as it demonstrated that the demon was unsure of the outcome and searching for some advantage. Radu blocked him and decided to engage defensively to goad the Butcher with stillness and calm. He knew he held the advantage if the Butcher's overconfidence drove his offense and made him mistake-prone.

Radu focused his mind. He would keep to fundamentals—nothing fancy. The Butcher would expect the aggression and showmanship Radu displayed in his youth. He scanned the pending outcomes and planned a simple three-movement finish: parry, slide through, strike from the back.

It would be over the moment it started.

The Butcher attacked in a flash, thrusting his blade down onto Radu, who parried, then slid past the dark warlock and cast his blade backward, intending to strike his spine. There was a crash, and sparks rained down over the combatants as the Butcher slung his blade over his shoulder and blocked Radu's blow.

He turned, facing Radu.

"Are we to fight like children?" asked the Butcher.

"I'm merely finding my pitch."

"Allow me to help."

The Black Butcher swung his blade wide to meet Radu's sword, then pulled the strike away and quickly jabbed his weapon toward Radu's head. Radu ducked and sidestepped, holding his blade outward as the Butcher did the same.

The tips of the blades met, exchanging white static across their central ridges as the two men circled one another.

Radu jumped forward with a stabbing jab, followed by another as the Butcher backed away, parrying the blows. The dark warlock moved with such precision and grace that Radu believed he was reading his mind—the Butcher's defense seemed impenetrable.

"It seems you have run out of mirrors and run out of time. Are we done with the games?"

"Only when you lie sliced in two!"

Radu leapt into the air with his blade extended high.

The Butcher raised his hand and cast Radu into the remnants of the stone table, his body cracking a thick portion of the slate upon impact. Radu groaned as he lay on the stone floor, trying to catch his breath, his demon blade hovering just out of reach.

Radu pulled the blade into his grip, faltering as he stood.

The Butcher marched toward him and thrust a powerful strike across his body. An intense shock wave lit the expanse as the blades met. Tired and injured, Radu forced all his weight against the attack, but the Butcher's strength was too much. Radu backed away, holding his blade firmly against the Butcher's weapon. The tips of the scimitars touched the table fragments, absorbing large portions of the stone.

Dust and rock fragments swirled around the combatants as they lunged, jabbed, and parried.

The Butcher continued his advance, pushing Radu toward the circular elevator shaft. Just as he stood at the threshold, there was a click and the dragon sconces lining the room recessed into the walls.

The stone floor lowered behind him.

Radu was pinned.

Nothing but a sheer drop to the dungeon corridor below. He tried to dematerialize, but could feel the Butcher constraining his ability to cast the spell.

The hooded warlock stood before Radu, his black blade pointed outward. Radu held his weapon in front guard position as he tried to center and calm his mind.

"Nowhere to run," said the Butcher.

Radu cast a quick glance backward, wondering if he had enough energy to summon a levitation spell and escape below, but he could feel the Butcher's power constraining him once more.

"No more spells, old man."

Realizing this was his last stand, Radu lurched forward, unleashing a series of desperate attacks.

The Butcher parried each, then struck a forceful blow that knocked Radu's sword from his hand. The blade hovered just above the stone floor, and as Radu reached for it, he realized he was frozen in his stance. A shower of red lightning from the Butcher's hand enveloped Radu, further constricting him.

The Butcher extended his free hand, and Radu's blade flew into it.

Radu was completely immobilized, struggling against the glowing red netting that entangled his body. The Butcher levitated him slightly and stood before him, crossing the blades against Radu's neck.

"So much for defense," said the Butcher. "Pity."

Radu struggled and grunted.

"I want to thank you, Radu. For everything you've done," said the Butcher as he walked forward and pushed Radu directly over the sheer drop to the corridor below. "All your scheming and lies through the centuries—dabbling in the dark to bring forth the light. You failed, and now I will take my prize. Your brother is mine."

"Strike me down and Elizabeth will be free."

"My dear Radu, you will die. But only when I am prepared. For now . . ."

Radu's body began to dissipate as the red weave constricted more tightly around him, crushing his essence into a fine speck of pink light. A final red blast flared and then Radu was gone.

The sheath of Radu's demon blade hovered in the air before it floated toward the Butcher and fastened itself to his waist. The dark warlock sheathed both scimitars and stood staring down the darkened shaft.

The key to his father's resurrection was now in his possession, and his enemy was routed at last.

*

"This way, quickly," cawed a raven as it swooped past Felix.

He was breathless and sweating, uncertain he could carry on. He leaned against a tree and took a moment to catch his breath as the howling echoed from behind.

The werewolves were close.

Felix stared up to the darkened silhouette of Čachtice Castle, wondering how he could breach the stone structure.

Three of Mary's ravens landed near the base of the castle, and Felix noticed the moonlight glistening off a stream running from a small inlet. The ravens cackled in unison and flapped their wings as the sounds of growling and snapping branches grew near.

Felix dashed toward the opening just as the shadows of three large werewolves crashed through the brush. All twelve ravens swarmed before him as he set his sights on the inlet. The birds banked upward and flew away as Felix approached. Realizing he had no time to navigate the opening, he dove headfirst into the gap, crashing hard into the rocky stream and bruising his buttocks as the rusty iron bars scraped along his backside.

A menacing growl came from behind him, and Felix turned to see the shadow of a massive wolf clawing at him from the opening. Even in the dark, he could make out its fearsome claws and jagged teeth as it snapped at him, trying to catch his ankle. Fortunately for Felix, the beast proved too large to fit its upper body through the opening.

Felix scrambled back on all fours as the stream soaked his garments, the werewolf still trying to force its body into the opening as it growled with thick saliva dripping from its mouth. Feeling the rocks underneath him, Felix grabbed the biggest stone he could find and thrust it directly into the wolf's teeth.

The beast yelped and backed away.

Felix sat in the dark, staring out through the opening and listening to the echoing sounds of struggle and the cawing of ravens. A quick whimper rose from outside, and the ravens shot into the opening, shimmering as they transformed into Mary, who slumped face-first into Felix.

He lay nearly submerged in the stream with Mary on top of him.

Breathing heavily and able to make out only her shadow, Felix could sense her face was inches from his.

"Hoo," said Mary.

"What?"

"Somebody needs a toothbrush," she said, laughing a bit as she climbed away.

"Seriously," said Felix, breathing into his palm and attempting to discern if he had bad breath.

"Just teasing," said Mary, extending her hand and pulling him up. "Wow, that was close."

"I'll say."

"Plucked out one of their eyeballs on my way in, so we'll consider it a small victory."

Felix turned and stared down the darkened tunnel. Low guttural growls stalked them from just outside the opening.

"There's a light ahead," said Mary, crouching as she walked forward.

Felix followed. They reached the decaying ladder and looked up to the torchlight emanating from above.

"Can you sense anything?" asked Felix.

"I'm really not the best at that, so no. Nothing. I could do my cockroach trick."

"Cockroach trick?"

Mary shrugged. "Basically, I transform into a bunch of cockroaches and do a bit of recon."

"Uhhh . . ."

"Agreed. Not the most attractive of my transformations. Hard to unsee."

"It's dark enough, but I like you in human form if possible."

Mary turned to him.

"Why, Your Eminence, are you growing sweet on me?"

Felix gasped quietly, trying to think of a reply.

"Forget it, lover boy. Wish me luck."

Mary planted a kiss on Felix's lips, then scurried up the ladder.

Felix stood in the dark, his heart racing, nearly forgetting he stood in a musty sewer outlet, being stalked by bloodthirsty werewolves.

"Felix, quickly!" came Mary's voice.

Felix proceeded up the ladder to find Mary standing in the torch-lit corridor before Radu, who lay against the brick wall holding his side, blood dripping over his hand.

Mary knelt to Radu as Felix dashed to them both.

"I'm sorry. I failed you," wheezed Radu, wincing a bit. "The Butcher has escaped."

"Here," said Mary, helping Radu from the floor.

Felix assisted Radu in steadying himself and noticed the warlock had two scimitars sheathed at his side. He wondered where Radu had acquired the second blade and what good it might do him with only one limb. He then looked to the long line of animal skulls with demon blades hanging below them.

"These are the blades you spoke of," said Felix.

"You figure that out all by yourself?" quipped Mary. "Here. Arm up." She moved to the wall and reached out to remove a scimitar.

"No, no!" said Radu. "The blades are too dangerous. Best let them be."

Felix sensed something suspicious hovering around Radu's aura.

"Sorry, big fellow," said Mary. "Overruled."

She slung a blade around her waist and handed another to Felix.

"You can fight?" asked Felix.

"Have you not been paying attention to the last eleven hours?"

"I meant with swords."

"I can do better than eighth place in my fencing class, if that's what you mean."

"Fair enough," said Felix, strapping his blade around his waist and scanning the shadowy corridor.

Torchlight glowed from an opening down the hall.

"Can you scale down the ladder?" asked Felix.

Radu did his best to stand upright and looked toward the glowing room.

"This way is better. Easier escape," he said, motioning to the sizable room, which appeared to glimmer with smooth walls. A rusty iron gate stood open at its entrance.

"I don't know, Radu," said Mary. "It looks—"

"Do as I say!" barked Radu. "And put back the swords. We cannot risk them falling into the wrong hands once we escape."

Felix was taken aback by Radu's sudden change in tone, and an eerie sensation crept up over the front of his ears.

"I'll take my chances," said Mary, scowling at Radu.

"This is the way," said Radu, motioning toward the corridor's end. "I'll follow. I am too weak to lead."

Mary shot a confused glance to Felix, who shrugged.

"I'll go first," said Felix, moving before her.

"Such a gentleman," said Mary, gripping her blade's hilt.

As they neared the iron bars on the entrance, Felix's stomach became overwhelmed with a gnawing sensation. He could now see that the room contained an open pit with a walkway encircling it and a plank leading to its center. At the end of the plank sat a slim metal cage with a pointy top attached to a chain that fed toward the room's ceiling.

His ears perked up at the sounds of low bass resonating from behind him.

Both he and Mary turned to Radu, who morphed into a dark figure wearing an eyeless executioner's hood and holding both scimitars toward them in long point.

"Now I have you," he said, kicking Mary into Felix.

She quickly unsheathed her blade and jabbed it at the Butcher.

The burly warlock blocked her strike as Felix sprung into action, removing his black scimitar and casting an overhead blow at the Butcher, who parried it with his other sword.

The darkened corridor flashed with white light as the Butcher heaved his weight onto his opponents and backed them into his dungeon.

"Time to walk the plank," said the Butcher, thrusting his weight into Mary and knocking her to the floor.

She shrieked and Felix glanced to her, realizing the entire dungeon was coated in silver.

"Mary!" he yelled while keeping all his weight pressed against the Butcher's advance.

White sparks flashed from their blades as the Butcher pushed him closer to the plank.

The dark warlock released his pressure, causing Felix to stumble forward. He then brought a mighty stroke down upon Felix's blade and knocked it from his hand. The blade hovered just above the silver floor and the Butcher kicked its hilt, sending it gliding along the curved walkway.

He pointed his blades at Felix's chest and Felix backed away down the plank, looking to the pit below, which bubbled with molten silver.

"Felix!" shouted Mary as she pulled herself from the floor, careful to ensure her flesh made no contact with the silver.

The Butcher extended his hand toward Felix, telekinetically pulling Felix's sheath from his waist and sending it flying to his blade, which hovered along the wall. He then thrust Felix into the silver cage at the end of the plank and locked him in. A rattling sound came from the walls as the cage was hoisted to the conical ceiling, where Felix found himself staring at another hanging cage containing Radu, unconscious within its silver bars.

"Radu, wake up," hissed Felix, kicking his cage.

Radu stirred, half opening his eyes.

"He's trapped us," said Felix. "Can you help?"

Radu shook his head. "What are you doing here? You were supposed to—"

"Forget about that. Mary's in danger."

Radu looked below, taking in the situation. "I'm sorry," he said breathlessly. "The silver has weakened me greatly."

Felix gripped the bars and peered down to the plank as Mary charged toward the Butcher, casting a series of forceful strikes—each appearing to catch the Butcher off guard as he backed toward the plank's end.

Mary continued her offensive, gracefully ducking under the Butcher's counterattacks, outmatching her larger opponent with each impassioned exchange. Step by step, she forced the dark warlock to the edge of the plank until he stood with the sheer drop behind him. Then she appeared to tire, breaking for a moment.

"Out of tricks, shape-shifter?" asked the Butcher as he regained his balance.

He extended his blades to Mary as she buckled over, catching her breath and appearing woozy.

"It seems the fumes have drained your strength."

"I'm just getting started," she said, out of breath.

Mary raised her scimitar high and cast a sweeping blow toward the Butcher, who disappeared into a fine black mist, causing Mary to nearly topple into the molten pool. Balancing herself, she spun around to see the Butcher materialize before her.

"My turn," said the Butcher, recoiling his powerful leg and kicking Mary in the stomach.

She yelped as she fell toward the molten silver below, striking the surface and slowly sinking into the depths. Her demon blade pierced the liquid vertically and sat with its hilt sticking from the shiny metal—a small whirlpool formed as it absorbed the silver.

"No!" screamed Radu.

"You son of a bitch," followed Felix, rattling his cage as he looked down to see the silver cover Mary's body entirely.

The torches encircling the room flickered as they burned low.

There was a high-pitched hiss, and a near-blinding white light glowed from the demon blade's jeweled hilt as the molten whirlpool grew in intensity. The blade suddenly evaporated—its jewel exploding and sending a powerful white shockwave through the chamber as the molten silver obliterated the demon trapped within its hilt.

"Impossible," muttered the Butcher, sheathing his blades.

His dark figure stood at the edge of the plank, watching as what remained of the ornate hilt sank into the silvery depths. He seemed to glare upward at Felix and Radu, who sat in their cages, shielding their eyes.

The room was once again lit only by the dying torches.

"You killed her!" shouted Felix. "I'll—"

The Black Butcher clenched his fist, delivering a remote blow to Felix's gut, silencing him.

The dark warlock then extended his hands and raised them upward as Mary's silver-encased body rose from the depths. She appeared to be caught in mid-fall with her arms and legs splayed haphazardly outward and a terrified expression on her face.

The Black Butcher extended his hand toward Felix's blade, which was hovering along the wall. The weapon sheathed itself and flew to his fist. He then turned to exit the room with Mary hovering by his side.

"Where are you taking her?" yelled Felix.

"A gift for the spider," said the Black Butcher as he slammed the bars shut. "Don't worry, Felix. You're next."

He pulled a lever in the corridor and a wall of pure silver lowered over the bars, sealing them in the dungeon.

"What do we do?" asked Felix.

Radu appeared sullen, staring listlessly into the molten pool as the torchlight flickered.

"Radu!"

Radu shook his head and looked to Felix. "The blade was destroyed. I—I can't believe it."

"Forget the damn blade! What about Mary?"

Radu slumped in his cage. "I'm sorry, Felix. Unless we can awaken what is within you, there's nothing to be done. I fear we've lost."

"Like hell we've lost. It doesn't seem to be affecting me, so come on—think!"

Radu looked Felix over as the torches died and the dungeon fell to the purest of black.

"Very well," said Radu. "Lesson number one. How to see in the dark."

*

"A bit more to the left," grunted Rurik as he sat upon Sebastian's shoulders and peered into a dirty glass window.

His hands gripped onto the sloped wooden shingles that hung from the second story's peaked roof. Sebastian shifted left, allowing Rurik a better view into the quaint Gothic building.

"Oh my!" he said. "It's a tavern. A gorgeous, lovely tavern."

He climbed down from Sebastian and landed upon the uneven cobblestone alleyway, careful to favor his wounded ankle.

"Well, that's a bit of an exaggeration. Looks like a real dump . . . but alcohol, buddy, alcohol!" Rurik slapped Sebastian on the thigh and grinned broadly. "I haven't had a drink in months. I'm all twisted up inside."

"Sebastian only drink water."

"Suit yourself, big guy," said Rurik, rubbing his hands together. "I'm going to have the tallest pint you've ever seen."

Sebastian nodded.

"Ugh," said Rurik, looking over Sebastian, who was wearing the ripped-open duffel bag over his head as a makeshift disguise. "Well," he continued, shifting the bag over Sebastian's head. "I had the best intentions with this. Was supposed to look like a cloak . . . Now you just look like a giant man wearing a torn duffel bag on his head."

"I like. I keep," said Sebastian, positioning the bag so it hung more over his brow.

"Your head, your choice. Shall we?"

Rurik tightened the straps of the hogweed canister on his back. He then limped down the alleyway and peeked into the street. Deciding it was clear, he motioned to Sebastian, who tiptoed awkwardly toward him.

They entered the rustic tavern, which was dimly lit by a candelabra center room and candle sconces lining the cedarwood paneling. The conversations ceased upon their entry, and Rurik counted up roughly fifteen patrons seated at various tables and booths. After taking a moment to inspect Rurik and Sebastian—but specifically

Sebastian, whose head nearly reached the rafters—the patrons returned to their conversations and a light chatter filled the room.

"Don't worry, pal," said Rurik, leaning into Sebastian. "Not the first time I've had to win over a strange tavern. Just wait. By the time we leave, they'll all be our best friends."

"Careful, Unk Rur."

An elderly woman with a terrible black mole upon the tip of her nose appeared behind the bar, which was adorned with a large wooden sculpture of a wolf's head.

"Nestojte len tam. Pod' dnu," said the old woman, waving to Rurik.

"Oh, right," said Rurik, leaning in again to Sebastian. "I forgot. We don't know exactly where we are."

Sebastian shrugged and they moved to the bar. The curious patrons glanced hesitantly at Sebastian's massive frame as they walked by.

"Do you happen to speak Russian? Romanian?" asked Rurik.

"Ruský?"

"Yes, yes! Ruský. Me Ruský." Rurik patted his fingers to his chest. The woman nodded.

"Áno. Áno, Rusky. Ale iba nepatrne. Only little bit Russian."

Rurik nodded. "Great. Áno is yes?"

"Áno. Áno—yes."

"I am Russian. My name is Rurik." Rurik exaggeratedly pointed to himself. "Rurik. Russian. And you?" He pointed back at the old woman.

She smiled at him, revealing her tarnished dentures. "Milena. Slovak."

"Ah, Milena. Nice to meet you." He leaned into Sebastian. "Looks like we're still in Slovakia."

Milena's neck craned backward as she looked up to Sebastian.

"I like the big man in fun hat," she said.

Rurik patted him on the arm. "This is Sebastian. Great man, this one. Quiet, but strong."

Milena shrugged, conveying she did not understand.

s and I are lost. What city are we in? Do you know city?"

Milena's face brightened. "Yes, city ... Hrachovište is our city."

"Wonderful!" said Rurik, looking to Sebastian. "See, I told you we'd figure this all out—now we just need a map and we can figure our way out of here. But first, some liquid." Rurik turned his attention to Milena. "Do you have vodka, by chance? You know . . . vodka?"

"Vodka, no. Beer only."

"Beer only!" Rurik reached into his pocket and pulled out one of Felix's gold coins. He held it to Milena between his index and middle fingers. "May I have a beer, then?"

Milena's eyes grew wide and she snatched the coin.

"Ó môj! Môžete mať toľko, koľko chcete," she said, smiling and nodding at Rurik. She held the coin high and leaned over the bar. "Tento muž je bohatý. nápoje pre vás všetkých!"

The patrons looked back at Rurik and broke into exuberant applause. One man seated near Rurik rose and patted him on the arm, then shook his hand, careful to steer clear of Sebastian as he returned to his chair.

"What happen?" asked Sebastian.

"I believe we just bought everyone a round of drinks."

"That good?"

"Very good, you'll see."

Milena returned with two large wooden pints and placed them before Rurik and Sebastian. Rurik quickly seized upon them both and pulled them before him. Milena regarded him curiously.

"Oh . . . my friend doesn't partake."

Milena scrunched her brow.

"Friend," said Rurik, patting Sebastian. "No drink."

"Ah," said Milena. She then leaned toward Rurik and whispered, "You and friend take care. You are safe here, but forest bad for stranger. Very many danger. You stay at inn upstairs and lock door. Leave at dawn."

"Leave at dawn," repeated Rurik. "Understood."

Milena walked away and returned to a wooden chair at the side of the bar.

Rurik looked up at Sebastian and pulled on his sleeve, causing the giant man to lean downward.

"Keep an eye out, will you?" asked Rurik. "We might be in trouble. I'll work on it."

Rurik wasted no time in bringing the first beer to his lips. He tilted his head back and chugged the liquid as quickly as he could, finishing the performance with a loud and exaggerated belch.

The bar patrons applauded and laughed, and Rurik took a bow.

"What did I tell you, big guy? Everybody loves a lush."

The door to the tavern suddenly swung open with a loud crash. The candles fluttered, and everyone turned to see an empty doorframe.

"That's odd," said Rurik, peeking into the darkened street.

The door remained open, and Rurik hobbled forward with Sebastian standing behind him.

Three seated patrons suddenly slumped to the floor.

Rurik's eyes widened as a clicking sensation reverberated across his rib cage. "Na—" he shouted as a thick, slimy substance struck him in the face. He fell backward as Sebastian stepped forward to catch him, placing him gently on the floor.

Chaos and confusion erupted inside the tavern as three blurs sailed through the entryway. The patrons jumped from their seats and dashed for the door as the bodies of three vámpir materialized and fell upon the unconscious patrons, tearing open their sternums and feasting on their hearts to the sounds of screams, breaking glass, and wooden chairs being scattered about the interior.

Sebastian growled and lurched toward the feasting vámpir as a fourth vampire appeared at the door and slammed it closed, trapping the fleeing patrons in the bar. It hissed at them and struck two in the face with its knockout venom while grabbing another by her neck. The vámpir squeezed the woman's neck until it loudly snapped. It tossed the woman's lifeless body on the floor as the rest of the patrons cowered against the back wall, crying and wailing.

Sebastian tore a feasting vámpir from its prey. He raised the monster to the ceiling, then slammed it back onto the floor. His ashen flesh glowed green as he forced his powerful hand into the creature's face and proceeded to crush its skull—its body dissipating to a smoky black ether.

The vámpir at the door turned its attention to Sebastian as the two feasting vámpir rose up and flanked him from his right.

Sebastian threw his arms wide and belted out a thunderous growl. The vámpir charged him, knocking Sebastian to the floor. One of the vampires gnashed its fearsome jowls and bit into Sebastian's forearm, quickly hissing and recoiling as his hogweed-infused blood began melting its mouth. The vampire fell backward and crawled away, screeching as the lower portion of its face continued to fall to the floor in darkened bloody chunks.

The two remaining vámpir forced Sebastian to the floor, and one of them wrapped its powerful clawed hands around his neck.

"Niemand tötet einen von uns!" hissed the vampire, slicing its sharp nail across Sebastian's neck. "Manfred, pass auf!" shouted the other, rising up and pushing Manfred off Sebastian, who grabbed his own neck and began healing his wound.

A plume of white gas enveloped the vampire on top of Sebastian as Manfred fell forward. Rurik was standing with his hogweed nozzle pointed forward while wiping the vampire saliva from his face. He turned to the wounded vámpir on the floor and walked a few paces toward the creature as it struggled to overcome its facial injury.

"Allow me to help," said Rurik, squeezing the trigger and coating the vampire in hogweed gas.

The vámpir howled as a bright green glow suffused its body, and its bones fell to the ground, slowly melting into green goo.

Sebastian stood, dripping with green vampire glop, and both men turned to confront Manfred, who opened his jowls wide and shot his saliva at Rurik.

Rurik raised his arm, blocking the liquid, but some of it found its mark, causing him to wobble a bit and fall forward. Manfred appeared ready to attack Rurik but was blocked by Sebastian moving between them.

The Red Baron glared at Sebastian and dematerialized into a black mist that broke through the bay window at the front of the tavern, sending glass flying into the cobblestone street.

Sebastian assisted Rurik from the floor and sat him in a chair while fanning his face.

"Wake up, Unk. Wake," he said, as Rurik's head bobbed about.

Rurik slowly regained his wits and looked up at Sebastian.

"Nice work, big guy." He blinked a few more times, then stood and looked around the bar. Two gored bodies lay upon the floor next to a luminous green puddle stacked with slowly melting vampire bones—the remaining frightened patrons still cowered against the wall.

"What do now?" asked Sebastian.

"I don't know. There could be more of them."

Rurik looked to the bar, but Milena was nowhere to be seen—only a tall, lovely mug of beer. He walked to the bar, wrapped his hand around the wooden pint, then proceeded to chug the entire contents. He slammed the mug on the bar and bowed to the patrons.

"Thank you very much, ladies and gentlemen. I am Rurik Kozlov, and this is my beautiful assistant, Sebastian . . . and that's tonight's show!" He grabbed Sebastian's arm. "Let's get the hell out of here."

Rurik hobbled along as he and Sebastian traversed the cobblestone streets, trying to find their way out of the village.

"This way," said Rurik, ducking into a side street. "Keep your eyes on the sky."

They navigated the slim side street and came into the town's central square, only to find the perimeter surrounded by dark shadows of men. Rurik stopped cold and turned to Sebastian.

"Wrong way," he said, pushing on Sebastian.

More shadows crept toward them from the side street exit.

Rurik and Sebastian backed away toward a fountain with a statue of a wolf holding a small girl, who was dumping a pitcher of water into its basin. The sound of the flowing water was soon overpowered by low growls emanating from the shadows as they neared.

Standing back-to-back with Sebastian, Rurik loosened his grip on his hogweed gun as the shadows of their pursuers became entirely apparent.

"Werewolves," said Rurik. "Why'd it have to be werewolves?"

*

The Black Butcher stood at the peak of Čachtice's tallest tower. He raised his arms into the night as dense clouds swirled above him like some gray, twisting inferno and periodic lightning illuminated the sky.

From his vantage point, he could see his werewolf minions scurrying from the dense forest that encircled the castle and even more gathering in the courtyard below.

"My children!" he shouted in Serbian, his voice echoing across the quiet forest.

Howls came from below as the pack gathered before him.

The Butcher was impressed by the sheer size of their pack. Many centuries had passed since he'd found a small band of gored and shackled werewolf warriors at the Romanian border, the last remaining survivors of a final and decisive battle against Vlad Drăculea's army of Nosferatu.

Werewolves were known as neutral guardians of the Veil, but after the Lycan High Council decreed that it would not intervene during the Inferno, a rift in leadership caused civil war. Those who chose to fight fled Serbia in hopes of finding a new home as they defended the supernatural from the Vatican's purge and thwarted Drăculea's heinous campaign against humanity.

Abandoned by their Serbian kin and hunted by Drăculea's Stovâjîk mercenaries, the wolves found refuge in the forest surrounding Čachtice on the pretense that they would guard the Butcher's sacred lands from outsiders in return for protection and sanctuary. But knowing full well the magick-enhancing properties of werewolf blood and bones, the Butcher had far more nefarious intentions.

From this small pack grew a fearsome army of protectors for House Báthory in the fifteenth and sixteenth centuries—remaining and guarding Čachtice long after the Butcher was trapped in the mirror and Elizabeth met her grim fate at the peak of Mount Hohenzollern.

Upon finally escaping his reflective prison in the early 1700s, the Butcher emerged in a state of shock. Drăculea had been vanquished, magick wielders were now cast into the shadows, and his allies and minions had been mostly hunted down and destroyed. Magick had seemingly devolved into mere superstition and humanity had somehow emerged the victor in this protracted battle to purge witchcraft.

Gravely weakened from his imprisonment, the Butcher returned to Čachtice to recover, pleased to discover his minions had hidden the demon blades deep within their family castle. When the time was right, Solomon's demons would be reborn. The Black Butcher would rise again and reveal his true identity to the world. He devised a plan not only to unleash the demons but to emerge the master of them all—even usurping his father, Bael.

The Butcher plotted his revenge against mankind, feeding on the werewolves to regain and surpass his earlier abilities. Over the centuries, his various identities wormed their way into several monarchies as advisors to the crown, shifting geopolitics to his advantage before finally settling on the German Empire with the coronation of Kaiser Wilhelm II.

An electric sensation surged through the Butcher as he stared down upon his lycan army. After centuries of setbacks and many sacrifices endured, all was now in alignment. The demon blade containing his father was in his possession, Radu cel Frumos sat imprisoned in his dungeon awaiting execution, and the reincarnation of Vlad Drăculea was a mere boy who would be tortured and bent to the Butcher's vile will.

The Black Sun would rise again.

"Tonight!" shouted the Butcher. "Tonight, I bring you wondrous news. News of my impending victory. Soon—no more will I live in the shadows. And no more will you cower in fear of further genocide among your kind. I have captured the liar and thief Radu cel Frumos. He now rots in this castle, imprisoned in my inescapable dungeon. But there is more, my children! The devil who slaughtered so many of you centuries ago . . . the beast I stood up to, saving your kind from extermination . . . Vlad Drăculea has been reborn!"

A growing chorus of angered growls came from the route of werewolves.

"Fret not! For in Radu's carelessness, I captured our enemy, who is now known as Prince Felix Yusupov. He too is my prisoner—trapped with no hope of escape, alongside his treacherous brother."

"Kill him! Slaughter him now!" came low voices from below.

"Now is not the time for revenge. Instead, we must strengthen our loyalty and trust in one another. For now, I will return to Germany and finish what I have started. And when I return, then you may exact your vengeance."

Silence.

Rage mixed with worry filled the Butcher, and the whirring clouds above began to fiercely churn with a palpable sense of agitation.

"Was it not me who shattered the shackles of your ancestors? Saved you all from certain and permanent destruction? Was it not me who allowed you to find sanctuary here—in the shadows of my family castle? Have I not delivered every promise upon which I have hung my hood? Are we not friends? I will finally give rise to a great and just Aryan nation. And through that, you, my allies, shall flourish."

The Black Butcher looked down to see the werewolves standing but offering no response.

"Alzbeta! Step forward."

A large female werewolf emerged at the front of the group that had gathered in the courtyard.

"Have you no gratitude for what our union has fostered?" asked the Butcher with concern in his voice.

Alzbeta looked to her pack and then up to the tower.

"We are eternally grateful to you, O Dark Master. You must forgive my pack, for this sudden news is shocking to us all. And you must understand our disappointment in being prevented from exacting a revenge we have waited centuries for."

"I have never—never—lied to any of you. My solidarity has never wavered. You must allow me to complete my motions. You must guard this castle with even more ferocity, for I am about to reveal myself to the world, and when I do, those who oppose us will turn craven and desperate. They will attempt to storm these walls to obtain what I hold within. Our alliance is paramount to victory."

The Black Butcher watched Alzbeta walk farther away from her pack and stand firm against the night sky.

"Then consider our resolve further strengthened," she said. "Our loyalty unbroken. We eagerly stand with our one true protector."

The Black Butcher stared down at them for only a moment longer before the cloud vortex disappeared, and his silhouette with it.

The stars shone in the night once more and a quiet enveloped the countryside.

Alzbeta turned to her pack as a larger wolf with gray fur upon his chest and a missing eye approached her.

"Why didn't you tell him about our captives?" he asked.

Alzbeta glared at him. "Back in line, General."

She fell on her haunches and tore into the forest, her pack following just behind.

PART III:
DIE REVOLVERHELDEN

Chapter 24

24

TOP SECRET—MI6 EYES ONLY

JOURNAL ENTRY RECOVERED FROM
LANCE CORPORAL JAMES HOLLAN
ARRAS, FRANCE, 1917

March 30, 1917

They come at night.

They come missing limbs with rotten, pale flesh hanging from their faces. I've seen some with mere skeletal limbs or no arms at all, trudging across no-man's-land with no awareness of their harrowing wounds. Some even move about with no eyes in their skulls, or with parts of their faces chewed or blown off. I've witnessed others with no lower bodies and entrails hanging from their torsos, clawing themselves along the mud and feasting on carcasses or limbs strewn about the battlefield.

With my own eyes I've seen soldiers who by any standard of reason should be dead simply rise up and feast on the flesh of their living comrades. At first, we thought the Germans had resorted to cannibalism, until we had a face-to-face encounter with these monsters.

We call them "berserkers" because of their fury and fearlessness. They can hardly be stopped and are so ravenous that sometimes they eat their own, who have become too decayed to carry on.

We're three days into our retreat, and every night they come for us. Over the trenches. Up from the tunnels. They seem to be some disease that keeps spreading. There are more

417

every night. Private Kennel, Lance Corporal Simmons, and I are all that's left of my squadron. The others are now among the undead. I was raised not to believe in ghosts or ghouls, but there is no other description for what these things are.

They mostly stay in the tunnels until dusk. But Kennel, who's a great shot, picked one off at about twenty meters yesterday afternoon. Blew the berserker's jaw clean off its face. Bastard didn't even flinch. Just turned to our position and fired its rifle, then ran toward us with no concern about being further wounded. Three of us unloading our magazines could not stop it, until Simmons finally landed a head shot. What I wouldn't give for a Lewis machine gun right now.

The command is lost. The French have deserted. Everything is no-man's-land. The only Germans we see are berserkers, and they hunt us down side by side with the undead French and British.

We fell back several trenches this morning at daybreak. How we survived last night I will never know. Private Kennel is very clever and devised a means of distraction that has likely extended our hopes of survival. Any kerosene we find or machinery that requires gas or oil, we light on fire at night. Fire seems to attract them and helps us keep on the move instead of engaging.

This morning we found a fortified open-air dugout a few trenches back and were finally able to sleep. The trenches are far too dangerous. They come from the tunnels, and since we're not familiar with these new lines, we don't want to be ambushed from below, not knowing the entry and exit points. What looks like a dugout for planning could be a nest of berserkers. We stumbled into one yesterday. They huddle together in the darkness, standing and swaying like some hive-minded mass. It's unnerving. Terrifying, actually.

Luckily, we were able to retreat before catching their attention. We believe they sleep during the day, but truly do not know if they sleep at all as some still roam in daytime. Kennel says they're scouts.

Three of the living from the Fifth Army happened upon us in the afternoon, and they were in no better shape. We shared our rations, but I wonder how many more days any sort of generosity will be felt among those of us left.

When I asked them how they had survived as long as we had, they told the most interesting story I have ever heard. It's a very tall tale. Perhaps it was delirium that led them to such crazed imaginings? But the way they told it stays with me.

It's a bit much to recall, but Private Hyde from the Fifth swears that just as they were trapped at the dead end of a trench by dozens of berserkers closing in, three Americans dressed up like rodeo cowboys arrived on the scene and mowed down the berserkers with an incredible display of marksmanship and sharpshooter acumen, with trick shots and all!

Can you imagine? I couldn't help but think back to an American moving picture I saw in London just before I was deployed. It had cowboys and Indians riding horses and a very elaborate train robbery. As for these mystery gunslingers, Hyde claimed they vanished into the night as quickly as they came.

The men from the Fifth are also saying that reinforcements are on the way. Even bringing landships, or tanks, as they call them. But I don't believe it will do any good. The berserkers swarm everything.

Simmons wants stand-to at dusk, but I have argued that we need to keep retreating. There's no stopping the berserkers. Fighting them is useless, unless you want to become one of them.

We have to keep moving south.

Simmons thinks that's just leading them closer to Paris, but I believe that with the tunnels the British have engineered across France, the berserkers will find their way to a more populated area regardless of our actions. Amiens is next in their path, and it's my hope that the civilians have received some word and already evacuated.

We're scavenging the best we can, but are starving and running out of ammunition. There is no hope in sight. I hold one grenade with me that is reserved for my final act. I fear this will likely be my last entry. The berserkers are growing in number, and we've dwindled to six. Thousands of infantrymen are now missing or dead, or walk among the berserkers. Those who abandoned their posts and retreated first were the smart ones. I see now that duty is overrated in situations like this.

The best we can do is hide and pray.

If you find this journal, pray for me. Pray for my wife, Carly, and my children, Ben and Sara. Pray for my soul. They say war is hell, but they have never experienced terror like this.

—L.Cpl James Hollan, Third Army, BEF.
[CONFIRMED DECEASED, MAR. 31, 1917]

*

March 30, 1917, 3:14 p.m.

Flight Sub-Lieutenant Arthur Roy Brown scanned the allied encampment in the distance as his biplane roared past Amiens' city center. He looked to the three haggard British soldiers crammed into the gunner's seat of his Armstrong Whitworth F.K.8. They huddled together, shivering and covered in dried mud.

"We'll be on the ground in minutes!" shouted Brown.

He steadied the plane and took one more pass around the encampment, noticing that just before the long line of olive tent barracks, a new corral had been constructed. Thirty or so soldiers sat inside the pen, which appeared to be guarded by other soldiers. He aligned his craft with the grass runway and pulled back on the throttle as he leveled for landing.

The plane bounced and bobbed as it touched down, and Brown guided it to the end of the runway where an officer stood flanked by four other soldiers. The officer planted his fists into his hips as Brown taxied toward them and killed his engine.

After a few loud pops, the plane fell to silence.

The three soldiers in the back climbed from the gunner seat and knelt on the mud as two soldiers broke the line and shuffled them off to the deserter pen. Brown sat in his cockpit, removing his goggles and gloves, then pulled off his leather helmet. He swung his leg over the plane and lowered himself to the ground to find himself face to face with the officer and the two remaining soldiers.

"Sir!" shouted Brown, standing rigid with his arms at his sides.

The officer stepped forward, and Brown noticed he wore the insignia of a major general.

What's he doing out here?

"Name and rank, pilot," barked the officer.

"Flight Sublieutenant Arthur Roy Brown, Number 9, sir."

"You the one who's been doing evac runs from Arras?"

"Yes, sir!"

The major general turned to the soldiers flanking him. "Tend to the prisoners, men," he said. "I'll handle this one."

"Yes, sir," said the soldiers, who ran back toward the deserter pen.

Brown looked over the officer, wondering how severe his punishment would be for appropriating his plane for unsanctioned rescues. From the officer's short mustache, curt expression, and the deep lines around his eyes and forehead, Brown assumed a stern lashing was imminent.

"You know me?" asked the officer.

"No, sir!"

"I am Major General John Frederick Charles Fuller."

Brown had never heard the name and wondered how to reply.

"You have some guts, kid," said Fuller. "How many of these runs have you done?"

"This is my seventeenth, sir. The situation in Arras is—"

Fuller raised his hand to silence him. "This I know. You saved nearly forty men. At ease. Walk with me."

"Sir!"

Fuller and Brown continued along the prisoner encampment. They walked toward a series of tents in the distance.

"Command is telling me they want all these men court-martialed," said Fuller, looking to the prisoner encampment. "Says they're cowards and deserters. What do you think?"

"Well, sir. I assume that includes me. I was surprised to see the fencing when I returned."

"Son, let me tell you. I happen to believe the stories coming back from Arras, and support what you have done here. Hell, I wish you could have kept at it, but the last batch you brought in caught the attention of the wrong figureheads. American mercenaries on the field of battle? Made some people at central command very unhappy. I was called in to inspect immediately."

"The Americans wanted to come here, sir. They specifically asked me to take them to the 'tank master.' You have any idea who that is?"

"I do," said Fuller. "He . . . is me."

Brown was surprised.

"You know what they're after, sir?"

Fuller stopped about twenty meters from the tents. "I don't. I only arrived just before you landed. I was hoping you could tell me. Apparently, they commandeered that tent over there and said they wouldn't meet anyone but me and would wait until the pilot returned. I told my men that we don't take orders from mercenaries, American or otherwise, but they were very hesitant to confront them. Almost like they were frightened to do so. I was chiding the hell out of those cowards as I heard your engine approaching."

Brown ran his fingernails over his scalp as he inspected the tent. "I know nothing, sir. They didn't say much. But they certainly seemed to know you'd be here."

"Curious," said Fuller as the two continued on toward the tent. "That all?"

"Well, it was still dark when I brought them in, but they were dressed like American cowboys and were . . . heavily armed."

"How heavily armed?"

"Guns and rifles strapped all over their bodies."

"Big guys? Gruff?"

"They were a bit smaller than me, sir. One of them was short. They all had masks over their eyes, so I didn't get a good look."

"Well, they've taken a keen interest in you. Any idea what that's about?"

"I don't, sir."

Brown and Fuller now stood before the tent.

"Think we need backup?" asked Brown, flipping open the button on his service revolver's holster and gripping the weapon.

"I don't think that will be necessary. If they meant any harm, they'd have done it by now. Button your holster, but stay alert."

*

Brown and Fuller entered the darkened tent and were immediately confronted by the pungent smell of pipe tobacco. From the available light flooding in from the door flap and a soft glow emanating from a kerosene lamp on a table to their left, they could see two of the Americans lying on some cots toward the back, and a third leaning up against a post at the center of the tent, smoking a fat brown cigarillo.

"Well, if it isn't Major General J. F. C. Fuller," said the cowboy against the post, wearing a mud-splattered gray trench coat and matching hat.

Fuller noticed the cowboy's Southern twang and that he seemed to be purposely lowering his voice.

"Yes, that's me. And who might you be?"

The cowboy flicked the cigarillo into an urn on the floor, then slowly raised a six-shooter to the brim of his hat and pushed it upward to reveal a black eye mask across his face. Then he reached up and pulled the mask away.

"Name's Phoebe Ann Mosey," she said, revealing herself as female. "But you can call me Annie."

She turned to the others on the cots, who sat up and leaned forward, placing their elbows on their knees and folding their hands together. Fuller could see they too were wearing eye masks beneath their hat brims.

"That right there is Martha, better known as Calamity Jane— and trust me, friend, she's earned the name. Over there, we have the one and only Stagecoach Mary but being a proper gentlewoman from the Deep South, you can call her Miss Fields."

"You're women," said Fuller, sounding surprised. "And she—she's a Black woman," he finished, pointing to Miss Fields.

Jane and Miss Fields chuckled softly, shaking their heads, as Annie walked toward Fuller and shoved her six-shooter in its holster.

She stood before him and crossed her arms. "Is woman hating a side effect of that saltpeter you soldier boys sprinkle in your rations?" Annie winked at Fuller. "We're out here saving lives, and everywhere we go it's the same story. Right, girls?"

"That's right," replied Jane.

"And as far as her being Black," continued Annie, "well, you best just clear your mind of it because believe you me, that one's got the ingredients."

"Ingredients for what?"

"Major General, you seem to be under the very erroneous assumption that because we're women, we can't fight," said Annie.

"Ma'am, I'm sorry. But women are forbidden on the field of battle. I must see to it that you are removed to safety."

The three gunslingers roared with laughter.

"Safety!" howled Jane. "Tell you what, Major General. How about you go ask your brave fighting men all tangled up in those fences out there about who's safe? Half those men we found curled up in a ball, crying with soiled britches, hanging onto their little peckers and praying to Jesus before we rescued them."

"Jane!" scolded Annie. "Mind your language."

Jane rolled her eyes and whistled sharply.

"*You* rescued them? Three women?" asked Fuller.

"Major General, do we need to quash this right here?" asked Annie. "The girls and I aren't going anywhere—other than back to Arras, to finish the job. You have some real ghouls out there on the battlefield. Kaiser's not playing fair any longer. Me, Jane, and Miss Fields were just hoping you might be the chivalrous type who'd lend three damsels, say, a few dozen of those tanks we've been seeing around lately? We're in need of some more firepower."

Fuller glanced at Brown, who stood slack-jawed, staring at Annie.

"What's the matter there, fly boy?" asked Jane. "You ain't never seen a lady with a gun before?"

"No, ma'am. I—"

"Relax, baby face. I'm just bustin' on you," said Jane. "You're the only one of them out there with stones in his sack, and we can use a fella like you on our raids."

Annie turned to Jane, shaking her head in annoyance.

Jane held out her hands and shrugged. "What? It's true."

"It is true," said Miss Fields.

"Excuse me, madam!" shouted Fuller, slapping his boot into the mud. "This is out of order. You! You are all out of order!"

Annie turned to him with a pursed smile and scanned him up and down.

"You know who you remind me of?"

Fuller stood stone-faced.

"President William McKinley. Mind you, he was heavier and a bit less bald. And more of a bush on his face than that pencil-thin mustache of yours . . . But I marched right into the Oval Office one day and told him point blank that if he wanted to end that Spanish-American War, well then, what he needed was a gang of female sharpshooters like us on the battlefield. We'd end that war quicker than a mare with a new set of horseshoes—"

"Madam, I am very sorry, but this ends here."

"Well, long story short, he didn't take me up on that offer. So a few years later when we heard what the Kaiser was up to, me and Miss Fields decided it was time to take matters into our own hands. We called up Calamity Jane over there and stowed away aboard the *Lusitania*."

"The *Lusitania*? That ship was sunk three years ago."

"Damn right it was," said Jane. "German spies got word of three gun-slinging witches from America on board and decided we weren't welcome in the European theater."

"Had to swim all the way to Old Head of Kinsale," finished Miss Fields. "And don't feel too bad there, Major. I don't think those Irish had ever seen a Black woman either. Especially not one so skilled with the iron."

Miss Fields pulled a six-shooter from her gun belt and twirled it several times around her finger before shoving it back in its holster.

Jane leaned over and nudged Miss Fields. "Truth be told," she said.

"Let's cut to it, Major General," said Annie. "You need us, and we need you. It's the only way anyone's surviving this."

"Madam, I don't know what you're referring to."

"Those pits on your ears, for one. You're no warlock, clearly, but you're what? A psychic? Clairvoyant? We know you've been communing with the Veil, which, by the way, we need to help you with. You're leaving your dirty fingerprints all over everything you been scanning."

Fuller swallowed, and his Adam's apple bobbed in his throat. He looked to Brown.

"Son, you'd better leave us."

Jane and Miss Fields stood behind Annie.

"He's in it now, Major General," said Annie. "So, how about we all take a seat and have a nice polite discussion about what can be done to rid ourselves of this undead menace once and for all?"

25

March 30, 1917, dusk

Hanne woke in a dark room.

"Back to sleep with you," came a hoarse feminine voice.

Hanne's mind fell to blackness, and she found herself once more pulling herself from the raging waters of the ravine and dragging herself across the muck until she reached grassy higher ground. She hissed and wheezed as she tore her helmet from her face and rolled onto her back.

The flesh was already melting from her arms and hands. Several of her finger bones were exposed.

Beware of moving water, came Vago's voice. *Every witch has a weakness.*

Hanne lay back on the grass, trying to catch her breath, and could feel her boots slipping off as her feet melted away to tiny nubs—bones and all.

"Help me, Mother," she wheezed. "Please."

I am here, child, came Elizabeth's voice.

Hanne rolled on her side, wincing from the pain as her body continued to decompose. She sensed Elizabeth's presence.

"Save me, Mother."

Elizabeth's ghostly apparition crept toward her, appearing like a blur of static.

You failed me.

Hanne grew too exhausted to speak. "No . . . I—" was all she could muster.

I warned you of the consequences if you failed. I knew I should have left you to rot in my web. Such a grave disappointment.

Hanne's world began to fade. "Felix Yusupov," she gasped. "I have made a discovery for you. The Kaiser's interest in him . . . Felix is the reincarnation of Vlad Drăculea."

Elizabeth's projection solidified for a moment as her ghostly voice projected into Hanne's mind. *And how did you come across this information?*

"I melded with his mind before Radu took me by surprise," wheezed Hanne. "Please . . . help me."

The banishment field makes that impossible. I can barely communicate with you now. Had you only killed Radu as commanded . . . pity. It seems soon you'll be nothing but dust. Die now, young Hanne. No further use do I have for failures.

With her quivering hand, Hanne reached to her throat and ran her fingers across her exposed thyroid cartilage and trachea—her facial flesh was largely melted away. She tried to extend her hand to Elizabeth's projection once more, but her arm fell limply in the grass.

Elizbeth's ghastly white image began to dissipate as the shadow of another person emerged from the woods.

Hanne snapped awake to the sound of a searing whistle.

She found herself stripped of her battle gear and lying upon a comfortable hay mattress in a compact room. A motion caught her attention, and she sensed the figure of a heavyset woman gathering a kettle from a small hearth along the hut's wall.

"Now you can wake," came the woman's voice.

Hanne sat up and could feel that her hands were mostly healed, save two knucklebones still sticking from her fingers. Tearing the covers from the bed, Hanne reached out with her mind to discover that her feet and legs were also intact.

"Moving water is a very common weakness among our kind. You must learn to be more careful," said the woman, bringing the kettle to Hanne's bedside. She poured its contents into a teacup that sat on a quaint wooden table next to Hanne. "Drink this. It will finish the healing."

Hanne reached to the cup, and an electrifying sensation warmed her body as she swallowed its viscous contents.

"Where am I? Who are you?"

"I am Boryana. You are in Slovakia."

"Your German is fluent."

"I speak *all* languages, child," said Boryana. "Going on twelve hundred years, this one. It all tends to sink in after a while."

"You saved me?"

"I healed your wounds. But saving you? Oh, child. You have a long way to go on that. You've fallen in with some very dark entities."

"Spare me the morality lecture."

"Elizabeth Báthory is not good company to keep."

Hanne glared at her, startled. "How do you know that?"

A glow came from Boryana's hand as she lit a pipe and sat smoking in a rocking chair next to the bed.

"My first impulse was to let you die, little girl. A proxy of that she-devil in my woods. But then I touched you. Sensed all that you've been through. Such a tragic story, young Hanne. I've been living in the shadow of Čachtice Castle for as long as I can remember. Do you have any idea what she used to do to children inside those walls? Innocent little girls?"

"You don't know anything," said Hanne. "Where's my battle gear? I'm leaving."

"You're free to leave anytime you choose," said Boryana. "But from what I gathered of your talk with Elizabeth down by the water, it seems to me that Mommy has abandoned her experiment. She left you to die. So where is it you think you're going? You don't have allies. Certainly not any friends."

"Old woman, I will strike you down right here if you—"

"Would love to see you try that," said Boryana, winking at her. "I'm old, yes. And I live alone in the woods. Nobody would ever know you struck me down in my own home. But you would be wise not to underestimate me. It seems you've been both sheltered and abused since you were a small child—not very wise to the world.

"Your new powers? Gave you a bad case of hubris. You were sloppy. Cast into a river by a dying warlock who should have been no match for you. Tsk, tsk . . . And that coven of yours? Elizabeth Báthory? They don't care about you. Never did. You've been tricked, little one. That mimic stole your bounty and threw him into an inescapable dungeon. You're officially out of the club."

Hanne grew agitated. As best as she tried to let Boryana's words pass, they cut right through her.

"You know nothing," she said again.

"Nothing? Well, see for yourself."

Boryana extended her hand toward Hanne, sending her into a trance.

Hanne's mind flashed to a dungeon where Radu and Felix hung in cages, watching as the hooded warlock from the bomber kicked their shape-shifter friend into a pit of molten silver. The vision faded just as the shape-shifter demon blade, submerged in the liquid, erupted in a flash.

"I never lie," said Boryana. "That mimic is in league with Elizabeth, half-siblings to be exact. You were nothing more than his pawn."

Hanne was silent.

"And that prince you came after. Felix Yusupov? Now that's a kind soul. If he happens to unlock what's inside him, well, you'd better just hope he never finds you. Angry young thing like you wouldn't stand a chance."

"We'll see about that," said Hanne, wobbling a bit as she stood from the bed.

She still felt powerful, but drained—and quietly panicked that Elizabeth's magick was waning.

"So, you're simply going to slaughter him? For what? To garner more power? To beg for favor from a no-good spider devil who's abandoned you?"

"I'll capture him and bring him back to her. I'll be rewarded. You'll see."

"Go right ahead. Seal your fate by wandering even further down a path of darkness from which there is no return."

Hanne grew enraged at the statement.

The old witch was correct—there was no return. She'd been betrayed and abandoned. The hooded warlock had used her, then captured her bounty. Hanne may have been rendered useless in these affairs, but she suddenly found it freeing, realizing she could exact any revenge she chose on all those who had harmed her.

She thought to Master Vakól's promise that she'd meet a beautiful dark enchantress sequestered on the mount. A powerful and wise entity extremely skilled in the dark arts, who would gift Hanne all her powers. Instead, she'd been greeted by a savage horror—a deranged psychopath on eight legs who had devoured every last bit of her innocence. Hanne felt bereft.

Look how this ends for any of those who feed on the dark, she thought, sensing that her own fate would only grow worse.

She'd been doomed since birth. And now she stood in her darkest hour, being mocked by a weak old woman. Hanne would have no more of it.

She hobbled to a table near the door, where the witch had placed her battle gear.

"Where are my garments?"

Boryana looked around the room. "Floating around here somewhere, I assume."

At that moment, Hanne felt a constricting sensation around her ankle as her spectral clothing began slithering up her leg and materializing on her body. She placed her deer skull helmet upon her head, strapped her blades on her back, and turned to Boryana.

"Now you will know fear," said Hanne.

"Ha!" Boryana forced her toes into the floor and rocked back and forth with zest. "My child, you look like a sad little doe."

Hanne reached up and unsheathed her blades, pointing them at Boryana.

The old woman stared at her with striking green eyes. "I see there will be no lessons learned here today. Do it. Strike me down. Fail another test."

Hanne let out a great wail and thrust her blades down upon Boryana, who disappeared in a burst of white light, followed by the entirety of the hut. Hanne's horned figure stood alone in the forest, her blades absorbing the earth at her feet. She swung around to sense Boryana standing in between two large trees with a large knapsack and her rocking chair strapped to her back.

"I tried to help you," she called. "But I see you are not ready."

"I don't need your help!" shouted Hanne.

Boryana let out a cackle. "We shall see, young one. We shall see. Best be careful in these woods. There are lycans about. Strangers don't last long here—mortal or otherwise."

Hanne marched toward Boryana as the old witch dissipated into a black mist.

431

Fail another test . . .

A hot rage welled inside Hanne as Boryana's words repeated in her mind. She scanned the ridge above and could sense the darkened outline of Čachtice Castle in the distance, cast against the oncoming night.

Hanne thought to her parents—to how stern and distant they were to her as a child. No matter her talent, no matter her successes, nothing she did was ever deemed good enough. When she had breached the mount, she had carried a silent longing that everyone—her parents, her coven, even Master Vakól—would now finally treat her with the reverence due to a witch of her stature. It was only a short time ago that thoughts of her parents showering her with praise filled her with a sense of purpose. But now they felt distant, meaningless—far away from her, where an icy wind blew a piercing whistle through the wasteland of her mind.

The loneliness that pervaded Hanne's life overwhelmed her, and her entire essence felt hollow. She was on borrowed time, and her new-found powers were likely diminishing. She was now a monster—horrifically scarred, with no sanctuary to call home and no hope of returning to the girl she once was. Her solitude would only continue to metastasize as she wandered the earth in search of solace that simply did not exist. Oblivion's frigid grip reached up and choked her, solidifying in her bones as she envisioned her very soul trapped in the belly of that wretched, evil spider.

She thought of Elizabeth leaving her to die on the riverbank.

Hanne would show her which of them was the failure.

Her figure dissipated in a flash and materialized on the grounds of Čachtice Castle.

Threw him into an inescapable dungeon, came Boryana's words.

Hanne sensed the opening before her and marched into the fortress. It was time to exact her revenge.

*

"Now, open them."

Felix took a deep breath and opened his eyes. The darkened dungeon reflected from his retinas in monochrome grays with striking contrasts of black and white.

"I don't believe it. I can see," he said, waving his hand before his face. "It's all black and white, though."

"You will learn how to see color in time," said Radu. "For now, breathe easy and master the technique. All esoteric learning is composed of building blocks. You've placed your first brick. Seeing reds and blues would be your next easiest step."

"What else? I want to know more."

Radu rested his back against his cage's bars and folded his legs. He placed his palms together and rested his fingers against his mouth.

"Let me think," he said. "Extrasensory perception, I believe. You seem to already have the skill, but simply cannot wield it."

"Then teach me."

Radu smiled and looked upward to the coned ceiling. "I'll admit the circumstances are not ideal, but this is a true joy for me, Felix— to feel you awakening again. You're certain you have no memories of your past life?"

Felix scrunched his face and closed his eyes. "I remembered the loch when Denis and I first arrived. But it felt like déjà vu. I didn't realize the significance at that time. Other than that, I can see a cloak, and then an older man's face . . . a friend, perhaps. But there's also a darkness about him."

Felix opened his eyes and looked to Radu.

"Hmm. That's difficult to interpret," said Radu. "The cloak— was it black? Like the Death Witch?"

"Yes."

"I believe that would be your ethereal garments, which are symbiotic entities that bond with witches. But let's not go down that path. Enchanted clothing is a study unto itself."

"I feel awfully funny trying to become a warlock wearing"— Felix looked down to Denis's garments—"well, these."

"Ha! For now, I think your clothing will be a benefit. No one will suspect a thing at first glance. I greatly wish I had a solution to unlock your former powers. Would save us decades of training."

"Decades? We don't have that long," said Felix.

"Indeed, we do not. I don't believe we're even granted days, considering the circumstances. If we can escape these walls, then we must get you to Poenari Castle hidden in the Carpathians. It was my brother's stronghold before he fell to darkness and took up residence at Loch Dracul. There is a powerful entity deep within the castle that may help reawaken what is locked within you."

"And what happens if Bael is resurrected before then?"

Radu let out a long breath. "A multitude of horrors—plagues, famine, genocides, mass enslavement, and whatever other devilish concoctions his wretched allies devise. We will have some time to oppose him if we can escape. Once he is freed, his powers won't be what they were to start. But it won't take long for him to recover."

"Can I face him?"

"Under no circumstances. Not until your former powers are unlocked."

Felix shifted in his cage and hung his legs through the bars. "That name she called me in the forest . . . Ve-hu something?"

"Vehuiah. Your archangel name. The spirit who attached itself to you when you were born as Vlad Drăculea. Those blades in the corridor? There are seventy-two of them in existence—well, now seventy-one." Radu gripped the bars and rested his chin on a horizontal support that encircled his cage. "As I divulged before, each blade contains the soul of a demon. In contrast, there are seventy-two archangels, and together, they balance the Ether between the Veil and the Void. Bael being your balance. And Vehuiah, which is you, being his. Each entity is as powerful as the other, and their symmetry brings balance to the universe."

Radu explained that during the Inferno, the angels, who were known in that time as a fraternity of warlocks called the Order of the Dragon, rid the earth of the demons by trapping them in blades' jewels. The Ether's balance shifted and leaned toward the light. The Order wielded the blades to defend the good and righteous, and also kept a watchful eye on their true enemies fashioned into their weapons. But the demons craved escape, and would find a way unless the blades were destroyed.

"We can drop them all in the molten silver," said Felix.

"It's a good idea . . . if we can actually escape. That was an amazing discovery. It was believed the blades were indestructible. Baphomet now has Bael in his possession. I can only assume he's devised a means to free him from the blade. Soon, all of the demons will be freed. With the souls of the archangels trapped in the belly of the spider Elizabeth, the balance of the Ether will tip to the Void. The Black Sun will rise once more, unleashing immeasurable suffering onto humanity such as we haven't seen since the Dark Ages. And now . . . you are all that stands against them."

"What about you?"

Radu also hung his legs from his cage. "I'm merely a warlock. I can fight, but my age is consuming me. I may be able to stand up to Elizabeth, but Bael will crush me. I'm stunned Baphomet allowed either of us to live. There are plans afoot here that we cannot fathom."

"Why didn't you just kill Elizabeth when you had the chance? That—"

Radu raised his hand to silence Felix. "Stop. I understand that to those of you uneducated in the art of witchcraft, it seems we always have the answers and know exactly what to do and when to do it. That is a fallacy. The mysteries of the Ether often present far more questions than answers, even to those of us skilled in communing with it.

"So, yes—in hindsight, I should have smashed that spider the moment I trapped her. But you need to understand, in that moment, I realized she still had seventy-one archangels trapped in her belly— not to mention the countless other souls she drank down on her hunt to eliminate the Order of the Dragon. Not knowing what would happen to them if I killed her outright, I decided a banishment hex was apt until I could decipher such complex magick. I made a poor and selfish decision. I failed. And now, it is very likely I will pay for that choice with my life."

Felix hung his head. "I understand. I'm sorry if I offended you. I don't know what I would have done in that situation either." Felix felt a buzzing sensation on the front of his ears. "I sense something." He turned his attention to the door.

Radu closed his eyes. "My powers are confined to these walls, but apparently yours are not. That's encouraging. What is it you sense?"

"I don't know. It's just a feeling I have."

"Excellent. Let's work with that. Extrasensory perception is akin to breathing for a warlock. It should feel natural and require no effort on your part. But we must train your mind to process the signals.

Now. Reach out. Feel the energy of the Veil surrounding you. Feel it in the echoes bouncing from the silver walls. Feel it in the rhythm of the bubbles bursting from the surface of the molten pool below. Make it one with your heartbeat, your breath—your very essence."

Felix sat cross-legged and placed his hands in his lap.

"I see . . . a deer," said Felix. "It's nearby. But something is . . . missing. Its heartbeat . . . its breath."

"Yes?"

"It has none. I can't quite conjure the image. I'm overwhelmed with the grief exuding from this poor thing. Am I sensing a dying deer?"

The torches lining the walls erupted in white flame and a loud reverberation echoed from the dungeon's door. Felix opened his eyes and swung around to see the tip of a black blade pierce the silver wall and begin to absorb the metal doorway in a whirlpool of cracked and broken metal.

"It's her!" said Felix.

Radu gripped the bars of his cage. "Then I'd like to congratulate you on sensing something I could not."

"Lot of good that's going to do us if she breaks through. Can you cast a spell?"

"I'm drained, Felix."

"What about me? Can you teach me something . . . quickly?"

"Nothing that would save us. Just remember: no matter the situation, you must call and rely upon your intuition."

Hanne burst through the remainder of the door and charged toward the end of the plank, her blades crackling and humming at her sides.

"Hanne!" yelled Felix in German. "Stop. You don't have to do this. We're not your enemies."

Her horned figure marched to the very end of the plank, and her skulled face peered up to Felix and Radu. She raised her blades over her head and cocked them behind her back, taking aim at the cages.

"Hanne, don't!" yelled Felix.

She screamed and cast the blades from her hands, sending them end over end into the molten pool below. The blades stuck into the liquid metal, churning the molten pool as their hilts grew white hot.

As Felix and Radu stared on from above, the blades evaporated in a blinding shock wave. Hanne was blown back several feet—the cages above rattled and shook with Felix and Radu hanging on tightly.

Felix pulled himself up and watched Hanne rise to her feet.

"Hanne! What are you doing?"

She tore her helmet from her head and glared at Felix with her pale, eyeless face.

"Taking my revenge," she replied, casting her horned helmet into the molten silver.

She raised her hands above her head and extended her fingertips wide. A metallic sound arose from the outside corridor. Felix and Radu watched as the demon blades floated into the room and encircled Hanne in a precipitous mass of glowing black metal. Round and round the dungeon they spun, until Hanne thrust her hands downward and sent the blades into the liquefied silver—the jewels on their hilts glowing white hot.

"Oh, no," said Radu. "Take cover."

"There is no cover," replied Felix.

The chains upon their cages rattled and shook.

Felix looked down to see Hanne's hands extended toward them. The cages snapped from their couplings and Hanne sent Felix and Radu flying into the corridor, breaking their cages open. She then set her energies upon the broken door at the dungeon's entrance, pulling the gate closed in a mishmash of twisted and rusty iron amid the sounds of screeching metal.

Felix grabbed his elbow and yelled at the lingering pain of striking the bricks. He crawled out of his cage and moved to Radu.

"You hurt?"

"I'm fine," said Radu, standing upright.

At that moment, a massive blast tore through the corridor, sending them both to the floor. Felix was nearly blinded by the light and a horrid ringing in his ears prevented him from finding his footing. He concentrated on his vision, slightly modifying the technique Radu had taught him to see in the dark, and the corridor before him slowly came into shape.

Felix dashed to the iron gate. When he reached the twisted metal, he began pulling and pushing on it, trying to break through.

"Hanne! Hanne, don't!" yelled Felix as he watched her rise up and move toward the end of the plank.

Her spectral garments hung tattered across her body and she was limping, missing a portion of her right foot and her left arm just above the elbow.

As Hanne reached the end of the plank, she turned and faced Felix.

"I left two of them for you," she said.

Felix reached out to Hanne through the bars.

"Please stop," he begged. "We can help you."

He could see Hanne's face clearly as a black tear fell down her cheek.

She smiled at him.

"You already did, Vehuiah. Now, go and save your friend. Then do what I could not—kill that wretched spider."

Hanne leaned backward and cast herself into the molten pool. There was no scream, no cry—only a soft metallic thud as her body sank and disintegrated into the silvery depths.

Felix stood, gripping the bars.

"I'm sorry, Hanne. I'm so sorry," he said, aware of a fluttering sound rising from the pit.

Felix's eyes widened as a kaleidoscope of black butterflies sailed from the pit and fluttered toward him. He stepped back a few paces with Radu just behind him. They leaned against the wall as the butterflies flew past them down the corridor.

The chrysalides flapped their wings, rising up the shaft in a shadowy vortex and entering the castle's main floor. They fluttered from the stone fortress, rising on a gentle breeze into the indigo sky—their black bodies finally melding into the night.

Felix slid against the wall and found his way to the floor, placing his head on his knees and wrapping his arms around his legs.

"I'm sorry," said Radu.

Felix looked up at him. "I can't explain it. There was something about her. She felt like a friend."

Radu knelt to him and placed his hands upon Felix's shoulders.

"And in the end, she was. Destroying those blades saved millions of lives. The first victory we've had thus far."

"I saw into her mind, you know. Back in the forest. They abused her as a child. Tricked her into becoming that . . . thing. She was a kind person deep down. I could feel it."

"You're awakening, my young friend. Just as you were before, you are keenly intuitive, and your empathy knows no bounds."

"Some good it does me."

"Come," said Radu, standing and walking down the hall. "We must ensure her sacrifice was not in vain."

Radu stood before an impala and ram skull. Below them hung the two blades Hanne had left behind for Felix and Radu.

"Ah!" said Radu. "She left us Duke Agares and Queen Vassago. Two terribly powerful entities." He pulled a blade from the wall and inspected its sheath. "These will come in handy. Which do you prefer? The wielder of earthquakes, or the soothsayer?"

"Neither. We should cast them in the silver."

"You are likely correct. And one day, we will do just that. For now, they are essential to our survival, and you will learn to wield them. But only one," said Radu as he strapped the Queen Vassago soothsayer blade around his waist. "Dimachaeri style is a bit advanced for you. Ready to cause some earthquakes?"

Radu pulled the remaining sword from the wall and held it out to Felix.

"I can cause earthquakes with this?"

"Wield it properly, and yes. But you must be careful and remember—the demons crave escape and are quite crafty. Be mindful in how you commune with it and learn to understand its power."

Felix stood and accepted the blade. He strapped it around his waist.

"Let's go save Mary," he said.

Chapter 26

26

March 30, 1917, night

Rurik drifted awake, surprised that he had slept until nighttime.

He pulled his glasses to his face and tried to find a discernible pattern in the shadows of the tree branches cast against the night sky, but lost interest as drowsiness overtook him. He turned on his side to find Sebastian sitting cross-legged, eyes closed, seemingly meditating, and thought back to the first time he met the giant fellow.

It was 1911—about a year after Sebastian's resurrection.

Rurik had traveled to Romania, attempting yet again to reconcile with Denis, and his first stop was the inn to check on Mary. He'd certainly heard Denis ramble on about his reanimation discoveries for most of their adult lives—even witnessed him reanimate a toad one evening. But the shock of seeing Sebastian sent his mind into a flurry of wonder. Even after all his dealings in the supernatural, Rurik looked upon Sebastian as if he were a creation of pure magick— created by a mortal, no less.

Thankfully, Mary had been in the room when Rurik entered the inn, intending to surprise her. Sebastian had initially confused him for Denis, growling and lurching at him. Even though Rurik did not bear Denis's scars, it took nearly an hour and multiple explanations before Sebastian was able to comprehend the concept of a twin, and that the two were not the same person.

A unique bond grew between Rurik and Sebastian from that point forward, and Rurik tried his best to visit Sebastian and Mary at least once a year at Christmas—even though he and Denis were barely speaking.

Rurik stretched his recovering ankle, pleased to feel its range of motion returning to normal. He'd be dead if it weren't for Sebastian—his giant, strange, kindhearted nephew of sorts.

Even as the werewolves had encircled them in the town center, Rurik felt surprisingly at ease when he stood back-to-back with Sebastian, knowing his chances of survival were far greater with the colossus near. He was still in awe of the memory of the large female wolf emerging from the pack and kneeling before Sebastian, and then the remainder of their pursuers following suit. Of all the crazy things Rurik had witnessed in his lifetime, a pack of rabid were-wolves kneeling before him was the very last image he'd ever expected to carry.

Hurt dog. I help, came Sebastian's words.

Four years ago, Rurik and Sebastian had taken an excursion to Gerlachovský Štít in the Carpathians, hoping to find Sebastian's Yeti clan. The memory of Sebastian mistaking a lynx for a "little kitty" and the mayhem that ensued almost caused Rurik to burst out laughing.

Sebastian still had a lot to remember, Rurik supposed, feeling sadness for him and hoping that one day he'd reunite with his Yeti family.

Last evening, as Rurik and Sebastian were led back to the were-wolves' caves, Rurik had been impressed by their well-hidden lair, which blended seamlessly into the surrounding crags. A few of the wolves were still openly hostile toward him, but by and large, the pack was kind and thankful—mostly to Sebastian for saving Alzbeta from the silver trap, but also to both of them for saving the villagers from the vámpir attacks. Some of the wolves even spoke perfect Russian, and Rurik thought to inquire about their relation-ship with the villagers, but held back. All he could surmise was there must have been some type of pact between the townsfolk and the lycans. He thought to Milena's warning at the tavern and the various monuments of wolves adorning the town, and settled on believing they must have acted as some type of buffer between the werewolves and any hapless travelers from the outside world.

Rurik and Sebastian had been confined for a few hours inside a wooden cage as the lycan council met. Alzbeta finally emerged from a cave and apologized for containing them. She then explained that they were welcome guests in their forest, but were to remain hidden and ordered to leave at next daybreak. The council had also agreed not to harm Rurik's traveling companions, if they had happened to survive the plane crash and were still in the area. But, Alzbeta warned, they must stay clear of a wolf named Tóth and his small band of loyalists, as they had voted to maul both Rurik and Sebastian.

Rurik now grew worried about Mary and the rest, realizing it had been over twenty-four hours since they were separated and hoping she hadn't crossed paths with Tóth.

He decided it was time to seek answers.

"Wake up, big man," said Rurik, pushing on Sebastian's leg.

Sebastian opened his eyes and yawned.

"Looks like we're both worn out. We way overslept."

"Sleep good. Much need."

Rurik ran his hands over the plush bed of leaves beneath him. "Tell you what, these werewolves are on to something. Who knew leaves could be so comfortable?"

"Sebastian don need. Rest in all place."

Rurik looked around the dense wood, wondering where the werewolves had gone. For a moment, he thought of walking to the cave in the distance, its mouth glowing with torchlight, but recalled Alzbeta's stern warning against venturing into the caves.

"I have word on your friend," came Alzbeta's voice in Russian.

"Ah!" shouted Rurik, standing up to confront her.

"Sorry. I forget mortals can't hear us approach."

"How do you do that, exactly?"

Even in the darkness, Rurik could make out Alzbeta's striking blue eyes.

"From my minimal experience with humans, I understand our power comes from what you call pheromones. We release them naturally—much like a skunk. Mostly when we hunt. Makes us invisible to your kind when close. We can also appear human, if needed."

"Really, just like that?"

"Just like that," said Alzbeta, morphing into a nude female.

"Hey!" said Rurik, covering his eyes.

"My apologies," said Alzbeta, returning to her wolf form. "Is that offensive to you?"

Rurik laughed. "No, not offensive at all, actually. But I'm—I'm a gentleman. Buy me a beer first."

"You want a beer from me . . . ? I don't understand."

"No. It's—never mind. What were you saying about our friend?"

"There is news," said Alzbeta. "About the shape-shifter."

Sebastian stood next to Rurik, bumping him out of the way.

"Watch it," said Rurik.

"Where Mary?"

Alzbeta looked up to Sebastian.

"Four of my pack picked up her scent yesterday, just after dusk."

"Why didn't you say something last night?" asked Rurik. "Was she mauled?"

"No. There's more to this predicament than I can disclose. Tóth and his clan tracked her and a companion for a bit, but she was not in human form. They managed to slip away. Good thing too or this would be a much more somber conversation."

"Was the companion Felix? Zazlov?"

Alzbeta looked to the ground. "I don't know. This Felix friend of yours? You're certain he is a good man?"

"He's my best friend," Rurik said, before quickly looking to Sebastian. "No offense, big guy."

"It OK. I like you number two. Mary one. Unk Rur two. Fele three. . . Zaz four."

"Good to know," said Rurik, focusing on Alzbeta.

"This . . . this is very complicated," said Alzbeta. "Does he also have the name Yusupov?"

Rurik's eyes widened. "Yes! You found him?"

Alzbeta turned away. "I've said too much."

"Wait. You have to know where he is. How do you know his last name?"

"I'm bound to secrecy, Rurik. I can say no more. Just the fact that you're standing here at the mouth of our home—alive—do you know how fortunate you are?"

"I do. We do," said Rurik.

"We slaughter outsiders. It's our way. How we survive. Had Sebastian not saved me . . . and even more—had you not saved the villagers we protect from those vampires, you'd have been mauled on sight."

"I just don't understand. Most of you have been so kind to us."

"We are good and kind—to our own. But our history is . . . you simply wouldn't understand. As for your friends, I can no longer promise the same protections offered to you."

"You're the leader, right? Can't you call them off? Let them know not to attack."

"I've done what I can. I must return to my pack. I suggest you rest until morning and we'll show you the way to the planes that landed nearby."

Alzbeta dashed off into the darkness.

Rurik looked to Sebastian. "She's definitely not telling us something."

"Agree. We follow."

*

"Can you see them?" asked Radu.

"I can't," said Felix, peering out into the forest. "But I can sense them."

Felix crouched against the sewer outlet's mossy brick. "Can you teleport us?"

"I can, actually. The fresh air has invigorated me a pinch, but I can't send us far enough to make a difference."

"What if you use some of mine?"

"Randomly teleporting can cause a host of horrid issues. I could end up popping us into a far worse situation."

Howls echoed from the forest and Felix squinted into the dark again.

"Can't see how it could be much worse than this."

Radu ducked his head and shimmied to the broken iron bars at the sewer's mouth. "Well, it's worse—they're here."

"Felix Yusupov! Radu cel Frumos! We know you're in the tunnel. We can smell you," echoed a gruff, masculine voice in clear and concise Russian. "Come out and face your fate."

"What do we do?" asked Felix.

Radu held out his hand. "Give me a second. I'm scanning their minds."

Felix waited for a long moment. "Well?"

"They're not going to kill us . . . not yet, anyway."

"So we simply surrender?"

"Under the circumstances, yes. I sense that would be wise. Negotiation is always the stronger hand."

Felix gripped his blade. "I say we fight."

"I admire your gumption," said Radu, staring into the forest, "but werewolves are not to be toyed with. They'll swarm us with great voracity. We won't last a minute."

"Teleport us, then. Somewhere. Fast—back to the ridge."

Radu turned to him. "They'll track us. Listen, I want you to close your eyes and focus on their minds. Tell me what you see."

Felix shut his eyelids.

"Same as before," said Radu. "Focus on the Veil's energy. Feel the night air, the forest . . . feel its vibration upon your skin. Sense their heartbeats, the blood pumping in their veins. Tell me. What do you envision?"

"I see a fire. I see . . . I see anguish and panic. Fear. I see fear."

"Fear of what?"

Felix opened his eyes. "Fear of me."

"My brother . . . technically you. Once you fell to darkness, you declared war on their kind and slaughtered them en masse. It was the Butcher who saved them and brought them to this refuge."

"I thought he was evil."

"Pure evil. He cares nothing for their kind, but they were frightened, pushed nearly to extinction, and their ferociousness was of use to him. So here we are—standing off against enemies you created long ago."

"I had nothing to do with it!"

"Good luck explaining that to them."

"That's exactly what I'll do."

Felix pushed by Radu and exited the sewer.

"Felix!"

Felix walked toward the tree line.

Radu reluctantly followed.

"This is dangerous," said Radu.

"We're in danger either way. You sensed they will not kill us. Let's see what they want."

"I said they won't kill us *yet*."

"Doesn't matter," said Felix. "We need answers. I sense they may have them."

Felix and Radu stood at the perimeter of the forest. With his night vision, Felix could see the large black bodies of several dozen werewolves. He reached down and undid the buckle holding his sword to his waist.

"Drop your sword," said Felix.

Radu followed.

Felix raised his hands and knelt to the ground.

"I'm here! It's me. We're unarmed. We mean you no harm."

The wolves crept from the forest on all four legs and surrounded Felix and Radu, their guttural growls raising gooseflesh across Felix's body. A black wolf with a silver patch upon his chest slinked toward Felix with a fresh wound in one eye, his other eye softly glowing yellow. Upon reaching Felix, he stood on his hind legs, revealing he was nearly as tall as Sebastian. Felix swallowed as he looked up at the beast's sharp teeth.

"Back from the dead, I see," said the wolf. "Where's the shape-shifter who took my eye?"

"The Butcher took her."

The wolf growled and shoved Felix to the ground. "Silence, Impaler."

The remaining pack continued to circle them, their growls and huffs growing in intensity.

"Grab their weapons," said the wolf.

Two of his pack crawled in, clamped the harnesses in their jowls, and pulled the hovering demon blades away.

The werewolf stared down at Felix, then fell to all fours and shoved his jaws mere inches from Felix's face.

"You slaughtered my mother and father. My baby pup. Tell me now why I don't gut you right here?"

Felix turned his face slightly as the wolf's breath overwhelmed him with the stench of rotten meat. He closed his eyes for a moment, took a deep breath, then stared into the wolf's yellow eye.

"I am not what you think."

"Liar! You're the reincarnation. My mortal enemy. Long have I waited to rip out your throat."

"Then slaughter me. If I can't find passage from this forest to save my friend, then I have no reason to live."

"Felix," said Radu, looking at him with a touch of scorn.

The wolf let out a low, growling chuckle.

"Always the trickster," he said, sitting on his haunches. "Now I am to believe you've come back as a force of righteousness?"

"Believe what you want. I mean you no harm. I only care about saving my friend."

The werewolf gripped Felix's face with his claws and forced him to the ground. Another wolf confronted Radu, growling at him. The beast hulked over Felix and pinned him into the dirt—warm saliva dripped from his mouth onto Felix's forehead.

"No harm, you say? Why, you foul—"

A sharp whimper filled the air and the wolf's weight was suddenly gone.

Felix sat up to see another wolf standing before his attacker, both of them growling and gnashing their teeth as they crept around one another in a tight circle.

"Stand down, General Tóth," the second wolf said in a feminine and commanding voice.

"Out of my way, Alzbeta."

"We're dead if you kill these men. Our orders are to wait."

"I have the Impaler in my sights. Stand away. I will have my revenge."

Felix sat up and scurried next to Radu. "What do we do?"

"This," Radu said, and got to his feet.

Three wolves circled him and Felix. General Tóth broke from Alzbeta and crept toward Radu as the mighty warlock stepped forward.

"The Butcher is the one who's been trapping you," said Radu.

The wolves' growls fell to silence.

"What did you say?" asked Tóth, creeping nearer.

"That wound on her leg," continued Radu. "It's from a silver trap, is it not?"

Alzbeta's blue eyes focused on Radu. "It is, yes."

"And who is it you think has been setting those traps?" asked Radu.

"Liar!" hissed Tóth.

"He feeds on your blood," said Radu. "He's been culling your pack for centuries. All the proof you need is within those castle walls—bones and pelts from your kind line the walls. Why do you suppose you're forbidden to enter?"

"More lies!" said Tóth, moving in toward Radu. "You were, are, and ever shall be false, Radu. Where were you when your brother went rogue and slaughtered my kind? You hid like a coward."

"Untrue," said Radu. "It was I who beheaded my brother and ended the reign of the Nosferatu. It was I who banished Elizabeth Báthory. And it was I who imprisoned the Black Butcher."

"He escaped your trap," said Tóth. "And so shall Elizabeth soon enough. You're old and weak."

"I tell the truth. The Butcher is not your ally. He uses you to guard his sacred property in his absence and supply him with the magical properties in your veins. You're merely his bloodstock."

General Tóth crept toward Radu, gnashing his great fangs. "Bring me Radu's weapon," he said to the wolf next to him.

"Stop this at once," said Alzbeta.

Tóth turned to her. "Back away, traitor. If we can't kill the Impaler, then let's see if his brother will," he growled as four other wolves gathered in behind him.

Alzbeta backed away and joined the remainder of her pack. "Don't do this, Tóth. It's treachery," she said.

Tóth stood upright and took Radu's sword from one of his wolves. He handed the blade to Radu.

"Someone is dying tonight," said Tóth. "Prove to us you're a man of your word. A man of principle. Strike down your brother once more and stop this menace before it starts. Kill him, and you may pass from our land. It's you . . . or him."

"Very well," said Radu, unsheathing the blade.

"What are you doing?" asked Felix.

Radu turned to Felix and winked at him.

The wolves backed away slightly as Radu stood and held the blade high.

"I think not," said Radu, lowering the blade and pointing it toward Tóth. "It was you. You're the traitor. You've known all along it was the Butcher doing the trapping."

"More lies!" growled Tóth.

Radu stepped forward, pointing the blade directly at Tóth.

"You forget, General," he said, "My power spawns from the Veil, and I see the unseen. Admit to what you have done. Aiding the Butcher in his crimes against your pack."

"Is this true?" came Alzbeta's voice.

"Tear him to shreds," commanded Tóth.

The werewolves surrounding Radu charged. As they leapt into the air, he ducked low to the ground, causing them to crash into one another, and swung his blade wide across Tóth's hind legs, amputating and absorbing them in one motion. Tóth howled in pain and fell to the ground, pulling himself away on his front claws as the other werewolves moved in on Radu.

"*Indo-talia!*" shouted Radu and vanished into the night.

Felix backed away on the ground as the confusion settled and the wolves turned their attention to him. He took one look at his blade hovering on the forest floor and extended his hand. The scimitar shot to him. Felix stood and unsheathed the weapon, pointing at the wolves encircling him.

A bright burst erupted through the forest, followed by the cries of General Tóth as Radu emerged once more from thin air and stuck his blade deep into Tóth's heart, absorbing the rest of his body with the strike.

The wolves cornering Felix turned to Radu, who held his blade toward them as he backed away and rejoined Felix.

The two stood back-to-back, staring down the wolves.

"Enough!" yelled Alzbeta as she came to the front of the pack and stood on her hind legs.

She turned her attention to Radu. "Is it true?" she asked. "What you said about the Butcher and Tóth?"

"You have my word. Enter the castle and see for yourselves," said Radu.

Alzbeta turned to her pack. "These two are to remain unharmed until I return. Juhász, Mészáros. Follow."

The three werewolves disappeared in a dark blur as Felix and Radu continued to hold their blades defensively against the remaining pack.

"Felix!" came a voice from the wood.

"Rurik?" questioned Felix, staring into the darkness. "Is that you?"

"It's me! Sebastian is here too."

Felix looked to Radu. "Now what?"

Radu shrugged.

Rurik and Sebastian walked toward them, and the lycan pack let them pass.

Felix sheathed his blade.

"So good to see you, old friend," Rurik said, embracing Felix tightly.

"I thought you were . . . ugh—"

The words were squeezed from Rurik's mouth as Sebastian picked them both up in a firm bear hug.

"So happy, Fele," he said.

"OK, big guy," grunted Felix. "Good to see you too. You can put us down."

Sebastian placed them on the ground.

"Sebastian, Rurik, nice to see you both still alive," said Radu, sheathing his blade.

"Any word on Mary?" asked Rurik.

"There is, but—" Radu motioned to the werewolves still surrounding them.

"What, them? They're our friends," said Rurik.

"Of course," said Felix, shaking his head.

"Everyone! These are the two I told you about," said Rurik, turning to the wolves.

The pack stared back at them, emitting low growls and grumbling among themselves.

"What's wrong with you?" asked Rurik. "These are my missing friends I was telling you about."

The wolves growled and backed away.

"What's going on here?" asked Rurik, looking to Radu.

"A lot has transpired. Best to wait for Alzbeta to return."

*

Alzbeta stood alone in the middle of a large circle of her pack.

"It is with horror in my heart that I tell you what Radu said is true."

A grumbling erupted among the circle.

"How can this be?" came a voice from the pack.

"Pelts of our missing hung like trophies. Bones of our loved ones strewn about a fire pit and ground into a crucible in his grand kitchen."

"Alzbeta speaks the truth," said Mészáros. "Juhász and I witnessed the same."

"We are no longer safe in these woods," said Alzbeta. "It is time we made our way back to Serbia—back to our homeland."

"Will our brothers in the Black Hand accept us?" asked Juhász, running his claws over his gray-haired chest.

"With General Tóth no longer in our ranks, I believe an attempt to mend our relationship with them stands a chance," said Alzbeta. "You know as well as I that we have lived far too long under the rule of that dark man. We turned to him in our weakness. I, as well as many of you, for too long looked away from what we knew to be true: the Butcher is a man of black character."

"But he is our protector," came a voice.

Alzbeta focused on the werewolf who had spoken. "My dear friends. He is anything but. We cannot turn away from our discovery."

*

"At least we finally solved the Rasputin mystery," said Rurik quietly to Felix. "I would have never guessed it in a million years."

Felix peered around Rurik into the short distance where Radu stood in the shadow of a large tree. Sebastian sat next to him, meditating.

"You and me both," said Felix. "But it's true." He gripped his scimitar's hilt to demonstrate his point. "Although I'm having a hard time accepting it."

Rurik leaned into Felix and whispered, "Told you he was playing a game none of us knew existed. Be mindful. We don't know what comes next. Remember—Cheshire Cat."

Felix nodded and they walked back toward Radu, whose eyes were focused on the council of wolves standing before the torchlit entrance to their lair.

Rurik stood next to Radu. "I still might call you Zazlov here and there until I am used to it. Still friends?" He extended his hand to Radu.

"You may call me what you wish, my dear Rurik," said Radu, shaking his hand. "Glad to see you have accepted the truth."

"I'm still getting there."

Rurik moved past Radu and lay back on his bed of leaves.

"Seems like everything is worked out," said Radu to Felix, who sat next to him.

"It's fine. He just wanted to hear it from me." Felix looked to the council. "How did you know Tóth was working with the Butcher?"

"I didn't know. I made it up."

"You what?"

"He was a grave threat to us. There was no way we were making it out of that situation alive unless he was eliminated."

"Radu—"

"At the time, several things were apparent to me. Firstly, I knew the Butcher was consuming their blood for its magical properties. Second, I sensed the friction and mistrust between Tóth and Alzbeta. I scanned the Veil to find her wound was from a silver trap. I then proceeded to connect it all in a narrative that enabled our escape."

"So you just slaughtered him?"

453

"I did. It was necessary."

"This won't go unanswered."

"Indeed it will. Those loyal to Tóth—what did you sense when I struck him down?"

"Anger at first. Then confusion . . . then relief. Even awe toward you."

"Exactly. You must learn to understand pack mentality. They witnessed me strike down an alpha. The rift in leadership between Alzbeta and Tóth is no more."

"It just feels . . . wrong to me."

"I need to shake you of this idea of black or white. Your next lesson for the evening—the true warlock survives in shades of gray." Radu sounded annoyed. He stood and walked closer to the pack, listening in as Alzbeta continued to soothe her pack's minds.

"Tóth was bad news," said Rurik, sitting up. "He advised Alzbeta and the pack to maul us even after we saved her and the townsfolk they protect."

"I understand," said Felix. "I'm just processing a lot currently."

Rurik nodded sympathetically. "So, now that you're magick, think you can conjure me up a bottle of vodka?"

Felix smiled. "I have a long way to go before I can do anything of the sort. But I did learn to see in the dark."

"Really? Wow! Congratulations, buddy. That's amazing." Rurik reached over and slapped him on the knee.

Felix was filled with embarrassment and hopelessness, feeling he was being over-congratulated like a child for completing a simple task.

"Thanks," he said, lying back on the ground.

*

Alzbeta woke them at dawn and led them to the clearing where the Jasta Eleven planes and one biplane sat abandoned. The Red Baron's triple-winged plane was gone.

"We killed all the pilots but one," said Rurik, looking over the planes. "Sadly, the big fish swims another day."

"You did well," said Radu, firmly gripping Rurik's shoulder. "Any disruption of dark plans such as these is a victory."

Sebastian stood next to Rurik. "Good job, Unk Rur."

Rurik looked up at him. "Thanks. Couldn't have done any of it without you."

The group turned to Alzbeta.

"Will you be all right?" asked Felix.

Her jowls sagged so that she appeared to frown. "I don't know, Felix. We have suffered so greatly for so long, but you—all of you—have given us hope. And shined a light to where there was only darkness. We now know the truth and will rebuild as we have always done."

"To Serbia, then?" asked Radu.

"I think so. Our kind has been fractured for too long between me and General Tóth, so thank you for doing what I could not. Lycan politics are . . . well, complicated. I am hoping that by returning to our homeland and to our kind, we may finally find peace."

Radu glanced quickly to Felix, then knelt before Alzbeta. "It is my honor to serve you, Alzbeta. You will always have an ally in me."

Alzbeta nodded and turned her large blue eyes to Felix.

"It's difficult for me to stand here before you, Felix. For centuries, we discussed what we'd do if the Impaler was ever reborn. But as I see you now, I can feel you are a good man. I trust you will remain that way during the challenges that lie ahead."

Felix placed his hand on his sword's hilt. "You have my word," he said, bowing his head.

Alzbeta came to stand before Sebastian. "And you," she said. "Thank you again for what you did." Her eyes shot to the ground. "You'd think after all these years we'd learn, but our hunger often makes us impulsive. If it weren't for you, I'd be a pelt hanging in the castle. From this day forth, you will always be one of us. Bless you, Sebastian."

Sebastian smiled and held out Dollie to her.

"Thank Dol-dol too. She help."

"And thank you to my little rabbit friend."

Alzbeta took a few steps back. "Godspeed to you all," she said. "I hope we will meet again under sunnier circumstances."

She took one last lingering glance at them before disappearing back into the dense forest in a fast blur.

The group walked to the resting craft and Felix ran his hand along the body of a matte black monoplane.

"I'll take this one," he said.

"Very well, Master Felix," said Radu.

 Radu turned to Rurik.

"You ready?"

"I am."

Radu placed his hand to Rurik's forehead and hummed softly. A nearly undetectable glow emanated from his palm as the pilot memories inserted into Rurik from Mary transfused into his mind.

"Quite good," said Radu, removing his hand. "The information really took."

"You can use it?"

"Once I familiarize myself with the aircraft, I think we will do fine."

"My turn!" said Felix, standing before Radu.

Radu placed his palm over Felix's forehead.

"Wow," said Felix, blinking repeatedly as the pilot's memories fused into his hippocampus. "That's really something."

The four men stood quietly for a moment, each knowing it was time to disband.

"Good luck, Radu. I hope this castle provides the answers you're looking for," said Rurik, turning his glance to Felix. "Train him well. I can't have my best friend turn out to be a bumbler."

Radu nodded and a half grin appeared at the corner of his lips. "You're a good man, Rurik Kozlov. I am honored to know you. I'm sorry for misleading you for so long. But now that you've had a sleep on it, can I assume I am forgiven?"

"Yes. Orna, though—I think she would have had a few harsh words."

Radu let out a bellowing laugh. "A few? My ears are burning just thinking of it. How I hid this from her for centuries will never cease to amaze me." He turned to Rurik's biplane. "Remember, you must land at the farm near Rabenstein, eighty kilometers southwest of Berlin. I have implanted the directions in your mind and called out to several associates along the way, who will assist in masking your flight path. You should be able to arrive unscathed. My colleague Albert will meet you once you are safely on the ground."

"Understood," said Rurik.

"My intuition rarely fails me. If we are to save Mary, I sense it centers on Berlin. Albert will help you with the rest—he's invented some incredible advancements in the craft."

The two men embraced.

"And you!" said Radu, turning to Sebastian.

Sebastian turned his back and walked to his airplane, where he placed his face against the craft and pulled Dollie close to his chest.

"Now, now—come on, big fellow," said Radu. "There is no need for sadness. Goodbyes are merely an opportunity for a future warm hello. We will meet again."

Sebastian turned and a green tear ran down his cheek. He picked up Radu in a great bear hug, then placed the warlock on the ground.

"And goodbye to you too, Dollie. Take care of my big, brave friend."

Radu walked off to his monoplane.

Felix patted his arm, and Sebastian reached out and swept him off the ground.

"I'll admit," said Felix, grunting, "I'm going to miss these giant hugs."

"I see Fele soon," said Sebastian. He placed him down, sniffling as he held back tears, then climbed into the bipane's gunner seat.

Felix and Rurik stood facing one another.

"You ever imagine when I showed up at the morgue . . . that one day we'd be standing in a werewolf-infested forest, trying to save the world?"

"That's what we do!" said Rurik, smiling. "And to think I almost turned you in."

"Really?"

"No. Not really, but it did briefly cross my mind. I had a sense about you, though—and look at you now."

Felix exhaled. "I don't know if I can do this."

Rurik stepped to him and placed his hands on Felix's shoulders.

"When I met you, you were an angry, spoiled, reckless boar. And now? Now I stand before a mighty warlock. Maybe not right now, but if you follow Radu's teachings, you will be great. You're still angry and reckless, by the way, but I am quite proud of you."

Felix laughed. "Nice to know you no longer think me spoiled."

"I've seen you eat beans from a can with your bare hands . . . hardly spoiled."

"Stay safe, Rurik. And call upon us the moment you find anything on Mary."

"You can count on it."

Felix nodded solemnly. "Well . . . this is it," he said.

"This is it."

"We'll see each other again. I can sense it."

"Then that's all I need," said Rurik. "Until next time, Mr. Warlock."

Both men turned and walked to their respective planes.

A few moments later, all three planes growled to life.

They shot into the morning sun, veering off in their perspective directions until swallowed by the puffy white plumes above—each team with its own perilous and harrowing agenda.

27

March 30, 1917, dusk

Wilhelm stood at a tall, oblong window overlooking the grounds of Huis Doorn, the German aristocracy's secluded safe house in the Netherlands. It was an open secret among the most powerful in the ruling elite that Huis Doorn was a well-traveled escape for illicit sexual excursions. Unknown to most was that the Prussian Secret Police also appropriated the structure at times as a black site prison and interrogation facility used against enemies of the German State.

Wilhelm had been visiting the modern Gothic mansion every June since his eighteenth birthday for an annual orgy celebrating the summer solstice and carried a genuine fondness for the grounds. He was quite pleased when Minister Schmidt recommended it as a temporary residence while the safety concerns surrounding Augusta's disappearance were sorted out.

The grounds were essentially state secret, moderately remote, and the structure itself was expansive—offering a luxurious, even palatial interior in which Wilhelm could relax and oversee his empire from a safe distance. He was also relieved that Ernest Louis had agreed to accompany him, but was still uneasy about the decision to bring along Nicholas.

After nearly an hour of heated debate, Wilhelm finally relented and agreed it would be best to hide Nicholas at Huis Doorn, where he and Ernest Louis would be able to indoctrinate the fallen tsar as they saw fit and oversee his communication with the newly converted Nosferatu thrall.

Wilhelm squinted as the last rays of sunshine sank beneath the heavily wooded forest that surrounded the mansion. It had been six hours since he had smoked a cigarette, and he kept his eyes firmly on the gate leading into the grounds, hoping his butler would be returning soon with a fresh carton.

Felix Yusupov.

Wilhelm believed that at any moment Schmidt or Hindenburg would contact him and inform him of Yusupov's capture. Then they would see he wasn't so crazy. By his own estimation, he was the most incisive man in Germany—if not the world—and he could barely wait to watch Hindenburg grovel when confronted with the truth. Wilhelm smiled as he realized he had outsmarted his personal seers.

Felix Yusupov was the reincarnation of Vlad Drăculea—of that, Wilhelm was certain. Radu cel Frumos had done it again. *Well*, thought Wilhelm, *not for long*. Blood was blood. And the moment Yusupov was imprisoned in Germany, Wilhelm would order his execution and—*voilà!*—a fresh new bottle of immortality.

With Nette deceased, Wilhelm considered who, if anyone, might be a good candidate for the new surrogate for his child.

Definitely someone of noble blood.

Anxiety flooded him as the thought reminded him of Augusta's disappearance. Their relationship had been strained of late, but in his heart, he still yearned to hold her near once more and know she was safe. He tried calming himself by thinking of the success in Arras and the further expansion of the Nosferatu hybrid program, reminding himself that Schmidt's gas would be deployed within the next forty-eight hours. The Parisian countryside would be overrun with his hordes within the week.

Paris will fall by April's end. Europe is mine.

But then there was the precarious situation surrounding Dmitri Pavlovich and Olaf. God, how Wilhelm despised Olaf. He'd ordered the warlock's termination after the failed Saint Petersburg operation and was surprised by General Hindenburg and Minister Schmidt's vehement objections. They'd maintained that the Russian witch was far too respected and feared to be assassinated—the retribution would be dire if such action were ever traced back to the Prussian Secret Police.

Wilhelm placed his hand in his pocket and leaned into the windowsill, questioning the wisdom of authorizing Dmitri and Olaf to travel to Bucharest to attempt to spawn the Nosferatu once more.

"Not one mark of my money goes into this operation! And I remind you that I retain supremacy when my child is born as the reincarnation of Drăculea—is that understood?" he said aloud, reenacting his firmness with Dmitri.

Schmidt was correct—Wilhelm had nothing to lose by sanctioning another attempt to respawn the Nosferatu under Dmitri and Olaf's command. In fact, he had everything to gain: it would only strengthen and reaffirm Germany's hold on the area, now that the Bucharest operation had run astray. Wilhelm was assured Vondling's assassination was a success, and Dmitri, along with his army of Nosferatu, could then rein in the Bucharest vámpir and employ them as useful tactical operatives in furthering Germany's operations in the region. Upon Dmitri's success, it was promised that Wilhelm's empire would retain hegemonic control of Romania and its surrounding nations indefinitely.

Wilhelm continued staring into the forest until the magenta and purple slivers of dusk settled into night and an eerie quiet crept over the grounds. A curiosity curled up in Wilhelm's mind when he noticed that the guards lining the high brick fence stood facing away from the forest—each equipped with gas masks on their faces and hogweed canisters strapped to their backs, never taking their goggled stares from his mansion's exterior.

"That's curious," he said. "Shouldn't they be watching the forest?"

Wilhelm jumped at the sound of several loud clicks, then forced his eyes closed and threw his hand outward to block the sudden light flooding the interior of his handsome mahogany study.

"What on earth?"

He quickly pulled the drapes closed and backed away from the window. The thick fabric still shone bright with a white-light corona bursting around the edges, illuminating the room.

"This will not stand!"

Wilhelm marched to his desk and pulled the telephone to his ear, only to find the line was silent.

"Hello? . . . Hello? . . . Damn thing!" He slammed the receiver onto its latch several times, nearly snapping the thin iron rods. "We will see about this!"

A short minute later, Wilhelm opened the front door to the mansion and strode onto the circular driveway that led to the main gate, shielding his eyes from the glaring spotlights. The gas-masked guards snapped into action, hooking their hogweed prods onto their belts and gripping the rifles strapped across their chests as they ran toward Wilhelm.

"Stop! Stop right there, Kaiser," shouted one of the masked men, raising his rifle to Wilhelm.

"How dare you point that thing at me!" screamed Wilhelm. "Put that down and turn out these damn floodlights! The entire inside is lit up like a . . ." Wilhelm paused, noticing that he was now surrounded by six other guards, all with their rifles pointed at him.

"What is the meaning of this?"

"My Kaiser. We must ask that you go back inside immediately. We are instructed to guard you and keep you on these premises."

"Keep me on the . . . why, you filthy . . . I can leave these grounds anytime I choose!"

Wilhelm forced his way through the line of guards and marched toward the gate.

A rifle shot rang out through the quiet, stilling Wilhelm in his stance.

He turned to see five guards pointing their rifles at him while a sixth slowly lowered his weapon after shooting it into the sky. From the corner of his eye, Wilhelm watched as another dozen guards ran along the fence perimeter and formed a line along the gate, all aiming their weapons at him.

Wilhelm was enraged. This was treason. He'd have their heads.

"Kaiser, this is for your own safety. We ask that you turn around and enter your residence immediately."

"Kaiser!" came a voice from the mansion.

Wilhelm turned to see Ernest Louis dashing toward them.

"Kaiser, please," he shouted.

The guards relaxed their rifles as Ernest Louis neared.

"Wilhelm," said Ernest Louis, breathing heavily. "You cannot be outside. Come. They're only following orders. No one is to leave the grounds."

"On whose command?"

"I must insist." Ernest Louis extended his hand. "Please, let's go back inside."

Ernest Louis pulled on Wilhelm's arm and guided him through the masked guards.

"And why aren't they watching the forest? Seems to me—"

"I'll explain everything once we're back inside. Too dangerous to be out in the open," said Ernest Louis, ushering Wilhelm into the mansion and closing the door.

*

"What do you mean the communication lines are downed indefinitely?" asked Wilhelm angrily.

That was it, he decided. They'd be leaving for Berlin first thing in the morning. Wilhelm would not stand for this and intended to punish each soldier who'd dared hold a rifle to him.

Ernest Louis crossed his legs and sat back in his chair, gazing at Wilhelm, who was seated behind his desk.

"My Kaiser, please. Let's just take a moment to calm down. We're stuck here for the time being—and it's a safer option for you until we locate Augusta and find those responsible for her disappearance. We need to ensure nobody knows you are here. Once that has been confirmed, then we can arrange to have you evacuated back to Berlin."

"Evacuated? This is madness. I'm the ruler of the German Empire! I will not be stuffed away like some . . . some . . . see? I'm all mixed up!" Wilhelm slumped back in his chair. "How am I to communicate with my advisors with no telephone? Not even a telegraph?"

"Such contingencies have been accounted for. We have a flock of carrier pigeons for—"

"Pigeons? Pigeons?" Wilhelm's face grew flushed. "I am to direct a world war with the use of pigeons? Have you lost all your sense?"

Ernest Louis pushed his palms outward. "Now, Kaiser. I understand it is not ideal, but you are in great danger and we must . . ." Ernest Louis tilted his head to the side. "Have I ever let you down, Wilhelm?"

No. If anything, Ernest Louis had proven himself loyal time and again. Wilhelm took in a short breath and relaxed.

"Prince Henry, Hindenburg, and Minister Schmidt are more than capable of handling the operations in your absence. I'll speak with the groundsmen tomorrow to see if anything can be done about the communication lines. Think of this time as a much-needed rest. You have been under a great deal of stress."

"Can I at least have my goddamn cigarettes?"

"Here," said Ernest Louis, pulling a near-crumpled pack from his breast pocket. "Have my last two."

Wilhelm reached across the desk and grabbed the pack, then pulled a cigarette from the paper box with his lips. He found his lighter and took a deep drag. The earthy smell of rich, dried tobacco filled the room as Wilhelm let out a great exhale.

"Ah, now, that is better."

"You see? Just calm your mind. We have more pressing affairs."

Wilhelm's eyes fell upon the curtained cage in the corner of his study.

"Are you awake in there?" he asked in Russian.

"I am," came Nicholas's soft voice.

Wilhelm gently tapped his cigarette into an ashtray, extinguishing the orange tip. He and Ernest Louis walked to the cage and pulled back the curtain to find Nicholas curled up at its base.

"Sleep well, cousin?" asked Wilhelm.

Nicholas nodded. "I'm starving," he said, vigorously scratching his head and face. "Feed me. I need it now. I burn all over."

Wilhelm crouched and stared into Nicholas's eyes.

"Only if you ask properly."

"Please! May I please have some blood?"

Wilhelm shot a wry glance to Ernest Louis.

"What do you think, Ernest? Has Nicholas been good?"

Ernest Louis smiled. "I think he's been a very good boy."

"Oh, I like that. 'Boy' . . . Well then, let's feed him."

Ernest Louis walked to the study's door and opened it. He leaned outside and muttered something to the guards.

A few moments passed and he returned to the cage carrying a seven-hundred-milliliter bottle of blood with a rubber neck and nozzle attached to it, akin to a hamster's feeding tube. Nicholas neared the cage bars on his knees and licked his lips as Ernest Louis affixed the bottle to a feeding slot at the side of the cage.

Nicholas seized upon the bottle, initially sipping from the metal tube and eventually ripping it off and guzzling straight from the bottle, spilling a good majority of its contents down the front of his already bloodstained garments. Nicholas licked his hands of the cruor—even lifting his blazer to his mouth and sucking the spilled gore from the fabric.

"Now," said Ernest Louis. "There is another bottle ready for you. But I need you to listen."

"Allow me," said Wilhelm, placing his right hand on his knee. "Nicholas, I know you want more blood. And I am happy to give you more. But you need to be aware of the changes your body is going through. After Minister Schmidt took your blood, we had it analyzed by the highest-level medical scientists within my admin- istration. They have told me that in the next few days, as you become accustomed to the country air, you might begin to hear voices in your head. You will even have wild dreams or waking visions of being on the battlefield and facing down the French and British. These are fever dreams due to your sickness and nothing more. When those voices cry out—if they cry out—you are simply to tell them to go away and continue to fight. The visions are a manifestation of your immune system fighting this horrid disease."

"Why visions of a battlefield?" asked Nicholas.

"I'm trying to help you, Nicholas. Trying to forgive you for betraying me and siding with Serbia and the Allies. But I am willing to put this behind us. You're very sick. Mentally and physically ill. These past few months have been a dire shock to your system. And this new disease of yours, my doctors have reported, is a rare form of stress-induced rabies, likely transmitted to you by Alexandra. They have told me that vivid dreams and visions of being at war are a common symptom of your illness. But you need to understand those voices in your head are not real. You must insist that they are to go away and continue to fight. Is that understood?"

"I understand . . . I think. But what about Alexandra? Alexei? When can I see them?"

"Very soon," said Wilhelm in a calming tone. "Very soon, in fact. My top men are working on extracting them from a remote area outside of Saint Petersburg. They are safe. And they want to see you very badly. Alexei is growing so big. All you need to do is listen to me and Ernest, and that will help us bring them to you sooner."

Nicholas nodded. "I will. I want to be healthy. I need to see my family. And I'm so sorry about Serbia, cousin. I am ashamed."

Wilhelm nodded graciously. "Very well, you are forgiven. And rest assured that I have my top doctors in Berlin studying your illness. We expect to have a cure very, very soon. For now, all you need to do is stay alive by feeding and listening to everything we tell you. I realize keeping you in this cage may seem cruel. But I am doing this to protect you. I am doing this out of love. I hope you see that."

"I do. Thank you, cousin. May I have more?" Nicholas raised his hands in supplication.

"Of course you may." Wilhelm nodded to Ernest Louis. "Bring the muzzle," he said.

Ernest Louis walked to the door once more and returned with two gas-masked soldiers. He held a bottle of blood in one hand and a muzzle with a dog leash and choker in the other.

"You sure about this?" asked Ernest Louis.

Wilhelm looked to Ernest Louis with confident eyes.

A Romanov will be your demise, came Franz Ferdinand's words. Well, not today. Not any day. The Kaiser already felt a blow to his ego when he agreed to come to Huis Doorn. He was not one to hide from conflict, yet here he sat—some six hundred kilometers from Berlin, hiding out while his secret police dealt with the matter of Augusta's disappearance. He had every intention of demonstrating his fortitude to Ernest Louis, reminding him of his fearlessness—knowing that everyone in the grand duke's inner circle would hear about how Wilhelm had hand-fed Nicholas.

"I am." Wilhelm accepted the muzzle. "Now, I need you to put this on," he said to Nicholas. "I must ensure you can be trusted."

Nicholas accepted the muzzle and slipped it on his face.

"Turn around," said Wilhelm.

Nicholas turned around and Wilhelm buckled the muzzle straps tightly to his head.

"We're going to let you out. But do you see those men behind me?"

Nicholas turned around and nodded.

"I want to remind you that those devices they're holding kill people with your illness on contact. If you act out in any way, they will be forced to spray you, and it will kill you instantly. Do you understand?"

"I do."

"Good."

Wilhelm unlocked the cage, entered, and strapped the choker around Nicholas's neck.

"This is made of the same wood as your cage. We have dipped it in candle wax so that you are not burned. But again, I warn you: if you act out, I will tug on it tightly and the wood will sink into your flesh and burn you. Will you be a good boy?"

"I will," said Nicholas, mumbling through his muzzle. "I'll be a very good boy."

"Perfect, now come along."

Wilhelm led Nicholas by his leash, and they stood before Ernest Louis.

"Down, boy," said Wilhelm, forcing Nicholas to the floor.

He sat in a chair with Nicholas on all fours by his side.

"Give me your hand and shake."

Nicholas's quivering hand reached to Wilhelm and they shook hands.

"Such a good boy," said Wilhelm, releasing Nicholas's hand and stroking his hair. "After this, we will give you a nice, hot bath. How does that sound?"

Nicholas looked to him with wide, terrified eyes and nodded.

"Such a good boy," said Wilhelm. "He's a good boy, don't you think?"

"Very good," said Ernest Louis, smiling.

"Now. I'm going to remove your muzzle, and Ernest is going to tip the bottle into your mouth. But I want you to drink it nicely. No more of your savagery. Can you do that for me?"

Nicholas nodded.

Wilhelm reached around his head and undid the muzzle. Noticing that Nicholas's bloodstained fangs were on full display, he firmed his grasp upon the leash.

"Go ahead, Ernest."

Ernest Louis uncorked the bottle and brought it to Nicholas's face. Nicholas looked to Wilhelm—his crow's feet framed eyes filled with shame. He peered to the gas-masked soldiers, then back to the bottle, slowly raising his hands to the glass. Gently wrapping his hands around the bottle's neck, Nicholas tipped it into his mouth and guzzled the cool, thick liquid.

"Very good, Nicholas," said Wilhelm, stroking his head. "See? I can be forgiving. Keep this up, and we can put Serbia far behind us."

Nicholas continued swallowing.

"Now, remember. We will care for you, look after you. Give you all the blood you want and all the warm baths you desire. All you need to do is tell those voices in your head—no matter what they say, or how real they seem—to stay away and continue to fight. The more they fight, the sooner you will be healthy again."

Nicholas finished the bottle and sat back.

"Can you do that for me?"

Nicholas bobbed his head, still licking his lips.

Wilhelm reached out and patted his matted hair.

"Such a very good boy," he said. "We're going to get along just fine."

28

March 31, 1917, midday

A dark mist materialized upon the grassy field that surrounded Mount Hohenzollern as the Black Butcher stepped from the Void with Mary's silver-encased body floating next to him.

He wrapped his hands around the hilts of the twin demon blades strapped to his waist and took in the gray wispy clouds above. His eyes traced the mount from its peak all the way to its base where a wide circle of Vago's undead coven stood before the briar patch, forming a human chain.

"She's been busy," he said, studying their rigid figures, which swayed slightly as they guarded the mount.

The Butcher took one step forward and a rushing sensation overwhelmed his senses, causing his organ of Corti to scream a high-pitched wail. Mary's metal body fell to the grass as he buckled over, threw his hands to his head, and growled at the painful vibrations. After taking a moment to catch his breath, the Butcher stood upright and shook his head. Over the centuries, the Void had spoken to him with such force only one other time—the day his father was imprisoned in the blade. He looked down to the blade containing Bael and found no unusual energies about the weapon.

It was something else.

His mind reached out to the Void for answers, and his vision was immediately thrust to the previous night's events at Čachtice Castle. The images rushed into his mind: Felix and Radu escaping, the werewolves discovering his deception, and finally, the image that sent his psyche into a fevered rage—Hanne casting the remaining blades into the molten silver.

The Butcher dropped to his knees.

"No," he muttered as saliva dripped from his mouth, wetting his hood. "No . . ."

He stayed on his knees, taking in the implications of the events and wondering how he could hide such malfeasance from his father once the demon was reborn. The Butcher scanned the Void for Felix and Radu's whereabouts and found a cluster of red pulsing globes surrounding their path. After picking apart the information, he knew they were headed back to Romania—to Poenari Castle, the former stronghold of Vlad Drăculea before his discovery of Loch Dracul.

"You fool," he said, cursing himself.

He silenced the imagery flooding in from the Void and called out to Olaf.

"Yusupov and Radu have escaped. I am back in Germany, preparing to resurrect my father. Before you journey to Loch Dracul, I command you to enlist Vondling and his armies. I am sensing Yusupov is heading to Poenari Castle. If he arrives, our plans are in grave danger. You must capture Yusupov and kill Radu."

Understood, came Olaf's voice directly into his mind. *But what of your sister? She will be freed upon Radu's death. That will complicate—*

"There is no other course. Do as I command," said the Butcher, standing and closing his connection to Olaf.

The Butcher waved his hand and Mary's body floated above the ground once more. He then marched toward the briar patch.

Vago's pale, zombified coven stood before him in their white and red robes, encircling the tangled branches. The Butcher emitted a strong psychic signal, alerting them to his dark powers and allegiance to Elizabeth. They paid him no mind as he broke through their lines and proceeded into the briar patch. The thorns clutched at him but crumbled to black wispy ashes the moment they touched his garments. Only another moment passed before the brambles slithered away from the dark entity and created an opening for him to pass. He continued on the path leading up the mount with Mary's shiny figure floating next to him.

*

"Hello, sister," said the Black Butcher, taking in Elizabeth's gruesome appearance.

Elizabeth crept toward him.

"Baphomet, is it really you? For too long I have wondered about your survival. Last we met was just before Radu trapped you in the mirror."

"It took some time, but I figured a way out."

Elizabeth now stood directly before his imposing dark figure.

"And after that time, did you ever think to find me? I've been waiting for you. Why is it you never breached the forest?"

"Everything that has transpired is a result of my planning."

"You left me to rot in here." Elizabeth sounded angry.

The Butcher felt pinned. He grew wary, even slightly nervous, as he remembered Elizabeth's psychopathic fits of rage. He could only imagine what centuries of seclusion might have done to her psyche. His hand made its way to the blade containing their father, and he considered striking her down. What did he need her for? The vessel for Bael's resurrection was here in the castle, and every other piece of his plan was firmly in place. Elizabeth's ambition and treacherous ways would only cause him trouble if left unchecked. Everything he'd been planning came down to this moment, and he sensed Elizabeth had pieced together his intention to keep her sequestered.

He had, in fact, left her to rot while he aligned the happenings to his advantage.

They had been at each other's throats since Elizabeth was a teen— she was constantly working to usurp his favor in the eyes of their father. But Bael would know. There would be no hiding it if he struck down his half sister for personal gain. The Butcher would be severely punished, perhaps even banished for the transgression upon Bael's resurrection. He would have to find some other way to contain her and use her unbridled evil to his advantage.

It was time to assert himself.

"What good would it have done?" he said. "The banishment spell was in place. And your hex on the forest, despite being breakable to me—and only me—was an excellent test for Vago's eugenic efforts. Your army of ghouls now guarding the mount, and your growing army of thrall on the western front? All because of me fostering Vago and leading him to believe he had a place in all this. I was the one keeping this area hidden and out of the minds of the ruling elite. Do not mistake my patience for treachery."

The Butcher waited, wondering if Elizabeth would lash out.

"You have always been a clever boy," she said with an unexpected warmth in her voice. "I see you've brought me gifts."

"Wonderful gifts." His hands gripped the hilts of the blades. "Where are the rest? I have seventy-two vessels waiting."

"Now is not the time. First Father. Then my mother." The Butcher gripped the blade containing Queen Kimaris—his mother's soul. "As we witnessed the last time our kind roamed free, too many rogue agendas weaken our objectives. Once Father's power is solidified, we can begin unlocking the more subservient demons as needed."

"Very well, but I don't believe Father will approve."

"He will do so with vigor. I have been communing with him via the blade."

The Butcher peered behind Elizabeth and noticed Vago hanging upside down, encased in webbing.

"Lovers' spat?"

"I discovered his treachery. He's the one who allowed Radu to breach our castle walls."

The Butcher walked to Vago, bent at the waist, and stared into his wide-open eyes.

"He never mentioned you were freed from the mirror," said Elizabeth, creeping near.

The Butcher gripped his sword's hilt, thinking she might strike. He turned to confront her.

"You can remove your hand from your sword," said Elizabeth. "I accept and understand your actions. It's simply one more lie Vago told to justify my actions against him."

Believing her to be sincere, he turned to Vago.

"Nice to see you again, Vago. My, my. It seems your backhanded ways finally caught up with you." The Butcher pressed his hand firmly into Vago's lower abdomen. "How does that feel? The notion that you are going to burst and yet will never find release? I can only imagine how hunger is ravaging your body. And your eyes. Your poor, withered, bloodshot eyes. What a relief it would be if only you could blink."

"Let him be," said Elizabeth.

"Are you growing soft on me, little sister?"

"Hardly. But I do, admittedly, from time to time, miss having him around to beg and plead just to be near me."

The Butcher spun around. "A fitting end for a disgusting syco-phant. I will enjoy watching him suffer over the centuries . . . and speaking of suffering, I brought something special for you."

The Butcher extended his hand, and from the castle's opening floated Mary's silver body. He levitated her figure and set it upon the ground just before Elizabeth's gangling front appendages.

"A statue?"

"No, sister. Not a statue. Contained within this silver is a gift be-yond your wildest desires—second only to breaking the banishment spell. I captured a shape-shifter. Consider it an offering, one of penitence and forgiveness. I hope we can put our sibling rivalry behind us and start anew." The Butcher dropped to his knee and bowed. "Forgive me for keeping you waiting for so long. I hope this will mend any torn flesh between us."

"If what you say is true, then it's a beginning." Elizabeth lurched over Mary and gripped her silver body with her front appendages. "Free her! Now! I must consume her."

"Patience. We are in need of this one. You may only drink from her. Take what essence you require to morph back to your human form. And then she will serve as your proxy in Berlin until Radu is killed. I have my top operatives hunting him down as we speak. It is only a matter of time."

Elizabeth backed away from Mary and positioned her body toward the Butcher.

"The effects of her blood will not be as long-lasting as her soul."

"You can finish what you started once we have completed our seizure of the German Empire and you are free of these walls. Until then, her blood is all I will allow."

Thick, clear liquid dripped from Elizabeth's fangs.

"Very well, I will do as you command."

The Butcher extended his hands and the silver coating Mary's body melted away, save two silver bands he kept around her wrists.

Mary lay unconscious and frozen upon the floor as Elizabeth loomed over her. She sank her fangs deep into Mary's abdomen and drank down her blood.

"That's enough!" said the Butcher, using his weight to push Elizabeth away. "We need her alive. Now—strike her with your stinger. She must be under your control."

Elizabeth shifted around and thrust the barbed tip of her abdomen into Mary's thigh, injecting her with trance venom. She then crept away, slowly raising and lowering her legs before her body slumped to the marble and began to jerk and contort.

The Butcher watched as her spider body tried to stand once more but became clumsy, swaying back and forth like some drunken fool. Elizabeth fell and rolled onto her back—all eight of her legs shivering as they constricted into her abdomen. Her white body glowed, and the Butcher held his hand before his face to block the searing white light. He closed his eyes and held them shut until the bright subsided.

Upon opening his eyes, the Butcher was pleased to see his sister standing before him in human form. Her nude figure strode toward him, her bare feet becoming covered in webbing. Elizabeth stood before her brother's hulking figure and looked up to his hooded face. She was exactly as he remembered—long, flowing black hair, bright green eyes, and slight facial features that suggested a pixie-esque innocence. Looking upon her, the layman would never guess the sheer bloodthirsty nature Elizabeth carried within her heart.

She stared at her hands and outstretched her arms while opening and clenching her fists. A tear fell down her cheek and she threw herself at the Butcher, embracing him.

"Thank you, Brother. Praise unto you."

"Welcome back to the living," said the Butcher, pulling a small leather pouch from within his ethereal garments. He tossed it to Elizabeth.

She caught the pouch and brought it to her face, inhaling the aroma of its contents.

"Werewolf dust?" she asked with a note of excitement in her voice.

"Open it and see."

Elizabeth untied the leather strap around the pouch to discover a small pocket of ground werewolf bones. She cast the powder into the air, stepping into the cloud of bone dust and inhaling deeply. Elizabeth stood shuddering as the invigorating high spread through her bloodstream and sharpened her senses, causing her to drool slightly.

"Thank you, Brother," she said, regaining her senses and calming her breath. "It's been so long since I've felt such exhilaration."

"Plenty more when you so desire."

Elizabeth stepped back a few paces and crossed her arms.

"And who is it hiding under that hood these days?" she asked.

The Butcher removed his hood, revealing a pale, featureless face akin to that of a fashion mannequin. His flesh rippled as the youthful face of Emperor Romulus Augustulus emerged, quickly morphing into that of Pontius Pilot, followed briefly by Emperor Constantine XI Palaiologos before finally settling upon General Paul von Hindenburg.

His black ethereal garments morphed into olive-green military attire.

"Who is this?"

"I have learned from my past endeavors. Rulers fall. I now prefer to arrange things from behind the curtain. I am now a German general and a top ally of your friend, Kaiser Wilhelm."

"Don't even speak his name! The foul, lumbering oaf."

"Then you'll be glad to know I have removed him from our purview. Our path to domination is nigh."

Elizabeth walked to Mary and stood over her.

"And what is her place in this?"

"Once Father and I return to Berlin, we must initially earn back the aristocracy's trust with an appearance of normalcy. Your participation in this will be key as I need her under your trance. But first . . ."

A piece of the Butcher's blazer peeled away, floated into the air, and slithered across Elizabeth's nude flesh, slowly expanding until she stood in a dress of the most radiant red with brown leather boots.

"I hope this will provide you with some comfort," he said.

Elizabeth looked down at the dress with a joyous expression.

"I adore it, Brother," she said, spinning and gripping the skirt in her hands.

The Butcher then waved his hands and the silver bands around Mary's wrists evaporated. She stood at once and looked at them both with eyes of the dullest white.

"Hello," Mary said to Elizabeth, her voice flat and monotone. "Are you my new mother?"

"I am," said Elizabeth. "And this is your uncle. We're so very glad to have you here with us."

Mary's face conveyed no emotion as she glanced back and forth between them.

The Butcher walked to Mary and removed a white glove from his hand. He gripped Mary by the chin and a soft glow radiated from his palm.

"Do you have it?" he asked.

Mary morphed into Augusta. "I do, Uncle. How do I look?"

"Like the spitting image."

The Butcher turned to Elizabeth and unsheathed the blade containing Bael. "Bring me a vessel. It's time for our father to return."

*

Five of Elizabeth's thrall children crept into the hall on all fours, raising their noses into the air as if they were searching for Elizabeth's scent.

"Come, my children. Come forward," she said, extending her hand.

The ghoulish youths clambered near and encircled her as Mary, in Augusta's form, stood to her right.

The Butcher looked over the children and extended his hand outward.

"That one. He's of the purest Prussian stock."

Elizabeth crouched down to Oskar Güterbach and stared into his eyeless face.

"You have been chosen, my beloved." She placed her index and middle fingers to her lips, then pressed them firmly to Oskar's forehead.

His pale face looked up to Hindenburg.

"Come forward, child."

Oskar slinked toward the Butcher with an air of mindlessness about him as the demon unsheathed the Bael scimitar and knelt to the child.

"You're certain he will not be absorbed?" asked Elizabeth.

"I am certain. The child is pure. His soul is a void. One void merged with another to unleash something new."

"And if you're wrong?"

The Butcher plunged the blade into Oskar's chest.

The child screamed and a shock wave burst from the blade's hilt, pushing the Butcher back several meters. Elizabeth ducked away and Mary stood motionless as Oskar's body levitated from the floor with the blade sticking from his chest—a black, glossy orb enclosed his gaunt figure.

The globe hovered above them, churning white and blue before growing red-hot. The red turned orange and the orb's surface cooled, crumbling and cracking to black ash like molten crust. A black, slimy substance oozed onto the floor, followed by the Masamune blade, which clanged to the marble sans its demon jewel.

The Butcher and Elizabeth walked toward the ebon pool, watching with wide eyes as it came alive and took shape. The ghastly material cracked and groaned, giving off the pungent odor of sulfur as it began to form an anthropomorphic shape, growing taller than the Butcher. He and Elizabeth knelt to the ground as the mass assumed the shape of their father.

Bael stood before them, breathing heavily. His muscular, lean body of the shiniest black sparkled and pulsed like some unholy oil-coated onyx. Ram horns grew from his head, curling down to a face that was part man, part beast.

He peered down to his kneeling children.

"Stand," said Bael, his voice low and hoarse.

Hindenburg and Elizabeth stood, taking in the dark majesty of their father.

"My children," said Bael. "Elizabeth and Baphomet. So long have I waited to see you both again."

Elizabeth rushed forward and wrapped her arms around her father.

"Praise unto you, Father. I have missed you so."

Bael placed his clawed hands upon her shoulders and pushed her away gently.

"I sense you have suffered, my child," said Bael.

Elizabeth nodded, then looked up to her father. "I have, Father. All in your name." Her chin quivered as she stared at the mighty demon. "And I would suffer through it all again to serve you."

"Dry your tears, my young beauty. For soon we shall have our revenge."

Elizabeth stood next to the Butcher, and Bael looked to the blade strapped to his waist.

"And I see you have brought your mother."

"I have, but not to resurrect her. Not yet. I will need this blade for our coming battle with our enemies."

Bael's black irises and striking white corneas moved along the blade's shape.

"Very well then. We will save her for when it is time to resurrect the rest of my clan. I trust you have kept the remaining blades safe?"

"I have, Father," said the Butcher, pausing. "They await anytime you say."

Bael took a mighty step forward, and the castle seemed to rumble under his hoof.

"Very well, Baphomet. You have performed flawlessly. May I have my shape?"

"With pleasure." The Butcher reached to Bael and gripped his muscular, blackened forearm.

Bael smiled and rolled back his eyes as he took in the information. "Excellent. Excellent."

Bael began to shrink as his new form took hold. Soon he was shorter than the Butcher.

"Will I pass?" asked Bael.

The Butcher studied Bael—now standing as Kaiser Wilhelm, complete with an ornate pickelhaube upon his head.

"Perfectly," said the Butcher. "Long live the Kaiser."

Bael took notice of Augusta standing lifelessly behind Elizabeth. "And I assume this will be my wife?"

"For the time being, until we can reincarnate my mother. As long as Elizabeth must remain here, this shape-shifter will be under her command until we locate and kill Radu."

Bael's mustache pointed downward.

"That name! It's been so long since I've heard its foul reverberation."

"There's more, Father. Vlad Drăculea has been reborn."

Bael's face snapped to him. "He must be destroyed."

The Butcher stood before him.

"Destroyed is one option—one I am currently pursuing. But you see, this woman, this shape-shifter portraying Augusta, I believe to be his true love. We can use her as bait to lure him. And once we do, he would be far more deadly under your command and in service of the Void. After you were imprisoned, the Vatican betrayed Vlad, and he became the darkest of warlocks the world has ever known."

Bael flashed his teeth. "What is the name of the vessel carrying the spirit of Vehuiah?"

"Felix Yusupov."

"Bring him before me. I will bend his will."

"As you command."

Bael looked to Augusta standing perfectly still and then to his children, who stared back at him with eager eyes.

"It is time, my loyal ones," said Bael, walking to a broken stained-glass window and gazing out at the German countryside below. "Now we will seize control of this German Empire. My Black Sun will rise again."

Chapter 29

29

March 31, 1917, night

Charles Vondling stood behind an ornate wrought-iron railing that encircled a wide, sweeping balcony overlooking the cobblestone avenue of Calea Victoriei at the base of the Royal Palace of Bucharest. The first-quarter moon shone brightly upon his crisp ivory military attire adorned with golden-yellow epaulets, his figure like a glowing white topaz against the drab-green uniforms worn by his accompanying officers.

"Oh, the pageantry! The pageantry!" shouted Vondling as two tanks grumbled past on the avenue below with soldiers hanging from its roof, saluting their emperor with their white-gloved hands.

Vondling clapped wildly as a garrison of perfectly aligned soldiers followed, hoisting Romanian flags above their formation—all with a black *V* painted over the blue, yellow, and red bars. Their boots slapping the avenue in unison echoed for several blocks as the sounds of an approaching marching band carried from behind.

Vondling raised his right hand in a forceful salute as his armies marched below.

"Simply magnificent," he said, clasping his hands together. "Oberst Gäntz!" Vondling turned to his commanding officer.

"Emperor!" replied Gäntz, saluting him.

"Nightly. I want an official decree stating that parades are to be performed nightly. Is that understood?"

"Yes, Emperor," said Gäntz, relaxing his salute. "But what of our plans to invade Berlin? These ceremonies put quite a drain on—"

"Did you not hear the part about nightly parades, Oberst?"

"As you command, Emperor. It will be done."

"Excellent."

Vondling leaned back over the railing as drumbeats anchored the sounds of trumpets, trombones, and a lone tuba filling the night.

"They're coming! They're coming," said Vondling, watching as the marching band veered off the avenue and gathered in formation in a grassy park across from the palace.

They continued on with their patriotic music as two armored trucks drove into view—each pulling a wide open-roofed cage with dirty and haggard human prisoners. The trucks growled to a slow stop and parked just below Vondling's balcony.

Vondling raised his hands into the air, then pulled his elbows downward and clenched his fists. The music stopped and the marching soldiers settled as the human prisoners cried out in a harrowing chorus.

"My subjects!" shouted Vondling. "Tonight we celebrate the birth of the most fearsome army the earth has ever known. Soon we will march north and annex Moldova. Then onward to Ukraine and Poland! We will conquer all in our path. Grow in numbers so fierce, so unstoppable, that the entire German and Austria-Hungarian Empires will cower under our boot! Bucharest and Berlin will fall. Then on to Paris and London, and then the world!"

Cheers erupted from below, drowning out the cries of the caged prisoners. A few scaled the bars to escape and were subdued when vampire soldiers struck them in the face with their rancid saliva. The escapees slumped to the cobblestones and were quickly pulled from Vondling's sight.

"But tonight! Tonight, we celebrate. To the fatherland! To Vonlandia!"

Vondling shot his arm into the air once more. The soldiers below and his officers on the balcony followed the gesture.

"Vonlandia! Vonlandia! Vonlandia!"

The chant carried on for several minutes until a quiet settled upon the parade.

"Well?" shouted Vondling. "What are you waiting for? Devour the human scum!"

The neat lines and orderly formations below devolved into a melee as the soldiers and marching band surged upon the caged prisoners, tearing them to pieces and feasting on their blood.

Vondling turned to his circle of advisors.

"What are you waiting for, gentlemen? Everybody loves a buffet."

His cabal leapt from the balcony and flew to the cages below.

Vondling gripped the railing and smiled as he took in the carnage.

"Vonlandia? Really?" came a voice from behind him.

Vondling turned to confront the stranger—his smile fell flat as his eyeglasses reflected the darkened silhouettes of three familiar men.

"Oh, no . . . not you," said Vondling, shaking his head. "Not you . . ."

Vondling turned and tried to fly off into the night, but felt a sudden force render him immobile. The invisible field turned him back around to face the men.

"You're not going anywhere," said Olaf, extending a gnarled claw as his invisible field gripped Vondling tightly. "We have plans for you."

*

Olaf stood with his back to Vondling as he took in the high, coffered ceilings of the grand ballroom.

"Forgive me, Charles," he said. "You seem to be under the impression that this is a negotiation."

Olaf turned and forced his fists into the pearl inlays upon the long, lean alderwood table.

"These are direct orders," said Olaf. "Count yourself fortunate that Wilhelm is off the game board, but fall any further out of line, and it won't be German elite forces who hunt you down. It will be me . . . and you are no match for my power."

Vondling swallowed and looked to Dmitri, who was seated to his left.

"Like it or not," said Olaf, "I'm the only friend you have. I suggest you listen."

Vondling curled his left cheek and wobbled his head in a manner of adolescent mockery, then stared into Olaf's dark eyes.

"Fine," he said. "But Vonlandia stands."

Olaf pursed his lips and glanced to the room's entrance, where Kir stood at the threshold with a hogweed canister strapped to his back.

"We have no problem with Vonlandia," said Olaf, glaring at Vondling. "So long as you understand who you serve."

Vondling crossed his arms and huffed out a quick breath.

"I serve the Black Butcher. *Heil der Doppelgänger.*" Vondling shot a lazy, mocking salute into the air.

Olaf nodded. "Very well, Charles. I am happy to hear you say that. Now," he said, rubbing his hands together, "who'd like some tea?"

"Ick," said Vondling.

"I'll have some," said Dmitri.

Olaf reached to the center of the table and picked up a delicate crème-colored porcelain teapot adorned with whimsical paintings of red roses. He poured Dmitri a cup, then one for himself. Olaf walked across the massive expanse to a hearth with no fire, took a long, lingering sip, then placed his teacup upon the mantel.

"There's no point to your endeavor," said Vondling. "The blackwood forest at Loch Dracul was burned to the ground. By—"

"Yes, I know. Felix Yusupov and Denis Kozlov."

"What are we going to do?" interjected Dmitri. "The Holy Upir need the trees to spawn."

Olaf took another sip from his cup.

"Mm," he said, savoring the hearty liquid and smacking his lips. "Just a smidgen of rosewater. Simply delicious." Olaf turned his attention to Dmitri. "Do you truly believe for one moment that I didn't come prepared for such circumstances? I can regrow that forest in a matter of minutes."

"Fancy you," said Vondling, rolling his eyes.

"Watch your tone," said Dmitri. "When I emerge as the prime vampire, my power will vastly exceed yours."

Vondling stared at him with an obvious smirk. "And who's the woman? Certainly you can't complete this without a female prime?"

"That is not your business," said Dmitri, staring down Vondling.

Olaf walked to them once more, attempting to cool the situation.

"Frankly, Charles," said Olaf, "we don't care what you do with your little vampire army once we have completed our task. But you would be wise to support our actions. Aside from this being a direct order from a dark warlock far more powerful than me . . . envision for a moment what you will achieve once we respawn the Nosferatu. Everything south of Romania—pardon me, Vonlandia—will be yours for the taking. The Butcher has expressed his interest in using you to command everything south of the fourth-fourth parallel." Olaf spread his hands wide and stared up at the ceiling. "You think this is fit for a king? Imagine what you could do with Cairo. The pyramids?"

Vondling nodded and stuck out his lower lip. "I like that very much, actually."

"Good," said Olaf. "I'm glad you have come to your senses. So I have your word then? There will be no marching on Berlin?"

Vondling held his hand behind his back and crossed his fingers. "I promise."

"How would you even do that, logistically?" asked Dmitri. "You can't march vampires during the day. Where would you roost?"

"What's the matter, Dmitri?" asked Vondling. "Still pouting over missing your shot at immortality?"

"Not for long," said Dmitri with anger welling in his eyes.

"And you are clear on your orders surrounding Yusupov and Radu cel Frumos? I predict they will arrive back in Romania tomorrow," said Olaf. "If they make it to Poenari Castle—everything we are working on will be cast into jeopardy."

"How is that my problem, again? If they were so important, the Butcher should have built a better dungeon. Or, oh, I don't know . . . killed them himself?"

Olaf scowled at Vondling.

"Fine!" exclaimed Vondling, rising from his chair. "I'll ensure they are captured the moment they land."

"Yusupov is to be captured. Radu killed," said Olaf. "But no games. No Shakespeare. And no parades. You and your minions are to kill him on sight. Your vámpir should have no problem overwhelming a warlock of his age. Is that understood?"

Vondling stood for a moment, looking back and forth from Dmitri to Olaf.

"With great pleasure," he said, and made an exaggerated curtsy.

30

April 1, 1917, 2:37 p.m.

After circling the area over Denis's farm three times to ensure the Germans had gone and the compound was indeed abandoned, Radu gave Felix a thumbs-up, indicating it was safe to land.

Felix pulled his monoplane alongside Radu's as they approached the landing strip near the barn. A heavy growl came from Felix's plane as he slammed on his throttle and barrel-rolled over Radu before taking the lead and descending to the ground.

Both planes taxied down the grassy field and killed their engines.

Felix jumped from his plane and removed his goggles while jogging to Radu's craft.

"That is the most fun I think I've ever had. We make it out of this, and I'm buying a fleet of these things."

Radu climbed from his pilot seat and stood before Felix.

"Glad to see you found a moment of levity in these trying times," said Radu, patting him on the shoulder. "Come, you'd better rest up a bit. Our journey is about to become far more challenging."

"I feel like I'm ready for anything," said Felix.

"Excellent. You'll be tested in every feasible way—physically, mentally . . . even emotionally. The path of the warlock is not for the squeamish."

Felix took a moment to absorb their surroundings. "Deserted as can be," he said, eyeing the smattering of tent canvases and trash strewn about the landing area. "I wonder where they went off to."

"My best guess would be Bucharest. All that matters is that they are not here. Let's scrounge you up some food."

"What about you?"

Radu smiled. "Another skill you will learn to acquire. I technically do not need to eat at all. Now, that doesn't mean I can't enjoy a fine meal. But I pull my energy from the world around me. And soon you will too."

"I don't know about that. I'm starving."

"Your body is just beginning to awaken. In time, it will be no challenge at all . . . save a delicious steak before you. I've yet to meet a witch who can resist that."

Felix suddenly snapped his head toward the forest.

"I sense something."

"Tell me."

Felix closed his eyes and held out his hand to the darkened woods. "It's Nima!"

Felix dashed toward the forest.

As he neared the wood, both Nima and Drina came galloping from the forest. Felix stood and watched as Nima trotted forward, stopping a few meters before him while nodding her head and huffing.

Felix wrapped his hands around her neck and squeezed her tightly.

"Told you I'd be back," he said, stroking her mane. He looked to Drina just behind her.

"Nice to see you too, Drina."

"Very good," said Radu, standing near them. "But search your mind. I do not think it was these horses that caught your attention."

Felix stepped away from Nima and stared into the forest—the front of his ears still agitated. Something else was there, something wicked.

"You're right," said Felix. "It's . . ." He turned to Radu. "It's Hanne's horse. What should we do?"

Radu crossed his arms. "We? I think what happens now will be up to you. What are your instincts telling you?"

Felix held his hand to the forest.

"I sense it is angry . . . but also afraid. What is it? Some kind of evil entity?"

"A Hellhorse. An animal come back from the dead, generally used and abused at the whims of its master. Stuck in a perpetual state of madness and torture. Not dead. But not quite alive either."

"Are they dangerous?"

"Extremely."

"Can we just let it go? Let it roam the forest until—"

"Until what? It grows hungry? Desperate? They are carnivorous and can be quite aggressive—even ravenous. Perhaps it wanders to a small farm and feeds on an unsuspecting child? It's not a creature to be left unattended."

"Then, what?"

"It's up to you to decide," said Radu, vanishing into a thin black mist.

"Great," said Felix. "Thanks for the help."

Felix stood, looking into the forest with steady eyes.

He understood that Radu was giving him a test—a test for which he had no answers. Closing his eyes, Felix extended his arm and called out to the Hellhorse with his mind. The animal emerged from the branches with great force, galloping toward Felix at top speed.

Nima and Drina whinnied and scattered off toward the barn.

Felix stood his ground.

The beast charged Felix, its powerful strides giving every indication it intended to crush him under its body.

"Stop," said Felix quietly, extending his hand further.

The beast did not yield as a mere twenty meters remained between the two.

Felix forced both hands forward. "I said, 'Stop'!"

The gallops grew louder and the whinnies more harrowing as the Hellhorse picked up speed with only ten meters remaining.

A burning sensation kindled in Felix's gut as a cold shiver ricocheted through his mind.

"Yield now!" he yelled, opening his eyes and thrusting his hands outward.

Felix felt the life force of the earth and grass beneath him, the thundering energy of the Hellhorse's hooves striking the mud, and all at once—the forces absorbed into his essence.

With only a few meters remaining, the beast crashed into an invisible field as Felix raised his hands and levitated it in the air. Felix fell backward onto the ground—the Hellhorse with him.

The steed reared its head around and stood once more.

Felix rose to his feet and stared at the beast's glowing red eyes, which glared back at him. It huffed through its nostrils and began thrusting its right hoof into the ground, conveying its intent to charge.

Felix walked to the ghoulish horse, extending his arms, seeming to calm the wild animal. He placed his hand on the Hellhorse's snout and scanned its mind.

Anger. Abuse. Malice . . . perpetual madness.

The emotions ran through Felix and in that moment, he knew what he must do.

Felix stepped to the side of the Hellhorse, unsheathed his demon blade, and slashed downward in one forceful motion, beheading the beast and absorbing a large portion of its neck. The mare's body took a few lumbering steps and slumped to the ground. Felix sheathed his blade and looked down to its face—its rotten gray tongue hanging limply from its mouth as the red glow in its eyes faded to darkness.

A calmness embraced Felix deep within his marrow.

While taking a series of short breaths through his nose, he looked off toward the barn to see Nima and Drina standing safely.

"You chose mercy," came Radu's voice from behind him.

Felix turned to him. "I levitated it. I—"

"You see? These powers are innately inside you."

"But I don't know how I did it. How can I ever do it again?"

"This is the way of the warlock. Each skill you acquire is another part of your neural network that is learning and connecting. It may take you several more attempts to do it again. And likely only under duress. To do these feats on command will take time. But it's time you must take. Shortcuts are the way of the Void. And it is the Veil you must learn to harness."

Felix looked down to the Hellhorse's carcass.

"It was suffering, but I still don't feel good about this."

"There is always a tear in the fabric of the Ether anytime a life is taken—even if that life was technically dead. You are becoming more sensitive to that energy field, and what you're feeling is justified. You released this poor creature from its suffering. Your actions were strong and just. I am proud of you, Felix."

Radu placed his hand on Felix's shoulder.

"Let's just scrounge up some food," Felix said, jerking his shoulder away from Radu and walking off toward Denis's home.

*

"They must have left in a hurry," said Felix, looking over Denis's sitting room. "Seems everything is still here."

"Can't imagine blackwood furniture has much value or use on the battlefield."

"For our battles it does."

Radu smiled. "For certain."

Felix sat on the sofa and reached to the goat skull helmet sitting on the table. He ran his hands over the metallic black surface, hoping it would kindle a memory from his past life.

"Nothing," said Felix. "Can't you just teach me some psychometry, so I can touch it and remember my past skills?"

Radu sat in a blackwood chair.

"If only it were so easy. When I saw you lying on the ridge, I could not sense my brother in you at first. Even now, I can feel only a small fragment of his power in you."

Felix felt a chill, uncertain what Radu was driving at.

"I'm still awakening," said Felix. "But I just levitated a horse. Certainly, my powers are coming back."

Radu nodded. "Indeed, some are. But I believe it's more complex. As I stated, you were only able to perform that feat under duress. Here—" Radu rose from his chair. "Levitate it."

"Come on. I can't just do it on demand."

"Try."

Felix closed his eyes and held out his hand, recalling the lessons he'd learned and focusing his energies on the chair. Sweat beads gathered on his brow as he took in deep breaths. After a short moment, the chair rattled and tipped over. Breathless, Felix opened his eyes.

"You see. You're not ready." Radu corrected the chair and sat. "I fear there was a tear in the Veil when I beheaded my brother so very long ago. His essence was within the bottle, which is why you are able to perform some magick feats, but I am now convinced that the spirit of Vehuiah did not fully make the transfer. It may have been trapped inside Vlad's corpse, or perhaps it is stuck in limbo. The entity at Poenari Castle should provide us with answers. But at the risk of overwhelming you—there is also a terrible danger."

"I'm already overwhelmed. Just say it."

Radu appeared sullen.

"There is a grave darkness in you, Felix. You are a good man—brave, earnest. But within you is an anger—one my brother carried, and one that can be easily manipulated by our enemies as it was in the past. It is my assumption that the Veil is thrusting you to confront and contain this darkness before the spirit of Vehuiah will fully awaken and attach itself to you."

"So, I'm only a fragment of an archangel."

"That's likely the best way to think of it."

Overwhelmed and wanting to change the subject, Felix placed the goat skull on his head. "I don't know," he said. "You sure this is my style? Scary helmet, farmer's clothes? Not sure this is the most intimidating look."

Felix removed the skull.

"We'll obtain your proper garments when we arrive at Poenari."

"The Order of the Dragon all wore these?" asked Felix, inspecting the head harness inside the helmet.

"They did. Spoils of battle, so to speak."

"How's that?"

"Once they trapped their opposing demons' souls in the blades, they took their skulls as helmets, as a reminder to all of their battle prowess. Each of the demons had a cloven-hoofed animal as its familiar, and took the animal as its natural state when not pretending to be human. Deer, impalas, rams, goats. That was Bael's skull before you beheaded and imprisoned him."

Felix stared at the skull. He let out a distressed sigh.

"I'm worried about Mary. How am I supposed to save her? I can't battle a demon—"

"Yet. You cannot battle a demon yet."

Felix nodded. "Even so. How am I supposed to kill the Butcher or Bael for that matter? You said they were invincible, so the soul spiders were the only means to contain their spirits."

"It does present a problem. Best put it out of your mind for now. It is my hope that once you can commune with Vehuiah's spirit, you will devise a method to vanquish Bael once and for all."

Tall order, thought Felix. But what choice did he have? He was too far down this path to turn back now, and knew he must continue if he was to obtain the skills to save Mary.

"Guess I'm in this for the long haul," said Felix with a rueful grin. He reached up and scratched his newly forming beard. "Isn't there some kind of spell I can cast to stop this from growing?"

Radu laughed. "There is, actually. But all spells come with a price. A wise warlock by the name of Julius Robert Mayer once proposed the notion that energy could not be created or destroyed. For every spell created, something must be sacrificed—even if it's a small energy transfer. Although you as an archangel may call upon the Veil for such energies, you should be wise in how you use such a gift. It would be considered poor etiquette to engage in such frivolity. Look at me." Radu pointed to his bald head. "Think I want this? Oh, you should have seen my locks when I was young."

"How old are you?" Felix asked.

"Let's see," Radu said, stroking his beard. "Embarrassingly, I've lost track. It's all rather the same once you cross seven hundred years. After that, most witches begin to show signs of aging. Although I once knew a witch who was two thousand years old and never seemed daunted in the least. Mind you, she dropped dead on her two thousand and first birthday, so . . ."

Felix laughed. "No rest for the wicked, I suppose." He reached up and scratched a bald patch on his lip.

"I've been curious," said Radu. "Tell me about that scar."

"This thing?" asked Felix, rubbing the bald spot. "Funny you should ask. Probably one of those life events that shaped me more than I gave it credit for. Started me off on my path as a loner."

"What happened?"

"Sledding accident. Happened when I was three or four years old."

Radu raised his eyebrows, waiting for more.

"Sorry. I don't like to talk about it."

Radu leaned back and rest his hook in the palm of his remaining hand.

"Fine," said Felix, letting out a sigh. "A bunch of royals decided to gather at some duke's retreat for the winter, so the children came too. I was always alone as a kid, so I was very excited. One day, we all suit up to go sledding, and the older kids take about ten of us to a hill on the property. It was probably just a small slope, but in my memory, it's this giant, snowy hill. Eventually, it's my turn . . . I remember being terrified, but I thought if I refused, then a hellfire of snowballs would rain down upon me from the older boys, and it felt really good to finally belong."

Felix shook his head and ran his fingers through his hair.

"I'm staring at the drop, ready to go, and that's when two of the older boys moved my sled about two meters to the left. Having never done such a thing, I thought nothing of the fact that they aligned me directly with a fat oak tree. They pushed me down the slope, where I sped right into that tree face-first. Knocked me out cold."

Felix leaned forward, placed his elbows on his knees, and folded his hands together.

"Next thing I know, I'm strapped to a stretcher with a sheet covering my face, kicking and screaming as my mother's voice is telling me to be calm. I can still remember looking down past the sheet and seeing my little boots flailing about, and the bloodstains on the fabric. It was only four stitches, I think. I don't remember the rest.

"But I think, deep down, it changed a part of me. I became far more withdrawn afterwards. Had a real problem trusting other boys—specially older ones. As time went by, I came to understand that they purposely placed me to hit the tree as some sick joke."

Felix clenched his fists.

"Even talking about it now fills me with vengeance. To this day, I can't tell you what I'd do if I ever saw those kids again. Even as grown men, I swear I'd knock them out. So, now you know why I like to keep shaved. I don't like being reminded of it. I wish I could let these transgressions go, but they fester inside me."

Radu leaned forward. "I'm sorry that happened to you. You must be mindful of your attachments and learn to let them go. Otherwise, they will consume you and push you toward the Void."

Felix nodded, considering Radu's statement. "It was for the best, I suppose," he said. "After I was taken away, apparently some madman emerged from the woods and struck down one of the older kids with a strange axe—took his arm clean off his body."

"That's quite curious," said Radu. "Did they ever find this man?"

"From what I recall, no. The search party yielded nothing. He just ran back into the forest and was never seen again." Felix paused. "What can I say? Rural Russia.

"I suppose I just need to let it go," he said, shaking his head and stroking his stubble. "Speaking of which, time for one last shave."

Felix proceeded up the spiral stair and left the room.

Chapter 31

31

April 1, 1917, 11:58 a.m.

A warm oceanic front crept high into the atmosphere, blowing from the English Channel and blanketing the crisp spring air across northern France. A thick, ominous cloud cover sat above the trenches just north of the Somme River near Amiens and spilled its freezing guts in a heavy downpour upon the small force gathering on the Allied side of no-man's-land.

It had been five days since Elizabeth's thrall had been unleashed upon the soldiers in Arras, and bit by bit, the ravenous undead grew in numbers, pushing south toward Paris. Of the several hundred Allied soldiers surviving the initial attacks, only seventy-eight were eventually evacuated to the south side of the Somme at Amiens.

Flight Sublieutenant Brown watched Major General J. F. C. Fuller exit his tent, pull binoculars to his face, and inspect the line of twenty-seven tanks rolling across a bridge over the Somme. Fuller removed his cap, closed his eyes, and seemed to briefly revel in the cool raindrops splashing his bald head before replacing his cover.

"I'll see a court martial for this," he said, looking to Brown.

"I'll be right behind you. But Annie's right. The brass will never believe the truth. Nor would they have the wherewithal to stop it. We're the last line of defense. If those monsters cross the Somme, then nothing stands in the way of them reaching Paris. Especially if they breach the south tunnels."

"So, the evac tunnels—think we just blow them to be safe?"

"Honestly, sir, I don't know what's right any longer. I've seen things in the past five days that have changed my entire perception of reality. All I know is I've faced those things and will give my life to stop them." Brown cleared his nose and spit upon the mud.

Blowing the tunnels on the German side—for certain. That was essential. Brown had battled the berserkers and knew they seemed to dwell in the tunnels. The ones leading to Paris central command? He couldn't say. Brown was a pilot, not a tactician. Although, he had certainly received a quick lesson over the past day while collaborating with Fuller and Annie on their pending offensive. Blowing the Parisian tunnels would put a burden on supply and infantry if they could only move aboveground. Plus, Brown assumed there would be no more hiding their actions from top command if they took that step. He and Fuller would be thrown in prison before they figured out what they truly faced.

"Might just be best to leave them open," said Brown. "We'll need them to evacuate in case of . . . well, I don't even know what the win is here."

Fuller puffed on his pipe, coughing a bit as the smoke irritated his esophagus.

"Six hundred infantry," he said. "It's all I could muster. Well, that and the tanks. Six hundred living, breathing men against what? Thirty, forty thousand undead berserkers? I'm sending these men to their deaths . . . or worse."

"They were briefed. They volunteered."

"Volunteered to fight German 'death soldiers.' They don't know what they're—"

"No matter—they've heard the tales from the survivors. All we can do now is fight. Whatever they're amassing behind those trench lines must be stopped. I think blowing their exit tunnel will be key. The tanks should handle that easily."

"If they can break the lines."

"They will. I've seen those gunslingers in action. They're scarier than the zombies."

Fuller forced a half smile. "They sure are something, huh?"

"That's one way to put it. They are certainly fearless . . . seem to actually enjoy the carnage. With a little luck, maybe—"

"Luck isn't a strategy, son."

Fuller squinted into the brightness of the whirring clouds as a lone beam of sunlight cracked through the gray and illuminated a grassy portion of the muck in the distance. He pulled out his pocket watch, shielding it from the rain.

"Stand-to in twenty-five minutes. Annie needs you in the air in thirty." Fuller looked up at the clouds again, his weathered crow's feet tightening. "These conditions are awful. Your pilots ready for this?"

"You're goddamn right we're ready," said Brown.

Fuller patted him on the arm.

"I like you, Lieutenant. Wish I had more of your caliber," he said, before reentering his tent.

Brown stood for another moment, feeling the freezing droplets on his face before jogging off to the biplane staging grounds where a mere six other pilots awaited his orders.

*

"Well, shit!" yelled Jane, exiting a covered dugout and walking into the trenches. She blinked repeatedly as the freezing rain pelted her mask-covered face. "Some damn vacation this is turning out to be."

"Language, please!" barked Annie.

She marched along the corridor with Jane and Miss Fields just behind her as the wooden planks beneath their feet wobbled and sank into the softening mud.

"Tell you what," said Jane. "I'd like to snap the neck of the sap who thought these planks was a good idea. They're more slippery than . . ." Three large rats scurried past their boots over the planks. "Hell, seems all they're good for is keeping the rats dry. What the Brits and French couldn't learn from some good old-fashioned American craftsmanship."

"Truth be told," affirmed Miss Fields.

A chubby soldier rounded the corner before them, his plump face staring down at a map. He looked up to see Annie and appeared startled as he stood to attention and saluted her.

"Put your hand down, Lieutenant Potts," said Annie. "We have no ranking command here."

"We're just lendin' you boys a little feminine geniality," said Miss Fields, gripping the brim of her hat and nodding.

"Yes . . . ma'ams? Is it ma'ams? Should I call you ma'ams?"

Annie smiled. "Call us whatever your pretty heart desires."

"Just don't call us late to battle," said Jane, flipping open her navy trench coat and showing off the six-shooters hanging from her belt holster.

"I was coming to let you all know that we're ready."

"Have your men been briefed?" asked Annie.

"Yes. Well, sort of. It took some time to convince them to take orders from women."

"Did it now?" asked Annie, looking back to Jane. "Well, let's just go see if our ladylike persuasion can't convince them a bit further."

"There's more," said Potts. "It seems the Germans are back to using human soldiers. We spied a group of them lining up big drums of something about four trenches back—all wearing gas masks and protective suits. Our reconnaissance team counted another seven snipers positioned along their front trench."

"Sounds like they're gearing up for a gas attack," said Annie. "Your boys have masks?"

Potts looked to the mud. "Unfortunately, no."

"Well then," said Annie, placing her hands on her six-shooters. "We better knock 'em back real quick-like."

"Snipers, huh?" asked Miss Fields.

Jane and Annie smiled.

"Let's definitely go see what we can do about that," said Jane.

The group rounded a corner to the main staging trench that led to no-man's-land to see a long line of olive-green-clad, mud-drenched soldiers lining the back wall. Some stood confidently while others appeared worried, shivering from the early spring cold snap. All stared at the three masked gunslingers from the United States with an undisguised expression of wonder.

Annie, Miss Fields, and Jane scaled the sandbags leading to no-man's-land and stood at the top of the trench.

"Um, Miss Mosey?" called Potts, pointing behind her. "The snipers?"

"That'll do, Lieutenant Potts," she said, leaning down to him.

Annie stood upright and thrust her fists into her hips. "Now listen here, gentlemen. Although you have my respect for volunteering for what is essentially a suicide mission, there's some things—"

"Suicide mission? What are you saying?" asked a worried-looking private as he stepped forward and squinted up at Annie—the dirt running down his cheeks as the rain pelted his face.

Annie reached over her shoulder and pulled a deep gunmetal-blue rifle from her back holster, leaned forward, and slung the weapon across her knee. She stared down at the soldier.

"It's not polite to interrupt a lady, there, junior," she said in a low, calm voice. "Back in line."

The fresh-faced soldier looked at the bullets wrapped across Annie's chest and encircling her right thigh. He then briefly inspected Jane and Miss Fields, taking in their muddy trench coats and bullet-strapped bodies.

"Jane?" said Annie.

"We're serious, sonny boy," said Jane. "Best you stand down. Plenty of time to embarrass yourself in front of your brothers once those berserkers rear up. Less'n you want me and Miss Fields here to deliver you a fine-ass whoopin' right in front of your brethren. Otherwise, shut up and listen."

Miss Fields stood forward and glared at the soldier, tilting her head and flashing a mocking grin. He looked back to the line of his comrades, who avoided eye contact. Defeated, he turned back to Annie and stared at the ground.

"We're going to have to play on the same team for a spell. Is that understood?" asked Annie.

The young man nodded and fell back in line.

Potts stepped forward again. "Ma'am, I really must remind you about the active snipers. They will spot you where you're—"

"That's the plan there, dingleberry," said Jane, laughing. "No wonder you boys are always getting your heads blown clean off. You know how you kill a rattler, Pottsy? You gotta snuff him out of the bush." Jane looked to Miss Fields. "Miss Fields? You mind showing these English tarts how we deal with snipers?"

"With pleasure," said Miss Fields, pulling a long matte black rifle from her back holster.

Jane removed her rifle from her back as Miss Fields raised hers into the air and fired off three consecutive shots—the blasts sounding more like tank concussions than rifle fire and the projectiles glowing with a dull luminescence as they popped from the barrel. The soldiers closest to Miss Fields threw their hands over their ears and watched as the gun smoke cleared around her silhouette.

"Just another moment," said Annie, pretending to check a nonexistent wristwatch.

"Now?" asked Jane.

"Now," said Miss Fields.

Annie and Jane knelt quickly to the mud and swung around with their rifles pointed across no-man's-land as Miss Fields jumped away and held out her hand, freezing six bullets in midair that were aimed directly at Annie's head. Miss Fields clenched her fist and the bullets melded together in a molten lead blob that fell to the muck. She knelt alongside Annie and Jane as all three fired off two shots each in rapid succession.

The gunslingers stood, slung their rifles over their shoulders, and stared down at the soldiers.

"Any questions?" asked Annie.

Nothing but blank, stunned faces along the line.

"And, Lieutenant," added Annie. "Tell your recon men there were only six snipers. Each of whom just took a bullet through the center of his forehead and right down the barrel of his gun. Back home, we call that a 'gentlewoman's handshake.'"

A grumbling in the distance caught Annie's attention and she watched as the line of Fuller's tanks plodded over the trenches and approached their position. Annie looked again to her nonexistent watch.

"Right on time, boys!" she cheered, placing her arm across her knee and leaning over the trench. "Now listen up—here's how we survive."

*

Potts ducked low as the tanks crawled across the trench overhead, knocking down some of the sandbags and damaging a good majority of the upper wall's structure. He looked to Annie and her crew, who leaned against the sandbag incline at the front of the trench—all puffing on cigarillos and paying no mind as the tanks grumbled past.

Annie listened as the tank engines moved a bit farther away. She flicked her cigarillo into the mud. Miss Fields followed.

"Which one of you gentlemen blows the little whistle?" asked Annie.

Potts raised his hand.

Annie winked at him. "No time like the present, brown eyes."

Potts pulled his whistle to his lips and a shrill pierced through the trench.

Disarray swept the muddy corridor as the soldiers yelled their battle cries and charged up over the trench, disappearing into no-man's-land. Gunfire echoed from the field above, and Annie turned to Jane, who was still relaxing against the sandbags, puffing on her cigarillo.

"You gonna suck on that thing all day? Or can we go knock some 'zerks?"

"Fine," said Jane, flicking away the smoke. "Just hate wastin' is all." She leaned forward, pulled her six-shooters from her holsters, and spun them around her fingers several times. "Let's do this."

All three gunslingers jumped over the trench wall and rushed into no-man's-land with enchanted guns blazing.

*

"Something's not right!" Annie shouted to Jane as they led the charge of tanks across no-man's-land. Most of the soldiers ducked behind the tanks as they slow-crawled across the brown sludge.

Jane knelt and fired off seven shots in various directions as human German soldiers with gas masks tried scaling their trenches and greeting the assault head-on.

"Where's the 'zerks?" asked Miss Fields.

Annie squinted into the distance where the shadow of the large exit tunnel led into the web of corridors connecting the German trenches.

503

"Maybe they need a wake-up call," she said, holding out her hand to stop a volley of bullets headed directly for her. The bullets plopped into the muck as she holstered her six-shooters and pulled her rifle from her back. "*Blasimus-mal,*" she said. The barrel of her weapon grew wider in circumference. Annie then fired a blue shock-wave toward the opening of the exit tunnel, causing it to rattle and shake upon impact.

She watched as the tunnel caved in slightly, then looked to Jane.

"Maybe we don't need these tanks anyhow?"

Jane shook her head. "You keep firing off like that and you'll be tuckered out in no time. Best save your energy."

Jane reached to a tank next to her and banged on its metal siding.

"You boys awake in there? Blast that goddamn tunnel!"

A series of bullets struck the tank before her, and the vehicle shook as it veered off into the tank next to it.

"What on earth?" said Annie as her eyes darted to the sky. She knelt to the mud. "Girls, we have bad company."

Jane and Miss Fields stood next to Annie, watching the sky as the shadow of a red, triple-winged biplane emerged from the ashen clouds.

"Where the hell is that Brown fella?" asked Miss Fields.

All three knelt and aimed their guns upward as the Red Baron dove and unleashed a dense smattering of gunfire across the line of tanks, causing eight of them to either stop cold in their position or veer off course as their caterpillar tracks were blown clean from their wheels.

Miss Fields stood and fired a glowing purple shot at the Red Baron as he roared past, missing him entirely as the vampiric pilot sensed the blast and took evasive action.

"Looks like we got a ghoul sharpshooter in the air," said Miss Fields.

"Truth be told," replied Jane, turning her attention back to the gas-masked German soldiers pouring over the trench lines, downing a dozen of them with a series of perfectly placed rapid shots.

"You sissies gonna fight or hide?" yelled Jane, craning her neck and grabbing an incoming bullet with her bare fist as she glared at a group of soldiers taking cover behind a tank. She dropped the slug and blew the gun smoke from her hand before turning her fire back toward the trenches.

The men behind the tanks moved into the clear and fired their rifles at the charging Germans.

"That's more like it," said Annie, joining the fight.

Gunfire and chaos erupted as the opposing forces engaged one another—dozens of limp bodies fell to the ground on both sides as bullets ripped through their flesh. Several tanks took position and fired shots at the exit tunnel, their projectiles either missing or slamming into the sides of the embankment but landing no direct hit.

Miss Fields shook her head. "These Brits can't shoot for shit."

"Enough," said Annie, taking aim at the tunnel with her rifle-cannon.

Before she could fire, Flight Sublieutenant Brown and his squadron of six other planes shot past, firing into the German trenches and taking out hefty pockets of soldiers.

"Attaboy!" shouted Jane, thrusting her fist into the air.

Annie watched Brown's squadron pop into the clouds. Her eyes widened as a series of smoke plumes rose from the German trench lines, firing what appeared to be large barrels toward their position.

"Now, what in tarnation is this?" asked Annie, tracing their trajectory.

The barrels landed all around them, blasting open and gushing a bright yellow gas into the surrounding area as three more smoke plumes rose from the German side, sending another series of barrels raining down upon them. Annie and Jane fired away, destroying six of the incoming barrels, which blasted open in midair, spewing saffron plumes.

The thick yellow smoke engulfed everything around them, causing Miss Fields and Jane to cover their mouths with their forearms and cough.

"Hoo-wee, that stinks," said Jane.

"This can't be good for mortals," added Miss Fields.

Annie watched as a group of soldiers to her left fell into the muck, choking and gagging as they rolled on their backs and grabbed their throats. It was only a moment before the purpose of the gas became apparent as the soldiers' faces became sucked of their essence, their eyes glowing a piercing yellow and fangs growing from their mouths.

"Girls?" said Annie, backing into Jane. "We got big problems!"

More and more British soldiers fell victim to the Nosferatu gas as a perpetual bombardment of barrels crashed down on them from the German side.

Annie leapt into the air, flipping backward onto the top of a disabled tank.

"Jane! Miss Fields! Up here!"

Jane and Miss Fields sailed toward her.

The three stood back-to-back and pointed their six-shooters downward into the sea of onrushing English berserkers. Annie aimed her rifle at the larger exit tunnel, hoping to blow it shut once and for all, only to see a swarm of Elizabeth's thrall gush from below like some rancid geyser.

Her eyes shot to the sky—the sounds of gunfire and explosions rang out above as the Red Baron engaged Brown's airmen, shooting down five of them in one fell swoop.

"Well," said Jane, watching the planes fall to the ground in a ball of black smoke and fire.

"Well, what?" asked Annie as she fired rapidly into the charging undead.

"Looks like we got ourselves in a little bit of a pickle."

"Just a tiny wiggle in the plan is all," said Miss Fields, smiling grimly as she unleashed a rapid barrage of glowing bullets into the oncoming berserkers. The luminous projectiles blasted their heads clean off their bodies, then continued to zigzag through several rows of the undead before splitting into smaller fragments and shredding through dozens more.

The growing mass of newly converted berserkers surrounded the tank, clambering up on the caterpillar tracks toward Annie and her crew. Miss Fields and Jane mowed down the front line of zombies with a series of powerful, repetitive blasts.

Annie turned to the rush of Elizabeth's thrall and noticed the human German soldiers retreating back along the trench lines— the mass of thrall allowing them to pass.

"Cowards," she yelled, firing her rifle and downing over twenty berserkers with a bright red shock-blast.

The low groans and guttural cries of the thrall rose over the gunfire into a cacophony of terror as they poured over the trench and their mass became one with the newly converted Allied berserkers—some firing their rifles aimlessly while others sprinted toward the gunslingers with unabashed rage.

"Goddamn it!" yelled Annie, watching the situation quickly devolve into madness.

"Hey," yelled Jane, grinning. "Language!"

Annie shot her a wry glance. "Kaiser's a bit more clever than we thought." She turned her attention back to the immediate mob swarming their tank.

"All right, girls," she said, strapping her rifle to her back and grabbing her six-shooters. Annie flicked her wrists and both guns shimmered as they morphed into double-barreled hand cannons.

"Let's show these 'zerks how we do it in the Wild West."

*

Flight Sublieutenant Brown and his squadron roared into the air, doing their best to navigate in the low visibility and windy conditions. During their preflight briefing, Brown had been certain to command his men to keep below the cloud line the best they could and focus the majority of their firepower into the German trench lines as the British tanks pushed through to the exit tunnel.

The six silver-painted biplanes flew low over the Allied trenches, steadying themselves and tightening their formation as the German trench lines came into targeting distance. Brown looked left and then right to ensure his pilots were in position. He peered down to see Annie and several hundred British soldiers engaging the Germans pouring over the trenches as his wingmen awaited his signal. Placing his fingers to his goggles, Brown then pointed his fingers forward, and all six of his crew dove lower across no-man's-land and unleashed a heavy round of fire upon the German soldiers below.

As they soared over the enemy lines, Brown looked back to see the Germans launch several projectiles across the field toward Annie. He raised his hand and made a circular motion in the air.

The small fleet shot upward, disappearing briefly into the cloud cover as they prepared to circle back.

"Damn it!" yelled Brown as they emerged from the clouds and descended back toward no-man's-land—the entire field was covered in a thick yellow fog.

Brown wiped the precipitation from his goggles with his jacket sleeve. He could see Annie and her crew standing on top of a disabled tank, firing wildly into the yellow gas as shadows of soldiers appeared to rush them.

"It's a goddamn mutiny," he shouted, targeting the field and preparing to fire his machine gun to cover Annie.

A blast to his right caught Brown's attention, and he turned to see three of his airmen's planes erupt in black smoke and perilously shoot downward into no-man's-land, crashing hard, engine-first, into a mob of the British berserkers and bursting into flame.

"Bastard!" yelled Brown as the silhouette of a triple-winged plane popped from the cloud cover perpendicular to him.

"If it isn't the Butcher of the Blue," he grumbled, feeling alarmed and slightly excited.

Brown traced the Red Baron's flight pattern as white flashes burst from the front of the red airplane. He thrust his yoke downward and his immediate wingman to his right did the same. The Red Baron's barrage struck two of the other pilots flanking his right side directly in their engines. One of the planes exploded instantly while the other wobbled and shook before entering a steep nosedive and heading vertically toward the earth.

Not wanting to see the plane hit, Brown searched his right side for the Red Baron and watched the red plane bank upward and conceal itself in the cloud cover.

"No way am I missing this shot," said Brown, looking to his remaining wingman.

Brown caught Lieutenant Randall's attention. He pointed his index and middle fingers to his goggles, then shot both fingers toward the clouds above, made a circular motion with his arm, and completed the signal by flattening his hand.

Randall nodded, pulled back on his throttle, and aligned his plane directly behind Brown.

"What I wouldn't give for a rear gunner right about now."

Brown looked behind. Deciding he was satisfied with Randall's position, he slammed the throttle forward and pulled back on the yoke, ascending nearly vertically into the clouds with Randall following.

The visibility was abysmal. Brown imagined he was flying through a blazing campfire's thick, sooty smoke. He looked backward and could barely make out the darkened gray lump of Randall on his tail. The two pilots continued to circle back over German territory, Brown constantly wiping the rain from his goggles with his sleeve as the downpour nipped at his chin like tiny wind-whipped nails. He squinted, searching for any sign of the Red Baron's shadow.

Deciding they were far enough away to avoid any potential artillery fire from the trench line, Brown pressed forward on his yoke and descended below the cloud cover, trying to adjust his foot pedals against a fierce side wind that was blowing him off track. He wiped his goggles clean once more and his jaw fell open at the sight of it.

Brown emerged several hundred meters beyond the German trenches, and in the distance could see a large airfield with hundreds of matte black monoplanes stationed in squares of ten by ten along a wide runway. He counted five such squares before turning to check on Randall.

"Come on, come on," he said, scanning the clouds above.

At that moment, a fireball erupted through the gray as fragments of Randall's plane tumbled to the earth. The Red Baron shot from the clouds, buzzing just above Brown, who immediately upped his throttle and banked low, cutting hard left in an attempt to turn around.

Taking one last look behind him, Brown watched as a series of monoplanes taxied to the runway.

"Let's see if you bastards can play in the dark," he said as he pulled up and entered the cloud cover.

Brown kept an erratic flight pattern, mostly on purpose, but also because he was fighting the stormy side winds that seemed to be gathering in might and unpredictability. He tried centering his breath as he continued to look backward for any sign of the Red Baron. Becoming aware of an additional engine growl, Brown looked up to see the red plane directly above him, descending rapidly.

"Is this guy crazy?"

The Red Baron positioned his plane mere meters above him, attempting to thrust his landing wheels into Brown's wings.

Brown dipped, emerging below the cloud cover.

With the Red Baron still directly above him, Brown killed his throttle and banked quickly upward. His plane tilted vertically in a fast air-brake motion.

The Red Baron barreled past as Brown leveled his craft and slammed the throttle.

"Now I have you."

Brown targeted the three-winged menace, firing relentlessly, but the Red Baron seemed to have an almost intuitive skill of avoiding the gunfire.

"Stay still, you Fritzie!"

Brown pulled on his trigger once more and watched as the Red Baron banked upward and disappeared again into the clouds—his engine whining so loudly Brown could hear it over his own.

"Not falling for that again."

He kept low as he sailed over the German trenches and barreled toward no-man's-land—Annie and her crew were nowhere in sight. A mass of berserkers rushed toward Amiens' town center. Brown positioned his nose slightly downward, targeting the undead and obliterating as many as he could before blasting past the Somme and sailing back to his landing area.

There was no pain at first, and Brown was surprised to watch his instrument panel splatter with red liquid. When he attempted to raise his left hand to wipe the liquid from the panel, his arm stayed limp. Blood spurted from a large bullet wound just above his knee—the lower portion of his leg was barely attached by a sliver of cracked bone and torn tendons.

"Fuck!"

Brown's left arm was hanging from his shoulder, which was largely blown off at his rotator cuff. Blood poured from the limb as he coughed, sending dark red gore streaming down his chin. The engine sputtered as the Red Baron again found his mark. Acerbic black smoke poured into the cockpit. As his vision began to fade, Brown watched the Red Baron soar triumphantly over him and disappear into the clouds.

"Keep it together, keep it together," grunted Brown as his vision narrowed to a darkened tunnel.

He could see the landing area in the short distance and knew a crash landing was eminent. With his right hand, Brown pulled back on the throttle and gently pressed the yoke forward.

The cockpit erupted in flames from the destroyed engine, igniting Brown's wool uniform as he continued to focus on the landing strip before him—the plane wobbling like a drunken moth a mere ten meters above the earth.

Coughing and gagging as the flames chewed into his flesh, Brown killed the throttle, undid his restraint belt, and fell unconscious onto his yoke. The plane smashed into the earth with a violent impact, breaking to bits and expelling Brown's flaming body into the soupy mud below.

*

"Hold the line!" yelled Annie.

"We *are* the goddamn line," replied Miss Fields, firing across a bridge near Amiens' town center and felling a pack of onrushing berserkers.

"This ain't working!" said Jane as she holstered her six-shooters and pulled her rifle from her back. "Rifles up, ladies."

Annie and Miss Fields followed her order and snatched their rifles.

"On three! . . . Hell! Do it now—blow the bridge."

All three gunslingers fired their rifles at the wood and stone bridge. Three white shock-blasts discharged from their barrels, collapsing the bridge in a shower of splinters and rock.

"How you like that?" shouted Miss Fields as a wave of berserkers continued rushing the bridge and fell into the river.

Several of the undead knelt at the banks and fired their rifles, the recoils knocking some of them back into the mud.

Annie quickly blasted off another shot that morphed into a fluorescent pink, horizontally flattened wave that tore into the first several lines of berserkers, slicing them in half and sending their bodies sliding into the rushing waters.

"Get some, you pansies!" yelled Jane, laughing as she made eye contact with Annie. "You gotta teach me that one."

"That's a Bill Hickok special. He calls it 'American hospitality.'"

"I miss that crazy old wizard," sighed Jane.

"Come on," said Miss Fields. "We gotta get Fuller out of here. Next bridge is a half mile up. This'll put them off for a bit."

They fired a few more illuminated rounds across the river, then turned and dashed through town, making their way toward the Allied staging area and landing field.

*

The three gunslingers arrived at the staging area just as a silver bi-plane descended erratically, spewing black smoke as it wobbled toward the runway.

The gunslingers rushed toward Brown's plane as it crashed into the field, ejecting his charred body into the muck.

"Oh, no," said Jane.

They came upon Brown to find him facedown in the mud, his body still aflame.

Miss Fields held out her hands and telekinetically extinguished the fire.

"Flip him over," said Annie.

She and Jane pulled Brown onto his back.

"My, my, my," said Miss Fields, taking in his wounds. "He still alive?"

Annie placed her hand over Brown's heart. "He is. All right, ladies, let's do this. Quickly now—another minute and he'll be scarred for life."

They stood in a circle around Brown and held hands.

Annie started chanting, followed by Miss Fields and Jane as their eyes turned entirely white. They raised their hands high and in one sweeping motion, thrust their fists downward as a blue dust devil swarmed upon Brown. The tiny tornado whirred around him, lifting his charred body into the air and enveloping him.

Annie and her crew stood back and watched as Brown twisted and turned in the turbulent mist, which finally dissipated and dropped his healed body back into the mud. All three slowly crept toward him, inspecting his body.

"Think that did it?" asked Jane.

"His body looks all right," said Miss Fields, leaning over Brown and taking in the contrast of his charred clothing against his healed flesh.

Brown suddenly opened his eyes and sucked in a deep pocket of air, coughing and gagging as he took in his surroundings.

"The Red Baron!" he yelled, still in a state of shock. "The airfield . . . hundreds of planes!"

"Now, now," said Annie, reaching down to him. "You just stay calm. Quite a hit you took."

Brown accepted her hand, and she pulled him from the ground.

"Thank you," he said, running his hand over his healed shoulder in disbelief.

"That's just how we do," said Miss Fields.

Annie turned to the encampment of tents and watched Major General Fuller exit his tent and dash toward them.

"Better late than dead," said Annie, as Fuller buckled over and attempted to catch his breath. "Bad news, Major General. The whole plan went pop."

Fuller looked to her. "Now what?"

Annie turned back toward Amiens, scanning to see if any berserkers had broken through.

"Well there, Fuller," she said, pausing.

"We have no goddamn idea," said Jane. "Best hustle to that south tunnel. Blow it and head to Paris as quick as we can. This little secret operation of ours is about to go public in a real nasty way."

Fuller stood upright.

"So be it," he said, his brown eyes becoming focused and stern. "In Paris, there are more . . . like me. We've been preparing for such an event for some time. Quickly. To the tunnel."

The group ran to an armored vehicle next to Fuller's tent and its engine roared to life. Moments later, they were speeding toward the Amiens tunnel that led all the way to Paris.

*

The berserkers overwhelmed Amiens in less than an hour.

The city was largely evacuated, but the monsters feasted upon those who remained, leaving no survivors. They marched across the Somme and amassed in the once-Allied encampment. The gas-masked human soldiers walked among the undead. They separated Elizabeth's thrall from the hybrid Nosferatu converted by gas and ordered them into divisions in preparation for their final march toward Paris.

A loud buzzing caught the attention of one gas-masked soldier, who lifted his goggled face to the sky and grinned devilishly beneath his veil.

The Red Baron emerged from the clouds and zipped overhead, followed by a hornet's nest of matte-black monoplanes, six hundred in total. The vampiric pilots flew the dark craft in perfect formation over the berserker encampment—the intrepid mass blocking out the very sky above.

*

From his triple-winged plane, Manfred sensed the divisions below and felt a surge of excitement at the never-ending wave of aircraft following him. He slammed this throttle forward and roared through the wispy rain clouds—for a mere one-hundred and thirty kilometers south, Paris awaited his wrath.

Nothing could stop him now.

For the Kaiser. For the empire. I am the omen of death.

32

April 2, 1917, dusk

Felix and Radu arrived at the foot of Poenari Castle deep within the Carpathian Mountains after pressing their horses hard for the past twelve hours.

Felix dismounted and stood on the rocky terrain, taking in the behemoth castle that appeared to jut from the rock itself.

"Incredible," he said, breathing deeply through his nose and looking to the dense surrounding forest and the deep valley below.

Radu positioned Drina next to Felix.

"You can see it?"

"Huh?" questioned Felix. "Oh . . . I meant the mountain air. But, yes. Of course I can see it."

Radu nodded and smiled. "Excellent. You're awakening by the moment. It's invisible to mortals."

Felix continued to study the stone fortress with rust-colored spires that rose proudly from several pinnacles at the top. He was hoping the structure might awaken some memory within him—alas, he felt nothing.

"Why did I leave this for the citadel at the loch? It seems heavily fortified and impeccably maintained."

"This castle is a source of light. A beacon of the Veil and to all those who speak to it. When you fell to black and discovered Loch Dracul, I can only assume you went there to commune with darkness and the Void. We, um . . . weren't on the best of terms during that time."

"So, before you beheaded me," said Felix, intending his words as a moment of levity.

Radu's lips tightened. "Let's change the subject, shall we?"

Radu nudged Drina, and she began a slow trot up the steep climb.

Probably shouldn't have said that, thought Felix.

A strange sensation crept up at the front of his ears, and he inspected the dense wilderness around him—his eyes scanning the evening's oncoming shadows.

Somebody's watching us.

"Young Master Felix!" came Radu's voice. "Come. Time is of the essence."

Felix inspected the surrounding foliage once more, then mounted Nima and followed Radu toward the castle's entrance.

*

Felix and Radu tied their steeds to two posts that stood before a stone stairway leading to an arched wooden door.

"Stay here, girl," said Felix, patting Nima's mane. He looked to Radu. "Will I need this?" he asked, placing his hand upon his goat skull helmet fastened to a strap on Nima's side.

"It is your helmet. Do with it what you will."

Felix looked over the helmet and imagined he'd look silly wearing it.

Maybe when I'm trained.

Felix decided to leave it behind. "What about the horses?"

"Ah, yes. Best to be safe."

Radu waved his hand and the horses disappeared.

"When can I learn that?"

"Actually, cloaking spells are quite basic. I wasn't thinking. We should have had you practice. Next time. Quickly, follow."

The pair walked up the stairs and stood before a heavy oak door adorned with a series of reinforced iron rivets. Felix turned and took in the sweeping countryside below just as the last remaining light sank below the mountainous tree line.

"What a view," he said.

"Since this castle is technically yours, you can enjoy it as much as you like."

"If we survive all this."

Radu nodded. "When we survive all this."

Felix studied the door, looking for a lever to open it.

"Is there a key or something?"

"Indeed there is, Master Felix."

Felix looked to him. "Where is it?"

"I'm staring at it . . . you're the key. Place your hand to the door."

Felix shrugged and reached his hand to the wood, placing it firmly against the polished surface. A click resonated from the other side and the door crept open to a darkened room.

"A bit dark in there. Can you do an illumination spell or something?"

"Again. I am looking at the illumination spell. Cross the threshold and see."

Felix extended his foot and placed it gingerly across the threshold. The immediate foyer lit up before him as the torches lining the walls erupted in flame. The castle seemed to come alive as he entered, flame beacons igniting throughout the rooms.

"Welcome home, Felix."

They were standing in a modest entrance with two stairways lining the walls that lead to a central walkway.

"It's rather quaint," said Felix.

Radu looked to the high ceiling supported by wooden beams and then to the stone floors. "Hmm. I suppose it is in comparison to the Russian palaces I've seen. Lots of space, though. Thousands of rooms. Mazes, puzzles."

"Puzzles?"

"This was your fortress for centuries, and you were a master of optical illusion. Quite an artist in many ways. Twists and turns abound to be discovered."

Felix walked a few steps forward and peered to the top of the walkway, noticing a series of seventy-two paintings that hung upon the wall. He began up the stair on the right as the front door swung shut and locked with a loud clang. Felix paid it no mind as he ascended the steps.

"Is this—"

"Yes. The Order of the Dragon."

"Wow," said Felix, studying the various portraits of shield and sword wielding knights that seemed to rise infinitely upward along the wall. "I recognize them."

"As well you should."

Felix's eyes bobbed back and forth as he took in the paintings. A sensation of longing mixed with sadness welled within him.

"Was this one was me?" he asked as his eyes settled on a painting of a long-haired warrior in pure white with a red dragon emblem emblazoned upon his chest. Felix stepped forward and stared at the image of his previous incarnation. The hair on his forearms stood rigid as if caught in some static field. Felix ran his hands across his arms as the chill subsided.

"That's some mustache," he said, stroking the stubble forming on his lip.

Radu let out an unexpected laugh.

Felix turned to him. "What?"

"Nothing. It's just comical that a mustache would catch your attention."

Felix shrugged. "I mean . . . it is quite a mustache."

"Indeed. And you were quite the warrior."

Felix shook his head. "I . . . I still have a hard time accepting any of this. I feel like I'm just going to wake any moment back in my palace bed."

"And I'm sensing you would much prefer that to your current predicament?"

Felix's eyes betrayed a sense of shame. "Yes, if I'm being honest. I really hope I'm up to this."

Radu smiled. "Come. I have something for you."

*

Felix whirled around in wonder as Radu led him through the various chambers of the castle. Enchantments abounded as they moved from room to room: stairs that bent and twisted in all directions, turning upside down and right side up, some appearing to lead nowhere; furniture that came alive and scurried away as they sauntered past; mirrors that reflected interiors other than the rooms they were in; candelabras floating through the air to light their way; and even the faint sounds of a pipe organ playing somewhere deep within the castle walls.

"This is more creepy than enchanted," said Felix, watching as a small hassock crawled alongside them, ducking and hiding behind various other furniture as it seemed to inspect Felix and Radu. "Hey there, little fella," he said, crouching down to the hassock.

The plush pillowed nymph jumped briefly into the air and scurried away into the shadows.

"Give it time," said Radu. "You will become accustomed to it . . . now!" He pushed open a double wooden door. "Your quarters."

Felix walked into the wide, round room with wooden beams supporting the domed ceiling. A warm fire burned in a hearth to his right, next to a glass door leading to a balcony.

"Nice digs," said Felix. "Cozy."

"You had a penchant for comfort in your previous iteration. That said, once your powers are unlocked, you could feasibly redo the entire interior to fit your tastes."

Felix placed his hands upon his hips and bobbed his head back and forth. "I quite like it, actually."

"Now then," said Radu, standing before a black monolith of a wardrobe. "Let's do something about those clothes."

"Oh!" said Felix, rubbing his hands together. "I thought this day would never come. What do you have for me?"

Radu opened the wardrobe, and Felix found himself staring into a deep blackness that appeared never-ending.

"It's empty," he said.

"Just wait," said Radu. "And you might want to remove your clothing."

"You mind?" asked Felix, spinning his index finger in the air.

Radu rolled his eyes and turned his back. "Boots too."

Felix removed his clothing and boots, wincing at his body odor. "I think maybe I should shower first."

A white sliver emerged from the black, slithering toward Felix with the air of a weightless serpent. He held out his arms as the wispy material crawled along his hand and expanded up toward his shoulder. Felix watched in amazement as the celestial filament solidified into fabric across his chest, then materialized into sterling chain mail over his shoulders, arms, and legs—covering him head to toe in the garments of a medieval knight.

"I'm not so sure about this," said Felix, turning to Radu.

Radu smiled at the sight of him. "You look incredible. A white knight of the highest order."

Felix looked down as bold red threading began stitching itself across his chest, finally displaying the emblem of a dragon.

Radu knelt before him. "As I served you in the past, it is my honor to serve you once more."

Felix blushed. "I'd prefer it if you stood."

Radu rose before him, appearing overjoyed at the sight of Felix.

"What? You look fantastic. See for yourself. Here, strap on your sword."

Felix strapped his demon blade around his waist and walked to a mirror.

"All right," he said, nodding and watching as his reflection in the mirror moved about on its own, showing off his new uniform. "I can approve of this. Rather wish it was black, though."

"You may change its color anytime you please. Well, once you acquire the skill. You can even morph it back to your farmer's clothing, if you desire."

"I think we'll leave those where they lie." Felix raised his arm and sniffed his new garments. "They even smell good."

"Ethereal garments are a powerful tool in a warlock's arsenal. They are symbiotes. Ones you must learn to commune with. The more you bond with your symbiote, and the more creative you become, the more your new suit will serve you. Endless possibilities, in fact."

Felix ran his hands over the red dragon emblem. "It feels warm."

"That, my young friend, is a lesson unto itself. A great power lies within that emblem."

"Show me."

Radu placed his hand upon Felix's shoulder. "Not tonight. Besides"—he looked to the ceiling—"hardly enough room in here for that spell. More of an open-expanse affair. Tonight we rest. Tomorrow, I shall introduce you to Mītaṭrūsh."

"Mit-a-what?"

Radu laughed. "Oh, yes, of course. The power I spoke of, deep within the heart of this castle. The ruling entity of Vehuiah—your gateway to the Veil."

Felix let out a sigh. "This is intense."

"Oh, Prince Felix!" came a voice echoing from beyond the castle walls.

Felix's ears perked up.

"Come out, come out—wherever you are!"

"This can't be good," said Felix.

He and Radu walked to the glass doors and emerged onto the wide balcony, their bodies illuminated by the nearly full moon.

"Oh, no," said Felix, looking down to the valley and taking in the massive conglomeration of shadows that lined the gorge below.

"Well, hello up there! So very nice to see you again," shouted Charles Vondling, holding a speaking trumpet to his mouth and standing atop a tank before a never-ending body of vampiric soldiers.

Several other tanks rolled into position next to him and aimed their cannons upward.

"We sent a welcoming party to meet you before you entered the mountains, but it seems you evaded our scouts. In any case, welcome back to Romania! Or as it stands—Vonlandia. I will be your tour guide this evening."

Vondling bowed to a series of cheers from his vampire soldiers.

"To your right, you will see the Wallachia border and its stunning array of deciduous trees," continued Vondling. "And over here on the Transylvania side, you will notice my illustrious army of vampires surrounding this fortress on all sides, who have come to eat your guts! Thank you very much for coming, and don't forget to exit through the gift shop!"

Vondling tossed his megaphone on the ground and leapt from the tank, landing at its side. "Blast them," he said, pounding the side of the tank.

"What do we do?" asked Felix.

Radu stared down into the shadows, taking in their predicament. "There's thousands of them."

Both men watched as the five tanks reared their cannons upward.

"Let's go!" shouted Felix, grabbing Radu's arm.

Radu stood still and pulled Felix back. "Stand your ground."

"Are you crazy?"

Blasts erupted from the tanks, filling the quiet mountain air with a thunderous roar.

Felix traced the projectiles heading directly for them. The artillery shells exploded at once upon hitting an invisible field just before the castle walls, causing Felix to duck as white shockwaves illuminated the dark.

Radu stepped forward and placed his hand on the stone railing.

"You're going to have to do better than that, Mr. Vondling. If you want a fight, then I'm afraid you'll have to come and find one!"

Felix stood next to Radu and traced Vondling's shadowed body as he reached to the ground and picked up his speaking trumpet.

"It's actually Emperor Vondling, thank you very much." Vondling flared his nostrils, appearing frustrated. "You know something, Felix? You have been nothing but one giant pain in my backside ever since we met! Do you have any idea the trouble you have caused me?"

Anger welled in Felix's stomach as he thought back to his initial encounter with Vondling on the train.

"You heard him!" yelled Felix, his voice echoing through the valley. "You want a fight? Then come and get it."

Felix looked to Radu and nodded.

"As you have just witnessed," shouted Radu, "this castle is impregnable. Nothing can breach these walls!"

Vondling pulled his megaphone to his mouth once more. "We'll have to see about that." He turned to his mass of undead. "You heard the prince," he bellowed. "Go get him!"

A great wail rose from below, and Felix watched a wave of vampiric shadows shoot into the air, eclipsing the moon and flying directly toward them.

"Oh, dear," said Radu.

"What? Won't the field hold?"

"There is no field," said Radu. "It was merely a quick protection spell, and I believe they've called my bluff."

Felix looked on in mute horror.

"Run!" yelled Radu, grabbing Felix's arm and casting a white flash to mask their escape.

They dashed into Felix's sleeping quarters and exited back into the castle's halls as the sounds of breaking glass and chaos followed.

*

"This way," said Radu, running down a long corridor that seemed to expand as he and Felix sprinted toward the end.

Upon reaching an ornate black wooden door, Radu looked behind them to see the corridor fill with vámpir rushing toward them—flying through the air and crawling along all sides of the hallway.

"I need you to focus," said Radu.

"On what?"

"Here," said Radu, pressing upon Felix's gut. "Quickly. Conjure the emotion."

Felix gritted his teeth and concentrated on his appendix. A burning sensation filled his abdomen as he watched the vampires close in.

"I have it," said Felix.

"Expand the hall."

"How?"

"Will it."

"Don't I need to say something?"

"We'll worry about invocations later. Take that energy in your gut and envision the hall growing longer, onward to infinity. Do it now!"

Felix stepped before Radu and pushed his hands outward.

The closest vampires were now a mere fifteen meters away and closing in fast.

Felix felt his heart pick up an irregular beat as the heat in his abdomen grew white-hot. He watched as the walls and flooring began to grow away from him, expanding the hallway and pushing the vampires farther away.

"Keep at it! As far as you can."

Closing his eyes, Felix thrust his palms out farther and more forcefully, concentrating on the warmth inside him and envisioning a train tunnel with a light far away in the distance. His mind kept pushing the light farther and farther away. The heat inside him dissipated. Felix opened his eyes to see the pursuing vampires slide away as the hallway continued to stretch far in the distance, sending their pursuers a good fifty meters away.

Radu gripped Felix on the shoulder.

"That, my young friend, was impressive."

Felix looked down to his hands. "It worked!"

"Quickly, this way."

Felix and Radu opened the door behind them and dashed down an iron stairwell that led to a large ballroom with a tall and wide mirror on the opposite side of the hall. The windows on both sides of the room imploded in a shower of glass as more vampires barged into the room. Felix unsheathed his blade and continued after Radu as he ran toward the giant mirror.

Radu was broadsided by three vampires who tackled him and forced him to the ground, gnashing their mighty teeth as they prepared to strike him. Felix jumped into the fray and beheaded all three with one swipe of his scimitar, sending their lifeless bodies slumping to the marble floor as his blade absorbed their heads. Radu stood, unsheathed his blade, and stood back-to-back with Felix. They continued to the mirror, facing down the mob of vampires that now surrounded them, backing them into the reflective glass.

Rabid, fanged faces glared at them as Felix and Radu placed their backs to the mirror.

"I thought these things were afraid of their own reflection," said Felix.

"I believe that's more of a deterrent than anything."

More vampires emerged from the stairs and crawled toward them along the ceiling.

"Sheathe your blade," said Radu.

"What?"

"Do it. Now. And grab the frame—tightly!"

Felix sheathed his scimitar and edged along the mirror, gripping the side of its ornate frame.

"*Sir'tolsur!*" shouted Radu as he spun around and smashed his sword into the mirror, shattering the glass entirely in a shower of reflective shards and revealing a massive black hole spinning within the frame. Radu sheathed his blade as the force pulled him toward the vacuum. He knelt to the floor, still sliding toward the black hole. Just as he reached the mirror's threshold, Radu stuck his grapnel into the bottom of the mirror's frame and grabbed on tightly with his hand. The force flipped him over and pulled his body into the blackness.

Everything within the ballroom suddenly plunged toward them, as if the room had been tipped on its side and its center of gravity was now the mirror's vortex.

"Hold tight!" yelled Radu as a fierce wind whipped through the expanse, pulling everything in sight toward the void within the mirror.

A wooden chair sailed toward Felix, who rolled closer to the hole to avoid being struck. The splinters flew into his face as it smashed against the wall and disappeared into the vortex bit by bit. Felix lost his hold, yet managed to regain his grip with both hands as his body hung into the vacuum. The sleeves on his ethereal garment enveloped his hands and grew outward over the frame, further cementing his grip. Felix peered over to see Radu clinging to the bottom of the frame as he too dangled into the blackness.

"I'm not sure this was the best idea!" shouted Felix as body after body of vampiric soldier shot past him—the black vortex absorbing everything into its nihility.

Radu pulled himself out of the frame and rolled low against the floor. Glass shards, hunks of marble flooring, and wooden planks whirred past as the turbulence devoured the contents of the room. He placed his back upon the floor under the frame and used his leg to shimmy toward Felix. Once he had reached Felix's side, Radu leaned face-first into the wall, crawled upward, and gripped Felix's forearm.

"Pull!" shouted Radu.

A portion of Felix's symbiote slithered up Radu's arm and wrapped itself around it snugly.

The two men grunted as Radu lifted Felix from the turbulent suction.

The giant crystal chandelier crowning the room tore from its base and flew toward them, followed by iron planks of the stairs that ripped from their screw settings. Radu wailed and used every bit of strength left in him to pull Felix from the void. They rolled out of the way and lay against the wall just as the crystal chandelier smashed into the sides of the frame—too fat to fit through the opening.

"*Reditus-tú!*" shouted Radu.

The whipping winds and chaos ceased.

Felix and Radu slid down the wall and crashed to the floor, followed by half the chandelier hanging out of the sealed mirror.

Felix stood and brushed himself off. "Holy smokes!"

Radu picked himself up and stood next to Felix as they stared into the mirror—slight imprints of clawed hands and fanged faces danced about its surface from the vampires now trapped within.

"Where'd you come up with that?"

"Old trick. Used it on our friend the Butcher once. Different mirror. Different time. Essentially the same technique."

"Too bad it didn't stick. Will this?"

More faint silhouettes of the vámpir appeared across the silvery surface as they attempted to claw their way from their reflective prison.

"Against vampires? Indefinitely."

Radu's eyes shot to the stair exit and then to the broken windows along the hall.

"More are coming," said Felix, peering out the windows.

Rumbling and gurgling grew in volume as more vampires scaled the castle walls and emerged from the stair exit.

"Time to meet Mītaṭrūsh," said Radu.

He thrust his fist into the marble floor and the tiles beneath them slid away, sending them falling into a dark tunnel. As if they were on some hinged device, the tiles re-formed upon the floor just as another wave of vampires swarmed into the empty ballroom.

*

Felix landed hard on a stone floor and groaned as Radu came down on top of him.

"Sorry," said Radu, pulling himself up.

"That hurt," said Felix, rolling over and taking in their sur-roundings.

They were in a large, circular room with a heavy iron door as its only exit.

Felix's heart sunk when he spotted a massive glowing jewel hovering near the ceiling that pulsed and shone red. A series of black and golden rings of various sizes surrounded its body and flipped around the jewel in a random and haphazard fashion.

"Is that—?"

"Yes," said Radu.

Felix became entranced by the jewel. He slid past Radu and stood directly under the florid entity.

"How do you say it, again?"

"Mīṭaṭrūsh, or Metatron in rabbinic texts. This is your gateway to the Veil."

Felix looked at him. "I'm not ready."

"Ready or not, it is the only way to discover why Vehuiah is not resonating from within you."

Felix was sweating. "Is it God?"

"There is no singular God. There is only the Ether split between the Veil and the Void. Nine such ruling energies exist to . . ."

Radu's words fell to a muted blur as Felix's pulse pounded his eardrums. Terror, excitement, and wonder surged through him all at once. Looking up to this strange energy force, Felix could sense its majesty—he felt as if he were staring into an eye that radiated pure wisdom. And then quietly, as if out of the Veil itself, Felix heard a voice. It had no speech but resonated with a near symphonic sound—low and rhythmic, communicating with Felix's mind. The message was clear. It was time. Time to calm his mind, time to trust in himself. He was to leave the doubtful, angry prince behind and face his fears to become his true self.

"I understand," said Felix, looking to Radu. "I know what I must do."

From the other side of the iron door came gunfire and the sounds of bullets striking the metal.

"They've found us," said Radu.

Felix stared up at Mīṭaṭrūsh.

"You're coming with me," he said to Radu.

"Sadly, I cannot follow," said Radu, watching the door.

The sounds of vampire grunts and banging rattled the iron door until it shook on its fat metal hinges. Felix considered their predicament and stood directly under Mītatrūsh as it pulsed a low sound wave through the circular room.

"They'll tear you to shreds," said Felix. "You must come with me."

"Only you can pass through Mītatrūsh."

"I'm standing with you. We leave together, or we don't go at all." Felix gripped his blade's hilt.

Radu backed away from Felix, continuing to face him. "This has been a long time coming, my brother. It's you who must live on if this evil is ever to be vanquished. My journey ends here and now."

The door began to pop off its hinges and the sounds of vampire howls ricocheted from the other side.

"Can they follow me?"

"Under no circumstances. Go, Felix. Seize your destiny. It was my honor to know you once more." Radu bowed his head.

Felix rushed to Radu and embraced him.

"Thank you, Radu . . . for everything. From my past life to this and on to the next—you will always be my brother."

Radu broke the embrace and placed his hands upon Felix's shoulders.

"It is I who should be thanking you. I know now that it was you who gave me a second life long ago. And for that, I am eternally grateful. Soon you will understand."

Felix wanted to ask Radu for an explanation, but the thought was broken as the door detached from its hinges.

"We'll see each other again," said Felix. "I can sense it." He backed away and stood underneath Mītatrūsh.

"Then I'd like to congratulate you once again on sensing something I cannot. Go. Call out to the Veil. Save yourself, save the world."

Radu unsheathed his blade. He turned and took a defensive stance as the vampires ripped the iron door off its hinges and rushed toward him.

Felix raised his hands to Mītaṭrūsh and quietly called out to the Veil.

The black and golden rings surrounding the jewel lowered to Felix, encircling him and raising him up into the glowing body. His last vision was of Radu standing firmly against the mass of on-rushing vampires with his blade raised high above his head. He slashed the blade downward with a vigorous strike as the monsters crashed into him and quickly overwhelmed the mighty warlock.

Felix's vision was flooded with red light.

Chapter 33

33

December 28, 1476, midnight

Felix looked down to his hands as the glowing red faded to darkness.

He stood in a grassy field. In the moonlight, Felix could see a drop-off in the short distance. He walked to the cliff's edge and watched as the moon's reflection rippled across the loch's surface.

"Not again," said Felix, turning around to see the massive black citadel rising high into the night sky, the shadowed blackwood forest of Loch Dracul extending behind it. Skeletal silhouettes of decayed and charred bodies hung impaled on a series of rusty poles that surrounded the citadel.

Felix recalled his vision of confronting Rasputin at the loch and wondered if this was another fever dream. But this was real—he could feel it deep within his soul and in the fetid air that blew across the smug-grass as a fierce wind picked up. From the peak of the black-stoned citadel, a solitary window flickered with torchlight. Felix could sense someone or something moving about at the top of the citadel.

He unsheathed his demon blade and marched toward the citadel.

*

Round and round, Felix climbed the thin stone stairwell that encircled the wall of the citadel, doing his best never to look down at the sheer drop to darkness below. Upon reaching the top, he saw an open door glowing with torchlight. He froze in his tracks as a low, guttural laugh emanated from the room—its echo seeming to absorb directly into Felix's flesh, chilling him.

"At last . . . at last, he's come," came a gruff male voice in Russian from the room.

Felix swallowed and wrapped his hand tightly around his blade's hilt, then crept up the remaining stairs that led into the room. The low cracking and humming of his scimitar gave him a modicum of comfort as he crossed the threshold.

The walls were adorned with torches, various ornate tapestries, and a long metal shield displaying the same red dragon emblem stitched on Felix's chest. Along the perimeter of the room sat corks and various bottles holding candles—all of which had a wax dragon emblazoned on their glass hulls. At its center knelt a long-haired man with his back to Felix.

"Who are you?" asked Felix, extending his blade.

The stranger knelt before a small altar that held a wide wooden bowl filled with water. He shook his head at Felix's question.

"Who am I, he asks," said the stranger as he cupped his hands into the bowl and brought the water to his face, gently splashing it across his forehead and cheeks. "Terror. Madness . . . oblivion," he whispered. "For these are who I have become."

Felix crept closer and inspected the stranger's long black hair, which flowed down his back over a dark leather cloak that covered his body.

"Face me," said Felix, pointing his blade toward the stranger's head.

The man appeared to float from the floor as he stood, keeping his back to Felix. He reached down and flipped open his cloak, revealing a demon blade hanging from his waist. The black-clad stranger turned around slowly and smoothly, as if gravity itself had acquiesced to his movements.

Felix gasped, standing back and taking in the one true image of darkness.

Facing him was none other than Vlad Drăculea. The tips of his fangs poked from his mouth, and Felix's reflection wriggled within his pure black eyes that contrasted against his strikingly pale skin.

"Hello, Felix," said Vlad, his voice low and calm. He unsheathed his blade containing Bael and pointed it toward Felix. "Shall we begin?"

Begin what? thought Felix, trying to understand why he stood before this dark power.

Sensing that Vlad might cast him down the citadel's shaft, Felix gripped his scimitar's hilt and positioned himself away from the chamber's opening.

The tips of their blades nearly touched and cast white static between the two weapons.

"Is this real?" asked Felix.

Vlad grinned and thrust a quick jab at Felix, who deflected the strike.

"Seems real," taunted Vlad.

Felix kept his back to the brick wall and crept closer to the sole arched window, calculating whether a leap from the tower would be his best escape. *Grass beats stone,* he thought, looking again at the shaft. He wished he knew of a spell to blunt his landing, briefly thinking back to his successes in levitating the Hellhorse and expanding the hallway at Poenari Castle.

It was too risky.

"Why am I here?" he asked Vlad. "How do you know me?"

"Oh, Felix—do you truly not remember?" Vlad appeared to smile in the shadows. "This is but a little dance that you and I must do every once in a millennium. The fate of which determines the world."

Vlad stepped forward, holding his scimitar across Felix's path to the chamber's opening—the tip of the demon blade absorbing parts of the wall as the bricks cracked and crumbled.

"We are one," said Vlad. "I have always known you, and deep within you is a darkness that has always been me. We are a dyad— in time and space . . . beyond."

Vlad pulled the blade from the wall and stood away from Felix, still pointing the weapon toward him.

"You're here for one very simple reason: I hold a power that you must reclaim. But Vehuiah is trapped within the darkest dungeon of my soul. It will never escape. And now you will join the mighty Seraph so that I may become whole . . . invincible. I was once master of the Veil, betrayed and left for dead. But I rose up against those who had forsaken me and spawned the Nosferatu. I now rule this time, and once I consume you—my lighter half—I will become the one black ruler of all the ages."

Vlad thrust his weight into Felix and their blades shot a flurry of flickering light across the circular room. Felix's back was nearly against the wall. He stared into Vlad's dead, soulless eyes, which projected a sense of mastery and calm.

"And should you manage to strike me down through sheer luck and absorb any portion of me into that blade, what then?" questioned Vlad. "It seems no viable bottle of my blood will ever make it to the future. You need all of my spirit within these veins—a fractured soul will not do. Save the world you might, but you will cease to exist."

Vlad jabbed his blade, forcing Felix to deflect the blow. Felix struggled to keep his footing as he was pinned to the wall.

Vlad suddenly relented and stood back.

"I knew this day would come," he said with a rageful tone. "I've communed with the Void, mastered it. I have seen my future spread across the great eons—a never-ending web of possibilities. I know that this very morning, my brother Radu will arrive as I slumber and behead me, then take my essence and give rise to you.

"But Mîțaţrûsh was mistaken to send you here, believing you could absorb Vehuiah and weaken me. You—so tender, so soft can never stand against me. Vehuiah is mine. A power I will feed upon, now and forever. Radu is too weak to defeat me. By the time he arrives, I will have consumed your essence. You, along with Vehuiah, belong to me."

Felix was panting. He moved to the window and peered to the darkened grass that was riddled with iron spikes jutting from the earth. The fall was too perilous. He was trapped. His only option was to fight.

Felix's mind raced with questions, and fear overwhelmed him.

He looked to Vlad, who stood confidently before him like some blackened dagger of evil.

"It's time, Felix. You cannot win. You never do. Drop your weapon. Submit unto me so that we may become whole. Save your friends and family from their future misery. Surrender so that my darkness will rule evermore."

If Vlad consumed his essence, all would be lost. Everything he and his friends had fought for would be doomed. Time itself would be fractured, giving rise to a future Felix did not have the acuity to fathom.

If he failed, would Vlad rule forever?

Would Felix's friends suffer no matter his choice?

"Never!" asserted Felix.

"Well then, Felix Yusupov. Our dyad, as it always does, ends here."

"I exist, don't I?" said Felix, standing firm. "You were defeated at one point. I can do it again."

Vlad stood, taking in Felix's remark, but said nothing.

Felix reached out to the Veil but received no answers . . . only a deep instinctual sense that he was not sent here to die. Yet, here he stood, facing down the one true master of darkness, who at one point had also commanded all the wisdom that Felix had still to learn.

Vlad stood within striking distance, but Felix believed he would react quickly to any sudden move. And if any portion of his soul was absorbed into Felix's blade, then what? Felix would cease to exist.

Thinking back to Radu's description of the blade's sharpness and its ability to expunge one's soul with the slightest cut, Felix reached down slowly and pulled the demon jewel from its pommel. The blade fell to darkness. Never taking his eyes from Vlad, Felix then placed the jewel near his ethereal garments, which swaddled the relic.

Vlad appeared amused. "Clever," he said. "It seems you intend to prevail. But you hear that, do you not?" Vlad pointed his long fingernail toward the peaked ceiling. "That is the sound of my children swarming in the night: an army of Nosferatu and my son—the Bloodchild. If they sense my demise, they will descend upon this citadel and tear you to shreds. I am the only thing keeping you safe."

Felix considered the implications. Even if he was fortunate enough to kill Vlad, certainly he would not survive against an army of Nosferatu with only a demon blade as his foil.

"You are cornered, Felix. It is over. Abandon your weapon and drop to your knees." Vlad removed the jewel from his blade and slid the gem into a pocket on his waist. "Two can play at this game. I will slice you open and devour your soul."

"You're a dead man," said Felix, standing back and positioning his sword low at his side for a wide strike.

Vlad laughed. "I've been a dead man for well over a decade."

The two men stood apart, each with his sword readied in strike position.

Vlad growled, gnashed his fangs, and swung his blade wide toward Felix's neck.

Felix sensed only a blur in the vampire's movement, and instead of attempting to block the strike, he too cast his scimitar outward toward Vlad's head. A white flash burst across Felix's vision. Everything around him seemed to buckle, shake, and slow, as if this confrontation, in this very moment, was bending the fabric of time itself.

Darkness. Vertigo. Cold.

A fierce freezing sensation pulsed through Felix's head as a pillow of icy dampness smothered him. He crashed into a deep snowbank, knocking the wind from his lungs. As he gathered his senses and crawled from the snow, he heard the laughter and yelling of children in the distance.

Felix stood and took in his surroundings, breathing in the frigid air as he noticed his blade was now sheathed and hanging from his waist. A large manor sat in the far distance, one he recognized from his youth. Agony gripped his heart as he took in the implication—Vlad had beheaded him. This was his hell.

He turned his attention from the hulking structure to a group of children on a nearby hill. The youths cheered as some heavily bundled teenagers placed a small boy on a sled and prepared to push him down the steep slope. A large, fat oak tree stood directly in the boy's path at the bottom of the hill.

Felix trudged through the snow, screaming for the teenagers to stop. They paid him no mind as they laughed and pushed his younger self down the hill.

The snow felt like a tar pit as Felix tried to dash toward himself and prevent the impending collision. But he was too late. He watched himself slide face-first into the oak. The older children howled with laughter, while a few of the smaller kids stood with shocked expressions.

Felix emerged from the sparse woods and stood over his unconscious self, watching as the fresh cut on his lip bled into the snow. White-hot anger grew inside him as he stared up the hill to the teens, who were still laughing.

"Hey!" screamed Felix.

The children in the group backed away as the four teenage boys folded their arms and stared down at Felix. "Nice outfit!" shouted the leader, mocking his armor.

Felix marched up the hill as the smaller kids ran away. The bullies remained, two of them casting snowballs that sailed past him.

When he reached the top of the hill, he could see three of the teens' expressions change to worry as the eldest stood unfazed.

"Go back to the woods, old man. You look like an idiot in those clothes."

Felix stood over the boy.

To this day, I can't tell you what I'd do if I ever saw those kids again.

Felix felt his better judgment slipping away as he stared down at the boy's mocking grin.

"What are you going to do? Beat up a kid?"

"Get out of here, you freak!" interjected another.

Felix unsheathed his blade and held it over the boy's head. The freezing sensation nipped at his brain once more.

Kill him, Felix. Do it, came Vlad's voice.

The boy shrieked and cowered, lowering himself to the snow and raising his hands in submission at the sight of the shiny black blade.

His cohorts dashed away toward the manor.

"We were just fooling around. Please don't."

Felix's heart was pounding. Decades of pent-up anger welled within.

He could crush this bully right here. Break the cycle. Finally have his revenge.

Struck down one of the older kids with some strange axe.

Felix paused, thinking back to his tale of the sledding accident.

Certainly, he wasn't the madman from the past.

Certainly, he could never strike down a helpless, unarmed boy.

But here he stood, towering over a frightened teenager with this *strange axe* in his hand, ready to cut the bully in two. Disbelief and confusion overtook his mind—as it must have been true. At some point in his past incarnations, he must have cut off the boy's arm and fled into the woods.

There is a grave darkness in you, Felix, came Radu's words.

A darkness that has always been me, finished Vlad.

Felix stared at the teen and felt an acute sense of shame that his anger had pushed him this far.

A tear fell from the boy's eye, and in that instant, Felix knew him. He stared deeply into the bully's watering eyes. He saw the merciless beatings from the boy's father, the cruel lashings from his mother, and the dark secret the boy held about the abuse from his uncle.

Felix relented.

"Go pick him up," he said, sheathing his blade. "Bring him to his mother."

The kid wiped the tears from his face with his snow-encrusted mitten, nodded, then ran to the bottom of the hill. He placed the younger Felix's unconscious body on the sled and dragged him up the hill, never daring to make eye contact with the oddly dressed stranger as he continued toward the manor.

Felix stood watching the boy's figure move through the snow and a sensation of calm took him. He placed his finger to the scar on his lip—the anger, the shame, had gone.

None of it mattered anymore.

Felix became dizzy as a fierce snow squall picked up, soon blocking his vision of the manor. He began trudging forward, and soon another building came into view in the distance as daytime fell to night.

As Felix approached, the building's shape became apparent— Yusupov Palace. He was home.

He continued through the blizzard toward the darkened palace, where light emanated from only one window on the first floor.

He peered inside to see his father's study, decorated with lavish cherry-colored patent leather furnishings and a roaring fire burning in the hearth.

From outside the room's entrance came the sounds of his mother screaming and his father yelling. Felix watched as two men, one older, wearing a black cloak, and the other burly and bearded, roughly pushed his parents into the room. The attackers shoved them toward the hearth and forced them to kneel before the fire.

Felix banged on the window. "Mother!"

They paid him no mind.

"Olaf, please!" begged Felix's father, extending his hands toward the cloaked man. "We have lived up to our part of the agreement. What's this about?"

"I need to send a clear message to Rasputin and inform him his time is running out," said Olaf, nodding to the burly man. "Do it, Kir."

Kir stood behind Felix's mother and unsheathed a taiga from his belt.

With one forceful whack, his mother's head was sliced clean from her neck. Her lifeless body slumped over, spurting blood onto the marble.

"No!" screamed Felix, banging on the window, attempting to break it.

"Zinaida!" moaned his father as Kir's blade sliced halfway through his neck.

The sheer horror on his father's face immobilized Felix as he watched through the window. Kir raised his arm again, this time lopping his father's head off his body.

Felix turned, unable to watch his body slump to the floor.

His hand found its way to his blade's hilt and he dashed toward the palace's entrance. Upon entering, Felix ran for his father's study to find a pool of blood soaking the floor and his parents' bodies aflame, shoved into the hearth.

Olaf and Kir were missing.

Felix knelt at the fire, desperately trying to pull his parents' bodies from the flames, catching his sleeves on fire and burning his hands as he gripped his mother's burning wrist. Felix yelped and sat back on the marble as his ethereal garments quashed the flames and repaired themselves.

This rage inside him was suffocating.

Felix would find these men and cast a mighty retribution upon them, no matter the cost. He stared into the hearth, growing nauseous at the sight of his parents' carcasses, crackling and popping as they burned to a crisp.

Lies.

Manipulation.

Betrayal.

For these were the hallmarks of Felix's life.

By no choice of his own, he was cast into these machinations from birth. And now he was dead, alone in his own personal purgatory—forever bound to walk the memories of this haunting netherworld from which there was no escape.

Felix shivered.

He pulled his knees to his face, wrapped his arms around his shins, and squeezed himself tightly, trying to calm the fury burning within.

He remembered Hanne—another victim of this dark malice, a kindred soul.

Felix wished he could travel back to Čachtice and cast himself into the molten pool. He was sitting with his head buried in his knees when the sound of a woman shrieking came from behind.

He stood to find his father's study empty.

Looking down at the pool of his parents' blood, Felix watched as the red liquid shimmered and cast a vision within the gore.

At first, he saw himself lying unconscious on a floor with Dmitri Pavlovich standing over him. He recognized the scene: this was the evening on which Felix had been betrayed and his beloved Irina murdered. Felix watched as Dmitri rose and stood before Rasputin, who held Irina in his clutches.

"Let her go!" shouted Dmitri, trying to free Irina from Rasputin's grasp.

Three other Black Hundred operatives who were in the room grabbed Dmitri and pulled him away, attempting to subdue him as

Dmitri struggled. They finally beat him into submission and re-strained him on the floor.

"This wasn't part of the deal!" shouted Dmitri, as blood dripped from his nose.

"You are in no position to question these events," said Rasputin.

"You promised you'd let her go."

"I promised that she would be freed."

Rasputin placed his hands on Irina's shoulders and forced her to the floor.

"But now, it is you who will free her. Prove your loyalty to me, Dmitri, or you will be joining her. Back away, men."

The Black Hundred operatives released Dmitri, who stood and stared at Rasputin for a long moment while Irina whimpered.

"If you want to walk among us, you must prove how far you are willing to go," said Rasputin. "Fail me and you will never be granted immortality. Are you one of us? Show me. Kill her. Now."

Dmitri scowled at the Black Hundred men behind him before walking slowly to Irina.

She looked up at him, her chin quivering. "Help me, Dmitri. Please."

Dmitri's posture was domineering, like that of a predator ready to feast. He puffed out his chest and held back his shoulders, clearly invigorated by a submissive woman kneeling before him.

"You brought this on yourself, Irina. I offered to give you every-thing, but you were too stupid to understand. You could have been with me—forever. But you never reciprocated. Forever loyal to that selfish boor." Dmitri looked to Felix's unconscious body. "Too bad he can't help you now. You should have chosen a real man. I wanted things to be different, but now I have no choice."

Felix stared into the pool, shocked at this discovery—Irina had always been faithful to him.

He then watched as Dmitri stood over her, wrapped his hands around her neck, and strangled her to death. Dmitri stood away as her lifeless body fell to the marble. He took one last look at her on the floor and quickly stormed from the room.

Rasputin knelt to Irina as great fangs grew from his mouth. Felix averted his eyes as Rasputin moved his clawed hands toward her body, tore open her sternum, and feasted upon her blood-engorged heart. The sounds of Rasputin's feasting still resonated, further torturing Felix. He slumped to the floor, and the vision within the blood dissipated.

"You've found another," came a feminine voice from the study's entrance.

In the doorway was Irina, in the same red dress she had worn the night of her murder.

"Irina!"

"You've forgotten me. Failed in your quest to avenge my death."

Felix was speechless as he took her in. He stood before her and embraced her.

"I'm so sorry, Irina," said Felix. "I've missed you so. I would do anything to make things right."

Irina stepped away but kept her arms on Felix's shoulders, staring into his eyes.

"There is something you can do."

"Tell me. Anything."

"I don't understand it all, but this seems to be some type of purgatory. I too am trapped here. I have been waiting for you before I can pass on. It seems we can only pass together. But, I fear it's too much to ask."

Felix felt a warmth ease him for the first time in a long while.

The last time he remembered feeling this carefree was when he and Irina were alone together before Dmitri's fateful party. That evening, he had stood staring out the window in his mother's favorite parlor and heard the sounds of breaking glass. He had turned to see Irina kneeling on the floor over a broken bottle of his most cherished scotch, her blouse soaked a light brown as the booze seeped into the fabric.

"It's not too much to ask, Irina. I just want to be with you—forever."

"You have to kill yourself, Felix. I can't ask for that."

"I think there's been a mistake," Felix told her. "I can't explain it, but I think I'm already dead. I don't know how I came to be in this place."

"That was your body. You must sacrifice your soul if we are to pass together."

Felix grew suspicious at her authoritative tone. "How do you know that?"

Irina appeared flustered. "I—I can't say. It just came to me. This place . . . it speaks to me. I have been informed that you must prove you are ready to pass into the Ether if we are to be together."

Felix's ears were buzzing. Something was amiss. Radu had warned him about holding on to attachments and their propensity to push one down a dark path. And with that thought, Felix knew what he must do—it was time to simply let go.

He stood back from Irina and unsheathed his blade as the freezing sensation grew once more in his mind. Felix forced a half smile and held his arm outward, placing the razor-sharp blade just over his forearm.

"This blade will release my soul. Just say the word."

"I love you, Felix," said Irina. "Make the sacrifice and allow your soul to pass. Do it for me. After you go, I will follow."

Felix nodded, accepting his decision and reminding himself how happy he once was with Irina. It felt like an eon ago. He looked to the blade resting against his flesh, then lifted his eyes to meet hers.

"Do you remember the last time we had a private moment together?"

"I do. I will always treasure it."

"You spilled my favorite vodka all over the floor. And I scorned you for not having it brought by the servants."

"Yes. I remember. And now we can finally be together again—forever."

Felix pulled the blade from his forearm.

"There is only one problem," he said.

"What is it, my darling?"

"You would know that I only drink scotch."

Felix let out a growl and swung the blade wide, cutting Irina's head clean from her body.

His father's study grew fuzzy as the walls appeared to melt into darkness. Felix soon found himself still standing in the citadel. Stunned, he leaned against the windowsill to take in the grim scene before him as Irina's headless body morphed into Vlad's corpse—a pool of blood gushing from his neck. His clawed hand still gripped the dark blade which rested on the stone.

Breathless as the shrieks of Nosferatu came from the window, Felix held his hand near his chest and found the demon jewel tucked into his garment. He placed it back into the blade's hilt and the weapon ignited.

Felix sheathed his scimitar and stood back from the pool of blood at his feet as a radiance shone from Vlad's body. It grew so bright that Felix closed his eyes and threw his palm over his brow, believing the light would blind him.

The glow subsided, yet remained.

Felix opened his eyes to see a luminous white body hovering over Vlad's corpse. It was vaguely anthropomorphic, with six wings extending from its slender body. Felix tried to speak but was too astonished by the phantasm's exquisite beauty. Vehuiah appeared as a perfect being—its every line and curvature gleamed within Felix's temporal lobe as geometrically pure, so that he felt he was staring into the core of the Veil itself. Perfect circles, precise lines, and impeccable arches meshed and merged in unison across its glowing aspect as Felix studied this holy creature.

He knelt upon the stone and bowed his head, trying to gather his senses and calm his racing heartbeat.

"Vehuiah," said Felix. "I am humbled before you."

The spirit spoke to him in a high-pitched cadence that was more song than speech, instructing him to rise.

Felix stood away from Vehuiah as the archangel raised its appendages above its angular head, which bore no discernible facial features. The stone within the chamber rattled, and the blood seeping from Vlad's body congealed and rose into the air. The darkened cruor formed into a ball of sparkling light, hovering just in front of Felix before condensing into a gilded ether and floating toward the wall. Felix watched in amazement as the wispy liquid gently fed itself into a green bottle with a red wax dragon symbol on its hull. A cork rose up from the floor and sealed Vlad's essence within.

The reverberations ceased and the faint sounds of celestial chimes echoed through the room. Vehuiah lowered its extremities and motioned toward the bottle. Felix moved to the wall and grabbed the vessel. He held it to a torch and inspected its contents—within the glass was a dark, viscous liquid that sparkled with golden, glittery flecks.

Felix's mind became awash with wonder as he stared at the bottle, knowing he held the nexus of his own existence in his very hands. Astonished, he turned and stared at Vehuiah. A sense of serenity swept through him. The spirit hummed once more and Felix understood that now was his time. He nodded in agreement, placed the bottle on the floor, and stood as Vehuiah floated toward him.

Felix nearly cried out as Vehuiah's energy passed through his cellular plasma membranes and absorbed into his being. The sensation was electric, absolute, as if a blaze born of purified, argent static had erupted from within his heart. The invigoration pulsed through him, growing to near delirium—a pleasure so frenzied Felix felt he might burst. The sensation of breathing air spawned from pure intelligence exhilarated him as the archangel's spirit fused deep within his mitochondria. His spine steeled and his muscles and tendons grew powerful and taut. He became versed in spells he never knew and fluent in languages he'd never spoken. The Veil called out to him like some mighty chorus of angelic sopranos—he knew the past and sensed the future as lifetimes of knowledge and book learning cemented within his neocortex.

Felix bent over, placing his hands on his knees as he tried to remain conscious, the overwhelming notion of infinite wisdom still buzzed within. He watched the ethereal clothing swaddling Vlad's corpse slither away and the jewel containing Bael roll to his boots. The black garment floated around Felix before finally melding with his own clothing. Felix held out his hands and watched as his medieval knight garb darkened to a black leather with metal fastenings protecting his heart and spine. A deep hood materialized over his head, followed by a flowing black cape that fell to his knees. Finally, a deep red dragon emblem stitched itself on his chest.

"That's more like it," said Felix, feeling grounded once more and taking in his new ensemble. When he looked up, he noticed that the sky was lightening outside the window. Dawn was nearly upon him.

Footsteps echoed from the shaft. Someone was ascending the stairs.

Felix moved over Vlad and unbuckled the sheath from his naked, shriveled remains. He then removed the darkened Masamune blade from Vlad's cold grip and collected the demon jewel containing Bael. After attaching the gem to the pommel and igniting the scimitar, he sheathed the weapon and retrieved the bottle of Vlad's essence. Felix stood center room, holding the bottle in one hand and the sheathed sword containing Bael in the other.

A hooded stranger entered the room.

The man held his iron sword toward Felix and cast back his hood to reveal a much younger Radu, who appeared shocked to see his brother lying beheaded upon the floor.

"Who are you?" asked Radu.

"It doesn't matter who I am. All you need to know is I am a friend."

Felix extended the blade containing Bael to Radu and knelt upon the stone. "Take this as my peace offering."

Radu sheathed his iron sword and accept the demon blade, quickly strapping it around his waist. He looked to the scimitar strapped to Felix's waist, then to Vlad's wilted remains.

"Did you do this?"

"No," said Felix, standing. "You did."

"I only just arrived. How could—"

"You did this. There are no other witnesses. You beheaded your own brother to save humanity, and that's the story you will stick to from now on. You then collected his blood in this bottle in hopes of redeeming him one day. And redeem him you shall. Take it." Felix extended the bottle. "I mean you no harm."

"Who are you, then?"

Felix flashed a confident grin from beneath his hood as a fitting quote from Faust rang through his mind.

"I am merely a part of the power that evil ever does; yet ever does the good," he said.

Radu appeared curious.

"Please, step forward," said Felix. "I am a friend."

After taking a moment to ponder the situation, Radu stepped forward and accepted the bottle.

"That is to remain in your possession at all times . . . until one day in the late 1800s, when a crafty young warlock by the name of Grigori Rasputin will come to you seeking apprenticeship. His intent is to steal this bottle. Allow him. On this, you must swear."

"I swear," said Radu, placing the bottle inside his ethereal cloak, which absorbed it into the fabric.

"The blade containing Bael will serve you well," said Felix. "Guard it with your life. The Veil will see to the rest."

From outside the citadel came the sounds of Nosferatu howling.

"You're not from this time, are you?" asked Radu.

"I am not."

"Well then, allow me to enlighten you," said Radu. "My brother, whom you have just slain, was one of the masters of the vicious army of Nosferatu that is certainly descending upon this citadel this very instant to defend their master."

"I am fully aware."

Radu again looked to Vlad's headless corpse.

"Considering you beheaded the darkest and most powerful warlock in the world, let's hope you're ready for what comes next."

"We must kill the Bloodchild of this era."

"You are well informed, my mysterious friend."

"Do you know where he might be?"

"It would be my guess that he is aware of his father's death and on his way to us."

"What about the mother?" asked Felix.

"She is not a threat. Only interested in feeding, not fighting. Shall we?" said Radu, motioning to the door.

Felix bowed and swung his arm wide to the door. "After you, my good Radu."

*

Felix and Radu exited the citadel as daylight crested over the mountain peaks in the distance. Peering into the darkened forest, they made out what appeared to be a never-ending cascade of stark white Nosferatu standing among the trees. At the very center of the front line stood a young man in his late teens, clad in black leather contrasted against his pale features.

"Traitor!" he yelled, when he saw Radu.

"Mihnea cel Rău," said Radu. "How big you've grown."

Mihnea and his front line of Nosferatu backed farther into the forest as a sunbeam cut a clear border: the forest on one side, Radu and Felix on the other.

Mihnea smirked, watching the light. "You are safe for now, Uncle. Only for now. It will be dark again soon, and we will hunt you. You and your hooded friend will pay for this."

Radu stepped forward and began to speak, but was silenced by Felix, who held his arm across Radu and stepped into the sunbeam.

"Young Mihnea," said Felix. "I believe it is you who will pay. Your reign of evil ends here and now."

"Show me," said Mihnea. "Come into the forest and fight."

"I think not," said Felix.

Felix focused his mind and called out to Vehuiah. His own question to Radu came back to him: *I can cause earthquakes with this?*

Felix unsheathed his blade, gripped the blade with both hands, and pointed the weapon downward.

"What are you doing?" asked Radu.

"Ending this."

Felix thrust the weapon deep into the dirt. Rage boiled within as he pushed all his weight into the hilt, the earth's magnetic resonance repelling the blade. His mind seemed to meld with the jewel, which began to grow white hot. A chorus of demonic chants filled his mind, and Felix began shouting, mimicking the diabolic chorus in his mind.

The skies turned ashen and the earth rumbled, jolting the very rock beneath them and shaking the forest so that the blackwood trees swayed and creaked. Vlad's darkened citadel began to crack to pieces. Large portions of stone fell from the base, weakening its structural integrity until the fortress caved in and crumbled to the ground in a shower of dust and blackened rock.

The Nosferatu flapped their wings and hovered as Mihnea steadied himself.

Felix focused his gaze on Mihnea, envisioning the ground tearing open before him. And at that moment, a crevasse opened beneath his blade and quickly splintered toward the young vampire.

"Freeze him!" yelled Felix.

Radu shot out his hand and froze Mihnea in position as he attempted to leap away from the fissure.

"Cast him in. Now!" shouted Felix.

Radu forced his hand downward and sent Mihnea deep into the crevasse.

Felix pulled his blade from the ground. The shaking earth calmed and healed the chasm, crushing Mihnea to death in its jaws.

Felix sheathed his blade and the jewel darkened. He stood next to Radu, and they watched as the army of Nosferatu shrieked while dissipating into a fine ether.

The sun cracked through the gray clouds, and all was calm.

"Incredible," said Radu. "How did you know the blade could do that?"

"Each of these blades has a magical property unique to the demon contained within its hilt. A Cheshire Cat enlightened me."

Radu appeared confused.

"Please. You must tell me who you are." Radu tried to peer beneath Felix's hood. "How did you acquire your blade? I've been searching for the rest."

"I am sorry, Radu. I cannot. If you know too much, it would place my future in jeopardy. Just keep the bottle and the blade safe. Follow my exact instructions. In time, you will see me again."

Felix stepped away and held his hands high, calling out to the Veil.

He ascended into the sky as his vision was smothered by a red, blinding light. His last vision was of Radu's young face, staring up at him as he melded into the air and disappeared from sight.

*

Felix landed gently on the stone floor in the heart of Poenari Castle.

He looked up to Mīṭaṭrūsh as the black and golden rings encircled the glowing jewel.

"Nice to see you again, old friend," said Felix, passing on the greeting from Vehuiah.

Mītaṭrūsh hummed and glowed in response.

Felix inspected the floor to find remnants of Radu's blood. He reached to the droplets and held his hand over them in an attempt to discern the outcome after he was transported away. His mind filled with images of vámpir rushing Radu and attempting to maul him as Vondling stepped into the room and commanded them to stop. Vondling placed silver fetters on Radu's wrists and his minions dragged the unconscious and battered warlock from the room.

Radu was still alive.

Felix dashed from the room, making it all the way to the castle's entrance, where he emerged into a bright sunny morning. No Vondling, no vampires—just a moment of peace and serenity amid the expansive forest of Wallachia.

At the base of the stairs stood Nima and Drina. Radu's cloaking spell had kept them safe.

Felix stared into the deep valley below.

He thought of his friends and the dangers at hand as he gripped the hilt of his demon blade containing the soul of Duke Agares, the bringer of earthquakes.

Radu would be rescued. Mary would be saved. Rurik, Sebastian— the world.

Bael and his cabal would be destroyed.

Felix unsheathed his blade, raised it high above his head, and roared into the sky as he expunged his anger and frustration. The rising sun cast its radiance upon him, and Felix appeared to shine against the deciduous mountain backdrop.

A great surge of warmth filled his body.

Felix sheathed his blade as his roar echoed back from the gorge. The angst and worry that once pervaded his mind were absent. The former Russian prince—once alone and wayward—now stood triumphant, the one great hope of a world poised on the brink of destruction. Confidence and wisdom beckoned to him for the first time in his life as he stood before the world as a powerful warlock.

For my friends, for the world. I am the harbinger of light.

Felix walked down the stairs toward Nima.

Squinting into the sun and relishing the light, Felix swore an oath that this festering darkness would crumble.

For soon, his enemies would come to fear his name—Felix Felixovich Yusupov, the Last Seraph.

TO BE CONCLUDED IN . . .
THE NOSFERATU CONSPIRACY, BOOK THREE:
THE LAST SERAPH

All out war!

With his friends scattered throughout Europe in perilous situations of their own, Felix must race to rescue Radu from the clutches of Charles Vondling and his bloodthirsty army of vámpir.

As forces of darkness move to conquer Paris, Dmitri Pavlovich and Olaf conspire to respawn the Nosferatu at Loch Dracul. All action centers on the diabolical plans of Elizabeth Báthory and her half-brother Baphomet as they work to rain terror upon humankind and conquer the world in the name of their father—the mighty demon king Bael.

Will Felix reclaim his full power in time to save his friends and defeat Bael?

Find out in *The Last Seraph*—the exciting conclusion to The Nosferatu Conspiracy series.

CONTACT THE AUTHOR

The author's site:
http://www.brianjamesgage.com/

The book series' site:
http://www.nosferatuconspiracy.com/

The author's social media profiles:
instagram.com/brianjamesgage
twitter.com/brianjamesgage
tiktok: @brianjamesgage

The book series' social media profiles:
instagram.com/nosferatuconspiracy
twitter.com/nosferatucon
facebook.com/nosferatuconspiracy
tiktok: @nosferatuconspiracy

ABOUT THE AUTHOR

Brian James Gage is a multi-award-winning horror author and aspiring classical pianist.

For more info, please visit:
http://www.brianjamesgage.com/

Notes

CPSIA information can be obtained
at www.ICGtesting.com
Printed in the USA
LVHW101214270722
724473LV00003B/96

9 780578 989631